DAVID
HEWSON

THE GARDEN OF EVIL
&
THE PROMISED LAND

PAN BOOKS

The Garden of Evil first published 2008 by Macmillan
First published by Pan Books 2008
The Promised Land first published 2007 by Macmillan
First published by Pan Books 2008

This omnibus first published 2011 by Pan Books
an imprint of Pan Macmillan, a division of Macmillan Publishers Limited
Pan Macmillan, 20 New Wharf Road, London N1 9RR
Basingstoke and Oxford
Associated companies throughout the world
www.panmacmillan.com

ISBN 978-0-330-54548-8

Copyright © David Hewson 2008, 2007
Map copyright © Kate Hewson 2008

The right of David Hewson to be identified as the
author of this work has been asserted by him in accordance
with the Copyright, Designs and Patents Act 1988.

For *The Promised Land* we are grateful to Warner/Chappell Music Ltd
for extracts from 'Swan Song' on page 47, words and music by Bruce Hornsby,
copyright © 1998 WB Music Corps., all rights administered by
Warner/Chappell Music Ltd, London W6 8BS.

1 3 5 7 9 8 6 4 2

A CIP catalogue record for this book is available from
the British Library.

Typeset by IntypeLibra, London Ltd
Printed in the UK by CPI Mackays, Chatham ME5 8TD

THE GARDEN OF EVIL

THE LITTLE DEATH

Part 1

THE LITTLE DEATH

– 1 –

Aldo Caviglia caught his reflection in the overhead mirror of the crowded 64 bus. He was not a vain man but, on balance, he approved of what he saw. Caviglia had recently turned sixty. Four years earlier he had lost his wife. There had been a brief, lost period when drink took its toll, and with it his job in the ancient bakery in the Campo dei Fiori, just a few minutes' walk from the small apartment close to the Piazza Navona, where they had lived for their entire married life. He had come to escape the grip of the booze before it stole away his looks. The grief he still felt only marked him inwardly now.

Today he was wearing what he thought of as his winter Thursday uniform, a taupe woollen coat over a brown suit with a knife-edge crease running down the trousers. In his mind's eye he was the professional man he would have been in another, different life. A minor academic, a civil servant, or an accountant perhaps. Someone happy with his lot and that, at least, was no lie.

It was 8 December, the feast of the Immaculate Conception. Christmas stood on the horizon, its presence finally beginning to make itself known beyond the tawdry displays that had been in store windows for weeks. Every

3

good Catholic would attend mass. The Pope would venerate two famous statues of the Virgin, in the Piazza di Spagna and at Santa Maria Maggiore. Catholic or not, families of all ages would flock to the city streets, to shop, to eat, to gossip, to walk around and enjoy the season. In the vast racetrack space of the Piazza Navona, which followed the lines of the Imperial stadium that had preceded it, the stalls occupied almost every last square metre: toys for the children, panini of *porchetta* carved straight from the warm pig's carcass for the parents, and the Christmas witch, La Befana, everywhere, on stockings and pendants, decorations and candies, a half-hideous, half-friendly spectre primed to dispense gifts to the young at Epiphany.

Caviglia gripped the handrail as the bus lurched through the traffic past the stranded temple ruins of Largo Torre Argentina, smiling at his memories. Theirs had been an uncomplicated, innocent marriage, perhaps because it had never been blessed by children. Even so, for Chiara's sake, he had left out a traditional offering for La Befana – a piece of broccoli, some sausage and a glass of wine – every year of their marriage, right to the end, when her life was ebbing away like a winter tide retreating gently for the last time. He had never possessed the money for expensive presents. Nor did it matter, then or now. The pictures that still remained in his head – of rituals, of simple, fond, shared acts – were more valuable than any lump of gold or silver could ever have been. When his wife was alive they served as visible symbols of his love. Now that he was alone, the memory of their giving provided comfort during the cold, solitary nights of winter. In his own mind Christmas remained what it always was: a turning point for the year at which the days ceased to shorten, Rome paused to look at itself, feel modestly proud of what it saw, then await the inevitable arrival of spring, and with it rebirth.

Even in the weather the city had endured of late – dark and terribly wet, with the Tiber at its highest for a quarter of a century, so brown and muddy and reckless it would have burst its banks without the modern flood defences – there was a spirit of quiet excitement abroad, a communal recollection of a small, distant miracle that still bore some significance in an ephemeral world of mundane fleeting greed. He saw this in the faces of the children spilling down the city streets and alleys, excited, trying to guess what the coming weeks would bring. He saw this in the eyes of their parents too, remembering their youth, taking pleasure in passing some fragment of the wonder on to their own offspring in return. Nor was the weather uniformly vile. Occasionally the heavy, dark clouds would break and a lively winter sun would smile on the city. He'd seen it drift through the dusty windows of his apartment that morning, spilling a welcome golden light onto the ancient, smoke-stained cobblestones of the alley outside. It had made him feel at home, glad to be a Roman born and bred.

Caviglia had lived in the *centro storico* all his life and worshipped in the Church of San Luigi dei Francesi around the corner. His wife had adored the paintings there, the Caravaggios in particular, with their loving and lifelike depiction of Matthew, at his conversion, during his work and finally at his death. One 8 December, twenty-five years ago it must have been, he had marked their visit by spending what little money he had from his baker's wages on a bouquet of bright red roses. She had responded by taking out the most beautiful stem and

5

pinning it into the strap of his floury overalls – he had come straight from work – then taking him in her arms in an embrace he could still recall for its strength and warmth and affection.

Ever since, even after she was gone, he had marked the day, first with roses, bought before breakfast from the small florist's store that stood close to the piazza, then a brief visit to the church, where he lit a single candle in her memory. He no longer attended mass, though. It seemed unnecessary.

A single carmine stem from Tuscany sat in the left lapel of his woollen coat, its supple, insistent perfume rising above the diesel odour and the people smell of the busy bus, reminding him of times past and how, in those last few weeks of her illness, his wife had ordered him, in a voice growing ever weaker, to mourn for a short time only, then start his own life afresh.

To the widowed Aldo Caviglia there was no finer time to be in Rome, even in the grey, persistent rain. The best parts of the year lay ahead, waiting in store for those who anticipated them. And in the busy, careless crowds of Christmas, flush with money, there was always business to be done.

He had an itinerary in mind, the one he always saved for the second Thursday in the month, since repetition was to be avoided. Having walked to Barberini for the exercise and taken a brief turn around the gallery, he had caught the 64 bus for the familiar journey through the city centre, following Vittorio Emanuele, then crossing the river by the Castel Sant'Angelo for the final leg towards

St Peter's. Once there, he would retrace his steps as necessary until his goal was reached.

Caviglia both loved and hated the 64. No route in Rome attracted more tourists, which made it a beacon for the lesser members of his recently acquired profession. Many were simply confused and lost. Aldo Caviglia, an impeccably dressed man in later middle age, who wore a perpetual and charming smile and spoke good English, was always there to help. He maintained in his head a compendious knowledge of the city of his birth. Should his memory fail him, he always kept in his pocket a copy of *Il Trovalinea*, the comprehensive city transport guide that covered every last tram and bus in Rome. He knew where to stay, where to eat. He knew, too, that it was wise to warn visitors of the underside of Roman life: the petty crooks and bag-snatchers, the hucksters working the tourist traps, and the scruffy pickpockets who hung around the buses and the subway, the 64 in particular.

He gave them tips. He taught them the phrase, '*Zingari! Attenzione!*', explaining that it meant 'Beware! Gypsies!' Not, he hastened to add, that he shared the common assumption that all gypsies were thieves. On occasion he would amuse his audience by demonstrating the private sign every Roman knew, holding his hands down by his side, rippling his fingers as if playing the piano. He had a fine, delicate touch, that of an artist, which he demonstrated proudly with this gesture. Before the needs of everyday life had forced him to find more mundane work, he had toyed with the idea of painting as a profession, since the galleries of his native city, the great Villa Borghese, the splendid if chaotic Barberini and his favourite, the private mansion of the Doria Pamphilj dynasty, were places he still frequented with a continuing sense of wonder.

The visitors always laughed at his subtle, fluttering fingertips. It was such a small, secret signal, yet as soon as one saw it there could be no doubting its meaning: the bus or the carriage had just been joined by a known pickpocket. *Look out.*

He was careful to keep records, maintained in a private code on a piece of paper hidden at the bottom of his wardrobe. On a normal working day, Aldo Caviglia would not return home until he had stolen a minimum of €400. His average – Caviglia was a man fond of precise accounts – had been €583 over the past four weeks. On occasion – tourists sometimes carried extraordinary amounts of cash – he had far exceeded his daily target, so much so that it had begun to trouble him. Caviglia chose his victims carefully. He never preyed on the poor or the elderly. When one miserable Russian's wallet alone yielded more than €2,000, Caviglia had decided upon a policy. All proceeds above his maximum of €650 would be donated anonymously – pushed in cash into a collection box – to the sisters near the Pantheon who ran a charity for the city's homeless. He prided himself on the fact that he was not a greedy man. Furthermore, as a true Roman he never ceased to be shocked by how the city's population of destitute *barboni*, many young, many unable to speak much Italian, had grown in recent years. He would take no more than he needed. He would maintain a balance between his activities and his conscience, going out to steal one or two days each week, when necessary. For the rest of the time he would simply ride the trams and buses for the pleasure of being what, on the surface, he appeared: a genial Good Samaritan, always ready to help the stranded, confused foreigner.

The bus lurched away from the bus stop. The traffic was bad, struggling through the holiday crowds at little more than walking pace. They had moved scarcely thirty metres along Vittorio Emanuele in the past five minutes. He stared at himself in the bus driver's mirror again. Was this the face of a guilty man? Caviglia brushed away the thought. Needs must, though, in truth, he could probably get a job in a bakery now he was sober. No one ever complained about his work. His late wife had thought him among the best bakers in Rome. There was a joke he now made to himself: these fingers can make dough, these fingers can take dough. It was a good one, he thought. He wished he could share it with someone.

'Needs must,' Caviglia emphasized to himself.

'You feel guilty,' said a quiet, inner voice, 'for yourself and the life you are wasting. Not for what you've done.'

He glanced out of the grimy windows: solid lines of cars and buses and vans stood stationary in both directions. The sudden joy of the coming holiday waned at that moment.

To his surprise, Aldo Caviglia felt a firm finger prod hard into his chest.

'I want the stop for the Vicolo del Divino Amore,' said a woman hard up against his right side. She spoke in an accent Caviglia took to be French, with a confidence in her Italian which was, he felt, somewhat ill-judged.

He turned to look at her, aware that his customary smile was no longer present.

She was attractive, though extremely slender, and wore a precisely cut short white gabardine coat over a tube-like crayon-red leather skirt that stopped just above the knee. Perhaps thirty-five, she had short, very fiery red hair to match the skirt, acute grey eyes and the kind of face one saw in advertisements for cosmetics: geometrically exact, entirely lacking in flaws and, to Caviglia's taste, somewhat two-dimensional. She seemed both nervous and a little depressed. And also ill, perhaps, since on second consideration her skin was very pale indeed, almost the colour of her jacket, and her cheeks slightly concave.

She had a large fawn pigskin bag over her shoulder. It sported the very visible badge of one of the larger Milan fashion houses. Caviglia wondered why a beautiful woman, albeit one of daunting and somewhat miserable appearance, would want to advertise the wares of the Milanese clothes crooks and, by implication, her own sense of insecurity. The bag was genuine, though. Perhaps €1,000 had been squandered on that modest piece of leather. The zip was halfway open, just enough to reveal a large collection of items – a scarf, a phone, some pens and a very large, over-stuffed wallet.

'I really need to find this place,' she said. 'It's near the Palazzo Malaspina, I know. But I was never very good at directions. I've only been there at night. I . . .'

For a moment he thought she was about to burst into tears. Then he corrected himself. She was simply absorbed, in something he could not begin to imagine.

Caviglia smiled, then reached over her to press the bell. A cloud of rich, somewhat cloying perfume rose from her body. French, he thought again.

'The next stop, signora, if you are willing to walk. I

will show you where to go. I have to get off myself in any case.'

She nodded and said nothing. When the bus finally came to a halt, Caviglia put a protective arm around her and pushed through the milling mob to exit by the front doors, as a local would, in spite of the rules, saying loudly as he forced his way forward, '*Permesso. Permesso! PERMESSO!*'

He waited for her to alight from the bus, his hands behind his back. She seemed even more frail and thin out in the brief bright light of this December day.

'It's ten minutes on foot,' Caviglia said. He pointed across the road. 'In that direction. There are no buses. Perhaps I can find you a taxi.'

'I can walk,' she said instantly.

'Can you find your way to the Piazza Navona from here?'

She nodded and looked a little offended.

'Of course!'

'Go to the end,' he instructed. 'Then turn right through the Piazza Agostino for the Via della Scrofa. Turn right again at the Piazza Firenze and you will find the Vicolo del Divino Amore on your left along the Via dei Prefetti.'

'Thank you.'

'You are entering an interesting part of my city. Many famous artists lived there. It was once part of the area called "Ortaccio".'

She looked puzzled.

'My Italian is bad. I don't know that word.'

Caviglia cursed his stupidity for mentioning this fact. Sometimes he spoke too much for his own good.

11

'It was an area set aside by the Popes for prostitutes. *Orto* may signify the Garden of Eden. *Ortaccio* signifies what came after our discovery of sin. The Garden of Humanity. Or the Garden of Wickedness or Evil. Or one and the same. But I am simply a . . . retired schoolteacher. What would I know of such things?'

The merest of smiles slipped across her face. Though almost skeletally thin, she was exceptionally beautiful, Caviglia realized. It was simply that something – life, illness or some inner turmoil – disguised this fact most of the time, stood between her true self and others like a semi-opaque screen, one held by her own pale, slim hands.

'A lot, I think,' the French woman said. 'You're a kind man.'

She stopped, smiled briefly again and held out her hand. Caviglia shook it, delicately, since her fingers seemed so thin they might break under the slightest pressure. To his surprise her flesh was unexpectedly warm, almost as if something burned inside her, with the same heat signified by her fiery hair.

Then she took a deep breath, looked around – seeming to take an unnecessary pleasure in the smog-stained stones of a busy thoroughfare Caviglia regarded as one of the most uninteresting in Rome – and was gone, threading through the traffic with a disregard for her own safety he found almost heart-stopping.

He turned away before her darting white form, like an exclamation mark with a full stop made from flame, disappeared into one of the side roads leading to the Piazza Navona.

Business was business. Caviglia patted the right-hand side of his jacket pocket. The woman's fat wallet sat there, a wad of leather and paper and credit cards waiting to be stripped. Experience and his own intelligence told him the day's work was over. Nevertheless, he was a little disturbed by this encounter. There was something strange about this woman in white, and her urgent need to go the Vicolo del Divino Amore, a dark Roman alley that, to him, showed precious little trace of divine love, and probably never had.

– 2 –

Aldo Caviglia strode towards the Campo dei Fiori and entered a small cafe located in one of the side roads leading to the Cancelleria, determined to realize his gains, then dump the evidence. This particular hole in the wall was a place he'd always liked: too tiny and local to be of interest to tourists, and one that kept to the old tradition of maintaining a bowl of thick, sticky mixed sugar and coffee on the bar so that those in need of a faster, surer fix could top up their *caffè* as much as was needed.

All the same, Caviglia had added a shot of grappa to his cup too, something he hadn't done for some months. This chill, strange winter day seemed to merit that, though it was still only twenty to eleven in the morning.

Within five minutes he was inside the tiny washroom, crammed up against the cistern, struggling, with trembling fingers, to extract what was of value from the bulging leather purse.

Caviglia never took credit cards and sold them on. Partly because this would increase the risk but also, more importantly, out of simple propriety. He believed people should be robbed once and once only – by his nimble fingers and no others. That way the pain – and there

14

would be pain, which might not simply be financial – would be limited to a few days or possibly a week. Nor would Caviglia look at the private, personal belongings which people took with them in their daily lives. He had done this once, the first time he had been reduced to thieving on the buses to make ends meet. It had made him feel dirty and dishonourable. His criminality would always be limited to stealing money from those he judged could afford it, then passing on the excess to the kind and charitable sisters near the Pantheon. As a Catholic in thought if not in deed, he was unsure whether this was sufficient to guarantee him salvation, if such a thing existed. But it certainly helped him sleep at night.

Caviglia attempted to remind himself of these facts as he wrestled with the purse in the extraordinarily narrow and confined space in which he found himself, increasingly aware that the large shot of grappa in his coffee cup had not been a good idea. Then the worst possible thing happened. The purse folded in on itself under the pressure of his clumsy fingers, turned over and spilled everything – notes, coins, credit cards and what looked like a European driving licence – straight onto the grubby toilet floor.

He lowered himself onto the seat and felt like weeping. Nothing could be left here. Every last item would have to be retrieved from the dark, grimy corners beneath the little sink, packed away again and rushed to the nearest litter bin. If a single item belonging to the woman was found, he would surely be identified by the youth behind the bar. There had been two cases against him already, occasions when his concentration had lapsed and he had tried to ply his trade in the presence of an undercover officer. A third would mean jail and with it the loss of the little apartment the two of them had shared as a couple for more than thirty years. Everything that was of value to him might disappear if he left one stray item behind on the floor of this toilet in a tiny cafe built into little more than a cave behind the Campo dei Fiori.

With a sudden determination to put the situation right he set about his work, recognizing a growing inward conviction, one he had noticed but never acknowledged before: his time as a Roman street thief was coming to an end. Tomorrow, or perhaps the day after, he would be back walking round the bakeries, looking to return to the world of early-morning heat and dust, and the fragrant smell of rising bread.

After a minute he looked at what he'd collected; there was no alternative in the circumstances. The woman's purse contained just under €400 in cash and a few coins, several membership tickets for cinema and arts clubs, three credit cards, a passport-size photo of a handsome, though unsmiling, dark-haired young man with a close-cropped beard, and, to Caviglia's shock, a single condom in a shiny silver sheath. Her driving licence gave her name as Véronique Gillet and an address in the 3ème arrondissement in Paris. The same name was also on an identity card for the Louvre Museum. She was, it said, a senior curatorial assistant in the Département des Peintures. The photograph was many years older than that on the driving licence, which showed a lovely young woman, perhaps in her student days, with shoulder-length lighter hair and a fuller, more contented face. She had an almost palpable air of happiness about her. It made his heart ache.

And you're sick, Caviglia thought immediately, feeling a stiff, cold weight of self-loathing begin to form in his stomach.

Something else had fallen out of the purse too, a small

pink plastic box, one that had puzzled him at first, and now, to his despair and mortification, was beginning to make sense.

He reached beneath the foot pedal for the water tap on the basin and retrieved it. The front had the universal emblem for medicine, a symbol Caviglia had come to know and recognize during his wife's illness. The caduceus, a kindly doctor had called it. Two serpents writhing round a winged staff. With a deepening sense of foreboding, he opened the lid. Inside was a collection of transparent foils containing tiny red pills, almost the colour of her hair, with a date and a time written precisely beneath each tablet. He peered at them. The next was to be taken at eleven thirty, just forty minutes away. And the next after that at three o'clock, then again four hours later. Whatever ailment the woman suffered from required, it seemed from the medication, six doses a day, at very exact intervals.

A small sheet of card sat next to the foils. He took it out and read there, in a very precise female hand, written in French, English, German and simple Italian, 'This medication is very important to me. If you find it, please call me on the number below, at any time. Even if I am unable to collect it, I will at least know I need to find some more. I will, naturally, be grateful.'

Aldo Caviglia leaned back on the flimsy plastic toilet seat and felt stinging tears – of rage and shame and pity – begin to burn in his eyes. The woman's face hung suspended in his memory, pale and damaged and in need. All because an idle old man would rather steal purses on the 64 bus than go out and earn an honest living.

He scooped up what he could of her belongings, gathered them into his pockets and stormed out of the cafe without pausing to utter a customary farewell. He had no phone but he knew where she was. Caviglia strode across Vittorio Emanuele without stopping, holding his arms outstretched, like a cross, like a figure in one of those church paintings he admired so much, utterly oblivious to the discordant chorus of angry horns and the stares of the astonished locals watching from the pavement.

– 3 –

No more than seven minutes later – he checked on his watch – he was in the Vicolo del Divino Amore, wondering how he could easily track her down. It was like many a city *vicolo*: narrow, dark, hostile to the outside world. Behind some of these plain doors and stone façades might lie entire mansions, busy offices, veterinary clinics or private clubs for visiting foreigners seeking female company. This was, he reminded himself, Ortaccio. But Rome's whores were no longer confined to a specific quarter on the orders of the Pope. Like all criminals, like Aldo Caviglia himself, they roamed freely, on the streets, in apartments and houses scattered throughout the city.

He strode along the dark, narrow alley, avoiding the badly parked scooters, scanning for a pencil-thin Titian-haired figure in a white gabardine coat. There was no one in the Vicolo del Divino Amore. Just dead grey buildings and the small church he half knew, locked, without a light inside, and, opposite, a long wall of plastic sheeting and scaffolding. A vague memory pricked Caviglia's imagination. The construction men were probably labouring to repair some distant part of the great Palazzo Malaspina, which sprawled through this part of the city, a vast monstrosity of Renaissance brick that was one of the last private palaces still in original hands in Rome.

This told him nothing. Without concern for the consequences, Caviglia dashed the length of the *vicolo*, then, when he reached the Piazza Borghese without seeing a thing, entered the nearest cafe, ordered a single *macchiato* out of politeness and commandeered the house phone. He fed a couple of coins into the machine and dialled the number she had given on the card, waiting as it ran through some invisible ethereal network he could not begin to imagine, from Rome to Paris and back again, finally delivering a ring tone after a good half-minute. All the while he fought to perfect his story, how he would explain what he had 'found' in the street and had immediately decided to follow her in order to return it.

But it was pointless. The ring tone went on and on. Nothing more. No message. No voice at the other end. He glanced out of the window, hoping her business was done and she might have gone on to the bright open space of the square behind the palace of the family that had once been known as the Borgias. She could be anywhere. If the pills were so important she should surely have left some answering service on her phone.

Except, Caviglia reminded himself, she was ill. Sick people, as he knew only too well, lacked logic sometimes. Towards the end they lacked any concept of care for themselves at all.

'Signora . . .' he said, to the woman behind the counter, then described the French woman in detail, thinking, as he did, of the way she was dressed, which was not casual, but careful, the kind of clothes a woman would wear for a business appointment. Or a date.

Nothing happens quickly in Roman cafes. The formidable middle-aged figure behind the counter discussed the possibilities with her husband, who was making panini for the lunchtime rush, with an elderly pensioner loitering over a cappuccino, then a workman in grubby blue overalls at the end of the bar, and finally three women gossiping over cakes.

Caviglia listened, feeling miserable. No one had seen a flame-haired pencil-slim woman in a pale coat and scarlet skirt.

'Why was your friend here?' the woman asked. 'We don't see many tourists . . .'

He thought of the identity card.

'She's in the art business. I think she had an appointment perhaps. Is there a dealer nearby? Or a painter?'

'You've missed the painters by four hundred years,' the woman laughed. 'They all lived here once, you know. Caravaggio had a place . . .'

'Where?' he asked immediately, for no good reason.

'It was a long time ago. Who knows?'

The old man at the end of the bar raised a skinny finger.

'There *is* a studio, though,' he said.

'What are you talking about, Enzo?' she barked at him. '*We* can barely afford to live here any more. How could some painter manage the rent?'

'I don't know. But he does. Opposite the church. The green door before all that damned – ' he stopped and stared at the workman at this point – 'noisy building work down there.'

The man in the blue overalls finished his coffee and laughed.

'If Franco Malaspina's offering money, do you think I should turn him down? How often does *that* happen?'

The pensioner tapped the side of his nose, ignoring the

question. 'I've seen artist types going in there. Brushes. A canvas. That I-am-so-much-smarter-than-you look all those arty-farty queers have.' He drew in a long, asthmatic breath to make one final point. 'They wear black all winter *and* summer long too.'

'Green door,' Caviglia repeated, and was out into the street immediately.

Sure enough, opposite the church was a flimsy wooden entrance the colour of cemetery grass, not to a house or office, but to a narrow alley, no more than two metres wide, running alongside what he took to be some rear extension to the Palazzo Malaspina. The door was unlocked. He walked through. The sunlight deserted him. It was cold and damp in this stone and brick slit cut between an ancient mansion and some nondescript building that could have been anything: a home, an office or simply some cheap storage place for the busy city centre half a kilometre away.

There was a single obstacle at the end: a bright shiny metal security door, the kind used to protect warehouses and places worth looting. Not expecting anything, his head in a whirl, knowing he was running short of options and ever more desperate to return the purse and the drugs, Caviglia strode purposefully forward and tugged on the handle.

To his surprise, it slid easily on silent runners, disappearing behind the wall to the right. Inside was darkness, a sea of black so unmarked by any visible feature it surely betokened a space of some size. He blinked, walked in and reached around both sides of the wall, hunting for a light switch, finding nothing. After a moment his eyes began to adjust. In the distance to the right he could just make out a slender line of yellow light, the kind of illumination that might fall beneath a distant door leading off to one side.

Aldo Caviglia felt for the woman's belongings in his pocket, seeking, with no good reason, some kind of reassurance from them. Then he edged gingerly forward into the gloom, hands in front in order to detect any high obstacle, hoping his feet wouldn't encounter anything low and hidden on the floor.

He was, he judged, halfway to the door when he heard her. The voice – high, pained, stretched by such an agony he could not begin to imagine what caused it – drifted through the damp, fusty air of the black space before him, pulsing with an exact and heart-rending rhythm, not that of a breath, but a blow of some kind, a persistent, continuous attack which drew from her a long, harrowing cry as if she were being tortured.

Wild, formless fears rose in Caviglia's head. He pressed on, more determined than ever, stumbling over stray bricks, feeling the right-hand wall to keep himself upright, watching the diagonal slant of light grow larger with each tentative, trembling step. There was a smell to the place too, organic, sweet and a little rotten.

Her repetitive, rasping sighs increased, in pitch and rhythm and volume. Through the wordless stream of anguish and stress there began to ring a single comprehensible word, spoken in French, the first consonant soft and breathy, the final silent, sounds so unlike the Italian.

'Jésus . . . Jésus . . . *Jésus* . . .'

He reached the stripe of yellow, unable to guess what might lie beyond. Some young thug bent upon rape? A vengeful lover turned violent? Madness in a dark and narrow urban street, unseen, unheard by passers-by, for whom this was simply another ordinary day?

Without thinking, Aldo Caviglia found himself shouting too, not knowing what he said, anxious, above all, to drown out the sound of her voice from his head, since it disturbed him greatly, in ways he could not fully comprehend.

'*Stop, stop, STOP!*' he screamed, throwing open the door, entering the room, glad that he had finally found a word to which he could pin some logical thread of thought.

It was bright in there. An artist's studio, as the pensioner in the cafe had said. An array of easels stood around a room that resembled a dusty, jumbled-up warehouse in which pots of paint had exploded in all directions and with extraordinary force. Colours ran everywhere: blues and blacks, reds and yellows, in golden streaks and white, white puddles, spattering the high brick walls, the floors and even the dusty, pale ceiling. Rays of winter daylight fell through the single long, grimy window. He wished it had never bothered.

Caviglia had to force himself to see through the bright, insane confusion there in order to work out what was happening, where the French woman, in her distress, might be. The moment he entered her screaming had ceased, instantly, in a way that was, he hoped, linked with his arrival, not some other dread event.

Finally, the sea of disparate, swirling pigment ceased to churn in front of his eyes and he saw her. Saw *them*.

They lay like a single conjoined beast in front of a large, brilliant canvas which served as a backdrop for their exertions, and was so bright, so full of some strange simulacrum of life, that he was unable, at that moment, to understand what he was seeing.

– 4 –

Véronique Gillet was stretched out naked, a thin pale skeleton of a figure on a dark red velvet chaise-longue drawn up beneath the painting, which itself seemed to feature some similar, though more bulky, nude form. Her head rested on the single raised arm of the sofa's head, lolling, inanimate. Her legs were loosely entwined around the torso of a standing man who wore a creased and bloodied red shirt and was positioned in front of her waist, still moving forwards at the hip with a dying, measured motion Caviglia now recognized as the cadence of her diminishing sighs.

The man's expression was crazed, that of an animal fixed on its prey, mindless, intent on one thing only.

Her face was turned towards Caviglia and the door, not out of some deliberate intent, he thought, but simply because that was the way her head had fallen. The eyes of Véronique Gillet were no longer the vivid, attentive grey of an exotic feline. They were dead and glassy. Her bright red hair was matted with sweat, so much that it clung tightly to her skull. Her attacker's hand held a knife tight to her throat, where it had drawn a dark red line, lazy and curving, out from her collarbone towards the base of her neck.

Caviglia ran forward, yelling, screaming, shouting as loudly as he could in the hope that someone in the street beyond would hear and come to his aid. Still, he was unable to concentrate on the point where his attention ought to lie – the man, the animal, the murderer – because his mind would not leave two incandescent burning points of visual focus in front of him.

He tripped on something, a can of paint perhaps, and stumbled to the hard floor, cracking the side of his skull hard on the ancient flagstones. The sweet stench of decay seemed to be everywhere, rising in his nostrils, filling his head with nonsense.

In these moments strange thoughts are born. He recalled what the woman in the cafe had said about the artists who had lived in this neighbourhood. Among them Caravaggio, who had painted so many vivid depictions of life and death in Rome: St Peter on the cross in Santa Maria del Popolo; David with the dangling head of Goliath in the Villa Borghese, where Caviglia would direct tourists looking for some peace in the city on a hot summer day. And the martyrdom of St Matthew, in his own Church of San Luigi dei Francesi, no more than a few minutes' walk from where he now scrabbled on a dusty, paint-strewn floor, trying to make sense of the nightmare that had risen from the dark Roman gutter to despoil this lustrous festival of the Immaculate Conception, when no one should have thoughts for anything but life and the world, children and the future, the coming shift of the season with its subtle, eternal metamorphosis from dark to light.

He blinked and when he opened his eyes again they were fixed, unfailingly, on the painting, unable to look anywhere else. What he saw made him catch his breath.

This was, in some cryptic, unknowable way, the very scene he'd just witnessed. The woman there, naked, surrounded by figures who attended to her in ways which were both loving yet inimical too, was gasping, through lips that were full and rosy and fleshy, brimming over with life.

The picture possessed a frightful beauty, one which burned so brightly that, once witnessed, could never be unseen.

Something real intervened in his view. The figure – Véronique Gillet's lover or murderer or both – had disentangled himself from her torso. He now stood above Aldo Caviglia. The bloody knife was in his hand, something the old, disgraced baker understood fully, without needing to look.

There was no point in fleeing the inevitable. He set his gaze on the canvas, marvelling at the full figure there, painted with such care and beauty and exactitude it was surely the work of a master. Her flesh seemed to pulse with warmth and blood, even on the point of an ecstatic epiphany so real, so violent it might take away the last, precious vestige of life itself.

'Be quick,' Aldo Caviglia murmured, and, against all instinct in the presence of such savage wonder, screwed his eyes tightly shut, waiting, one last, taut breath held close inside.

Part 2

THE VICOLO DEL
DIVINO AMORE

– 1 –

Gianni Peroni didn't fit in a bunny suit. He wandered round the overcrowded storeroom looking faintly obscene, the white plastic overall clinging tightly to his large frame, its colour almost the same shade as his face. He was angry too, and willing to make this plain to anyone who came in close proximity, from Inspector Leo Falcone down.

It was now mid-afternoon, two hours since the Questura got the call about suspicious cries coming from the address in the Vicolo del Divino Amore. A routine visit by a uniformed officer had rapidly escalated into a full-blown murder inquiry, with Falcone deputed to lead the team. It was, Nic Costa felt, a little like old times. Teresa Lupo and her chief morgue monkey, Silvio Di Capua, were poring over two bodies, both the apparent victims of violent attacks. Scene of crime officers were starting to pick their way around a room that looked like a forensic team's nightmare: spatters of wild colour, blood and dirt and dust were everywhere, on the floor, on the walls, on the grubby tables and chairs. It seemed much like an artist's studio. There were easels and used pots of paint, some commercial household brands, some artistic. There

31

was also what appeared to be a substantial canvas some way behind the two bodies positioned on the floor, now outlined by white chalk, and tended by Teresa and her team of acolytes. Costa knew that he would have to see that before he left, but for now he would leave it as it was, hidden under a green velvet coverlet so large it draped down both back and front, obscuring it from view entirely.

Some things had changed, though.

'Sovrintendente.'

Falcone's voice echoed clear and commanding in the cold empty space. Costa daydreamed. He'd spoken to Emily on the journey over. She was in a class at the architectural school in the Piazza Borghese, no more than two minutes' walk away. Costa had mentioned his destination, though not the purpose. From the warm, inquisitive tone of her voice he knew what she'd do: walk down into the narrow, dark lane and try to take a look for herself. She still hankered after law enforcement, even though her architectural career seemed about to blossom, thanks to an internship with one of the city's largest partnerships.

'Sovrintendente,' Falcone repeated, more loudly.

The old inspector was now almost fully recovered from a recent gunshot wound. He had a slight limp, little more. Inside the Questura, Falcone was, if not the top dog, a substantial intellectual force once more, the officer to whom the awkward cases fell. He was also a man at peace with himself again, apparently happily alone after a short, odd romantic entanglement. And, like Peroni and Teresa, utterly delighted to have attended the brief civil marriage ceremony at which Costa and Emily Deacon became man and wife three months ago to this day.

The senior officer leaned over and whispered into Costa's ear, 'Nic!'

'I'm sorry,' Costa found himself stuttering.

It had been a remarkable year. The tragedy of a child lost in a miscarriage, a wedding and then, returning to the Questura the previous Monday, discovering his promotion had come through while he and Emily were on a too-brief weekend break in Sicily.

'Sir,' he added.

'And so you should be,' Falcone complained. 'Your vacation is over, Officer. Pay attention, please.'

While he spoke, Falcone was watching Gianni Peroni fulminate by the side of the two bodies, spitting complaints in the direction of anyone within earshot. The inspector was wondering perhaps what the big man, once an inspector himself, was making of his partner's rise through the ranks. It was certainly a subject which had occupied Costa's thoughts since he returned to work, and one he had to discuss with Peroni, soon.

'What would you do in my shoes?' Falcone asked, eyes sparking with interest, hand on his trim silver beard.

'Seal the room and keep it sealed,' Costa said instantly.

Falcone nodded.

'Why?' he asked.

'It's going to take days before forensic manage to sweep this place properly. It's a mess. We'll need to bring in experts we don't know about at the moment, and if that's to mean anything we must make sure there is no unnecessary disturbance. Also . . .'

He glanced at the manpower crammed into the cramped and jumbled space around them. There were thirteen people there, including two photographers and three civilians from the media department, two of them trainees, who were preparing what to say to the press and TV. Only seven people were serving police officers. This seemed to be the way of things lately. The investigative process was becoming muddied, mired in procedure, dictated more by lawyers on occasion than the need for the fast, clear discovery of facts and culpability.

'I think we need to keep the numbers down as much as possible. There's a lot of material in here. I know everyone's careful. But all the same . . .'

The inspector grimaced.

'We do these things by rote these days, Sovrintendente. The first act, always, is to pick up the manual and read what it says. You're right . . .'

Having little truck with politeness, the inspector brusquely ordered the media team to get out and watched them slink towards the door, casting mute and furious glances in their wake. Then he folded his long arms and glanced towards the two corpses in front of him, a thoughtful finger momentarily stroking his silver goatee, a familiar expression of wry amusement in his angular, tanned face.

'On the other hand,' he added with nonchalant ease, 'it would appear to be a relatively straightforward matter.'

A man of late middle age, wearing a smart suit and an expression frozen halfway between horror and simple mute fury, lay curled on his side, clutching his stomach, gripping himself in the taut, terrified agony of a vicious death. The black wooden shaft of what Costa suspected would turn out to be a large kitchen knife protruded from beneath his ribcage, staining his white shirt with a ragged patch of dark, congealing blood. Next to him was the naked corpse of a much younger woman, so thin her ribcage was showing.

The contrast between the two was marked. The woman's face, which had a still, bloodless beauty that transcended life, was almost peaceful. She lay on her back, legs slightly raised and akimbo, in a position that could, possibly, have been post-coital. She had short fiery red hair, which was disarrayed, as if by some kind of violence, and somewhat greasy, maybe from sweat. There was a wound to her throat, perhaps a hand's span long and probably from a knife, logically the same one that killed the man. The cut ran down towards her breastbone, though it was not deep, it seemed to Costa, since there was much less blood than appeared on the shirt of the other victim. Her pale grey eyes, like those of her apparent attacker, were wide open, though much more distended, as if through some kind of medical condition. They stared fixedly at the ceiling in an unwavering gaze.

Her lips were a cold shade of blue, starting to resemble the same dull tone he could see in her dead eyes.

'He didn't do it,' Peroni insisted.

'He?' Falcone asked.

'He,' the big man responded, stabbing a fat finger in the air. 'Aldo Caviglia. I've put him in court once for stealing on the buses. I've warned him twice too. He's a petty thief. A sad, confused little guy. He steals . . .' Peroni looked pale. He was never happy around death. 'He *stole* wallets for a living, for God's sake. The last time I caught him he promised he'd give up.'

Costa noticed something about the dead man's appearance: a bulge in his jacket. He knelt down beside Teresa Lupo, receiving a warning glance from the pathologist along the way.

'Touch nothing without my permission,' she warned.

'The pocket?'

She looked, saw what he was getting at, then reached into the man's jacket and withdrew, in her gloved fingers, a woman's expensive leather purse.

Peroni swore.

'Sometimes people lie, Gianni,' Teresa said. 'It's shocking, I know. But at least . . .'

She was sifting through the contents and dropping each item one by one into an evidence bag.

'He's given you some ID for her.'

Teresa stood up and showed them the card. The three men read it.

'French,' she said. 'Might have known.'

'Why?' Falcone asked immediately.

'You really don't notice much about women, do you, Leo? Alive or dead? She's wearing mascara, so beautifully applied I can't quite believe it. She still has perfect make-up, despite all that's happened here. The only other thing she has on are a couple of diamond earrings too beautiful for most of us to contemplate. Also . . .'

The pathologist nodded towards some large white bags beneath the paint-stained window.

'She was wearing a winter outfit that must have cost a fortune. And the shoes. In this weather. I ask you. This was not someone out for a day's sightseeing, I can tell you that. She was dressed up for an occasion. A job interview. A date.'

'Were the clothes torn?' Costa asked.

'Not in the slightest,' Teresa said. 'They were folded up nice and neatly, the way you do before you go to bed.'

She glanced again at the card.

'Perhaps she was doing business on behalf of the Louvre.'

Falcone coughed into his fist.

'Sorry, sorry,' she added. 'That's your job, isn't it?'

'Very much so,' Falcone agreed. 'Did they have sex?'

Teresa got up, placed the card in the evidence bag, passed it to Di Capua and frowned at the sight of the dead Caviglia on the floor.

'These two? No. I am guessing here. I'll tell you more later, once we have them back in the morgue. But some sneaking feminine intuition tells me that couples who expire post-copulation rarely do so with one partner naked and the other fully dressed and looking like he's going to an interview with the bank manager. Even his zip's done up, Leo. Think it through for yourself.'

'She *is* naked,' Costa pointed out.

'I said "they" didn't do it. She did. Quite rough, though not necessarily rape, I'd venture. There's minimal bruising. Unprotected, though. I'll have your DNA sample ready first thing in the morning. A good dinner says it isn't that of our light-fingered friend here. Nor,' she added quickly, 'do I think she killed him. It's just meant to look that way, and not well orchestrated either. Someone was in a hurry. Look at the details. She's on the floor. And there's a perfectly good chaise-longue over there. Why would they get down to it here? We would also have to assume that she killed him first, then expired herself. Remarkable in itself, and even more so if she then managed to lie down flat, quite unclothed, on a cold stone floor, all ready for the grave. No—'

Falcone held up a lean, tanned hand, demanding silence.

'Enough,' he said quietly. 'Leave us something to do. Please. Clearly we are meant to believe something here.'

'Aldo Caviglia couldn't hurt a fly,' Peroni insisted. 'Why would someone pick on a poor old soul like him?'

'That's what we're supposed to find out,' Costa said automatically, and was shocked that it sounded like an admonition.

'Thank you,' Peroni said quietly. 'Sir.'

'Blue lips,' Costa murmured, ignoring him.

Teresa was staring at the dead woman's face, interested, but worried also, it seemed to Costa, by the distance there had to be between a *sovrintendente* and an *agente* who was more than twenty years his senior.

'Quite,' she said. 'Do you notice the smell?'

Costa imagined they all had and put it down to the presence of death.

'I thought this whole place smelled bad,' he said. 'Drains.'

She grimaced, as if she'd missed something important.

'It does stink, you're right. But she has a particular smell. A little like sweaty socks, in case you're too polite to say.'

'Is it unusual?' he asked.

'Not around any cops I know,' she answered. 'But on a woman like this?'

Watched by Falcone, Costa knelt down and leaned over the corpse. It was obvious: direct and pungent.

'It takes an hour or so to degrade that much,' Teresa said.

'What does?' Falcone demanded.

'Amyl nitrate.'

'A sex drug?' Costa asked, astonished.

'Hold on there,' she cautioned. 'Amyl nitrate is a very useful pharmaceutical in the right circumstances.' She was staring directly at Costa, challenging him to think. 'It's relief for angina. And emergency revival in heart cases.'

'Blue lips,' he said again.

'Quite.'

She was grinning.

'No wonder you promoted him, Leo.'

Falcone sighed.

'So this woman died of a heart attack,' he said. 'During sex? And the drug was there either for stimulation or to revive her?'

'I am merely a pathologist,' Teresa replied. She held out a hand. Peroni took it and helped her to her feet. 'If I'm to help you with the rest I need to get these two out of here and safe and warm to my lair. We have everything we're going to get in situ. Silvio can stay behind and supervise the rest. I want her medical history from Paris for one thing. You don't mind if we handle that?'

'No,' the inspector said, nodding. 'Just the medical side. You agree?'

'Of course,' she concurred, smiling pleasantly.

'I told you he didn't do it!' Peroni pointed out.

She smiled and patted his arm.

'So you did. Good for you.'

'He stole her wallet, though,' Falcone added. 'He came here for some reason. He saw something . . .'

The room had gone quiet. The other officers who'd been working alongside the forensic team waited, except for two of them who seemed to be lifting some loose masonry close to the rotting iron window.

'Perhaps he saw this,' Costa suggested. Then, unable to wait any more, he walked over to the large easel behind the corpses and, very carefully, removed the green velvet drape, exposing the canvas there.

Not a word was uttered for a good half a minute. Not a breath even, it seemed.

'Perhaps he did,' Teresa whispered, breaking the silence.

No one could take their eyes off the painting. Even the presence of two corpses, one clearly murdered, the other dead through strange and suspicious circumstances, did nothing to distract their attention from the canvas at that moment.

Falcone walked over to join Costa, his gaze fixed on the shining naked form, three-quarters life-size, in front of them.

'I need to know who owns this property,' the inspector ordered. 'I want Caviglia checked with the rape unit just in case. Sovrintendente?'

Costa was lost in the swirl of the painted flesh, the extraordinary expression on the subject's face, and the entire artfulness of the work, with its stylistic flourishes, the names of which came back to him from the lost years when he'd spent most of his endless, empty free time in the city's galleries. *Sfumato, chiaroscuro, tenebrismo* . . .

'*Sovrintendente!*' Falcone repeated, unamused this time.

'We need to find an art specialist as well,' Costa replied eventually, finally able to turn his attention away from the painting. 'And good security.'

'This is a murder scene,' Falcone snapped. 'Of course we need good security.'

'I'm not an expert. But this is either a genuine and unknown Caravaggio, or an excellent attempt to forge one. Either way, I think . . .'

Falcone glowered at the canvas. Since Costa had

unveiled it there hadn't been a moment's activity in the room.

'The painting can wait,' the inspector grumbled, then strode over to the easel and roughly dragged the green velvet drape back across the frame and the tantalizing figure of the woman.

'Sir?'

It was one of the pair who had been working by the window. He looked shocked and a little pale. The three men went over to look.

The officers had laid out what they'd found. It was a collection of photographs. Costa picked up a couple of them.

'These didn't get printed in any lab,' he said. 'This is cheap, thin paper. The kind you use at home on a printer.'

Peroni leaned over his shoulder.

'No lab is going to develop those now, are they?' he observed.

'Where did you find them?' Falcone asked.

'There was a loose flagstone beneath the window,' one of the officers replied. 'We just looked. These are just a few. There must be fifty or more in there.'

'Keep looking,' Falcone ordered, then took the photos and spread them out on a dusty chair.

Costa stared at the images on the flimsy, home-made prints. It was clear that they had been taken in this very room. There was the same stone floor. In places he could see splashes of paint, and even a pot and a brush. In one single picture there was the corner of the green drape used for the canvas they'd uncovered too.

There was the link. Every photo portrayed the upper torso of a naked woman. Most of them looked foreign.

Some were black, with the overblown hair and excessive make-up of the African hookers who worked the suburbs.

It was impossible to judge the expressions on their faces. It could have been rapture, sexual or spiritual. Or pain in the final moments of life.

He turned to Peroni, who knew vice intimately and before his indiscretion had been one of the most effective inspectors working the illicit sex scene in Rome.

'Do you know any of them, Gianni?' Costa asked.

'What the hell is that supposed to mean?' Peroni roared.

Costa cursed his own stupidity. The big man's career had collapsed because once – just once – he'd slept with a vice girl himself.

'I'm sorry. I phrased that very badly. You worked vice for many years, and very well indeed,' Costa explained patiently. 'I think these women look like hookers. But if you thought so too it would mean a lot more.'

Peroni sighed, then shrugged apologetically.

'They look like hookers.' He glanced back at the body of the French woman, now surrounded by attendants making the body bag ready. 'She doesn't, though. She . . .'

Peroni stared at the photos again. Then he picked one of them up in his gloved hand.

It was a muscular black woman with a head of long hair, artificially straightened and glossy. She seemed to be trying very hard to look as if she was in the throes of ecstasy. All the women in the photographs did.

'I've booked her,' Peroni said. 'Nigerian. Quite a nice kid.'

He stared out of the grimy window for a moment. Then he spoke again.

'She's on the missing persons list. Has been for a few weeks. I saw it on the board. I recognized . . .'

Falcone was cursing under his breath again, and this time Costa was sure there was something specific behind his reaction.

Then, before he could ask, there was a brief pained scream from the team raising the flagstones. Costa looked at the men. They were standing back from the area on which they were working. The blood had drained from their faces entirely. One of them looked ready to throw up.

Falcone was there first, even with the limp. He took one look at what was emerging from beneath the damp, algaed stone.

'Doctor,' he said, just loudly enough to bring Teresa Lupo to his side. Costa and Peroni moved forward to look. Then the big man swore and walked away.

Something wrapped tightly in semi-transparent plastic, like a gigantic artificial cocoon, was emerging from the grey, damp earth beneath the solid floor of the studio. Costa glanced at it and started to walk, rapidly, around the room. There were several areas where the grey flagstones appeared to have been moved recently, sometimes hidden by paint pots, sometimes by empty easels or furniture.

When he got back to Falcone, Teresa Lupo was hovering over the discovery with a scalpel in her hand.

'I don't think this will be pretty, I'm afraid,' she said firmly. 'Those of a delicate nature should retire now.'

Costa stayed and watched. He and Falcone were the only police officers who did. The face beneath the plastic was grey and dirty, and, in spite of the substantial period that must have passed since she was killed, undoubtedly that of the Nigerian woman Peroni had recognized. The stench that rose the moment Teresa made the incision would, he thought, live with him for a long time.

'I don't think she's alone,' Costa said, catching Falcone's eye, realizing, to his dismay, that the old inspector did not, for some reason, appear to be surprised. 'We have to—'

There was a sound from outside. Not in the alley, somewhere else. Costa glanced behind the painting. There was a dusty door there, beyond an ancient dining table covered in paint stains, half hidden behind some old sackcloth drapes. It was ajar.

'He's still here,' Costa muttered, mainly to himself, as he leapt the table and headed for whatever lay beyond, out in the cold grey day.

It was a courtyard of a kind, a messy place of junk: old wooden cases, discarded furniture, a couple of tall metal filing cabinets rusting to nothing on the green cobblestones. A man could easily hide here. A single narrow corridor, dank with moss and decay, led off in the far corner, inwards, through the heart of whatever greater building – the Palazzo Malaspina, Costa's memory wanted to tell him – sprawled across this hidden enclave of the city, then, he assumed, onto the street. And freedom.

Falcone was barking orders into his radio, demanding immediate action from the officers outside in the *vicolo*. Costa wanted to tell him this narrow, malodorous alley didn't run that way. It burrowed deep into the labyrinthine palace itself. Stumbling out into the grey daylight of the yard, he could hear the crush of bodies behind him, Peroni's voice in the lead, above the tense chatter of men working themselves into the state of mind that went with a pursuit.

Costa stopped and took his bearings, thinking. Why would a murderer wait so close to the scene?

Some did. Some couldn't resist it.

One of the officers who'd found the buried corpse appeared at his side. With the automatic instinct that seemed to come with the job for some, he'd taken out his gun and was now holding it in front, uncertainly, wavering between a couple of the high filing cabinets, an obvious place for someone to hide, and a pile of old furniture near the wall.

Costa pushed down the barrel of the weapon.

'No guns,' he insisted. 'It could just be a kid.'

And that was a stupid thing to say, he thought. Kids wouldn't mess around places like this. It was all too dark and dank and scary, particularly if you peeked in the windows and saw what was going on inside, beneath the placid gaze of that naked woman on the canvas.

The grimy yard was at least ten metres on each side, and half of it filled with material, some of it looking as if it had been thrown there years ago. The surrounding building rose a good six storeys high, past grimy barred windows, a line of scarred, black brick leading to the leaden December sky, filled, at that moment, by a flock of swirling starlings.

Costa looked up and didn't see a single face at any of the rain-streaked panes of near-opaque glass in the storeys above. Then he stared down the long narrow corridor leading to God knows what. It was empty, and towards the end turned into a tunnel, a pool of darkness formed by the overhanging building above. A tiny square of dim daylight was just visible at the end. There wasn't time for a man to escape them so quickly, surely. Nor could he have got there without making a sound.

'Assume he's here,' he said quietly. 'We'll go through the junk piece by piece until we find something or he moves. Assume—'

There was a voice. Peroni was bellowing. Behind a rotting wooden desk, its metal legs like skeletal limbs made of rust, was the shadow of a figure, crouching, only the shoulders, torso and legs visible.

Something struck Costa the moment he saw it. The man wasn't trembling. He was as still and calm as a statue.

'You have to come out of there,' Costa said calmly, walking forward, signalling to the officer with the revolver to keep it trained down towards the stones just in case.

'Sovrintendente,' Falcone yelled.

Costa ignored him and continued walking forward.

'You need to come out now, sir,' he added in a voice he hoped was low on threat but brooked no argument. 'This is a crime scene and we have to talk to you.'

The figure was no more than three or four strides away. He didn't move.

'Start moving,' Peroni bellowed.

Costa glanced back at the men behind him. Falcone was silent now. It wasn't like him.

'Out!' the big man roared, and that did it. The long dark form – the intruder was dressed in dark khaki, some kind of military-style top and trousers, with black boots tied tight around the ankle, just like a soldier – was starting to move.

'Stand by the wall,' Costa ordered. 'Hands above you. This is just a routine matter. Just a . . .'

He didn't go on. The figure had worked its way free, with an agile athleticism that gave Costa pause for thought. He still couldn't see a face. Just a long, lithe body, muscular and fit, at ease in the anonymous military clothing.

'Damn it,' Falcone shouted, pushing his way through the crowd of officers jamming the free space in the courtyard. 'This is my investigation, Costa. You do what I tell you.'

'Sir . . .' he said, and watched the figure in khaki emerge from behind the rotting folded carcass of a mattress, pink and grey stripes hanging down in ragged tatters from the burst mouldy body.

The man wore a black, full-face gas mask with a glass eye shield that revealed nothing at all. He had a repeating shotgun in his right hand, held tight, with a professional deliberation, and, in his left, some kind of canister that was already beginning to smoke at the handle.

'Weapons!' Falcone cried.

Costa wasn't really listening. Sometimes these things came too late. The smoking canister was already spinning in their direction, turning in the air, releasing a curling line of pale fumes that carried before it the disgusting, noxious smell Costa knew from the last riot he'd had the privilege to attend.

The thing burst with a soft explosion and a dense white cloud enveloped them. Coughing, eyes streaming, he possessed just enough mind to stumble clear, down towards where he expected the exit corridor to be, eyes tight shut, a handkerchief clutched across his mouth and nose.

Gasping for clean air, aware of the curses and screeches of the men trapped in the noxious fumes behind him, Costa was sure of one thing: Falcone would haul him over the coals for the way he had handled this particular encounter. Perhaps with good cause.

Then, as he half knelt, half fell against the grubby courtyard wall, something brushed his shoulder.

He looked up. The khaki figure was standing there, still in his mask, which hid, Costa guessed, a broad, self-satisfied smile.

The shotgun was pointed directly into Costa's face, the barrel no more than a hand's length away.

Costa coughed, tried to look the man in the eye and said, 'You're under arrest.'

Then he watched, feeling a little baffled and not, for a single moment, frightened.

Nothing happened. Costa looked again. Somehow the fabric of his would-be killer's military gloves had got caught up in the gap between the trigger and the metal guard, preventing the firing of the weapon through nothing more than a shred of fabric and luck. It was a small and temporary thing to keep a man alive, but Costa wasn't much minded to think on it. Instead he kicked out hard with his right leg and caught the individual painfully on the shin. The shotgun tilted up towards the sky and fired, with an explosive screech that rebounded round the black brick and sprayed hot pellets through the air. A soft lead rain dappled the ground around him.

Then the gas returned, and this time it was in his eyes, stinging like wounds from a million crazed bees, sending tears streaming down his cheeks, bile rising in his throat.

Costa swore. Behind him men were screaming. He rolled out of the smoke haze drifting his way and saw the long, brown-clad figure disappearing down the corridor, into the dark pool of shadow, towards the grey patch of light at the end.

With an aching reluctance, he lurched down the slippery cobblestones, coughing, choking, realizing there was no one from the team behind in much of a state to help him.

The memory of the shotgun barrel poking in his face burned as badly as the tear gas. He took one more look down the corridor. Whoever it was had got a good head start on them all.

The military form emerged from the shadows and fell into the bright light at the distant wall, then stopped, turned, ripped off the gas mask, hitched the shotgun up to his shoulder and stared back at him.

He wore a black military hood beneath, the kind the anti-terrorist people wore, tight black cotton with two tiny slits for eyeholes. It was too far to take a worthwhile shot from this distance. The man was, surely, making some kind of point.

Costa watched as the hood contorted around the mouth, the lips closed, then formed a perfect 'O', and those distant hands closed round the trigger.

Somehow he could hear the single word he was mouthing, even though that was impossible.

Boom, the man said, and then laughed.

What happened next came so naturally Costa didn't even have to think about it. He ripped the service pistol out of his shoulder holster, took some vague aim down the brick corridor ahead and let loose four rounds in rapid succession.

The figure in khaki had fallen back against the wall, twitching and shrieking in a way that Costa, against his own instincts, found satisfying.

But it wasn't a wound. It was shock and fear and some kind of outrage that he should be a target in the first place. The man hauled himself to his feet and dashed a vicious glance back down the alley before he stumbled to the right and out of sight. But at least the brief moment of fear Costa had instilled in him redressed the balance a little.

Without waiting to see what condition the others were

in, he dashed towards the brick tunnel ahead, lurching like a sick man, holding the weapon loose and impotent by his side, dimly aware he had only a couple of rounds left in it now, against a furious, murderous individual with a repeating shotgun who was surely about to try to bury himself inside the middle of Rome on a busy holiday afternoon.

There was no time to radio for assistance. He wasn't sure he had the voice to make the call anyway. All Costa could do was run and, with the old skills he still retained from his marathon days, he found that rhythm almost instantly.

When he emerged from the cold black overhang of the building at the end of the passageway he blinked at the sunlight, and the location. He was now just round the corner from the Piazza Borghese. As he squinted his stinging eyes against the sudden sun, he saw a khaki figure limping towards the square, then took three good breaths of city air, as clean as it could get.

Inside his jacket his phone was ringing. He recognized the special, individual tone. It was Emily calling. She'd have to wait.

– 3 –

The rain had left the cobblestones of the Piazza Borghese greasy and black. This was one of the few open spaces between the Corso and the river. Every day hundreds came here to park, leaving vehicles everywhere: cars and vans, motorbikes and scooters. A few students from the nearby colleges were gathered in one corner, arms full of books and work folders, laughing, getting ready for lunch. He couldn't see anyone of interest, no athletic, brown-clad figure with a shotgun anywhere. Just a few shoppers and office workers walking the damp pavement.

Costa scanned the square, wondering where a fugitive might run in this part of Rome. There were so many places. South towards the Pantheon and the Piazza Navona was a labyrinth of narrow alleys that could hide a hundred fleeing killers. West lay the bridge over the river, the Ponte Cavour, and escape into the plain business streets beyond the Palace of Justice. And both north and east . . . street after street of shops, apartment blocks and anonymous offices. He didn't know where to begin.

There would be backup soon. The officers from the studio, Gianni Peroni, a furious Falcone.

Costa took one last good look around him and sighed.

Then the phone rang again. That familiar tone again. This time he answered it.

'May I take it you're hunting for a gentleman wearing a Rambo outfit, a very suspicious-looking expression, and trying, rather poorly, to hide the fact he's got a rifle or something on his person?' she asked.

Once an FBI agent, always an FBI agent.

'Just tell me where,' Costa ordered quietly, seriously.

'I've followed him to the Mausoleum of Augustus. I could be wrong but I think he may be headed down into the grounds. Good place to hide, among all those bums.'

Costa knew the monument, though not well. Roman emperors got mixed deals when it came to their heritage. Hadrian's mausoleum turned into the Castel Sant'-Angelo. Augustus, one of the most powerful emperors Rome had ever known, came off much worse. His burial site had been everything from a pleasure garden to an opera house over the centuries. Now, after Mussolini laid waste to it in preparation for his own tomb, one he never came to occupy, it was a sad wreck of stone set in its own rough green moat of grass, half hidden between the 1930s Fascist offices set behind the Corso and the high embankment by the Tiber. The scrubby city grass was a favourite sleeping place for local tramps. The interior was a warren of dank, crumbling tunnels, so unsafe the public had been barred years ago.

'Thanks,' he said. 'Now go get a coffee. Somewhere a long way away.'

He didn't wait for an answer. He started running north, towards the river. There was building work everywhere. The authorities were creating a new home for the Ara Pacis, the altar of peace, one of the great legacies of Augustus, and a sight that had been withheld from Rome and the world for too long. But for now the area was a mess of construction work: cranes and closed roads, angry traffic and baffled pedestrians wondering where the pavement had gone.

He rounded a vast hoarding advertising the new Ara Pacis building and found himself facing the southern side of the mausoleum, with its locked entrance and steps leading down to the interior. It looked more dismal and decrepit than he remembered: a rotting circle of once golden stone falling into stumps at the summit, crowned by grass and weeds and stray shrubbery. A couple of tourists hovered near the padlocked gate, wondering whether to take photos. Beyond the railing Costa could see a bunch of itinerants huddled around the familiar objects that went with homeless life in the city: bottles of wine, mounds of old clothing and a vast collection of supermarket carrier bags stuffed full of belongings.

Then, as he was about to dial in for assistance, his eyes came upon something worryingly familiar: a blonde woman in a long black winter coat. Emily was beyond the railings, just inside the mausoleum grounds. Costa briefly closed his eyes and murmured, 'Wonderful.'

His wife was sitting on the wall of a weed-riddled flower bed just the other side of the tourists, trying to look like a visitor who'd plucked up the courage to vault the fence. And, to his eyes, doing a very bad job of it. She was too animated, too interested, to be genuinely absorbed by the miserable sight in front of her. As he was realizing this, she turned, caught sight of him, nodded down towards the green ditch in front of her and mouthed a single word: 'Here.'

At that moment a vast lorry bearing construction equipment roared in front of him and stopped with a sudden deliberation that meant, Costa knew instantly, it wasn't moving any further. He dashed round the rear, a long way, heart pumping, found the temporary barrier for the works by the very side of the Ara Pacis, taking out his gun, reminding himself there were now just two shots in the magazine, and probably no time to hope to reload on the move.

When he rounded the timber hoardings the tourists were still there. Emily was gone. His breathing halted for a moment. The police phone shook in his pocket. He took it out with trembling hands. It was Falcone.

'Where *are* you?' the inspector demanded.

'Augustus's mausoleum. He's inside. There are people around. We need to approach this carefully.'

'That goes without saying,' Falcone answered abruptly, and the line went dead.

'Indeed it does . . .' Costa murmured to himself.

He walked over to the tourists and told them to go somewhere else. They looked at his face and his weapon, then fled. After that he climbed over the railings and scanned the area. The tramps were getting interested. One of them wandered over and demanded money. Costa brushed him aside. He came back. One sight of the gun took care of it.

'There's a woman here. And a man in brown. Where?' he asked.

One of the seated figures, huddled in an ancient black overcoat, nodded round the corner, past some green and dingy buttress that looked ready to collapse.

'Thanks,' Costa said, and walked on, knowing, somehow, exactly what he'd see.

All the same, his heart froze the moment he found them.

They were no more than twenty metres away. The figure in khaki had met her – lured her maybe – into some dark dead end up against the deepest part of the moat, a place with no easy exit. He had his arm round Emily's neck. She was struggling as he dragged her backwards. The gun hung loose over her chest, its dull barrel hard against the black fabric of her coat. He was dragging on the hood as he fought to contain her.

Costa let the weapon fall to his side, walked forward and tried to count his options. A thought occurred to him.

Emily knows you now.

The khaki figure dragged Emily all the way to the stone wall of the mausoleum. There was nowhere else to go. Costa walked forward until he was no more than five paces from them. His wife's face was livid with rage. She never took lightly to violence. The shotgun had been hard at her throat for at least part of their journey into this dark, shadowy alcove in the masonry. She looked mad and ready to act. The figure in khaki had no idea the woman in his grasp was a trained law enforcement officer, one who'd learned how to deal with hostage situations, skilled in self-defence, one who possessed, in all probability, more knowledge and experience of dealing with this kind of problem than Costa himself.

'Half the police in Rome will be here any minute,' Costa said quietly. 'So how bad do you want this to be?'

'I really don't mind.'

The voice behind the black hood was interesting. Cultured. Haughty. Local.

'Everyone minds in jail,' Costa said. 'Ten years or twenty. It's a big difference.'

He laughed and Costa got the feeling, again, that this was someone outside the normal criminal mould.

'I'm not going to jail,' the man responded, without a trace of doubt in his voice. 'Not ever.'

The gun was still tight across Emily's chest. There was fury in her eyes, and a part of it, he knew, was aimed in his direction for taking this gentle, firm approach, not trying to nail everything down with force and some unbending iron will. Officers possessed different styles, Costa thought. This hoodlum also had his wife, and a shotgun at her throat. All the training in the world meant nothing, sometimes, out in the cold light of day.

'Please . . .' Costa said, and held out his empty left hand in a gesture of pleading.

'Don't beg, Nic,' Emily spat at him. 'You *never* beg. It's the worst thing you can do. The *worst* . . .'

He should have expected it. In one swift movement, Emily lifted her right leg and twisted it behind her, raking the man's shin with her sharp, hard heels. Then she arced her elbow back and jabbed it hard into his left shoulder, finding the most tender patch there as she fought free.

Costa took one step forward, raised the pistol in his right hand and aimed it straight at the black hood, straight into those dark unseeable eyes.

Emily had hurt him. He was crying with pain from the vicious scrape to the leg, hugging the shotgun to himself the way a child clung on to a toy.

'Let go of the gun,' Costa said slowly, 'or I will, I swear, shoot you.'

He stole a glance at her. Emily was to his right, just a

step away, not close enough to be seized again, not with the gun trained on him.

'Emily,' Costa said firmly. 'This is not your place. Go back to the entrance. Now. Everybody will be here in a moment.'

He could feel the heat in her gaze. This wasn't the way she thought things ought to be done.

'I'm fine. There's nobody else here, Nic. Can't you see?'

The man wasn't whining any more. He was watching the two of them from behind the hood, his head cocked slightly to one side, listening, taking this all in. Taking in the fact they were more than mere acquaintances. Costa just knew that.

He hadn't moved the shotgun an inch. It still lay in his arms like some evil infant. Then he mumbled something.

'What?' Costa asked.

'Pretty white girl,' the man in brown said.

He laughed, and it was more like a giggle.

He leaned forward, looking conspiratorial.

'You *know* her.'

The way he said the word 'know' was deliberate, with intent.

'The gun,' Costa emphasized.

The hood nodded.

Slowly he held it out with both hands, one on the barrel, one on the stock, parallel to his body. He didn't do anything else.

'Drop the damned gun!' Costa yelled, and found his own weapon stiff in his outstretched hand.

What came next was a shrug. A gesture so Roman Costa had seen it a million times. When a street seller didn't have the change. When an errant motorist got caught for speeding. On all those small occasions when a tiny tear appeared in the fabric of an ordered life, and everyone, the culprit, the victim, the witness, just wished above all else they could pretend it had never happened, had never been seen.

'Pretty white girl,' the hooded figure murmured again, in a different voice, one lower, one more serious, a voice that made Costa feel a chill run down his backbone.

He could see it now. The gun was horizontal in his hands, of no threat to anyone ahead, apparently unusable. But the thumb of the man's right hand – a thumb enclosed in the black cotton of a soldier's glove – was hooked through the trigger piece, ready, poised.

And the barrel had a certain, intent direction.

'Em . . .' Costa whispered, and was immediately aware that something – some bellowing, inhuman roar – wiped out the final syllable of her name.

Part 3

FUNERAL RITES

– 1 –

A bright winter's day, sunlight streaming through the bedroom windows of the farmhouse, pigeons cooing noisily on the roof, the buzzing drone of a distant jet turning for Ciampino.

Costa woke and in that shifting, formless space between dream and reality was briefly disoriented as he struggled towards consciousness. From downstairs he could hear a soft, familiar feminine voice calling his name.

Still half asleep he dragged himself to the door and walked to the head of the stairs.

'Nic,' she said. 'It's time. You have to get dressed. There are people here.'

Pepe, the small terrier that had accompanied his youth, now approaching sixteen and refusing to accept his frailty, sat at Bea Savarino's feet, quiet and calm, staring at him placidly from the foot of the stairs. Bea wore black, just as she had for his father's funeral, after all those long months of nursing him through the final stages of his illness. On the low table next to her sat a pile of unopened Christmas cards, most still with two names at the top of the address.

'Of course,' he said, glad his head was finally clearing.

A person did not disappear easily. Emily was dead. It

didn't mean that every trace of her being, her sharp, keen personality, had departed the house. Bea had patiently, subtly taken her clothes to the charity shop during the ten days since the shooting, had cleaned the house, reorganized it so that his life did not fall apart any more than was necessary. There was an excuse, naturally. Her own apartment in Trastevere was undergoing some work which made it convenient for her to stay at the farmhouse again, with Nic's permission, which he gave willingly, not quite thinking or understanding much at the time, for a simple and obvious reason: inside he felt dead, utterly detached from anything that happened around him.

In his work he'd told so many bereaved relatives that it was impossible for their loved ones to be given speedy funerals because they were the victims of crime. He'd said, always, he understood their grief. Now he really did, and it wasn't what he'd expected at all. Had Teresa Lupo not intervened with a clear-cut statement that she would not, under any circumstances, permit Emily's body to lie in the police mortuary any longer, since there were no evidential or scientific grounds for its retention, the agony would be continuing, as it would have for most civilians. Instead, for him, came a fixed point in the calendar, a date on which the remains of his wife of a few, too short months would make one final journey, then disappear behind a pair of velvet crematorium curtains. After which her physical presence would be gone forever, leaving a chasm in his own existence which seemed to grow with each passing hour, not diminish.

It was the week before Christmas and he was a widower before he'd turned thirty. Costa hadn't wept yet. He'd still to find the key to that particular secret. It had eluded him from the moment he recovered consciousness after the figure in khaki clubbed him to the ground during those few, agonizing seconds by the Mausoleum of Augustus, a sequence of events that continued to replay themselves inside his head with a cruel, vivid authenticity when he least expected it.

That, and the possibilities. What if she'd taken his advice and gone for a coffee, against, he knew, all her innate instincts? Or he'd shot the bastard straight away when there was the slightest hesitation, an act which, Costa understood, was equally contrary to his own character? As these images revolved around his head, endlessly, never resting, her death seemed to swim in what-ifs and alternative endings. One more prominent than the other, and he could hear the words uttered from his own throat, as if he'd had time to say them directly to that figure with the black hood and the unseeable eyes: *Shoot me instead. Take my life because it's so much less worthy, so unimportant next to hers, which is bright and smart and leading to something she has yet to imagine for herself.*

And that was the harshest thought of all. Because inside it lay something Emily Deacon – he'd never really thought of her with the married name – would not have brooked for an instant. Self-pity. Defeat. The tantalizing, appealing black pit of gloom into which it was so easy to descend, a place he knew already, a dark haven that beckoned him, in a bottle, in a wallowing morass of despair. Which was why the white lie about the apartment in Trastevere was invented, why his father's former carer – and perhaps one-time lover – moved in so quickly to try to save him.

*

'Nic!' the familiar female voice said again, with that half-scolding tone he'd come to know so well.

Bea walked upstairs carrying the black suit from the cleaners, a white shirt ironed so perfectly it seemed new and a dark tie she must have bought for the occasion.

He took them and said thank you.

Bea, pretty Bea, the stiff-backed elegant woman he'd loved, in a way, as a child, stood in front of him, her eyes full of concern and a little glassy. She had a tan from a winter break in South Africa. The customary gold necklace hung around her neck. There were wrinkles on the tanned skin now as she approached sixty, though she looked as beautiful as ever in an expensive dark funeral dress and shoes.

'You must come,' she said, and put a firm, warm hand to his cheek.

'I will, I promise,' he replied obediently.

She had something on her mind and was reluctant to come out with it.

He stared at her, waiting.

'For pity's sake, Nic, let a little of this grief go,' she pleaded. 'God gave us tears for a reason.'

It was a strange thing for a lapsed communist, even one as middle class as Bea, to say.

'I didn't think you believed in God,' he observed.

'I don't know what I believe in any more. Do you?'

Four hours later they were back, meandering around the table of food Bea had prepared, chattering in the idle, restless, uncomfortable way that happened after funerals. People he knew. Strangers from America, who were distant with him, for good reason. This was the first time they'd met Emily's Italian police-officer husband. It would be the last too.

Teresa Lupo had hardly spoken a word. She was in the kitchen, a disconsolate, untidy figure seated on a chair at the table, not eating or drinking, Peroni holding her hand, watching the tears pouring down her cheeks. The pathologist had been fine in the crematorium. It was the farmhouse, the place the four of them had spent so many hours, that got to her. Teresa worked with death, was comfortable with its presence in the surroundings where it belonged. In a house, one that had briefly been Emily's home, everything was different.

Costa walked over from the living room, placed a hand on her shoulder, saw the way she wasn't able to look into his eyes, then received a knowing nod from Peroni. There came a time when there were no more words of consolation left, for any of them. This was that time. Emily was gone. He'd spent days in some curious limbo where bureaucracy – formal identifications and death certificates – mixed with the ludicrous long hours dealing with funeral directors. And, in between, when he found the opportunity, trying and failing to convince Falcone to let him return from compassionate leave to work on the case.

Instead the inspector had insisted he stay away, placing a car at the end of the drive to keep the determined army of curious media out and, Costa knew, him in. Emily had told him what the newspapers were like. A photogenic death was always front-page material. She'd been proved right, and the lurid facts of the case had only served to feed the frenzy. The beautiful wife of a Roman police officer was dead, murdered in front of his eyes by a killer who'd fled a crime scene where, it later transpired, several other women, one of them an upper-class French art historian, had died. The story contained all the elements the media loved: attractive women, vicious crimes of a sexual nature and an apparent inability on the part of the police to locate a single potential suspect, in spite of a huge, and national, hunt.

Costa had ordered every important newspaper, had watched most of the daily news bulletins and had followed the case on the web, the way Emily had showed him. Two things continued to nag at him. It was impossible, surely, to believe the police had not come across a single lead in a case so rich with forensic evidence. And no one ever mentioned the painting, the image of which had yet to be entirely displaced by the shocking memories of what came after.

He waited until people began drifting away. Then he watched Leo Falcone detach himself from the company he was keeping. The inspector had arrived with Raffaella

Arcangelo; the two seemed so friendly that Costa wondered if that romance had returned. A sudden death altered the landscape. Falcone was a man who enjoyed his own company, but had found something else during the time Raffaella had cared for him the previous year. Now that he was fit and active in the Questura he had no need for her physical support. But emotionally . . . Costa wondered, as he watched Falcone slyly remove himself from the dwindling crowd, find the back door, then disappear into the garden.

He excused himself from the kindly American relative who stood next to him, running out of words, and followed Falcone outside. There had been a time when the man would have been smoking one of his foul-smelling cigarettes. That habit had disappeared. He was seated by the decrepit wooden table that looked out over the bowed, blackened vines, a place where Nic and Emily had entertained all four of them – Falcone and Raffaella, Teresa and Peroni – often the previous summer.

Costa took a seat next to his boss and stared at the land. Everything – the house, the garden, the fields – seemed larger somehow. Emily's absence magnified the world and its emptiness.

Falcone cast a quick look back through the French windows, into the lounge.

'I'd smoke if only I could get away with it. Women . . .'

Costa briefly closed his eyes and stifled his astonishment – which should not, he knew, have been so great – at the man's lack of tact.

'You and Raffaella . . . I don't want to pry, Leo.'

'Oh.' Falcone kicked at some pebbles on the ground. Sometimes he was alarmingly childlike. 'That's back on. I called her.' He turned to look at Costa, as if asking for some kind of reassurance. 'I needed to, Nic. Not just to make arrangements for today. I wanted to see her. Everything seemed so cold otherwise. It wasn't that I felt alone, you understand.'

Costa made some sympathetic sound.

'God . . .' Falcone shook his head with a sudden bitter fury. 'I miss Emily. I miss that bright mind. And talking to her. She didn't think the way we do. I could listen to her throwing an idea around for hours. It's all so . . . futile.'

He turned to Costa and made this next point with that familiar, long index finger.

'Had that architect's career not worked out, I would have got her into the police, you know.' He sighed. 'Lord knows we need officers who see things differently. Particularly today.'

'Leo . . .' Costa said a little testily.

'What?'

'Is this your version of sympathy? Do you behave this way at all funerals?'

'Most funerals I avoid!' Falcone replied, hurt. 'What do you mean?'

'I mean, you're saying what I'm supposed to say. And I'm listening to what you're supposed to listen to.'

'Oh.' He nodded. Perhaps there was a vestige of comprehension there. '*That* kind of sympathy.'

Falcone reached over and patted Costa's knee. His avian face had a winter tan, the silver goatee newly trimmed, and eyes that were full of intelligence, understanding and a firm, unbending friendship.

'You surely know how I feel, Nic. How we all feel. Do I really have to spell it out? I'm not a man for wasted words. I never have been. If you need me, you know where I am. The same goes for Gianni and Teresa, though I imagine they've told you that ten times over, because that's their way, and good luck to them with it.'

They hadn't, in fact. Costa understood why. In some strange way they were now so close to one another that they had no need of these spoken reassurances. Those were reserved for outsiders.

'So?' Falcone asked.

'So what?'

'So when would you like to come back to work?'

'I'll be back the instant you want me.'

'Good. There's an attachment coming up in Sicily just after the holiday. It would be an excellent opportunity under any circumstances. People-smuggling. Rome needs some expertise there.'

'Sicily.' Costa groaned.

'Sicily,' the inspector agreed.

Costa waited, searching for the words.

'This is what friends are for, Leo. I have never exercised that friendship until now. I want the case. You have to give it to me.'

A swarm of dark crows danced on the horizon, near the distant circular outline of the tomb of a long-dead Imperial matron, Cecilia Metella. Falcone watched them for several long seconds, then said, 'I can't do that. I find it grossly unfair of you to exert personal pressure in this way. Compassionate leave could stretch to a month or more if you want it.'

'I'd be even crazier after a month. This is enough. Besides, I have every right . . .'

The crows lost their importance. Falcone turned to him, a flash of anger in his face.

'You have no rights whatsoever, other than those of any other bereaved civilian. Don't be so ridiculous. An officer investigating his own wife's death? What do you think the media would make of that? Or those clowns on the seventh floor?'

Costa steeled himself. He was prepared to argue.

'It's an investigation into several murders. I would leave my own feelings to one side.'

'Who do you hope to fool there? Me? Or yourself?'

He didn't have a good answer, only pretexts, and now, faced with Falcone's stubbornness, he knew they wouldn't work.

'I have to do something.'

Falcone shook his bald head. It gleamed under the low winter sun.

Costa sought the words. These thoughts had dogged him ever since her death. They wouldn't go away easily.

'I can't bury her, Leo. Not in my head. Not properly. Unless . . .' He sighed. 'I need to work. Otherwise everything just keeps going round and round.'

Falcone shrugged.

'Then work in Sicily.'

'I have to do something here.'

'I hate personal issues,' Falcone grumbled. 'You feel responsible. It's understandable. Anyone would. It's the way we're made. It will pass.'

'No,' Costa murmured. 'It won't. Not on its own.'

'And what if you fail?' the older man asked severely. 'What will that do to you?'

'I won't fail.' That thought had really never occurred to him.

Falcone sniffed, took a sly look back at the house again, slipped a small cigar out of his pocket, then lit it.

'You have no idea what you're asking. We are more than a week into this investigation, yet I have nothing . . .'

He scowled. Some thought, some irritant, affected him at that moment.

'. . . nothing concrete to show for all the work we've done. Frankly, several aspects baffle me more every time I look at them. With you gone and Peroni drooping around the place like a dog that's lost its best friend . . . we're not on top form to be honest. They're already whispering upstairs that perhaps we should hand over everything to the Carabinieri. If I could do this, Nic, do you honestly believe I'd turn you down?'

'You can find a way,' Costa replied. 'You always do.'

Falcone was up on his feet, with an easy swiftness that showed the injuries that had troubled him since the shooting in Venice were now surely in the past. Falcone could do it. His standing in the Questura was high again. He could do anything he liked, if he wanted.

And now he was angry. The heat suffused his walnut cheeks.

'Damn it!' he barked, just loud enough for a few faces at the window to turn in their direction. 'What kind of occasion is this to start throwing professional demands at me?'

'It's my murdered wife's funeral, sir,' Costa replied with a flat, cold disdain.

- 3 -

Half-recognized faces, people he hadn't seen for years. Funerals always brought them out, and Costa had never been good with names. They were almost all gone within thirty minutes, leaving Bea clearing away the plates and glasses and Costa talking to a somewhat embarrassed Raffaella Arcangelo alone in a chair in the dining room, stroking the ancient, half-slumbering dog.

'You'll have to go and speak to him, Nic,' she said. 'It's freezing cold out there, he doesn't have a jacket, and he won't come in of his own accord.'

'It's like dealing with a child,' he complained.

She nodded.

'I have very little experience of children but I must admit it does sound very similar. All the same . . .'

Costa stormed outside, ready for another argument. Falcone was back at the decrepit wooden table, puffing on another cigar, blowing the smoke out towards the dead, hunched vines waiting for spring and a reawakening.

He watched Costa sit down, then said, 'You'd have to work over Christmas.'

'That,' Costa replied, exasperated, 'is hardly an obstacle.'

Falcone nodded.

74

'I hate Christmas too. Welcome to the club.'

The last few people were drifting outside, Raffaella among them. They couldn't, he knew, leave without saying goodbye. This had to be brought to an end.

'What am I supposed to do, Leo?'

The sharp eyes flashed at him again. There was an unmistakable expression of self-doubt in them, something Costa had rarely seen in the man. Falcone reached into his jacket pocket, withdrew a copious set of keys and removed two from the ring.

'These are for my old apartment in the *centro storico*, in Governo Vecchio. You know it?'

Costa had never been invited there. The place predated Raffaella and the apartment she had shared with Falcone. But he knew the location, just a stone's throw from the Piazza Navona.

'I had been planning to move back there now I can walk properly,' Falcone went on. 'But Raffaella prefers Monti. Here.'

He gave Costa the keys.

'I have a home,' he noted, waving a hand at the house.

'Bea can look after it. In three days' time I want you to pack your bags. Expect to be gone a week or more. And – ' the finger jabbed at him – 'don't tell a soul where you're going.'

This was interesting, Costa thought.

'Teresa is due to deliver some kind of news to me then,' Falcone continued, before Costa could ask a single question. 'She never hurries, naturally. You have a reason to be at that meeting. Take it. We are due at that damned studio for her theatricals. Afterwards you will return to compassionate leave. In my apartment. I will explain later.'

He looked lost for a moment, staring at the grey horizon, as if seeking answers.

'Finding a criminal is only half the challenge,' he added cryptically. 'Don't make me regret this, Nic.'

Costa didn't have time to answer. A voice drifted from the door. It was Raffaella. Falcone dipped the cigar down below his waist and flicked it into the vineyard with a long, agile finger.

'You have some identification for these dead African women?' Costa asked in a quiet voice.

'What do you think?' Falcone grumbled. 'If a man wishes to commit a crime, best commit it against the underclass. Their families are too scared to complain. Or . . .'

He didn't wish to go on.

'Someone has to be able to ID them, Leo.'

'You'd think . . .' he replied with a bitter, ironic smile. 'Fake names. Fake identities. These are illegal immigrants desperate to stay out of our way. Even when we do find them . . .'

He shrugged as if it were helpless.

'There must be—' Costa insisted.

'Nic. Please. No more. I have two officers in Nigeria at this very moment, following up the only real lead we have. It could take months of work, even if people there are willing to speak to us, and that is an assumption I am not inclined to make. Do not equate your absence in all this with a lack of effort on our part. Nothing could be further from the truth.'

Costa shook his head.

'I never meant it that way,' he murmured. 'I don't understand.'

'None of us understands. Perhaps Teresa will shed a

little light on matters when we meet. But there's something else you must do first. The painting we found in that studio. I will make some calls. You must either tell me it's important or let me forget about it altogether. An art expert attached to the Barberini is due to start looking at it shortly. I will arrange an appointment for you, before we meet in the Vicolo del Divino Amore. I happen to have made her acquaintance before. She comes to you recommended. The woman's name is Agata Graziano. The gallery has a laboratory close to the Piazza Borghese. She's the best apparently. And there's another surprise . . .'

He elaborated no more and simply gazed at the still-smouldering cigar on the cold winter earth.

'I want whoever did this, Nic. Just as much as you.'

Part 4

THE BARBERINI'S EXPERT

– 1 –

It was raining when he drove out of the farmhouse three days later, leaving Bea performing some unnecessary cleaning, and issuing persistent queries about where he was going and why. Costa had no sensible answers. He had a suitcase full enough for a week away, as Falcone had demanded. He felt glad to be out of the place too, to be moving. Inactivity didn't suit him, and perhaps the inspector understood that only too well. The previous night he'd barely slept for thinking about the case, and Falcone's strangely gloomy assessment of what had been achieved so far. It was highly unusual for the man to be so pessimistic at such a relatively early point in an investigation.

The city was choked with holiday traffic. The narrow lanes, now full of specialist shops selling antiques and furniture and clothes, were cloaked in skeins of fairy lights twinkling over the crowds. It took ten minutes to find somewhere to park near the Piazza Borghese, even with police ID on the vehicle.

Costa's opinion of the canvas had not altered since the black day of 8 December. In truth he felt little had changed since the moment Emily was snatched from life.

It was as if his world had ceased to move, and in this sense of stasis remained a certainty about the work he had first seen in the studio in the Vicolo del Divino Amore. Either it really was an unknown Caravaggio or somehow they had come across an extraordinary fake. There had been plenty of copyists over the years, both genuine artists working in his style by way of tribute and con men trying to hoodwink naïve buyers into thinking they had chanced upon some new masterpiece. At home, alone, trying to think of something other than those last moments by the mausoleum, Costa had taken out his old art books, delved deep into the images and the histories there, welcoming the respite he could take from the imaginary world that enveloped him. The dark, violent genius who was Caravaggio had lived in Rome for just fourteen years, from 1592 until 1606, when he fled under sentence of death for murder. Every genuine homage that Costa could find had made it plain through some reference, stylistic or by way of subject, that it came from the brush of another. Every fake was, by dint of the original's extraordinary technical skill, modest in reach, an attempt to convince the potential buyer that it came from Caravaggio's early period in Rome, when he was open to quick, cheap private commissions, though even then only on his own terms and for subjects of which he approved.

As he remembered it, the canvas from the Vicolo del Divino Amore seemed to fit neither of these templates. It was bold, extraordinarily ambitious and far more substantial than some ordinary collection piece thrown up on a brief commission in order to pay a pressing bill. It stood more than two metres wide and half as high, housed in a plain gilt frame that had faded to the dark sheen of old gold. Even with the briefest of glances, Costa had been able to detect tell-tale signs of the man's individual style. Seen from an angle to the side, close to where the body of Véronique Gillet lay on the grey flagstones, still and deathly pale, he had been able to make out the faintest of incisions, preparatory guidelines cut with a stylus or sharp pen, similar to those etched into plaster by fresco painters, a technique no other artist of the time was known to use on canvas.

The *sfumato*, a gradation from dark to light so subtle that it was impossible to discern the blend of an outline or border, appeared exquisite. Taken as a whole, the abiding style of the piece went beyond mere *chiaroscuro*, the histrionic balance of light and shade first developed by da Vinci. During his brief life, Caravaggio had taken da Vinci's model and emboldened the drama with a fierce, almost brutal approach in which the core figures were set apart from the background and the characters around them by a bright, unforgiving light, like a ray of pure shining spirit. The effect was to heighten the emotional tension of the scene to a degree hitherto unseen in the work of any artist. There was a technical term for the style Caravaggio had pioneered, *tenebrismo*, from the Latin *tenebrae*, for shadows, and it was this that made paintings like the conversion of St Paul and the final moments of Peter on the cross so electrifying, so timeless.

He found his vivid recollections of those canvases racing through his head as he followed the directions Falcone had given him for the laboratory outpost of the Galleria Barberini. When he got there he realized it could have been no more than half a kilometre from the studio in the Vicolo del Divino Amore itself, though the distance was deceptive, since a straight line would run principally through hard Renaissance brick and stone, unseen halls and buildings hidden behind high, smog-stained windows.

Both the laboratory and the studio appeared to be part of the black lumbering mass that was the Palazzo Malaspina, an ugly façade for what was reputedly one of the finest remaining private palaces still in original hands. No one set foot inside the palazzo itself without an invitation. But it was no great surprise, Costa thought, that areas of the vast edifice were rented to outsiders. Shops, apartments, offices and even a few restaurants seemed to find shelter in varying parts of the area covered by its sprawling wings.

The small, almost invisible sign for the Barberini's outpost was in a side alley off the relatively busy Via della Scrofa. He rang the bell and waited for at least thirty seconds. A guard in the blue civilian uniform of one of the large private security companies opened the door. He had a belt full of equipment and a holster with a handgun poking prominently out of the top. There were valuable paintings here, Costa reminded himself. One perhaps more valuable than anyone else appreciated.

Before he could say a word a short slender figure in a plain billowing black dress emerged from behind the guard's bulky frame.

'I'll deal with this, Paolo,' she declared, with a sureness of voice that sent the man scuttling back to his post next to the door without another word.

The woman was perhaps thirty, dark-skinned, with a pert, inquisitive face, narrow and pleasant rather than attractive, with round gleaming brown eyes beneath a high and intellectual forehead. A large silver crucifix hung on a chain around her neck. A black garment which Costa thought might be called a scapular was draped around her slight shoulders. She seemed somewhat anxious. Her full head of black shiny hair hung in disorganized tresses, kept untidily together by pins. In her left hand she held on to a couple of creased and clearly old supermarket plastic bags bulging with papers and notes and photographs, as if they were some kind of replacement for a briefcase.

It took a moment for Costa to understand.

'I'm sorry, Sister,' he apologized. 'I'm looking for the Barberini laboratory. I have an appointment.'

She reached into one of the plastic bags, took out a very green apple, bit into it greedily and, still eating, asked, 'You are Nic?'

He nodded.

'Come in. You don't look like you do in the pictures in the papers,' she replied, turning, then marching down the long corridor with a fast, deliberate gait, her heavy leather shoes clattering on the wooden floor.

He followed, hurrying to keep up. There was a brightly lit room at the end.

'You read the papers?' he asked, surprised.

She turned and laughed.

'Of course I read the papers! What am I? A monk?'

They walked into the chamber at the end. It was like entering an operating theatre. The canvas sat on a bright new modern easel beneath a set of soft, insistent lighting that exposed every portion of it. Costa stared and felt his breath catch. The painting radiated light and life and an extraordinary, magnetic power.

The nun sat down and finished her apple in four bites. Then she placed the core back in one of the supermarket bags, took out a wrinkled paper handkerchief and patted her lips. Costa had little experience of dealing with the city's religious community. There was rarely any need.

'I've an appointment with Signora Agata Graziano,' he explained. 'Will she be long?'

She folded her slender arms and stared at him.

'Are you a detective?'

He shuffled on his feet, stealing glances at the painting.

'Rumour has it,' he muttered.

'Then tell me what you make of this. You have an appointment with a woman. You come here. I am a woman. You see me.' Her skinny arms opened wide, a look of theatrical disbelief spread across her dark face. 'And . . . ?'

Costa blinked.

'I never thought you'd be a nun.'

'I'm not. Sit down, please.'

He took the chair next to her.

The woman's alert, dusky face took on the patient, if slightly exasperated, expression of a teacher dealing with a slow pupil.

'I am a sister, not a nun. I took simple vows, not solemn ones. It's complicated. I won't trouble you with this.'

'I'm sorry, Sister.'

'Agata, please. When I am here, I am here as an academic. When I am at home, there you could call me "Sister". Except there you are not allowed in my home. So the point is moot.'

'I consider myself both enlightened and chastised.'

She laughed.

'Oh . . . a *sarcastic* detective. I like that. Convents lack sarcasm. Throw it at me as much as you like. Now, your first question.'

'Is it genuine?' he asked.

She rolled her large brown eyes and threw back her head. Then, to Costa's amazement, something akin to a curse, albeit a very mild one by Roman standards, escaped her lips.

'Nic, Nic, Nic,' Agata Graziano complained. 'When I walk outside my convent I'm a historian first and a lover of art second. I don't make rash judgements. I need to ask some scientific people in here to examine paint and canvas samples. To take X-rays and consult with others of their ilk. Also, I need to look further at what records we have from that time.'

The painting was so near he could almost touch it. Costa was enjoying the ability to see it close up again, under decent light. Nothing there changed his original opinion.

'The records won't tell you much,' he suggested.

She stared at him, another teacher-like look, this time of exaggerated surprise, and said, 'I'm sorry.'

'If this is a private commission of Caravaggio's, the chances are there won't be a mention of it anywhere,' Costa went on. 'From what I've read the only reliable records are for his church works. It makes sense. They had to be paid for with public money. That had to be accounted for. When he was employed by individuals, he might have had nothing more than a letter. Perhaps not even that.'

'I was under the impression art was the responsibility of the Carabinieri,' she observed.

'I was under the impression the Barberini employed its own people.'

She delivered up a jocular scowl, one that said *touché*. Then nothing else.

'Why *are* you here?' he asked.

'Because they believe I happen to be the best person for the job. Their usual suspects are in New York, supervising some coming show at the Metropolitan Museum. My luck. And – ' she emphasized this point with a sharp look at the painting – 'they are right. There are a few things I don't know about our mutual friend Michelangelo Merisi da Caravaggio. But they are just a few and on those no one else is any the wiser either. There. Immodesty masquerading as frankness. I have one more thing to confess.'

She hesitated.

'And you?'

'I'm just interested. That's all,' Costa said.

'I meant about something to confess.'

He didn't know what to say.

Agata Graziano screwed up her brown eyes with a sudden embarrassment so real Costa wondered what to do.

'Oh, I'm sorry. I read the papers. I'm an idiot. I apologize.'

'For what?'

'For treating you like this. You lost your wife and here I am making jokes.'

Costa wanted to utter something about the way the world ran on, regardless of individual tragedies. Instead he said, 'I came back to work because I wanted to. I'll deal with what that brings.'

'A brave idea,' she observed. 'A wise one? What do I know? I'm just an academic who thought this was purely business when clearly it isn't.'

'This is business,' he emphasized.

'If you insist. I am not very good at sympathy, I'm afraid.'

'There's no need to be. You don't know me.'

'Is that relevant?' she wondered. 'In any case I am saddened by your cruel loss. I cannot begin to imagine how it must feel.' She paused, a little uncertain of herself. 'Can we consider that done with now?'

'Please. There's one other reason to think you won't find a record,' he said quickly, wishing to change the topic.

'That being?'

'Paintings like this weren't for public viewing. They were commissioned for some special room in the house. Only to be seen by a wife or a lover, or a male friend one wanted to impress.'

He stopped, wondering whether he was blushing. Years ago he had read widely about this type of work in an effort to understand how much of Caravaggio's output, and that of his peers, might have been lost. The depressing answer was: a lot. The famous canvases of naked young boys – works that, some believed incorrectly, had led him to be accused of being a homosexual – fell precisely into this category. They were daring, at the very edge of acceptability in a city where sexual crimes could carry heavy penalties and sodomy itself was deemed worthy of a death sentence. Such paintings only survived because they had entered large and well-maintained collections early in the seventeenth century. Lesser, or more obscure, works were often destroyed or reused by later artists for their own purposes. Countless examples from private collections of the period, by Caravaggio and his contemporaries, had been lost forever, recorded, if at all, only in the private correspondence and diaries of those who had been lucky enough to see them. He was unsure how to elaborate on these delicate matters with a woman who called herself a sister.

'So you think it might be genuine?' he asked again.

'Persistence,' she answered. 'You are a detective after all. I have a confession. When your inspector called I was able to obtain a dispensation from my normal duties in the convent. Most, anyway, and only for a few days. So I have a little spare time on my hands, which I spent yesterday examining this painting, then this morning looking at what archival material I can lay my hands on easily. They kept very good records in the sixteenth and seventeenth centuries, by the way. You should be grateful. The Uffizi owns a letter from a contemporary of Caravaggio's, the poet Giambattista Marino, which may refer to a canvas very like this one. In 1599 he writes that he saw a painting of Caravaggio's which was so consummate in execution, and so reckless in subject, he doubted anyone dare show it, even to those closest to him. Least of all the man who commissioned it, who was a cardinal in the Church.'

'Then how come this Marino character got to see it?'

'Where's your imagination?' She seemed a little disappointed by his comment. 'Marino was a poet. He lived in Ortaccio, just as Caravaggio did. They probably got drunk together all the time.'

'Ortaccio,' he replied. So much was coming back from the days when he spent every waking hour with a book about Caravaggio and his world. 'The cardinal was Del Monte?'

She clapped her small brown hands in delight. The noise rang around the empty room, loud and happy.

'Bravo! I think you are a well-informed detective.' She was idly fidgeting with the crucifix on her chest as they spoke and seemed, to Costa, utterly without guile, without a single layer of self-awareness sitting between her and the world.

'I read in the paper that your father was a communist,' she went on. 'I imagined you would know nothing of a churchman such as Del Monte.'

He felt a little disturbed by the degree of interest she had taken in him since Falcone had, presumably, called her the previous day to ask for assistance.

'Communism is a kind of faith too,' he replied.

'The wrong one. But I imagine a misplaced faith is better than none at all. What do you think?'

'I think Del Monte was no ordinary churchman,' Costa replied. 'He had arcane tastes. He was a cardinal, a favourite of the Pope. But he also dabbled in alchemy and obscure science. There were rumours of homosexuality and licentiousness.'

'It was Rome!' she cried. 'There are always rumours, just like now.'

'I agree. It was a bohemian court at the time. Galileo was one of his hangers-on while Caravaggio was there. A work such as this would not be out of place, though one can see why it was not on general show.'

She nodded, watching him with those gleaming brown eyes.

'Even a sister knows the sexual content would be a little rich for the time,' she agreed. 'Perhaps for these times too. There is one more thing we know from this letter. Marino writes that Caravaggio "took Carracci's whore and turned her into a goddess". Any ideas?'

'None.'

She beamed. 'Well, I'm pleased I can tell you something new.'

Agata Graziano led him across the room to a computer screen on a nearby desk, then sat down and began typing. Almost instantly a painting appeared on the screen, one similar to the canvas in the room, but paler, cruder. It was clear from the style and execution that the artist was not Caravaggio.

'You can see this in the Uffizi today when they feel like showing it. Just a few years later, dear old Annibale was painting the ceilings in the Palazzo Farnese and declaring himself the most pious creature in Rome. And here you have him depicting . . .'

She stared at him frankly

'What, exactly, do you think?'

Costa was still trying to grasp the implications of the canvas on the screen. It was like the Caravaggio, but unlike it.

'Pornography?' she asked simply, when he remained silent.

'If it was pornography, I doubt it would be hanging in the Uffizi.'

'Pornography masquerading as art, then,' she observed. 'Which would be worse, since therein lies hypocrisy.'

'I really don't know,' Costa said, and meant it.

'Tell me what you *see*, Nic,' she insisted. 'Spare me no details.'

Her skin was so dark he wondered whether he truly saw a blush there.

The computer told him the plain facts. The painting by Annibale Carracci was known as *Venus with a Satyr and Cupids.* It depicted the goddess half reclining on a rich velvet bed, her back to the viewer, a crumpled sheet discreetly covering her midriff, then winding round her torso until her right hand gripped it, in a gesture, perhaps, of fading bliss. A dark-skinned Dionysian satyr leered in front of her, bearing a bowl overflowing with grapes. Behind her head a small cupid played, gazing out of the frame of the canvas. Another small figure was depicted at the bottom left of the scene, and it was this that lent the work its curious, half-obscene nature. The creature's face was positioned by the thigh of the goddess, as if it had recently been close to her, and, in a gesture of astonishing frankness, a small, stiff, muscular tongue protruded lasciviously from its mouth. Its eyes were wild and rolling. While the body of the goddess seemed to hint at intimacy – in the stiffened muscles of her abdomen and the arched position of her legs – her face was calm, almost detached. It was as if the expression Carracci wished to paint on her had been transferred, instead, to the cupid between her thighs in some final failing of courage.

Costa said this all out loud, keeping his eyes firmly on the canvas.

'Good,' Agata complimented him. 'But let's leave the inferior. What do you think of this?'

She gestured at the canvas on the modern easel. Costa took a step towards it, trying to force himself to think carefully, logically.

An art teacher at school had once told him, 'Always begin with the name.' The title of a work was not some simple label. It described both its direction and ambitions, and its origins too. So he dragged his attention away from the canvas itself and looked at a small golden plate in the middle of the lower horizontal arm of the frame. It bore the same words as the Carracci, this time written in carved, archaic capitals: VENUS WITH A SATYR AND CUPIDS.

The work was like its inferior relative in some respects, perhaps even inspired by it, since the canvas in the Uffizi was dated *circa* 1588, when Caravaggio was seventeen and merely an apprentice. But in execution it was entirely different, more adventurous, more competently delivered, and infinitely more erotic, too, though in a subtle, almost sinister way. The artist had produced nothing explicit. Instead he placed the onus of interpretation entirely upon the viewer. An innocent might see this as some strange classical idyll, a mythical female beauty surrounded by her admirers. But a more mature – more carnal – interpretation was hidden inside the exquisite strokes of the artist's brush. Caravaggio had played this trick often enough, daring the beholder to imagine what deeds and actions were taking place just out of view or obscured behind some foreground object. Never had he done it with such elusive wit and cunning skill.

There were clear references to another Caravaggio work Costa knew only too well, and had often visited in the sprawling palace of the Doria Pamphilj in the Piazza del Collegio Romano, perhaps a ten-minute walk away. The model for Venus was surely the same as the beautiful red-haired woman in *The Rest on the Flight from Egypt*. But she was not slumbering with the infant Jesus in her arms, unknowingly listening to a lustrous angel playing the violin to sheet music held by a grizzled Joseph. Here she was entirely naked, back half turned to the viewer, as in Carracci's work, recumbent on some scarlet sofa, and attended again by two cupids and a more dominant leering satyr, central to the composition behind the woman. Like Joseph in the painting in the Doria Pamphilj, this larger figure had in his hands a piece of music, single notes this time, distinct on the stave, with impenetrable lyrics in Latin beneath. The cherub in the sky to the right held a jug from which some pale liquid fell slowly, carelessly into a silver goblet in his left hand, poured, one imagined, for the goddess. The second cherub in the left-hand corner lay lazily on one elbow, mouth open, singing from the satyr's notation, and with a tongue that protruded only slightly, not with the rigid, suggestive vigour of Carracci's satyr, though once again it seemed to carry some reference to the earlier work, with its fleshy, almost obscene grotesqueness. The creature carried a perfect golden apple in its right hand. In the background were more trees, some bearing fruit, and a scene reminiscent of a classical Renaissance garden, a subject Caravaggio had never, to Costa's recollection, depicted in any other work.

Costa examined the satyr's face closely and felt, for a moment, dizzy with a sense of revelation. The bearded individual there, inquisitive, prurient, unable to draw himself away from the scene though a part of him found it disturbing, was uncannily similar to the several self-portraits Caravaggio had inserted in everything from the famous martyrdom of St Matthew in Luigi dei Francesi to the late, spectacular beheading of John the Baptist in Malta. At that moment Costa felt he was staring into the very features of the stricken, violent genius who had died on the beach at Port'Ercole in 1610, a hundred kilometres from Rome, on a futile final journey home spurred by a papal pardon for the murder of an enemy in a street four years before.

'It has to be authentic,' he murmured.

'Then what is it?' Agata demanded. 'Caravaggio was beneath copies, even when he was starving.'

Costa saw her point. The central figure in the painting – he recalled now the name of the volatile Ortaccio whore, Fillide Melandroni, used by Caravaggio as a model for biblical and mythical characters – was quite unlike the Venus in Carracci's version, remote, distanced, controlled, almost detached from the scene. On the canvas before them she had been transformed by a knowing adult imagination. Alive, engaged, ecstatic, she ceased to be an unreal mythical goddess at play in paradise and became a living woman, one in a familiar state for those able to recognize it. The canvas was innocent until seen by someone who was not.

Even so, it seemed distant from the grim and seedy serial murder into which he had unwittingly led Emily, with such terrible results.

'I don't know exactly,' he murmured. 'Do you?'

Her small, round mouth screwed up into a childlike half-grimace.

'I told you,' she replied. 'I'm thinking. Slowly. There's no other way. How can I call you?'

She took a small notebook out of the nearest plastic bag and stared at him. Costa once more had the feeling that he was a schoolboy in the presence of the brightest and sternest teacher. The encounter was over, he realized, with some relief. In truth it wasn't a meeting at all. More a test, an interrogation so subtle he had scarcely noticed.

Wondering how well he had done, Costa ringed the mobile number on his card and passed it over.

'Just use this for the time being. You won't find me in the Questura.' He had to ask. 'And you?'

The throaty musical sound of her laughter echoed around the room once more.

'I've taken vows of common and personal poverty and that includes business cards. I have no phone of my own, mobile or otherwise. You may pass on a message through the convent. Here.'

He watched her scribble something on a sheet of paper and rip it from the pad.

'But if you should need me once this present dispensation is over, do not call between 5.45 a.m., when I rise, and 9 a.m., when I finish breakfast. Or lunchtime. Or after 4.30. If I decide to go out, it will be later.'

'You can do that?' he asked automatically. 'Go out?'

There was, finally, something akin to sympathy in her half-pretty, half-plain face, the face, he realized, and admonished himself for the thought, of a shop girl or waitress, a million young working-class women with lives that had somehow escaped this curious individual in the cheap black dress, a member of some religious order whose name he hadn't thought to ask.

'Occasionally,' she answered, still laughing. 'There. Something else we share in common along with poor Michelangelo Merisi da Caravaggio. You see me in my prison. And I see you in yours.'

Part 5

THE EKSTASISTS

It was a short walk from the studio to the Vicolo del Divino Amore, a brief journey blighted by memories of that final pursuit of the figure in the black hood, with the shotgun hidden beneath his khaki jacket. Snatches of that last dark day assaulted him with a cruel alacrity that had not yet diminished with time. This was no great surprise. The conversation with Agata Graziano, which was both amusing and, when it fell to the subject of the painting, a little disturbing, had proved a distracting interlude. But Emily still lay there in his imagination, waiting. In spite of her sheltered background, Agata had seen through him from the outset. This was not entirely business. There was a settlement, a resolution to be made. It would be difficult to feel quiescent about the end of their life together until that was reached.

The section of the street outside the studio's green door was still cordoned off, with three bored-looking uniformed officers stationed outside. In front of them stood a small crowd of the curious: men and women in winter coats, looking disappointed to discover that the scene of the most infamous crime to have occurred in the city in years appeared so mundane from the outside.

Costa could see at least two press photographers he knew, and ducked through the small huddle of bodies quickly in order to avoid them. There was, he thought, precious little in the narrow alley for the prurient. Short of more discoveries, the Vicolo del Divino Amore would surely soon return to some kind of normality.

He showed his pass and went in, preparing himself for Teresa Lupo's performance. She usually had a theatrical touch to her revelations. Even so, she must have asked them back to the place for a reason. The studio was not as he remembered it, resembling more an archaeological dig than a crime scene. Forensic officers were still busily working there. They had set out a secure walk-through area, outlined by tape, across the worn flagstones. Beyond the yellow markers a small unit of specialists in identical white bunny suits – the same now worn by Falcone's team – were bent over an array of careful excavations in the floor, each marked out by more tape, some carrying spades and pickaxes, others with evidence and body bags and scientific equipment.

Teresa herself stepped out from behind the barriers the moment Costa walked in, followed by her assistant, Silvio Di Capua. Falcone led the way, followed by Peroni, Costa and, a little behind everyone else, a woman officer, Inspector Susanna Placidi, who was introduced as the head of the sexual crimes unit. Accompanying her was the last person Costa expected to see: Rosa Prabakaran, the young Indian detective who had been attacked and injured during an investigation the previous spring. After which, Costa had come to believe, she had disappeared from the Questura altogether.

The smell still lingered, pervasive and disgusting, a cloying foul stink.

Teresa Lupo glanced at him with a sad, sideways look in her eyes, then said to them all, in a calm, formal manner, 'Thank you for coming. I asked you here so that you might appreciate a little of the magnitude of the task ahead of us. We are not one-tenth of the way into it. What I will tell you today are simply a few initial findings. I hope for much more in the way of answers, but I can't give you any time-scale about when or how they will come. This place defies conventional analysis in many ways. It was, I think, a real art studio once. It was also . . . something else.'

She glanced round the cold interior.

'Something I don't quite understand yet.'

'So long as we have a start,' Falcone observed without feeling. 'Some facts, please?'

He eyed the excavations.

'Facts,' she grumbled, and cast her round, glassy eyes over the excavations in the stone floor. 'They were all women, all black. Battered to death from what I can work out. Nor are they all accounted for. There is female DNA here that doesn't match that of any of the victims. Blood mainly, which means either they got killed and taken somewhere else, or they escaped or were allowed to leave for some reason. The most recent corpse dates from less than a month ago. The oldest, maybe twelve or fourteen weeks. Beyond that . . . we have a wealth of potential forensic material, but nothing that is linked to any existing criminal records, or . . .'

She allowed herself a somewhat caustic glance at Susanna Placidi here.

'. . . anyone fresh to try them out against.'

Costa was beginning to appreciate Falcone's despair.

'Wouldn't it have been obvious there were corpses

here?' he asked. 'Surely someone would have noticed? The smell . . .'

Falcone intervened, as he'd promised.

'Sovrintendente is here out of courtesy,' the inspector announced. 'We all share in his grief, though none of us can conceive of its depth, of course. I asked him to attend this one meeting so that he could appreciate that fact, and see how hard we are working to find those responsible for these crimes, and the murder of his wife. After which he will return to compassionate leave.'

'Thank you,' Costa muttered, embarrassed. 'The smell . . .'

'Normally you'd be right, Nic,' Teresa replied, and seemed relieved that the conversation had moved on to practical matters. 'But our friend – or friends more likely – had a plan. A little scientific or industrial knowledge too. You recall how the first victim we found looked?'

Costa thought it would be a long time before he forgot. The corpse had seemed to emerge from some kind of semi-transparent cocoon.

'They were stored in some way?' he asked.

'Out back he had a machine,' Teresa explained. 'It's exactly the same kind of device they use in industrial locations or packing plants. Anywhere you need to shrink-wrap something so that it's airtight. It wasn't going to keep that way forever. But it did a damned good job in the time they had.'

'He's clever. He had everything covered in advance,' Susanna Placidi added. She was a neurotic-looking individual in plain clothes – tweed wool jacket and a heavy green skirt – and a broad, miserable pale face that looked as if some unseen disappointment lurked around every corner. The body language between her and Rosa seemed distant and difficult.

'We found a stolen van around the corner,' the younger officer added. 'Not a large one. Just big enough for a corpse. There was a very expensive bouquet of lilies in it. And a coffin. Plain wood.'

'It was for the French woman,' Teresa said immediately. 'What other reason would there be?'

'The French Embassy is more than anxious for news,' Falcone went on. 'What am I supposed to tell them?'

'What about Aldo Caviglia's family?' Rosa snapped. 'Don't they feel the same way? Do you need to be white and middle class to get attention around here?'

Peroni whistled and looked at the ceiling. Teresa gave the young woman detective a filthy look.

'Everyone gets dealt with around here,' she said patiently. 'Caviglia was murdered. Until you people find the man who did it, there's not much more to say. The French woman's different. Silvio?'

Di Capua shuffled over, a short stocky figure in his bunny suit, bald-headed, with a circlet of long, lank hair dangling over the collar of his top. He was carrying a set of papers and a very small laptop computer.

Teresa took some of the documents from her colleague and glanced at them.

'You can tell them she died of natural causes. If it's any comfort, I don't imagine we will be using those words about anyone else who's expired hereabouts. The French won't argue. I spoke to her consultant in Paris and he's amazed she lived as long as she did, and frankly so am I. Congenital, incurable heart disease. Plus she had full-blown Aids, which was unresponsive to any of the very expensive private treatments she'd been receiving for the past nine months. They kept away the big day for a while but not for much longer. She saw her physician the week before she died. He told her it was a matter of weeks. Perhaps a month at the most.'

'We've been through this before,' Peroni objected. 'She still had a knife wound.'

'A scratch,' Di Capua said, and called up on the computer a set of colour photographs of the woman's neck and face, then her pale, skeletal torso. They all crowded round to stare at the images there, frozen moments from a death that took place a few steps from where they now stood. Even Peroni looked for a short while before he turned away in disgust. Costa could scarcely believe what he was seeing. Perhaps time or the light in the studio had played tricks. Perhaps the curious painting had disturbed his powers of observation, amplifying everything – the light, the atmosphere, his own imagination. When he'd first seen the body of Véronique Gillet on the old grimy floor he'd been convinced she, like Aldo Caviglia, was the victim of some savage, un-thinking act of violence. In truth, the knife mark barely cut through her white, flawless skin. Now the thin, straight line of dried blood looked more like an unfortunate accident with a rose bush than a meeting with a sharp, deadly weapon.

'She died of heart failure when he attacked her?' Peroni suggested, coming back into the conversation, pointedly not looking at the photos. 'It's still murder, isn't it?'

'Oh, poor sweet innocent,' Teresa said with a sigh. 'Take a deep breath. It's time for me to shatter a few illusions about our pretty little curator from the Louvre. As I told you when we first arrived here, she had intercourse shortly before she died. And no, I don't think it was rape. There's nothing to indicate that really. No bruising, no marks on her body. No skin underneath her fingernails. This was consensual. Sex on the sofa, in front of that spooky painting. With a knife to add a little spice to the occasion.'

Peroni looked out over the stinking holes in the flag-stones to the dusty window. It was raining: faint grey streaks coming down in a soft slanting veil onto the smoke-stained stones of the *centro storico*.

Susanna Placidi, furious at this idea, glowered at the two pathologists.

'How the hell can you know that?'

'Evidence,' Di Capua said simply. 'Here. Here and here.'

He pointed to the photos. Elsewhere on Véronique Gillet's body, on the upper arms, on the smooth plateau of her stomach, and beneath her breasts, there were healed cut marks too and a network of shallow but visible scars from some earlier encounter.

Teresa Lupo went through them, one by one, indicating each with a pencil.

'These are indicative of some form of self-inflicted wound, or ones cut by a . . . partner, I imagine that's what we'd have to call it. Human beings are imaginative creatures sometimes. If you want specialist insight into sadomasochistic sexual practices I can put you in touch with some people who might be able to help.'

'They could be just . . . *cuts*,' Placidi objected.

Falcone sighed.

'No. They are not simply cuts. One perhaps. Two. But . . .'

Costa forced himself to examine the photos carefully.

In places the light scars criss-crossed one another, like a sculptor's hatch marks on some plaster statuette. And something else too, it occurred to him, and the thought turned his stomach.

'There are too many,' Costa said. 'Also . . . I don't know if there's a connection, but Caravaggio made this kind of mark in many of his paintings. His incisions are one way people use to identify his work.'

He looked hard at the photographs. The small, straight cuts on the woman's flesh, mostly healed, but a few still red and recent, were horribly similar. He tried to remember where they were on the canvas they had found: on the naked goddess's upper arms and thighs. Just as with Véronique Gillet.

'The painting—' Costa went on.

'Is a subject for another conversation, and another officer,' Falcone interrupted, and gave him a quick, dark glance. This was not, it seemed, an appropriate moment.

'I know nothing about art,' Teresa Lupo said. 'But I can tell you one thing. She came here to die. Or, more precisely, to make sure that when she died, it happened here, which would suggest to me that she knew this place, knew the people, and certainly knew what went on.' Her bloodless face, expressive in spite of her plain, flat features, flitted to each of them in turn. 'But what do I know? You're the police. You work it out.'

'And the man?' Falcone asked.

'Six stab wounds to the chest, three of them deep enough to be fatal on their own,' Teresa replied straight away, and watched Di Capua take out a folder of large colour photographs, ones no one much wanted to look at. Blood and gore spattered Aldo Caviglia's white, still-well-ironed shirt. 'This is extreme violence I would put down to a man. Women tend to give up around the third blow or go on a lot longer than this. A couple went into the heart.'

'Aldo was not the kind of man to get involved in nonsense like this,' Peroni protested. 'Creepy sex. It's ridiculous . . .'

'You don't know that, Gianni,' Costa observed. 'How many times did you meet him?'

'Three? Four? How many does it take? He wasn't that type. Or a voyeur or something. Listen . . . I've talked to his neighbours. To his sister. She lives out in Ostia. She works in a bakery. Like he used to.'

The big man didn't like the obvious doubt on their faces.

'Also I spoke to the woman in the cafe down the street. She said someone who sounds like Aldo came in, white to the gills, desperate to find some skinny, red-haired French woman. He was *trying* to find her. He had her wallet. OK. It's obvious how that came about. Per-haps – ' Peroni struggled to find some explanation – 'perhaps he just changed his mind and wanted to give it back.'

'Pickpockets do that all the time,' Rosa suggested sarcastically.

'He was not that kind of man,' Peroni said, almost stuttering with anger.

To Costa's astonishment, Rosa Prabakaran reached out, put her hand on Peroni's arm and said, 'I believe you, Gianni. He was a good guy. He just couldn't keep his hands to himself, but that's not exactly a unique problem in Rome, is it?'

'You're in the wrong job,' Peroni replied immediately, pointing a fat finger in her face. 'You have something personal going on here. I'm sorry about that, Rosa, not that I imagine it helps. But you should *not* be on a case of this nature. It's just plain . . . wrong.'

The forensic people were starting to look uncomfortable. So was Teresa Lupo. Her people liked to work without disruptions.

'Why is it wrong?' Rosa asked him, taking her hand away, almost smiling. 'There are plenty of officers on this force who've been robbed some time, or beaten up in the street. Does that mean they can't arrest a thief or a thug. Is innocence of a crime a prerequisite for being able to investigate it now?'

'That's just clever talk,' Peroni snapped. 'Everyone here knows what I mean.'

The room was silent for a moment. Then Leo Falcone folded his arms, looked at Peroni and said, 'We do. And in normal circumstances you would be absolutely right. But these circumstances are anything but, I'm afraid.'

He cast a brief glance at the young policewoman, a regretful look, and was silent.

'You bet this isn't normal,' Teresa agreed. '*Normally* I'm fighting to find material to work with. We're positively dripping in the stuff here. I've got blood and semen. DNA aplenty. Silvio? Fetch, boy . . .'

Di Capua went to the rear door, where a pile of transparent plastic evidence bags was beginning to grow waist high. He came back with a swift selection. They looked at what lay inside.

'We haven't had time to take it all away yet,' Teresa continued. 'We've been too busy digging. There are whips. Flails. Knives. Masks. Some leather items that are a little beyond my imagination. We have a wealth of physical evidence here the likes of which I have never seen in my entire career. We could nail the bastards who did this with one-tenth of this material. Just point us at a suspect and we'll tell you yes or no in the blink of an eye. This is the motherlode of all crime scenes. All we need from you is someone to test it against.'

The room was silent.

'*Well?*' Teresa asked again, somewhat more loudly.

'Let's take this outside,' Falcone murmured.

- 2 -

It was freezing cold in the control van parked at the head of the street, by the Piazza Borghese. The interior stank of spent tobacco smoke. It came from a large middle-aged man in a brown overcoat who sat on one of the metal chairs awaiting their arrival. He introduced himself as Grimaldi from the legal department and then lit another cigarette.

Peroni was the last to sit down at the plain metal table in the centre of the cabin. He took a long, frank look at Falcone, who wasn't meeting his gaze, then at Susanna Placidi, who'd placed a large notebook computer in front of her and was now staring at the screen, tapping the keyboard with a frantic, uncomfortable nervousness.

'Shouldn't we have a few more people in on this conversation?' Peroni asked. 'Six people murdered. The press going crazy. Is this really just down to us?'

'What you're about to learn is strictly down to us,' Falcone replied, and cast the woman inspector a savage look. 'Tell them.'

She stopped typing and said, 'We know who they are.'

The utter lack of enthusiasm and conviction with which she spoke made Costa's heart sink.

'You know who killed my wife?' he asked quietly.

'We think we can narrow it down to one of four men,' Placidi replied, staring hard at the computer screen.

'And they're just walking around out there?' Peroni asked, instantly furious, with Teresa beginning to make equally incensed noises by his side.

'For the time being,' Falcone replied, and nodded at Rosa Prabakaran.

Without a word she reached over, took the computer from the uncomplaining Placidi and began hitting the keys. She found what she wanted, then turned the screen round for them all to see.

It was a photo from the Caravaggio exhibition Costa had worked on the previous winter, organizing security. Four men stood in front of the grey, sensual figure of *The Sick Bacchus*, which had been temporarily moved from the Villa Borghese for the event. This was a self-portrait too, a younger Caravaggio than that seen in the religious paintings, and in the *Venus* now undergoing scrutiny under the expert eye of Agata Graziano. Dissolute, saturnine, clutching a bunch of old grapes the same colour as his sallow skin, staring at the viewer, like a whore displaying her wares showing a naked shoulder; despite this, the only focus of hope and light in the entire canvas.

The men in front of it didn't look much different. One, vaguely familiar, seemed more than a little drunk. He stood on the left of the line, with his arm around the shoulders of the man next to him in a tight proprietorial fashion. The other two stood slightly apart, looking like friends in the process of turning into enemies for some reason.

'They call themselves the Ekstasists.'

Costa couldn't take his eyes off them. He gazed at the

blank, cruel masculine faces on the screen, trying to imagine what each would look like inside a black, military hood.

'Him,' Costa said eventually, indicating the one on the far left, the man with his arm around the shoulders of his companion.

The two women officers exchanged glances and said nothing.

Grimaldi, the lawyer, finally shuffled his chair up to the table and took some interest.

'The man wore a mask,' he pointed out. 'How can you be sure?'

'I'm not. I'm guessing. You can still bring him in on that.'

Grimaldi sighed and said, 'Ah. Guesses.'

'He has the same build,' he insisted. 'The same stiff posture. As if he used to be a soldier. This—'

'This,' Grimaldi cut in, 'is Count Franco Malaspina. Who was a soldier once, an officer during military service, for which he received some decoration. He is also one of the richest and most powerful individuals in Rome, a patron of the arts and of charity, an eligible bachelor, a face from the social magazines, a fine man, or so a casual scan of the press cuttings might have one think.' Grimaldi hesitated and cast his sharp dark eyes at each of them.

Costa knew the name. He'd surely seen the man's picture in the papers. As far as he was aware, Malaspina continued to own the vast private palace with his family name, which sprawled through Ortaccio, embracing both the Vicolo del Divino Amore and the Barberini's studio. Was simple chance recognition why Costa had pointed the finger of blame?

'I'm sorry,' he said. 'Perhaps I was just remembering the wrong thing.'

'Perhaps,' Grimaldi agreed. 'Let me tell you a little of this man all the same.'

The lawyer didn't even need to refer to notes. He simply spoke from memory as Costa stared at the photo on Rosa's screen, an image of a tall, athletic twenty-eight-year-old merchant banker with an eponymous family palace in Rome, homes in Milan and New York, and, said Grimaldi, enough files in the Questura to fill an entire lifetime for most hoods, every last one still open. Malaspina was heir to a fortune that had been built up by his clan over more than three centuries, one that began with the bank-rolling of a Pope. He was a true Roman aristocrat of a dying breed, and came from a family with unusual antecedents. Unlike most of the city's nobility, the Malaspinas had embraced the era of Mussolini, seeing in the dictator opportunity, and not the coarse, proletarian Fascism most other ancient families detected and instantly despised. His grandfather had served as a minister for Il Duce. His own father had been a rabble-rouser on the fringes of right-wing politics, and consequently had been deeply disliked in Rome, a city that was temperamentally left-leaning, until his death in a plane crash five years ago.

Costa had no recollection of Franco Malaspina being involved in machinations around the parties that formed the continuing, argumentative coalitions at the heart of the Italian state; only the vague memory that he was a notorious player in the money world, one who sailed so close to the wind that the financial authorities had investigated him more than once. Not that these probes had resulted in any form of action, which meant that Mala-spina was either innocent or so deeply powerful no one dared yet take him on. There were good reasons for caution. Men of his kind liked to build up fortunes before turning to the Senate and Parliament to lay wider, deeper foundations for their power.

Rosa identified the others in the picture; they were strangers to him, though two names were familiar. Giorgio Castagna was the son of the head of a well-known and notorious porn empire, a Roman playboy rarely out of the showbiz magazines. Emilio Buccafusca was the owner of an art gallery that specialized in some of the more outré areas of sculpture and painting. He had frequently clashed with the law over the public display of work that bordered on the extreme. The previous winter his gallery had provoked public outrage for exhibiting several 'death sculptures' by a Scandinavian artist supposedly consisting of genuine human body parts encased in clear plastic.

After a field day in the media, a worried Questura *commissario* had dispatched Teresa Lupo to the gallery to investigate. She'd denounced the organs as demonstrably animal in origin, probably from slaughtered pigs. Buccafusca had laughed out loud at the time; now he didn't seem in the mood. Both men appeared somewhat inconsequential next to the aristocratic Malaspina, though they were all of similar stature, dressed in black, Castagna and Buccafusca with similar pinched and bitter faces.

There were more photographs too, from other arts events. Malaspina's expression – self-satisfied, confident, powerful – was constant throughout. In the early photos the others looked much the same way. Something had happened over the previous few months to change that. There, Costa knew, Falcone would see his opportunity.

The fourth figure, a man completely unknown to Costa, usually skulked close to the background, and seemed somewhat out of place in such company. He was short, sandy-haired and chubby, about thirty, with a florid, slack face, possibly from ill-health or drinking, and an expression that veered, in these photos, from boredom to a visible, subservient fear.

'Being an avid reader of junk magazines,' Teresa Lupo said, staring at the same image, 'I feel I've met most of this eurotrash already. But who's fat boy?'

'Nino Tomassoni,' Rosa Prabakaran answered. 'He's the only one here who doesn't have much money as far as we can see. He's an assistant curator at the Villa Borghese.'

Tomassoni. The name sparked a memory for Costa, one he couldn't place.

'The man is probably on the periphery of all this,' Placidi added. 'Perhaps he's barely involved at all.'

Falcone scowled at her. It was exactly this kind of imprecision in detail that he hated in an officer.

'His name is on the list,' Falcone pointed out. 'If that means nothing, it means nothing for the rest of them.'

'The list?' Peroni wondered. 'You're accusing these men of some pretty nasty stuff. They are people who like to wear nice suits. And all you have against them is a list?'

Placidi sighed, then pulled a sheaf of printed papers out of the folder in front of her and stacked them on the table.

'They're more . . . messages really,' she said. 'We got another this morning.'

'You did?' Falcone was clearly unaware of this latest missive and displeased by that fact.

'It arrived just before I left for this meeting,' she answered with a sudden burst of temper. 'I can't be held responsible for keeping everyone informed about every damned thing. This is the same as the others. An untraceable email from a fake address. Nothing the computer people can work with.'

She placed the paper in front of them, not looking at the words. It was a standard office printout.

Placidi, you cow. What ARE you morons doing? Do I have to spell it out? The Ekstasists. Castagna. Buccafusca. Malaspina. And that stupid helpless bastard Tomassoni. Are they paying you scum enough to let them get away with this? Does it turn you on or something? Can you sleep at night?
PS Whatever you think THIS IS NOT FINISHED.

'That's it?' Costa asked. 'That's a case?'

'No!' It was Rosa Prabakaran, angry. 'It's not it. We have messages like this detailing a string of vicious attacks on black prostitutes, throughout the city, covering a period of almost four months. Where and when and how. We've tracked down some of the victims. The poor women are so scared they won't tell us a thing. It's true. Everything. And now – ' she nodded back down the alley, towards the studio – 'we know why. Those are the ones who survived.'

'Let me get this straight?' Peroni cut in. 'You have a string of sexual attacks and not one of these women will sign a witness statement?'

'I had one,' Rosa answered. 'She described everything.

The men. Four of them. What they did.' She paused. 'They took it in turns. The point . . .' She stopped for a moment, embarrassed. 'They wanted to see her in the throes of an orgasm. Not faked, the way hookers did. The real thing.'

Costa thought about the photographs they had found in the studio: shots of women in the throes of either agony or ecstasy.

'And if they didn't get what they wanted?' he asked.

'Then things turned violent. Very violent. These people weren't paying for sex. Not in the way we know it. They wanted to see something on the faces of these women. They wanted to know they put it there, and capture the moment somehow.'

She paused. This was difficult.

'The one who talked said they had a camera. They filmed everything. Her cries most of all. When they felt she was faking . . . they beat her.'

'All hookers fake it,' Peroni pointed out with vehemence. 'What kind of lunatics would do something like that? What do they expect?'

Costa looked at his friend. Peroni had spent years in vice. He must have seen some dreadful cases in that time. The expression of shock and distaste on his battered face told Costa he'd never heard of anything quite like this.

'Obviously they don't know hookers,' Costa suggested.

'They've known plenty of late,' Rosa continued. 'These are sick bastards. Clever bastards too. I thought I had that girl. Two days later she walked out of the hospital and disappeared. Maybe dead. Maybe back home with money. There's no way of telling.'

Falcone couldn't take his eyes off Susanna Placidi.

Costa knew why. A witness in a case like that should never have been allowed to flee, whatever the circumstances.

'Who do you think the messages are from?' Teresa asked.

The two female officers glanced at each other. Grimaldi was silent again, staring at the photos on the screen.

'We don't know,' Placidi admitted. 'Probably someone we don't know about. Someone on the periphery who thinks it's gone too far. Or Tomassoni . . .'

'It sounds like a woman, don't you think?' Teresa asked. 'Listen to the words. "Placidi, you cow!" I've been called a bitch a million times by some jerk male. But never a cow. They don't talk to you like that.'

'A woman, then!' Placidi screamed back. 'How the hell am I supposed to know?'

Teresa leaned over, impatient, close to anger.

'I said it sounds like a woman. Perhaps it's meant to. In which case they are clearly over-estimating our abilities somewhat. What does it matter? We've got DNA. We've got forensic coming out of our ears from that creepy room of theirs. Just go and arrest them and leave it all to me.'

Falcone sat back, folded his arms and waited for Placidi to respond. Grimaldi had adopted precisely the same position.

'We've tried to arrest them,' the woman inspector admitted. 'We've been to the lawyers more than once. The trouble is . . .' She scattered the emails over the table. 'This is all we have. The women won't talk. We can't . . . The evidence we have is all so vague.'

Her miserable eyes fell to the table again.

Teresa turned her attention to Falcone. 'Leo . . . Give

me an hour with these people and a bag of cotton swabs and I'll put them in a cell before bedtime. There's a bunch of dead bodies here and they're itching to talk.'

He looked at her and shook his bald, aquiline head.

'Why not?' asked Peroni.

Falcone picked up the sheets of messages on the table.

'Inspector Placidi told you. These are all we have,' he said. 'If they are what they appear, they clearly come from someone inside the group, someone who's apparently frightened about what they're doing. One imagines some-one whose name does not appear on these lists, though I wouldn't wish to rule that out.'

'So what?' Costa wondered.

'So alternatively they may be some kind of practical joke,' Falcone went on. 'Tomassoni apart, these people are often in the public eye. Publicity attracts cranks. We all know that. They could be innocent.'

Susanna Placidi banged the table with her fists.

'They are not innocent, Leo! These sons of bitches are laughing at us.'

'She's right,' Rosa said quietly, confidently. 'Taunting us is part of their fun, I swear.'

'That's hardly going to get anyone in court, is it?' Falcone observed severely. 'A policewoman's instinct.'

'Whoever wrote these emails knows the places!' Rosa screeched. 'They know the women, unless you think they've been making it up and putting themselves in hospital too.'

'I am aware of all this,' he replied coldly. 'I don't think for one moment that these are crank messages. From the point of view of Malaspina and his friends, though . . .'

'It's a good story,' Costa agreed. 'They will attract cranks.'

Falcone nodded, grateful for his support.

'Furthermore—'

'No!' It was Teresa Lupo, livid and ready to lose it. 'I do not wish to hear any more of this. I've told you we have the evidence. You've told me you have the suspects. Bring them in and leave it to me.'

She watched their faces. No one spoke until Grimaldi, the lawyer, took a deep breath, then said, 'If only it were that easy . . .

'I am here to tell you a simple truth,' he went on. 'Inspector Placidi and her team have attempted to do this very thing and failed. Unknown to me or anyone in my department, they arrested all four men named in these messages, without sufficient evidence or adequate preparation. Then they threw these anonymous, unconfirmed allegations at them in the absence of the slightest evidential corroboration, and . . .'

Placidi's face was reddening.

'Now we have to live with the consequences, which are damaging in the extreme,' Grimaldi concluded.

'I had to do something!' Placidi objected. 'I had to take the risk. The women wouldn't talk when it happened and two weeks later they were gone. We had nothing *but* these messages. Did you expect me to sit on my hands until some smartarse from elsewhere came up with something better?'

Falcone cast a fleeting sideways look in her direction, one Costa had seen in the past. He wondered if Placidi understood how dangerous was the ground beneath her.

'These are intelligent, important, well-connected men,' he pointed out. 'Did it not occur to you that perhaps that was part of their enjoyment too? Feeling untouchable, beyond the pathetic efforts of the law?'

She said nothing.

'They were never going to throw their hands up in the air and offer you a confession, Susanna. Had you thought about it for one moment, you would surely have known that.'

'There were women getting raped!' Placidi pressed.

'It now transpires there were women getting murdered,' Grimaldi declared. 'Which is all the more reason to do the job properly. Instead, you offended some very influential people so much they turned on us, very professionally too.'

Teresa Lupo's eyes start to dilate with a sudden, growing fury.

'You also forewarned them of the police investigation,' Falcone continued, 'without sufficient evidence even to substantiate a temporary arrest. They now understand fully what we will look for in the way of concrete evidence and can prepare for that eventuality.'

Placidi was close to tears.

'I wasn't to know . . .'

Falcone looked at the rest of them and then Grimaldi.

'You'd best tell them,' he suggested.

The lawyer took out a notebook from his jacket and consulted it.

'Two weeks ago, after being approached by Inspector Placidi's team, a team of lawyers representing all four men went before a magistrate, in camera,' he said. 'We had insufficient notice. Malaspina knows the legal system. He winds it round his little finger. He has the advantage of being extraordinarily rich and in league with some important figures in the organized crime world too. It is a winning combination.'

'And?' Teresa demanded.

'By the time we were able to assemble a competent team he was already challenging the legal rules through which we may and may not demand any physical evidence, both fingerprints and DNA specimens, from people who refuse to give them willingly.'

The pathologist's large face turned a shade paler.

'Rules? *Rules?* We know what the rules are. Either they give us a sample willingly or I get a piece of paper and force it out of them.'

It was that straightforward. All Costa needed if any subject refused a DNA sample was the approval of a senior officer in the Questura to take one by force if necessary. Most suspects ceased to resist once they realized they'd be compelled to provide a sample within a matter of minutes if need be.

Grimaldi's scowl was that of a man denied something he dearly craved.

'Thanks to Malaspina's lawyers, and our own ineptness, the rules have changed,' he said. 'From now on we may only obtain physical material against the will of a suspect on the basis of a judicial order. So if they object strongly enough we have to go before a magistrate, where we must make our case. We are, in a nutshell, screwed.'

The pathologist let loose a stream of Roman epithets.

Grimaldi waited for her to draw breath, then went on.

'The standard routine you have all grown accustomed to using in these situations is now out of the question should any suspect refuse. Unless you can find sufficient firm and incontrovertible evidence to put to a magistrate.'

Grimaldi picked up the papers, then dropped them on the table.

'Which, having spent the last hour going through what you have here, I must say you do not possess.'

Teresa's mouth hung open in astonishment.

'You mean I can pick up any amount of beautiful physical evidence I like and we can't match it to a suspect unless he or she deigns to cooperate? These people are criminals, for God's sake. Why should they do us any favours?'

'They won't,' the lawyer agreed. 'Unless they know they're innocent. We're trying to appeal the finding, but to be honest – ' he frowned – 'the question of human rights is rather fashionable at the moment.'

'What the hell about the rights of these women?' Teresa demanded.

Grimaldi's eyes widened with despair.

'Why are you arguing with me on this point? It is useless. This is now the law. I wish it were otherwise, but . . .'

'I could always organize for one of these nice gentlemen to bleed on me a little,' Peroni suggested. 'Or steal one of his coffee cups.'

The lawyer shook his head.

'Anything gathered by subterfuge will not only be inadmissible but may well damage our chances of a successful prosecution should we be able to gather sufficient evidence by other means. This is a general observation, by the way, one we must now apply to every case from this point forward, not simply to these charming gentlemen who call themselves the Ekstasists.'

A bitter, almost despondent look appeared on Falcone's lean, tanned face.

'Welcome to modern policing,' he said. 'I'd hoped to escape this particular phase. What Grimaldi has explained to you will be standard practice in all cases from this point on until we can successfully challenge it. Other officers are having this change in policy explained to them privately over the next few days, though not the reasons for it. We would like to keep those to ourselves.' He grimaced. 'At least for a little while.'

Teresa Lupo glowered at the female inspector across the table.

'You did this? Your cack-handed blundering has put the onus on *us* to prove bastards like these need to show us they're innocent? That's half our working practices dumped straight out of the window. Just because you barged in there without doing your homework first.'

'No!' Susanna Placidi screeched back at her. She pointed at the photos on the screen. 'I did my best. Malaspina is responsible for this. That man—'

'Not good enough,' the pathologist yelled. 'You're not good enough. This is—'

'Ladies. *Ladies!*'

Grimaldi had a loud and commanding voice. It silenced them, for a little while at least.

Costa waited for the temperature to fall a little, then said, 'In that case, you'd better start looking for some proof.'

'Where?' Susanna Placidi demanded.

Grimaldi stared at Falcone and raised an interested eyebrow.

'That,' the inspector announced, 'is something you no longer need worry about.'

He shook his head, stared at the desk, then at her.

'This case . . . appals me, Placidi. We have lost a dear friend. There are women who have been attacked and worse in this city of ours, while it was your responsibility to protect them. Your laxness and incompetence have cost innocent people their lives. You have damaged our ability to unravel the dreadful mess you have left behind. And all you can say is . . . you did your best. If that was the case, it was sorely lacking. You can go home now. This case no longer concerns you.'

He reached over and dragged the computer to his side of the table.

'Nor any in the future if I can help it. Breathe one word to a soul about what we have discussed here and I will, I swear, drag you in front of a disciplinary tribunal and finish what's left of your career for good.'

Grimaldi took an envelope out of his pocket and placed it in front of her.

'These are formal suspension papers. I will confirm the notice was properly delivered.'

She was speechless, red with rage, her eyes brimming with tears.

'I will give you a lift home, signora,' Grimaldi offered.

'I have a driver and a car!'

'Not any more,' he replied.

– 3 –

Falcone waited for them to leave. Then he went and checked the door. There was no one else in earshot.

'This is my city,' he went on. '*Our* city. It's got its problems, God knows. But I always thought a woman could walk safely on these streets. Any woman. Black or white. Legal or illegal. I don't care. I will *not* allow that to change. Not under any circumstances. Whatever the cost.'

It was Peroni who broke the silence. He was laughing, just for a moment, and with precious little mirth.

Falcone's grey eyebrows rose.

'Well?'

'I love it when the word "cost" comes into your conversation, Leo,' Peroni observed pleasantly. 'It always suggests life is about to turn interesting.'

Falcone ignored the taunt. He looked relaxed. Determined too. Costa knew this kind of mood. It meant someone was about to wander outside the usual rules.

'Look at us,' Falcone said, smiling, opening his hands in a wide, expansive gesture. 'Two careers in autumn. Two careers in spring. And the best criminal pathologist in Italy.'

'No praise, please,' Teresa protested. 'You know how uncomfortable that makes me.'

'It's true! What better time for you to test your skills?' Then, more grimly, 'What better time for us?'

His eyes drifted to the computer screen and caught the image of Franco Malaspina there, frozen by some paparazzo's camera. The man had frizzy dark hair and the features of a Sicilian, an angular, handsome face almost North African in its dusky hue. His bleak, black eyes glittered back at the photographer, staring at the lens intently, full of the easy wilful arrogance of a certain kind of Roman aristocrat.

'This man thinks he and his friends are unassailable,' Falcone said. 'I have close to one hundred officers in the Questura on this case, two in Africa seeking earlier victims as potential witnesses, and I have put out every appeal I can think of to our friends in the Carabinieri. This is not a time for rivalries and they know it. These are the kinds of crimes none of us ever expected to see in Rome and we must do all in our power to bring these men to face justice. Yet . . .'

He wrestled his slender hands together in frustration.

'I cannot tell any of them the names we have here. If I did that, these men would know. Their lawyers would return to court again, screaming harassment of the innocent, without, on our part, the least tangible evidence to support our efforts. Tame politicians would be dragged out of their beds to hear their complaints. We all know how these things work. We would lose what little we have, perhaps forever. There is an army of officers, good men and women, who will do everything they can to find some conventional – some might say old-fashioned – evidence that might break this case. Yet they must work in the dark, since I daren't share with them a word of the information you have heard here. They will fail, with dignity and professionalism, but it will be failure all the same.'

'Leo—' Costa began.

'No,' the inspector protested. 'Hear me out. Unless they have left some obvious and stupid form of identification in this hellhole of theirs, Inspector Placidi's incompetence means they have every right to feel untouchable.'

He glanced at Teresa Lupo.

'Am I mistaken, Doctor?'

'I told you, Leo. We are swimming in forensic. In proof.'

'What? A business card? A letter? A driving licence?'

'*Proof!*'

'By which you mean scientific proof. DNA and prints. The two primary pillars of our investigative process today. You heard Grimaldi. They are useless. Proof means nothing if I can't take it before a judge. They have us gagged and bound, don't you see? Without some miracle I cannot foresee, the only ones who can establish their guilt are these men themselves. All our conventional means of attack are worthless. I can do . . . nothing.'

He placed his long forefinger on the photograph of Franco Malaspina and stared at Costa.

'And I want them, this creature most of all. He is not some Renaissance prince who can flaunt himself on these streets regardless of the law.'

Falcone glanced at his watch.

'At twelve thirty the four of you will meet in the Piazza Navona, outside the Brazilian Embassy, for convenience. I will arrange for lunch to be brought round to my apartment at one.' He glanced at Costa and Peroni in turn.

'The place has only two bedrooms, I'm afraid, so you two can fight over the sofa between yourselves.'

'I'm staying in your apartment?' Rosa Prabakaran asked, astonished.

'Until further notice,' Falcone declared.

Teresa Lupo's arms flailed in the air in protest.

'And I'm supposed to walk out of the biggest murder case we've had in years and throw in my lot with some private underhand snooping of yours?'

'If there is one thing I have learned about you in recent times,' Falcone replied, 'it is that you will do what you feel like regardless of anything I say. I invite you along to listen and then decide. Given that no one, not God himself, seems privy to either your working methods or your diary, I doubt you will have much difficulty being engaged simultaneously in both your conventional work and a task that is a little . . . different, and something else besides for all I know.'

Teresa was momentarily speechless, then muttered, 'Was that a compliment or not?'

'I will not rest until these bastards are in jail, and neither will you,' Falcone continued, ignoring the question. 'I have gone through what passes as Placidi's investigation log on this case. There is a strand of evidence no one here knows about, an odd, possibly worthless thread. Susanna Placidi certainly thought so, which was why she buried it at the bottom of the pile.'

The grey eyes travelled over them all and fell on Rosa Prabakaran.

'We have an appointment with a statue,' Falcone said cryptically. 'After that you are on your own.'

Part 6

INCRIMINATING VERSES

– 1 –

'Statues can't talk,' Peroni insisted.

The five of them – Costa, Rosa, Teresa, Peroni and Falcone – stood in the tiny open space known as the Piazza Pasquino, named for the battered three-quarters statue of a man with no arms and an unrecognizable face turned as if to look towards some vanished companion. The inspector had arrived on time, then marched them there immediately. They were in a busy narrow street which fed off the sprawling Piazza Navona. The rain had halted for a while.

'This one can,' Falcone replied. 'Unfortunately the only police officer who had the wit to listen was Agente Prabakaran.'

Smiling at that, Rosa walked forward, pointed to the worn, stained stone on which the statue known as Pasquino stood, and explained, 'The anti-racist people told me. They found it first.'

The base of Pasquino was covered with posters, hastily pasted there, most in frantic, badly written script, though a few were printouts from a computer and even had simple photographs and cartoons on them.

Costa remembered this place from his schooldays.

Pasquino had been plastered in anonymous messages for centuries. In recent times most were anti-government, posted there by left-wing or anarchist groups, or ordinary citizens who wanted to vent their anger without revealing their identity. He couldn't recollect ever seeing any racist material. It was rare in Rome in any case. The sight of Pasquino jogged another memory, though Rosa got there first.

'There are other statues that used to serve the same function,' she said. 'They placed messages on those too.'

'Not now,' Falcone interrupted, and ushered them down into the narrow medieval street of the Governo Vecchio. His apartment was a hundred metres or so along from Pasquino's piazza, on the first floor next to an upmarket shop selling expensive fountain pens and propelling pencils. The place was huge and beautifully furnished in a modern fashion. Falcone was clearly proud of it, judging by the brief, modest tour he insisted upon – out of the practical consideration that they would now be closeted there for some time, naturally. There was an elegant living room decorated in plain, modern taste, two bedrooms, a well-equipped kitchen with a small balcony and a line of healthy pot plants glistening after the morning's rain. It was spotless, with the smell of recent cleaning. He had prepared for this moment. There was also a case full of smart clothes, sent by Bea from the farmhouse, which Falcone passed over without a word of explanation.command.

He beckoned them to the table, opened the briefcase he'd brought and took some photos out of a folder.

'More statues,' he said, and glanced at Prabakaran. 'Agente?'

She pointed to the representation of a muscular man

built into a brick wall. He wore a beret and was holding a barrel over a drinking fountain. Water still trickled from the cask, though the work looked centuries old. 'This is Il Facchino. The porter. It's in a side street off the Corso, near the Piazza del Collegio Romano. And this . . .' She removed another photo from Falcone's folder: a weather-worn full-length statue of a Roman noble in robes, stand-ing on a plinth against a grime-stained marble wall.

'I recognize that,' Peroni said instantly. 'It's in Vittorio Emanuele, next to the church, Sant'Andrea della Valle. I chased off some classy girls doing business there years ago. It's also – ' the big man glanced at each of them, to make sure they would be impressed – 'the scene of the first act of *Tosca*.'

Teresa blinked. 'You know opera?'

'One of the girls told me. I said they were classy. I didn't hear any statue talking, though.'

'He's known as Abate Luigi,' Rosa continued, ignoring the distraction. 'Pasquino still talks today. I thought even you might have noticed, Gianni. It's always covered in cryptic slogans. Usually, if you can understand them, ones that insult the same few people in the government.'

'I know it!' Peroni insisted. 'What the hell has this got to do with us?'

Costa intervened. 'The talking statues were a way of making a point that could have got you into trouble if your name was attached to it. Perhaps a political point. Perhaps just ratting on a neighbour.' A memory troubled him; it came with a mental picture of Emily, lovely in a shirt and jeans by the side of the gleaming lagoon, that lost summer eighteen months before. 'In Venice they used to do it privately, by posting unsigned let-ters through those lions' mouths I once showed you. In

Rome, we prefer something a little more public. But only on Pasquino these days. You say there were messages on the others?'

'Exactly,' Falcone said, and removed a large envelope from his case and spread the contents on the table: sheet after sheet of words, jumbled together in the random yet semi-logical way a madman might have worked. He glowered at the messages and pointed at a set of enlargements of the head on each of them. 'Placidi didn't even look closely enough to see this.'

Magnified, it was clear there was a crest on the top of each, an ancient coat of arms of some kind. When he caught the direction of Costa's gaze, Falcone threw a photographic blow-up of the emblem onto the table.

Three dragon-like creatures were depicted there, limbs writhing, talons clutching at the screaming torso of a female figure entangled in their scaly embrace. The beasts possessed vicious, grinning features, half human, half beast. The expression on the woman's face might have been pleasure or pain, rapture or the final rictus of terror.

A title ran above the chilling emblem in contorted medieval script: *The Ekstasists*.

The verses weren't written but formed from headline words and letters cut out of newspapers and magazines, then pasted together to form cryptic poems.

Rosa began to sort them into three separate piles, then read out one from the first.

'You baboon whores, beware the bad thorn's prick.
It's blood he lusts for, not the thing between your legs.'

'Malaspina,' Costa said. 'The bad thorn.'

She nodded. 'That was stuck on Pasquino the morning after a hooker was left for dead near the Spanish Steps. Right next to another talking statue they call the Baboon.'

'That's a hell of a stretch, Rosa,' Teresa complained.

'So everyone told me. But there's a pattern once you see it. The messages each make some cryptic reference to one of their pleasant little club. We've a total of thirteen: four each for Castagna and Buccafusca, five for Malaspina. Here's another one for you.'

She picked out a sheet from the second pile.

'Run quick, poor Simonetta!
The mountain chestnut spills its spiny seeds regardless.
And snakes are deaf to your black cries.'

'The chestnut being Castagna?' Peroni asked, knowing the answer.

'That one was left on Il Facchino *before* the event,' Rosa explained. 'The following day a black woman was raped, then beaten with a wooden club in the Via dei Serpenti in the Monti district, close to the Forum. We couldn't possibly have understood the reference to snakes and mountains beforehand, of course. They're not stupid. They're not trying to lead us to them. It's some kind of a joke. A tease.'

'Who the hell is "Simonetta"?' Teresa asked.

'You'd know if you moved in art and history circles,' Rosa replied, looking at Costa.

So many memories were coming back to him at that moment, from his single days when much of his free time was spent in art galleries, staring at the works on the walls, trying to understand what he saw there and link it to his native city's past. And, too, from the delightful time he'd spent working security for the exhibition in the Palazzo Ruspoli, when he and Emily had finally decided to marry. An entire room there had been devoted to the Medici dynasty.

'Modern academics believe that the first Duke of Florence, Alessandro de' Medici, had a black slave for a mother,' Costa said. 'It was kept secret, as much as possible of course. But there were so many reports it's generally thought to be true. The woman's name was supposedly Simonetta.'

'The Medicis were black?' Peroni asked, amazed.

Rosa smiled. 'A little. Millions of people are, you know. Where's the surprise? White Italians have been screwing us for centuries. Simonetta, incidentally, didn't come from Florence. She was from near here. Lazio. Collevecchio. Thirty minutes up the A1. It's a little too chi-chi for coloured people these days. But the woman they attacked worked the motorways. She was picked up from the Flaminia service station by three men she said she couldn't identify. Flaminia is the nearest service point to Collevecchio, which means . . .'

She left it there.

Teresa, astonished, asked, 'You really think they'd go to those lengths to make some kind of obscure point? Why, for God's sake?'

Falcone didn't let her answer.

'To see how long it would take us to read what they were doing. She's right. This is a game, a test. The kick they get out of taunting us is as much a part of their pleasure as the act itself.'

He stabbed a long finger at another message. This time Costa read it.

> *'The mouth of darkness truly bites.*
> *Unlike the mouth of truth.*
> *Ask dirty sweet Laeticia.'*

'The mouth of darkness is presumably a play on the name Buccafusca,' Falcone said. 'This one was pinned to Abate Luigi the day after an Angolan illegal immigrant, Laeticia Candido, was visited in hospital when the staff – not the woman – called the Questura. She'd been found unconscious near the Bocca della Verità. The mouth of darkness and the mouth of truth.'

He appeared stiff with visible outrage.

'The woman had several bite marks on her breasts and other parts of her torso. The bites removed substantial amounts of flesh. She will be scarred for life. The only thing she would say about her attackers was that they carried a camera and filmed her throughout.'

Peroni gazed at the pages on the table and let loose a long, pained sigh.

'When Susanna Placidi's people asked for a statement,' Falcone continued, 'she wouldn't even file a complaint. If it weren't for the message we wouldn't know how there was a connection at all, which is one more reason why they send us these things. Now she's gone. Home probably. I have the Angolan police looking and some of our officers on the way to help. I am not hopeful.'

Costa had a sudden picture in his head: the Bocca della Verità, where lines of happy tourists queued patiently to place a hand into the gap of an Imperial-era water-culvert cover, believing a spoken lie might snap it off, just as Gregory Peck promised Audrey Hepburn in *Roman Holiday*. This was central Rome, out in the open, next to the busy Lungotevere, an area where street safety had never been an issue.

'How the hell can this happen, Leo?' Teresa asked, outraged. 'Why didn't someone pick it up?'

He frowned. 'Susanna Placidi didn't have the experience, the imagination or the learning. Or the witnesses. We believe those who survived were paid off, as was Laeticia Candido. We don't have a single signed statement, one we could use in court. As far as we know, most victims have returned home, doubtless carrying the kind of money they wouldn't pick up working the streets. Or they're dead in that hellhole in the Vicolo del Divino Amore. What does that leave us? A few anonymous emails mentioning this odd and inexplicable term, the Ekstasists, and some strange, vile street graffiti that seemed unconnected until Rosa here put two and two together. Meanwhile, Placidi ignored everything of use and simply marched in on those grinning aristocrats, thinking they'd hold out their hands the moment they saw a badge.'

'Why did she do that?' Costa asked. 'She must have had evidence.'

He caught the dark thunder in Rosa Prabakaran's face.

'It was a routine follow-up. We had Malaspina's number plate caught on CCTV. Nothing more. We were just going through the routine and . . .'

They waited. She shook her head.

'You need to meet him to understand. He laughed at us. It was subtle. He didn't say an incriminating word. He didn't need to. I was there, with Placidi, and both of us understood it was him on the spot. He wanted us to know. It was what he intended. And . . .'

She raised her slender shoulders in a gesture of frustration.

'Then she did what Malaspina wanted of us all along, I guess. Brought in everyone, demanded DNA, warrants, the lot. We had nothing except a number plate and a smirk on that stuck-up face. It was impossible. Unbelievable. They walked free because we lacked the evidence, and we never even tried to lay these messages at their door.'

Falcone reached for the photograph of the man, drawing a finger over his fine, dark features.

'It's not unbelievable at all. It's the sequence of events he had in place for the moment we came for him.'

Rosa said something caustic under her breath.

'I know, I know,' Falcone said with a pained sigh. 'You tried to tell Placidi. But this is a highly unusual case, and we are temperamentally inclined to struggle with anything that lies outside the norm. Would I have made the same mistake if you'd come to me? I'd certainly have wanted some answers. The rape unit doesn't have that stretch of the imagination. It's about rape. And this – ' his eyes drifted to the window – 'is about a lot more than that somehow.'

He stared at the messages.

'The Ekstasists. Why would wealthy, powerful young men wish to capture some poor street prostitute reaching a moment of rapture? Educated men like these?'

'Educated?' Rosa asked, visibly inflamed by the word.

'Educated,' the inspector repeated. 'Listen to the words. *Listen*. They think they're writing a kind of poetry.

They believe they're taking part in some kind of perform-
ance, one that's not quite real, maybe. I don't know.
These people aren't born criminals . . .'

'You wouldn't say that if you saw some of the women
they left raped and bleeding in the road,' Rosa spat back
at him. 'And they were the lucky ones.'

'They're not ordinary criminals,' Falcone insisted.
'Which means we cannot hope to apprehend them using
ordinary means. If we treat them the way the want us to
– the way, I suspect, we would temperamentally prefer –
then we will surely fail once more. Teresa will ensure her
people rake over every last stone and speck of dust in that
dreadful place to find some link with these men beyond
the prints and DNA we can't use for the moment. I have
officers on two continents trying to find someone who
will put their names in a statement.'

He stared at them in turn, to emphasize the point he
was about to make.

'But if we put them under formal surveillance with
what little we have, they can and will go back to their
lawyers and start taking us to court for harassment, and
they would win. I do not intend to let that happen.'

Teresa Lupo pulled the set of photos in front of her
and put a finger on Franco Malaspina's swarthy, smug
face.

'You think you know what's going on here, Leo. It's
time to share.'

He sighed and shook his head.

'I know very little. This is guesswork, and guesswork
alone. I can't broach it in the Questura. You all know the
politics of the department at the moment. We have a new
commissario, the man who turned up from Milan last
week. I have scarcely discussed this case with him yet.

That's the way things are. Management comes before crime. Do not expect me to fight a battle I can't hope to win.'

'What are you thinking?' Teresa persisted.

He took a deep breath.

'I can only imagine that this is some kind of strange brotherhood, a rite of passage with its roots in their mutual affection for art, since that is the only thing they have in common apart from breeding. I believe Véronique Gillet was a part of it, an active member who came here to die in that place, at the hands of one, perhaps more, of these men, willingly. The unexpected arrival of Aldo Caviglia changed all that. They now no longer have this killing room of theirs or the painting which may have had some special significance. So what do they do?'

'They give up,' Costa said straight away. 'They go back to being rich, ambitious private citizens, who keep quiet company with their criminal friends but do nothing wrong in public, not a thing. And then . . .'

It was so obvious and so simple. None of this happened through need or some conventional criminal urge. If Falcone was right – and he usually was – the entire deadly interlude was just a game, a bloody prank. Once the risk became too real, the men went back to leading apparently blameless lives, smug and safe inside their remembrance of the evil they had achieved, and their certain understanding that this was known to the authorities too. Their lawyers killed what past suspicion might damage them. The police struggled to find a single new act with which to pursue the case.

'That would be my guess,' Falcone agreed. 'So in the circumstances we can only tread water, or be . . . a little creative.'

They were silent. There was a look in his eyes Costa now knew well. This was the moment the case went beyond the usual. This was why they were here.

Falcone walked over to the long modern sideboard and came back with a new laptop. He placed it on the desk and turned it on. Very quickly three photographs appeared on the screen: live video, fed from cameras that must have been high up on a wall overlooking the street.

The lenses were focused on three figures everyone in the room knew by now: Pasquino, Il Facchino and Abate Luigi, three grubby stone statues, damp, malformed shapes in the winter rain. Falcone pressed some more keys. The screen was covered in row after row of tiny video images, from all the CCTV cameras in all the familiar places every *centro storico* cop had come to know from past investigations.

'Obsessive men respond to obsessive acts. Count Franco Malaspina isn't the only one who can write messages,' Falcone murmured, and threw on the table a sheaf of pages, each surmounted with the small obscure crest of the Ekstasists at its head, and covered in the large, spidery writing that Costa recognized as Falcone's own.

– 2 –

Three hours later Costa walked in silence with Leo Falcone to the Palazzo Doria Pamphilj, wearing the suit, white shirt and tie that had been brought from home, thinking about what he'd heard. Teresa had returned to the Questura to continue the difficult – perhaps hopeless – hunt for some clue in the wealth of material she was retrieving from the Vicolo del Divino Amore. Peroni and Rosa were mastering the surveillance system which Falcone had begged from some acquaintances in the security services. It was sophisticated, quite unlike anything Costa had seen in use by the state police. Falcone must have pulled some important strings. In addition to the existing surveillance network, each of the talking statues was covered by three cameras, all capable of night sight. The computer logged a video frame from each every second. Whenever anyone approached a statue close enough to be expected to post a message on it, the monitoring system kicked in and generated an audible alert. That way whoever was on duty could be in touch with what was happening in the different locations without having to keep his or her eyes glued to the screen. It was better than standing out in a doorway in the miserable winter weather.

There was plenty of other work besides. Falcone had retrieved every last document in existence on the three suspects, from newspaper clippings to private internal reports held by the police and security service archives. The public information was depressingly predictable. A few traffic incidents apart, the newspapers had no evidence to suggest that Franco Malaspina, Giorgio Castagna and Emilio Buccafusca were anything other than the rich, privileged individuals they purported to be on the surface. In private, however, Malaspina – and he alone – had been the subject of no fewer than five investigations by the police, the Carabinieri and the Direzione Investigativa Antimafia. Each had ended in failure after intense legal threats and new-found silences among potential witnesses. He was a man who knew how to work with the system. In some ways he seemed to think he owned it.

In the Piazza del Collegio Romano Falcone stopped. This was where they would part: the inspector back to the Questura; Costa to meet Agata Graziano, at the inspector's request, in the gallery set in the sprawling private palace that lurked behind the busy shopping street of the Corso.

'Are you happy with what I'm doing?' Falcone asked. 'Be frank.'

'I'm happy.'

'You're involved. You probably feel that's not enough. But this may be a long game, Nic. We need to improvise. We have to shake them out of their lair. Inside their rich men's homes, locked up with their lawyers . . . they're untouchable. If we can get them into the street they're on our ground. There we might take them.'

*

After they left the apartment the two of them had walked round to two of the statues, Pasquino and Abate Luigi, and, when there was a gap in the passing pedestrians, posted the scrawled message, with the Ekstasists' copied insignia on the top.

It was Falcone's wording, an adaptation of some doggerel from Dante in a book from the inspector's own shelves.

Behold the solstice, brothers!
With it the shadows shorten,
On chestnut, thorn and darkening mouth.
Now the light of truth falls on love, divine and profane.
Now you lose your Venus forever.

It was an obscure message for obscure criminals, one Falcone had to explain to Gianni Peroni, who remained sceptical. The winter solstice was three days away. From that point on the days lengthened, and the noon shadows began to abbreviate. The message for the Ekstasists, all three principals spelled out by name, was, the inspector hoped, cryptic but couched in their own kind of language: what had happened in the Vicolo del Divino Amore would soon be revealed. Furthermore, the painting, seemingly the talisman for their acts, was out of their hands, and would remain so.

'These are arrogant men,' Falcone had observed after the last message was posted. 'Arrogant and, in the case of some, I suspect, scared. With luck this will prompt a response. Someone may panic. Perhaps even put up some reply of their own.'

'You think they'd take the risk?'

The inspector frowned.

'Risk is a part of the thrill. Or so it seems to me. Why else do they keep taunting us? It's like a bullfight. The closer they are to the horns, the more they feel alive. They will want to respond in some way. I'm sure of that. They like those talking statues because they're public and that feeds their own vanity. No ordinary criminal would advertise his work that way. This scum think they're special. Perhaps if we give them a little of their own treatment in return . . .'

He glanced at Costa with a mournful expression.

'There was nothing you could do about Emily, you know.'

'How can you be certain of that?' Costa answered with a swift, unintentional brusqueness. 'You weren't there.'

'I know because I know you,' Falcone replied instantly. 'If something was capable of being achieved you would have achieved it. Not that any of this will help in the present circumstances. It's only natural you blame yourself. I just hope that with time you can find some way to release your grief.' He frowned. 'I speak for us all, Nic. You have friends. We care for you. We're concerned that you must let this grief out from inside.'

Costa didn't know what to say. Falcone was a cold man by nature. None of this could have come easily.

'I'll mourn when I'm ready,' he said simply. 'When I have the time?'

'Don't count on the time,' Falcone replied.

'Meaning?'

'Malaspina is a man with many friends. People like that can come up with tricks you'd never dream of, not in a million years. Don't ask me to explain.'

Money and position mattered in Rome, and always

would. Falcone could not pass up any opportunity, or the chance to create one. Costa appreciated that.

'Why am I meeting Agata Graziano again?' Costa asked. 'Is she allowed out whenever she pleases?'

'Not at all. She has a temporary dispensation,' Falcone replied. 'Didn't she tell you? Agata Graziano is a remarkable woman. I know that for a very good reason.'

He waited. Falcone had given something away, uncharacteristically, and now regretted it.

'Do I find out?' Costa asked.

'I suppose I'll have to tell you now,' Falcone sighed, something like a blush staining his cheeks. 'Though I do not wish this broadcast at large. A little over twenty years ago my marriage was collapsing, through my own stupid fault. It became clear to me I would never become a father. I wasn't the only one,' Falcone hurried on. 'It was a kind of tradition among a few of us in the same position. A little charity on the side sometimes made it easier to get through the day. So in that sense my generosity was selfish. Just as it is for Franco Malaspina.'

'I never imagined.'

'Quite. I suppose you never imagined people knew about your habit of giving money to beggars every day too.'

'That stopped,' Costa admitted with a little shame.

'You got married. You found a partner. You were looking to start a family of your own. It was only natural. I . . .' Falcone laughed at his own embarrassment. 'They said I had to sponsor a particular girl in the convent orphanage. They chose her for me, naturally. As luck would have it, they chose Agata Graziano, though I'm still not sure she ever really was a child. I first met her when she was nine years old and she was just as serious and awkward and curious about everything as she is now.'

So that was the connection. Costa would never have guessed.

'Did she have to become a nun?'

'Sister! She belongs to a different order.'

'Sorry. Sister.'

'No,' Falcone replied with obvious care. 'She could have done anything she wanted. In a sense she did, with university and her studies. I observed in silence from the wings, visiting her three or four times a year. Taking her on trips occasionally. Watching her grow, which was wondrous, but no more so than for any other child, I imagine. I knew she was remarkable from an early age. Then . . . I imagine everyone thinks that.'

His sharp eyes glanced at Costa.

'In twenty years I haven't heard her express the slightest desire to leave that convent and I never once questioned her decision. Agata has enough difficult ideas rattling around that intelligent head of hers without you adding to them.'

'I'm sure you're right.'

'I am. Remember it. If anyone can get to the bottom of that painting of yours it's her. Why do you think I asked for her in the first place? Always use someone you know if you can, Nic. Remember that when everything gets more complicated in the years to come. Make the most of Agata's knowledge. And . . .' A brief expression of doubt and inner concern passed across Falcone's tanned, lean face. 'Take care of her. I fear she's not as resilient as she believes. I must go now. Really . . .'

Costa was thinking of the clothes Falcone had sent for

from the farmhouse, insisting he wear them for the evening. They were the best he had.

'Why am I getting dressed up like this to go to a gallery, Leo?' he asked.

The inspector coughed into his fist.

'Didn't I mention that?'

'No.'

'Ah. After the gallery there is an event. The Barberini's staff party. I thought you might enjoy it.'

Costa's mind went blank.

'A party? You want me to go to a party?'

Falcone ducked his head for a moment, an expression of momentary guilt.

'It's not just a "party". It's in the Palazzo Malaspina. You will be there as a civilian. A guest. No one can complain of harassment. It's just a little idea I had . . .'

Costa nodded, beginning to understand.

'He will be there. Malaspina.'

'I expect so,' Falcone admitted. 'Oh . . .'

He half turned as he strode away.

'Have fun, won't you?' he ordered, and was gone.

Part 7

THE SONG OF SOLOMON

- 1 -

He found her in the Saletta del Seicento, exactly where he expected: in front of the central painting on the long wall, Caravaggio's sumptuous depiction of *The Rest on the Flight into Egypt*, with its elderly Joseph holding the music for an ethereally beautiful angel, who bowed a violin to a slumbering Virgin and Child. Agata Graziano was accompanied by a slender man with bright golden hair and a face not unlike that of the divine being with the violin, though somewhat older and a little careworn. Both he and Agata were, however, intent on studying the painting to the work's left: another Caravaggio, this time the slumbering penitent Mary Magdalene.

She turned to smile at him as he arrived.

'Riddles,' she said. 'Nothing but riddles. Do you recognize the woman here?'

'Fillide Melandroni,' Costa said straight away.

'Quite. One of the busiest ladies of her time, and here she is, the model for both the Magdalene and the Virgin herself. And – ' a flicker of puzzlement crossed Agata's dark, energized eyes – 'the woman in our own mysterious canvas. Do you wonder Caravaggio wound up being run out of Rome? Even if he'd never murdered that man in the street.'

Her gaze fell on the slumbering Magdalene, a portrait so exquisitely human in its portrayal of both physical and spiritual exhaustion that its subtle, intense power made Costa's mind reel whenever he saw it.

'Here's another thing,' she pointed out. 'You see what she's wearing? These are the clothes of a Roman prostitute. An Ortaccio whore. This is what Fillide looked like when she went about her business.' That glimmer of self-doubt ran across her face again. 'Not that I'm much qualified to offer you an opinion there. Caravaggio would have produced these about the same time, working no more than a five-minute walk from where we stand. You can see it in the colours, the people, the style. The life, more than anything. This was perhaps 1596. Michelangelo Merisi was still young, undamaged by the harsh reality of everyday Rome. He had just entered the household of Del Monte, painting by day, listening to philosophers and alchemists in the evening. And Lord knows what else . . .'

She glanced at him.

'Still, that's not my territory either, is it? Here's something else.' Her hand pointed to the scroll of music held by the elderly Joseph, listening, in wonder, to the angel's violin. 'Music. *Real* music. Alexander?'

The man next to her looked at Costa and grinned. Then he began to sing, a slow wordless melody detailed in a perfect alto voice, halfway between a choirboy and a diva.

When he stopped he grinned at Costa's discomfort.

'Don't worry, we won't get thrown out. This is one of my party tricks. Alexander Fairgood. I run music events here from time to time.'

'Ah,' Costa replied, understanding. He walked forward and examined the sheet of music in the raddled Joseph's worn and elderly hands. 'I always thought it was just . . . notes.'

'That's what riddles are for,' Agata pointed out. 'Making you think. Tell him, Alex.'

He was American but spoke Italian in the easy fluent way foreigners did after a few years in the city.

'This is what's known as a Marian motet. A form of medieval religious music dedicated to the Virgin Mary. This particular piece is an extract from a work by an obscure Flemish composer, Noël Bauldewijn. The words are from the Song of Songs, 7:6 to 7:12. I have this from memory, in Latin or Greek, Hebrew or English. Lord knows I've sung it enough.'

His clear, firm voice rang throughout the chamber and the corridors beyond once more, timeless and in perfect, controlled pitch, now declaiming a set of rich and sonorous verses precisely, word by word.

The man's voice had an ethereal clarity that stilled every other sound in the gallery. Costa didn't understand a word.

'It's Latin,' Fairgood announced, looking a little testy. 'No problem. I'm used to translating it for Romans. The price is you get it in English. It sounds more alluring that way. Can you manage?'

'I'm fine with English,' Costa said, knowing somehow he didn't have to ask this question of Agata.

'*Come, my beloved, let us go forth into the field; let us lodge in the villages.*
Let us get up early to the vineyards; let us see if the vine flourish, whether the tender grape appear,

*and the pomegranates bud forth: there will I give
thee my loves.'*

Fairgood grinned.

'That was the King James Version. Pretty racy for an
old Protestant Scot, don't you think?'

'It's a love poem?' Costa asked. 'An *erotic* love poem?'

'It's the Song of Songs!' the American replied, astonished by Costa's ignorance. '*The* erotic love poem. And
this other thing you gave me to look up . . . Not that I
know why, though I might guess.'

He glanced at Agata, hoping for clarification.

'When I can tell you, I will tell you, Alex,' she said
sweetly.

'I should hope so,' he grumbled. 'It's the same piece
of music but with a different verse set to it. One Bauldewijn never put there in the original.'

He took a slip of paper out of his pocket and, this
time, spoke the words in his relaxed Italian.

*'His left hand is under my head, and his right hand
doth embrace me.
I charge you, O ye daughters of Jerusalem, by the roes,
and by the hinds of the field, that ye stir not up,
nor awake my love, till he please.'*

Alexander Fairgood stared hard at the canvas in front
of them, a wan smile on his handsome face.

'You know,' he said softly, 'I always used to think this
was the most sensual thing I'd ever seen in my life. The
way that half-naked angel has his feathered wings turned
towards you, making you ache to stroke them.' He

indicated the lazy, knowing eye of the donkey behind the grizzled head of Joseph, its gaze taking in everything. 'I always wondered what would happen if Mary woke and discovered this vision there, next to the old man who wasn't even the father of her child.'

'I've told you a million times,' Agata said patiently. 'The subject – or at least *one* subject, because there are many here – is the same as the Song of Songs. Does love stem from spirituality or sexuality? Will one beget the other? And where, in the balance, lies the love of God?'

He eyed her, his expression coy, teasing.

'It's sex wrapped up as religion, Agata. If you spent more time out of that chaste little nunnery of yours you'd know it.'

'I *am* spending more time out of it, in case you hadn't noticed,' she answered testily. 'Thanks to a dispensation.'

'Temporary only, then,' he murmured with a frown. 'What a pity.'

'Thank you, Alex,' she said, and glanced at the door.

'Oh,' he said. 'I have overstayed my welcome.'

She folded her small arms and said nothing.

He took one last look at the painting in front of them. Like the work in the Vicolo del Divino Amore, it seemed to pulse with a vibrant life of its own, though one softer and more gentle.

'I never tire of coming here,' the American added. 'Particularly in such interesting company. But this other painting I heard about . . .'

His voice was transformed in an instant into a disembodied plain chant that sent a shiver down Costa's spine.

'*His left hand is under my head, and his right hand doth embrace me,*' Alexander Fairgood sang, then stopped, delighting in the resonance of his own voice as it echoed through the Palazzo Doria Pamphilj's labyrinthine galleries.

'It's real,' she said, in a low, excited voice when the musician was gone. She gripped his arm, her small fingers tight on the cloth of his coat. 'I knew it when they first brought me to it. But that was instinct. This is fact. See here for yourself. This is the same model. Fillide. The music has the same antecedents. The style, the artistry, the feeling of the thing . . . I can sense Caravaggio in the paint for pity's sake. Can't you?'

'Yes,' he said quietly, and felt a pang of concern.

'And yet . . .' She breathed deeply, unhappy with her own bemusement. 'What does it mean? Why a subject he never broached before or after? He must have understood how wonderful it was. Why stop there?'

The same questions kept nagging at him.

'He produced our painting while he was in the employ of Del Monte?'

She nodded energetically.

'I think so, but towards the end. If you look closely you can detect the man's age, his moods, his grow-ing anger and depression in the strokes of the brush. In the early years when he produced canvases like these he was as happy as he would ever be. This was before the churches began to hire him, before the gloom and the fear we see beginning to rise in the Contarelli Chapel and the Matthew cycle. Before death and decay began to infect his mind. He lived with Del Monte, with those poets and magicians and alchemists, their whores and their boyfriends, and somehow, somewhere along the way, a patron – perhaps Del Monte himself – came along and showed him that inferior Carracci, put some money in his pocket and said . . . what?'

'Be better and more daring,' Costa replied immediately.

'More daring?' she asked, astonished. 'He was trying to out-paint even himself. He was trying to put on canvas something, some moment, human, divine, diabolic, I don't know . . . except that it had never been painted before. And when it's finished . . . nothing. Except for that brief mention in the journal of Giambattista Marino, it may well have never existed. From the moment of its creation it's been some kind of secret. Who's kept it? Why has it never been displayed, discovered, sold? Where has it been? In Rome, surely. But where?'

Some unfathomable inner knowledge threw an idea into his head at that moment.

'In the hands of someone, some family that never needed the money,' Costa suggested. 'Or the public acclaim of owning it.'

Agata Graziano scowled.

'That's guesswork. It offends me. Besides, what rich family would own a painting like this and *not* show it? Those people delight in letting the rest of us know how blessed they are.'

'I'm a police officer,' he replied, shrugging. 'Sometimes guesswork is all I have.'

'Then I pity you.' She took his hand, turned the wrist and glanced at his watch. Timepieces, it seemed, were another possession Sister Agata Graziano avoided. 'I can't stay here any longer. My head will burst.'

In spite of herself, Agata found herself turning again to the wall, this time to the smaller canvas of the Magdalene to one side: Fillide Melandroni, asleep, slumped, dressed in the rich costume of a late-sixteenth-century Ortaccio whore.

'Do you ever hear their voices?' she asked softly.

He knew instantly what she meant.

'When I look at the paintings, of course,' Costa answered honestly. 'That's Caravaggio. These aren't idealized human beings. They're the people he met every day, and when we see them we realize they're the same as those we meet too, just like you and me. They're not history. They are us.'

'They *are* us,' she agreed, and there was some grim note of self-reproach in her voice. 'Still. I know where they lived and where they died. I walk the same pavements, pass the same buildings, stay awake at night over the same fears and doubts.'

Her attention never left the canvas on the wall for a moment: Fillide Melandroni, long-dead, sleeping, gripped by a deep, exhausted fatigue that verged on mortality itself.

'Sometimes,' she said slowly, 'I imagine I see a man in the street, a dark-haired man, with that incomplete beard and a sad, shocked face. He is staring at me from the other side of the road, not seeing the traffic, not noticing anything except the faces and the pain and the same bright, damaged humanity he saw there too.'

She gripped his arm more firmly.

'We inhabit their world. They inhabit ours. Why else would a man want to paint, except to live forever?'

Her dark glittering eyes studied him before returning briefly to the painting of the sleeping Fillide. 'And . . . Alexander said it. He would kill to see a painting like that.

Someone has. People have died. The reason you wish to talk to me is that you believe I can tell you why.'

'I hope so,' he replied.

'Will that help you, Nic? You?'

There was no similarity whatsoever between Emily, his lost wife, and this eccentric woman whose life was so distant from anything he could imagine that she might have come from the moon. Nothing except their mutual insistence on one subject alone: the truth was there to be faced, however terrible it might turn out to be.

'I don't know, but I hope so,' he answered, and found himself following the line of her gaze, straight to the slumbering female figure on the canvas on the wall.

Something caught his attention on the face of the Magdalene, a detail he had never seen before. He blinked, then looked again. At first it appeared to be a flaw, a rip in the canvas, exposing some tiny bright, white element beneath the paint. Then, as Agata noticed what he was seeing, he moved closer, so close it seemed improper, yet he was propelled by her insistent arm.

Nic Costa had lost count of how many times he'd walked through the doors of the Doria Pamphilj, how many hours he'd spent in its glorious corridors, over-whelmed by the beauty of its collection, and the open, everyday way in which it was displayed, as if in a home, not a museum. He had never before seen this minuscule speck on the cheek of the sleeping woman. Agata Gra-ziano had taught him something: how to look. Now he felt transfixed by the revelation, so small and yet so large: a single element, infinitely human, depicted with the rudimentary perfection of an unconscious genius.

A single glassy tear was caught, frozen in a discrete

moment of time on the cheek of the slumbering Fillide Melandroni. As she slept, in the guise of the once-fallen Magdalene after the Crucifixion, aware of the tragedy that had newly entered the world, a part of her, the soul, perhaps, wept. The sight of this infinitesimal secret ripped at his heart, dragging out its own dark tragedy from the depths, as it was meant to.

'You're learning,' Agata whispered, casting him a glance that seemed to contain some distant, studied admiration.

– 2 –

They walked through the *centro storico*, Agata pointing out the streets he thought he knew well, now realizing how mistaken he had been. She understood them so much better, and in so many different dimensions: where the painters they both adored had lived and fought and died. It was like a lesson from the freest and frankest of university professors. Agata talked of the society – rich, violent, hedonistic and yet, in a sense, deeply religious, even moralistic – that had first nurtured Caravaggio, then, as his behaviour worsened, began to reject him, finally delivering the death sentence for the killing that dispatched him into exile. As she spoke Costa realized there was something he had never really sought before: the spirit behind the brush, the burning creative animus that had driven one lone rebel, with little in the way of formal education or tuition, to redress the focus of painting and seek the divine in the mundane, the thieves and prostitutes, the criminals and the vagabonds who walked the streets of Rome.

It was all, she said, a question of *disegno*, which, for the painters of Caravaggio's generation, meant not simply 'design' but, as one of his contemporaries put it, '*il segno di dio in noi*', the sign of God in us.

'Do you see the sign of God anywhere today?' she asked.

'No,' he replied, and shrugged. 'Sorry. Do you?'

'Everywhere! You must learn to look properly. I will deal with this lapse.'

They strode past the grand home of Caravaggio's one-time patron, Agata speculating about the behaviour of the eccentric Archbishop Del Monte and his bizarre household in what was now the genteel home to the Senate, guarded by innumerable uniformed Carabinieri. Then they made their way across the busy Christmas traffic bickering to fight its way through the perennial jam at the Piazza delle Cinque Lune as she talked constantly, about the past in the present, daring him to sense its nearness. No more than three minutes away, towards the Corso, stood the Piazza di San Lorenzo in Lucina, the place where Caravaggio fell into the deadly street fight that led to his exile from Rome. The same distance towards the river, beyond the Via della Scrofa, which led towards the Vicolo del Divino Amore, lay the Tor di Nona, the tower where some of his fellow ruffians had been imprisoned after the pitched knife battle, perhaps with the wounded Caravaggio among them, until, with the aid of some of his aristocratic admirers, he was able to flee the executioner.

'They are here, Nic,' she insisted. '*He* is here. You simply have to look and listen. Come.'

They turned the corner into the small cobbled piazza. The early Renaissance façade of the Church of Sant'-Agostino stood above them, its pale travertine, visibly plundered from the Colosseum some five hundred years before, now luminescent in the orange street lights. He followed her up the long, broad flight of stone stairs, through into the vast echoing nave. Instinctively, he turned to his left, towards the painting he'd seen countless times, and knew would see anew through her eyes.

'No,' she said, and took his elbow, guiding him away. 'I didn't bring you here for that.'

The Madonna of Loreto, an exquisite Caravaggio Virgin with the infant Jesus in her arms, the holy pair framed in the doorway of a simple stone house, staring down at two grimy pilgrims, stood in the gloom at the edge of his vision, like a sombre, glowing beacon.

'If he worshipped,' she said, 'and I believe he did, he worshipped here. They all came to this place. The artists and the poets. And worse. This was an altar for the fallen. They had need of it most of all. Where would the Church be without sinners?'

She turned to face the entrance and he did the same, seeing the sculpture there, a pale study of two figures illuminated by a sea of candles.

'This was the whores' church, too,' Agata Graziano went on. 'The seat of worship for what was once Ortaccio. The mistress of Cesare Borgia is buried here. So were some of the most famous prostitutes of Rome, not by the Muro Torto, where the law dictated. You won't find their tombs here any more. All gone, out of a sense of . . .'

She frowned.

'. . . decorum. I'm just a humble sister with a fondness for art. I know no more of your world than I wish to. But this puzzles me. That men should want a thing so badly, and then feel filled with shame when they achieve it. Fillide felt none. Why should she? Look, Nic, look well . . .'

He'd never spent much time on the figures there at all, though a dim memory told him that they had some special significance for the ordinary women of Rome. Sometimes, when visiting the Caravaggio, he'd seen them slip up to the larger statue, the Madonna, almost furtively, place an offering in the box, light a candle, cross themselves. Then, with one last sideways glance, step gently forward and touch the silver slipper that protected her foot.

He stared at the placid, beautiful woman carved from stone, seated majestically beneath the half-shell cupola of the alcove, with the child standing, one leg on her lap, one on her throne. Costa wondered how he could have been so blind. Above her hair, lit by the forest of blazing candles in the niche, rose a starry halo. Around her chest, tight beneath her breasts, ran a silver garland. The child was magnificent, rising to face the world, a bright, brave metal robe girding his waist. Wreathed in light, surrounded by flowers and mementoes, messages and photographs of children, so many of them, she was beyond Christian iconography, timeless, like Venus displaying the infant Cupid, a prize, a miracle in her arms.

'What do women pray for when they come here? When they touch her feet like that?' he asked.

'Again, you are asking the wrong person. This is *The Madonna del Parto*, the Madonna of motherhood, of birth. It's an idea that predates my faith. That through womanhood comes the fecundity of mankind. So I imagine they pray for the child they are bearing or hope to.'

She hesitated.

'Even the likes of Fillide, perhaps, though a Christian sensibility gave her generation the notion, the mark, of sin too.'

He thought of the painting hidden in the studio, its message lurking beneath so many surface deceptions. And he remembered Emily and the child they had lost. There were no prayers to ease that pain, no candles and flowers, or the worn, comforting touch of a statue's silver foot shining in the gloomy belly of an ancient church marooned in its own quiet piazza, a few steps from the choking bustle of modern Rome.

'When they came here,' Agata asked, speaking in a loud, firm voice, the way the priest did, when all else whispered, 'what do you think they saw? Del Monte and Caravaggio. Galileo and Fillide Melandroni. What did they seek?'

'*Disegno*,' he replied simply.

The design of God in us.

He was unable to avoid her fixed, interested stare.

'You are a good pupil, Nic Costa,' Agata Graziano declared with a sudden serious turn. 'I only wish I were a better teacher.'

He began to object.

'No,' she interjected. 'A good teacher would have some answers.'

'I could ask an easier question,' he suggested. There was a moment's thought before he found the courage to say it. 'Who are you? Where did you come from?'

All sense of amusement departed her face. This dark, austere yet pretty woman, hugging herself tightly in the long black coat of the nun she was not, looked back at him, uncertain of herself.

'What interest is this of yours?' she responded.

'I'm curious. It's part of the job. Most of the job, to be honest with you.'

'Well, there is nothing to know. I was one abandoned child among many. They thought my mother was a woman of the kind . . .'

She looked around the church.

'. . . who would once have dreamed she might enter a place like this, and doubtless never have been pretty enough or rich enough. My father was a seaman. He was African, I believe. From Ethiopia. That is all I know and all I wish to know. The sisters took me in, raised me, and then, when they saw something worth cultivating, set me on this present course through the simple medium of education. My story is wholly unexceptional, for which I am grateful.'

A shadow of doubt crossed her face.

'Now, for a day or two, I am something else. One of you. Thanks to your inspector.'

'Another of Leo's gifts.'

She looked a little cross.

'He told you?'

Costa was aware that he had done something wrong.

'Just the basics.'

'Why on earth would he do that?' she asked, not expecting an answer. 'In another man I would have said it came from misplaced pride. But not him. Never. How strange.'

She pointed a short, commanding finger at his chest.

'What Leo did was charity, and charity is best performed in silence. I am grateful for it, and wish to hear no more.'

She gazed at the statue: the bright, gleaming Madonna, an older goddess too perhaps, with the magical child in her arms. There was something there, he thought, that was beyond even Agata Graziano.

'We are done with the dead,' she said, and set off for the door. 'For the time being anyway.'

Costa hesitated, staring at the statue, thinking of

Emily. Thinking of what it might be like to be in the same room as the man who had taken her life so casually.

Leo Falcone demanded a high and difficult price of everyone he knew. Costa wondered, for a moment, whether he could meet it, whether he could enter a room with the men he knew to be the Ekstasists and act as if nothing was wrong.

'Nic?' Agata asked from the door. 'Are you coming or not?'

He had never said this to Falcone, but the suit the inspector had ordered to be brought from the farmhouse was the one Costa wore for their wedding.

'I'm coming,' he said.

Part 8

THE PALAZZO MALASPINA

– 1 –

Thirty minutes later they stood on the steps of the Palazzo Malaspina. The entrance dominated much of the narrow seventeenth-century street that led, in a few short minutes, to the Mausoleum of Augustus, a place Costa had yet to find the courage to revisit. The Vicolo del Divino Amore was even closer around the corner, as was the Barberini's small external studio, where the canvas of Venus with her satyrs now resided. Everything about this case, it seemed to Costa, was contained in the small, secretive warren of dark, dingy alleys here, the labyrinth that was once Ortaccio.

They stopped at the foot of the curving stone staircase. A heraldic decoration ran the length of each side: a stone shield half a metre high, divided into two halves, one stippled, one plain. A bare angular tree in the centre with three short horizontal branches on the left and two on the right. From each emerged sharp spines, top and bottom of the branches. *Mala spina*. The bad thorn.

Agata Graziano looked at him, a shadow of guilt in her charming face.

'I lied a little, Nic,' she confessed. 'This isn't simply the Barberini's Christmas party. We're sharing it with one of the private galleries too. It's about money, of course. We can't afford it on our own any more.'

He thought of Falcone and realized he should have expected this.

'Let me guess. The Buccafusca Gallery.'

'Yes,' she replied, impressed. 'You're quite the detective. How did you know?'

'Falcone told me. After a fashion.'

'Ah. He is an . . . interesting man. He likes you. I can see that.'

'Interesting,' Costa agreed.

'I merely wish you to know that some of the things you see here will be Buccafusca's,' she added. 'Not ours.'

'I can't wait,' Costa replied, and then followed her through the front doors into a grand, marbled reception area set beneath an alcove with a carved scalloped half-shell many times the size of that over *The Madonna del Parto*. He watched the private security men, who seemed to know Agata Graziano, nod gravely and take off their caps before ushering the pair of them into a square, echoing hall of pillars and shining stone façades, an extravagant lobby more in keeping with that of an embassy than a private home. A palace like this was, for Costa, a rare blank sheet. The home of the Malaspina dynasty – now occupied, as far as he knew, by its lone surviving member – was a sprawling complex that covered a vast area of this part of Rome, and never opened its doors to the public, not even for a day.

The place was a wonder; the crowds would have flocked there. Smaller mansions, such as the Palazzo Altemps, had been acquired by the state and turned into grand museums, former aristocratic homes that were as much exhibits themselves as the rich and varied collections they held. The Malaspina clan had escaped such a fate, and maintained their secret, hidden lives behind the soot-blackened walls of a city fortress that was dark and forbidding from the outside and full of light and beauty within.

Beyond the entrance was a vast cobbled courtyard, with a large statue of Cupid stretching his bow at its centre. On all sides rose three floors, the first two open to the elements, with an arched colonnade on the ground and a balustrade balcony on the first. Lights blazed from every level, silhouetting a sea of bodies talking animatedly, members of a society to which Costa knew he would never belong. He felt hopelessly out of place, and perhaps she saw that, because Agata Graziano took his arm for one brief moment, almost slipping hers through his, and said, 'Don't worry. I'll look after you if you look after me.'

'Agreed,' he murmured, and then they pushed their way through the first ground-floor hall, where a noisy throng of people gossiped. The Buccafusca Gallery insignia, a black mouth, open, in greed or ecstasy, it was unclear which, appeared everywhere; all the objects surrounding them appeared modern, and ugly.

'*Salut*,' Agata declared, grabbing two glasses, orange juice for her, prosecco for him, as a scantily clad waitress fought her way through. 'I may join you in that before long.'

He cast his eyes around the room: bright, shiny people, beautiful in the main, fixed on each other, looking as if they owned the world.

'So this is how the upper classes live,' he observed. 'I always wondered what I was missing. Perhaps . . .'

He fell silent. He could see them now, across the

room, and the sight of them blended with the images in his head: of Rosa Prabakaran's photographs, and that dreadful experience close by a long-dead emperor's tomb, just a short walk away from where they now stood in this strange, artificial party.

Looking at the four – Malaspina, Buccafusca, Castagna and the stocky, uncomfortable Nino Tomassoni by their side – he realized that any of the taller men could, in theory, have been the figure behind the hood. But there was something about Malaspina – the commanding, stiff stance, the natural assumption of superiority – that convinced Costa he was the man, could only be the man.

'Are you comfortable with the aristocracy?' Agata Graziano asked, watching him.

'I don't have much experience,' he admitted.

'Well,' she said, shrugging, and beginning to fight her way through the sea of silk-clad bodies with a jabbing elbow and a forceful determination, 'let's start.'

– 2 –

'Christmas,' Franco Malaspina declared, 'the same thing every year. A party for the Barberini. A line of cheques to be written. Everyone presumes on my charity, Sister Agata. Why did I do this? Tell me. Please.'

Agata laughed. It was a deliberate taunt, cheerfully delivered, though Costa felt the atmosphere was not as cordial as Malaspina pretended. The three men by his side had shambled away when they approached. The men seemed unhappy, uncomfortable, as if they had been bickering, stopping simply because of the arrival of company.

Malaspina possessed the kind of too-perfect Mediterranean tan that seemed to be *de rigueur* for a certain kind of young Roman aristocrat. His craggy face, marked by a prominent Roman nose, was intelligent but disengaged, as if everything around him was of no great significance. Buccafusca and Castagna were of similar build but somewhat less striking in appearance, with the dark hair and pale, serious faces of bankers or bureaucrats, and a manner that was diffident in the extreme. Tomassoni, short, overweight and sweating visibly under the hot lights, looked as if he didn't belong in the place, and couldn't wait to get out. All three of them had now reassembled a few metres away, close to another strange modern sculpture, talking quietly, furtively among themselves.

'You do this because you are a good man at heart, in spite of all your pretences, Franco,' Agata replied happily. 'One day you'll be married and have children of your own. Then you'll think differently. Then you'll remember Christmas as it was when you were a child.'

Malaspina looked her up and down.

'I spent Christmas with servants,' he complained. 'It's not the same. Besides, of course I'm a good man. Don't you read the papers? I can show you the accounts if you like.' He hesitated, staring now at Costa. 'So why have you brought a policeman to interrogate me?'

'I'm not here to interrogate anyone,' Costa replied politely. 'Sister Agata and I were working together. She merely suggested I come along. If this offends you . . .'

'Why should it offend me?'

'Some people are not fond of us . . .'

'Not me!' Malaspina raised a glass. 'To law and order. But *order* most of all. You'll drink to that, won't you?'

Costa sipped his prosecco, unable to take his eyes off the man. Franco Malaspina was not what he expected. In flesh, close up, he seemed amiable, larger than life, and yet ill at ease, with them and with himself, both forthright and subtly reticent. Costa had, he was forced to admit, no idea what to make of the man. The voice didn't ring a bell. The physique, the posture . . . these could have matched many in Rome.

'Of course, Agata,' Malaspina continued, 'if I marry, I should marry you. Imagine the publicity. I finally find the last worthwhile virgin left in Rome.'

She said nothing.

Malaspina looked at Costa and tapped the side of his nose. 'Agata is a fan of Dante, as are we all, though for different reasons. She sees herself as Beatrice. Beautiful, chaste, alluring. And dead.'

He laughed at his own joke. He was alone.

'You are too intelligent to make such a foolish comparison,' Agata objected. 'You know Dante as well as any of us. He loved Beatrice, and she died. Through that he discovered there was a greater love than the physical. A spiritual love.'

Costa caught his breath. Something in Agata's words had produced a moment of bleakness in Franco Malaspina's eyes. It was only there for a second, but it was unmistakable, and also unreadable. Anger? Sadness? Grief even?

'You sound like the Pope,' the man groaned. 'This is Christmas. Even for a pagan like me, it's not a time to talk of death.'

Agata nodded in agreement.

'I'm meant to sound like the Holy Father, aren't I?'

'No. It's a waste, Agata. A beautiful woman. Someone with feelings. I know you have them. You know too. We're all human, the same little animals with the same desires and fears. What's the problem?'

He stared into her eyes.

'Be like the rest of us, bold now and chaste afterwards,' Malaspina murmured, watching her draw back to stand closer to Costa. 'Who's to know? Is that all your god is? Just a spy in the bedroom?'

She shook a small fist at his chest, laughing still.

'He does this to me all the time,' she told Costa, half serious, half joking. 'It's one of his tricks.'

'Tricks,' he answered softly. 'You bring a policeman

into my palace and accuse *me* of tricks.' Franco Malaspina gazed at Costa, still and confident of himself. His teeth were unnaturally perfect. His eyes, bright, unafraid, glittering, held him. 'Why are you here?' he asked.

'I told you,' Costa insisted. 'I was invited to a party. Nothing more. If it's a problem . . .'

The man took a deep breath, as if disappointed by the mild reply.

'You're the one whose wife died. I saw it somewhere. In the paper, I believe. They took pictures of you at the funeral. How does that feel?'

'Franco!' Agata intervened. 'Don't be so rude.'

'But I'm curious,' he protested. 'He has no need to answer. Not if it offends him.'

'I'm not offended,' Costa cut in. 'How does what feel exactly?'

'Being followed by scum like those reporters. Nosy bastards, invading your life. When you've done nothing wrong. I've had them too.'

'Not like this,' Costa replied sourly.

'No.' And the man had changed again. He seemed genuinely upset. Almost penitent. 'It was wrong of me to presume in that way. I'm sorry. To lose the woman you love . . . I should never have asked. It was rude of me. Here . . .'

Malaspina's right hand, the one Costa believed, when he entered that room, had taken the life of Emily, was extended now.

'Shake, please,' the man said. 'Accept my apologies and my condolences. It's the lot of everyone to be bereaved one day.' That strange, lost expression crossed his face once more. 'I am merely fortunate never to have lost anyone who mattered to me. An absentee father scarcely counts.'

'Thank you,' Costa said, and took his hand. He had an extraordinary grip, strong and insistent. And then it was gone, and Malaspina stood rocking on his heels, seemingly embarrassed by his own actions.

'You know a little of Caravaggio, then, do you?' he asked, as if it were small talk.

'A little,' Costa confessed.

'Only the art, I imagine. Not the man. The life. What made him.'

Costa agreed.

'Only the art.'

'*"Nec spe, nec metu"*,' Malaspina said quietly.

Costa shook his head. Agata came to his aid.

'Oh, not that rot again, Franco. "Without hope or fear". It was the motto of a certain kind of Roman individual in those times.' She glanced across the room, at Buccafusca and Castagna, or so it seemed to Costa, then turned back to Malaspina.

'So you've read Domenico Mora, Franco?' she asked him. 'Or do you just spout what the others tell you?'

'I read,' he answered immediately, though a little taken aback by the question. 'We all do.'

'You've lost me,' Costa confessed.

'They have a certain little club, Nic,' she explained. 'Men without girlfriends often do, I believe. They think it's their duty to behave like stuck-up pigs when they feel like it because that is what a true Roman gentleman does, and has done for five centuries or so.'

'A knight offends fearlessly,' Malaspina interrupted, sounding as if he was quoting something. 'For therein, and only therein, lies true distinction.' Then he smiled, as if it were all a joke. 'But only in the right circumstances. Most of the time I'm am absolute angel.'

Agata Graziano looked at him the way a teacher would regard a stupid child.

'So was Caravaggio, yet he spent the last four years of his life fleeing a murder charge and squandering his talent,' she observed. 'Violence in the name of honour. What did it get him?'

'We're still talking about him, aren't we?' Then, with no warning, he turned to Costa and asked, 'Are you part of this investigation into the death of Véronique Gillet and those street women?'

'I'm not part of any investigation,' Costa said simply. 'I thought I'd made that clear. Tonight . . .'

He raised his glass again.

'. . . I'm merely happy to drink your wine. Why?'

'Because I knew her, of course,' Malaspina responded. 'We all did.'

'Poor Véronique,' Agata added. 'I met her once or twice, only briefly. This is a small world. Not that she said very much. I never did understand why she visited Rome so often, to be frank. The Louvre never bought anything or lent much in return either.'

'The French stole what they wanted two centuries ago,' Malaspina muttered. 'What happened?'

'I have no idea,' Costa answered with a shrug. 'As I said, that is not my case.'

Agata shook her head.

'She was murdered, surely? What other explanation is there?'

Malaspina sighed, then said, 'Véronique was a very sick woman. She didn't have long to live in any case. She told me so. Perhaps she was no innocent party, Officer. Have you thought of that?'

'I've thought of nothing.'

That answer displeased him.

'Then offer an opinion. You have one, don't you?'

'An opinion?' Costa drained the glass and handed it to the passing waitress, refusing another. 'From what little I know, I would guess she was involved. But I doubt one woman could achieve such a succession of deaths on her own. Someone must have helped her. Perhaps instigated what went on.' He glanced at Agata, wondering whether to say what he wanted, then reminding himself that some-times duty came before tact. 'She had sex shortly before she died.'

'Well, that's a comforting thought anyway,' Malaspina said. 'Tell me. Is that painting genuine, do you think?'

'You've seen it?' Costa asked.

Malaspina laughed.

'Of course I've seen it!' he responded. 'The money I give to the Barberini . . . If they didn't call me in to get a private view of something like that I'd want to know why.' He enjoyed Agata's discomfort. 'Oh dear. You feel some misplaced sense of ownership towards the thing. That's a pity.'

He leaned down to peer into her pert face.

'It's called "privilege" for a reason, dearest. So . . . is it genuine?'

Costa decided to interrupt.

'The painting is part of a serious investigation, sir. While this is none of my business, I would suggest that is not a question one should address publicly. For reasons of—'

'I'll address it,' Agata interrupted. 'Professionally I will not be able to say this for many weeks. All the obvious signs are there. We had some results for the pigment tests and the canvas this afternoon. They date very well to the late sixteenth or early seventeenth century. The X-rays show it is a virgin work, with nothing of any import underneath except some preliminary sketches. All the trademarks . . . the incisions, the stylistic peculiarities we associate with the artist. More than that – ' she smiled at Costa openly, with some visible affection – 'when I stand near a Caravaggio I feel something. A little faint, a little excited, and more than a little scared. Don't you agree, Nic?'

He nodded. 'Exactly.'

'And I don't?' Malaspina asked angrily. There was heat in his cheeks now, visible anger in his expression. The transformation was immediate and astonishing. 'You think I am somehow less perceptive than the two of you. Well?'

'I have no idea, Franco,' she said sweetly. 'Your true feelings about anything are entirely unknown to me. When I see evidence of them, I shall judge.'

Malaspina nodded at the room around him. 'Best be nice to me, Agata. That way you can hope to come and see it here if I happen to be feeling generous. This will be one Caravaggio the hoi polloi won't sully. The Palazzo Malaspina is not the Doria Pamphilj. You'll have to beg to get in.'

Both of them stared at him mutely for a moment. It was if a different man were now talking to them.

'What do you mean?' she asked eventually. 'The painting is in the custody of the Barberini. No one's mentioned it may be moved elsewhere.'

'They will. Soon too. Didn't I tell you? I'm amazed the police haven't found out yet. The hovel where they found it belongs to us. The Malaspina estate has been unchanged for three centuries. We never sold off one square metre. I own so much around here I find it tedious to keep track of it all. There's a whole precinct near the Piazza Borghese we picked up from a Pope somewhere along the way. Gambling debts or a woman, one or the other. What's new?'

'Ownership of the studio in the Vicolo del Divino Amore scarcely makes the painting yours,' Costa pointed out.

'No? Talk to my lawyers.' His sharp, black eyes held Costa. The man was laughing at them now, with enough force to ensure they knew, and sufficient vague subtlety to make them wonder if they could believe what they were hearing. 'If this painting isn't mine, then whose is it? In the absence of proven title, ownership falls to the landlord. I checked with the idle little agent we employ to look after these matters. The place hasn't been rented out for years. As far as that idiot knew it was empty, which rather begs the question why he wasn't seeking to rent it. If no one else can claim it, the thing is mine.'

'That may be the law,' Costa agreed. 'But possession—'

'You are not listening to me,' Malaspina barked, becoming animated for the first time since Costa had been introduced to him. 'Lawyers. The more you have, the more you gain. Now that I know Agata's opinion, I will stake my claim tomorrow and see if anyone dares come to court to argue. I doubt it will be a long wait. You should be grateful for that, shouldn't you? One less thing for you to worry about.'

'I wouldn't expect any early judgements,' Costa replied, scanning the room, wondering what the others were doing.

'It's mine!'

Malaspina's voice had risen to a shriek.

Costa stared at him.

'It is not yours, sir. Not yet, if ever. It is evidence in a murder case in which several women have died through extreme violence. Possibly crucial evidence. That we shall see.'

'Lawyers!' Malaspina yelled. Agata took a step back. Costa stood his ground. 'I will drown you in lawyers. I will send them to your home. I will have them throwing stones at your windows when you lie in bed alone at night. The painting is mine.'

'One day, possibly,' Costa acknowledged. 'But not now. And not soon. Whatever case you may have for title, we are the police and we have ultimate claim when it comes to matters of physical evidence.' The thought came from nowhere and it pleased him to say it. 'That which we have in our possession already, to hand.' He paused, for effect. 'Identifiable and tagged.'

'You—'

'As long as this murder investigation stays current,' Costa interrupted, 'that painting will remain in police custody, secure and out of sight of everyone. Once we can put someone in jail for these terrible crimes – ' he smiled at Malaspina – 'perhaps you can see it then.'

The man swore and with a sudden, strong flick of his wrist sent the contents of his glass flying into Costa's face.

'You do not know with whom you are playing, little man,' he spat viciously.

Costa took out a handkerchief and, with no visible sign of anger, wiped the drink from his face.

'I think I'm beginning to get an idea,' he observed calmly.

He looked into Malaspina's eyes and wondered what he saw there. A kind of fury, surely. But an irrational desperation bordering on fear and despair too. This man did not simply desire the painting they had under lock and key in the Barberini studio. He craved it, like an addict longing for his fix.

– 3 –

'Oh dear,' Agata groaned after Malaspina had stormed off. 'We've upset a sponsor. I must say, he's more touchy than usual tonight. He didn't like you being here, Nic.' Agata peered at him. 'I think something upset him, don't you?'

'Who knows? Is his behaviour always this erratic?'

She thought about the question.

'Sometimes. Franco doesn't much like anyone, I think. Himself most of all. There's a sadness about the man I don't understand. You know, one time he actually made some reference to the colour of my skin. As if his is much different. All this wealth. What more could a man ask? And yet . . .'

The smile disappeared.

'You see the world of art from the outside and think it is nothing but beauty and intellectual rigour. Those things do exist. But so do ugliness and jealousy, obsession and some bitter rivalries on occasion. We're living, breathing people too, and while I try to avoid all that as much as I can, it is not entirely possible. In order to work, one must be strong enough to face down these problems. Véronique Gillet . . .'

She hesitated.

'What about her?'

'She was a very strange, very sad woman. She frightened me a little. There was something *so* compulsive about her, about the way she needed to be with *them* all the time. She was very strong and determined about something, I don't know what. And lost too.'

Her dark head of unruly hair had nodded in the direction of Malaspina and his acquaintances, then she gazed straight into Corso's face.

'I'm not a worldly woman, but I must say this. Somehow, I would not be surprised had Véronique been part of Franco's pathetic little band of hooligans.'

She stiffened inside her shapeless black dress and began to toy with the crucifix around her neck.

'Do you know what they do?' he asked.

Very quickly, with the acuity he was beginning to expect, she was suspicious.

'No. Why should I? I do hope you and Leo aren't playing me for a fool. I promised to try to help you get to the bottom of that painting. Nothing more.'

'Nothing more,' Costa agreed.

She still didn't look convinced.

'Franco and those idiot friends of his are simply late-developing teenagers, playing a stupid game. Véronique was different. Darker, somehow. I promise you. I've known Franco for five years or more. He's variously infuriating or charming, depending on his mood. He gives generously to the Barberini every year, and other charities too, I believe. That's the man. He is an aristocrat. He feels he can behave as he wishes. You live with it or . . .'

She glanced around the room. The strains of a string quartet began to drift through from an adjoining corridor.

They were playing some kind of odd, atonal jazz. For Malaspina, Costa thought, nothing could be quite how one supposed.

Her glass was empty. He picked up a fresh one from a passing waitress. She took it from him, smiled, then exchanged the orange juice for prosecco from the tray.

'. . . or you will never enter his world.'

'What kind of game?' he asked, and was dismayed by the obvious discomfort this question caused.

'A secret one. I don't know. Anyone can speculate. Is it hard? Women. Drink. A little upper-class football hooliganism perhaps, since I believe this is fashionable among the aristocracy once more. When he comes into the studio, Franco talks about what he's been up to in a roundabout way. I think it's part of his pleasure. Seeing how far he can go with a humble little thing from the Church like me. It doesn't work. I'm not ignorant.'

Her eyes were bright and intelligent.

'How can I hope to do the work I do and be blind to human frailty? Or evil. I meant it about the Mora book. All these ridiculous notions of virtue through violence. This is nothing new. Men like Malaspina and the rest have been behaving this way in Rome for centuries. Millennia even. For some it's almost a duty.'

It must have been the expression on his face.

'You've never heard of Domenico Mora, have you?'

'Should I?'

She grinned.

'If you want to know a certain kind of male you should. Domenico Mora was a Bolognese soldier. He wrote a book called *Il Cavaliere*. It was a response to a treatise on courtesy, *Il Gentilhuomo*, by Girolamo Muzio. Mora, being a soldier, took a different view. His thesis was that the true gentleman was beholden to no one, and best served his position by letting that be known at every possible occasion. By confrontation, violence, rudeness and arrogance.'

'Towards women too?'

'Women weren't important in Mora's world, except for the obvious purpose. What mattered was one's status. Mora said something to the effect that the source of the pleasure one acquires in insolence towards others is the feeling that, in the injury you inflict, you claim an exceptional superiority over them. For the likes of Caravaggio and all those other young blades, this was a way of life. Arguments, duels, death even.' She hesitated, thinking of something. 'The remarkable thing about Michelangelo Merisi is that, when it was over, he went home and painted such exquisite scenes of beauty that I must forgive him his excesses, as did the Pope in the end, though too late. Some other, greater idea still nagged away at the man. *Disegno*. It was in him, he knew it, and I think that caused him pain. He would have been far happier without it. He would never have painted a worthwhile canvas either, of course.'

There was sudden, raucous laughter from the far side of the room: Malaspina swaggering through the crowd, glass held high, dark face contorted with some brief manic pleasure. Costa could just catch sight of Nino Tomassoni at the edge of the crowd, staring at this man with an expression of fear mingled with hate.

'It doesn't make them happy,' Costa said.

'Is unhappiness a rarity? Caravaggio must have been the most miserable man in Rome, yet he had glimpses of heaven too. Franco and his thuggish friends will see the light. Today they toy with those ridiculous ideas. In five years' time they'll have wives, be fathering children, and getting apoplectic about the wayward state of society. It's a passing phase. That's all.'

More laughter, this time from some of the women, in their bright, expensive evening dresses, listening to Malaspina tell a crude joke at the top of his voice, so that everyone might hear.

'I can't imagine being married,' Agata continued quietly. 'It seems such a . . . loss of identity. We spend so much time trying to find out who we are. Then we throw it away on a whim.'

Agata Graziano looked at Costa, something unfamiliar – indecision, perhaps even fear – in her face.

'I need to be presumptuous. Before you turn red in the face and refuse to answer, you should know this: I am not asking out of idle curiosity. The question pertains directly to this strange painting you and Leo brought me. Well?'

He wondered if there was anything, any part of the human experience, this woman didn't want to understand, even if she refused – through fear, reluctance or some inner conviction – to be a part of it herself.

'Ask away,' Costa replied.

'Which came first when you met your wife? The spiritual side or the physical?'

The words were so unexpected he burst out laughing, freely, with a sudden, involuntary rush of emotion he hadn't known since Emily died.

'I have no idea.'

'Then think about it. Please.'

'I can't. It's not a conscious decision, one before the other. Love is . . .'

He was blushing, and he knew it.

'. . . unplanned. Perhaps a little of both, I imagine.'

It was a good and interesting question and he wished, with all his heart, she hadn't asked it because the thought would, he now knew, nag him forever.

'The two seemed . . . inseparable. I don't know how you'd divide one from the other.'

Her sharp eyes sparkled, watching him.

'If it's not conscious, where does it come from?'

'Atheists fall in love too,' he replied, understanding where she was going.

'Which proves nothing. A blind man cannot see you or me. Does that mean we don't exist? So tell me. What comes first?'

He shook his head, exasperated.

'You can't ask that question. I can't answer it. Nothing's quite that straightforward.'

He tried to think of an explanation, one that might make sense to him and to this inquisitive, quick-witted woman from a different life.

'Something happens,' he said. 'You only see it afterwards, I think.'

'Something happens? Specifics.'

'A moment. A word. A look. A thought . . . A recollection. The memory of a gesture. The way someone picks up a cup of coffee or laughs at a terrible joke. A smile. A frown. It . . .'

Nic Costa sighed and opened his hands, lost for something else to say.

'I'm sorry.'

'Why?' she asked. 'You gave me my answer.'

Agata Graziano glanced nervously at her feet and asked, 'Does it also happen at that moment, Nic? The

197

one depicted in the painting? Is that when you truly know?'

'No,' he said straight away.

'You're blushing very profusely,' she pointed out.

'What do you expect? This is not a conversation . . . not the kind of thing you talk about. With anyone. Least of all . . .'

But the Ekstasists wanted to capture that intense, private instant for themselves. That was why they raped and murdered on the streets of Rome. They needed to understand something. So, though she was reluctant to admit it, did Agata Graziano.

'You mean least of all someone like me?' she replied. 'I would have thought I'm the obvious person. Someone who's utterly disinterested in the matter.'

'All I can tell you is the truth as I see it.'

She shook her head, cross all of a sudden, and with herself this time. Her dark hair glittered under the lights of the bright chandeliers.

'This infuriating painting is designed to drive me mad. It's a game, a joke, a riddle, like Franco and his stupid gang. Why did he never paint anything like it again? Not because he couldn't. And what on earth does it really mean? Caravaggio was not Annibale Carracci. He wouldn't paint pornography for anyone who came along bearing a full purse.'

An abrupt flash of displeasure crossed her face, and it was directed at him.

'It would all have been so much easier if you could have answered yes to that last question.'

'Why?'

'Because then it would have had some personal dimension? The discovery of God in some small intimate, physical moment. But it's not. It's more than that. Or less. Oh . . .'

A modest curse escaped her lips.

'I blame this on you. And Leo Falcone. And now . . .'

She took hold of his wrist again, turned it and checked the watch there.

'It's late and I'm in trouble. That hasn't happened in months. I'm none the wiser too, which is worse. Men!'

He liked her anger. It made her more vulnerable somehow.

'I'm sorry if your carriage has turned back into a pumpkin.'

'Unlike Cinderella, I have no need of a carriage. Or fairy stories. Furthermore, my sisters adore me, which is why they are so indulgent. Therefore your analogy is very poorly chosen.'

'I'm a lot wiser,' he added. 'I know we have a painting that appears to depict a woman, no ordinary woman, some kind of goddess, in the moment of ecstasy. That she is surrounded by men, one of whom is singing a refrain from an erotic poem, the Song of Songs. I knew none of that this morning. All I knew was – ' it came out before he could halt the words – 'that somehow, in some strange way, this has to do with Emily's death. That perhaps, if I appreciated how, I would understand that better also.'

She folded her arms and gazed at him.

'You will never give up, will you?'

'Not until I know,' he replied without a moment's hesitation.

'Know what exactly? Simply a name? An identity?'

Costa shook his head.

'No. More than that. I want to understand what caused this. I want to see the instant this darkness appeared, from nowhere – ' this thought depressed him, even as he uttered it – 'to infect us.'

'That is an interesting quest,' she said quietly, nodding to herself, thinking.

Then she grasped at his sleeve and checked the watch again.

'We have time for one more viewing,' she insisted. 'There's only so much trouble a sister can get herself into in a single night.'

'We're going back to the studio?'

'Exactly.'

'Why?'

'Because you are a genius.'

'I am?' he asked.

'I believe so. Let's put this conundrum to bed once and for all, I hope. Are you with me?'

She knew there could only be one answer. Costa tried not to look back as they left, remembering Falcone's words. It was important not to give them any more excuses to run to their lawyers. Even so, he wondered whether they would be watching, Malaspina and Buccafusca, Castagna and the short, insignificant man he knew to be Tomassoni, a name that continued to stir some distant memory he could not yet place.

But they were nowhere to be seen and that was strange. This was Franco Malaspina's home. In a sense it was his party. Yet Costa had the distinct feeling that the man had left, with his fellow Ekstasists, venturing together out into the dark Roman night.

Part 9

REVELATIONS

- 1 -

Gianni Peroni didn't need a machine to tell him something was wrong. He'd stayed glued to the screen most of that evening while Rosa went through some personal documents on Malaspina and his circle sent round by Falcone. Teresa Lupo was now in the kitchen making dinner, grumpy at the lack of progress in the studio in the Vicolo del Divino Amore. Nothing had advanced during the day; her team was still awash in physical evidence, but lacked a single item that could directly link the crimes there to any one individual.

'Stop being some grubby Peeping Tom,' Teresa ordered, and returned to the table with three plates brimming with gnocchi covered in tomato sauce and cheese. 'You can't stay watching that thing all night. Besides, Leo told you . . . it would bleep if anyone came near the statues.'

'I can bleep for myself,' Peroni objected, and took a big forkful without looking, a good portion of which went straight down the front of his white shirt.

'Sorry,' Peroni murmured, then put a fat finger on the computer screen.

When he took it away they could just make out the

image of a figure, shadowy and unidentifiable under the street lights.

'Him,' he said simply.

It was a man in a dark coat, collar up, face indistinguishable in the night. That was the problem with CCTV, the police system, and these special cameras Falcone had organized. They were surveillance devices, not identification systems. There wasn't enough detail for Peroni to see what the man really looked like.

The two women abandoned their food and came to sit either side of him.

'What about him?' Teresa asked.

'Listen to someone who knows how to read these streets of ours. I have spent a lifetime watching Romans walk around this city and I know when something's amiss. It's a freezing cold night in December. Spitting with icy rain. No sane person stays outside in that weather. Except him.'

'Has he done anything, Gianni?' Rosa asked.

'No . . .' the big man replied, in that deliberately childish way he used when he was trying to argue. 'That's the point.'

Teresa grabbed a forkful of food, most of which made it to her mouth, then said, still eating, 'So he's just standing there. Where is this?'

'Abate Luigi,' Peroni replied immediately. 'The first act of *Tosca*. Remember?'

'If you continue to throw opera at me like that I'll take you to one of the damned things.'

He turned to stare at her.

'This is work,' Peroni objected.

'He's a man in the street,' Rosa said. 'Just standing there.'

'It's not a street,' he insisted. 'It's a dead end that doesn't go anywhere. And yes, he's just standing there, though I swear he keeps looking at the statue too.'

He took some more food, then said, 'He wants to see it, but he daren't. For all they know, there's a different message on every damned statue. This is one of Malaspina's bunch. Maybe the man himself. I'm telling you. I can feel it.'

Teresa slapped him cheerfully around the head.

'It's a man in the street who's probably waiting for one of those high-class hookers of yours. Get real. And remember, Leo said just to look and see where he went. Nothing else.'

'Nothing else?' Peroni answered, aghast, and that got a supportive squawk out of Rosa too. 'Look at the picture on this stupid thing. It's night. There's no moon. We can't identify him. As long as we're sitting here we're useless. Maybe – ' he flicked a finger at the screen – 'we could try and see where he went using all these other cameras Leo's got us wired up to. But I don't believe it. This is just some idiotic pile of plastic crap. It doesn't catch criminals for us. It can't pick up the phone and scream for backup. It's . . .'

He stopped, displeased with himself, wishing he felt confident enough to think he was off duty and able to open a beer.

'We all want to do something, Gianni,' Teresa said, then, to Rosa's embarrassment, she took his battered face in her hands and planted a noisy kiss on his lips.

'I *will* do something,' he insisted. 'Watch me.'

Teresa pounced with another theatrical kiss. When it was over Rosa groaned, took her eyes off the screen and said, 'Not now. Our friend's leaving.'

Peroni swore.

'Did he do anything?' Rosa asked.

'Not that I saw . . .'

It was the whining tone again.

'Then what—?'

'I was just imagining,' he interrupted, feeling as miserable and dejected as he had done the day of the funeral. One pressing thought continued to nag Peroni: if he felt this way, what emotions still ran through Nic Costa's sensitive soul on a daily basis? 'You eat. I'll watch.'

'Food . . .' Teresa said, and shoved the plate in front of him.

He pushed it away and muttered, 'Later.'

Gianni Peroni wasn't much of a one for instinct alone, least of all that gained through the artificial medium of a night-time surveillance camera watching some ancient statue in a tiny, grubby piazza by the side of a church off one of Rome's busiest streets. Nevertheless, he found he didn't much care for a beer any more, not even when the man with the upturned collar walked right out of sight of the camera, heading north, back towards the Piazza Navona. There was another camera there, part of Falcone's covert surveillance scheme that was, he understood implicitly, also hooked into the *centro storico*'s CCTV system through an arrangement made outside the Questura's normal channels.

That was the way things were, and the way they would remain until these men were brought to book.

He was happy with the idea. Simply uncomfortable with pursuing it in the cosy remote warmth of Leo Falcone's apartment, with a plate of good gnocchi going cold by his side.

'North,' Peroni said, knowing that this would take the

figure in the dark towards the most visible of those statues, Pasquino, which stood at the very end of the street in which they were now located, perhaps no more than a minute away on foot if he ran as quickly as he could manage.

He keyed through the cameras along the way and saw nothing. There were so many narrow back alleys, so many cobbled channels through this part of the city. This was the Rome of the Renaissance, not a place built for stinking modern traffic or the eager lens of some video camera perched in a private corner, its grey monocular eye fixed permanently on the shifting, ceaseless world below.

This remote, soulless form of policing was stupid. It could become an obsession, and was, he thought, for Nic already, which only made things worse.

'Eat . . .' Peroni muttered, and took a big forkful.

Then he turned the camera to Pasquino, not expecting to see a thing except a few midweek diners wandering through the drizzle, debating where to eat.

The fork stopped a finger's width from his mouth. Tomato and garlic, gnocchi and cheese, dripped onto the computer keyboard in a steady thick rain.

'Gianni,' Teresa said uneasily.

'He's there. Look. It's him.'

There must have been hordes of men wandering the street that night with their collars turned up, their faces hidden away from the rain.

'You don't know . . .' she began, then he snatched some of the photos from across the table and laid them out over the keys.

'Tall, well built, young . . .' Peroni murmured. 'It could be any of them. If only he'd move into the light so we could see his face.'

'It could be any number of people,' Teresa replied, and didn't sound so convinced.

They watched the figure in the wet raincoat wander towards the statue at the end of the road, against the wall of the cut-through to the Piazza Navona. Falcone's taunting poem had been there four or five hours now. The email boasting about it had gone out around the same time. It was a crazy idea, Peroni thought. Any sane criminal would never have risen to the bait. But Falcone understood these men somehow, understood that this was all some kind of tournament, a challenge, a deadly diversion the enjoyment of which depended, surely, on the degree of risk.

The man in the gleaming coat walked steadily towards the statue of Pasquino, a 2,000-year-old torso damp in the rain, strewn with messages, one of them very recent.

'Do it,' Peroni said. 'Do something. Anything.'

He walked past the statue and the posters, his head scarcely turned there. Nothing happened. Nothing.

'Shit,' Teresa grumbled. 'Are you going to eat your food or not?'

He didn't take his eyes off the screen. Something was going on. The figure had turned back, as if unable to stop himself. He was now over the low iron railings that protected the statue from nothing but badly parked cars.

The three of them watched. With his back to the camera, he took something out of his pocket and, in a series of crazed, violent movements, scraped at the paper on the stone, casting anxious sideways glances around him.

'Show your face,' Peroni muttered. 'Show your face. *Show your face . . .*'

There was one last stab at the stone, and a scattering of paper tumbling down to the rain-soaked pavement.

Peroni was fighting to get inside his coat before anyone could say a word. By the time he'd got it around his big frame, Rosa was ready to leave too.

It wasn't the kind of thing he did normally. But at that moment it seemed appropriate. Gianni Peroni retrieved his service pistol from its leather holster, slammed out the magazine, checked it was full and slammed it back.

'Wonderful,' Teresa moaned. 'What am I supposed to tell Leo if he calls?'

'Watch the screen.' He grabbed the earpiece of his mobile phone and stuffed it into place. 'Try to see if you can make out where he's going now.'

'And Leo?' she asked again.

Rosa was at the door.

'We go to Navona,' Peroni ordered. 'When we're there, we decide.'

He kissed her quickly on the cheek. There wasn't time to register the concern, and the fear, in her eyes.

'Tell Leo this time the bastard doesn't get to run away so easily.'

– 2 –

The night was cold. There were no lights in any of the adjoining buildings. The Barberini's outpost was set in an external block of the Palazzo Malaspina so distant from the main building he couldn't even hear the sound of the music he knew must be there, and the voices too: men and women looking forward to the Christmas holidays, and a break from work, a time for family. There was, as far as he could see, no one else in the entire block except the armed guard from the private security firm, the same man who had let him into the building that morning, and now did so with a cheery, unsurprised enthusiasm.

'Sister Agata,' the man chided her. 'You work too hard. You and your friend disturb my sleep.'

'Go back to it,' she said quietly. 'But don't snore.'

Then, silent, thinking, she led him ahead, still carrying the two over-filled supermarket bags full of papers and reference material that she had left with a puzzled cloak-room attendant at the Palazzo Malaspina when they arrived. They walked into the long, dark corridor that ran past closed offices to the room with the painting. Costa felt detached at that moment, full of random thoughts and emotions, about the case and what had happened, about himself and his loss. Had Malaspina and his group really left the palace? He had no idea, and that realization in itself felt awkwardly distant somehow, making him appreciate he had not yet found his way back into thinking like a police officer. Emily's death still stood in the way, and he had no idea how long that obstacle would remain, or whether, in truth, he wished for its removal.

There were many places Malaspina and his friends could have disappeared to in that bright, sprawling palace. But if Falcone had done his job, they now had something on their mind. A taunting message on the talking statues, its presence relayed to the Palazzo Malaspina through an anonymous phone call. Costa's own presence in the man's very private home. Could these have explained Malaspina's tense and aggressive demeanour?

It was possible, he knew. It was also possible that Malaspina was talking to his lawyer already, trying to stir up some new harassment accusation. Costa had done his best to avoid that possibility. The way Falcone had engineered their meeting meant that there would be no formal instructions on hand in the Questura to support any such charge. Nevertheless . . .

A part of him was already beginning to wonder how he might feel if these men succeeded in escaping responsibility for their acts. Like every active police officer, he recognized the pulse, the temperature of an investigation. The tell-tale signs were there. The presence of Grimaldi the lawyer, with his sour face that said, 'This is going wrong already.' The constant concern in Falcone's eyes, the way the inspector was willing to work outside the rules, not caring about any personal professional risk to himself and those he was using . . . All of these indicators told Costa that failure was by no means a remote possibility. If the Ekstasists simply sat back and did nothing remotely illegal again, there might be precious little chance of apprehending them.

Nor, some small inner voice whispered, would anyone else die, or be snatched from some squalid street assignation and taken to a dark, dismal corner of the city and subjected to a brutal ordeal, simply for the gratification of a bunch of playboys and their hangers-on. That would be a kind of result, and he retained sufficient detachment, even at that moment, to ask himself the all-important question: how much was he seeking justice, and how much vengeance?

What was it Bea had said the day of the funeral? *For pity's sake, Nic, let a little of this grief go.* He hadn't wept, not truly, not yet. The taut dark tangle of loss and anger remained locked inside him. In the company of Teresa and Peroni, Falcone too, up to a point, it was easy to pretend it wasn't there, until they started subtly introducing the subject into the conversation. Talking to Agata Graziano, a woman of the Church, quite unlike any he'd ever met, that inner act of delusion was possible too. But the knot remained, begging for release, like some bitter black tumour inside, waiting to be excised.

Then Agata reached the door of her room, the focus of her tight, enclosed universe of intellect, and turned on the light. Costa found himself dazzled once more by the painting, which, under the glare of the harsh artificial bulbs, seemed to shine with a force and power that burned even more brightly than they had during the day.

She walked over to the computer and called up a familiar painting on the screen: a stricken man on the ground, an executioner standing over him, clutching a knife.

'What can you tell me about this?' she demanded, returning, so easily, to the role of teacher.

'*The Beheading of St John the Baptist*, Valletta, Malta. Caravaggio painted it while he was in exile from Rome, trying to be a knight, and failing.'

She looked unimpressed. 'In order to become an apprentice knight of the Order of St John, he would have had to swear an oath that went something like, "Receive the yoke of the Lord, for it is sweet and light. We promise you no delicacies, only bread and water, and a modest habit of no price." Bit of a comedown after the Palazzo Madama and Del Monte's bohemian crowd. No wonder the poor boy didn't stick it. You're giving me history, Nic. Facts, for pity's sake. I can get those from a book. I want more. I want insight.'

He felt tired. He didn't want to go on. Costa needed sleep, needed a break from this world that Agata had dragged him into. It possessed too many uncomfortable dimensions. It was the universe that Caravaggio had spun around himself, and it was too real, too full of flesh and blood and suffering.

Nevertheless, the memories were there. He'd spent so much of his life, before the arrival of Emily, in the company of this man. It was impossible to lose that kind of bond now.

Costa sighed and pointed at the stricken Baptist, dying on the grimy stone of the prison cell, his executioner about to finish the act with a short knife drawn from behind his back.

'He signed it,' Costa said wearily. 'It's the only painting he ever put his name to. It's in the blood that flows from the saint's neck.'

'Really?' she asked. 'You've been to Malta? You've seen his name there?'

'I can't go everywhere there's a painting of his, Agata. Can't this wait until the morning?'

'No.' She frowned. 'I've never been to Malta either. They won't let that painting travel. It's the only one of his important works I've never seen. One day perhaps. But now. Look!'

She hammered at the computer keys and zoomed in on the focal point, the dying man, and then, more closely, the pool of gore running in a thick lifelike flow from his neck.

'Use your eyes, Nic, not second-hand knowledge. There is no name. You picked that up from a book, like everyone else. Paintings are to be seen, not read. What Caravaggio writes in the saint's blood is *f. michel*. Which, depending on your viewpoint, means "frater" Michelangelo – to denote his joy at becoming this trainee knight. Or, perhaps, *fecit*, to denote his authorship of the painting. I know which I believe. Three months later he was expelled from the order, from Malta entirely, "thrust forth like a rotten and fetid limb" they said in the judgement, which they delivered to him in front of this selfsame masterpiece. There's gratitude.'

He shook his head.

'I give up. I am tired. I am stupid. I do not see the connection.'

She took hold of his wrist and dragged him back to the luminous canvas that dominated the room.

Costa stood in front of the naked red-haired woman, who seemed so close she was real, her pale, fleshy back towards him, her mouth open, legs tantalizingly apart, sigh frozen in time, watched by the leering satyr with

Caravaggio's own face, holding music that clearly came from the same brush as that in the Doria Pamphilj earlier in the day.

'You will stand there until you see something,' she ordered. 'Concentrate your attention on the area beneath this lady's torso, please. I offer that advice out of more than mere decorum. Now I must fetch something.'

With that she left the room.

He closed his eyes for a moment, trying to concentrate, then focused on the painting. The nude female form swam in front of his eyes. It was the most seductive, the most dreamlike of compositions, from her perfect, satiated body to the lascivious satyr and the two cherubs – *putti*, common symbols in religious Renaissance painting, though here they had a more earthly and lewd aspect, each fixed on the woman's orgasmic cry. One sang from the left-hand corner. The second perched in a perfect blue sky, carelessly pouring some ambrosial fluid from a silver jug, the thin white stream spilling into the goblet below, then – he could see this now he had learned to stand close – running over the edges, down to a hidden point behind and beyond the central figure's fulsome torso.

It was hard to concentrate on the area she had indicated. This part of the canvas contained nothing: no object, no intriguing swirl of pigment, no depth or the slightest attempt to create it. What he saw, beneath the gentle curve of the nude's ample thighs, was a patch of vermilion velvet, lacking the sheen and texture of the remaining fabric around her, the coverlet on which she lay.

He stared and he thought. When she came back, carrying something he didn't dare look at, Costa said, 'This isn't right.'

'Go on,' Agata urged.

'You told me it had been X-rayed. That it was impossible it had been under-painted and over-painted.'

She was doing something with her hands, down at her
waist. He still lacked the courage to look.

'For a policeman you are remarkably imprecise at
times. What I said was that it was clear this had not been
painted over another work.'

'Perhaps it's been restored.'

She shook her head.

'There isn't the slightest sign of any general restoration. My guess is this canvas has been in storage for
years. Centuries perhaps. Even when it was on display it
would have stood behind a curtain, which would have
blocked out any daylight, were people stupid enough to
position it near a window. It's never needed restoring.
What you see, for the most part, is what Caravaggio
painted a little over four hundred years ago.'

For the most part.

'Here,' he said immediately, and pointed to the plain
flat patch of paint. 'I thought it had to be restoration. It
lacks anything. Depth or substance, interest or any deliberate withdrawal of interest, which is what I'd expect of
an area of the canvas that he didn't feel was of great
importance.'

She said nothing, simply gazed up at him with that
pert dark face, smiling.

'I could have painted that,' Costa said. 'And I can't
paint.'

'You can learn though,' she replied, grinning.

Finally, he looked at what she was doing. He found it
hard to believe.

'What's that?' he asked, knowing the answer. 'What
are you doing?'

'This is white base and ammonia,' Agata said, dipping the small, strong brush she held in her right hand deep into a tin pot of pale paste which had a distinctive and pungent smell.

She moved in closer to the surface of the canvas, her eyes focused on the area beneath the fleshly sweep of the nude's thighs.

'What does it look like I'm doing? I'm removing some paint.'

– 3 –

Peroni ran towards Pasquino, feeling his ageing legs complain beneath him. He wasn't fast enough any more. By the time he made it to the battered statue, now with newly shredded scraps of paper scattered over the litter at its base, there was no sign of their man in the steady winter rain, no dark figure hurrying through the vast, nearly deserted stadium of the Piazza Navona.

Rosa, keeping up easily with his pace, gave him a sideways look, one he recognized because Costa did it a lot these days too. It said: *I'm younger than you, and quicker. This is my call.*

'Teresa,' he barked at the neck mike of the phone. 'Did you see where he went?'

He still wasn't happy about Rosa being on the case. She was inexperienced. She was angry at the way her insight into the investigation had been ignored by Susanna Placidi. More than anything, in Peroni's view, she was still marked by the grim Bramante affair that previous spring, a dark, brutal investigation in which the young *agente* had been attacked by a man who had played the police with the same cruel skill the Ekstasists now appeared to possess, and the same relish, too.

'What am I?' the voice in his ear snapped back. 'Surveillance now? Of course I didn't see. These cameras aren't everywhere.'

'Look north,' Rosa suggested. 'He wouldn't have gone into Navona if he wanted to head in any other direction. He'd have been doubling back on himself.'

She'd keyed herself into the conference call. Peroni should have expected that. All the young ones were so bright when it came to playing with toys. So were Malaspina and his men. But toys didn't protect you forever, no matter which side you were on.

'I'm looking,' Teresa answered. 'This would all be so much easier if we could call in for support.'

'We can't!' Peroni yelled. 'You know it.'

The line went quiet for a moment.

'I know, I know it. I was just saying. I don't want you racing round Rome on foot, pretending you're a teenager. You're old, you're unfit and you're overweight.'

'It's pissing with rain, I am looking for a murder suspect and I have no idea what to do next,' he snapped back. 'I am so honoured to receive your personal views on my physical state at a moment such as this.'

He was gasping for breath, too, and his heart was pounding like some crazy drum. She was right, and he wished there was some way he could hide that fact.

'Well?' the pathologist asked.

Rosa could probably outrun even Costa, he thought. Nic was a long-distance man, built for endurance, not speed.

'Find him and Rosa can go ahead.'

He looked at the young woman in the cheap black coat. If he'd been back on vice he'd have been wondering why exactly she was out on the street on a night like this, flitting through the trickle of late-night shoppers and revellers brave enough to dodge the rain. She was listening to every word, eyes gleaming with anticipation.

'You do nothing without my permission,' he ordered, jabbing a finger in the air to make the point.

'Sir,' she said, with a quick salute.

Peroni heard a familiar sigh of relief in his earpiece.

'There,' Teresa declared. 'That was so easy. I picked him up a moment ago. At least I think it's him. If it is he did go north. He's not running. He's walking nice and slowly. I imagine he thinks he's passing for one more idiot getting wet out shopping for the night.'

'Where?' Peroni yelled.

'Going right past that funny old church, Sant'-Agostino. You know, if I was a betting person – and I am – I'd say he's headed back to where this all began. The Vicolo del Divino Amore. Or thereabouts. What did Nic call it?'

'Ortaccio,' Peroni murmured, remembering. Then he watched Rosa Prabakaran set up a steady, speedy pace north, out past Bernini's floodlit fountain of the rivers, picking up speed to put a distance between them he'd find hard to close.

There were still a few stalls left out from the Christmas fair. Men were putting away sodden cloth dolls of La Befana, the witch, dragging in sticks of sugar candy from the wet, covering up the stalls of Nativity scenes as they were buffeted by the choppy winter wind. He looked up and saw the moon caught between a scudding line of heavy black clouds. A spiral of swirling shapes, starlings he guessed, wheeled through the air. It was Christmas in Rome, cold and wet and pregnant with some kind of meaning, even for a failed Catholic like him.

There were times, of late, when Gianni Peroni wished he could remember how to pray. Not the actions or the words. Simply the ability to reconnect with the sense he'd once possessed as a child that there was some link, some bright, live fuse, that ran from him to something else, something kind and warm and eternal. Meaningful and yet beyond comprehension, which made it all the more comforting for the solitary, insular child he had been.

After one quick curse at the rain, he began to follow, heart pumping, head searching for solutions.

- 4 -

It was like watching a surgeon at work. Agata Graziano pulled over an intense, white lamp and bent down to the base of the canvas, applying the paste in small squares, one at a time, with a compact paintbrush, then removing it quickly with another solution that smelled of white spirit.

She worked slowly, patiently, with a hand so steady Costa couldn't imagine how such precision was possible.

And as she laboured something began to emerge from beneath the pigment that had been dashed on, then revarnished, to hide it.

He lost track of time. She sent him for some water, for her, not the process. When he came back he looked at this woman. He'd not met Agata Graziano before that day, yet now he felt he knew her, in part at least. There was an expression in her eyes – excitement, trepidation, perhaps a little fear – that he connected with, and that connected the two of them too. This painting contained something she needed to know, had to know, with the same relentless hunger he felt. There was a shared desperation between them, and he wondered what pain on her part had placed it there.

'I can't work with you hovering over my shoulder,' she said after a while.

Beads of sweat stood on her brow, like lines of tiny clear pearls. She wore a taut, serene expression of absolute concentration. When she finally beckoned him over he looked at his watch. She had been working on the canvas for no more than twenty-five minutes. It had seemed like hours. What he saw when he came to her side was something new and entirely unexpected. Agata had not simply uncovered a signature. She had found something else, something that took a moment to make its identity clear, because nothing he had seen, in any work of that period, by any artist, bore the slightest resemblance to what had been painted there by the artist in the original version.

It was the size of a child's hand, a pool of white, milky liquid, the same colour as the stream that fell from the cherub's jug, and spilled over the lip of the silver goblet set by the nude's pale thighs. The feature sat with the same sticky intensity he had seen in the puddle of gore flowing from the dying Baptist's neck. The trickles that ran from it formed letters in the same flowing, erratic hand as on the canvas in the co-cathedral in Valetta: the writing of Caravaggio himself.

'What is it, Nic?' she asked, her voice trembling. 'That substance. I need you to tell me.'

'It could be . . . milk. I don't know. I've never seen anything like it.'

'This was a private painting. It was kept behind a curtain. Perhaps in a master's bedroom. Perhaps in the palace of Del Monte, where Lord knows what occurred. Milk?'

He understood the question – and the answer. Agata

had told him earlier that day what kind of trick the artist was playing here, putting flesh on the ideas that had been forming in his own head. This canvas was challenging the viewer to make his or her interpretation of what it portrayed, daring the beholder to transform a scene that was, at first glance, almost innocent into something else, something that became illicit, secret, intensely intimate, but only through the presence of a living human being to provide the final catalyst.

'It's the aftermath of sex,' Costa said. 'In Malta he wrote in warm blood. Here, he wrote in . . .' He stared at the leering satyr's face, Caravaggio's face. 'He wrote in a simulacrum of his own semen.'

She took his arm. Costa bent down to read the words as she spoke them aloud: *fra. michel l'ekstasista.*

'Brother – there can be no doubt about that here – Michelangelo Merisi, the Ekstasist, a made-up word,' Agata said. 'This is impossible. It makes even less sense than before. What is an Ekstasist, for pity's sake?'

He couldn't speak. He didn't have the courage to tell her.

She threw the damp and now misshapen paintbrush onto the stone floor and swore once more. Then she placed her small fists together and, eyes closed, looked up at the ceiling.

'Why does this elude me? Why?'

This close there was something else he noticed, and he knew why Agata had missed it. All that interested her was the canvas. Everything else was irrelevant. He remembered his old teacher's words again. *Always look at the title.*

Costa walked over to the table where she kept her tools and implements, found a small chisel and returned with it to the canvas.

'What on earth do you think you're doing?' she demanded.

He placed the chisel beneath the nameplate. There was the smallest of gaps there.

'If we're going to take this thing apart, we might as well do it properly. When you made me stand here staring at that part of the painting I noticed something else. This isn't right either.'

He forced the chisel blade beneath the plate, twisted and forced away the wood there.

Agata came to join him, looking, staring, entranced.

'Oh, my God . . .' she whispered.

– 5 –

This wasn't her kind of work. Teresa Lupo found it hard keeping her attention on ten or more tiny video screens at one time, each showing the same kinds of figures, people in dark winter coats, struggling through rain that was starting to turn sleety and driving. The man – if it still was him – had continued to head north, through the labyrinth of Renaissance alleys that had turned into the shopping streets and the offices of modern Rome.

It was getting ridiculous. Rosa was racing these black streets in vain. Peroni was breathless, trying to keep up with her. Even if Teresa could have picked up the phone and brought in support, she doubted they'd have much chance of tracking down a lone figure, in a dark coat, face unseen, on a night like this.

Then, to her astonishment, she saw him. *Him.* It was the centre screen on the monitor. He was stopping to take cash from an ATM machine in the Via della Scrofa, his black frame captured perfectly by the surveillance camera situated to keep an eye on the location. She watched. The machine coughed up. Lots and lots of notes that went straight into his coat pockets. Not the kind of amount you'd take out for a night on the town. He had a scarf up tight around his face. She couldn't see who he was. But this was the same man, Teresa knew. It had to be: the stance, the clothes, the shifty way he kept his head down . . . Instantly, she was on the line to Rosa, sending her in the right direction, with Peroni, breathing heavily down the phone line, some way behind.

Then, as she heard Peroni's rasping, loud voice bellow something she couldn't hear, the landline handset on the table rang. She knew she ought to ignore it. But this being Leo Falcone's apartment, the man had to have one of those new-fangled phones with a little panel on the top that told you the number of the person calling, and the name if you'd put it into the address book.

It was flashing at her now and it said: *Questura – Falcone.*

Typical. He even keyed in his own office phone number.

'What?' she yelled when she picked it up.

There was a pause. Falcone never liked shouting unless it came from him.

'I was merely calling in to enquire about progress.'

'We have him, Leo,' she yelled back. 'He came along and tried to scrape that stupid poster of yours off the statue.'

'You saw him? Who he was?'

'No! Do you ever look at these little toys of yours before you give them to other people to play with? You can't see people's faces very well. Particularly when they've got their collars turned up. Have you see the weather out there?'

The brief silence that followed was so typical of the man she wanted to scream. Leo Falcone had many talents, and one of them was the unerring ability to hear something in your own voice you desperately didn't want him to detect.

'I told you to try to identify him, either visually or by tracing where he went,' he said. 'Nothing more. Well?'

'Peroni's going crazy, Leo. Emily died, remember?' she screeched. 'We can't all just bottle up our emotions like you . . .'

It was uncalled for, unfair and, quite simply, cruel. Falcone felt the loss as much as anyone. Perhaps his inability to show that made it worse. She would never know.

'I'm sorry—' she began.

'Where is he?' the calm, distanced voice interrupted. 'Where's Peroni? And Prabakaran?'

She rattled off the street names in an instant. Then the phone went dead without another word.

'You're welcome,' Teresa murmured, and stuffed the mobile headset back on. It took a moment before she realized both Rosa and Peroni were screaming for directions over the crackly line.

'He's leaving a cash machine in the Via della Scrofa, still going north,' she said without thinking. 'Towards the Palazzo Malaspina. Anywhere in that area. Also, I suspect Leo's on his way too, so be careful.'

Peroni said something quite unlike him. He sounded old, she thought. Old and thoroughly pissed off with the job. And that wasn't just because of Emily or the mess that had followed.

'Be careful,' she murmured again, to no one, and then went quiet. 'He's taken some money. A lot of money.'

A thought came to her: it was only intuition, but it had seemed, for a moment, as if this was a strange, foreign act. A man taking out cash from a street machine, something he didn't do often. Then putting all that money straight into the pockets of his coat, not a wallet.

'I think it's Franco Malaspina,' she said quietly. 'Or someone else who isn't in the habit of keeping a lot of cash about his person. The rich are like that, aren't they?'

The figure in black had stopped under a street light. She watched as he paused, took out a packet of cigarettes from his jacket and lit one. It made a small white point of light on the monochrome screen. He seemed so calm, so certain of himself. For a second the light of a passing vehicle caught his face. With a flash of her fingers, she stopped the video, rewound a couple of frames and froze the picture. It might be Malaspina. There wasn't enough in the way of detail to tell one way or another.

No more traffic came along to help. The roads were empty. It was getting late.

The figure stood back from the rain-filled gutter as a dark and shiny new van drove up. It stopped by the side of him. A man got out. He wore a hooded anorak, the top close around his head. Unrecognizable in their similar clothes, the two of them exchanged words.

She watched what happened next and felt her mind go numb.

The second man went to the rear of the van, took out something the length of a child's arm and began to examine it under the street light. He passed it to his colleague. Quickly, with the swift, professional skill she'd expect of a soldier or a cop who'd spent too long in weapons training, the first man in black bent back into the open van rear and removed a stack of cartridges, loaded several into the repeating magazine, then tucked the sawn-off shotgun beneath his coat before slamming the door shut.

Then the two of them got back in the van and began to drive away. North. Towards the Palazzo Malaspina. Towards Ortaccio.

'Gianni!' she yelled into the neck mike. 'For Christ's sake! Peroni!'

Her voice rang around Leo Falcone's empty dining room. Nothing came back from the phone but static.

– 6 –

He could feel his heart pounding against his ribs, his breath coming in short, painful gasps. Peroni was running along some dark, nameless alley leading off the Via della Scrofa, seeing Rosa's short, dark frame ahead, steadily adding to the distance between them.

'Leo?' he barked into the neck mike. '*Leo?*'

The walls were high around him: five or six storeys of apartments set over stores that were full of Christmas gifts, lights dimly twinkling over jewellery and paintings, upmarket clothes and furniture, all the pricey individual glitter that took place at ground level, in public, in this part of the city.

Even so, he found himself yelling out loud, looking like a madman to anyone watching, screaming into the blackness, at nothing but his neck mike, 'For Christ's sake, man. There are two bastards with shotguns wandering out here. Forget the rules. Call in backup.'

There was no reply. Teresa had already told him Falcone had left the Questura for the scene. Was he bringing support? The sight of two armed men wandering through Rome at night was certainly good reason to do so. But if they were from the Ekstasists . . . Peroni knew enough about the labyrinthine workings of the Italian legal system to understand why Falcone might have reservations. With good lawyers and bottomless pockets, it might be easy to get away with a simple fine for possession of a weapon in a public place, and bury forever the prospects of a conviction for Emily and the dead of the Vicolo del Divino Amore.

A good minute before, Rosa had turned a corner, heading left, straight into the web of ancient twisting lanes that led towards the place where those women had been dug out of the cold grey Roman earth, retrieved from the rubble of centuries, wrapped in plastic like still, dark grubs trapped inside a tight cocoon.

He listened to the lilting sound of another female voice, excited, breathless over the open comms line, chanting the names of streets so old, so obscure, he'd never really understood what they meant.

Gasping for breath, cursing his age, he leaned against a wall that was damp from the rain and black with grime and soot.

'Wait for me,' he panted.

'How long?' she demanded.

'Tell me where. It's the studio, isn't it?'

'No,' Rosa said anxiously. 'I thought so too. But they turned away from that one block away. They're going around the back of the Palazzo Malaspina. Towards the Piazza Borghese. Maybe . . .'

She hesitated.

'Are we sure these are the right people?' she asked. 'This looks like a robbery or something.'

It was Teresa who answered. Peroni felt remarkably grateful for the simple sound of her voice.

'It's them,' she said simply over the line. 'Leo? For God's sake, are you there?'

Silence.

'Wait for me,' Peroni ordered, and began to run again, his legs leaden from the effort, his body soaked in a cold and clammy sweat.

– 7 –

Costa stared at the title he'd uncovered with the chisel. Agata had let go of his arm now. She was crouched down, examining the words with a magnifying glass she had retrieved from the set of tools on the table behind.

The letters appeared carved in an archaic script that was similar to those on the title plate that had been used to cover them, though these were more elegant, more individual. It occurred to him that the two had, perhaps, been contemporaneous, the second placed over the other shortly after the painting was completed, as if to hide it from view, perhaps in a hurry.

The words read: *Evathia in Ekstasis.*

'It means nothing to me,' he confessed.

'It means everything,' she murmured, and he could hear the trepidation in her voice.

She lifted the glass so that he could see the words more closely. As he did so he realized they weren't carved at all. That was simply a trick of the artist. They were painted onto the wood in a style designed to imitate the cut and gouge of a chisel. There were scratch marks there too, fine lines, just as there were on the painting.

'He painted the title?' he asked. 'Caravaggio? Why would he do that? Surely it was beneath him?'

'He did it for the best reason of all. No one else would. No one else dared.'

Costa stepped back and had to fight to turn his attention away from the canvas. The woman there, her mouth half open in that eternal sigh, seemed so lifelike he felt that he would touch warm flesh if he was rash enough to reach out and place a single finger on her pale, perfect skin.

'This was a private painting,' he said. 'For a man's bedroom. Kept behind a curtain. I still don't understand why he'd have to put a name on it himself. And why that would need to be covered up so quickly.'

She'd gone back and retrieved the glass of water he'd fetched for her, and was now sipping it, eyes sharp and thoughtful, shaded a little with fear.

'Evathia is the Greek for Eve. *Evathia in Ekstasis* means Eve in Ecstasy. This isn't Venus at all, though there is a tradition in some quarters to associate the two of them. Remember *The Madonna del Parto*? Mary with Jesus on her lap. Or Venus with Cupid. It's hard to tell the difference sometimes. They're both associated with the spring, with birth and fecundity.'

'So?' he asked.

'So imagine, Nic. Imagine that the owner of this painting realized how dangerous it was, even hidden behind a curtain. To protect himself he had the artist put a new name on it and afterwards, unless you knew the secret, your perspective was changed. The painting was tamed. We were tamed. Not him, surely. Or . . .'

Her eyes never left him.

'. . . those who came after and knew what this really

was, those who owned it in the years that followed. When someone outside the secret is allowed to see the canvas, we see the new name, not the real one. We behold the beautiful satiated woman and the apple and assume this is Venus with the fruit Paris gave her. Not something else, the elemental gift Eve plucked from the tree. We see this bearded, lascivious figure and assume he is some kind of satyr. But where are the horns? Where are the goat's legs? This isn't a satyr at all. This is . . .'

Her eyes lost their focus. She was thinking to herself, and deeply shocked by what that revealed.

'. . . blasphemy. And pornography.'

His head whirled with images, other canvases, other works by Caravaggio, as his mind fought to find some comparison with what he saw now, so close he felt could sense Michelangelo Merisi's presence alive in the room.

'We're meant to witness what only God saw before, Adam and Eve at their first coupling,' Agata murmured, almost to herself. '"And Adam knew Eve his wife." Genesis 4:1, directly after their expulsion from the Garden of Eden. The Lord said, "Behold, the man is become as one of us, to know good and evil." Full of that knowledge, they make love, and the world loses its innocence. Seven verses later Cain kills Abel. Lust and evil with all their consequences are set loose on humanity. Caravaggio paints the very instant the world turned, when, with that single sigh of ecstasy, Pandora's Box is opened, and everything we now think of as good and bad comes flying out, never to be confined again.'

It was cold in the studio, and deathly quiet. She glanced at Costa, guilt and fear etched in her dark features.

'This is the moment of the Fall. The instant no one

ever dared depict before because it was too intimate, too shocking,' she murmured. 'Caravaggio seeks to be both sacred and profane at the same time, and to engage us in his guilt for doing so, since this canvas only becomes each of those things because of our presence here, our shared part of that original sin.'

She shook her head, then glared at him.

'Why did Leo Falcone give me this? Why me?'

If she was right – and it seemed impossible to think otherwise – this surely was the worst sight to confront a woman like Agata Graziano. It was something a sister of the cloth was never supposed to face. Perhaps – and he realized this was a thought that had been dogging him since they first met – it stirred doubts, about herself, her calling, even her religion, that had been swimming around that intelligent head for years.

She deserved the truth, he thought.

'Because Franco Malaspina's gang of thugs call themselves the Ekstasists,' Costa said quietly, feeling sick with guilt. 'Because we need to stop them.'

Her hair flew furiously around her shaking head.

'What? *What?*'

'I'm sorry, Agata. We never knew.'

'This dispensation is done with,' she spat back at him, livid, her eyes bright with rage. 'Take me back to my convent. None of this concerns me now.'

Her arms gripped her small frame tightly. Costa didn't know what to say or do to comfort this woman. He could only guess at the whirling conflict occurring inside her at that instant. And yet . . . she couldn't take her eyes off the canvas. It would not leave her easily.

'I'll drive you,' he said. 'Please . . .'

Then there was an unexpected sound, one that made

them both start with shock. His phone had sprung to life, shrieking in his jacket pocket with a harsh, electronic tone that was out of place in the studio, an unwelcome intruder from another world.

Costa took it out and tried to listen.

Something got in the way. It was the growing noise of voices, angry voices, shouting, bellowing, from outside the door, down the long dark corridor where the security guard in the blue suit had been gently dozing, a revolver at his waist.

As they listened, too taken aback to speak, the roar of a weapon rent the air. Costa felt seized by a sudden spasm of cold dread. He recognized the precise timbre of that sound. He had heard it once before, in the muddy grass at the foot of the Mausoleum of Augustus, the moment Emily had been ripped from the living.

Agata was walking towards the door, furious.

He raced to intervene, grabbed her roughly around the waist and stopped her forcefully. Two small brown fists beat on his chest. Agata Graziano's tear-stained eyes stared at him in rage and fear.

He was an off-duty cop, chasing the ghost of an idea, with nothing in the way of official police backing. That meant many things. But at that moment, more than anything, it meant he didn't have a gun.

'We need somewhere to hide,' Costa said, scanning the room.

A second explosion burst down the corridor, echoing off the thick stone walls of this distant, half-forgotten outpost of the Palazzo Malaspina. Afterwards the air was filled with the rank dry smell of spent ammunition, and the sound of a man in agony.

– 8 –

There were too many dark streets, too many disturbing possibilities running through Leo Falcone's head. He'd heard Peroni's bellowed call over the open voice link. Then he'd issued a single order before sending his Lancia screaming hard across the black slippery cobblestones of this tangled quarter of the *centro storico*.

The two men weren't heading for the Vicolo del Divino Amore but for Agata's laboratory. That could only mean one thing. They wanted the painting.

He had pushed his luck to the limits, setting up a private, possibly illegal, covert operation with the sole aim of placing unauthorized surveillance on Malaspina and his accomplices. He could put up with the heat from that if he had a conviction, certain and guaranteed, lying down the line. If there was the slightest doubt, the tiniest crack through which these most slippery of men might wriggle, then he would be lost. They would escape once more, for good in all probability. His career would be over, alongside that of Peroni and possibly Costa and Rosa Prabakaran too. He had no great concern about his own fate; he surely did not wish to share it with others. However loudly Peroni yelled, Falcone was determined he would not call in for assistance until he was certain it was both necessary and would result in success.

The long, sleek car sped along the Via della Scrofa, now just a minute, perhaps two, away from the half-hidden lane where the Barberini's outpost lay.

There was one other cop in the vicinity too, Falcone remembered, at the party in the palace nearby. He was reluctant to involve him, given the history. But they were short-handed. They needed help.

He barked Costa's name into the voice-operated phone. A single word was all he needed.

'Nic?'

Waiting for an answer, he wondered what it had been like to spend an evening with the pretty and charming Sister Agata Graziano in Franco Malaspina's extravagant palace, one of the few grand mansions in Rome Leo Falcone had never visited in his entire career. Costa deserved some time in pleasant company, a few hours to take his mind off the pain Falcone knew would be there, and would remain, until this case was closed.

It took an unconscionable number of rings for an answer to come. Falcone listened to the snatched, breath-less conversation and heard, with a growing dread, the line go silent halfway through.

'Where are you?' he barked. 'Where *are* you?'

His head alive and confused with myriad possibilities, he spun the vehicle sharply round to perform a U-turn in the Piazza Borghese, knocking over the stand of a news-paper vendor packing up his stock for the night. Sheets of Christmas wrapping paper flew into the air.

He fought to get the vehicle under control, and finally managed to manoeuvre it hard and fast the wrong way down the narrow alley that led to the studio.

Braking sharply, he brought the Lancia to a halt a few metres short of the entrance to the Barberini's office. Falcone flew from the vehicle, took out his handgun and held it high and ready. To his relief, two familiar figures were coming up the alley from the south, one fast and young, the second older, out of condition and struggling.

There was a van parked there, badly, blocking the street entirely. Its back door was open. The interior was empty.

A menacing smell reached him from the door: spent ammunition. Somewhere, beyond the light in the open doorway, he heard the sound of a man's weak cries and, more distant, angry, violent shouting.

He was still considering this when the two of them arrived, almost together. Peroni's face was pale and troubled; his breath came in snatched gasps.

'Sir . . .' Rosa Prabakaran began.

The big man pushed her to one side.

'We need to get in there,' he urged, then somehow found the strength to drag out a weapon and hold it low by his side. 'Now, for God's sake. Nic's there. You left the line open, you old fool. We all heard it.'

Falcone wondered, not for the first time, about these lapses. They seemed to happen with increasing frequency; everyone was getting older.

'I did,' he said, and nodded, remembering now. Conference calls on the private system they'd used stayed there until they were closed. That was doubtless what sent Peroni racing here, too fast for his own good.

Falcone looked at the weapon in Rosa Prabakaran's hand. It was obvious she had never used a gun in anger before. The pistol trembled in her fingers.

'Stay behind me,' he ordered. 'Do what I say always.'

241

He made the call he knew was inevitable now, and wondered how long it would take for them to respond. On a quiet, wet night before Christmas, the Questura was scarcely at its most alert, even when an inspector demanded urgent assistance at a shooting incident. The most recent statistics had shown that it took between ten and twenty minutes for uniformed cars to arrive at incidents outside the centre of the city, where the tourists were. No one would be patrolling these dead, silent streets as a matter of course. This was his to deal with, no one else's.

Leo Falcone entered the dim light of the Barberini outpost's door with a steady, determined stride, and became aware, the moment he crossed the threshold, of the distinct and pervasive stink of human blood.

– 9 –

There was a storeroom. It took all his strength to drag her there, as she kicked and fought, his hand over her mouth, his arms tight around the rough fabric of her black dress. The door was ajar. Costa levered it open with his foot, grabbed her more tightly and dragged the two of them through into the darkness.

She struggled all the way, wrestling in his arms. They fell against the shelves. Cans of paint tumbled to the floor, old easels, dusty, unused for years.

'Nic!' she screeched.

He pulled the door shut, then, in the meagre light that fell from the cracks above and below, he pushed her to the end of the small, enclosed chamber and held her close. In the gloom her eyes glittered with emotion.

'They have weapons,' he said simply. 'They kill people. We keep quiet. We wait.'

She stared at him and withdrew from his grip, standing back against the shelves he could just make out in the stripes of yellow illumination from the room beyond. They contained the junk of ages: fusty books, small canvases wrapped in sackcloth and palette after palette of long-dried paint.

'Why did you bring me into this?' she whispered with obvious bitterness. 'What did I do?'

He glanced at the door.

'You knew enough to unlock the painting,' he answered immediately. Then, before she could say another word, he placed his finger to his lips.

They were there, outside, moving swiftly, arguing. Angry voices. Two. And a further sound too: a man in pain, howling, pleading for help. The security guard surely, from along the entrance corridor.

One voice, more than the other, seemed familiar from the Barberini's party that evening. Franco Malaspina. Agata surely thought so too. She listened in shock and covered her mouth with her small, dark hand.

The noise of them grew louder. It was obvious what they wanted. The painting. The canvas was large, perhaps manageable by one man, but much easier for two. They were talking about how to remove it, what to cover it with, how to proceed.

And they were different: one confident, masterly, the second scared, fearful.

Finally, the other, weaker one spoke up.

'You shot him,' he moaned in a high-pitched, almost feminine whimper. 'You *shot him*. For God's sake.'

'What do you think we brought these things for?' the second voice snapped.

'He's alive!'

There was a pause. Costa watched Agata. She seemed ready to break.

The bolder intruder spoke.

'I'll deal with that on the way out. Don't squawk. You can wash the blood off later. Now help me move it. We don't have time . . .'

Agata's eyes went glassy. She stumbled. Her elbow caught something – a box file, covered in dust – teetering on the edge of the shelf. As it balanced in the darkness, she reached for it, caught thin air, her flailing fingers sending more old and grubby objects tumbling noisily to the floor, a tell-tale cacophony of sound announcing their presence.

The room beyond became silent.

Then a voice, the one he thought he knew, said loudly and full of confidence, 'I wondered why the lights were on. Careless . . .'

– 10 –

It was more than a year since Leo Falcone had fired a weapon, and that was on the firing range, on the routine duty he regarded as an administrative chore. Inspectors didn't shoot people. If he could help it, none of these officers did either. That was not why the police existed.

He tried to remember what he knew about how to enter a building safely. It wasn't a lot. So he clung to the walls of the entrance corridor, with its ancient, smoky ochre walls. The plaster was peeling from the damp beneath the old stone of the palace in which the corridor lay like an afterthought, tucked into the hem of a sprawling pile of dark masonry that sat, unvisited and unknown, in this strange and, for Falcone, increasingly inimical part of the city.

Right arm out perpendicular to his body to ensure Peroni and Rosa stayed behind, Falcone took a series of rapid strides, hard against the wall, seeing nothing, hearing voices ahead. A bright light indicated the studio where he had first approached Agata Graziano and asked for help, a decision he now regretted deeply. There were no more shots, though. That gave him some satisfaction. Then he moved forward again, gun held high, ready and visible, and beckoned the two figures behind him to dash safely into the alcove on the right, where Falcone dimly recalled the presence of a middle-aged security guard.

Rosa went first, squeezing behind his beckoning hand. Falcone stared down the corridor and briefly turned to nod at Peroni to wait. Then they looked at one another, a familiar expression of shared dismay in each man's eyes. Rosa had let out a sudden, high-pitched shriek. Falcone turned, spat something low and vicious in her direction, hoping it would shut her up, and crossed the corridor.

There was a figure in uniform on the floor, brutally wounded, sitting upright against the wall clutching his bloodied stomach with both hands, a look of intense fear in eyes that were fast fading towards unconsciousness.

Falcone listened to him say something that might have been, 'Help me.'

'There are people on the way,' the inspector said, and, feeling a rising tide of fury enter his head, stormed back into the corridor with a firm intent, weapon in front of him, not knowing whether the female *agente* and Gianni Peroni, his only support at that moment, were following on behind.

– 11 –

Costa took a deep breath, then stepped in front of Agata and looked around him, seeking something, anything, that might count as a weapon. He was still searching when the old wooden door that separated them from the studio exploded in a roar of heat and flame. The shotgun blast came straight through it, just a metre or so from where he stood, hoping to protect her. A thin, scattering cloud of lead shot fell around them, ricocheting off the high walls, peppering their heads and shoulders with tiny searing balls of fire.

Agata was screaming. Something caught Costa in the eye: dust or a shard of wood. He was aware of the barrel of the weapon crashing through what remained of the door and a figure there, following it: all in black, with the familiar hood.

He had the weapon crooked in his arms. The eyes behind the slits stared at them, dark and malevolent. The man was fumbling in his jacket for more shells, which he casually stuffed into the maw of the gun as if he were on some idle weekend game shoot.

The entry didn't take more than a moment, too little time for Costa to attack.

Instead he held his arms wide open, fingers grasping into the darkness, a gesture that meant nothing.

'You don't need the woman,' he said firmly. 'Take me if you like. But not her. She's no idea what this is about. She's no idea who you are.'

Without realizing it he'd backed all the way to the end of the storeroom. She was trapped behind him, trembling, crouched against the wall.

The long, deadly shape of the weapon rose, loaded now.

'That bitch always had a sport in the blood,' the figure said, in a low, dead voice, half recognizable, half lacking any human feeling at all.

He brought the gun up easily, with the kind of familiarity a hunter used, as if it were second nature.

This was all a question of timing, Costa thought, something it was impossible to know. He wasn't even sure what his hand had found on the shelf, only that it was hard and heavy and easy to grip.

As the gun moved towards horizontal, he took tight hold of the metal handle and swung it in front of him with as much force as he could muster. The can of ancient paint flew off the shelf, towards the shape in black, who had moved forward sufficiently to be silhouetted against the bright studio lights behind. It crashed into his face, the lid bursting open as it met the woollen hood.

A flow of pigment the colour of ancient blood flooded over the black fabric. The can crashed to the ground. A cry came from behind the covered mouth. It was something, Costa thought. It was . . .

. . . nothing.

Before he could attack again, the man took a step back, wiped the paint from his face with one elbow and stood there, madder than ever, the weapon swiftly back between his hands.

Costa threw something else from the shelf, something not so heavy or awkward. It bounced off the wall just catching the barrel of the gun as it exploded.

Fire and heat and a terrible, deafening noise filled the air. Something took hold of his left shoulder and flung him backwards with an agonizing force. Feeling giddy, and aware of a growing, burning pain racing through his body, he tumbled into Agata, whose slender arms managed, almost, to break his fall to the hard ground.

One more time, he thought, knowing what was happening now without needing to look. That was all. The man with the gun was getting closer, intent on finishing this for good.

Costa turned, ignoring the searing, spreading ache from his shoulder, and threw himself forward. He caught the barrel, placed his right hand, palm down, over the two gaping holes there and forced it up towards the ceiling, waiting for the moment when the agony would begin again as the shells tore through his flesh and perhaps gave them a few more brief moments of survival.

– 12 –

Falcone saw a tall, muscular figure dressed in black, hooded, struggling with the painting, weapon on the floor. He barked the first words that came into his head, in a voice that was loud and forceful and brooked no argument. The man raised his arms over his head and started to talk, in a falsetto babble riddled with fear.

'Shut up!' Falcone yelled, then ordered Rosa to keep her gun on him.

Something was happening at the far end of the room, in an annexe that lay beyond the canvas and the bright, piercing lights that stood above it.

Peroni came to his side, weapon raised.

'How well can you shoot, Leo?' he asked.

He didn't dare answer, and instead watched in despair as three figures tumbled through the door, the first all in black too, with a shotgun held in the air by Costa's struggling arm as the young officer, his left shoulder covered in blood, his coat ripped by pellets, pushed the intruder out into the light.

Agata Graziano was fighting just as hard, kicking and punching and screaming at the faceless attacker.

It seemed to take an interminable time for Falcone and

Peroni to join them, with Rosa continuing to cover the second man on the inspector's orders. One armed individual was enough to deal with. These situations deteriorated into chaos so easily. As Falcone raised his pistol towards the head of the first angry figure wrapped so tightly into the mêlée of bodies in front of him, he realized this was not a solution that would work at all. They couldn't fire because they couldn't safely distinguish one from the other in the sea of flailing arms, the tight grip of bodies, they'd become.

For a second, no more, there was an opportunity. Costa was down, hard on the floor, his legs kicked from beneath him by the taller, stronger shape in black, but able, along the way, to drag the long grey profile of the shotgun's barrel with him, finally hauling the whole weapon from the grasp of those powerful dark arms as he did so.

Falcone made a mistake at that moment, and knew it in an instant. He looked at Costa, and had to stop himself asking the obvious. *Are you all right?*

By the time he'd dragged his attention back to where it mattered, everything had changed.

The man in black had Agata Graziano tight in his arms, terrified and furious. The barrel of a small handgun was hard against her temple, pressing into her olive-coloured skin, making a clear and painful indentation. The second intruder glanced at Rosa Prabakaran, then, without any protest on her part, limped over to the storeroom doorway and stood there by his side, silent, submissive.

Falcone kept his own weapon directed straight ahead, towards the one who mattered.

'You will let her go,' he said simply.

It was the best he had and he knew immediately how

weak it sounded. Something happened then that made him feel old and stupid and out of his depth.

In a room with four police officers, three of them armed, one of them wounded, though not badly, it appeared to Falcone, this masked and murderous creature laughed, easily, without fear. As if none of this touched him, or ever would.

He dragged Agata Graziano closer to his chest, holding her like a shield, in a tight, avaricious grip. With his free arm around her throat, he turned the weapon in his right hand abruptly to one side, ninety degrees, away from the threat ahead.

Before Falcone could say another word the man pumped two shells into the skull of the hooded figure next to him.

She struggled helplessly, eyes white with terror, feet almost off the ground in the power of his grip. Costa, who had been slyly working his way across the stone slabs in the direction of the man's legs, stopped on the instant. The small black revolver's barrel was back at the terrified woman's temple.

'If the painting isn't outside in thirty seconds,' said the voice behind the hood, a calm, male voice, controlled, patrician, 'I will blow these bright brains straight out of her skull.'

– 13 –

It was raining. There were still no police cars. Just Falcone's Lancia and, a little way along the narrow alley, beneath a single street light, the van, with its rear doors open.

Falcone and Peroni had the canvas in their arms and followed the hooded man, who was dragging Agata roughly, the gun never leaving her forehead. Rosa, on Falcone's instructions, followed behind.

There was nothing any of them could do. Agata was a hostage, held by a man with no desire for negotiation. Costa clutched his aching shoulder, feeling the lead shot biting into his flesh, the blood from the wound making his clothes stick to his skin. Unseen by the figure in black, he'd picked up a weapon, snatching the gun left on the floor by the dead intruder. It felt useless in his left hand, the only good one, and there wasn't a sound from anywhere, not a siren, not a tyre squeal in the night.

'I prefer the car,' the voice behind the black wool mask said, and his arm tightened around Agata's neck, holding her so hard that her face was taut under the pressure. 'Keys.'

Falcone took one hand off the painting and removed

them from his pocket, holding them out in the cold night air.

'You,' the man barked at Rosa.

'I'll do this,' Costa said, then, ignoring the pain, tucked the gun back into his waistband beneath his jacket before stepping in front of the young *agente* to take the keys from Falcone, keeping his eyes on the man and Agata all the time.

'In the ignition,' the voice behind the hood ordered. 'Engine running.'

Costa opened the driver's door, sat briefly in the seat, brought the potent engine of the Lancia to life first time and got out.

A large delivery truck had come to a halt at the top of the alley, blocking that exit. There was only one way out, past the abandoned van the intruders had brought. The exit route was narrow. Not easy. As he walked away from the vehicle, Costa stopped, stared into Agata's eyes, hoping she might understand. There was, perhaps, one final chance.

Falcone lifted the rear hatch and, with Peroni's aid, manoeuvred the canvas into the interior as Costa stood his ground, no more than a metre from the masked man and Agata, now still and tense in his tight grip.

'I can go in her place,' he said again, not moving.

'You're not so much fun.'

Costa raised his bloodied right arm and pointed at the face behind the mask.

'If there is so much as a scratch or a bruise on this woman when next I see her, I will kill you myself.'

There were words he didn't catch. Then the man in black pushed Agata through the driver's side, ordering her to climb into the passenger seat, holding the gun to her head all the time, scanning the four cops by the vehicle constantly, waiting for any kind of movement. There was not, Costa knew, a single opening. It was well done. Finally, when she was in the seat, he let himself fall deftly into the car, working his feet onto the pedals, taking the wheel with his free left hand.

The door closed. Costa heard the electronic locks slam shut. He wondered how many times Agata had been inside a vehicle in her entire life. She lived in the centre of Rome. She was, in her own eyes, a working woman, one who took buses and the metro, not expensive cabs and cars.

He doubted she had the first clue how to open a door held shut by central locking, even if she knew where to find the switch.

The hooded head hung out of the open window for a few seconds.

'Follow me and she dies,' he said in a firm, low voice which betrayed not the slightest degree of trepidation.

– 14 –

Costa turned and walked away, limping a little, conscious of the blood draining from his shoulder, intent on moving towards the abandoned van. As he did so, he surreptitiously removed the weapon from his belt, letting it hang loose in his left hand. Before the Lancia could begin to move he was squeezing down the narrow gap between the van and the stone wall, barely wide enough for one person, a slender space in the darkness into which he could disappear. On the other side . . . he was praying the gunman hadn't worked this out yet. He guessed there was room – just – for Falcone's car. But only if it negotiated the gap carefully, in first gear, and with some manoeuvring.

The high-powered saloon's eager cylinders roared with sudden life. Its tyres squealed on the cold, damp cobblestones of the lane. The shining vehicle reversed. From his position in the pool of black by the van, Costa saw what he expected. The driver had been focused on more important matters than the traffic. When he looked behind, he saw the truck at the head of the lane blocking the obvious exit. There was only one way out: past the van. Past *him*.

The Lancia edged forward, towards the space on the far side. Costa waited, moving further forward behind the open rear door, heart pumping, trying to summon what strength he still had.

He was aware that there was a second or two during which he might act, nothing more.

From the far side of the vehicle came the teeth-jagging racket of metal screeching against metal as Falcone's prized possession began to squeeze into the narrow gap between the van and the far wall. He heard the wheels squealing over the stones as the driver locked and turned them, trying to negotiate a corner that was near impossible.

Gradually, the gleaming hood began to emerge, and Costa knew he had one slim chance, the moment when the passenger door would be briefly free before the body of the vehicle cleared the obstacle and they would gone, flying into the night, to a place and a fate he could only guess at.

The Lancia lurched forward, almost free. He could hear the powerful engine growling with anticipation.

'This I will not allow,' Costa muttered to himself, then judged the timing instinctively, seeking the precise instant he saw the full length of the passenger door by his side before extending his wounded arm, screaming as he did so, 'Down! Down! Down!'

He saw her face frightened but alert through the glass and that single exchanged glance was enough. She was ready. She was quick. He watched her wayward head of her hair dive towards her lap, then turned the weapon in his good hand towards the dark figure at the wheel, placing a single shot through the very top of the side window, praying it would hit home.

There was a bellow of gunfire and the shattering of glass. Splintered shards jumped up into his face, sharp and stinging. He thrust his good hand through the window, then, with the shaft of the pistol, raked at the break there to make it larger, dashing the weapon round and round, screaming words he couldn't hear or understand. It was enough to get his bloodied right fist through and find the lock. Except she was there already, before him. The passenger door of Leo Falcone's police car swung open, took him in the chest, sent him reeling backwards, as another body flew out, into his flailing arms.

'Nic . . .' she yelled.

'Behind me . . .'

The others were squeezing their way through the narrow crack by the side of the van. There wasn't enough room for them to gather. He couldn't get the picture of that sawn-off shotgun out of his mind either. He had failed Emily this way once. Twice . . . It was unthinkable.

'*Behind me,*' he bellowed, and felt her slim body squeeze past his aching, screaming shoulder, to some place that might count as safety.

The Lancia revved angrily. The figure behind the wheel was alive, and furious.

But not stupid enough to engage in a battle that was lost.

He managed to loose off one more shot with his weak left hand. By then the car was forcing its way out into the open alley, unmindful of the damage caused by stone and metal. Once free, it found a sudden and violent life. Tyres spinning wildly on the black shining stones, it careered off the far wall and leapt out into the open space. He watched, the gun loose in his hand, his fingers too tired, too pained to think of another shot, as the vehicle disappeared in a wild, torque-driven arc, disappearing into the warren of streets he had come to think of once more as Ortaccio, a web of twisting ancient passageways that could lead almost anywhere in the city.

Costa leaned back on the door of their truck and closed his eyes.

He felt weak and stupid, almost paralysed by the aftershock and the wound to his shoulder. But more than anything he felt elated. This time the man in the hood, with his deadly shotgun, had failed.

'You're hurt,' she said, sounding cross, as if it was his fault somehow. 'Where are the doctors? Leo? Where are the doctors?'

'Coming,' Falcone said.

When he opened his eyes again the inspector stood next to her, bending down to look at his shoulder.

'He'll live,' the inspector added. 'Now, Agata . . .'

'He'll live! *He'll live!*' she roared. 'What kind of thing is that to say?'

'I'll live,' Costa broke in, and stared at her, still only half able to believe she had possessed the speed and the wit to take the minute possibility he had created.

'Agata . . . Did you recognize him?'

She stopped, and glanced at both of them.

'Recognize?'

'Was it Franco Malaspina?' he asked, and noticed a sudden, disappointed intake of breath on Falcone's part when he heard those words.

'How do I know, Nic? I never saw his face.'

'The man knew you,' he pointed out.

'He did,' she agreed. 'Still . . . All I heard was that muffled voice through the mask. Perhaps. I don't know.'

Her bright eyes gazed at him through the steady rain,

asking a question she didn't want answered. Why he needed this so much. Half suspecting, he knew, the answer.

'We know it's Franco,' he said quietly, not caring what Falcone thought any more. 'I told you. *They* are the Ekstasists, Malaspina and the rest. They killed those women in the Vicolo del Divino Amore. My wife. We *know*. The man's so rich and powerful and clever, we can't prove a damned thing. Not without a start. Not without some small concrete piece of evidence. Something that will force his hand.' He knew it was the wrong thing to say. Provocation. Leading a witness on. He didn't care any more. 'A simple, positive identification would do that.'

Falcone was staring at his shoes. Peroni and Rosa were walking around the other side of the van towards them. Costa knew where they must have been. Inside. A place that seemed, briefly, almost irrelevant at that moment.

'Is this true, Leo?' she asked. 'That you suspected Franco all along? You involved me in this, knowing what manner of man he is?'

Falcone held out his arms, pleading.

'I was desperate, Agata. We all were. I'm sorry. If I had thought for one moment . . .'

'Is it true?'

Falcone's eyes were back on his feet.

'This is not the way we do these things,' he said in a low, despairing voice. 'There are procedures and rules about evidence. Placing ideas in a witness's head . . . If I were to use you as a witness there would be the issue of protection. He is a dangerous man.' He hesitated, reluctant to continue. 'More dangerous than you can begin to know. I don't want to hear any more of this. I won't.'

She didn't wait long.

'It was Franco Malaspina,' she said. 'I am sure of it. I know his voice well. I heard him speak my name. There. Use it. I will say this in court. Use it, Leo!'

The inspector shook his head and sighed. 'Don't go down this road. There's no turning back.'

'I will say this to you. Or to anyone else in Rome who wishes to hear.'

Falcone took out his radio and put out a call for the immediate arrest of Malaspina, Buccafusca, Castagna and Tomassoni, with all caution to be taken when approaching men who might be armed and dangerous.

'A doctor too,' Agata Graziano insisted. 'For Nic. And those men inside.'

Peroni coughed into his big fist.

'Those men inside are beyond doctors,' he said. 'I think you can cross Emilio Buccafusca off that list too. Judging by the wallet on the corpse in there, he's out of this already.'

A distant siren broke the silence of the night. From somewhere in the direction of the Mausoleum of Augustus a blue light flashed down the alley, like some mutant Christmas decoration newly escaped from the tree.

Part 10

THE NEW COMMISSARIO

- 1 -

Within fifteen minutes the entire area around the Barberini studio was flooded with a tangle of police vehicles and officers stretching as far back as the Piazza Borghese. A city-wide alert had been issued for Falcone's stolen vehicle, so far without results. Costa had been seen by the duty medical officer and dispatched, with Agata insistently by his side, to the hospital for treatment for his wounded shoulder. Scene of crime were preparing to seal off the studio and start work on the body of Emilio Buccafusca, under the supervision of Teresa Lupo, who had found her own way to the scene, and taken control of her team without a single order from anyone. There was an excess of activity and resources, one suspect dead, one missing, both with clear links to the earlier cases in the Vicolo del Divino Amore.

Falcone should have felt happier than he did. It was Franco Malaspina behind the mask. He was sure of that. But Agata's identification under pressure from Costa was so vague, and came about from crude prompting. Even in a mess like this, with evidence available everywhere, a rich, powerful Roman aristocrat would retain some friends, and – possibly – sufficient influence to disrupt the momentum of the case at the very point at which it appeared to be about to break.

There were still too many unknowns, and one of them was striding through the rain towards him at that moment, a tall skinny figure about his own build, but with a full head of wavy black hair damp from the weather, not that the man cared much. Falcone had spent little time with Vincenzo Esposito since the man arrived from Milan to take up the position of *commissario* in the Questura. He had no idea what to make of him, and nor had anyone else, since he was utterly unlike any of the officers – all Roman, all risen through the local ranks – who had preceded him. A few years short of Falcone's own age, quietly spoken, sharply intelligent and – to the dismay of active officers – keenly interested in the minutiae of the investigative process, Esposito was a mystery to those he commanded, and seemed happy to keep it that way.

Falcone had looked through newspaper cuttings after his appointment. There was nothing there except an illustrious though quiet career, one that had included busting a clan of the 'Ndrangheta crime organization while working in Reggio di Calabria, and bringing about the successful prosecution of several state officials for bribery in connection with public works contracts in his native city. These were the actions of an ambitious officer. One, Falcone hoped, who had limited time for authority when a little leeway was called for. It was possible he would find himself suspended, alongside those he had inveigled into the illicit surveillance operation against the Ekstasists, once the dust of this night had cleared. It was also possible he could talk his way out of things, for a while anyway.

Only the morning before he had met Esposito in a corridor in the Questura, between a conference with the primary team working on the bodies in the Vicolo del Divino Amore and the visit to his own apartment to brief Peroni, Costa, Teresa Lupo and Rosa Prabakaran. There had been a brief exchange of words – the kinds of sentiment that officers expressed in the middle of difficult cases.

And Falcone had let something slip, quite deliberately, knowing that Esposito was aware of the interest in Malaspina, and the difficulties that caused.

The man had listened and said simply, 'The rich are with us always, too. Sadly.'

After which he had excused himself, then, with a backwards glance, headed off down the corridor to one of the endless management meetings that always reminded Falcone why he didn't want to be a *commissario*.

Esposito didn't look displeased at being dragged out of bed. He seemed energized, interested, even a little amused.

'You do spring surprises on me,' the man observed cheerfully. 'I've just been chatting to that young Indian officer of yours. I thought we had one investigation. Now it transpires we had two.'

'I had intended, sir—'

'No need,' the *commissario* interrupted. 'I don't expect to be told everything. Unless it's absolutely necessary.' He stomped his feet and clapped his hands together. It was an act. The night wasn't that cold. 'Well. Is it?'

'I don't believe so at the moment.'

'Good. No one has seen your car. Don't you find that odd?'

'Very,' Falcone grumbled. There had been a single sighting of the vehicle, on the Lungotevere by the new museum for the Ara Pacis. The police car which made the identification was blocked behind another vehicle on a red light in a side street. By the time it reached the main road, the stolen car was nowhere to be seen.

'Unless it's in that damned palace round the corner, eh?'

'It's big enough,' Falcone admitted. 'That would seem rash, surely. An underground car park would be the obvious place. If he was a criminal, I would suggest he might have easy access to some truck used for car theft. Someone could simply drive up a ramp and it's out of sight.'

Esposito seemed amused by this idea.

'*If* he's a criminal? I read the file. These animals have murdered at least seven women and attacked God knows how many more, just to get their dirty pictures . . .'

'I'm not sure it's quite as simple as that.'

'I am. Malaspina murdered the wife of one of our own officers. And one of his brothers in arms tonight, in front of you. *If.*'

'I meant if he were a career criminal. Part of some organization.'

'A criminal's a criminal,' the *commissario* noted cryptically. 'So your suspect is gone. And that painting he loves too.'

'I will find this man,' Falcone insisted.

'I should hope so. And this young officer of yours? Costa? Is he badly hurt?'

'They will be picking shot out of his shoulder for a few hours. It won't be pleasant. It won't be fatal either. He is a very . . . persistent individual. Rather too much for his own good sometimes.'

'So I'd heard. Then he should rest. He never took sufficient compassionate leave in the first place.'

'I know.'

Esposito watched him keenly.

'You have ideas, Ispettore?'

'A few. For later. They are insufficiently developed.'

'And now? Think about this. It's important. Are you sure it was Franco Malaspina? Absolutely? We can't play fast and loose with a man like that. One more screw-up and he's probably free for good.'

'We have a positive identification from Sister Agata Graziano, a woman of the Church.'

Falcone was aware of the hesitation in his own voice. So was Esposito.

'Of a hooded man who said very little indeed from what Prabakaran tells me,' the *commissario* observed.

'It will put no one behind bars. But perhaps it will unlock enough doors for us to find the evidence that will. Though I hope to have something better before long.'

Esposito looked at the sea of bodies and vehicles around him, the forensic team climbing into their white bunny suits, the organized mayhem that followed any major crime incident, a necessary flow of procedures and bureaucracy set down so firmly on paper that every senior officer knew it now by heart. He didn't seem much interested.

'I'd be a damned sight happier if we simply picked up this creature behind the wheel of your car,' he complained. 'That would make everything so simple, which is doubtless why it won't happen. Do we really need all these men and women earning expensive overtime at this hour of the night?'

'Those who are not involved in the crime scene are waiting, sir.'

'For some magistrate who's been dragged out of bed to give you carte blanche to charge through the Palazzo Malaspina?'

'Good God, no,' Falcone answered, aghast. 'That's what he'd expect. If Malaspina's there it means he's fixed some alibi already. If not . . . it's irrelevant. His lawyers have us wrapped in cotton wool. We can't apply for a warrant without notifying them first, and that would extend any hearing until the daylight hours at the earliest.'

The *commissario* beamed. For the first time in a while Leo Falcone felt quite cheered. Something told him he wouldn't necessarily be fired. Yet.

'So?' Esposito wondered.

'So I have applied for warrants to enter the homes of Giorgio Castagna and Nino Tomassoni. Castagna lives in the Via Metastasio, two minutes to the south from here. Tomassoni has a house in the Piazza San Lorenzo in Lucina. It's just as close.'

Esposito looked pleased.

'I know Rome. No need for directions. We could walk there. But we won't, of course. I want this done properly.'

'Sir . . .'

'In fact . . .'

He put a gloved finger to his lips, thinking. Vincenzo Esposito had a pale, softly contoured and elongated face, that of one of the Piedmontese peasant farmers Falcone used to see as a child when he was on holiday in the mountains, or in the bloodless, idealized paintings so popular in the north. It was difficult to imagine the man in the flush of anger or engagement.

'You take Tomassoni,' he ordered. 'I shall visit Castagna. With Agente Peroni by my side. Is that agreeable to you?'

'Well . . . as you wish,' Falcone replied, a little staggered by the directness of this intervention. 'Peroni?'

'An interesting man. I have read his file. I have read all your files.'

Falcone said not a word.

'I like this city of yours,' Esposito declared. 'Now, may we go and arrest some criminals, do you think?'

- 2 -

Their destination was in another dark, narrow alley in a part of Rome that Gianni Peroni was beginning to dislike. He felt tired and worried. He was concerned, too, about this new *commissario* who seemed so friendly and had picked him out by name, even going so far as to pat him on the shoulder as they rode to the address that was registered for Giorgio Castagna.

Commissario Esposito took one look at the dingy street and the shiny door, that of a single house, not the apartments one would not normally expect.

There were ten other men with them, one of them a *sovrintendente*, Alfieri, who was less than pleased to discover Esposito didn't appear to regard him as his most senior officer around.

'Why are you an *agente*?' the *commissario* asked idly as they looked at the door from down the lane, thinking of their mode of entrance.

'Because the people in charge at the time got sentimental,' Peroni replied immediately. 'I should have been fired. I was an inspector. They found me in a cathouse when it got raided. My life was a little . . . strange at the time.'

Esposito said nothing.

'Why are you asking this?' Peroni demanded. 'Since you clearly know it already if you've read the papers.'

'Sometimes it's better to hear things than read them. Don't you agree?'

'Of course . . .'

'And also because . . .' Esposito shrugged. 'I have to make a decision when the dust has settled. Do I throw the book at you all for running this little show outside the rules? Or . . .'

The *commissario* looked at Alfieri, who was shuffling on his big feet, and standing in front of some muscular *agente* Peroni didn't know, one who was passing a large, nasty-looking implement from hand to hand, somewhat impatiently.

'We are talking, Officer,' he pointed out. 'A private conversation.'

'S-sir,' the man stuttered, 'we have someone here who has done the new entry course.'

Esposito raised an eyebrow at the large metallic implement in the hulking *agente*'s grip.

'No more mallets, eh? Isn't progress wonderful?' He turned to Peroni. 'What would you advise?'

'Nic and Rosa had nothing to do with this. He's still in mourning. She was just obeying orders.'

'I meant what would you do here?'

It was obvious. Anyone who'd worked Rome for a couple of decades would have known the answer from the outset. But the new generation, men like Alfieri, were formed by the courses they went on, not by what they saw about them on the street.

'The house is terraced,' Peroni pointed out. 'I know this area well enough to understand there is no rear exit.

It simply backs onto whatever lies behind. They didn't build passageways out the back in those days.'

'So?' Esposito asked.

'If it was me, I'd ring the doorbell,' he answered.

Esposito nodded across the street and ordered, 'Do it.'

Grumbling low curses, aware he was exhausted and his temper on a short fuse, Peroni wandered down the alley, stood in front of the house, looked at the bell and the upright letter box built into the centre of the old wooden door.

He pressed the buzzer, then popped a fat finger through the letter box and lowered his head down to its level as best he could, trying to peer through. To his surprise there was a light burning brightly on the other side.

After that he went back across the street and looked at Alfieri.

'I'd use your toy instead.'

'Sir!' the man answered, with a burst of bitter sarcasm.

But he went eagerly all the same, ordering the heavily built young *agente* in front of him, taking obvious satisfaction as the metal ram began to work on the door.

Peroni stayed with Esposito, who wasn't moving.

'That was decisive of you,' the *commissario* noted.

'It was indeed. Were you listening? When I said all that about Nic and Rosa not really being a part of Leo's little freelance venture? One's still in mourning, the other's still green.'

Esposito stared at him, puzzled.

'I always listen, Agente.'

The metal toy was starting to do its work. The ancient wooden door, which might have sat there for a century or more for all Peroni knew, was trembling on its strong hinges like a tree falling under the axe of some relentless, vindictive forester. Dust – clouds of it – was starting to hang around the entrance as the frame began to come away from the plaster and brickwork that held it in place.

'There's no rush,' Peroni said, putting a hand on this odd new *commissario*'s arm as they crossed the street, successfully slowing their progress.

'Why?' Esposito asked straight away.

They were nearly through and Peroni was beginning to feel guilty. He could see what would happen. The heavy planked wood would fall backwards, as if there was a hinge on its base, straight down onto the stone floor he suspected must lie behind.

The two of them were no more than a couple of strides away when it finally began to go. Esposito was free of him, walking quickly towards the action. Some bosses always had to be there first, Peroni reminded himself.

It came loose with a whip-like crack. Peroni watched it go over, trying to calculate, as best he could, the effect it might have on what he believed he had seen through the letter box.

Gravity wasn't his fault. Nor the over-enthusiasm of a bunch of officers newly returned from a course on how to smash their way into private homes.

'Why?' Esposito turned to ask again as he marched to join the others.

Peroni stopped. The massive wooden slab tumbled back-wards. Plumes of plaster and brick dust rose from around its frame as the old and once-solid structure that held it in place collapsed under the blows it had received from Alfieri's strongman. Whatever lay behind the door . . .

This wasn't a conversation Esposito had allowed to develop.

Led by the *commissario* in his black raincoat, the team pushed into the brightly lit space that now appeared before them, making the grunt-like noises of enthusiasm men tended to do on occasions like this.

It didn't last long. Someone – Alfieri, Peroni suspected – screamed. Then the entire pack of them retreated in haste, waving their hands in distress that, on the part of a couple – though not Vincenzo Esposito – appeared to border on horror.

A pair of naked legs – a man's, and he was pretty sure of the identity – flapped down onto them, pivoting from some unseen point above, pushing gently against their faces and hands. The body had been given some brief renewed life by the force of the door as it came off its hinges and fell backwards, piling into the corpse somewhere above the knee.

Peroni walked forward, cocked his head through the doorway, looked up and saw what he'd expected all along, ever since he got a glimpse of those white, dead legs through the narrow slit of the letter box. The pale, misshapen naked body of a man was suspended there, hanging from a noose which appeared to be thrown across an ancient black beam that ran, open and horizontal, across the entrance space at the first floor.

'Because of that,' he said.

– 3 –

Falcone knew the Piazza di San Lorenzo in Lucina well. It was a small, very old cobbled square by the side of the Palazzo Ruspoli in the bustling shopping street of the Corso, with a porticoed church that looked more like an Imperial temple than a home for Catholics, and a handful of houses that must have gone back centuries.

It was an expensive location for a lowly official of a state art institution. As he stood with his men at the edge of the cobbled square, their flashing lights reflecting on the damp stone, the racket of their engines bringing activity to the windows of the surrounding apartments, Falcone found himself thinking, not for the first time, of Costa's insistence that the key to this case somehow lay in the past. A past that might, perhaps, be unreachable through any conventional means. More and more, Falcone felt himself to be a player in a drama that was taking place in another era, another century altogether, one in which he lacked sufficient understanding to follow the rules, or even begin to comprehend them.

This had to change. They owed that to all those dead women, Emily included. Yet for all the progress he felt sure they ought to make over the next few hours, Falcone felt unsure of himself. Out of caution, he had placed a call to the Palazzo Malaspina, enquiring whether the count was at home, only to be told that he had left the palace after the party for 'private business' and had yet to return. Even without Agata's questionable identification this was sufficient to make it possible for Malaspina to have been at the scene in the Barberini studio. Still, it was too soon, Falcone felt, to exert any pressure on the man. If it was him behind the black, all-covering hood, he was surely closeted with his lawyers now, concocting some alibi. Or else he had fled the city altogether.

In the absence of usable physical evidence, could one man possess sufficient money and influence to bury his direct involvement in several bizarre murders forever? This question had nagged Falcone ever since he became aware of Malaspina's background. He loathed to think that it could be true. Yet he knew enough of the ways of those who lived at the summit of society to understand that they did, from time to time, abide by rules and mores which would never be allowed to the masses living further down the ladder. Bribery, corruption, casual acquaintance with criminals . . . These failings occurred in all walks of life, in business, in local and national government, and, on occasion, in the law enforcement agencies too. Could they extend to turning a blind eye to the vicious deaths of a series of unfortunate women?

Only in the minds of a privileged few, such as Franco Malaspina and those he had assembled around him. Men like Nino Tomassoni, who was now, perhaps, in bed in his home, an ancient building, decrepit and untouched by recent paint, just a few short metres from the neon lights of the Corso, with its ribbon of stores, some with the Christmas lights still winking, even in the dead of night.

What was it Susanna Placidi had said? Tomassoni was the weak one, perhaps the original source of the emails themselves, a peripheral player at the very edges of this drama. If so, he was there for a reason, and it was one Falcone felt determined to discover.

He turned to look at the team he had assembled: four armed men, one with the necessary equipment for taking down the door to the house, should that be needed.

'Follow me,' he ordered, then walked directly to Nino Tomassoni's front entrance, put his thumb on the bell push and held it there. After ten seconds, no more, he nodded at the entry man to begin taking down the door.

There was no time for niceties. Besides, Tomassoni, if Susanna Placidi had got just one thing right, was a small man who might possibly be cowed by a show of force.

'When you're in,' Falcone commanded the men around him, 'I want you to make the noise from hell. I'll deal with the neighbours.'

That seemed to go down well. He watched the door fly off its hinges in a cloud of dust.

'Everyone goes inside,' he ordered. 'The man may be armed and accompanied.'

He was the first to step through the cloud of dust that followed the final hammer blow. And the first to come to a halt too, amazed by what lay beyond the threshold.

When the grey cloud cleared from the forced entry he found himself faced with a scene that seemed to come from a different century. The interior of Nino Tomassoni's home – the residence, Falcone already knew from intelligence, of a solitary man unknown to his neighbours, one who had inherited his expensive central address from parents who had emigrated to the USA years ago – was like nothing he had expected, more a film or theatre set than a home fit for the twenty-first century.

Though it was now past three in the morning, gas lights flickered inside glass bulbs down each of the long walls of the narrow entrance room, casting a faint orange glow over the interior. Paintings in gold frames hung alongside them. On each side stood a pair of ornate carved gilt chairs, worn antiques with tattered red velvet seats and backs, and a shaky aspect that probably made them unfit for use. The floor was dusty stone, unswept for ages. From somewhere came a dank smell, the kind Falcone associated with the ill-kempt homes of solitary, impoverished bachelors, places that reeked of rotting food, stale air and solitary habits.

'This is creepy,' someone said from behind him. 'Like a museum or something.'

That was right, Falcone thought. Just like a museum, and the idea gave him some encouragement, though he was not quite sure why.

'Room by room, floor by floor,' he ordered quietly. 'I do not understand the layout of this place. It's . . .'

From another time.

The words just slipped into his head.

'I want someone to take a look at the back to see if there's some way out there, and that way blocked if it exists. I want—'

His phone rang. It was Vincenzo Esposito. He sounded shocked, a little out of sorts, which was probably a rare experience for the man.

Falcone listened, absorbing the news. Esposito would remain at Castagna's home for the rest of the night, and he had ordered a permanent guard for Agata Graziano to be sent to the hospital in San Giovanni where she had gone with Costa.

'Don't lose any more witnesses,' the new *commissario* ordered, his voice low and grim over the phone.

'No, sir,' Falcone replied, and cut the call.

The house had three floors and no rear entrance, simply a blank wall, without windows on any level. The gas lights seemed to be intermittent. In other areas, weak yellow bulbs, usually hanging from the ceiling by a single wire, without a fitting or shade, provided the illumination. There were no carpets and little in the way of furniture, no sign of a human presence.

Many riddles continued to nag him about the nature of the Ekstasists. The studio in the Vicolo del Divino Amore was just one of them. It was, Falcone felt sure, a place they used only occasionally, *in extremis*, when their games moved beyond some norm that was simply deca-dent into a realm that was more dangerous, doubtless more tantalizing. They were an organization, one that needed a home. Malaspina was too intelligent and circum-spect to allow it to be inside his own palace. Buccafusca and Castagna were well-known men in the city too, likely to arouse comment and suspicion if their illicit activities took place on premises with which the public were famil-iar, an art gallery, or the porn studios out near Anagnina where Castagna's father based his grubby empire. So Nino Tomassoni, a quiet, insignificant minor bureaucrat in the gallery of the Villa Borghese, who lived a solitary life in a house a short walk away from everywhere in what was once Ortaccio, offered a solution of a kind.

The ground floor was occupied by nothing more than storage space crammed with junk: old furniture, discarded boxes of papers and magazines, many pornographic, and several bags of household rubbish. On the first they found one large bedroom, with a dishevelled double bed, and sheets that looked as if they hadn't been washed in weeks, and a smaller room with a single mattress and no sign of recent use. The floor above contained a small study, with a computer that was still on when Falcone touched the keyboard, open at an email application. He called for one of the younger officers to come forward and start using the thing.

'Can you see what's been sent from this recently?' Falcone asked.

The man flailed at the grubby keyboard.

'There are four months of old messages, in and out,' the *agente* replied after a couple of seconds.

'Good. Call in the forensic computer people. Tell them to take it away for analysis. But . . .' He stopped the man before he left the grimy seat at the table on which the machine sat. 'First tell me if there are any messages to Susanna Placidi here.'

The keyboard clattered again. Several emails came up on the screen. They were familiar. Falcone smiled and patted the officer on the shoulder.

'Progress,' he said. 'Now there's a word we haven't heard in a while. Let's take a look at the next floor.'

He led the way up the narrow, steep stairs and was aware, from some hidden sense, that this place was different, in a way that made him take out his weapon instinctively and hold it in front of him in the darkness.

The door was open, the entire floor beyond a space without so much as a stick of furniture from what he could see. A single skylight stood off-centre in the pitched, low roof. Through it a wan stream of weak moonlight fell, revealing nothing but bare, worn planks in the centre of the room.

Falcone felt for a light switch. It took some time for him to realize there was none. But there was the smell of gas, faint yet discernible, and as his eyes adjusted they found the shapes of the same glass bulbs he had seen on the ground floor. He had no idea how to turn on gas lights, and no desire to find out.

He took a torch from one of the officers behind him and cast it around the pool of darkness that lay impenetrable in front of them. There were shapes, familiar ones. And from somewhere, he thought, the sound of faint movement, of someone disturbed by their presence.

'Fetch more light,' Falcone ordered in a loud, confident voice.

Two officers went downstairs, out to the vans for gear.

Falcone strode into the centre of the room, dashing the beam of the torch everywhere, taking in what it revealed.

He should, perhaps, have expected this. In front of him lay an array of paintings, canvas upon canvas, each stored leaning against the next, protected by some kind of cloth covering, stacked in a fashion that was half professional, half amateur.

The corner of one piece of cloth was incomplete. Falcone lifted it and ran the beam across what lay beneath. He saw pale flesh, naked women, bodies wrapped up in one another. And a kind of style and poise that spoke of skill and artistry.

'What is it, sir?' the officer who had worked at the computer asked.

'Fetch me more light and we'll see.'

Falcone still recalled well the time he had spent working alongside the Carabinieri art unit in Verona, with the pleasant major there, Luca Zecchini, who would spend hours showing him the vast register of missing artworks which every officer on the unit would be required to inspect from time to time. The size and richness of it amazed him, and the fact that there was a market for works which could never, in normal conditions, be shown to a single living soul because of their fame.

The new brighter floods arrived. He ordered the sea of searing brightness they created to be turned towards the piles of paintings, then walked around them, throwing off the covers, hearing the low buzz of excitement grow behind him.

'I know that,' someone said after a while.

'It's one version of *The Scream* by Munch,' Falcone explained. 'I believe it's been missing from Copenhagen since 2004. This . . .'

He stared at another work, a smaller, older canvas.

'. . . looks like Poussin, I believe.'

There were pictures here he thought he recognized from Zecchini's register, works perhaps by Renoir, Cézanne, Picasso, and a host of earlier artists beyond his knowledge, unless they were all very good fakes.

He moved towards the furthest corner, an area where not the slightest mote of moonlight fell, and one which was still in shadow from some large canvas under wraps covering the entire diagonal of the space there.

'What we have here, gentlemen,' Falcone went on, 'is a storeroom for stolen works of art, one that seems to have been sitting beneath our noses, in the centre of Rome, for years.'

Falcone stopped and kept a firm grip on his gun.

'It would be fitting,' he added, 'if we could match up these objects with their so-called owner, don't you think?'

In one quick movement he threw aside the sackcloth over the painting and stepped behind the frame. The man was there on the floor cowering, hands around his knees, head deep in his thighs, not saying a word.

Nino Tomassoni was wearing a grubby pair of striped pyjamas and stank of sweat and fear.

'This is a fine collection,' Falcone said drily. 'Would you care to tell us where it came from?'

The figure on the floor began rocking back and forth like a child.

'I asked a question,' Falcone added.

The man mumbled something.

'Excuse me?'

'He will k-k-kill me . . .' the crouching man stuttered.

The expression in his bulbous eyes was more fear than insanity. Falcone wondered how long Tomassoni had been hiding here, and how he had come to know the events of the night. There was so much to ask, so many ways in which this strange little man could provide the means by which they might make their way, finally, into the depths of the Palazzo Malaspina and close the door on its owner forever.

'No one will kill you, Nino,' he said calmly. 'Not if we look after you. But all these paintings . . .'

Falcone cast his eyes around the room. This was a miraculous find in itself. He could scarcely wait to call Vincenzo Esposito to tell him the news.

'I fear this looks very bad.'

Out of interest, he lifted the sackcloth on a small canvas to his left and found himself staring at a jumble of

285

geometric shapes and human limbs that seemed to him, perhaps erroneously, reminiscent of Miró.

'Did he bring the painting here?' he asked.

The man said nothing and stayed on the floor, holding his knees, mute and resentful.

'The Caravaggio?' Falcone persisted. 'After he stole it from the studio tonight, and killed your friend Buccafusca along the way, did he bring it here? If so, may I see it?'

'That animal was not my friend,' the figure on the floor muttered, still rocking.

'This is your decision,' Falcone observed with a shrug. 'We will find out in any case. I was merely offering you an opportunity to demonstrate your willingness to cooperate. Without it—'

Tomassoni stabbed an accusing finger at him from the floor.

'The Caravaggio was mine! Ours. It always has been. Since the very beginning.'

This was beyond Falcone.

'I do not understand.'

'No! You don't! It's *ours*!' He glanced around the shrouded canvases mournfully. 'It's the only one that is. And now I don't even have it. Now . . .'

He stopped. Falcone smiled. It was an answer of sorts. These interviews always began with a small, seemingly insignificant moment of acquiescence. It would suffice.

'Perhaps you would like to get dressed,' he suggested. 'This is going to be a long day. I think pyjamas are not the best idea. You should bring some of your other things too. Whatever you want from this home of yours. I believe you will be in custody for a while. Safe and secure, I promise that.'

The man shuffled to his feet. He was short and overweight, perhaps thirty-five. Not Malaspina's class or kind. Nino Tomassoni must have offered something different, something particular, for him to have moved in those circles.

'And thank you for those messages,' Falcone added. 'The emails you sent to my colleague. They will work in your favour. As to the postings on the statues . . .'

He didn't like the look on Tomassoni's face. It was vicious and full of spite.

'What about them?' he asked.

'Were they your work too?'

'For all the good it did me,' he replied. 'I'll get my things.'

'Excuse me.'

Falcone bent down and retrieved the object he had noticed on the floor from the start. It was a specialist radio, and when he turned it on it was easy to see the unit was tuned to a police frequency. It wasn't hard to understand how Tomassoni had worked out what had happened that evening. Buccafusca's death had been broadcast on the network. The threat to himself must have been obvious after that.

'This is illegal too,' the inspector noted. 'I hope I shall have reason to ignore it.'

The little man swore again and shuffled through the mill of bodies, then hurried downstairs a floor and walked into the bedroom, closing the door behind him.

He got there so quickly Falcone was several steps behind, and fuming at the way the officers on the landing simply let him through.

'Rossi,' he yelled at the man closest to the door, 'what the hell do you think you're doing letting a suspect slam a door in your face like that? Get in there and watch him.'

He knew what had happened the moment he heard the noise: a loud, repetitive rattle that seemed to shake the very fabric of the ancient, fragile building in which they stood.

'Get down!' Falcone yelled, and pushed the nearest man he could find to the floor, watching the rest of them follow, terrified. A storm of dislodged plaster began to descend on them. The ancient wallpaper rippled beneath the deafening force of gunfire.

The nearest officer to the door got a foot to it, then retreated back behind the wall. Falcone could see – just – what was happening beyond the threshold, and imagine in his mind's eye how this came about.

He had left the vehicles outside unattended, needing every man he had. Now someone was standing on one of them, possibly the Jeep that was directly beneath the window, and letting loose with some kind of repeating weapon – a machine gun or pistol – directly through the glass, straight into the dancing, shaking body of Nino Tomassoni.

Flailing across the floor, intent on avoiding the hail of shells that was pouring into the building, Falcone rolled towards the staircase, found it, then, followed by two other men who had the same idea, half fell, half stumbled down the steps to the ground floor. Clinging to the damp wall, he made his way towards the entrance, and the collapsed door they had brought down earlier.

'Behind me,' Falcone ordered, and watched the shining cobbles and the dim street lights, gun in hand, wondering what this might be worth against the man outside.

The noise had stopped. By the time he felt the cold

night air drifting in through the empty space at the front, another sound had replaced it: an engine at full revs, squealing across cobbles.

'Damn you,' Falcone swore.

He threw himself out into the street, men yelling at his back, screaming at them to keep cover.

The figure was no longer on the roof of the Jeep. Falcone had no idea where he'd gone to. A black slug-like Porsche coupé was wheeling across the greasy cobbles, describing a fast arc in the space in front of the old church.

As he watched, it disappeared behind the group of police vehicles, and Leo Falcone found himself running again, with men by his side, good men, angry men, weapons in their hands, heat rising in their heads.

'Behind me!' he bellowed again, and forced them to fall back behind his extended arm.

A single raking line of repeat fire raged through the night air on the far side of the convoy of blue vehicles. He fell below the window line of the van in front, aware, as he did so, that thin metal was no protection against a modern shell.

It lasted a second, no more. They were going. This was a warning, not an act of intent. Falcone raised his weapon and pointed it across the open space of the Piazza di San Lorenzo in Lucina, back towards the Christmas lights still burning in the Corso, conscious that the men around him were doing the same.

'Do not fire,' he said firmly. 'Do *not* fire.'

In the distance, walking down the road, struggling to get out of the way as the Porsche found the street and roared off towards the Piazza Venezia and the open roads of Rome, was a straggling group of revellers, with stupid Christmas hats on their heads, a bunch of happy young party-goers looking for the way home.

'Get the control room on this,' he ordered, barking the number plate of the black vehicle at them as he returned towards the door. 'As if they won't know already.'

He raced up the stairs and found the bedroom. The place was beginning to stink of gas.

'Find the source of that smell,' he barked at the nearest officer. 'The last thing we want in here is an explosion.'

Nino Tomassoni lay on the floor of his squalid bedroom, open-mouthed, eyes staring at the ceiling, his blood-soaked, shattered body strewn with broken glass.

'There goes the witness,' Rossi observed with a degree of unhelpful frankness Falcone found quite unnecessary. 'Do we have any more?'

'Just the one,' Falcone murmured. 'Franco Malaspina will not touch her, I swear.'

Part 11

THE VIA APPIA ANTICA

- 1 -

When Nic Costa opened his eyes he was somewhere that smelled familiar: the scent of flowers and pine needles.

People, too, in a room that wasn't meant for a crowd.

Christmas, Costa said to himself, waking with a start, then sitting upright in his own bed, in the house on the edge of the city, his head heavy, his mind too dulled by the hospital drugs to think of much at that moment.

He reached for the watch by the side of his bed, aware that his shoulder felt as if it had been run over by a truck, and saw that it was now almost four on the afternoon of 23 December. He'd lost more than half a day to sleep and medication. Then his eyes wandered to the room and stayed fixed on the single point they found, the person there.

Franco Malaspina was wearing a grey, expensive business suit, perfectly cut, and sat, relaxed, on the bedroom chair where Emily used to leave her clothes at night. He stared back at Costa, legs crossed, hands on his chin, looking as if this were the most natural thing in the world.

'What in God's name . . .' Costa found himself muttering, wondering where a gun might be in this place that was so familiar, so private, yet at that moment so profoundly strange to him.

Malaspina unfolded his legs, then yawned, not moving another muscle. He had strong, broad, athletic shoulders, those of a powerful man. In the bright daylight streaming through the windows, his dark, Sicilian features seemed remarkably like those of Agata Graziano.

'This was their choice, not mine,' the man protested in his easy, patrician accent. 'Take your anger out on them.'

Costa's attention roamed to the others in the room. All eyes were on him. Some he knew. Some, mainly men in suits like Malaspina's, were strangers, as was a middle-aged woman with bright, close-cropped blonde hair who wore a black judicial gown over her dark blue business jacket and sat on a dining-room seat in the midst of the others, as if she were the master of proceedings.

'What is this?' Costa asked.

'It is a judicial hearing, Officer,' the woman said immediately. 'Your superiors felt it so important we come here and wait for you to wake up. This was their prerogative. My name is Silvia Tentori. I am a magistrate. These men here are lawyers representing Count Malaspina. The Questura has legal representation . . .'

Toni Grimaldi stood next to Falcone, with Peroni on the other side. None of them looked happy.

'I thought he didn't like being called Count,' Costa found himself saying immediately. His head hurt.

Agata Graziano sat next to Falcone, looking frail, bleary-eyed and unusually upset.

'You know the judiciary,' Malaspina observed. 'Very well, I imagine. It's all formality, even these days. You can call me Franco.'

'Get out of my house . . .'

He tried to move and couldn't, not easily, not quickly. It was Agata Graziano who rose from her chair, picked it up and came to sit by him. Costa couldn't help noticing the pain this caused Leo Falcone.

'Nic,' she said quietly. 'I'm sorry about this. It was never meant to happen.'

She glared at Malaspina.

'His lawyers made it so. If there was some other way. If I could prevent this somehow—'

'You could just tell Signora Tentori the truth,' Malaspina interrupted. 'Then – ' he looked purposefully at his watch – 'I might be able to go about my business.'

'The truth,' Costa murmured.

'The truth?' Malaspina echoed in an amused, nonchalant voice. 'Here it is. After the festivities I hosted on behalf of this ungrateful woman's gallery, I spent last night in my own home, until eleven, when I went out to meet a companion, who will vouch for me. After that, I received a call saying the police were making enquiries. So – ' he shrugged – 'I did what any good citizen would. I went to the Questura. And sat there. From a little before one in the morning until five, when Inspector Falcone here finally managed to find the time to see me.'

'I did not know—' Falcone butted in.

'That is not my fault,' Malaspina responded.

'The others,' Costa said. 'Castagna. Tomassoni.'

Malaspina's dark face flushed with sudden anger.

'My friends, you mean? And Buccafusca too. They are dead, murdered, and you sit here pointing the finger at me when you should be out there looking for whoever did this. I wish to see their families. I wish to help them make arrangements. Yet all I hear are these stupid accusations. Again. I tell you . . . there is a limit to what one man will bear before he breaks, and you have crossed that limit now. To be told one is under suspicion in these circumstances. Of crimes committed when I am sitting in your own Questura, offering whatever assistance I can . . .'

Costa could read the look in their eyes. It was despair. He could only guess at what the night had brought them: death and disappointment. Malaspina believed he had won again, and this informal judicial hearing, with his rich man's lawyers hanging on every word, was surely some formality he hoped to use to seal that fact. And to take pleasure from the act of entering the home of a man whose wife he had murdered. It was there, plain in his face.

Still, his timing was not perfect.

'Emilio Buccafusca was murdered . . . this painting was stolen . . . before you went to the Questura,' Costa pointed out.

Malaspina leaned forward, like a school teacher making a point to a slow pupil.

'While I was at a private dinner. With someone who can vouch for me.'

One of the grey men in grey suits said, 'It offends my client that you waste time on this nonsense when you could be looking for the real criminals in this case.'

'It offends me that the man who shot my wife is sitting in my bedroom, smiling,' Costa answered immediately. 'Ask your questions, then get out of here. But this I tell you . . .'

He pointed at Malaspina.

'I am not done with this man yet.'

The woman with the robes around her shoulders

sighed and said, 'After that I wonder if there is really any point in going on. From a serving police officer . . .'

'One who was shot in the course of duty last night,' Peroni pointed out. 'By this bast—'

A look from Falcone silenced him.

'The point of this proceeding,' the woman went on, 'is to discuss the police application for papers which will allow you to search the Palazzo Malaspina freely, and take specimens from Count Malaspina. Or is there something new you wish to add to that list now, Inspector?'

'That will suffice,' Falcone replied. 'It's all we need.'

The woman picked up a briefcase and took out a substantial wad of papers.

'At a previous hearing I established that you will not be allowed to ask Count Malaspina for specimens without firm and incontrovertible evidence linking him to these events, which you have so far failed to provide. There are rules about harassment. There are avenues open to an individual persecuted by the state.'

'Four men died last night,' Falcone pointed out. 'One of them an innocent security guard. Sovrintendente Costa could have been killed. Sister Agata—'

'This is irrelevant to Count Malaspina unless you have proof,' she declared with a peremptory brusqueness. 'How many times do I have to say this?'

'I don't know,' Falcone barked back. 'Given that it always seems to be you who deals with these requests when they are made, possibly many, many more.'

Grimaldi put a hand to his head and emitted a groan. The woman turned and glowered at him.

'Are you letting your officers accuse me now?'

'There is only one person in this room we accuse,' Grimaldi answered. 'Please address the point, Falcone.'

'I merely note that,' the inspector added icily, 'I find it intriguing that whenever the subject of prosecuting Franco Malaspina comes before us, the name of Silvia Tentori invariably appears on the sheet. It is . . . illuminating to discover that the judiciary works so efficiently these days that it is able to supply us with magistrates who seem already to be familiar with the case we wish to bring before them.'

'This will not take long,' the woman muttered. 'Sovrintendente?'

Costa nodded at her, taking in Falcone's bitter, resigned expression.

'What do you want to know?'

'In spite of yet another application for discovery and specimens concerning Count Malaspina, your colleagues can supply no evidence linking him to these crimes. Nothing except this identification from you and Signora Graziano last night. Tell me. You are certain of this?'

Costa glanced at the seated aristocrat, who watched him, relaxed, waiting for an answer, a finger to his lips, something close to a smirk on his face.

'I am certain of it.'

'How is that?' she asked. 'The man was hooded.'

'I recognized his voice. The tone of it. The way he spoke to Sister Agata.'

The lawyer in the grey suit leaned forward.

'You had not met the count until last night, and then spoke to him only briefly. We have witnesses for this.'

'I spoke to him once before. When I followed him from the Vicolo del Divino Amore, the day he murdered my wife.'

There was a chill in the room and an awkward silence. Then the lawyer added, 'Another hooded man, in another hurried situation. Furthermore, if this was true, you would surely have reported the fact to the Questura immediately. Not returned to the Barberini studio to look at this painting. All the more so because of the personal nature of this so-called identification.'

He was not going to pursue this. It was pointless.

'And what lying bastard was he supposedly dining with last night?' Costa asked. 'When he stole that painting and killed Emilio Buccafusca?'

The lawyer sniffed.

'The count dined with me, at home, just the two of us. My wife is away. We were together from eleven until twelve forty-five, when his household contacted us to say the police had enquired after him. After that I accompanied him to the Questura immediately in order to offer whatever assistance was required.'

'Then,' Costa replied, 'after I am done with his lies, I will deal with yours.'

Silvia Tentori glared at him, furious.

'Thank you, Officer. That is enough. I reject this identification entirely. It is clearly based on nothing more than personal animosity.'

'It is based on the truth,' Costa insisted.

'I doubt that,' the woman said. 'This leaves one so-called identification alone. Signora Graziano.'

'Sister . . .' Agata corrected her quietly. A surge of anger in Silvia Tentori's eyes indicated she did not appreciate this.

'You say you can identify Count Malaspina as the man you saw in the studio last night?'

All eyes in the room were on her.

'I believe so.'

'You believe so?' the magistrate demanded. 'What does

that mean? We know you never saw his face. How is this possible?'

'I have known Franco for several years. I know his voice. I recognize the way he speaks to me.'

Silvia Tentori nodded, listening.

'And were you helped in this identification?' she asked. 'Did one of these police officers suggest to you this man whose face you never saw, whose voice you only heard in the course of a violent robbery, was Count Malaspina?'

She shook her head.

'No. I mean . . . Nic and I . . . talked.'

'You talked. When? What was said? The details, please.'

Agata looked so exhausted. Nic felt like screaming at them all to get out of the room.

'Sister Graziano was the victim of a violent attack herself,' Costa pointed out. 'You have to expect her to be hazy on some details.'

He knew it was a stupid thing to say the moment the words were out of his mouth.

'Quite,' the magistrate observed with visible pleasure, then openly, as if she didn't mind, glanced at Malaspina, who was studying his nails, and added, 'but this is a very serious accusation to base upon a few barely heard words from a man whose face she never saw.'

'I *know*,' she insisted. 'Say something for me, Franco.'

Malaspina took his attention away from his fingers and stared at her.

'Say something?'

She didn't flinch.

'Say, "That bitch always had a sport in the blood."'

He thought for a moment, then uttered the words in a precise, considered, aristocratic Roman accent, one both like and unlike the voice they had heard the previous night.

'Well?' Silvia Tentori asked. 'Am I supposed to infer something from this?'

'It was him,' she said, 'I know it. He knows it. We all do.'

Malaspina shook his head, then got up and walked to the window, with its view out onto a bleak grey winter's day and a field of slumbering vines. He placed his hands easily on the sill, looking at home, as if he owned the place.

'This is ridiculous, Agata,' the man said. 'I know you have always resented me. You're not alone. Envy is every-where. But to manufacture an accusation like this. Here . . . Let us see how far you will go with this mindless vendetta.'

There was a bookshelf behind him. Half the titles in the bedroom were still Emily's, English and American literature, old books, about history and travel and classic stories she must have read time and time again. The rest were Costa's or the family's, a collection of texts that hadn't been looked at for years, Gramsci and Pinocchio, the hard-boiled 1940s thrillers his father loved, and more modern *gialli* by Italian writers.

One more book, too, its pages unopened for years.

Franco Malaspina pulled the ragged family Bible off the shelf. His father had insisted on having an edition in the house, in spite of his beliefs. He would refer to it from time to time, and not always to prove a point.

The man threw the black, battered copy, with its dog-eared and torn pages, across the room. It landed on her lap. Reluctantly, she took hold of the thing to stop it falling to the floor.

'Look me in the eye, Agata, and swear on that precious object of yours that you know it was me last night.'

She had her eyes closed, unable to speak. The faintest outline of a tear, almost invisible, like that of the Magdalene in the Doria Pamphilj, began to roll slowly down one cheek.

It was all lost. Costa knew it.

Painfully, he dragged himself out of the bed and sat on the edge looking first at her, silent, remorseful, then at Malaspina.

'Get out of my home,' he said again, and, with a glance at the magistrate and the lawyers, added, 'and take your creatures with you. When I come for you, Malaspina, you will know it.'

'That is a threat!' Silvia Tentori screeched. 'A blatant, outright threat to a man against whom you have not the slightest evidence! I shall report this. I shall report *everything* here. We do not live in a police state where you people can go around terrorizing any innocent citizen you choose.'

There was a steady, dull ache at the back of his head, but Costa knew somehow this signalled the return of his faculties, not the failure of them. Life, his father had said from time to time, often depended upon the ability to drag oneself off the floor and learn to return to the fray anew.

'No, signora,' he said quietly. 'We live in a world where the law has become an instrument that protects the wicked, not the innocent.'

A memory rose from the previous day, a single useful fact, prompted by Rosa Prabakaran, one he had filed, wondering if it would ever be of use.

' "Run quick, poor Simonetta!" ' Costa recited. ' "A

sport in the blood." You hate black women, Franco. Why is that? Would you care to tell us?'

It hit home, and that felt good. Malaspina's swarthy face turned a shade darker.

'I would guess,' Costa pressed, 'that it stems from something personal. Some experience. Some knowledge. Some grudge . . .'

Agata stirred with a sudden interest by his side. Smiling, she rose and walked towards Malaspina, placing her face close to his, examining his features with the same curious, microscopic interest she would normally reserve for a painting.

'Something personal? Why, Franco?' she asked. 'The Malaspinas are cousins to the Medici, aren't they? Is that the line? Oh! *Oh!*'

She clapped her hands with glee.

'I think I see it now. In Florence, in the Palazzo Vecchio, Giorgio Vasari has a wonderful full-length portrait of Alessandro de' Medici. The first son. A dusky man, Franco. With his helmet and his armour and his lance. And a black slave, Simonetta, for a mother.' She hesitated to emphasize what was coming. 'Which gave him his hatred of anyone who reminded him of his blood line. Is that you too, Franco? Are you more a Medici at heart? Is the blood you hate most really your own?'

The effect was astonishing. Malaspina rose from his chair, livid, out of control, and began to bellow a stream of vicious threats and vile obscenities, so violent and extreme it was his own lawyers who raced to silence the man and drag him still screaming from the room, down the stairs and out into the garden, where he stood for a good minute or more, yelling up at the window.

Every sentence seemed like a blow to her. Agata

Graziano had surely never experienced words or threats like this, or expected that her idle taunt would generate such a response.

She listened, shocked, pale, glassy-eyed, until she could bear no more and placed her small, flawless hands over the wayward hair above her ears.

– 2 –

Five minutes later, after Silvia Tentori had left the bedroom issuing warnings and threats in all directions, Peroni
brought coffee for them all provided by Bea and said, 'We
could arrest him for that performance. Threatening words
and behaviour.'

'For how long?' Costa asked. 'You saw those lawyers.'

Agata still looked shocked, and a little ashamed, at the
effect her words had had on the man. The hearing was
over. They had lost everything, in conventional judicial
terms. And yet . . .

'You touched something,' Falcone suggested. 'But
what?'

'I have no idea,' Agata answered. 'I was simply being
mean and horrible. Taunting Franco. The Malaspina clan
was related to the Medici. Everyone knows that. They
survived when the Medici died out. He makes the odd
racist comment from time to time. It always struck me as
odd. There had to be the possibility of some distant link
with Alessandro, and that meant he had some black blood
himself. All the same. The idea he would respond so
violently . . .'

She shook her head, thinking.

'I should stick to paintings,' she said. 'This is all beyond me.'

'You should,' Costa agreed.

The idea raised a wan smile.

'Good. Can I go home now please? I'm tired and there are many duties I have missed. There's nothing more I can do for you.'

Leo Falcone looked at her frankly.

'I'm afraid that's impossible. Commissario Esposito will be here shortly with Dr Lupo. We will review the case. Perhaps you should join us, for part of the conversation at least.'

She laughed.

'I'm a sister who agreed to help you identify a single painting, Leo. One you have lost, which means my work is done. I have more menial chores now. I do not belong here.'

Falcone frowned, looking uncomfortable.

'Agata, you're the only material witness in an investigation where every other one has been murdered. Those guards the *commissario* put in place last night were not temporary. They are outside now. They will remain there as long as I say. You cannot return to the convent until this is over. We cannot protect you there. You must be somewhere that is private, easily secured and accessible.'

'Then – ' she threw her small arms open wide – 'where?'

The old inspector said nothing and simply glanced guiltily at the floor.

'*Where?*' she asked again.

Costa tried to catch Falcone's eye. It proved impossible.

– 3 –

'No,' he said again as they sat together at the dining-room table, after Bea had thrust more coffee and cakes at them, then taken Pepe out for a brief walk. 'I won't allow it. This is a private home. Known to Malaspina. Also . . .'

The reason was personal in a way that made it difficult to share with these people. Perhaps it was the presence of Commissario Esposito. Perhaps the problem lay inside himself. It felt awkward having Bea in the house at times. Another woman . . .

'Nic,' Falcone broke in, 'in case you hadn't got the message by now, Franco Malaspina has many allies, and bottomless pockets. He could find anywhere we chose to keep Agata, if it came to that. This place has a long drive, easily guarded, and we know it.' He hesitated. 'We've done this before. It worked. Until you broke the rules.'

'Will you kindly stop talking about me as if I'm some kind of invalid?' Agata broke in. 'What am I supposed to do here for however long this sentence is meant to be?'

'What do you do normally?' Teresa asked out of interest.

'Sleep, pray, think, eat, write . . .'

Teresa shrugged.

'You can do those anywhere. There's Nic's house-keeper here, Bea. So you have a chaperone.'

'A chaperone?' Agata asked, outraged. 'Why would I need a "chaperone"?'

'I just thought . . .' Teresa stuttered. 'Perhaps it would make it easier with the Mother Superior or whoever it is you take orders from. I'm sorry. I'm not good around nuns.'

'She is not a nun,' Falcone interjected wearily. 'Nor does she need a chaperone. But you do require some-where safe and secure. And – ' he took a swig of Bea's strong coffee – 'I hope this won't be for long. We have . . . avenues.'

None of them, not Teresa, Esposito or Falcone, looked much convinced of that.

'Your painting's gone, Leo,' Agata pointed out again. 'You've just been sent away with a flea in your ear by the magistrate you hoped would give you carte blanche to enter the Palazzo Malaspina and take whatever you want. Unless I have misread the situation, you have no scientific evidence in this case—'

'We're drowning in scientific evidence!' Teresa cried, aghast. 'Unfortunately it now applies simply to dead people. Buccafusca, Castagna and Tomassoni, who did things in that dreadful house in the Vicolo del Divino Amore a woman like you couldn't imagine.'

'I am a sister in a holy order, Doctor,' Agata said coldly, 'not a child.'

'Well, *Sister*,' Teresa retorted, 'let me tell you this. I have had hardened police officers throwing up in that hell house these last few weeks. Don't play the heroine until you've been there. The plain fact is this. I have more than enough for what I would need in normal circumstances.

But a fingerprint, a fibre, a DNA record . . . they don't mean a damn thing unless I am allowed to match them with something else, in a way that will stand up in court.'

Agata folded her arms and looked at each of them in turn.

'So I could be here for months.'

It was Commissario Esposito who intervened.

'We have plenty more possibilities to look at now. There were seventeen canvases in Nino Tomassoni's hovel in the Piazza di San Lorenzo in Lucina.'

She blinked and asked, seemingly amazed, 'Where?'

'In the man's house,' the *commissario* replied. 'Seventeen canvases. Eleven we have identified from the stolen art register. These are works that have been taken from museums as far away as Stockholm and Edinburgh. Tomassoni – and, by implication, one assumes Malaspina – were seemingly part of some illicit art smuggling ring working on a massive scale. Perhaps this explains why our interesting count finds it so easy to gain access to the criminal fraternity when he has call for their talents. He is simply dealing with his own.'

'Tomassoni's house? I didn't know where he lived. It was in the Piazza di San Lorenzo?'

She looked directly at Costa when she spoke. Once again, the name nagged at him.

'Yes,' Falcone agreed. 'Is this important?'

'I'm nothing but a humble sister, Leo. What would a little woman like me know?'

Costa was trying so hard to remember.

'The name means something,' he said. 'And I can't remember what.'

They fell silent, all of them, and looked at Agata Graziano, waiting.

'You're asking me?' she said eventually. 'I thought I was just supposed to be the silent house guest.'

'Yes,' Costa prompted her. 'We are asking you.'

'What a strange world you inhabit,' Agata Graziano observed. 'With your procedures and your science, your computers and your rigid modes of thought. Does it never occur to you that if an answer does not manifest itself in the present, that is, perhaps, because it prefers to do so in the past?'

She looked at Costa.

'What did I tell you, Nic? When we were walking through those streets last night? Those ghosts are with us, always. Only a fool wouldn't listen to them.'

'We're police officers,' Falcone grumbled. 'Not hunters of ghosts.'

'Then perhaps I'll be here forever. This is not acceptable to me, Leo. I shall allow you a week to bring Franco Malaspina to book. After that I return home, to some form of sanity. Or now, if you do not agree.'

Falcone's thin, tanned face flared with shock.

'No! That is impossible. You cannot set time limits on such things. Who do you think you are dealing with?'

'I've just watched Franco Malaspina tell me that. I'm a free woman. I may do as I wish. Best start working. Perhaps if you hammer those computers of yours a little harder. Or find some newer science for your games . . .'

'It's an old name,' Costa interrupted, hoping to cool the temperature. 'Tomassoni.'

'It is an old name,' she agreed. 'Here is one more fact I doubt any of you know, for all your wonderful toys and resources. I would have told you, but it seemed irrelevant until today. Possibly it still is.'

Agata got up and walked to the line of bookshelves by

the fireplace. Volume after volume from the days of Costa's father sat in rows, gathering dust along the walls. She picked up two substantial editions, both bought years ago, books on art, then brought them back to the table, where she began to leaf through the pages as she spoke, looking, surely, for something she knew was there already.

'It is a known fact,' she said, 'that Caravaggio lived in the Vicolo del Divino Amore for some time. Not during the happier part of his life either. This was after he left the hedonistic paradise of Del Monte's Palazzo Madama. He had little money. He kept bad company. Very bad. This was Ortaccio, remember. The Garden of Evil.'

She found what she wanted in one of the books, placed it in front of them and covered whatever lay there with a napkin from the table.

'I have walked every inch of Rome in that man's footsteps,' Agata added. 'I know where he lived and ate, where he whored and fought. No one can be sure of this precisely, but you must remember something, always. In Caravaggio's days, men kept records. They noted down details of crimes and property transactions, small civil disturbances and matters of money and debt. Many of those papers are with us still.'

She smiled at them.

'Out of your reach, true, safe in archives in the Vatican, in a country where you people have no jurisdiction. But a small and curious sister of the Church, with a little interest in history . . .'

Costa found himself transfixed by her, and he wasn't alone.

'You looked up the records for the street?' he asked.

'Of course I did! When Leo first told me the painting had been found there. Who wouldn't?'

'Well . . . ?' Teresa asked.

'The house where Caravaggio lived was either that same property or one of the two to either side. I cannot be more specific. The street had a different name then, different numbering. But there is a record in the church register which names Caravaggio as a resident in 1605, with a young boy – a servant, a student, a lover, who knows? He was reduced to poverty. He was constantly in fights and brawls and arguments.' She paused. 'It was his home when he murdered the man whose death forced him to flee Rome.'

They were silent and, Costa apart, dubious.

It was Peroni who spoke first.

'Agata,' he pointed out, with good grace, 'this was hundreds of years ago.'

'Caravaggio took that man's life on 28 May 1606, while he was living in what we now know as the Vicolo del Divino Amore. Within days he was gone from Rome forever, travelling ceaselessly – Naples, Malta, Sicily – dependent on the help of allies and patrons to feed him and keep him from the executioner.'

'A long time ago,' Falcone repeated, staring at the book on the table, wondering, like the rest of them, what it contained.

'They fought in the street,' she went on, ignoring him, 'over what we don't know. When it was over, the man was dead. His name was Ranuccio Tomassoni. He died in the house where he and his family had lived for almost two centuries, and for all I know continued to live thereafter. It was in the Piazza di San Lorenzo di Lucina.'

Costa closed his eyes and laughed.

'How on earth did I forget that?'

'You forgot it,' she said instantly, 'because you

regarded it as history and irrelevant to the present. As I may one day tire of telling you, it isn't. These are not the stories of people turned to dust. They are our stories, and in some curious way they became the stories of Franco Malaspina, Nino Tomassoni and the rest.' She shook her head. She looked exhausted, but immensely energized by her subject too. 'Something has placed them alongside what happened then. Perhaps that painting that means so much. Perhaps . . . I don't know. Look . . .'

It wasn't the picture they were expecting, but another from the second book.

'Caravaggio painted this while he was in Malta.'

It was a dark study of an elderly man, half naked on his bed, writing. St Jerome. Another of the canvases in Valletta that Costa knew, one day, he had to see.

'At this time of his life, Caravaggio chose what he did for a reason,' she went on. 'Money. Survival. The passing friendship of influential men. We know for a fact that this particular work was painted at the request of someone who helped him escape from mainland Italy and reach the temporary safety of the Knights Templar in Valletta. A few months later Michelangelo Merisi was fleeing once more after committing some other crime, which the Knights hid for fear it shamed them too. This patron continued to assist him. In Sicily. All the way to the end, when he returned to the mainland and sought to come back to Rome.'

She took a sip of water from a glass on the table.

'That man's name was Ippolito Malaspina. I have never raised this fact with Franco. But I know for sure that he must be a direct descendant. The man had many children. The castle Franco continues to own in Tuscany, from which he has lent the Barberini works for display from time to time, was the property where his ancestor lived with his family before leaving for Malta with Caravaggio.'

Her dark eyes stared at them.

'There was a connection between the Medici and the Malaspina clans. Perhaps Franco's fury stems from that. What more do I have to show you? Are these subjects you will pass on to some young police officer and hope they can comprehend? Even I don't understand them. Perhaps in time.' She glanced at Costa. 'With help and insight. But . . .'

She sat back, closed her eyes for a few seconds, then folded her arms and glared at Commissario Esposito.

'You will provide the books I need. A computer. An officer who can carry out external research and fetch and carry when I require. Tomorrow I shall see this house of Tomassoni's. And the place in the Vicolo del Divino Amore . . .'

'It's not pretty,' Teresa observed, shaking her head.

'As I keep telling you, I am not a child. You will do these things and I will help you. And if it's no use, then what's lost?'

They were silent, even Costa.

'Commissario,' Agata declared. 'I will not stay here and learn to knit. The choice is yours.'

'Very well,' Vincenzo Esposito snapped. 'Indulge Sister Agata as she requires. You will organize security, Falcone. Agente Prabakaran will act as go-between for anything the sister demands. The details of these visits outside will not leave this room. Franco Malaspina is a far more dangerous individual than any of us appreciated. If his talents run to tame magistrates and international art smuggling, then he will know men who are capable of anything. As is he.'

'Good,' Agata said, then removed the napkin from the page of the second book, an old biography of Caravaggio, one of Costa's favourites, and held it up for them all to see.

They found themselves looking at the black and white photograph of a portrait of a gentleman, round-faced with a pale complexion, a double chin and large, very bulbous eyes. He sat on a velvet-covered chair and wore rich, sumptuous clothes, as if he was of some importance.

Agata ran a finger over the man's unattractive features. 'You must excuse me in a moment. I'm tired. I need to rest. I expect some time on my own. This is by Caravaggio from his Malta period,' she said. 'It was in the Kaiser Friedrich Museum in Berlin from the early nineteenth century on. Unfortunately the work was destroyed when the city was retaken at the end of the Second World War. What you see is a portrait of Ippolito Malaspina painted by Caravaggio shortly before he fled Valletta.'

Costa stared at the portly, bloodless individual in his faintly ridiculous court clothes. He had the face of a weak and lascivious civil servant. It was tempting to see some sarcasm or ridicule of the subject in the face; such sly, slight jokes were not unknown to Caravaggio.

'This pasty-faced idiot doesn't look anything like that pig we had here!' Teresa said, jabbing a finger at the portrait.

'Precisely,' Agata replied quietly, then snapped the book shut.

- 4 -

At eight in the evening Bea was standing at the foot of the stairs, tapping her feet, looking mildly cross.

'A part of me wishes to say this is the worst girl you have ever brought back, Nic,' she muttered, perhaps only half joking.

'I wouldn't call her girl to her face,' he said. 'Nor do I think it accurate to say I brought her back.'

'No,' she grumbled. 'More like putting her in prison really, isn't it? And I'm the warder.'

Bea didn't like the men at the bottom of the drive. Some urge within her made it essential she take them coffee and water and panini from time to time. On the last occasion she had encountered Peroni, who was singing a bawdy Tuscan song at the top of his voice. Costa understood this was as much to keep up morale as anything. It was Peroni's way; to try to lighten the situation and keep a team going. He couldn't expect Bea to understand such an idea, and so there had been a chilly encounter between the two of them.

'Also . . . she hasn't yet had a bath. She may be a genius, but to me the poor thing's positively feral in normal company.'

'Normal company being us, naturally. Agata does not live the way we do. If you want to return to your apartment . . .'

'Don't be ridiculous. You can't expect a woman like her to be alone in a house with a man. It wouldn't be right. Also . . . someone shot you last night, in case you forgot.'

'Buckshot,' he answered. 'Water off a duck's back really. You know the Costa breed. We feel nothing. Seriously. It's uncomfortable. Nothing more.'

'The arrogance of men . . .' she muttered. 'There will be food on the table in five minutes. I would be grateful if someone turned up to eat it. I've called several times. Not a word in return. You speak with her. I give up.'

With that she marched back to the kitchen, leaving Costa at the foot of the steps, wondering.

This was an awkward situation, but it was his house.

He went upstairs, along to the largest guest room, which had been hastily cleaned by Bea, with new sheets found for the double bed, and towels and soap for the bathroom. It was a beautiful room, his brother's when he was young, with the best view in the house, an undisturbed one back to the Via Appia Antica, and scarcely a sign of modern life, no roads, just the single telegraph pole leading to the property, visible in the very corner, beyond the vines and the cypresses lining the drive.

He knocked on the door and said, 'There's food.'

'I know.'

Nothing more.

'Are you coming?'

'Yes.'

He was about to go when she added, 'Come in, Nic. Please. I want to ask you something.'

With a sigh, he opened the door. Agata sat in front of the dresser staring at herself in the mirror, an expression of puzzlement and fear on her face. She was wearing a white cotton shirt and black slacks. Her hair was tied back tightly, drawing the rampant curly locks away from her face, which, now he saw more of it, was angular and striking. This was the head of some artist's model, not beautiful in a conventional sense, not even pretty necessarily, but one that was fated to be looked at, stared at even, because it contained such an intensity of life and thought and – the word did not seem inappropriate – grace.

'Look what they've done to me,' she complained. 'I asked for books and information. They bring me these clothes too and say I must wear them to look less conspicuous. Why?'

'Castagna, Buccafusca and Nino Tomassoni are dead,' he pointed out. 'Like it or not, you're our only material witness. These precautions—'

'Franco simply hates anyone who's black. Even half black. We all saw that today.'

She couldn't stop looking at the image of herself in the glass.

'We don't have these big mirrors at home,' she murmured. 'Or private rooms with beds large enough for four. And this house . . .'

She stood up and walked to the window.

'I can't even see a light from here. Or hear a human voice or a car or bus.'

'Most people would think that an advantage.'

She turned and stared at him, astounded.

'What? To be denied the sounds of humanity? I've lived my entire life in the city. I know it. Those are the sounds of its breathing. Why do people wish to run away from everything? What are you frightened of?'

'Tomorrow,' he replied, shrugging. 'Today sometimes too.'

She laughed, just.

'Well, thank you. That's one trick you've taught me. I never feared anything until you people came into my life. Now I see a man with a gun round every corner, and I look at a painting – a painting by Caravaggio – and wonder if it should shake my faith. Thank you very much indeed.'

'This is the world, Agata,' he replied meekly. 'I'm sorry we dragged you into it. I'm sure, some day soon, you will be able to go back to where you came from. Just not now.'

She was silent for a moment, seemingly reluctant to speak.

'And you?' she asked in the end.

'I will find my own way,' he answered. 'By some means or other. Provided I eat from time to time. Now, will you join us? Please?'

– 5 –

At nine fifteen Rosa Prabakaran delivered the items Agata had demanded, then left for the night. Costa watched Agata carefully unpack what had arrived, taking immense care over several ancient academic tomes and a notebook computer bearing the stamp of the Barberini on the base, and very little notice indeed of two plastic supermarket carrier bags with what she said were her personal items from the convent.

Bea stared at the paltry collection of cheap, well-worn clothes and asked, 'Is that it?'

'What more am I supposed to need?'

Bea walked out of the room and came back with her arms full of soft towels, some so large and suspiciously fresh Costa wondered if she'd bought them that afternoon, along with boxes of soap and other unidentifiable cosmetics.

'The plumbing in this place can be difficult sometimes,' she declared. 'When you are ready I will introduce you to the mysteries of the bathroom.'

Then she went upstairs.

Agata watched her leave.

'What is Bea to you, Nic?'

'A family friend. She and my father were . . . very good friends once upon a time. That died. The closeness remained.'

'Does she think I'm odd?'

'Probably,' he admitted.

'Do you?'

'You're not the normal house guest.'

'Who is?'

He groaned. Agata did not give up easily. She had insisted she wanted to retire to her bedroom to work. Yet now . . .

'I have to speak to the men outside. You have your belongings. Is there anything else I can provide?'

'Yes. There is a room with some art materials in it. Along there . . .'

She pointed to the rear of the house and the place he hadn't entered, not since Emily's death.

'What is it, please? I couldn't help but notice earlier. I may need something.'

'Let me show you,' he said, and led the way.

The studio was clean and tidy, though it smelled a little of damp, as it always did when the place went unused and unheated for any amount of time. Emily's work was everywhere: line drawings of buildings, sketches, studies, ideas, doodles. 'Your wife was an artist?' Agata asked.

'An architect. Or she was hoping to be one. When she finished her studies.'

'You can't learn to build well overnight,' she countered, picking up a sketch from the nearest pile. It was of the Uffizi in Florence, from the weekend in October when he'd found the time to take a break from work, the first since their wedding in the summer. He didn't find it easy to look at now.

'She could draw,' Agata commented. 'Very well. Art and architecture go hand in hand, but then you know that. I'm sorry. I shouldn't treat you like an imbecile.'

She looked around the room and shivered. It was cold. She was wearing just the cheap, thin white cotton shirt and the equally inexpensive slacks that came from the convent. The Questura budget hadn't run to clothes, though Rosa had told him quietly she intended to correct this in the morning. In some strange, subtle way, they were beginning to adopt Agata Graziano, form a protective, insular wall around her, and not simply as a way of keeping out Franco Malaspina and his thugs. A part of her seemed too delicate to be allowed to wander free in the world the rest of them inhabited. Costa wondered whether this was fair, or even an accurate reading of the facts.

'I shouldn't be in this place, prying. It's private. I'm sorry.'

'It's just a room,' he said, and smiled. 'You're welcome to use it as much as you wish. Before Emily had it, my sister worked here. She is an artist too. It needs . . .'

The white walls were now a little grey and in need of paint. He remembered the sound of voices in the house when he was growing up, and how he would come in here for peace sometimes, watching his sister work at some strange, abstract canvas he would never understand.

'It needs company,' he murmured, and found the thought began to bring a sharp, stinging sensation to his eyes.

She noticed and said quickly, 'Goodnight, Nic. I must see what Bea has to teach me about this bathroom of yours.'

– 6 –

He waited at the foot of the stairs, thinking, wondering whether he should stay nearby in case there was some difficulty between the two. But after a while he heard their voices from above, happy voices, followed by the running of water, then, drifting down the steps, the smell of soap and shampoo.

If Bea had had a daughter she would have been about Agata's age. He had seen that glint in her eyes the moment this bright, dishevelled young woman had walked through the door. *The poor thing's positively feral.*

Costa found himself amused by the description. It was both apposite and ridiculous somehow too. Agata was an extraordinarily sophisticated woman. She simply chose not to show it on the outside.

He found his coat, walked down the drive and went to the men in the marked car blocking the entrance. It was a cold, clear night, full of stars, bright with the light of a waxing moon.

Peroni was there with an officer Costa didn't recognize. They were listening to the radio – old, bad Italian jazz, the kind Gianni would force on anyone given half the chance – and drinking coffee from a Thermos.

'Is there anything I can get you gentlemen?' he asked as they wound down the window.

'Some ladies, some wine, some food,' Peroni responded instantly. 'Actually, just the food will do. Got any?'

'You know where the kitchen is. I'm going to bed.'

'How's the shoulder?' Peroni asked, suddenly serious.

'Aching. But it's not worth worrying about. Is everything OK here?'

'It's good,' Peroni said, nodding, meaning it. 'Better than it looked. You know, when that bastard stormed out of here all smug and knowing this afternoon, I didn't think so. I thought . . . there you go. Some rich jerk is going to walk all over us again. But I don't now. I have no idea why. It's probably the early onset of mental degeneration. I just think . . . we will nail him, Nic. We're here. There are a hundred good men or women or more on the case back at the Questura. This new *commissario* is on our side too. It will work out. Somehow or other. I promise.'

He turned and stared out of the car window.

'You know what makes me so certain? It's that awful detail Rosa got out of the hooker who went away. The idea that these animals photographed those women like that. You know. Just when . . .'

He did know. Costa thought he understood why too. It was the precise instant captured in the canvas. Agata described it exactly: *the moment of the fall.* In the cries of those women, however unreal, however they were brought about, by sex or violence or – and he had to countenance this – the imminence of death, lay some secret pleasure the Ekstasists craved to witness.

'I don't believe in God,' Peroni went on, 'but I'm

damned sure that men like that will not walk away from us, not in the end. It's only Malaspina now, and we will have him.'

Costa agreed.

'We will,' he said, then went back to the house, poured himself a small glass of the Verdicchio, which was barely touched, and found the chair by the fire, once his father's, always the most comfortable in the house.

The dog was there already, a small, stiff furry shape curled up in front of the burning logs, slumbering.

There was a photo on the mantel. He reached up and took it in his hands, wishing, in the futile way one did, that his father could have seen this before he died.

He and Emily stood where newly married couples often did on their wedding day in Rome, by the Arch of Constantine, next to the Colosseum, in their best clothes, Emily with a bouquet in her arms, smiling, happier than he had ever seen her, he in a suit Falcone had helped him buy, the best he'd ever owned, a perfect fit, now consigned to Teresa's evidence pile, torn apart by Malaspina's pellets, stained with Costa's own blood.

Lives were drawn together by invisible lines, unseen contours that joined way-points one never noticed until they were already fading in the receding distance of memory. From the moment captured here to Emily's death was but a few brief months, and nothing could have told him that then, nothing could ease the ache he felt now, the pain, the regret over so many unspoken words, such a proliferation of deeds and kindnesses that never took place.

Time stole everything in the end. It had no need of an accomplice, some arrogant, deranged aristocrat hiding behind a mask and a gun.

From above him he heard a sound, one he struggled, for a moment, to recognize. Then it came . . . laughter. Bea and Agata, happy together, their amusement running like a river, almost giggling, the way that children did, or a mother and daughter, joined by some mutual amusement over something that would never, in a million years, reach his ears.

This was how it was supposed to be. This was how it should have been.

He closed his eyes and held the photograph in its frame close to him.

God gave us tears for a reason.

Perhaps, he thought. But something stood between him and Emily's pale, remembered face, still alive, still breathing in his memory. It was a figure in a hood, one that now possessed a voice and a face and a black, evil intent that was not yet sated.

Part 12

FRAGMENTS FROM
THE PAST

– 1 –

They left the house at midday, in a convoy of three vehicles, Agata and Costa in the centre, with a specialist driver at the wheel, an arrangement Commissario Esposito said would be standard practice until Franco Malaspina was in jail.

Agata had risen early, spending most of the morning alone in the studio with her books and the computer, coming out only for glasses of water, saying nothing. Halfway through the morning Rosa had arrived with fresh reference works . . . and new clothes. Agata had snatched at the former and scarcely even noticed the latter. When she emerged for the conference at the Questura she had, it seemed to Costa, no conscious knowledge of the fact that she was now wearing, probably for the first time in her life, the kind of apparel most Roman women would regard as standard, half-elegant office wear: smart grey slacks and a matching jacket, and a cream shirt. With Bea's help, her hair now seemed relatively under control, snatched back in a band. The dark, angular lines of her face made her look a little older, a little more businesslike perhaps, though the effect was somewhat ruined by her insistence on wearing her old shoes, a pair of worn, black, deeply scuffed half-boots that looked as if they had marched over most of Rome several times over. She continued to carry two over-stuffed plastic bags, one so heavy it gave her a marked tilt.

Agata said nothing in the car, and walked through the Questura, catching curious, occasionally admiring looks along the way, as if heading for some routine academic conference, not a desperate convocation of law enforcement officers struggling to find some way back into a case of multiple murder, one in which she might be the only worthwhile witness.

Finally, at one o'clock, as sandwiches were passed around the table, the meeting began, with a summary of the case from Falcone and the forensic from Teresa Lupo. Costa, with Agata on one side and Rosa Prabakaran on the other, listened avidly, hoping there would be some lacuna in the exposition of what he knew by heart, some gap or flaw in what they had done which would give them some new foothold that would lead into the Palazzo Malaspina.

He heard none. Falcone described at length the extended Questura investigation into the murders in the Vicolo del Divino Amore and of Emily. Rarely had such resources been brought to bear on a single investigation in recent history, in part because of the continuing media and public outcry over the case. There was shock that such dreadful events could be uncovered in Rome. The newspapers were outraged at the lack of progress and ran editorials daily, lamenting the seeming impotence of the police. At the same time they were – with the lack of logic allowed to the journalistic profession at times – beginning to question the expense of the operation, with its thousands of officer hours and overseas trips, which now extended beyond Angola into Nigeria and Sudan, all without the least sign of progress.

Nor was the usually productive route of forensic making much of a contribution. The new rules brought into force following Malaspina's legal applications made most of the conventional processes – the accidental, covert and deliberate sampling of DNA in particular – unusable. The deaths of Castagna, Buccafusca and Nino Tomassoni the previous night left Teresa Lupo's team swamped with work, and would doubtless provide a sea of evidence which might one day prove useful. But neither she nor Falcone had any fresh material which linked Malaspina directly with the case outside the forbidden area of genetic identification.

Malaspina's lawyers had dispatched the Questura back to the age of intellectual deduction, with little recourse to science. Castagna's suicide would, Teresa felt sure, soon prove to be fake. There was, however, no calling card from Malaspina, not a phone call or a speck of physical evidence that could connect him with the man's death. The two were acquaintances, perhaps even friends. This was only to be expected among two leading members of Rome's younger glitterati. A magistrate like Silvia Tentori would not give a moment's consideration to a name in a contact book or a few bland emails on a computer. They were, for the moment, entirely reliant on the relationship Malaspina had with the reclusive Nino Tomassoni, and there, Falcone said, something different surely existed.

In the way of Italian law enforcement, it had only that morning come to light that both men's names were on Interpol's list of art-smuggling suspects, which had been handed to the Carabinieri's specialist team in the field. That same list, Falcone had gleaned from his contacts within the Carabinieri, also identified Véronique Gillet as a suspect, to the extent that there was active discussion about whether to question her shortly, an act which would inevitably have led to her suspension from the Louvre.

'Sick, out of work and on the verge of getting busted,' Teresa interjected. 'No wonder she was feeling a touch suicidal.'

'Isn't that enough to get us a warrant for Malaspina on its own?' Rosa asked.

It was Esposito who intervened.

'Not at all. If Gillet or Tomassoni had named him, of course. But since they are dead . . . Malaspina is simply one name on a long list, the result of anonymous information. Rich men attract this kind of gossip all the time. On its own it's worthless. We need more than tittle-tattle.'

They stared at one another, and Agata Graziano eyed them in turn, waiting.

'So?' she asked in the end. 'Is that it?'

'There may still be some room for opportunity here,' Falcone suggested. 'We know he was obsessed with that painting in the Vicolo del Divino Amore. If we can prove some connection there . . . We don't need evidence of the other crimes. It's a stolen artwork like the rest, even if it's not on the list. We can proceed on that basis alone.'

She glanced at Costa and he knew, immediately, why.

'That painting wasn't stolen, sir,' he said.

'What are you talking about?' Esposito snapped. 'Of course it was stolen. We have seventeen like it from Tomassoni's house. Positive identification for fifteen of them now. Every one taken from some European art institution over the past decade. You're telling me this one is different?'

Agata's small hand banged the table.

'Of course it's different.'

Teresa Lupo wore a sly smile.

'It was in a different place, gentlemen,' she said. 'It was on a stand, out there to be viewed. Those others were items of trade, in storage, awaiting a buyer. I believe our sister here is right.'

'Thank you,' Agata murmured, with the briefest of glances at Teresa as she spoke. 'I am. This painting cannot have been stolen, not in the same way, for one very simple reason. As far as any of us knew, it didn't even exist. Explain that to me, Leo. I am listening.'

'So what did happen?' Esposito asked, looking prickly when Falcone stayed silent.

'I have no idea,' she replied, shrugging her small shoulders. 'I'm simply telling you what didn't happen. Isn't that important too?'

Teresa nodded.

'Very. But if it wasn't stolen, where the hell has it been for these past four hundred years?'

'Here,' Agata cried. 'In Rome. Where it belongs. Where else? If it had been sold or gone abroad, we would have known. Who could have kept quiet about a work like that? An unknown Caravaggio, with a secret no one might guess at?'

'A secret?' Falcone asked.

Costa sketched out the details of the hidden signature and the alternative title. They looked baffled. This was beyond conventional policework.

'All of which means what exactly?' Peroni asked in the end.

Agata sighed and looked at Costa hopefully.

'I'm not sure,' he admitted.

'It means,' she said abruptly, 'this was a private work of art for a gentleman's bedroom. One that had a certain moral ambiguity that came from the artist, and was not, I suspect, part of the original commission, or indeed noticed by the men who owned it. For them, it was a kind of pornography. For Caravaggio, it was a discourse on the nature of love, a question for the viewer, asking him or her to define an attitude towards the origin of passion. Did it come from earthly flesh or was there some divine intent, some holy, sacred plan there, daring you to find it?'

'And this is important?' Peroni asked.

'For Franco Malaspina,' she said quietly, 'this painting is the most important thing in the world. Why else would he risk so much to regain possession of the work? He needs it. So did Véronique Gillet. Castagna. Buccafusca. Everyone except Nino Tomassoni, who was a quiet, sad little thing, I think.'

'He said something,' Falcone pointed out. 'Tomassoni. Before he died. "The Caravaggio is mine. Ours. It's the only one that is."'

'Then Franco took it from him,' Agata responded. 'To enjoy what it brought. Which was . . . you tell me.'

They were looking at each other, wondering who would be the first to say it.

'I cannot assist you if I don't know the facts,' Agata complained. 'You are all very bad liars, by the way. So kindly stop.'

Costa took the leap.

'We have evidence that the Ekstasists took photos of women while they were having sex. That they tried to capture the instant of passion, not that it was passion, of course, but that doesn't seem to have mattered.'

She took a deep breath and asked, 'You have the photos?'

'We have a few,' Teresa replied. 'Some of the victims are among those who died in the studio. Others . . . they don't seem traceable.'

'What do they show?' Agata asked.

Costa intervened. 'They show women in the throes of sexual ecstasy or some kind of torture, or perhaps even a fatal spasm. There's no way of knowing.'

Agata took a sip of water from the glass in front of her.

'They wish to experience the moment of the fall,' she said quietly. 'The transformation Caravaggio's painting describes. The very second the world turns from Paradise into what we know now. If they do that, they become part of that moment, something witnessed only by God. They celebrate their own power over everyone, over these poor women. Over you and me. This was Franco's doing, not the others'.'

The slight, dark woman ran her fingers through her hair, exasperated.

'You should surely realize this for yourselves by now. He is an obsessive human being. This is not just a painting for him. It is a hunger. An object of worship. A need. Something that acts as a catalyst to deliver what he wants.'

Costa looked at her. He had an objection.

'They didn't know about the other title,' he pointed out. 'Or the signature beneath the paint.'

'They must have known. Perhaps Tomassoni had passed it on as some family history. Perhaps they simply read it in the canvas itself. This is art of the highest order. That painting was designed to be some cunning kind of mirror.

It gave back to the viewer what he himself sought in it. For someone like Franco that would be the equivalent of turning the key in some dreadful lock. He found what he sought. Caravaggio painted it that way deliberately. Were I writing some dry academic paper I'd be tempted to hypothesize that this was his revenge on the commissioner, if you like, since he clearly wasn't in the habit of painting this kind of material, and probably didn't enjoy it. He was paid to produce pornography. In return, he created something infinitely more subtle. Crude and lascivious to those who wished to see that. Subtle and spiritual and didactic – a warning against lasciviousness and decadence – for those who sought that. And perhaps . . .'

She stopped in mid-thought, looking lost for a moment.

'. . . a little of both for those who deem themselves "normal". Do you understand what I am saying now? Or do I have to spell it out?'

No one spoke.

Agata groaned.

'Franco and his friends needed to see this voluptuous Eve because what they did became more important, magnified, by her presence. I know nothing of these things, but I know what ecstasy means. Is it possible that this work would so infect a man that, in its absence, he was unable to achieve that state? And perhaps Véronique Gillet too? I am asking you this because I cannot know. Is that possible?'

They were all silent, until Teresa Lupo wrinkled her nose and said, 'One thing you learn in this job, Sister, is that it's amazing what pushes some people's buttons. I think you just put your finger on our man. Not that it helps. In fact, it makes him scarier than ever.'

Agata smiled.

'Does it? I thought it made him more human. Now I would like to go to the Vicolo del Divino Amore, please.' She waited, staring at Commissario Esposito. 'Unless someone has a better idea . . .'

'You have helped us enormously,' Falcone interrupted. 'We're very grateful. Now, please, return to the farmhouse. You will be safe there. We will provide what you want.'

'What I want,' she said bitterly, 'is to help. How can I do that if you treat me like a prisoner?'

'Agata . . .' Falcone began.

Esposito waved him down.

'She's right,' he conceded. 'We need all the help we can get. Costa, you take her with your team, since you all seem to know each other. Falcone and I will stay here and go through what little we have so far.'

He stared at Agata Graziano.

'There is a condition, though.'

She listened, arms folded.

'You will do as you're told, Sister. In particular what Agente Prabakaran advises, since she will be by your side throughout.'

Agata nodded and said simply, 'I know a little of obedience, Commissario. You have my word.'

– 2 –

Thirty minutes later Agata sat in the back of the car with Costa, sorting through the contents of a supermarket bag: books, notepads, pens and pencils.

She didn't say much until the vehicle rounded the Piazza Borghese and came to a halt at the top of the little alley, some twenty metres short of the small crowd of spectators and a couple of photographers who stood, bored and stationary, outside the yellow barrier of tape now beginning to look old from the rain and mud.

'This city seems different from a car,' Agata mused. 'I prefer walking. Don't you?'

'No sane person drives in Rome,' he replied with feeling.

'In that case this is a city of lunatics,' Rosa Prabakaran cut in from the front seat. 'Sister Agata, do you mind if I make a suggestion?'

The car had stopped. The two guard vehicles were either side, front and back. Officers were getting out, checking the area, as was Rosa, with a professional, calm intent Costa liked.

'You can't drag your life around with you in a carrier bag,' Rosa said suddenly, then passed something over from the front seat. It was a smart new satchel in black leather with a shiny silver buckle. 'Please take this. A gift from the Questura.'

Costa caught her eye. This was surely not from the police fund. The thing had all the hallmarks of the cheap yet serviceable goods Rosa's father sold to tourists from his stall near the Trevi Fountain.

'I'm worried you will lose something from one of those carrier bags,' she added. 'This is purely practical . . .'

Agata took it from her and stared at the shiny leather, sniffing it for a moment, and wrinkling her dark nose at the smell.

'Carrier bags have served me well for a very long time,' she noted.

'You're not walking from the convent to work and back, a few minutes each day. Not any more.' Rosa was adamant. 'Please.'

Agata shrugged and took the thing, flipping up the buckle, then preparing to empty the entire contents of one carrier by the simple act of turning it upside down over the bag's open mouth.

She stopped, staring inside, then reached in and delicately removed a black metal object there. It was a small police-issue handgun.

'What is this?' she asked. 'No. That was a stupid thing to say. I know what this is. Why do you want me to have it? That's impossible.'

'Guns are not useful in the hands of people who don't know how to use them,' Costa remarked. 'What on earth are you thinking, Agente?'

'Commissario Esposito spoke to me before we left, sir,' she replied. 'He wants Sister Agata to have this and for me to give her instructions on how to use it, if necessary. It won't come to that. Nevertheless . . .'

Agata held the gun in front of her, touching the black metal gingerly, as if it were something poisonous.

'Those are your orders, Rosa, not mine,' she muttered.

'Why did Commissario Esposito suggest this?' Costa asked, furious the man had never raised the subject directly.

'Operational reasons.'

The duty guard officers were beginning to mill around the car door, anxious to move. Costa persisted.

'What operational reasons?'

Rosa frowned.

'Sister, do you have any idea what the Camorra is?'

She shook her head. The hair didn't move any more. The crucifix around her neck, lying on the cream business shirt, and the bulky, scruffy boots apart, Agata Graziano no longer looked the woman she still felt herself to be.

'Should I?' she asked.

'There is no reason whatsoever,' Costa snapped, angry that Esposito, for some reason, had not used him to approach Agata on such a sensitive matter. 'The Camorra are criminals.'

Agata stared at him, wide-eyed, curious.

'Just "criminals"?'

'They're a criminal fraternity based in Naples, though they have arms, tentacles, everywhere in Italy, and in Europe and America too,' he went on. 'Imagine a kindred organization to the Sicilians, the mafiosi. I imagine you've heard of them.'

'As I told you once before, I am not a monk.'

'Quite,' he answered. 'What on earth has this to do with us?'

Rosa wasn't taking the proffered gun from her.

'They're good Catholics too, mainly,' she said. 'At

least they think of themselves that way. We heard from Naples this morning that one of them, a man who is occasionally friendly with the police there, wanted to warn us of something he'd heard. That a Roman, one unidentified, at least someone he was unwilling to name, was seeking someone to carry out an attack, and looking to pay well for assistance.' She gazed at Agata, a mournful look in her brown eyes. 'He said the target was to be a Catholic nun.'

'I am not a—'

Rosa put her hand on Agata's tightly clenched fingers.

'We know. But the name he had was yours. This is good news, Sister, trust me. At least we are forewarned. We also know that no one accepted the commission. The man was appalled by the very idea and believed those in the Camorra would feel the same. But they are just a few criminals among many. Franco Malaspina knows more and he has money that shouts very loudly. So please . . .'

The police woman pushed the weapon back over the seat.

'Do this for me,' she added. 'I will show you how to handle a gun safely should the need arise. But it won't. We will protect you. Nic and I and – ' she indicated the officers beyond the door – 'all of us. This will not be necessary. It's simply a precaution.'

Agata uttered a small, slight curse and, with pointed disdain, placed the weapon back where it came from.

'I like the bag, Agente,' she conceded with a curt brusqueness. 'Thank you for that.'

- 3 -

The last piece of physical evidence had been removed from the studio in the Vicolo del Divino Amore. But the smell of death – sweet, noxious, sickly – remained. Agata feigned not to notice. Rosa Prabakaran and Peroni, on the other hand, both made excuses to stand outside. Costa understood why. Something – perhaps the work in lifting the floors or the exposure of so much dull, dark earth itself – made the stench worse than it had been at the moment the first body was found.

There was, surely, nothing left of interest to be removed from the charnel house that had been the lair of the Ekstasists. Nevertheless, Teresa Lupo, as she guided her visitor around its interior, explaining its grim, dark secrets, insisted each of them wore the standard white forensic suit and moved within the tapes while she went through each and every victim with painstaking care and in exact detail.

Agata listened, asking questions only rarely, eyes wide open in wonder mostly, occasionally misted with shock and dismay.

'What do you know about these women?' she asked when Teresa had finished her main exposition. 'Who they were. Where they came from.'

'Not much,' Teresa said sadly. 'Not real names. Not history. They worked the streets, probably in the rougher parts of town. That much we know. Not a lot more.' She hesitated. 'You understand what Aids is?'

'Of course,' Agata answered with a sigh.

'Four of them were HIV-positive. One possibly was developing Aids itself.'

Agata shook her head. She looked oddly young in the white bunny suit.

'Poor things . . .'

'They weren't alone in that,' Costa pointed out. 'Véronique Gillet suffered from Aids too.'

'What a world you inhabit,' Agata murmured. 'And you think that of Caravaggio was primitive by comparison. Did you find any artist's materials that didn't seem to be modern?'

This was a subject that clearly didn't interest the pathologist.

'There was some paint and a small number of brushes that were a few years old. They hadn't been used in a while.'

Teresa glanced around her.

'This was a studio, though, wasn't it? You can see how it would be suitable for that purpose? Tell me I'm correct, Agata.'

'I think so,' she answered.

'Caravaggio's studio?' Costa asked.

Agata gave him a stern look.

'You can't give me firm answers about events that happened here in the past few months. Yet you expect me to illuminate you on matters that may or may not have occurred four hundred years ago?'

Teresa folded her strong arms.

'Yes, Sister, we do. Otherwise why are you here?'

Agata laughed.

'Very well. Let me tell you what I read about last night, in the deadly quiet of Nic's lonely farmhouse. Caravaggio did live in this street, right up until the moment he fled Rome after killing Ranuccio Tomassoni in a brawl, involving several others on both sides and knives. It's difficult to be more precise than that. In those days this street had a different name. It was the Vicolo dei Santi Cecilia e Biagio – don't ask me why it changed, I have no idea.'

She turned and stared around the room.

'When Caravaggio fled, the authorities made an inventory of his home. Most of the possessions, one assumes, were his, not those of his boyfriend or servant.'

A look of brief dejection crossed her face.

'Reading the list of his belongings, you wonder what he had come to. It was pathetic. A guitar. Some very old and poor furniture. Some weapons, of course, among them a pair of duelling swords in an ebony case, possibly the most valuable things he owned.'

She stared at them.

'That was the man. He saw everything, lived everything. Good and evil. The touch of grace, the absence of it. He simply wished to paint it all, every last detail. But here?'

Agata Graziano held out her small arms in empty despair.

'I don't know. Perhaps he lived and worked in the same room. Many did when they were poor. The street name has changed. The numbers have changed. I have no idea. Did you find nothing?'

'We were looking for evidence from now,' Teresa

answered. 'We're forensic scientists, not archaeologists. Of course we found other material. We were digging up bare earth.'

'Old brushes? Papers? Anything with writing on it?'

Teresa brightened a little and said, 'Let me show you what we have.'

They followed the pathologist over to a set of bright red plastic boxes stacked four deep. They were positioned next to the rear exit to the yard behind, a sight that brought back too many memories for Costa, so that he turned and looked away for a while, wondering if it was really possible to feel the past, to detect the presence of an extraordinary human being through some odd sixth sense that defied explanation.

When he turned, Agata was rummaging forcefully through the boxes, turning over broken crockery and trash, and piece after piece of unidentifiable rubbish accrued across the centuries in the black Roman dirt.

'A brush,' she said, and threw something on the floor at his feet. 'It's probably of the period. But it could be anyone's. This is a waste of time. There's nothing . . .'

She stopped. Costa and Teresa watched in silence as she withdrew an object from the box and put it to one side. Then she tore into the second box with flailing hands, raked through the contents for a minute or more before finding something else and removing it.

They scarcely had a chance to see what she had found before both items went into her bright new shiny black satchel.

Agata Graziano gazed at her small, silent audience.

'I don't care to remember things that happened months ago,' she declared. 'It seems to me a waste of my time to dwell too much on the immediate past. But . . .'

There was a sharp glint of excitement in her eyes.

'I do recall a conversation I had with Véronique Gillet one night when they were opening that exhibition at the Palazzo Ruspoli, the one that had so much Caravaggio material from abroad.'

Costa closed his eyes. He had worked security for that event. He and Emily had decided, at its close, to marry.

'I teased Véronique. She was French, for pity's sake, and the French demand it. Besides, they have stolen so much of ours, and do not even deign to share it either. This was – ' she pointed at them to emphasize the matter – 'the subject of our little playful argument. There was a painting that ought to have been there. *The Death of the Virgin*. The Louvre wouldn't allow it out of their grasping hands. Some excuse about security or preservation or whatever. It should have been in Rome, not sitting in Paris, gawked at by tourists who haven't the slightest understanding of what they see. Listen to me now. Caravaggio painted from life. Always.'

'I'll try,' Teresa replied. 'And the point you're making?'

'There was an outcry when he delivered that painting of the Virgin. The Madonna was swollen and lifeless. She was dead, after all. Very obviously human, not some goddess awaiting the call to divinity. Worse, there was a widespread belief that he painted her from the corpse of a common Roman whore recovered from the Tiber. I believe this too. It's there for the world to see. In the way she looks. In the sympathy with which she is regarded by the figures around her – a common sympathy. *Disegno*. He sought the sign of God in all of us.'

She stared into space, not seeing anything, intent only on the questions racing through her head.

'We know precisely when that work was executed

because it was a Church commission. There are records. If this was Caravaggio's studio, that corpse must have lain here,' Agata said finally, staring at Costa with eyes that brimmed with both shock and a terrible knowledge. Her fingers pointed to the ground. *Here.* Four hundred years before your poor black street women . . .'

'If . . .' Teresa murmured.

Agata shook her head free of the forensic suit's hood and started to struggle out of the white plastic.

'I wish to go to the Doria Pamphilj immediately,' she declared, then, still fighting with the bunny suit, swept through them, marching for the door. No one moved.

'I can phone Commissario Esposito if you like,' she shouted, turning to face them, beckoning with her short, skinny arms.

'So you could,' Costa groaned, and followed.

They stood in the Piazza del Collegio Romano, in mild winter drizzle, six police officers crowding around the small figure of Agata Graziano, who was huddled inside a raincoat Rosa Prabakaran had spirited from nowhere. The gallery was closed for the afternoon. Costa took it upon himself to phone to the Doria Pamphilj internal office, but by the time he'd finished the call the door was open and a beaming attendant was waving them in. Agata had spoken a few words into the intercom; that was all it required.

'Sister, Sister!' the middle-aged man in the antiquated uniform bleated. 'Come in! Please! Out of this awful weather.' He stared at the army of police officers and Teresa Lupo stamping her big feet on the doorstep. 'And your . . . friends too.'

'Thank you, Michele,' she answered, and stomped into the dark hallway, then marched directly up the grand flight of stairs, to the first-floor gallery.

It was hard to keep up. By the time they got to the top of the stairs, Agata had gone through the public entrance, walked quickly through the Poussin Room and the Velvet, and was passing the ballroom, seemingly picking up speed with every step. Then she almost ran through the closed bookshop and turned right, towards the series of chambers that included, in its midst, the sixteenth-century room and the two Caravaggios they had come to visit just a couple of days before.

She was standing rigid, fascinated, in front of the smaller canvas, the penitent Magdalene, when they arrived, her shoulders moving, some unexpected emotion gripping her small, taut body.

Costa felt concerned. Then he realized what was happening. She was laughing quietly, to herself, not minding what anyone thought at all.

'Agata . . .' he said gently.

'What?'

Her sparkling eyes turned on him. Her mouth broke in a bright, white smile.

'Is everything all right?'

'Everything is wonderful. And I am an idiot. We are all idiots. Here. Take a look at this . . .'

She reached into the black leather satchel and took out the first object he saw her retrieve from the red box in the Vicolo del Divino Amore. Surreptitiously, she must have been working at it in the car on the way to the gallery. It was no longer a dusty, unrecognizable shape. What Agata held in her hands was a glass carafe of the kind used for water or wine, one with such gentle curves it could only be hand-made and very old.

Agata rubbed the sleeve of her raincoat hard against the edge.

'Tell me that's not evidence,' Teresa said, alarmed.

'It's wonderful evidence. The best I could ask for. Not for you, though. For me.'

They watched as she held the flask next to the slumbering

Magdalene in the painting. An identical glass object sat close to the figure's feet, next to some discarded jewellery, evidence of some regretted tryst, or a life that was in the process of being abandoned.

'It's the same jug,' Agata said firmly.

'It's *a* jug,' Teresa pointed out.

'No. He painted from life. He had no money most of the time. Perhaps he was sentimental too. Throughout his life the same objects reappear – props and models. He used what he was familiar with. The items he loved . . .'

She glanced at the painting with the deepest of affection.

'. . . he tried to keep. Caravaggio painted this work while he was in the Palazzo Madama under the patronage of Del Monte, alongside bohemians and alchemists, geniuses like Galileo, and vagabonds and quacks from the street. In the seven years between the Magdalene here and that squalid pit in the Vicolo del Divino Amore he rose and fell, to become the most acclaimed artist in Rome and then a hunted criminal, wanted for murder. Why? *Why?*'

'It's a jug,' Teresa said again.

'A poor man growing poorer sells what's of value to others and attempts to hold on to what is of value to himself,' she declared. 'This is the flask. It was like everything else. He used it more than once. I can show you the paintings if you still doubt me. *Bacchus* in the Uffizi. *Boy Bitten by a Lizard* in London. Nothing later. Nothing after he fled Rome.' She stared at them and her eyes didn't brook any argument. 'Because he didn't have it.'

She held up the glass for them to see. There was a distinct stain, like old blood, in the base.

'Wine, I imagine,' Agata added. 'There's another reason to keep it. He could paint it. He could drink from it too.'

She noted the scepticism in their faces.

'If Caravaggio lived in that house,' she went on, 'Franco Malaspina must have known. He said it himself. It's part of the Malaspina estate, the poorer part, in Ortaccio, but property all the same. These families keep records for everything. Most of what we know about painting in the sixteenth and seventeenth centuries comes from the book-keeping of either the Church or the aristocracy.'

'Even for me,' Teresa remarked quietly, 'this is stretching things.'

'Nic! Tell them what we discovered on that painting before Franco stole it from us. *Tell them!*'

'We saw a signature,' he said. 'Caravaggio's. It said . . .'

He paused. All the paintings they'd seen, all the same faces, the same objects . . . these were alive in his head and intermingled, one with the other.

'It said,' Agata interjected, '*fra. michel l'ekstasista*. Michelangelo Merisi, the Ekstasist. Franco did not pluck the name of his murderous, thuggish gang out of the ether. He picked it out from history. Or it picked him. What he and Buccafusca and Castagna and poor, stupid Nino Tomassoni did came from that act, and it destroyed them in the end. Look . . .'

She pointed at the beautiful slumbering woman with the tear shining on her cheek like a transparent pearl.

'We know her name. Fillide Melandroni. A prostitute, a violent one too, a woman who had been to court for marking her rivals by slashing their faces with a knife to make them less saleable. Here she is the Magdalene.

Elsewhere Judith slaying Holofernes, Catherine leaning on a wall before her martyrdom. *Here!*'

She indicated the adjoining painting and the figure of Mary, with the infant Jesus in her arms, on the flight to Egypt.

'A holy whore,' she said quietly. 'And note the dress.'

She pointed at the rich olive fleur-de-lys brocade of the sleeping Magdalene's flowing halter gown.

'This was the costume of a moneyed Roman prostitute, the kind of woman who slept with cardinals, then talked art and philosophy with them afterwards, before going out onto the streets of Ortaccio at night and . . . what? Making mayhem with Caravaggio and his friends.'

To Costa's astonishment, Agata reached out and touched, very briefly, the soft, pale skin of the sleeping woman on the wall.

'Both good and evil, and each to excess,' she said quietly. '*Nec spe, nec metu.* Without hope or fear. She was surely with them. Franco Malaspina did not invent the Ekstasists. He merely revived them, brought back from the dead the ugly gang that included Caravaggio and Fillide before everything fell apart so terribly.'

Agata took her attention away from the wall.

'Here is a word I thought I would never utter,' she said again. 'I read what records there were of the case against Caravaggio last night. They disclosed that one possible reason for the fight was that Ranuccio Tomassoni was Fillide's pimp. The man who sold her to others. Is that right?'

She closed her eyes for a moment.

'No, no. I know it is. This is all part of your world, not mine, but yours intrudes, I can't avoid it. Tell me also. Is it possible this was Véronique Gillet's relationship to Franco Malaspina too? Accomplice. Lover. Muse. Fellow criminal. Could that be true?'

Costa was lost for words. Watching Agata struggle with these ideas – ones that seemed to make so much sense to him – he could see the mix of excitement and distress they caused.

'They recreated something we still don't understand,' Agata went on. 'Something to do with that painting. With Tomassoni, perhaps, or some link with Franco's own lineage.'

Her eyes scanned each of them.

'This much I do know from what I've read. Ranuccio Tomassoni was the *caporione* of his quarter. The boss of it. The man who ran the gangs, who ruled the streets, and handed out vengeance and a kind of justice as he saw fit. Just as Franco is today. For a while Caravaggio was with him, alongside Fillide. Somehow . . .'

She squeezed her eyes tight shut again, trying to concentrate.

'Franco and Nino Tomassoni found out about this, and recreated it around that painting. Then, with Véronique's assistance, they made everything so much worse. How? Why? I have no idea.'

Teresa shook her head and sighed.

'If this is true, it still doesn't give us enough evidence to put Franco Malaspina in front of a magistrate. Even if we could find one who wasn't tame. They'd look at us as if we were crazy.'

'It's a question of time,' Costa insisted. 'And work. The more we know, the closer we get to this man. Sooner or later . . .'

'Nic,' Teresa objected. 'It's a piece of very old glass and a lot of interesting connections that may or may not add up.'

'No, it's not,' Agata said, and reached into her bag again.

She took out something else and rubbed it hard against her sleeve. Dust and dirt fell from it onto the Doria Pamphilj's polished floor. Then she held the object next to the painting on the wall for all to see.

It was a fragment of fabric, a square, deliberately cut, about the size of a hand.

Agata kept it there and no one said a word.

'A memento,' she suggested, 'of love at a time when Michelangelo Merisi was happy, inhabiting a world full of light. And later, an item of comfort, a reminder of that abandoned past, when he himself lived in permanent darkness and violence and blood. *Look!*'

It bore the same fleur-de-lys pattern as the fabric on the dress of Fillide Melandroni, sleeping as the penitent Mary Magdalene. Costa reached out and touched it with his fingers. The cloth felt thick and expensive.

If one imagined away the dust and the dirt of centuries, it would surely exhibit the same olive colour too.

Part 13

THE EKSTASISTS' LAIR

– 1 –

'Nino Tomassoni can wait. Show me this statue you looked at,' she asked as they left the Doria Pamphilj. 'It's not far.'

'It isn't,' Teresa agreed from the front seat. 'But don't hold out your hopes. We've scraped everything we can off these damned things, looking for something that might link us back to Malaspina. Paper. Ink. Spit. You name it.'

The pathologist sighed. She looked exhausted too. There was a nervous tension about them all, one that spoke of desperation and failure.

When they were about to get back into the car, Costa had taken a call from Falcone in the Questura. The legal department was getting restless. Toni Grimaldi, never the most forthcoming of colleagues, was suddenly saying nothing at all.

'We've tried the other statues too,' Teresa added. 'We could spend months working on that material. Perhaps we will. I don't know ... We would need something extraordinary, something direct. Plain DNA won't help us. We still run up against the same brick wall. We can't get a thing to corroborate it with.'

They waited for the other cars to stop and the officers

to crowd round Agata's exit. Then they got out and stood in front of the crude, worn statue of Pasquino underneath a grey winter sky. Dusk was descending over the city, and black clouds full of rain, their bellies dotted by the slow-moving starling flocks that circled endlessly high above them.

'This is ridiculous,' Agata hissed under her breath. 'Why would anyone wish to kill me? The magistrate has already thrown out my evidence.'

'If we find more evidence, we can reintroduce you as a witness,' Costa argued. 'Also . . .'

He didn't want to say it now, but she was staring at him intently.

'Perhaps he thinks you're the person who might see something the rest of us will miss. That would worry him deeply.'

'He's wrong there, isn't he?' she grumbled. 'I can't even uncover the truth of what happened to Caravaggio and I've been studying him for years.'

Like her, he'd read so many books, so many biographies. None of them gave any good answers about what happened the day Ranuccio Tomassoni died, or why.

'Why don't we know?' he asked, with a genuine curiosity. 'It was a criminal case. There were records, surely.'

'Nothing reliable. Caravaggio fled. Most of the others too, and when they returned everything was hushed up, damages paid, reputations mended. I simply don't know. What information we have comes from contemporary accounts by partial bystanders. Caravaggio's friends. Or his enemies. By rights there should be something in the Vatican archives. I have contacts there. I've looked. The cupboard's bare. Perhaps they incriminated someone important. Del Monte himself even. What's the point in speculating?'

She took one step forward towards the statue, then reached out and touched the stone. It had been scraped clean recently by the forensic team. Even so, the posters had returned, with their customary vehemence. There were five messages there, all in the curious scrawl of a computer printer, artificial letters posing as handwriting. Three seemed to be nonsense. One castigated a senior politician as a criminal. The final poster was a foul-mouthed rant, calling the Pope any number of names and comparing him to Hitler.

'So much hate in the world,' Agata said quietly.

She stared at the statue's battered face, barely recognizable as a man.

'Why do the police spend their time looking at things like this?'

'Because sometimes it's worth it,' Rosa cut in. 'It was here, in the end. Though normally – ' she shrugged – 'it's just racist or political material. We need to keep tabs on that kind of information. Where else would you find something that . . . frank?'

'Where else?' Agata echoed, not taking her eyes off Pasquino for a moment. 'Where were the others?'

Rosa told her. Then the small, slight woman in black pushed her way back through the huddle of officers, finding the middle car, only to sit there, waiting, engulfed by her own private thoughts.

When he got in, Costa found her staring at him.

'Tell me about these statues, Nic,' she asked. 'I must have walked past them a million times. I'd like to know.'

It was good to discuss something that was not to do

with paintings or Caravaggio or, directly, Franco Malas-pina.

So Costa told her about Pasquino, Abate Luigi and Il Facchino, and some of the other lesser-known statues he'd discovered in his recent research, the curious encrusted figure of Il Babuino beyond the Spanish Steps, Madama Lucrezia in the Piazza San Marco, and Marforio, once Pasquino's partner, until the displeased authorities of the Vatican moved the recumbent figure of a sea god to the Campidoglio.

She laughed at his stories, a little anyway, and then, in a few short minutes, they were in the Piazza di San Lorenzo in Lucina, where she ceased to laugh at all.

– 2 –

The Tomassoni house was wreathed in barriers and yellow tape. A lone press photographer hung around outside. For no obvious reason he pulled out an SLR and began firing it the moment the three-car convoy arrived. The officers from the front car leapt out and were around him in an instant. Costa ordered Rosa to take Agata straight to the house. While she was doing that, as quickly and efficiently as her charge would allow, he walked over to confront the individual with the camera.

'What the hell do you think you're doing?' Costa asked the man, who was struggling and swearing in the arms of two plain-clothes officers.

'Earning a living,' the photographer barked back in a southern accent. 'Or trying to. What do you bastards think you're doing? This is a public street. I can do what I like.'

'ID,' Taccone, the *sovrintendente* in charge of the first car, said, and it wasn't a request. He was pulling the card out of the man's wallet already.

'All you had to do was ask,' he moaned. 'This is persecution. We've got rights.'

Costa took the wallet and looked at the photograph and the bare details there.

'Carmine Aprea,' Costa read off the state identity card. 'Well, Carmine . . . where are your press credentials?'

'I don't work inside the system, man,' Aprea answered.

'Then how do I know you do what you say?'

'You call any of the papers. Give them my name. They know me. Maybe they don't like me, but what the hell? So long as they're buying . . .'

He nodded at the house.

'Normally I take pictures of the living. But all these dead people you've got around here. It's been a while since I took a few stiffs. A man needs a change from time to time.'

'*Paparazzo*,' Taccone muttered, and spat on the ground. 'There are no bodies for you in this place. Go find some cheap little actress to pester.'

'How much are you making, moron?' Aprea retorted, looking Taccone up and down. The old *sovrintendente* never was much one for sartorial elegance. It was almost a joke in the Questura. 'I could buy you with one picture, man . . .'

At that point Peroni intervened and his big, scarred, ugly features made the small, pinched-faced individual with the camera go very quiet.

Peroni snatched the bulky black Nikon from Aprea's hands and held it in front of the man's face, lens uppermost, fat metal barrel just a couple of fingers from his swarthy nose.

'Do you know what an endoscope is, Carmine?' he asked.

Aprea screwed up his swarthy features, baffled.

'Kind of, it's—'

'Wrong. This – ' Peroni barked, pushing the Nikon right into Aprea's face – 'is an endoscope. If I see your plug-ugly face again, I'll shove the thing so far up your arse you'll be taking pictures of your own throat. Now get the hell out of here.'

It didn't take another word. Aprea snatched the camera and was walking quickly away, muttering, just loud enough for them to hear, 'Big guys. Big guys. So really big . . .'

'Get out of here . . . Hey!' Peroni yelled.

The photographer had turned and was firing away at them as he walked backwards. Except the lens wasn't aimed in their direction. It was going to the door of Nino Tomassoni's house.

Agata was there, looking at the exterior and the cobbled street, as if trying to recreate some scene in her imagination.

'Inside!' he yelled at Rosa. 'Like I said.'

Peroni started to move. Aprea stopped shooting, just long enough to call out to the two women by the door, '*Grazie, grazie!* I will make you both look beautiful tomorrow.'

Then he turned on his heels and ran, faster than a man of his age ought to, a bulging black shape disappearing into the web of lanes that fed towards the river.

'Leave it,' Costa barked at Peroni.

'We didn't even check . . .' the big man began.

'I said . . .'

He stopped. There was a bigger argument going on and it was coming from the door of Nino Tomassoni's home.

The tall, skinny woman from the city council waved some kind of card in his face as he entered, yelling, 'You will not touch a thing in this house or I'll call my superiors and have you in court for cultural terrorism before dinner.'

Costa looked at her ID. She was from the city heritage department and seemed quite senior.

'Signora . . .' he said calmly. 'We are in the course of a very serious investigation. One that involves multiple murder. Please . . .'

'You are not allowed to knock down protected buildings,' she shrieked.

'For Christ's sake, I keep telling you! I don't want to knock it down.'

Silvio Di Capua was in a white bunny suit that didn't look very white any more. It was covered in mortar and dust. He was holding a sledgehammer in his hands. It looked as if it had been used.

'What do you want to do?' Costa asked.

'Just rip it apart,' Di Capua pleaded. 'A little bit. Not much.'

'You cannot . . .' the woman began.

Agata Graziano had placed her small body between Di Capua and the council woman. There was clearly some recognition there.

'Signora Barducci! Please. You know me. This is important. Listen to these men.'

'You're that nun from the Barberini,' she said. 'What are you doing here?'

'Helping,' Agata replied, and not bothering to correct her. 'Making sure there is as little disruption as possible. This house . . .'

The downstairs hall was covered in the detritus of a police forensic team. Even so, the place was remarkable, like the faded set from some historical movie, with battered furniture and paintings, and a musty, damp smell that spoke of age and solitary occupation.

'Are those gas lamps?' Agata asked.

'The very thing,' said a voice coming down the stairs. It was Teresa Lupo, and she appeared to be covered in even more brick dust than her deputy.

She shook some of the muck off herself, then smiled.

'And that,' she said, 'is why we have to take down the wall.'

The woman waved her long arms in the air.

'No, no, no! I will not permit it.'

'Show me,' Costa ordered, and they followed Teresa up the winding staircase.

THE GARDEN OF EVIL

– 3 –

It was a simple conundrum: there were gas lights on the ground floor and the top. On the landing of the middle floor the lights were electric, though very old indeed.

'This means?' Costa asked.

Teresa glanced at Di Capua.

'He's the building freak. You tell him.'

'It means there's something wrong,' he explained. 'This landing abuts the house next door. This place is such a mess it's hard to tell whether you're up or down half the time. There are no building plans we can refer to. Nothing formal at all . . .'

He cast a vicious look at the woman from the council.

'Not even among the preservation people.'

'It's preserved!' she said. 'The place is sixteenth-century, for God's sake.'

'It's preserved,' Costa agreed. 'What's wrong?'

Di Capua picked up the sledgehammer and, ignoring Signora Barducci's shrieks, tapped it lightly on the wall to the left, then to the right.

'That.'

They all heard it. A distinct, resonant tone came from the right wall, one that had to indicate some space behind.

'The gas line runs up the original right-hand wall,' Di Capua explained. 'There are so many twists and turns on this narrow staircase, it's hard to make out what's happening here. But this isn't the same wall, and that's why it doesn't have it. The mains goes straight up from the ground to the top floor, and into that room over there . . .' He pointed to the single door across the landing. 'But not here.'

Agata walked up and tapped the wall with her knuckles.

'It's still brick,' she said. 'If you're right, this predates gas surely. These houses are from ancient and difficult times. The *caporione* lived here. A man who might have been involved in crime. It would not be unusual to have some private, secret storage place. Most houses of this kind would.'

'Precisely,' Di Capua agreed, and lifted up the sledge-hammer again.

Costa tried to think this through, aware that he felt tired and his shoulder was beginning to ache again.

'But . . .'

Di Capua was getting ready to strike a blow.

'If it's a hidden compartment,' Costa pointed out, voice rising, 'there has to be a way in.'

The hammer stopped in midair. He was aware they were all staring at him, as if expecting an answer.

'Maybe,' Di Capua suggested, 'there used to be a door.'

Teresa swiped him around the head.

'In that case, idiot, it wouldn't have been much of a secret, would it?'

Signora Barducci pushed her way forward, then stood in front of Di Capua, between his hammer and the wall.

'This is another reason why you can't start knocking things down. This and . . .'

She began to reel off a seemingly endless string of statutes and orders, laws and conventions, all to do with her own city department, each demanding prior written permission before a single brick of a protected building in the *centro storico* could be touched.

'Also . . .' she added happily, 'does it possibly occur to you for one moment that this wall might be structural? That by removing its support you could bring this whole house down around our heads? It's happened. I've seen it.'

Di Capua blinked and shook his bald head from side to side. He was wearing his remaining hair long again these days and the locks deposited dust everywhere as they moved.

'Structural?' he asked. 'Structural? Of course it's not structural. If it was, don't you think . . .'

He stopped. They all went quiet, even the Barducci woman. There was a sound, a new sound, at that moment, and it took a few long seconds for Nic Costa to appreciate its source.

Someone was behind the wall, making scrabbling noises, like some gigantic rat rummaging around in the dark.

'What the hell . . .' Teresa began to say.

And then stopped. There was a human being behind the brick and she was screaming.

'Agata,' Costa murmured.

He looked upstairs, closed his eyes for a moment, swore and then took the steps to the upper floor three at a time.

*

There were two forensic officers in the big open room and they retreated behind a couple of paintings when he stormed in.

'Where is she?' Costa shouted.

'Went in there,' said the first one, who looked like a student fresh from college, with bright yellow hair and a terrified expression.

'Where?'

The woman was pointing at a large, long, fitted wardrobe running almost the entire length of the wall. It wasn't difficult to work out this had to stand over the suspect area on the floor below.

'We gave her a torch,' the other forensic monkey added plaintively, as if that was some excuse.

Costa was at the door by then, staring into a Stygian pool of inky darkness.

'Wonderful. Do you have a spare one for me?'

They shrugged in tandem.

He stepped through into the wardrobe and almost immediately found himself struggling to stay upright.

'Agata? *Agata?*'

It was like yelling into a black hole that lurked somewhere beneath him, its dimensions unseeable in the dark. Costa stumbled, and managed to hold onto something made of old, dry wood. The hatch, he guessed, and it was up.

'Where are you?'

His right leg found whatever chasm led down to the floor below, and he began half testing, half lunging for some kind of step.

'Nic?' said a small, frightened voice from below him.

Then a yellow beam of light worked its way back towards him and he saw, for the first time, what she'd found. There was a trapdoor, and steep, almost vertical steps, virtually a stepladder made of worn, old wood, though there was little in the way of dust, as if this place was used regularly.

'It's all right,' he said, reaching the bottom of the stairs. 'I'm here. Walk towards me. Bring the torch.'

The light turned further towards him. She kept it low to the ground always. He couldn't see her face, but soon she was close enough for him to sense her presence. Her hands found his and thrust the torch into his fingers. That brief touch told him she was shaking like a leaf.

'It's all right,' he said again automatically.

'No,' she whispered into his ear. 'It's not.'

Voices began to clamour from behind and above. Teresa had found the entrance too. Costa called up for them to await orders.

The place was a narrow rectangle, perhaps two metres wide and longer than he expected, a good eight metres or so. Big enough to be a child's bedroom, but that wasn't the purpose. She had understood what this was for from the beginning, understood too that there had to be some way in that wasn't obvious, and it could only be from above or below.

At first glance there seemed to be nothing there but battered cardboard boxes that looked many years old and, at the very end, some kind of tall cabinet reaching up two metres.

'I thought the painting might be here. I don't know why. I dreamed . . .'

That she would be the one to find it. He understood that urge on her part. In some way she felt responsible for its loss.

She pulled away from him. He felt, briefly, the touch

of her cheek. It was damp with tears, and she must have realized he'd noticed, since she was soon wiping them away with her sleeve, as she'd wiped away the dust on the glass jug in the Doria Pamphilj.

'It was here,' she insisted. 'Look!'

Her firm, determined fingers forced the beam to the left wall. Costa looked and found his breath locking tight in his lungs.

It was the same shape, surely. The same size. Dust stood around the paler wall where the canvas had hung, undisturbed, for years, centuries perhaps. Above the missing frame, scribbled in pencil, in a hand that looked ancient, someone had scribbled *Evathia in Ekstasis*.

Costa looked at it and thought: that was how they knew. A line of pencil, scribbled God knows how long before, gave Tomassoni the insight into the true nature of the painting, one he passed on to Malaspina with such terrible consequences, ones that were now visible and very real.

Something had taken the place of Caravaggio's work. Knowing she wouldn't look too closely, Costa walked forward and peered at the items that were stuck there. They were the same kind of photos they had found in the studio in the Vicolo del Divino Amore, colour shots from a computer printer, of poor quality, as if snapped by a phone or the cheapest of digital cameras.

There were perhaps ten in all, stuck there with drawing pins. Each depicted a close-up of a woman, all apparently foreign, all seemingly in the throes of ecstasy or pain or the onset of death. Tomassoni may have been reluctant to take part but he clearly liked to watch, then spill out his fears in anonymous emails to the police afterwards.

'The canvas was here all those centuries,' Agata said,

with a cold, sad certainty in her voice. 'Then Franco
found out and took her. He heard what she said to him.
He wanted to. That was Caravaggio's point.'

'We mustn't touch anything,' he insisted. 'This place
must soon be crawling with forensic. Teresa . . .'

'I'm waiting,' said an enthusiastic voice from above.

Agata took the torch from him. Then she strode to the
back of the chamber and the cabinet there. The black
wooden door was ajar. She'd looked already. It was this,
Costa understood, from the way she steeled herself, that
had made her scream, not the shocking photographs in
the space that had once held the painting.

She stopped, her wary eyes urging him to go on.

'Please. I have seen and wish to see no more.'

Costa walked past her and opened the door.

There was a figure there dressed in an archaic tattered
and rat-gnawed velvet jacket, an ancient shirt the colour
of ochre visible at the point that had once been a human
neck. It was merely a skeleton now, dusty bones and the
familiar rictus of death set in a crooked skull.

Costa paused for a moment, thinking. Some kind of
notice sat on the bony chest, held there by dusty string
tied around the back of his head.

He picked it up and read out loud the archaic, awkward words, knowing they sounded familiar.

> '*Noi repetiam Pigmalion allotta,*
> *cui traditore e ladro e paricida*
> *fece la voglia sua de l'oro ghiotta.*'

'I know that,' he said, not expecting a reply. 'Almost.
It's familiar . . . and strange too.'

'Everyone's favourite poet,' she murmured. 'Around here anyway. Dante. From *Purgatorio* if I remember correctly. You probably read the modern translation. Most schoolchildren do.

> *Then we tell of Pygmalion,*
> *Of whom a traitor and thief and parricide*
> *Made his greedy lust for gold.'*

Agata reached out and touched the notice, seeing, with her historian's eye, something that had been lost on him.

'There are two lines through the word *paricida*,' she pointed out. 'What do you think that means?'

He looked. She was right. It had been crossed out the way a teacher would mark a mistaken word in a piece of homework.

'Perhaps that part at least is untrue. They regarded him only as a traitor and a thief.'

'Good,' she said, nodding. 'I would see it that way too. They were like Franco. They enjoyed showing off their so-called learning, even when it was in part inappropriate.'

She had recited the words with the perfect precision of a poet herself. He recalled what Malaspina had said in the palazzo that night: *She sees herself as Beatrice. Beautiful, chaste, alluring. And dead.*

'I'm sorry. I thought I would be some use to you. All I do is make everything murkier. I bring you more puzzles when you need more light. It's a waste of time. Put me somewhere safe if that's what Leo wants. I won't complain.'

'I will,' he said, shifting the sign to one side, looking

at what lay beneath it, resting on the grey bones of the rib-cage that was visible through the ripped fabric of the shirt. 'We need you.'

'Why?' she asked softly. 'So that you can bury your wife, finally? Is that what I'm supposed to do for you?'

Costa turned and looked at her. In the yellow half-light of the torch she seemed, for the first time, he thought, a woman, much like any other. Not part of some different life he couldn't begin to comprehend.

'No,' he replied simply. 'I'll do that myself, when I'm ready.'

'Then what?'

The heat rose in her eyes.

Costa put a finger to his lips. This once, she obeyed him and became silent. He walked to the steps, barked a few questions at Teresa Lupo and Silvio Di Capua, then had them throw down a couple of clear plastic evidence bags.

'You may not want to watch this,' he said when he got back to the cabinet.

'Why not?' she demanded. 'What have you seen? Tell me!'

'This . . .'

He moved the sign to one side and indicated an area on the left of the corpse's chest. There was an object there, some kind of round medallion, dull dark metal on a similarly coloured chain, but with the outline of the emblem at its centre still visible, still comprehensible.

Three dragons, limbs thrashing, talons wrapped around the figure of a woman who writhed in their grip, screaming, eyes rolling wildly.

'This is the same symbol we found on the notes the Ekstasists placed on the statues,' he said. 'Now we know where that came from. It's a link. A tentative one, but I'll take whatever I can get.'

'A link,' she grumbled, and folded her arms.

'And this . . .'

He pushed aside completely the yellowing paper bearing Dante's words and shone the torchlight directly on the portion of the velvet jacket next to the dull black medallion. At first it had seemed a wild guess. Now, under the fierce beam, it was unmistakable.

'You don't recognize it, do you?' he asked.

It was a heraldic badge: a shield divided into two halves, with a skeletal tree bearing three short horizontal branches on one side and two on the other, dotted with spines.

'I don't notice much except paintings,' Agata replied with a frown. 'Usually.'

'It's all over Franco's beautiful palace. It's his family crest. The bad thorn.'

In this small, stuffy room that was cold and damp, Agata Graziano laughed.

'That's impossible!'

'Take a look.'

She did and shook her head.

'Who on earth is this? What does it mean?'

'Finally,' he said, 'you're asking me a question.'

'Yes.'

He nodded.

'Then, as a police officer, I would guess this is a murder victim.'

'I know that . . .'

'Given the identification, one who was once known as Ippolito Malaspina.'

She put her fingers to her mouth with shock.

'That's impossible! How could you know?'

She stopped, thinking, eyes glittering.

Everything connects in Rome, he reminded himself. Past and present. And in this case the crimes of four centuries before.

'I can't. But I can guess,' he said emphatically. 'You showed us the portrait that was supposed to be Ippolito in Malta, several years after he left Rome. You said yourself, it was nothing like the description of the man in all the reference books you found . . .'

'That doesn't mean . . .'

'He had a family,' Costa interrupted. 'Was that before he left the city with Caravaggio or after?'

'Before. Afterwards he travelled constantly and never . . .' She stopped and stared at him. 'He never returned home. Never went anywhere he had been before, as far as I recall. They inherited everything when he died. And . . .'

He watched her turn this over in her bright, constantly active mind.

'Is it possible,' he asked, 'that they inherited everything without ever seeing him again? That Franco Malaspina is descended from the real Malaspina, but the man who went to Malta with Caravaggio was an impostor?'

'Yes,' she answered in a low, firm voice. 'From what I've read . . .'

'Good,' Costa said, then took out the plastic envelope and stared at the grey, dusty skull in front of him.

'What are you going to do?' she asked.

'Find the evidence to put Franco in jail.'

'From a corpse that's four hundred years old?'

'Why not? We can't go near him. But he is an aristocrat. His lineage is there, set down in the state archives. If the DNA of this corpse is related to that we have from the Vicolo del Divino Amore, all we have to prove is that this gentleman – ' he prodded the velvet jacket with his forefinger – 'is Ippolito Malaspina. It won't put his descendant in the dock. But it would make it damned hard for a court to refuse a few tests to prove the truth one way or another, and that's all we need.'

She didn't look scared any more. She looked fascinated.

'You can do that?' she asked. 'Take a sample from a skeleton that's nothing but . . . bone?'

'No!'

The loud female voice made them both jump. Costa couldn't work out how Teresa Lupo had found her way down the stepladder without their noticing. She barged her way in front of him and stared at the skeleton. Then she snatched the envelope out of his hands.

'But I can,' she said with a grin that was wide and friendly in the yellow light of the torch.

The pathologist leaned forward. In her gloved hand was an implement very like a small set of pliers. She gazed at the skull's open mouth. The left-hand front tooth was missing already. Teresa fastened the pliers to the remaining one, then, in a swift, twisting movement, snapped it free and dropped the object into the bag.

'You're coming home with Mummy,' she added, greatly pleased with herself. 'Right now.'

She stared at the pair of them.

'And you two should go home as well. You've done enough for one day.'

Teresa held up the bag.

'There is a time for happy conjecture and a time for science, children. Tomorrow is Christmas. Come back and see what La Befana and her little elves have for you.'

Part 14

THE NIGHT BEFORE CHRISTMAS

- 1 -

La Vigilia was already stealing over Rome; Christmas Eve, a pause from the rush and chaos of everyday life. The convoy drove back to the farmhouse through streets that were dark and deserted. There was no need for the fairy lights any more, no cause to be anywhere but home, in the company of family and friends. Teresa and her team might relish the idea of spending the night poring over the contents of Nino Tomassoni's secret lair, trying to decode the genetic fingerprint hidden inside the tooth of a skull of an unknown man who just might – Costa knew this was a stretch – turn out to be Ippolito Malaspina. But for the rest of the city this was a time for reflection and enjoyment.

And food: *seven fishes*. No real Roman ate meat at La Vigilia. It was always fish, by tradition seven types, one, his father used to say, for every Catholic sacrament. Even in the Costa household, which, during his childhood, was more solidly communist, and atheist, than any he knew in Lazio, it was impossible to separate La Vigilia from the custom of the seven fishes.

The godless needed rituals too from time to time.

As they reached the drive and the two guard cars

peeled off to block the entrance behind them, Costa wondered why this memory had returned at such a time. Then, dog-tired and ready for bed, just as Agata clearly was too, he opened the door for her to enter and a succession of aromas and fragrances wafted out from the kitchen beyond, ones that took him back twenty years in an instant and sent a strong sense of urgent hunger rumbling through his stomach.

Bea stood there in her best evening dress, wearing a huge white, perfectly ironed apron. By her side, Pepe the terrier sat upright, a red ribbon round his neck.

'Happy Christmas,' Bea said, welcoming them with a bow, then making to take their coats.

Agata's face lit up. She sniffed at the rich and exotic aromas drifting from the kitchen.

'What *is* this?' she asked.

'And you a Christian,' Bea scolded her. 'It's La Vigilia. Christmas Eve. And I am a spinster with much time on my hands and a fondness for the old ways. So you will sit down and dine with me. Do not try to play the vegetarian here, young man. I've seen you eat fish.'

'Seven?' he asked.

'Of course,' she replied, as if it were an idiotic question. 'Now go upstairs and change. This is a special occasion. If the dog can dress for it, so can you.'

Agata ran her slim fingers over the black, hand-me-down coat.

'I am fine like this, Bea. I have nothing . . .'

Bea wiped her hands on her apron, then helped Agata out of the coat, holding it away from her, as if it were a thing of no value.

'Sometimes La Befana comes early. Even for those who come home late. Now go upstairs! Shoo! Shoo!'

The dog barked.

'La Befana?' Agata gasped, eyes glittering.

Bea watched her ascend the stairs quickly, like a child.

'See,' she said quietly, 'she is only human after all.'

They sat around the long table in the dining room, Bea at the head, guiding them through the spread of food, which seemed to grow with every passing minute: cold seafood salad, salt cod, mussels, clams, shrimps, a small lobster, then, finally, the delicacy his father always insisted on, however much it cost, *capitone*, a large female eel, split into pieces and roasted in the oven wreathed in bay leaves.

Agata sat there, astonished, eating greedily. Somehow, during the shopping, Bea had found time to buy her a new white shirt and plain blue trousers. She wore them, with the customary battered crucifix around her neck, and within minutes had sauce and debris spattered everywhere, on her clothes and on the table. Bea gave up staring in the end. It was of no consequence.

'This is obscene,' Agata cried when the eel finally appeared.

'Compared with what we've seen . . .' Costa observed quietly.

'No work,' Bea snapped. 'I didn't sweat in that kitchen for hours to listen to you two moan about your day. That is the rule. La Vigilia! Eat! And then . . .'

She went to the kitchen and came back with a plate of sweet cakes and a bowl full of small presents wrapped in gold paper.

'Then what?' Agata asked.

'Then we choose from the bowl,' Bea responded. 'What do you normally do at Christmas, for pity's sake?'

Agata shrugged, then picked up a large piece of eel, stuffed it in her mouth and said, while chewing, 'Pray. Sing. Think. Read.'

'And?' Bea asked, ignoring the warning glance Costa hoped he was sending her way.

'And . . . take a little wine before midnight mass.' She cocked her head towards the window. Her hair was now so different. She was different. Costa wondered whether he ought to feel guilty for that change.

'Can you hear the cannon from the Castel Sant'Angelo when they fire it?' she asked brightly.

'No,' he answered. 'Sorry. We could find it on the television perhaps.'

'It wouldn't be the same.'

Bea carefully refilled their glasses with prosecco.

'Is a cannon important?' she asked.

'It means midnight mass is not far away,' Agata responded immediately. 'I love midnight mass. More than anything. I love the little shows the churches have, with their manger and their infant, Mary and the shepherds. I love the way people look at one another. Another year navigated. Another year to come.'

She put down her knife and fork, then wiped her hands with her napkin.

'There are churches nearby,' Agata said hopefully. 'Beautiful ones in the Appian Way. Do you think I could go? How many people would be there in a desert like this? You could come with me.' She glanced at Bea. 'Both of you, I mean, naturally. I would not hope to evangelize. You've shown me your world. Can I not show you a little of mine?'

Bea coughed into her fist and stared at her plate.

'Do you think Leo Falcone would allow that?' Costa asked. 'A church is . . . a very open place.'

'It's supposed to be,' she said quietly.

There was silence. Then, after a while, she added, somewhat downcast, 'I've never missed midnight mass. Not in my whole life. Or the sound of that cannon for as long as I can remember.'

'I'm sorry.'

She smiled at him.

'But you would do it if you could.'

'Certainly.'

Agata was watching him in a way he found vaguely unsettling.

'What would you have done?' she asked. 'Before? With Emily?'

He had to think.

'Last year we had a meal with Leo and his friend, Teresa and Gianni,' he said, when he finally managed to recover the memories. 'In the city.' He nodded at Bea over the table. 'It wasn't a patch on this food.'

But this Christmas it would have been different, more private, spent at home, just the two of them. Emily was his wife, finally. Had they not lost the child she was carrying in the spring . . .

This thought – another of those painful, hypothetical leaps of a cruel imagination – assaulted him. Had Emily kept the child, she would have given up college by now. There would have been no reason for her to have been lurking near the Mausoleum of Augustus on a dull December day, no energy left to be wasted following a fleeing fugitive the way her old skills from the FBI had taught her.

There would have been two new lives in the old farmhouse at that moment. *If* . . .

Costa blinked back something in his eye. The two women were watching him. He wondered whether to make an excuse and leave the table.

'I'm sorry,' Agata murmured. 'I should never have asked that.'

'No,' he replied emphatically. 'You can't undo the past by ignoring it. What has happened has happened. I don't want anyone – ' he glanced at Bea – 'to let me pretend it can be undone somehow.'

The two women exchanged a brief look. He could see they hoped he hadn't noticed.

'It's the silence,' Agata said, changing the subject rapidly. 'To me it shouts. Is that strange? That I miss the noise of the traffic? The buses? The people outside my window who've had a little too much to drink and sing so loudly, so badly, I have to laugh beneath my sheets?'

'Of course not,' he answered. 'You miss what you're familiar with. It's only natural. You miss the background of the world you know. You miss what you love.'

'Just like you,' she said quickly, without thinking, glass in hand, her eyes bright with life and interest now. 'I'm sorry. Just like . . .'

Her fingers flew to her face. She had drunk the wine too quickly, too freely. Something in her firm reserve, which had been so resolute ever since he first met her in the Barberini's studio at the back of the Palazzo Malaspina, was now crumbling visibly.

'I didn't meant that,' she stuttered. 'It's the food, the drink. It's me. Oh . . . *Oh* . . .'

Agata ran from the room, tears welling in her eyes, and raced into the corridor beyond.

Costa blinked.

'What did I say?'

Bea sighed and declared, 'Nothing.'

'Then . . . what?'

'Oh, try to think, Nic. The poor child's not seen anything like this. She's not used to family. Or the idea two people can talk honestly with one another. Damn the Church for doing that to someone. I doubt she's had that much decent food and prosecco in her entire life. That and God knows what you've shown her. It's my fault. I'm sorry. This meal was an idiotic idea.'

'You cannot judge her like that,' he said, with a sudden brief burst of anger.

Bea put out her hand and touched his cheek.

'I don't. Believe me. I was trying to help. To show her what it's like outside that prison of hers.'

'She doesn't see it that way. It's none of your business. Or mine either.'

'Isn't it?'

The day had been too long. There was a surfeit of ideas and images and possibilities running round his exhausted head. His shoulder hurt. His mind felt bruised from over-activity.

'You really don't have the faintest idea, do you?' she asked tartly.

'No . . .' he answered softly, a vague, disturbing thought rising from somewhere he wished it had remained.

Bea held out the bowl with the tiny presents in it.

'You might as well take one anyway.'

He did. It was what had always happened, even when he was a child. The rules, the laws that governed this game, demanded one small box be empty and as usual it was his.

'This is not your day,' Bea declared. 'Go to bed now, and leave everything – including our young friend Agata – to me.'

– 2 –

He knew the house so well he felt he could hear the old stones breathing as they slept. When he awoke the clock by the bed said 3 a.m. and someone, elsewhere, was awake.

Costa pulled on a dressing gown and went downstairs. She was where he least expected, in the studio, and it didn't look anything like he remembered.

From somewhere – Rosa had brought them, he guessed – she had found a series of photographs of the missing painting. Caravaggio's sensual, fleshy image of Venus – or Eve, he was unsure which any more – stood on several of Emily's easels, in full frame, close up, and very fine detail in several of the shots too. Agata was perched on the single artist's stool by the desk, staring at the biggest photo, a finger on her cheek, thinking, seemingly as alert as ever, a large pile of documents and what appeared to be an old book by her side.

'It doesn't really look like that now, though,' he said.

She jumped, surprised, perhaps a little embarrassed, by his appearance. She still wore the clothes Bea had found for her, the shirt spattered with food. She hadn't been to bed at all.

'How do you mean?' she asked, placing her elbow over the papers, as if she didn't want him to see.

'You found the signature. And the real name.'

She frowned.

'You found the name. Besides, now I've had the chance to think about it, I'm not sure it's as important as all that. Caravaggio was playing a game with them. Painting something they thought they could keep to themselves because it was so shocking . . .'

She pointed to the face of the satyr, the artist's own.

'He was part of it too. One of the Ekstasists. The man had a sense of humour, you know. He was laughing at them, and perhaps at himself as well.'

Costa came and stood next to her. The photograph did not do the painting justice. The work seemed distant somehow, lacking in the force and meaning that were so powerful, so unavoidable, when the canvas was in front of one's face. It possessed something that could not be conveyed through the modern medium of a camera.

'It doesn't mean he was a part of whatever they did. Perhaps he simply knew them and accepted the commission.'

'Oh, don't talk such rubbish.' She gave him a withering look. The teacher in her had returned. 'Remember the way he signed it? Why would he describe himself as an Ekstasist if he was outside the club? How would he even know the name? Don't blind yourself to the truth, Nic. Michelangelo Merisi was part angel, part devil. Like most men, only more so. We know he was involved in cruel and criminal acts. In the end it cost him everything. He was with them. I can feel it. Nothing else makes sense. I just wish . . .'

She stopped and scratched her head.

'Why are you still awake?' he asked.

'How can I sleep?' she complained, still unable to take her attention away from the photographs. 'I miss everything about my home. The noises. The female company. The routine. The fact I'm safe there. I don't have to worry about all these troubles that bother you . . .'

'You will return,' he assured her. 'As soon as possible.'

'I hope so,' Agata replied, but not with much conviction. She stared at him. 'Tell me. If there was some way I could find out why it all went wrong that first time round, with Caravaggio and Tomassoni. Why some stupid, juvenile band of thugs degenerated into murder and bloody hatred. Just as it did with Franco. Would that help?'

'You still don't understand this, do you?' he declared, almost exasperated. 'What it is that we do?'

'You establish facts and then act on them. Of course I understand that.'

Costa shook his head.

'No, you don't. Sometimes the facts lead nowhere. You have to fill them out with guesswork, imagination.'

'That idea offends me. It's not scholarly. Not scientific.'

'Is the Bible?'

'It's scholarly.'

'As is Teresa's laboratory, but Franco Malaspina has denied us that. We don't have those luxuries any more. Emily and those women are dead. Franco Malaspina and his accomplices were responsible somehow. What we need are plain, ordinary, unassailable facts that link him to them. We can't find any. So instead . . .'

'Guesswork,' she grumbled. 'But would it help if you understood about the Ekstasists?'

'I have absolutely no way of knowing. Why?'

She hesitated and eyed him nervously.

'I was just curious. I'm sorry about tonight,' she said in a low, nervy voice. 'Sometimes I speak too freely.'

'Too much wine.'

'That was an excuse. I hardly touched the wine. I simply . . .' Still she wouldn't look at him. 'I don't belong in a place like this. It's mundane and close and personal in a way that's beyond me. I know that's selfish. I'm sorry.'

'It doesn't matter.'

'Don't say that. It does. All that beautiful food. The care Bea took.' She shrugged her slender shoulders and wrapped her arms around the stained white shirt. 'I never expected to be a part of such an evening. I didn't even know anything like it ever existed really . . .'

Agata walked rapidly over to the desk, which was still littered with Emily's drawings.

'Do you think I'm wasting my life?' she asked him from across the room. 'Be honest.'

'Do you?'

'It's very unfair to answer a question with another question. Answer me, please. Look at what your wife did. She drew, she thought, she tried to create things. One day I imagine you would have had a family. And I . . .'

She scowled, an expression of moody dissatisfaction spreading across her face.

'I stare at paintings and try to find life in them. Why? For myself. Because I daren't face the real thing. It's egotistical, obsessive, unnatural.'

'I can't give you an answer,' he said.

'Why not?'

'Because I don't know you well enough. And even if I did it would be presumptuous. To ask another human being whether there's value in your own existence . . . that's for you to judge.'

She thought about this.

'But you placed a value on Emily's life,' she pointed out. 'You still do. I see her in your eyes, like a mist that's always there. Her memory drives you, more than anything I have ever seen in another person. I can't imagine what you'll feel if this need you have to bring Franco Malaspina to justice isn't satisfied.'

'That won't happen.'

'It might.'

She walked over and stood in front of him again.

'You're trawling through grey dust and old bones for an answer now. How desperate does a man need to be to do that?'

'I prefer to think of it as determined.'

Agata laughed. Not in the way she did when they first met. This was open and happy and carefree.

'You know,' she murmured, 'I used to stare at people in your world and pity you all. So much pain. So much to worry about.'

She pulled a dissatisfied face.

'And so much life too.' Her hands came away from the silver cross on the chain. Nervously, she tucked a stray strand of hair behind her ear, then looked him straight in the eye and said, 'I had to ask myself tonight whether I really wanted to go back to the convent. Whether this life – your kind of life – wasn't a more honest one. I've never really faced that question before. It's been there. Before any of this happened. I recognize that now.'

'Agata . . .'

Her dark eyes burned with the keen curiosity that was never far away.

'It's very late, Nic. I think I should go to bed.'

His head felt heavy. He was unsure what to do, what to think.

Then the lights came on in the corridor, and he heard the sound of feet on the old wooden floor, and not long after the yapping of the dog.

Bea appeared at the door and turned on the big bright floods Emily had installed in the ceiling of the studio for her work. Costa stood there, blinking in the glare.

'I . . . I'm sorry,' Bea stuttered, embarrassed. 'I heard voices. I didn't know—'

'No matter,' Agata cut in swiftly. 'We had business to discuss. Now that's done I shall sleep. Goodnight.'

She walked away from him, kissed Bea on the cheek and left the room.

'Goodnight,' Costa said to the small, slight figure disappearing towards the stairs.

Part 15

A SPORT IN THE BLOOD

– 1 –

Christmas Day was grey and wet, the cloud so low it almost touched the tops of the jagged monuments littering the horizon of the Appian Way. Costa woke late, his shoulder hurting. The women were downstairs already, dressed and ready for whatever the day would bring. Peroni was with them, looking thoroughly miserable.

'Coffee,' Agata ordered, raising her cup. '*Buon Natale!*'

The smell of Bea's cappuccino could wake the dead. He gulped it down gratefully with some fruit and pastries. Then Bea went through the ceremony that had been interrupted the night before: the bowl and the little gifts.

This time round he got a tiepin. Peroni picked out a cheap keyring with a tiny torch attached to the chain and managed to look extraordinarily pleased with it. Bea grabbed one of the remaining two boxes – and didn't open it – then pressed the final one on Agata.

'This seems like a fix,' she murmured, but took it anyway.

There was a small silver crucifix inside.

'It's beautiful,' Agata said gratefully. 'I will wear it on

special occasions. It's too good – ' she wrinkled her nose – 'for anything else.'

'Whenever suits you,' Bea said easily, and opened her box. It possessed something similar, doubtless from the same collection: a brooch in the shape of a butterfly. She looked at the two men. 'Now go away, you two, and have the conversation you want to have. We don't wish to hear.'

'Conversation?' Costa began, and found Peroni dragging him off to the sitting room, his face like stone.

They sat down. Peroni pointed back towards the kitchen.

'That is the most stubborn, pig-headed woman I have ever met in my life. She makes Teresa look like a saint, for God's sake. I can't believe—'

'Bea?'

'Not Bea.'

'I've been sleeping, Gianni,' he said quickly. 'And you speak in riddles. Please . . .'

Costa listened, and wished, for a moment, he didn't have to.

Even mafiosi celebrated Christmas. The tentative tip-off from the informer in Naples had been superseded. The previous evening one of the most senior capos in the same city had taken an equally senior police officer into his home for a traditional La Vigilia supper. In the course of the meal, the crime boss had told his acquaintance that a contract on the life of Agata Graziano was now in place, in the hands of the 'Ndrangheta from Calabria, secretive men, rarely penetrated by the police, professional criminals who took on commissions from outsiders only rarely, and usually saw them through.

'You told her?' Costa asked.

'Of course I told her,' Peroni answered. 'How can you keep something like that secret? Falcone has made all the arrangements. We have a safe house in Piedmont she can use. If necessary we could come up with some kind of new identity, a place in the witness protection scheme . . .'

'Agata won't agree to that. Not for an instant.'

'Why not?' Peroni demanded. 'These are serious people. Malaspina wants her dead. We can't protect her properly here. Falcone has decided. She must go. Today. Now.'

He folded his arms.

'Tell her. I have. She refuses. She says if we keep on nagging she'll take a cab back to that convent of hers and send us the bill.'

'You could try making her,' Costa suggested.

'Don't play the smartarse with me, sir. We can't make her. If she wants to walk straight out of here and wander round Rome till she's dead there's nothing we can do to prevent it. She's a free woman.'

'I'm not sure that's really true,' Costa found himself saying.

'We can't stop her. She's adamant she wants to be part of the next conference we have. Teresa has called one at the Tomassoni place for two. After that we have to go to the morgue. Like an idiot, Falcone told her.'

'She's helped us, Gianni,' Costa pointed out. 'We'd still be arguing with Toni Grimaldi if it weren't for her.'

'She won't be able to help us much if she's dead. Besides . . .'

Costa stared at the damaged, miserable face of the man who'd come to be one of his closest friends over the past few years. There was more to Peroni's sorrowful state than the steadfast refusal of Agata Graziano to disappear from Rome.

'Besides what?'

'We are still arguing with Grimaldi. There are bad noises coming from above. The kind people make when they are facing nasty decisions.'

Peroni's big farmer's face, scarred in ways Costa barely noticed any more these days, fell into a deep, miserable scowl.

'Such as?' Costa asked.

'I don't know, but I have a rotten feeling we're about to find out. Malaspina is starting to affect us in all kinds of ways. Other forces are starting to become involved. The Carabinieri are on the line constantly. I imagine that is just what he wants. There are investigations everywhere crawling to a halt because of evidence problems. The word is getting out there, Nic. These hoodlums understand all they have to do is cross their arms and say no to a swab or a fingerprint and everything goes into the queue with the lawyers.'

'How the hell do they know?'

Peroni looked at him as if he were an idiot.

'Because we're in Rome. Because people are human. There's talk. What's new? Everyone's starting to realize what the problem is. If we can't corroborate what we have, Malaspina will simply prance up and down in front of us, waving his fingers in the air, and there's not a thing we can do about it.' Peroni's sharp, piercing eyes didn't blink. 'Those men from Calabria will get their chance and then they'll be gone, without a single footprint back to the Palazzo Malaspina. We've lost enough people already. Let's not lose any more.'

Costa got up and walked into the kitchen to find Agata sitting on a stool, her attention deep inside the pages of one of Bea's women's magazines. She looked bemused.

'I think there's something important we need to discuss—' he began.

'The answer's no,' she cut in. 'I called Leo and told him again while you were talking. He is . . . acquiescent. This meeting with Teresa is at two. I would like to visit my sisters briefly along the way, if that is permissible.'

She looked up at him and smiled: a different woman, the same? He wasn't sure. There was something in Agata Graziano's face at that moment he didn't recognize, though in another woman he would have called it guile.

'So shall we go?' she asked, picking up the black leather bag Rosa Prabakaran had provided the day before, one that looked as much at home on her now as it would have done on any young woman in Rome.

– 2 –

She spent an hour in the convent, a grey, anonymous building close to the river and the bridge to the Castel Sant'Angelo. No men were allowed past the high wooden door, so Rosa Prabakaran and two other female officers accompanied her, and came out none the wiser. Agata had simply gone to her room and the chapel, spoken to some other sisters, entered the library to consult some books, then returned in just enough time for them to make the meeting with the forensic team.

The terraced house in the Piazza di San Lorenzo in Lucina was unrecognizable. Half the square was now blocked off to allow forensic officers clear access. The ancient, moth-eaten furniture from the ground floor had been removed. A sanitized plastic tunnel now ran through the front door for visitors. In the space between plastic and wall, men and women in white suits were on hands and knees performing a fingertip search of every last crack in the ancient floor, every mote of dust in the corners. The route led through the entire central, twisting staircase, a sterile cocoon through which they would pass until, Teresa said, they got to the top floor, where the work was essentially done and there was enough room for a meeting.

Halfway up Agata stopped and stared at the area where, the day before, she had found herself face to face with the skull of the corpse Costa prayed would turn out to be Ippolito Malaspina. This section of the building was transformed. Silvio Di Capua had clearly won his battle with the city planning authorities. Gigantic iron supports had been brought in to run from floor to ceiling, and workmen had removed the wall brick by brick, revealing the rectangular hidden room behind. Open to view, it seemed much smaller. The cabinet was still there, now empty. The boxes of documents that he had seen lining the far wall had disappeared too.

He knew Teresa's methods well. She was a woman who was directed, always, by priorities, and possessed an instinctive grasp of what was worth seizing first. Forensic on the strange skeleton Agata had found would surely be uppermost in her mind. But she understood, as well as any, that this was no straightforward case, no hunt for incriminating evidence. They had that already. What they needed was a link – a connection that placed Franco Malaspina in this dingy, rotting building, and made him a part of the Ekstasists, in such a firm and undeniable way that even the most sceptical or malleable of magistrates could not ignore it.

Whatever hopes he had in that direction faded the moment they entered the top floor, where the canvases were now stacked neatly to one side. Toni Grimaldi stood close by in a grey suit, a short cigar in his hand and a sour expression on his face.

'Oh, wonderful,' Peroni murmured, rather too loudly for comfort.

'Merry Christmas, gentlemen,' Grimaldi announced with a yawn before lifting the sackcloth on one of the canvases, squinting at what he saw and adding, 'They say this stuff is worth millions.'

Agata strode over and threw the sackcloth off entirely.

'Poussin,' she declared, with the briefest of scowls. 'At least it's supposed to be. Leo?'

Falcone came away from the window, where he'd been staring idly into the piazza.

'Poussin it is,' he agreed. 'If you think it's a fake best tell the people in Stockholm now, because they have other ideas.'

'It's their painting,' she replied, then stared at the newcomer.

'How goes your case, Sister?' Grimaldi asked under the heat of her glare.

'I don't have a case.'

He shrugged.

'Maybe you're not the only one. Let me make my position clear. Today . . . Christmas Day . . . I listen to what they have to say. Then I decide whether to allow you to put it in front of a magistrate. Once again. Think of me as that man or woman of the judiciary. Before you can convince them you must convince me. Should you fail . . .'

He bestowed a humourless smile on all of them. Grimaldi almost always wore the expression Costa associated with Questura lawyers, the one that said, *I will stop you doing anything stupid because I know I can*. He was also one of the smartest and most assiduous men they had, a decent, dedicated police official who would work every minute of the day to get a conviction when he thought there was a chance of one.

'Franco stole all these paintings, didn't he?' Agata

asked, raking her slender arm around the room. 'Isn't that enough?'

'Prove it,' Grimaldi replied.

Falcone's long, lean face wrinkled with displeasure.

'You know we can't. Yet. But look at the circumstantial evidence.'

'I've looked at little else for weeks,' the lawyer answered. 'Let me summarize. Nino Tomassoni was involved in an art theft ring. So, the French would have it, was this Véronique Gillet. Malaspina knew both, socially, perhaps intimately in the case of the woman.'

'He slept with her,' Costa said. 'He told me so.'

'Sleeping with a suspected criminal is an offence?' Grimaldi asked, throwing his big arms open in a theatrical gesture.

Peroni spoke up.

'Toni, we have known each other for many years. I understand your caution—'

'This is not caution. This is plain common sense and good practice. You have nothing. Even those dreadful photographs you found here. Have you a single woman to interview as a result?'

The colour rose in Falcone's face.

'They're either dead or back in Africa. Give us a chance, man. A little time.'

'You don't have time, Leo. This investigation has cost the Questura a fortune in legal fees alone. And where are you? Malaspina has all of us tied up in knots. You can't ask him to take the most basic of scientific tests because he's used your ham-fisted investigations against you—'

'Not ours,' Falcone cut in.

'The law does not distinguish between competent

police officers and incompetent ones. You're all the same in the eyes of the magistrate. That is why you cannot use your swabs on this man. Or anyone else who is unwilling, if they know about this loophole. Please, you have made us enough work already. Do you know what *our* priority is at this moment?'

'To put this murderous bastard in jail?' Peroni asked, as livid as Falcone now.

'Live in the real world, Gianni,' the lawyer retorted. 'In the absence of an impending arrest, our priority must be to overturn this judgement in principle that Malaspina obtained against you.'

Falcone turned and looked at him.

'"In principle"?' he repeated.

'In principle. Must I spell this out?'

Agata, clearly baffled, said, 'For me you must.'

'Very well,' Grimaldi agreed. 'If I try to attack the individual ruling that Malaspina won, then I open up every nasty black bag of worms you people have provided him with. The harassment. The unproven and unprovable allegations. The use of evidence that does not meet the most basic of legal rules. The very personal nature in which you pursued this investigation.'

'The man is a crook and a murderer,' Falcone complained.

Grimaldi was unimpressed.

'And an aristocrat with more money and connections than most of us could dream of in several lifetimes. Think about it. See this through our eyes.'

Costa was starting to get a sick feeling in his stomach.

'Through your eyes?' he asked.

The lawyer hesitated. He didn't appear to enjoy his position any more than the rest of them.

'We may have to make choices. Unless you can come up with something very soon. Such as today. Or tomorrow at the latest . . .' He coughed into his big fist, embarrassed by what he was going to say. 'Without that I'm going to have to recommend to the *commissario* that we scale down this investigation, take the heat off this man and hope we can come to some kind of arrangement.'

'What the hell does that mean?' Peroni bellowed.

'It means . . .' Grimaldi looked deeply unhappy. 'I have to be practical about this. If you can't nail him, I must ask myself a broader question. Shouldn't I be thinking of the future instead? Of all those men like him who'll get away using the same trick? If I can cut a deal with Malaspina so that he leaves us alone to close that loophole, and we don't make it retrospective, which might be hard anyway . . .'

There was silence in the room. Even the handful of scene of crime officers had stopped work and turned to stare at the large lawyer in the grey suit, astonished, appalled.

'It's not as if Franco Malaspina is going to go out there and start his tricks again, is he?' Grimaldi looked like a man at bay. 'You people tell me what the right thing to do is. Fail to imprison some murdering bastard who's finished killing? Or find a way to try to hit the sons of bitches out there who are about to start?'

The man appealed to Teresa Lupo.

'You're forensic. You tell me. What would you rather have? Him on the streets, not daring to touch another woman in his life, and the way it all was before? Or him on the streets and you still trying to do the job with your hands tied behind your back. Well?'

It was Agata who spoke.

'I'm just a sister,' she said, staring at him. 'But I think you can only judge a man on what he's done, not what he might do. These crimes . . .' She caught Costa's eye. 'If one turns a blind eye to them, what sense of justice is there anywhere?'

'Fine!' the lawyer yelled. 'I deal in the law, Sister. I leave justice to priests and nuns like you.' He stabbed a finger at Teresa Lupo. 'Tell me, do you want your toys back or not?'

The pathologist just stared at him and shook her head.

'You know,' she said quietly, 'just when I think I'm working my way out of the habit of wanting to hit people, someone like you comes along. Will you shut up and listen for a moment? I'm greedy. I want both. Let's run through the small business here quickly, then go to the morgue and stare at some bones. And if that fails—'

'Then I go home to my family,' Grimaldi cut in. 'So do you have anything that links Malaspina with this place? Anything at all?'

The two forensic scientists stared at one another, anxious and, for once, silent.

There was, in truth, very little to tie any of it to Malaspina. A set of stolen paintings worth tens of millions of euros, looted from a variety of public institutions throughout Europe over a period of seven years. Some documents, found in the boxes in the hidden room, indicating that Nino Tomassoni acted as a kind of warehouseman for whatever gang was involved in the thefts. The photographs from the gap in the wall where the Caravaggio had once stood. One single piece of paper that linked the late Véronique Gillet to the loop: an email sent from her Louvre address, revealing the movement of a Miró canvas from Barcelona to Madrid, a journey during which it had been stolen. Finally the clear evidence that it was Tomassoni who had been sending messages to the Questura in an anonymous effort to draw the police's attention to the crimes.

'This is it?' Grimaldi asked. 'Not a trace of Malaspina in the house. Not a fingerprint. Not a single document . . .'

'The emails Tomassoni sent to the Questura name Malaspina,' Teresa pointed out.

'Uncorroborated gossip from a dead man,' the lawyer observed.

'Give us time,' Falcone pleaded. 'We're inundated with material. We can't cope with what we have. It could be weeks. Months.'

'You don't have months, Leo,' Grimaldi replied with marked impatience. 'I wish I could say you did. This happens to be my professional opinion. But it's more than that. It's a political issue too these days. The justice people are calling. Everyone is calling. The wheels are starting to come off everywhere, not just with us, with the Carabinieri, the local police, the customs people . . . Everyone is affected by this and I'm the one who gets the phone call. The criminal fraternity *know*. Very soon every last one of them will understand they can, in the absence of other hard evidence, duck a fingerprint or a swab. Fifteen years ago we didn't even have these things and we put people in jail all the time. Now it seems that, without them, we're screwed.'

Costa thought he could hear Esposito's voice in all this. The new *commissario* was a pragmatic man, one who would not wish to be tied by the mistakes of others.

'We've a wealth of material,' Teresa said confidently. 'We're working as quickly as we can. There are reams of documents downstairs . . .'

'You said they were historical,' the lawyer retorted.

'They are,' she answered, uncertain of herself.

'So what use is that?' Grimaldi flung his hands in the air. 'This is here. This is now. If you want me to prosecute Franco Malaspina I need evidence from this century, not the scribbles of a few ghosts.'

'And if a ghost could talk?' Agata asked quietly.

'I'd look even more of an idiot trying to sell this farrago of loose ends to a magistrate.'

Agata took the black bag off her shoulder and Costa realized, at that moment, what was wrong. The thing was heavier, and had been since some time the previous day.

She retrieved a large, thick book from its interior, one bound in dark leather cracked with age. Agata opened it and they all saw what was on the page: line after line of scribbled script, broken into paragraphs with dated headings. A journal. A diary from another time.

'You took this from that room?' Costa asked. 'Without my seeing? You stole it before I even got there?'

She'd been reading it, too, when he'd walked into Emily's studio the previous night. He recognized the book. It had been by her side.

'There goes any possibility of introducing it as evidence,' Grimaldi moaned. 'Not that I believe for one moment—'

'You have the evidence,' Agata interrupted. 'You've told me that. Time and time again. What you want is the link, isn't it?'

Teresa walked over and placed her gloved fingers on the cover.

'Prints,' she said. 'Silvio. Arrange it. God knows . . .' She glanced at Agata. 'We'll have to take yours to exclude them from anything we get.'

She held up her hands. They bore white forensic gloves just like Teresa's. They must have been in the bag as well, and she had slipped them on as she withdrew the volume.

'I stole these from your forensics officers,' she said. 'Now, do you wish to prosecute me for petty theft? Or would you like to know what I found?'

– 3 –

It was a diary, one that covered a period of nine years, from 13 June 1597 to 29 May 1606, the day after Ranuccio Tomassoni's murder. She had spent much of the previous night reading it, but parts had still, Agata said, only been skimmed. She had focused on those that appeared to contain the most activity. Then, when she had made the excuse to visit the convent, she had consulted with another sister there, one skilled in documents of that period and capable of translating some of the words and terms with which she was unfamiliar.

There were many. Agata Graziano's dark complexion hid her blushes, mostly. The front page of the book bore the title, in ornate gilt lettering, *Gli Ekstasisti ed Evathia – The Ekstasists and Eve*. It concealed the private chronicle of the Ekstasists themselves, a week-by-week account of a secret male brotherhood that began as a prank of wild young men and developed over the years into something darker, more malevolent. The contents were, to begin with, frank and boastful, the record of a private gang of talented and often moneyed men who spent their days in the bright, chattering intellectual society of Renaissance Rome and their nights in the bleak, hard, physical violence of the Ortaccio underclass. There were wild tales of sexual adventures with society women and prostitutes, and practices among the members themselves that could have attracted a quick death sentence had the truth become known to the Vatican. There were sketches, pornographic cartoons and ribald, obscene poems. And the pages recorded rituals too: ceremonies only hinted at, but, Agata said, with pagan and alchemical antecedents.

Among the ancient scribbles were preliminary drawings for paintings, at least some of which were the work of Caravaggio.

'Here,' she said, indicating the strange rough outline of three naked muscular figures seen from below, set around a globe. 'This is a sketch for his only fresco, commissioned by Del Monte for the casino of the Villa Ludovisi. It's still there today. Jupiter, Neptune and Pluto, although in truth these are allegories for the triad of Paracelsus, an alchemical conceit . . . sulphur and air, mercury and water, salt and earth. The casino was used by Del Monte for dabbling in pursuits the Vatican would have regarded as heretical. Possibly with Galileo at his side.'

She turned to the beginning of the book and another sketch, one occupying two full pages as the frontispiece.

'*Evathia in Ekstasis. Eve in Ecstasy.* The moment those worldly sins they worshipped in secret entered our lives.'

They all crowded round to see. Even this sketch, in crude ink, took Costa's breath away. It possessed the finished work's subtle play upon the mind, the ability to shift in perspective and daring, depending on how the viewer gazed on the rapturous woman's tense and highly physical moment of bliss.

'She,' Agata said quietly, 'was the goddess of them all.

Mother and wife. Whore and slave. Bringer of both joy and damnation. This was what they worshipped. *This –* ' her fingers traced the sensuous outline of the female nude on the page – 'is what Franco Malaspina worships today. Like his ancestor.'

There were, she said, seven of them, never referred to by name, only by trade or position: the Painter, the Caporione, the Merchant, the Servant, the Poet, the Priest and, more often than any, 'Il Conte Nero' – the Black Count. This was Ippolito Malaspina, she believed, while Ranuccio Tomassoni was the Caporione, Caravaggio the Painter, and the Priest someone in the service of Cardinal Del Monte, the artist's landlord at the turn of the century.

'How do you know about the Priest?' Falcone demanded.

'It was – ' a sly smile flickered in Costa's direction – 'guesswork. I was in luck. The records of Del Monte's household still exist. In these days of modern miracles I can even examine them in the Vatican repository on Christmas Day, at two in the morning, on someone else's computer. There was a name there . . . Father Antonio L'Indaco, son of an artist recorded in the annals of Vasari, one who had worked with Michelangelo. This was a bohemian household.'

'And it was him . . . because?' Costa asked, half knowing the answer.

'Because at the end of May 1606 Antonio L'Indaco disappeared and was never seen again. Why?'

They waited, listening, all of them, the police officers and the lawyer, and scene of crime people in their suits. 'He is the one who went to Malta with Caravaggio and pretended to be Ippolito Malaspina, while the man himself was dead, inside this house, murdered in the violence that also brought about the death of Ranuccio Tomassoni.'

Costa touched the pages. The paper was thick and felt a little damp. It was not hard for him to imagine Caravaggio and the other Ekstasists standing over this book, scribbling down the details of their exploits, and small sketches, almost doodles, in the margins.

'Why did he die?' he asked. 'Do you know?'

'I can guess,' she answered with a marked, quiet reluctance. 'This book covers nine years. A substantial part of many a man's life in those days. In the beginning – ' she frowned – 'it's nothing more than a game. Drinking and fighting and women. The way it began for Franco, I think. Until something – the "sport in the blood" – took hold of him. Then . . .'

She flicked to a page with a yellow bookmark, towards the end of the book. They crowded round and gazed on what was there: an ink drawing of a terrified woman naked on her back, surrounded by grinning, laughing men . . .

He followed the line of her extended finger. In the margin of the page was written, 'God forgive me, for I know now what I do . . .'

The flowing, easy writing, sloping, somehow almost regretful in its very nature, was the same as that on the missing painting, the same as that of Caravaggio himself.

– 4 –

'You can see them fall apart,' she went on. 'Over the final two years. I am certain that it is Antonio L'Indaco who writes most of these entries. There are phrases and terms he uses that would be natural to a priest and to no one else. Here . . .'

She turned to a page dated 16 November 1604. There was no illustration this time. The entry described the abduction of an Ortaccio prostitute and her removal to a private place, 'in front of the Goddess', where she was subjected to a humiliating series of sexual acts, each described in precise detail, though in a fashion that led the reader to believe the author of the account did not approve – or perhaps witness – what had happened.

'It became worse, and it was Ippolito Malaspina and Ranuccio Tomassoni who led this throughout. Time and time again. It is here in these pages. A steady downward cycle of despair and abasement until . . .'

Another yellow bookmark kept the place. Agata opened the page. It was dated 27 May 1606, one day before the murder of Tomassoni.

'Read it,' she ordered.

The hand of the writer must have been shaking, with

fury or terror or both. In large, uncharacteristically inelegant letters, he shrieked:

> The Count is mad! He and Ranuccio run to the Pope and blame us! And believe they may win over some corrupt and crooked officer of the 'law' by giving him the Goddess! There is no justice in Rome. No hope. No life. We flee for our lives. We pray for God's forgiveness and his eternal damnation on the Black Count, who has forced this shame and humiliation upon us. Hear me now, O Lord! With your hand I defend myself!

Agata glanced towards the window.

'The following day, out there, Ranuccio Tomassoni was slain by Caravaggio and the others. In here, I believe, Ippolito Malaspina died. The two of them were about to betray their brothers, using that painting they all adored as a bribe to shift the blame from themselves. This is how the Ekstasists disintegrated, in blood and hate and murder. Remember the sign around the corpse's neck?'

'A traitor and a thief,' Costa said, recalling every word.

'Lines from Dante . . .' she added. 'Who better than a priest to remember them? These were ordinary men in the main. Ranuccio had brothers, good, honest citizens, who were not involved with the Ekstasists as far as I can see. The records show that they fled Rome a few days after these events, but were allowed to return and remained here, handing their property on to their heirs. As it has been ever since, until poor, weak Nino Tomassoni. I suspect the brothers were ashamed of what had been done in the family's name. I believe they gave assistance to Caravaggio too. They kept the painting.

They stored the body of Ippolito as respectfully as they could. Meanwhile, Antonio L'Indaco assumed the guise of the dead count, escaped alongside Michelangelo Merisi, then wrote letters, copious letters – we have some still – from Malta and the other parts of Italy where he lived thereafter.'

She slapped her finger hard on the page.

'It is here. It is all here!'

Grimaldi sniffed, then looked at his watch.

'I don't doubt that, Sister. You may have solved a crime that is four hundred years old. Unfortunately, that is outside my jurisdiction. Now—'

'Nino Tomassoni knew that room,' she cried. 'It was a secret, handed on from generation to generation. One he shared when he began this second career as an accomplice to Franco's art thefts! Here! Look!'

She turned to the final page of the book. There, in what looked like modern ink, scrawled with the casual ease of graffiti, stood four names, each in a different hand: *The Pornographer, The Merchant, The Servant* and *The Black Count*.

The word 'black' was underlined in Malaspina's entry.

'Four hundred years on they saw that painting and decided to revive the brotherhood. They read this book. They followed in the footsteps of Ranuccio Tomassoni and Ippolito Malaspina.' She hesitated. 'And sad, lost Michelangelo Merisi too.'

Something bothered Costa.

'Franco had this obsession with black prostitutes,' he pointed out. 'Did they before?'

'No,' she replied, a little hesitantly. 'Not at all. The street women of the time, those who lived in Ortaccio, were primarily white. We see that from their portraits, from the records we have. Simonetta was a kitchen maid in Florence, almost a century earlier. A slave effectively. I suspect the real Ippolito Malaspina would have thought it beneath him to mix with a woman of colour. He must have been like Alessandro de' Medici. Ashamed of his heritage. Like Franco too . . .'

Teresa Lupo looked the lawyer in the face.

'There. Something modern. Something that goes from there to here.'

'Which means what?' Grimaldi asked. 'Tell me.'

'It means,' Agata suggested, 'that something happened to light a fire in Franco Malaspina's head. Something that turned this idea into an obsession. Though what?' She uttered a long, despairing sigh. 'This defeats me. It was always a joke in company. That he had a touch of the African in him. I remember . . .'

She stared at the page on the book, trying to think.

'I remember perhaps a year or so ago that it became a joke one no longer made. Franco's sense of humour had disappeared on this subject.' Her slender, dusky fingers stroked the page. 'Yet I can see nothing here that would have proved this connection at all.'

Teresa Lupo glanced at her assistant.

'It's in the blood, you know,' she said quietly. 'I just might be able to help.'

– 5 –

Thirty minutes later they were in the Questura morgue, with Grimaldi glancing constantly at his watch, still looking as if he didn't understand why he was listening to history when he could have been home with his family. Teresa stood over the skeleton that lay on the shining table at the centre of the room, a collection of grey bones now covered with labels and brightened in areas by obvious examination.

'The first thing to say,' Teresa began, indicating the skull, 'is that everything I see here supports Agata's interpretation of events. This man was murdered savagely.'

She indicated a gaping, shattered rent in the skull above the right temple.

'It's a pretty typical sword wound and would have been deep and serious. But – ' her gloved fingers ran over the arms – 'there are any number of defensive injuries here, on both limbs. Stab wounds to the ribcage. A broken femur. He was attacked and murdered, probably by more than one person.'

'Could this have been a fight?' Falcone asked.

Teresa shook her head.

'No. He was fighting them off with his arms. The balance of possibilities is that he was struck down by several men. And also—'

Peroni was staring at the skeleton with a gloomy expression on his long, pale face.

'They did that,' he cut in, and stabbed a long, fleshy finger at the largest obvious wound, one a good hand's length long that ran down the left of the chest and tore open several ribs.

'Someone did,' she observed with a long sigh. 'But not in the way you think. This happened after he was dead. Technically it's what's called a post-mortem ablation of the heart. It was a known, though not common, funerary practice in some medieval communities. The heart was removed for – ' she shrugged – 'worship usually. You know the kind of thing you get in churches? Here are the saint's remains. Pray for his soul . . . and yours. This is how it was done.'

'He wasn't a saint,' Agata pointed out.

'No,' she agreed. 'I think that much is clear. But it was done for famous men too sometimes. Kings. Lords. Dukes.'

'Where would they put the heart afterwards?' Costa asked.

'I can tell you where it was meant to be,' she replied immediately. 'Silvio?'

Her assistant came over with a series of large blown-up photos. They showed in detail the cabinet in which the skeleton had been found.

'This was specially made,' Teresa said. 'When they killed him, they meant to preserve him. The skeleton didn't get this way by natural decay either. It was boiled. Sister Agata isn't the only one who's been looking at the

Tomassoni family. Do you know what the brothers did for a living?'

Di Capua flung a few more photos on the table next to the bones. They were medieval prints depicting some kind of charnel house, men working hard to dismember a corpse.

'They were undertakers,' he revealed. 'Specialist knowledge would have been around in a profession like that. They would have boiled the body in a mixture of water and vinegar. We can still detect traces of it. It must have taken a couple of days. There would have been some evisceration too. It's nothing compared with what the Egyptians did, but still pretty impressive.'

'And the heart,' Teresa interjected, 'surely sat here.'

She indicated a hole in the base of the cabinet, one that looked as if it had been purpose-made for some kind of box.

'Whatever was in there has gone missing. And recently,' she added. 'We can tell that from the lie of the dust. It must have disappeared around the same time as whatever stood on the wall where Nino stuck up his dirty pictures.'

'Franco took it,' Agata said straight away. 'This was his ancestor.'

'That's one explanation,' Teresa said hesitantly.

'Can you make the connection?' Falcone asked simply.

'I think we know the answer to that already,' Grimaldi moaned. 'Otherwise we wouldn't be listening to this rambling dissertation.'

'I can make some connections,' she answered quickly. 'Whether our friend here thinks they're enough . . .'

'I . . .' Grimaldi looked around at them. He knew when he was outnumbered. 'I will listen a little more.'

'Excellent,' Teresa replied, and didn't take her beady eyes off him. 'I have four individual examples of male DNA from that hellhole in the Vicolo del Divino Amore. Three of them come from semen, on the corpses of those women, on the floor, that sofa they used. One has no sexual connotation at all. It is primary physical contact of an everyday nature. Fingerprints and sweat, the kind of evidence anyone would leave walking around a place and touching things.'

'Nino,' Agata intervened. 'That was him.'

Teresa nodded. 'Good guess.'

'I knew these men,' she objected. 'Not well, but I saw them quite often. Franco was their leader. Castagna and Buccafusca were his henchmen. Nino was subservient to all of them. This nonsense Franco believes in, about the life of the knight, his right to behave as he wishes . . . Nino was a frightened little man. He couldn't have felt that way for a moment.'

'We have no evidence Nino Tomassoni took part in any of the sexual acts or the murders,' Teresa confirmed. 'It's undeniable from the pictures we found in that house he was there. Maybe he was a bystander.'

'And the rest?' Falcone asked.

Silvio Di Capua picked up a couple of folders of reports from the nearest desk and waved them in front of him.

'We have Castagna and Buccafusca identified without a shadow of doubt.'

'Two dead people,' Grimaldi moaned. 'Thanks . . .'

Silvio Di Capua clenched his small fists and let out a brief scream.

'For Christ's sake, man. Use your imagination. We have one sample that remains unidentified. It has to be Franco Malaspina. All we need is a chance . . .'

'Imagination?' Grimaldi shrieked. 'We're on the brink of getting sued for harassment as it is and you want me to go in front of a magistrate and talk of history and imagination? When will you people learn? We can't screw around with this individual any more.'

'We should know our place,' Costa said quietly.

'I didn't say that!' the lawyer objected. 'Do you think I like this? Do you think I want to defend this monster? He's a murderer and a crook and I'd give my right arm to see him languishing in a cell for the rest of his life. The only way we can do this is through the law. What else do we have?'

Agata looked at him and smiled, a quizzical expression on her face.

'The law is an ass. Who said that?'

'Every last stupid cop who thinks I should be able to close a case he can't,' Grimaldi snapped. 'Give me something to work with. Something that isn't several hundred years old.'

'Like most lawyers, Toni, you have a very closed mind,' Teresa Lupo observed in a censorious tone. 'Silvio? Let us talk genealogy.'

- 6 -

Di Capua walked over to the main desk. They followed and watched him unroll three long family charts, two of them clearly printed and official, the third scribbled in the tight, clear hand Costa had come to recognize as the forensic scientist's own. Di Capua was the department magpie; if an avenue of research existed that didn't interest him, Costa had yet to see it.

'Alessandro de' Medici. The Moor,' Di Capua said, and threw a photograph on the table. It was the portrait of a pale-faced scholarly individual dressed in black. He appeared to be drawing, unconvincingly, the face of a woman on parchment with a metal stylus. The man might have been a cleric or a philosopher. His young face was solemn and plain, with a skimpy beard. His skin . . .

Costa leaned down and looked more closely. Agata was there with him instantly, smiling, pleased, it seemed to him, that someone else had been looking at paintings for a change.

'Do you know this?' he asked her.

'Am I supposed to be familiar with every work of art there has ever been? No . . .'

'It's in Philadelphia,' Di Capua explained. 'You're the expert. What do you think of the pose?'

Agata frowned. 'It's a joke. This man was the capo of the Medici dynasty, as ruthless and venal as any. Here he is pretending he can draw, as if any of these great people could do that. Their talent lay in sponsorship, if at all . . .'

Di Capua produced another photograph: the same man, seated this time in a suit of armour, with a lance on his lap, his face only half seen, turned away from the artist and the viewer, his skin again oddly underpainted, as if the artist had refrained from finishing the final tone.

'A sport in the blood,' she said firmly. 'This is the one I know. Giorgio Vasari. It's in the Uffizi. Vasari's timidity is even more obvious in the flesh. They wouldn't dare admit it, would they? You know the story. We all know the story.'

'Yes,' Grimaldi agreed. 'It's a story. His old man had an affair with a black kitchen maid and the bastard got to inherit the family silver.'

Agata scowled at the lawyer.

'His "old man" was Giulio de' Medici, who became Pope Clement VII. Not that Giulio admitted it. He got his cousin to put his name to the child. It was inconvenient for a Pope to take his offspring to Rome. We know this for sure.'

'How?' Costa asked.

'Someone like me can go places police officers can't,' she said, smiling. 'The Vatican keeps records.' The body of the crucifix played in her fingers for a moment. 'This all happened just sixty years before Caravaggio came to Rome. It's my job to know. If this cadaver is Ippolito Malaspina . . .'

She reached out and touched the curving line of the ribcage, close to the point where it had been torn apart.

'He is the grandson of Alessandro de' Medici, the great-grandson of Lorenzo, the Duke of Urbino. He comes from a line that produced three Popes and two Queens of France. Do you wonder they took out his heart, even though they killed him for a traitor and a thief?'

'Can we use any of this?' Falcone asked.

'It's fact,' Agata insisted. 'I can give you the names of any number of historians who will swear to it in court. Alessandro was the son of a future Pope and a black kitchen maid. But the idea that the Malaspinas were in part the Medicis' illegitimate line . . . It was just rumour. Gossip among the nobility. Centuries old.'

'No,' Di Capua insisted, and pointed to the second family tree, that of the Malaspinas, running from the 1400s and ending three centuries later. 'It wasn't rumour. See this woman . . .'

He pointed to a name: Taddea Malaspina.

'She was Alessandro's mistress. It's documented in the Medici archive. Gifts. Love letters. He wasn't the most faithful of men. But he loved her. This painting – ' he pointed to the Philadelphia portrait – 'was given to Taddea as a gift.'

Agata looked impressed.

'That must have meant something. Alessandro was murdered, if I recall correctly.'

Teresa stepped in.

'He was slaughtered by his own cousin, supposedly on the way to some bedtime appointment. They smuggled out his body in a carpet and even I can't give you DNA from that. But . . .'

She jabbed a finger down hard on the Medici chart. Agata laughed and clapped her hands.

'They opened the tombs a few years ago,' she declared. 'I read about it in the papers.'

'Correct,' Teresa answered. 'In 2003 the Florence authorities began a methodical examination of the Medici tombs in order to check the structural state of the building. At the same time they let in a few friendly scientists to look at the bones.' She stared at them all. 'The remains of Alessandro are lost. His father, Lorenzo, is buried in the chapels, in a tomb by Michelangelo. There can be no mistake about his identity.'

She gave a set of papers on the side table a sly glance.

'It took a little persuasion with those damned Florentines. However, I now have their reports, and preliminary tests back on the DNA from the remains we recovered here yesterday. They need confirmation before we can put them into a form that is good enough for a court. But what I can tell you is this . . .'

She paused, for obvious effect, then ran her finger along the skull of the skeleton in front of them.

'This dead man was a descendant of the duke in the Medici chapels. The unidentified DNA found in the semen on all of these murdered women is a part of the same line.' Her fingers rattled on the cadaver's ribs as if they were child's musical instrument. 'These bones belong to the line of Alessandro de' Medici. That semen comes from the same recognizable dynasty, ten, fifteen, twenty, who knows how many generations on . . . Who cares?'

Grimaldi smiled for one brief second, then gave a brief nod, as if to say 'well done'. This was, Costa thought, the most enthusiastic sign he had displayed all day.

'And there's more,' the pathologist added. 'Silvio?'

'Do you see this?' The assistant was pointing at the open jaw. 'Both front incisors are missing. We only took one. We only need one. Someone else snatched out that other tooth, and they did it recently. You can see that from the socket.'

'Why on earth would someone take a dead man's tooth?' Grimaldi asked, bemused.

'For the same reason we did,' Teresa butted in. 'The same reason the heart was removed. To find out whether the rumours were true. Look . . .'

Di Capua produced a printed report bearing the name and crest of an American medical institute in Boston.

'If you want to find out about black heritage from DNA there is only one place to go,' he went on. 'This lab specializes in tracing African ancestry from the most minute of samples, however difficult it might seem. They've built up a database over the years, tracking down slave movements from all over Africa to the rest of the world.'

Agata rolled her eyes in amazement.

'So they could even find my father?' she asked.

Di Capua nodded.

'With a match. With two samples. Even from just yours they could look at the DNA and tell you whereabouts in Africa he came from. We contacted these people yesterday and sent them the preliminary results of our own tests. They looked them up for us. This is still early. As Teresa said, we need to work on the confirmation. But this corpse and the semen sample from the Vicolo del Divino Amore show clear connections with female DNA from the Bamileke tribe in what we now call Cameroon, an area plundered regularly for slavery for centuries.'

He threw an indecipherable scientific graph, covered in

lines and numbers, on the examination table next to the bones there.

'This is the mark of Simonetta, the kitchen maid some Tuscan aristocrat impregnated in Florence in the autumn of 1509.'

'I told you,' Agata sighed, her eyes full of wonder and elation. 'They are us. We are them.'

'It's in this skeleton,' Di Capua went on, regardless. 'It's in the semen on those dead women. The reason we got to know that so quickly . . .'

He flashed a covetous glance at Teresa.

'It was your call, Silvio,' she said gently.

'He was there before us. Franco Malaspina first sent the heart, hoping they could work with that. It was too old. The man knew nothing about forensic pathology and what was required of remains this old. So later he took that tooth, on the direct instructions of the only laboratory in the world you'd go to if you wanted to trace some black ancestry from a sample of ancient DNA. They already had the work done. They could fingerprint the black strand, and come up with some rough geographical location too. It was just a matter of looking up the records.'

No one said a word.

Di Capua made a *faux*-modest little bow, then took out one more sheet from his folder and placed it next to the skull.

'One final thing. I found this in the archives of the Art Institute of Chicago. It's by an artist called Pontormo.'

Agata was poring over the image in an instant, holding it in her shaking hands.

'Jacopo Carrucci . . .' she murmured.

'Pontormo,' Di Capua corrected her.

'It's the same man,' she said, smiling, and placed the object in front of them. 'I have never seen this before.'

'It's certified that it was painted in 1534 or 1535,' Di Capua went on. 'The work is recorded in the Medici archives. This is a genuine representation of Alessandro de' Medici, the only one that ever acknowledged who he really was.'

They began to crowd around the image. It was a full-face portrait of a young and apparently sensitive man, clearly the Alessandro of the two earlier images, but this time seen at close quarters, where there was a baleful, almost malevolent look in his eyes, and some militaristic metal brooch at his neck. His skin was almost the colour of Agata's, darker than any native Tuscan, and his lips were full and fleshy.

'It's Franco,' Agata whispered. 'It is *him.*'

Costa stared at the painted face of this long-dead aristocrat and felt an icy shiver grip his body. The hair was different and the skin had been lightened a little, even in this frank depiction of the man. But the resemblance was obvious and disturbing.

Falcone turned on the lawyer.

'Is this not enough for you?' he demanded.

Grimaldi shrugged.

'A picture? Some old books? And many, many circumstantial connections? Of course it's not enough . . .'

Teresa swore.

'All the same,' he added quickly, 'this business in Boston. It's here. It's *now*. If I can prove he was in contact with them, that he dispatched first the heart, then the tooth on their instructions . . .' Toni Grimaldi burst into a broad grin that changed his countenance entirely and made him look like a grey-suited Santa shorn of his beard. 'If we have that, then we are home. It places Malaspina in the Tomassoni house, at the centre of everything, with undeniable knowledge of those stolen paintings. I will push the swab into his mouth myself. After which we will throw so many charges at the bastard he will never walk free again.'

'The swab is mine,' Teresa said softly.

'So,' Grimaldi added, beaming, 'these people in Boston will provide an affidavit. A statement. We can take such things by email these days. If I have that tomorrow, I go before a magistrate immediately.'

The two pathologists stared at each other.

'When I say it came from Malaspina,' Teresa continued carefully, 'what I mean is we know it came from Rome. A year ago. It was a very expensive business. Not something one would do lightly.'

The lawyer's smile disappeared.

'Did they give you his name?' he asked.

'The lab said it came from Rome. Who the hell else could it be?' she pleaded. 'How many other people here had the motive, the money and the opportunity?'

'I need his name,' Grimaldi emphasized. 'On a piece of paper.'

'This is medical research! There are ethical issues! Of course they won't give me a name.'

The man in the grey suit swore.

'Ever?' he asked.

'Show a little faith,' Teresa pleaded.

'This is not about faith. Or justice. Or anything other than the law.'

'The law is an ass,' Agata repeated quietly, staring at the bones on the table.

'The law is all you have,' Grimaldi muttered. 'I have

wasted Christmas Day. As have you. Excuse me. I will leave you to your bones and your books and your fantasies.'

'Sir,' Agata said, and stood in his way.

She had the photo of the portrait from Chicago in her hands.

'Look at him,' she implored. 'We all know this face. We all know what he's done. There is a man here – ' she glanced at Costa – 'who lost his wife to this creature, and I am only here thanks to this same man's courage. Do not abandon us.'

Grimaldi's face contorted with a cold, helpless anger.

'I abandon no one. Give me a case and I will work day and night to put Franco Malaspina in the dock. But you have none, and these officers know it. I have a duty to those who will be harmed in the future by this paralysis he has created in our investigative procedures. It cannot be allowed to continue.'

He turned and looked at them all.

'In the morning I must tell Commissario Esposito the truth. I have no confidence we can bring this man to book. We should . . . sue for some kind of peace that lets us go back to catching fresh criminals the way we wish. We draw the line with Malaspina. In return we negotiate to be allowed to bring back the old evidence rules he has removed from us, with no retrospective clause applied to him. I am sorry. Genuinely. That is my decision.'

'Toni . . .' Peroni began.

'No. Enough. We do not have the resources or the evidence to defeat this man's money and position. There comes a time when one must admit defeat. I see it in the eyes of all of you, yet you refuse to let it enter your heads. This is your problem. Not mine. Good day.'

Teresa Lupo watched him walk out of the door, then muttered something caustic under her breath.

'No.' Falcone was holding the photograph of Alessandro de' Medici and spoke in a quiet, dejected voice. 'He's a decent man who has the courage to tell us the truth. We've done what we can and we've failed. Malaspina has defeated me as surely as he defeated Susanna Placidi. Money . . .'

'Tomorrow—' Costa said firmly.

'Tomorrow this all becomes history too,' Falcone interrupted him. He pointed a long bony finger at Agata Graziano. 'Tomorrow you will go to that safe house in Piedmont. Until we have concluded these discussions with the man. I will make your safety a precondition, naturally.'

'You will not negotiate with this evil creature on my behalf, Leo,' she shouted. 'How can you even think of such a thing? *How?*'

He waited for her fury to subside.

'If we cannot prosecute this man, then negotiating something quietly, through a third party, is the best we can achieve.' He cast a brief glance in Costa's direction. 'I'm sorry, Nic. Truly. That is the way it must be. Now, go home all of you, please. It's Christmas. We should not spend it in a place like this.'

Part 16

THE MADONNA'S TOUCH

- 1 -

Two years before they had dined together on Christmas Day: Falcone, Peroni, Teresa and Emily, all of them at the farmhouse on the edge of Rome, watching a rescued Iraqi orphan build a snowman among the vines outside the back door in the fields that led to the tombs and churches and monuments of the old road into the city.

It seemed a memory from a different lifetime. The streets were deserted by the time they climbed into the cars of the convoy, and a steady drizzle fell on the cobblestones of the *centro storico*. A chill wind was now beginning to build from the north. There would be no snow, not even a little. Costa felt sure of that, and a part of him regretted the thought, because he would have liked to show Agata Graziano the Pantheon in that kind of weather, would have enjoyed the look of wonder on her face at the line of soft flakes swirling through the oculus.

He felt tired. His wounded shoulder hurt. It wasn't mending as quickly as he'd hoped. Over the past few weeks Costa had become conscious of some rising, interior knowledge within himself; he was getting older, now a widower, one who would be unable to put Emily's memory to rest for a long time.

It may have been the doubt and distance on his face that prompted her remark. As they fell into the back of the centre car, Agata Graziano looked him in the eye and asked, 'Do all policemen give up this easily?'

He closed his eyes and tried to laugh.

'I don't think anyone would call this easy,' he replied. 'We've worked for weeks. Susanna Placidi was there before us. All told we've spent months spent trying to bring this man to justice, and we've failed. Leo is right. As usual.'

'The arrogance of men.'

'We have nothing to put in front of a magistrate, Agata. That's the truth. Accept it.'

The car began to move. Her eyes turned from him. She stared out of the window, at the rain and the gleaming, empty cobbled streets.

'I do,' she sighed. 'And I shall go to Piedmont as Leo dictates.'

She looked at him, a quizzical frown on her dusky face.

'Will you really negotiate with a man such as Franco? After all this?'

'We negotiate with terrorists and kidnappers in Iraq if it saves a life sometimes. In the end, if you want peace you talk to your enemies. Who else is there?'

'And then they kidnap someone else because they know they have you.'

'Perhaps,' he answered with a shrug. 'But would you like to explain that to the relative of someone in their custody? That the life of a man or woman they love should be sacrificed in order to save other, unknown human beings in the future?'

'No,' she said instantly. 'I would not like that responsibility.'

The car turned into the Corso. There was not a single

Christmas light in the shop windows, not a soul on the street.

'Why do you do this?' she asked. 'Why do you take on the pain of others?'

The question puzzled him.

'We don't, do we? It's just a question of . . .'

He remembered his father, and the routine round of charity, money to men and women without homes, without hope, quiet donations, often to Church institutions a good communist was supposed to avoid.

'The point is . . . we don't walk away. We don't stop. We don't give up. Not until . . .' He thought of Teresa and her forensic people working through the night; Falcone bending the rules, agonizing over what might work and what might make the situation with Malaspina worse. 'Not until it's hopeless.'

'And then?'

'Then I go home, open a good bottle of wine and drink myself stupid.'

'Nic!'

Her small hand dashed across his knee.

'That is shocking,' she cried. 'You will not do this tonight. Bea will have cooked another wonderful meal for us. Then tomorrow I expect a personal escort to this hovel in Piedmont Leo has in mind for me, and that will be no pleasure at all if you have a thick head.'

'Sir,' he said, with a mock-salute.

She reached into her bag. He wondered, for a moment, what other surprises might lurk there. All that came out was a small, very modern mobile phone.

'That looks like a possession to me,' he pointed out.

'One more gift from Rosa. It's better than a gun, isn't it?'

He listened to her make a single, short call to the convent and wish someone well. Then, as they were turning onto the Lungotevere by the river, she said, 'Please turn round. This is important.'

'What is?' he asked.

Her bright eyes held him, pleading.

'I can't go through this entire day without entering a church, Nic. Please. Sant'Agostino would be suitable. It is open. I know.'

She watched him, waiting.

'We'd allow in an atheist, you know.'

He spoke to the two guard cars on the radio and ordered them to turn round. It didn't take long. There was scarcely another vehicle on the damp, shining roads.

'As long as you're under our protection,' he answered, 'you'll have to let in more than one.'

– 2 –

The church was deserted except for a lone priest extinguishing candles and tidying chairs. He didn't look pleased to see seven men in winter coats march into his church at that moment.

'We're closing,' the man said, scurrying towards them in his long black robes, causing them to halt. 'Please, please. Even a priest deserves some time at Christmas.'

Then he stopped, seeing Agata Graziano, and put a hand to his mouth.

'Sister Agata,' he murmured. 'Are you . . . well? I hear all these stories. About you. And the police.'

'The police,' she said, and waved a hand at Costa and his colleagues. 'See, I am on business. Perhaps it touches them too.'

'Oh,' the priest answered hesitantly, then added, 'You won't be long, will you? I'm hungry. It's been a tiring day.'

'We won't be long,' Costa interjected. 'Will we?'

'No,' she murmured, and immediately went towards the altar, small feet making light echoing steps in the vast empty belly of the nave.

On his orders four of the men followed discreetly, in

the dark shadows of the aisles on both sides. Agata stopped, crossed herself and fell slowly to her knees. Costa stayed with the priest, his eyes straying, as always, to Caravaggio's *Madonna*, the child in her arms, the simple peasants in front of her. The pencil-thin halo above the Virgin's head seemed brighter, more obvious than he'd noticed before.

'The painting's about her,' he noted quietly. 'I never realized before.'

The priest laughed.

'It is called *The Madonna of Loreto*. You should always read the name on the frame.'

'I should,' he agreed. 'This whole church – ' something, some revelation, hovered out of reach – 'is about women somehow, isn't it?'

'Primarily,' the man observed, 'I would have said it was about God. But then, I'm biased.'

She was done. Agata was walking back towards him again, head down, face serious. She couldn't have prayed for more than a minute.

Costa thought of Fillide Melandroni taking much the same steps on the selfsame flagstones four hundred years before. Making some compact with the Church, then striding out into Rome in the company of Caravaggio and Ranuccio Tomassoni and Ippolito Malaspina for a different life, one of surfeit in the name of the Ekstasists, one in which she would take a knife to the cheeks of her rivals simply to earn a little more money for her favours. Men and women enduring lives steeped in the cruel reality of everyday existence, still seeking spirituality wherever, whenever they could find it. Watching her slim, dark shadow slip towards him through the nave Costa understood at that moment that Agata Graziano was their diametric opposite: a bright, engaged mind that had never, until late, considered anything of the earthly world at all.

He glanced at the Caravaggio, wondering what to say.

She didn't arrive. The priest next to him uttered a short, shocked sigh. Costa turned.

Sister Agata Graziano stood in front of the milky-white statue of the Virgin in the scallop-shell alcove, triumphant beneath her starry halo, a silver circlet beneath her breast, the child standing on her knee, loins girt with metal like a tiny warrior from some distant Greek myth.

Tentatively, with an expression on her face that was part anticipation, part fear, she reached out and touched the lustrous argent cap on the Madonna's foot, placing her fingers on the shiny worn object as untold numbers of Roman women – Fillide Melandroni among them – must have done before.

'Now that is something new,' the priest whispered.

It only took a moment. Soon she was walking towards the door.

'Please excuse the rudeness,' Costa said, preceding her. The rain had halted. The long sweep of steps in front of the church gleamed like yellowing dirt-stained ivory. The three cars were at the foot. He went ahead, Agata behind, with the men at her back.

When he got to the bottom he found Taccone there, fuming.

'Damn it!' the tall, broad-shouldered *sovrintendente* yelled out into the piazza, apparently at no one.

They stopped by the middle car. Costa was conscious of the large, familiar shape of Peroni by his right side, standing in front of Agata, trying to guide her towards the rear door.

'That stupid photographer we saw yesterday,' Taccone grumbled. 'The one outside Tomassoni's house. He was here too. I swear. He went past on a scooter. Looking.'

The *sovrintendente* turned to face them.

'Don't scum like that ever take a day off?'

Peroni's eyes caught Costa's.

'What the hell would a photographer be doing out here on a night like this?' the big man retorted. 'Where is he? What—'

'Let's get inside . . .' Costa started saying, then heard his words drowned out by the roaring, whining sound of a two-stroke engine, coming somewhere from the right.

He caught Agata by her slight shoulders, gripped her hard and dragged her down to the damp, dirty stones behind the rear doors. From the corner of his eye, fast approaching the three vehicles, lined up together, locked in formation, he could see the scooter roaring into the piazza.

There were two men on it, both hooded. The passenger sat backwards on the pillion, one hand tight on the rail by the seat. In his other sat a weapon, black, with a long barrel and a long magazine.

– 3 –

Costa tore at the door, forced it open and managed to bundle her inside, ordering her to keep low on the floor of the big police saloon. Then his words disappeared beneath the chatter of a machine pistol, barking repeatedly into the black night, its metallic voice echoing off the old stone façade of the church.

As Costa looked up, Taccone caught a shot to his upper torso and fell back screaming onto the steps. Peroni was yelling at the others to get down behind the vehicles. There were seven men there. Enough, surely. But it was night. It was Christmas. They weren't expecting any of this. This was Rome. Not some gangster town on the Ionian Sea in Calabria, where Malaspina had surely hired his deadly 'Ndrangheta thugs.

Hide or fight.

It was that choice again. The only choice.

He looked at the stricken Taccone, crawling across the steps to try to find some safety from the constant horizontal rain of machine-pistol fire raking the piazza. For a brief second, he found his attention straying to another figure at the head of the stairs: the priest, upright, hands to his face again.

Peroni had the man in view already and was yelling at him, a long, angry sentence filled with the kind of curses a Roman priest rarely heard, and a final threat, that if the man didn't get indoors soon a police officer would likely shoot him instead.

'Gianni . . .' he barked over the noise, and then found himself catching his breath.

The piazza had gone quiet. All he could hear was the pained groans of the wounded *sovrintendente*, the anxious breathing of Peroni by his side, and, like distant echo, the faint reverberation of remembered gunfire rattling around his head.

Peroni peered hurriedly around the car for a second, then got back to safety and shook his head.

'He's changing magazines, Nic. We have to—'

Costa didn't wait. He lunged over to the wounded Taccone and snatched the weapon from the man's hand. Then, with both his own and the borrowed gun firm in his grip, he stood up and walked out from behind the long, dark shape of the unmarked police Lancia, pointed both barrels at the two figures on the bike, the gunman struggling with the machine pistol, the rider looking anxiously around, jerking at the throttle.

He didn't waste time with procedure, with a warning. They were five, eight metres away at most. Costa walked forward, firing loosely at both men, intent on getting as close he could, and aware that others were beginning to follow him. His own body surely blocked their shots. At that moment, he really didn't care. There was nothing else that mattered on the planet but these two men, in the familiar black hoods he'd come to associate with Franco Malaspina and his works.

A cry of pain broke the brief silence between two shots.

The figure in black on the pillion jerked, threw his hands in the air and began to fall sideways. The machine pistol rolled out of his hands and clattered on the wet cobble-stones. The engine whined madly and the scooter's front wheel jerked towards the black coverlet of the sky before the vehicle shot forward, leaving its wounded passenger behind, racing for the web of streets beyond the Piazza Navona, cutting a fast, direct path into the confusion of lanes and dead ends and alleys that was Ortaccio.

He kept firing, one gun after the other, until every shell was gone and he found himself pulling hard on dead triggers. He flung the spent weapons to either side and kept walking. Across the square the figure on the scooter got smaller and was gone.

Peroni appeared at his side. All the others were soon there too, even, barely able to stand, Taccone, who was shivering, teeth chattering with cold and fear and pain.

Costa took one look at the injured man.

'Get him an ambulance,' he ordered.

He watched them take the *sovrintendente* back towards the broad steps of Sant'Agostino. Peroni walked over to stand by the bent, broken body on the ground, still staring in the direction of the disappeared scooter.

'You know,' he said, when Costa got there, 'you always told me you were a lousy shot.'

The man on the shiny cobblestones lay on his back, eyes wide to the sky, mouth gaping open to show two lines of badly cared-for teeth. There was a wound in his left temple the size of an espresso cup, bone and gore around the edges.

'I guess,' Peroni added, 'our friend Aprea here might not agree.'

'We could have used a witness,' Costa grumbled. 'That bastard gets all the breaks.'

Peroni was going through the dead man's clothes, pulling out nothing but money and ammunition.

'We could have used a real name too,' he replied. 'It certainly won't be Aprea. If he's one of our Calabrian friends, I doubt we'll even get to know.'

'Damn,' Costa muttered. Then louder, 'Damn, *damn*!'

He strode back to the car. The men stood in a huddle around Taccone, who, to Costa's amazement, was clutching his wounded shoulder with one hand and sucking on a cigarette with the other.

'I like the first aid treatment,' he said to them caustically. 'What is the point of all this training exactly?'

They didn't answer. They had the expression junior officers wore sometimes, the one he'd come to recognize since promotion, one that, at this instant, filled him with dread. The look was furtive and it spelled guilt.

'Where is she?' he asked.

He stormed over to the centre vehicle and threw open the rear doors. The back seats were empty.

'Where is she? Where in Christ's name . . . ?'

'She'd gone, boss,' Lippi, the youngest of the officers said straight up. 'She must have run off while we were trying to help you out there.'

Furious, Costa scanned the piazza.

'She could be anywhere by now,' the *agente* added unhelpfully.

Costa spun round on the slippery marble pavement and found himself roaring her name into the darkness.

'Agata! *Agata! AGATA!*'

All that came back in the night was the echo of his voice off the marble façade of the church and the clatter of unseen pigeons, invisible wings rising into the black, enveloping sky.

Part 17

THE COMPANY OF GHOSTS

- 1 -

Hours later Costa was sitting in Falcone's office in the Questura, dog-tired, head fuzzy from the painkillers the medic had given him to take away the hurt from his throbbing shoulder. They'd pulled in men and women from everywhere, once again dragged officers from the warmth of a family Christmas, and sent them out onto the damp, cold streets of Rome, looking for a lone woman of the Church who had disappeared into the dark.

It was almost as if she had never existed. There were no relatives to visit, no friends to check out. The city was deserted. The stream of officers dispatched into the *centro storico* by Falcone could find scarcely a soul to question, and anyone they did come across had no recollection of a slight young woman in black making her way through the rain to some place Costa could not even begin to guess at. Falcone had stationed a team at the house on the Via Appia Antica, and further officers were scouring the roads leading to it, looking for some leads. Rosa Prabakaran had visited Agata's convent and talked to the women there, pleading for help, getting nothing but sympathy and bewilderment. Agata had vanished into the heart of a city that was empty for the holiday. Finding a missing person in the overcrowded metropolis of a normal day was difficult enough. Locating her in this strange, deserted labyrinth of ancient streets, alleys and dead ends was even worse. She had, surely, either gone to ground somewhere or been taken by a different set of Malaspina's men, seeing their advantage when Costa led the response to the armed attack by the man who had called himself Aprea.

That idea – the thought that his own wilfulness had left Agata exposed – tore at his conscience. When he closed his eyes he saw another incident, another time. On the feeble winter grass and mud of Augustus's mausoleum, where a hooded man with a shotgun had his arm round Emily's neck, her voice in his ear, then, now, always . . .

Don't beg, Nic . . . You never beg. It's the worst thing you can do. The worst . . .

But begging was what a man resorted to when the stakes were high, when he was desperate and there was no other option left. He would have begged for Emily's life, given his own in exchange. And the same for Agata. Instead . . .

He screwed his eyes tight shut and tried to force these thoughts from his head. A firm hand on his shoulder brought him back to the real world and shook him awake.

It was Peroni, his broad, ugly face creased with concern.

'Why don't you go home?'

'Yes,' Falcone added from across the desk. 'Go home. You look terrible.'

'She was my responsibility,' Costa shot back at both of them furiously. 'I go home when we find her.'

Falcone flicked through some papers in front of him on the desk.

'The truth is this. Agata walked away from that church of her own volition. It's not possible she was snatched. That priest would have noticed.'

'The priest didn't notice a thing,' Costa pointed out.

Falcone scowled.

'That's what he said. These Church people stick together like glue. You'd think we were the enemy sometimes. Agata did this for a reason. Perhaps she just can't take any more. When she wants us to know, we will.'

'That's comforting,' he grumbled.

'In a way,' Peroni said thoughtfully, 'it is. Better than some of the alternatives anyway. Now go home. You're no damned use to us here. Besides, nothing's going to happen tonight now, is it? This is something we're going to have to pick up in the morning. It would help us all if you were halfway awake by then.'

'In the morning,' Costa pointed out, 'Grimaldi plans to offer Franco Malaspina a pardon.'

'Then Agata will have nothing to fear at all,' Falcone pointed out without emotion.

'Do you think she'll be happy with that idea?' he asked.

'Since when was this job about happiness,' Peroni grumbled. 'Get out of here. You're starting to become tedious.'

He nodded. Peroni was right.

'True,' Costa agreed, and walked out of the Questura, out into a bleak and empty Rome.

2

He didn't want to go home. He wanted to think, not sleep. Costa walked from the back street in which the Questura stood out into the broad, open Piazza Venezia and, this once, strode straight across the cobbles without seeing a single vehicle tearing maniacally from one side to the other. From the ugly white wedding-cake monstrosity of the Vittorio Emanuele monument he went on to the Via dei Fori Imperiali, Mussolini's flat, broad highway through the heart of ancient Rome, with the Palatine and the jagged ruins of the old forums on the right, and the terraced ranks of Trajan's markets, red-brick walls leading up to the Quirinal Hill, rising in a semicircle to the left. Even close to midnight on Christmas Day the lights set amid the monuments were burning brightly, cutting out soft yellow silhouettes of a different city from a different time. Rome looked beautiful. He knew, at times like this, he could never live anywhere else. This was home. It was a part of him, and he a part of it. Weary, he strode on to find the low bench seats by the side of Caesar's Forum, a place he had often visited as a child with his father, listening to all those tales from history, building in his own imagination a picture of the solemn night that saw the cremation of the dictator there. He could name without thinking the buildings that sat in the space beyond, a collection of wrecked columns and porticoes bearing such grandiose names they seemed eternal, the temples of Castor and Pollux, of Saturn and Vesta, the forums, of Augustus and Nerva, the great Arch of Titus . . . relics of a race of men and women with whom he still felt some kind of affinity. In their struggles against their own dark nature, their endless striving to attain goodness, justice, in a world that seemed, at times, hopelessly fallen, Costa sought some kind of comfort, some distant sign of grace.

He had sat here sometimes with Emily, talking, listening, and wondering in silence. All those moments were equally precious to him now. Yet the vista that stretched before him was simply old stone, as Caravaggio's paintings were in essence nothing but ageing pigment on ancient canvas. Without the presence of humanity, without imagination and the gentle touch of another – a gesture that said *I see, I feel, I hurt, I love too* – they were nothing. That was what the artist was saying in the painting that had come to obsess Ippolito Malaspina and, four centuries on, his descendant too. Beyond the mundane and the physical lay another experience, one that could be reached only through the selfless route of compassion and surrender.

It must have been the night. Stray dust in the wind. Something pricked at his eye. Costa wiped it away, a single, stinging tear, from the corner. Then he saw he was not alone. By the low, feeble bushes at the edge of the pavement overlooking the small, once-holy place where a famous man had been turned to ashes, a woman sat on the ground with a child on her lap. She wore the heavy clothes of an immigrant: bulky yet exotic once, with a patterned headscarf that might have been colourful years ago, and a flowing, grubby dress beneath a man's winter parka.

The child could have been no more than five or six, so tightly wrapped against the cold or rain it might have been a boy or a girl, there was no telling. In front of them lay all the usual signs of the lost and destitute, the illegal and starving, carried around the city. *We are hungry. I look for work. Have pity.*

And a cardboard box full of small objects, barely visible, glittering under the bright illumination of the forum.

He got up, walked over and retrieved one of the items. It was fashioned from rubbish: foil and silver paper tightly wrapped together to make something that approximated to a piece of jewellery, a brooch perhaps. This was how they spent their day, he guessed. Trawling through litter bins trying to turn the detritus of the city into a handful of small change, enough to buy a little bread.

Costa put the thing back in the box. The woman was staring at him, silent. Afraid, he thought. It was late at night. They were on their own. Sometimes, rarely but it happened, a band of racist thugs might emerge from the suburbs and beat up people like these, just for the hell of it.

He took out his wallet, leaned down and gave the woman a fifty-euro note.

'Happy Christmas,' Costa said, and some dimly remembered line from a song repeated in his memory with a cruel insistent irony . . . *War is over*.

'Thank you, sir,' the woman said in a heavy Middle Eastern accent.

The child's eyes stared at him, shining, puzzled, fearful.

'You don't need to be out in this kind of weather,' he said, reaching for something else in his wallet. 'There are places . . . the Church . . .' His voice seemed to be breaking. 'Nuns . . . sisters . . .'

He threw down the card he'd kept for years, the one he hadn't handed out to anyone for a while because the old routine, the one he had inherited from his father – a gift a day, always to a stranger – had disappeared from his world altogether somehow.

'Please . . .' he croaked.

The woman looked up at him, a shadow of a smile on her wide face, which was, he suspected, both tanned and dirty, and said, 'I am Muslim, sir.'

'It doesn't matter to them,' he snapped. 'Does it to you?'

The tone in his voice alarmed them. He could see it on their faces. They were frightened, of him, of what he stood for.

'I'm sorry . . .' he stuttered. 'I didn't mean to sound like that. The point is . . . there's help. Please. Go. Tomorrow. Please . . .'

He took out the wallet again, opened the flap, turned the thing upside down, let all he had – notes and cards and scraps of paper that no longer meant a thing – fall out, mumbling incomprehensibly as he did this, not even knowing himself what the words were.

Everything tumbled down to lie in the grimy fabric between her knees, so much, so loose in the wind, it spilled over onto the pavement and began to scatter on the breeze.

They were more frightened this time.

'Too much, sir,' the woman said.

'It's not too much. It's nothing. It's . . . meaningless.'

It wasn't the night. Or dust on the breeze. Costa was crying, his eyes so full he could scarcely see. Everything was a blur – the lights on the ragged lines of ruins, the white wedding cake of the Vittorio Emanuele monument.

He staggered back to the stone bench and sat down, head high, staring through these tears, choking, sobbing, feeling, at that moment, as if the world had ceased to matter.

He didn't know how long this went on. It came to an end when the child walked over and tapped his arm. It was a boy, with a face as innocent as an infant in one of the paintings Costa loved so much. In his hands he carried the cash that had fallen from the wallet – most of it – and the cards and the notes. And a small brooch made of tinfoil and the lining of a cigarette packet.

'*Grazie.*'

'*Prego,*' Costa mumbled, and looked at it, unable to raise a smile however hard he tried.

At that moment his phone rang. The boy retreated, back to his mother. The living world returned.

'*Pronto* . . .' Costa said in a voice he didn't recognize.

'Nic? Are you all right. You sound—'

'Where are you?' he asked. Just hearing her voice made his throat well up with emotion once more.

'It doesn't matter. I'm safe. Listen to me. This is important.'

He did listen. He wasn't sure he heard the words correctly. He wasn't sure he understood anything much at that moment.

Besides, there was something he had to say, something so important it couldn't wait, whatever Agata thought.

'No—' he interrupted her in mid-sentence.

'You must listen to me,' she insisted, 'carefully.'

'Where are you?'

There was a quiet, impatient silence on the line. Then . . .

'I told you this before,' she said with a clipped, angry precision. 'There are places I may go where you cannot.'

'What kind of an answer is that?'

'It's the best I can do.'

'*No!*'

He was getting to his feet, screaming like a madman on Mussolini's deserted highway under the silhouetted skeletons from another time.

Out of the corner of his eye he saw the woman get up, grab her son and bundle the child away, stumbling down the broad pavement, carrying their belongings, the cardboard box, some plastic carrier bags – the sight of them ripped at his feelings – and a huge roll of grubby bedding.

'Where I come from,' he said as calmly as he could, tears rolling down his face again, warm and salty, welcome in some strange way too, 'you do not run away. You do not abandon people as if they mean nothing whatsoever. In my world there is nothing worse.'

That silence again, and he wondered how it was possible to interpret nothingness, to sense in this absence of sound that she was listening, shocked, baffled, wondering what to say.

'In my world,' Sister Agata Graziano replied eventually, 'I have never had to think of things like that. You must do as I ask. Please. Alone. That is the only way. I will call.'

She said no more. The line was dead. Costa was utterly alone, wishing, more than anything at that moment, that there was something he could say to the woman on the street and her frightened child, fleeing into the night, afraid of what he had become.

But, all too quickly, they were gone, out towards the Piazza Venezia, and the places where the homeless gathered together for safety when winter closed in: the Pantheon and the Campo dei Fiori, the riverside haunts by the Tiber where he and Emily had once helped save one – just one – young foreigner from the night.

The tears still pricked at his eyes.

Costa wiped them away with the sleeve of his jacket, then he limped across the empty dual carriageway of the Via dei Fori Imperiali, found one of the cheap flophouses off the Via Cavour and got a hard, cold single bed for the night.

Part 18

THE GARDEN OF EVIL

- 1 -

At 8 a.m., when the noise from the neighbouring room woke him, Costa walked out into the street and found stallholders in white jackets firing up charcoal braziers for hot chestnuts, panini stands getting ready for the day. A lone tree, sprinkled with artificial snow, stood erect at the entrance to the square. Next to it was some kind of musical stage at the foot of the Vittorio Emanuele monument, complete with a gaggle of bored-looking musicians and a troupe of skimpily dressed girl dancers shivering, clutching at their bare arms, trying to find some protection against the weather. A bright winter sun did nothing to dispel the bitter, dry, bone-chilling cold. A trickle of people wrapped in heavy clothing meandered past the moody entertainers on to the broad pavements of the Via dei Fori Imperiali, spilling out into the traffic lanes now closed to all but pedestrians, as they were every Sunday.

It was still Christmas in Rome, just. The place felt unreal, expectant somehow. Costa walked down the middle of the road, where a thousand cars and vans normally fought each other daily, thinking, praying for his phone to ring. Then, when he got near the foot of the tree, close enough to see the low illumination of the fairy lights still lit even in the brightness of the day, a familiar unmarked blue Fiat worked through the barriers and came to a halt next to him. Peroni was behind the wheel. He looked bemused. But not unhappy.

The big man pushed open the passenger door and said, not quite angry, 'You left your ID card in that crummy hotel. Amazingly they phoned to tell us. You'd better get in.'

Two minutes later – far more quickly than he could ever have expected on a normal day – they were parked in the Piazza Navona, the place empty save for the pigeons. Peroni said little along the way, except for murmuring a couple of cautious remarks about his looks. Costa ignored them. He felt distanced from everything, as if this was all part of a waking dream. As if . . .

They got out and walked round the corner towards the statue of Pasquino.

Costa's heart skipped a beat. There was a slender figure in black there, back to him, facing the battered, misshapen statue, staring at some fresh sheet of white paper stuck on the base.

He ran, ignoring Peroni's anxious calls from behind.

A sister, a nun. He didn't know the difference. He no longer cared.

When he got there he placed a hand gently on her shoulder. The figure turned, smiled at him, then stepped backwards, primly removing herself from his touch.

She was a woman in her forties, with a very pale and beautiful face, light grey eyes and silver hair just visible.

'I'm sorry,' he muttered. 'I thought . . .'

His attention was divided between her and the poster on the statue. A poster she'd fixed there the moment before. There were other figures in black nearby too.

They had pieces of paper in their hands and rolls of tape. They were placing the sheets everywhere, on walls, on shop windows, carefully aligning each at eye level to make them as visible as possible.

'They're all over the city,' Peroni said, catching up with him. 'On the other statues. In the Piazza Venezia. This lady asked for you in particular.' He glared at the woman in black. 'Which is all she'd say.'

'Not true,' the sister objected. 'I wished you a good morning and happy Christmas too. You should be flattered. Normally I would say nothing at all.'

'Sister,' Peroni replied, 'Agata Graziano is missing. We would very much like to find her. There is no time for these antics.'

She shrugged and responded with nothing more than an upturned smile, a worldly gesture and very Roman. Much the kind of response Agata would have given if she'd wished to avoid the conversation.

He read the poster, a new message for the talking statues, one they were determined to post everywhere, as Falcone had posted his, though this was very different.

'It was Agata's idea?' he asked quietly. 'Sister . . .'

The woman's grey eyes returned his gaze, unwavering, interested and, he thought, marked by an inner concern she was reluctant to reveal.

'You're Nic?'

'I am.'

'This is true,' she replied. 'You are as she described.'

The woman looked at Peroni and began to motion with her hands, saying, 'Shoo, shoo, *shoo*! This is for him. No one else.'

Under the fierceness of her stare, the big man backed off, towards the large public square behind.

She waited, then retrieved an envelope from the folds of her black cloak.

'Sister Agata sends this. For you and you alone.'

He ripped it open and read the contents: a single sheet in a spidery academic hand. Unsigned.

'God go with you,' the woman said quietly.

He took one more look at the words on the poster beneath the malformed, crumbling statue. His childhood studies, literature and art, had never really left him. The quotation was recognizable. Given the book, he could have found it. The words were an adaptation from Dante again, with a message, direct and personal, tagged on the front.

Costa read the words out loud, listening to their cadence, hearing her voice in each syllable.

'Franco, Count of Malaspina. Do you not know that, for all your black deeds and black blood, you are like all of us "worms born to form the angelic butterfly"? For Emily Costa and all those murdered women whose lives were taken by your sad anger, God offers forgiveness. Take it.'

The sister watched him impassively as he spoke, her head tilted to pay attention to the words.

'He's not looking for salvation,' Costa noted, stuffing the letter into his jacket pocket, then taking out his gun, checking the magazine was full, and thinking ahead of what might lie in wait.

Agata was attempting to force Malaspina's hand, both by revealing his guilt and by what she believed to be the secret he hated most: his ancestry. It was . . . Costa wished his head was functioning better. It was wrong, he felt, though he was unable to be precise about his reasons.

The woman in the black robes eyed the weapon with a baleful expression.

'Everyone is looking for salvation,' she murmured with a quiet, simple conviction. 'Whether they know it or not.'

He wasn't in the mood for distractions. Peroni came over, looking hopeful.

'I have to do this on my own, Gianni,' Costa said, ignoring the woman.

'But—'

'But nothing. That's how it is.'

The sister's smug smile was becoming annoying.

'Arrest these women for fly-posting,' he ordered. 'Keep them inside under lock and key until this evening.'

She began to protest, and her colleague across the way too.

'Sister,' Peroni interrupted, 'you have the right to remain silent. Or call the Pope. But he might be busy today.'

'You've no idea how many women there are in Rome like us,' the senior one hissed at him. 'None at all.'

He didn't. Nor was it important. There was only one thing that mattered.

Costa started running north, back into the narrow streets and lanes beyond the Piazza Navona, back into the streets of Ortaccio, letting the long-forgotten rhythm of his movement across the cobbled streets of Renaissance Rome remind him of a time before this pain, a time when he was nothing more than a single, insignificant *agente* in a city full of wonders.

- 2 -

By nine thirty Gianni Peroni was sick of seeing nuns and sisters. It seemed as if an army had assembled on the streets of Rome, every last woman in a religious order who could walk, flocks of them, no longer scampering through the streets quickly, discreetly, like skittish black-birds brought to earth, but instead throwing off their shy invisibility to stomp around the deserted city with one idea only: putting up Agata Graziano's curious message in places even the most adventurous fly-posters would never dare to venture. Her adaptation of Dante, with Franco Malaspina's name and crimes now attached, was plastered on some of the most famous and visible build-ings in the city.

Copies ran like a line of confetti across the roadside perimeter of the Colosseum, to the fury of the architec-tural authorities, who had interrupted the peace of their holiday break to call the Questura in a rage. All the other talking statues were now covered in them too, as was the statue of Giordano Bruno in the Campo dei Fiori and the stone sides of the Ponte Sant'Angelo, the pedestrian pilgrims' bridge across the Tiber on the way to the Vati-can. A handful of sisters had even managed to attach

468

several to the front of the Palazzo Madama, the Senate building where Caravaggio once lived under the patronage of Del Monte, an act that had brought down the tardy wrath of the Carabinieri, who now, the TV stations said, had fifteen sisters and nuns in custody, for vandalism against public, though never Church, buildings throughout Rome.

The Questura, Perroni was alarmed to discover on his return with the two silent, smug women from the Piazza Pasquino, was in possession of no fewer than twenty-three, which was why Prinzivalli, the duty uniform *sovrin-tendente* at the front desk, threw up his hands in horror at the sight of Peroni leading two more through the door and wailed, 'What are we doing, man? Collecting them?'

Peroni turned and looked behind him. The quieter of the two women he had apprehended was patiently taping a poster to the notice board in the public waiting room. She seemed to have an entire roll of them stuffed inside the voluminous dark folds of her gown. He found himself wondering at the idea that a community of sisters should have a photocopying machine, then cursed his own ignorance. All along, Nic had understood something that had eluded the rest of them. These women were not shy and weak and unworldly. Some, perhaps. But not all. Many had a determination and a conviction that escaped the daily population of the city who nodded at them on buses and in the street, never thinking for a moment there was much life or interest beneath that drab uniform. Yet they possessed a certain kind of courage, needed it to withdraw from conventional humanity in the first place.

When that resolution was tested . . . Peroni checked himself. They were still women on their own, and Agata Graziano a defenceless sister, seemingly alone in a city where at least one 'Ndrangheta thug remained on the loose and looking to take her life.

Falcone bustled in. The inspector looked bright-eyed, full of vigour . . . and damned angry.

'What is this?' he demanded, ripping the sheet from the wall, staring at the words as if they were in a language he couldn't understand. 'Well?'

'Don't ask me,' Peroni answered. He nodded at the two by his side. 'Ask them.'

'I've been asking their kind all morning. All they do is stare back at me, smile sweetly and say nothing. Well?'

The two women smiled at him, sweetly, and said not a word.

'Damn it! Where's Costa?'

'He had a message,' Peroni replied, fully expecting the storm to break, and utterly without a care about its arrival. 'Sister Agata passed it on through this lady here.'

Falcone asked tentatively, 'And?'

'He's gone. He didn't say where. She—'

'I don't know,' the older sister interrupted. 'So please do not be unpleasant. You will only make yourself more choleric.'

Falcone's eyebrows rose high on his bald, tanned forehead. The door opened and two uniformed officers walked in with four more women in long flowing winter robes.

'Arrest no more nuns,' Falcone ordered. 'Put that out on the radio, Prinzivalli.'

The *sovrintendente* nodded with a smile, made some remark about this being one of the more unusual orders he'd had to pass to the control room of late, and disappeared.

'Sister,' Falcone went on, standing in front of the

woman who had delivered the message to Costa, 'you must tell me where Agata Graziano is. Where our officer is too. I don't understand what she's doing, but it is a distraction, perhaps a dangerous one, in a case of the utmost seriousness. I cannot allow her to be dragged in any further. I regret bitterly that I allowed this involvement at all.'

The woman's grey eyes lit up with surprise and anger.

'You arranged it in the first place, Falcone.'

The inspector's cheeks flushed.

'You know my name?'

'Naturally. Sister Agata spoke to us at length last night. We broke our own rules. We were awake long past the due time.' She smiled at Peroni. 'We know about you all. And more.' Her face became serious. 'We know you have no case, Ispettore. This man . . . Malaspina. He has defeated you. He has money and the law on his side. He is one of those nasty, thuggish Renaissance knights Sister Agata told us of, a man who has – ' to Peroni's astonishment she stabbed Falcone in the chest with a long, hard finger – 'bested you entirely. For all your power. All your – ' this time her eyes flashed in Peroni's direction – 'men.'

'That is an interesting observation, Sister,' Falcone barked. 'Now, where the hell are they?'

'You think God has nothing to do with justice?' the woman asked, seemingly out of nowhere.

'If he has,' Falcone answered immediately, 'he's been doing a damned poor job of it lately. If . . .'

The tall, lean figure in the slick grey suit went quiet. Peroni hummed a little tune and rocked on his heels. It was a remarkably stupid – and quite uncharacteristic – comment for such an intelligent man to make.

The long, bony finger poked at Falcone's tie again.

'God works through us,' she said. 'Or not, as may be the case.'

'Where are they?' he asked again.

She took his wrist and turned it so that she could see his watch.

'All in good time.'

Then the woman took one step back and exchanged glances with the others there, all of whom had listened to this exchange in silence. She was, it seemed to Peroni, the senior among them, and they knew it.

'There is one thing,' she said with visible trepidation.

'What?' Falcone snapped, but not without some eagerness.

'Sister Agata told us your coffee isn't like our coffee. From powder. In big urns. She said . . . your coffee was . . . different. May we try some? It is Christmas.'

Falcone closed his eyes for a moment, then took out his wallet.

'The Questura coffee is not fit for animals,' he declared. 'Take these women out of my sight, Agente. If you can find them somewhere that's open, buy them whatever they want.'

– 3 –

Ten minutes later they were in the nearest cafe that was open, a place famed for both the quality of its coffee and cakes and its foul-mouthed owner, Totti, a middle-aged bachelor now stiff with outrage behind his counter, like a cock whose territory had been invaded by an alien species.

'It's not right,' he confided to Peroni behind his hand, as they stood at the end of the bar, a little way away from the gaggle of black-clad women sipping at their cups of cappuccino and tasting cornetti and other cakes as if this everyday event was entirely new to them, as it probably was. 'It's bad enough when there are more women here than men. But these women.'

'They are just women,' Peroni grumbled.

He didn't like Totti. The man was a misanthrope. If there had been anywhere else within walking distance that was open . . . But the coffee was good. From the expressions on the women's faces, it was a revelation.

'A waste of a life,' Totti replied. 'What good does that do any of them? A couple would look decent scrubbed up and in a dress too.'

Peroni gave him the stare, a good one. There were, he reflected, decided advantages to being an ugly brute at times. Totti's toothbrush moustache bristled and, without a word, the man walked off to polish, half-heartedly, some beer glasses by the sink.

Each of the sisters now possessed a half-brown, half-white cappuccino moustache above her top lip. Oblivious to something they seemed not to notice even on one another, they were gossiping, the way all Roman women did, but quietly.

He walked over, trying to make sense of the thought that kept bugging him.

'Ladies!' he said cheerily, picking up one of the empty coffee cups. 'So, how was it?'

'Very rich,' the senior one said immediately, for all of them, that was clear. 'Enjoyable but a luxury. Perhaps once a year. No more.'

'Once a year is better than once a lifetime, Sister,' Peroni observed.

'Before Rome, I worked in Africa,' she answered tartly. 'They would have been happy with once a lifetime there.'

'Happy?' Peroni echoed. 'I doubt it, don't you?'

'I never realized a police officer would be so precise about words. Sister Agata said you were remarkable. The three of you. So what now?'

He beamed at them.

'Now you clear your debts. You tell me something.'

'Falcone paid,' she said. 'He's not here.'

'It's a small thing and, being sisters, you believe in charity. It is this.' He had checked with Prinzivalli while Falcone was berating them in the Questura. It had seemed, to him if not to Leo Falcone, an obvious question to ask. 'You've performed Sister Agata's bidding on most of the prominent buildings in the *centro storico*. It's an impressive feat. You must have been very busy.'

'What is?'

'The boss sister you just met told us. We've failed. The law's failed. All the ways we have of dealing with situations like this . . . They're done with, busted, and Agata knows it. The best we can hope to come out with at the moment is a green light from Grimaldi to start using Teresa and her magic DNA machine again on anyone except Malaspina. That's the pay-off . . . and your cunning little sister thinks she has another way.'

He didn't hear an instant explosion. That was good.

'Five good men,' he added hopefully. 'An unmarked van. An hour or two. No more. I don't think we'll need it.'

'I don't have—'

'If she's in there she will surely need our help before long. Whether she – or they – know it or not. Do you want to leave that to a phone call and the off-chance we might have a spare car to send round from the Questura. Would that make you happy?'

Falcone uttered a quiet, bitter curse, then added, 'For a mere *agente* you have a lot to say.'

'Nic's there. I rather like Agata too. What do you expect?'

'Wait outside,' he ordered. 'And don't let anyone know what you're doing.'

– 5 –

She had specified the place, and the location filled him
with dread. It was the area behind the studio in the Vicolo
del Divino Amore, the dank cobbled yard full of junk and
stray weeds where he had first encountered Malaspina,
hooded, armed and deadly, before chasing him out into
the open streets, towards the Mausoleum of Augustus.

Towards Emily.

Costa stopped for a moment as he entered the narrow
brick corridor from the street, the place where Malaspina
had turned and made that perfect 'O' shape behind the
fabric, murmured 'boom' and then dodged his fire in
return. After that . . .

He didn't want to think about it. There wasn't time.
He retraced his steps down the alley, wondering where
she might be, whether he was too late already. The place
seemed different. Smaller. Even more squalid. Looking
everywhere, half running, close to the wall, trying to move
with as little noise and visibility as possible, he went on
until he got to the small, enclosed yard at the end.

The sight of the junk, and the vicious, clear memory of
Malaspina hidden behind it, brought back such bitter
recollections. For one fleeting moment he could see

Emily's face rising in his imagination, staring at him, angry, determined, the way she always was when danger threatened.

Then a sound, thankfully, sent her ghost scattering from his head.

Agata emerged in the far corner of the yard, creeping out from behind some discarded mattresses leaning against the blackened stones of the grimy terrace that had once been the home of Caravaggio. She was trying to smile. There was something in her hand he couldn't see.

Her clothes were ordinary: a simple black nylon anorak and plain jeans. The kind the convent probably gave out to the poor, he thought. She looked like many a young woman in Rome at that moment, except for the expression on her face, which was excited, with a fixed resolve that worried him.

He walked over and stood in front of her.

'You will come with me now,' Costa said forcefully. 'You will leave this place and go to the Questura. Even if I have to carry you.'

'Do that, Nic, and you lose forever. Franco Malaspina will walk free. He will negotiate with that lawyer of yours. His guilt will be forgotten in return for allowing you to establish that of others. Do you wish to bargain with the devil? Is that who you are?'

'Agata—'

'Is it?' she demanded, her dark eyes shining.

'I lost my wife to that man,' he said quietly, hearing the crack in his own voice. 'I don't wish to see another life wasted.'

'Don't fear on my account. That's my responsibility. How did he come here for those women?' she asked. 'Did you think about that? He's a well-known man. He wouldn't walk in the front door. It was too obvious. Nor . . .'

She turned her head briefly to the brick corridor.

'. . . would he have risked that. It opens out into the Piazza Borghese. He would have been seen there too. People notice. You hardly ever meet Franco out in the open, in the street. It's beneath him.'

'This is all too late.'

She leaned forward, smiling, her pert, smart face animated as always.

'He owns everything. Every square metre. Every last brick and stone. He came through his own house.' She glanced towards a shadowy alcove half hidden behind some discarded chests. 'You never looked. It never seemed important. After all, you couldn't enter his palace anyway.'

Costa struggled to find the words to make her understand.

'Malaspina wants you dead.'

'No.' She shook her head. Her dark curly hair flew wildly around her with the violence of the gesture. 'That's only a part of it. What he wants is to forget what he is, where he came from. All those black women. Women like me. "The sport in the blood." He's ashamed of his lineage, as were Ippolito Malaspina and Alessandro de' Medici before him. There is your resolution, if only you knew it. Franco Malaspina is at war with himself and flails at everything in order to hide that simple fact.'

He sighed. 'I don't think so,' he said.

'So what, then?'

Something still didn't ring true, however hard she tried.

'This is all conjecture,' he answered. 'Useless and dangerous.'

'No,' she insisted. 'It's not.'

'Did you ever stop to think for a moment how we all felt when you ran away?'

'Nic,' she whispered, black eyes sparkling, her mouth taut with emotion and something close to fear. 'This is not about me.'

'I lost my wife . . .'

'I'm sorry. I didn't mean to hurt you. I never meant that.'

'You don't know what hurt is. You're too afraid to feel it. You're terrified something real might penetrate the cocoon you have built yourself.'

'That's not fair . . .'

'I don't care about fair any more. I just want you to live. Please. Let me take you out of here.'

He held out his hand for her. She looked up at him, scared, resolute too.

'You really think I can go back into my shell now?' she asked, amazed, perhaps resentful too. 'As easily as that?'

'I think—' he began.

'It's impossible,' she cut in, shaking her head. 'You made it so. You and Falcone.' She hesitated. 'You more than any.'

He took a step forward. She shrank back against the wall, put a hand out in front of her. He saw now what she'd brought. Another large carrier bag with the name of an economy supermarket on the front lay at her feet. An object he couldn't quite make out protruded from the top.

'Wait . . .' Costa ordered.

Before he could go on she had ducked away from his

grasping arms and was running behind the discarded chests into the shadowy alcove.

He followed. When he got there she had the crowbar in the bottom half of a small, battered wooden door black with soot and grime. The top had been splintered already. Agata had found a way into the Palazzo Malaspina earlier, before his arrival. She was, as always, prepared.

'This is madness,' he muttered. 'I should call the Questura now. Why take such risks when you have your sisters all over Rome putting up that poster about the man?'

She leaned hard on the crossbar. The lower half of the door refused to budge.

'Because of what Falcone says,' she answered. 'You pile on the pressure, you see what happens. Franco will not walk out of this place for you, will he? But with a little force here . . . a little force there . . .'

She had known Leo Falcone longer than he had. It was, he thought, only natural that she should pick up his ways.

'The question is,' she went on, 'will you come with me? Or do I go into his palace on my own? There are – ' she leaned hard on the crowbar again, to no effect – 'no other alternatives. Can't you see that? Your law won't help you. Nor your grief.'

Agata gave up on the door and looked at him. Her face shone in a stray shaft of winter sun.

'All we need is the painting,' she insisted. 'Where else can it be?'

He muttered a quiet curse, walked over and took the metal bar from her. It was a strong door, in spite of appearances. But after the third attempt the old wood cracked and they could see beyond, into the interior of this distant wing of the Palazzo Malaspina. There was darkness there, nothing else. It was prescient of her to bring along the torch in the carrier bag. It now sat in her hand, extending a long beam of yellow light into the gloom.

'I go first,' Costa said. 'What are you doing?'

She was pressing the keys of the mobile phone Rosa had given her, dispatching a text message with the speed and enthusiasm of someone who did this every single day.

'Talking to my sisters,' Agata replied cryptically, then pushed past him, torch blazing, into the black maw behind the door.

Costa followed quickly. From the wall above a red light blinked persistently. He reached forward, took her hand to guide the beam towards it. There was a security camera there, a single glass eye, blinking. There had to be hundreds in a place like this. He turned round and looked back at the door. There was no entry detection device that he could see. Costa knew how difficult such large and sprawling buildings were to monitor. There was no way of knowing whether they had been seen or not; the probability was that no one had yet been alerted to their presence.

All the same he picked up the crowbar off the floor and dashed the forked end hard into the lens of the camera, stabbing at it until the glass broke and he was able to lever the unit off the wall.

She watched in silence. In the half-light she looked afraid.

He took the torch from her hand. There was no protest.

'Stay behind me,' he ordered, and strode forward into the gloom.

– 6 –

It was bitterly cold inside whatever remote, deserted wing of Franco Malaspina's palace now enclosed them. They walked in single file down a long, straight, narrow corridor, then came directly to a plain grey wall, windowless, nothing but old stone and mortar.

'This must be the rear wall of the palace proper,' she whispered. 'That was how they built in those days. The master's part would be erected on its own. The rest – the quarters in the Vicolo del Divino Amore, everything that wasn't integral to the palace itself – would be added later. We must be in some kind of access corridor between the buildings. It's—'

'Quiet,' he whispered, placing a finger to his lips.

Agata stopped speaking instantly. Her eyes, whiter than usual in the bright, unforgiving light of the torch, betrayed her fear.

She can hear it too, Costa thought.

Footsteps. Heavy and echoing, with a loud, insistent rhythm.

He flashed the beam around both sides of the junction. They were trapped in a slender stone vein deep within the bulky mass of the palace. The sound danced around them deceptively. There was nowhere to hide, no easy way to discern the source.

Before he could think this through, she tugged on his arm and then did something so strange, yet so obvious.

Agata placed one hand on her left ear, then one on her right, dividing the echo from its origin, measuring which was stronger. Quickly, decisively, she pointed to the left and arced her arm over to indicate the opposite direction.

Costa looked behind her, at the corridor they had already traversed. A way back to freedom. She cast him one brief, withering look, then snatched the torch from his fingers and was moving, down the right-hand side, in the lead, brushing vigorously through thick grey cobwebs with her arms, away from whoever was on their trail, or so she hoped.

He kept pace behind, continually glancing backwards, seeing nothing. There were no alternatives, no other route to follow, and very soon they found themselves in another constricted stone channel, this time wide enough only for a single human body, one that curved with a regular, geo-metric precision, as if tracking a circular room beyond the wall. He had no idea what the interior plan of the Palazzo Malaspina looked like. Costa had only seen the first, public rooms, which covered a tiny proportion of the total site. Great Roman palaces often contained many surprises: private chapels, baths, even a secret place for alchemical experiments, like the private casino of the Villa Ludovisi, where Caravaggio had painted for Cardinal Del Monte. It was impossible to judge in which direction they were headed, impossible to see anything except the grimy walls of uniform stones laid almost five centuries before.

The other sound quickened, became louder, and was now identifiably behind them. And closer.

Costa caught up with Agata, felt for his gun to make sure it was safe to hand, and found himself brushing against her, accidentally, inevitably, before realizing why.

The corridor was narrowing. In the space of a few steps it became so slender his shoulders rubbed against the walls as they moved, half running. Then the change in dimensions stopped. It would, he thought, stay this way for a while. He caught her arm, stopped her and mouthed, *Go ahead*.

Her sharp eyes flared with anger and she whispered, 'No!'

All the same, when she resumed her pace he managed to drop behind, just a little, enough to stay inside the penumbra of the torch beam that trapped them in this confined, enclosing space.

Whoever was following was near. He was sure of that.

Costa took out his gun, held it tight, trying to work out some strategy. He blundered on in the semi-darkness, weapon in hand, wondering what the possibilities were in the belly of this stone leviathan, where the chances of anything – a scream, a forlorn message on the police radio – reaching the world outside were infinitesimal.

No easy answers came. None at all. Then abruptly, with a force that made him apologize automatically, he found himself barging into her small, taut body, which was locked in an upright position, hard against stone.

She had stopped. Her breathing was so rapid and so shallow he felt he could hear and feel every gasp she made. The corridor had come to a dead end. It led nowhere, which seemed impossible. The only way was back.

'Stay still,' he murmured.

She wasn't listening. She was turned to one side, as

stationary as the stone that trapped them, and, when his eyes adjusted to what he now realized was a new kind of light, he understood why.

The corridor ended in a bare stone wall, but down one side stood a long, musty drape that flapped into his face as the hand she had wrapped tightly in its folds began to shake. This was an entrance into another room, one that, as he began to look, was huge: a circular chamber, bathed, incredibly, in light so bright that even this side view made his head hurt.

In the centre, beneath a domed glass roof that let in the piercing rays of a low winter sun, stood the painting. *Evathia in Ekstasis.* It shone under the incandescent illumination pouring down from above, the central fleshy figure, frozen in Caravaggio's pigment, seemingly alive, energized, almost exultant as she opened her throat to release that primal scream.

In front was a couch, a chaise-longue much like the one they had found in the squalid studio of the Vicolo del Divino Amore. On it Franco Malaspina, still in a business suit, his trousers hitched halfway down, heaved and groaned over a naked African woman, her skin the colour of damp coal, her eyes wild with terror.

Malaspina's long, strong body strained over her. They could hear his panting, whimpering, grunting, and the obvious desperation behind the pained sighs. When Costa looked more closely, he could see the man's eyes flickering between the floor and the figure in the painting, never to the woman beneath him.

'Sweet Jesus,' Agata moaned. 'What's wrong, Nic?'

He didn't answer. He was thinking of the steps behind. Or trying to.

'What's wrong?' she demanded. Then, when he

remained silent, she answered her own question. 'Even with the painting he finds no . . . gratification. That's it, isn't it? Even now?'

They were watching the man who had murdered Costa's wife struggling to reach some kind of satisfaction with another woman snatched from the street, another pawn in his desperate, pitiless manoeuvres.

Agata shook her head. Her face seemed full of self-doubt, self-hatred even.

'We have to get out of here,' he insisted, casting a glance through the small gap created by the portion of curtain she was holding.

As they looked on, Malaspina let out a long, pained bellow of misery, then stood up from the couch, clutching his trousers to himself, refastening them. Costa's fingers tightened on the gun, but the woman was quick. While Malaspina remained absorbed in his own misery, scarcely noticing her presence, she fled, as many must have done before, scampering from him in fright, snatching some clothes off the floor and then leaving, Costa noticed, by an open door that lay almost exactly opposite from where they now stood.

It was an opportunity. If the two of them could escape alive, he'd be happy, he thought, and wondered how many 'Ndrangheta men Malaspina had in his service. One was dead already. If luck was on their side, perhaps that left no more than a single hired thug to guard the Palazzo Malaspina on this quiet, lazy day after Christmas.

'I pity him,' Agata murmured, taken aback by her own surprise. 'I . . .'

He heard the metallic sound echo down the corridor and recognized immediately what it was. The checking of a magazine. One last prerequisite before violence.

THE GARDEN OF EVIL

'Get out! Get down!' Costa ordered, pushing her rapidly, roughly through the drape, into the sea of light beyond and, he knew, the presence of Franco Malaspina.

A deafening burst of automatic fire burst deep within the stone vein back along the route they had stumbled. Sparks flew off the walls around him. Costa rolled forward to follow Agata, loosing off a wild succession of shots back into the gloom as he fell.

– 7 –

Gianni Peroni sat in the passenger seat of a white Fiat van bearing the name of a drain-clearing company on the side. It was parked a hundred metres from the main entrance to the Palazzo Malaspina. The place looked dead. The double doors at the top of the front staircase were closed. Not a soul had come or gone in the twenty minutes since they'd arrived. The four other officers with him – men he didn't know, men who were deeply unhappy about having their holiday leave interrupted and didn't seem too keen to accept his assumed authority over them – were starting to grumble the way cops did when boredom took hold.

'I sat outside some place on the Gianicolo for four days once,' the one behind the wheel, a skinny, tall individual with a Florentine accent, complained. 'Turned out it was the wrong house. Belonged to a big – and I mean big – woman opera singer and we thought we were staking out the *capo* of some Sicilian family. Four days. You take that with you to the grave.'

'Did you hear her sing?' asked a voice from behind.

'Yes . . .' the driver answered in a petulant whine.

'So why didn't you check?' another one demanded. 'I

mean . . . a *capo* doesn't normally have opera singers around, does he?'

'Hindsight,' the driver moaned. 'Every smartarse I ever met has it running through his veins.'

'It's a fair question,' another voice from the back piped up.

'We checked! It was someone else's fault.'

'It usually is,' Peroni observed. 'May I make a request, gentlemen?'

They went quiet and listened.

'Shut up and watch, will you?'

'Watch what?' the driver asked. 'And why? You're just an *agente* now, Peroni. You're not the boss.'

Gianni Peroni muttered something obscene under his breath, then caught the dark figure in the distance, slowly making her way down the cobbled street towards the palazzo.

'Watch that,' he ordered.

And they did.

It was a nun – or a sister, Peroni had no way of telling which – on the oldest scooter he had ever seen, one that belonged in a museum, not on the road, since it was probably illegal: rust everywhere, bald tyres, a cracked exhaust that, even from this distance, sounded like a flatulent pigeon recovering from the night before.

'What the hell is this?' wondered a puzzled voice from the back.

'Watch,' Peroni ordered again.

She made her way slowly down the street. Then, outside the palazzo, she stopped. The woman wore black, flowing robes, so long and billowing he wondered whether they might catch in the spokes. If she'd ridden a two-wheeled vehicle before she didn't show much sign of it. She was perhaps sixty, tall, skinny, awkward. A bright red cyclist's helmet sat over the black and white headgear he had come to associate with the uniform of a nun in Rome.

'It's Evel Knievel's grandma,' the driver joked, and the rest of them snickered, until they caught sight of the displeasure on Peroni's battered face.

The woman struggled to flip down the stand, got there eventually, then dismounted. After that she reached into the flapping folds of her robe and withdrew a large kitchen knife.

'You may not be too wrong there,' Peroni murmured.

They watched as the woman looked around to check no one was watching, then bent down and started stabbing at the front tyre with the kitchen knife. It deflated in a matter of seconds; the wall must have been paper thin.

After that she walked up the broad, semicircular stone staircase of the Palazzo Malaspina, found the bell by the shining wooden double doors, put her finger on the button and kept it there.

'Next time I go undercover I go as a nun,' one of the voices behind muttered, and there was more than a modicum of admiration in it too.

Finally the door opened. Peroni squinted to get a good look at the man there. He was relieved by what he saw. Sister Knievel might have pulled one of Malaspina's 'Ndrangheta thugs. Instead she got a flunkey, a tired-looking middle-aged individual of less than average height, one who didn't look too smart and had probably been called away from cleaning the silver.

He didn't seem much interested in helping a stray

sister whose ancient scooter had developed a flat tyre. The way the woman was talking at him, she plainly meant to ensure he didn't have much choice. At one point she took hold of the collar of his white cotton servant's jacket and dragged him out onto the steps. Peroni watched, impressed. He could almost hear the conversation.

Sir, I am in a hurry for mass. I am only a sister. You must help.

Yes, but . . .

SIR!

Reluctantly, with a very Roman shrug of his hunched shoulders, the servant gave in and walked down the broad steps, followed her to the rusty machine, bent down and started looking at the flat. Naturally, he left the door ajar. This was a rich man's residence. No one expected opportunistic thieves. Nor could the servant see what the woman was doing as she stood over him – namely, beckoning to someone around the corner, half hidden at the top of the street.

The five police officers in the drain-clearing van watched what happened next in total silence. Peroni couldn't even find the space in his head to raise a laugh. It was so . . . extraordinary. And also so obvious. What the police needed, they clearly knew, was an excuse to enter the Palazzo Malaspina. They had spent weeks trying to find that through myriad means: forensic and scientific investigation, detective work and an exploration of Franco Malaspina's ancestry.

They hadn't counted on the cunning of a bunch of scheming nuns who, doubtless under Agata Graziano's tuition, had spent the night preparing to penetrate Malaspina's fortress in a way no law-enforcement officer could possibly have imagined, let alone entertained. They would bring in the police by the very simplest of expedients: committing the small crime of trespass themselves.

They flooded round the corner, an entire flock, black wings flapping, running with the short, straitened gait their robes forced on them. Perhaps twenty. Perhaps more. A giggling, excited mass of sisterhood raced down the street and poured onto the steps of the Palazzo Malaspina, scampering upwards, to the door, not stopping to heed the cries of the servant, who was no longer staring at the flat tyre on the crippled scooter because its owner had swiftly departed to join her fellows, leading them exactly where Peroni expected.

Through both doors, now the intruders had thrown the second one open, the black tide flooded happily into the interior of the Palazzo Malaspina, as if this were some schoolgirl jape, the most amusing event to have occurred in their quiet, enclosed lives for years.

Peroni gave each of the men a look that said . . . *stay here*.

Then he slid out of the passenger door and strode down the street.

The servant was starting to flap and squawk, his pasty face red with outrage, lost for words, unsure what to do. He looked scared too. Peroni didn't need much imagination to guess that Franco Malaspina wasn't the nicest of bosses.

The man didn't take a single step towards the black mass of figures pushing into the palace on the steps above, either. Peroni understood why. They seemed a little scary too.

'Sir,' Peroni said, pulling out his police ID card, 'I'm from the Questura. Is there a problem?'

'A problem?' the man squawked. 'What the hell do you think?'

Peroni glanced at the pool of women. It was diminishing. Most of them were in the palace by now. He could see their silhouettes moving alongside the windows on both sides of the entrance as they ran in all directions.

'You know,' Peroni observed, 'this has been a bad day for nuns. It's shocking.'

'What the . . . ?'

'This is why you pay for a police force. To create order from chaos. To save ordinary citizens from . . .'

He glanced at the steps. The last black-clad figure was struggling through the doors.

'. . . the unexpected.'

'Oh, crap,' the man moaned. 'Malaspina will go crazy.'

Peroni leaned down and put on his most sympathetic face.

'Would you like me to go inside and deal with this for you?' he asked in a noncommittal fashion. 'Discreetly of course.'

'Yes . . . But . . . *But* . . .'

Peroni wasn't listening. He had what he wanted: a legitimate invitation to enter the Palazzo Malaspina, one prompted by a bunch of nuns and sisters who would surely impress any court.

He turned and beckoned to the men in the van. Four burly police officers jumped out, looking ready and eager for action.

The servant groaned, put his hands to his head and started to mumble a low series of obscene curses.

'You can leave it to us now,' Peroni shouted cheerfully down the street as he walked towards to the staircase, wondering what a private Roman palace looked like from the inside, and where on earth, within its many, rambling corridors, he might find Nic Costa and Agata Graziano.

He paused on the threshold. This really was not his kind of place. Then, out of politeness more than anything – since he had no intention of waiting – he placed a call to Falcone, explaining, in one sentence, what had happened.

There was a silence, pregnant with excitement.

'We're in, Leo, and I am not leaving until I have them,' Peroni added, walking through the door, almost blinded by the expanse of shining marble that glittered at him from every direction. 'Send me all the troops you have.'

– 8 –

It was like the Pantheon in miniature and that brought back memories. Costa rolled on the hard stone floor, hurting already, worked out where Agata was and dragged himself in front of her. They were right up against the wall of a room that formed a perfect circle marked by ribbed columns, each framing a fresco, each fronted by a plinth with a statue. The ceiling was glass held by delicate stone ribs, incandescent with dazzling sunlight. The floor seemed to be sunken and above it, no more than the height of two men, ran a balustraded gallery, like a viewing platform for some contest that would take place on the stage below.

It took a second or two for him to adapt. The gun was still in his hand. That was some consolation. He got to his knees, then stood up, glancing at Agata, understanding the shocked expression on her face, guarding her with his body as much as he could.

She had reason to be silent, to be shaking with fear behind him. This was Franco Malaspina's most private of sanctuaries and it was dedicated to a kind of classical pornography that defied the imagination. Behind the still-confident figure of Malaspina stood a marble Pan, larger than life and so beautiful he might have been carved by Bernini, laughing as he raped a young girl, every crude physical detail of the ravishment laid bare for the beholder. To their left stood a warrior in silver armour, painted to resemble Carpaccio's St George, savaging the maiden at the stake as the dragon lay bloodily at his feet. Equidistant around the circular chamber stood figures that were semi-human, beasts and men, half-real creatures and everywhere naked, vulnerable women, young, virginal, portrayed as if they were on the precipice of some revelation, afraid yet desperate for knowledge too, lips open, ready to utter the primal scream of joy and release that Caravaggio had placed in the throat of Eve in the painting at the heart of the room.

These were all plays on known works of art, paintings and statues he recognized, transformed by an obscene imagination, and they were old, as old as the Palazzo Malaspina itself, perhaps even more ancient, since Costa believed he could see some that must have preceded Caravaggio's enticing goddess, the original Eve, in the ecstatic throes of the original sin, taunting them with a conundrum – carnal love or divine? – that was lost, surely, on most of those who saw it.

Franco Malaspina stood next to the canvas watching them, unconcerned, amused.

As Costa struggled to consolidate his position – Agata behind him, protected, silent, astonished by what she saw – the count strode forward. He was unarmed but Costa could see where his eyes had drifted before he took that first step. Around the room at set intervals – there surely to enforce the impression that this was a knight's secret lair, a chamber of the round table dedicated to the sexual power of men – were collections of armour and weapons: swords and daggers, gleaming, clean, ready for use.

'Do you like my little temple?' Malaspina asked, stopping a short distance in front of them, smiling, bowing, unconcerned.

'Consider yourself under arrest,' Costa retorted, his voice hoarse from the dust in the corridors. 'The painting's evidence enough for me.'

The man laughed and took one more step forward.

'You can't arrest me here. No one can. This place belongs to me. To us. To my line. To my ancestors.' He caught Agata's eye. 'You are merely insects in the walls. Nothing. Does it not interest you, my little sister? Did you see me well enough from your little peephole?'

'What is this, Franco?' she murmured.

'This?' Malaspina replied, still moving slowly forwards. 'This is the world. The real world. As they created it. Those who came before. My ancestors and their friends. Artists. Poets. And lords to rule over them all.' His face turned dark. 'The world has need of lords, Agata. Even your Popes understood that.'

'Raping black women from the streets is scarcely a sign of class,' Costa observed, casting a nervous glance at the curtain to the hidden corridor, wondering what had happened to their pursuer, praying that one of his shots – how many remained in the magazine he'd no idea – had hit home.

Malaspina stopped and looked at them, his cruel, dark, aristocratic face full of contempt.

'Be honest with yourself, Costa. Given half the chance you would have stayed and watched too, then said nothing. That small, dark demon is in us all. Only the few have courage to embrace it. The Ekstasists have been here always, in this place, in this city. My father was one. His before him. When I have a son . . .'

It was clear. Costa understood the truth implicitly, and it horrified him, the idea that such a cruel and vicious decadence might be passed on through generations, though surely not with such savagery.

'Your father didn't kill people, did he?' he asked, trying to work out a safe way to reach the door by which the woman had left earlier. 'He didn't murder some penniless immigrant on a whim.' He nodded towards the canvas on the easel in front of the couch, its cushions still indented with the weight of Malaspina's body and that of the woman they had seen. 'He didn't need to place that painting in some squalid little room to hide the blood and the bones.'

'Black blood, black bones,' Agata murmured behind him.

'It was just a sick game before,' Costa went on. 'A rite of passage for a gang of rich, bored thugs. Then Nino showed you that painting and it became something worse.' He clutched the gun more tightly. There was a noise from near the curtain. 'Why was that?'

He backed her more tightly against the wall. The thunder in Malaspina's face scared him. The man didn't care.

'I will kill you first,' he said without emotion, then nodded towards Agata cowering behind Costa's shoulder. 'Then I will have her. This is my domain, little policeman. I own everything. I control everything. When I am done, what is left of you will disappear forever, just like those black whores. This . . .'

He strode over to the wall and took a long, slender sword, a warrior's weapon, real and deadly, from one of the displays there, tucking a short stiletto into his belt for good measure.

'. . . is why I exist.'

Costa held the gun straight out in front of him. He didn't care about the consequences any more, or whether some bent lawyer or magistrate would one day accuse him of murder. He had the man's cold, angular face on the bead and that was all that counted.

Then Agata was screaming again, slipping from beneath him. Costa's attention shifted abruptly to the drape and a figure crawling through it, bloodied, wounded, dying maybe.

It was Malaspina's man and in his gory hands he clutched a gun, clinging on to the cold black metal as if it were the most precious object in his life.

The 'Ndrangheta never gave up, never stopped till the job was done.

One brief rake of fire ran low against the circular boundary wall. He could feel Agata's small body quaking behind him. Before the man could find energy for a second run, Costa directed his gun away from Malaspina and released a single shot straight at the bloodied figure wrapped in the curtain, struggling to get upright. The shock of the impact jerked the stricken figure back into the drape, back into the dark chasm at the mouth of the corridor. He didn't move again.

Grinning, Malaspina took two steps forward, slashing the blade through the air in an easy, practised fashion.

'This is for my wife, you bastard,' Costa murmured, and drew the short black barrel of the Beretta level with the arrogant face in front of him, keeping it as straight and level as any weapon he had ever held, with a steady hand and not the slightest doubt or hesitation.

He pulled the trigger. The weapon clicked on empty.

- 9 -

Gianni Peroni had never been in a building like it before. There were women in black robes, nuns and sisters, wandering everywhere, lost once they had gained entrance, puzzled about what to do. And there were so many rooms: chamber after chamber, some grand, some small and functional, many looking little used in this sprawling palace that was home to a single human being detached from the reality beyond his domain.

Any servants around clearly had no desire to make themselves known. Perhaps they realized the Malaspina empire was crumbling under this strange invasion and knew what that meant. As he raced through the building, screaming out that they were police and demanding attention, Peroni became aware he was simply becoming more and more lost in some glorious Minotaur's maze, a travertine prison in which Franco Malaspina lived as solitary ruler of an empire of stiff, frozen grandeur. It was like hunting for life in a museum, like seeking the answer to a riddle from yet another riddle, a journey that wound in on itself, circling the same vistas, the same monuments and paintings and galleries.

The men from the Questura followed him, just as

bemused. Twice they met sisters and nuns they had encountered before, and got nothing from them except a shake of the head and equal puzzlement. The women's brief, it seemed to Peroni, was simple: find a way into the Palazzo Malaspina and breach its invisible defences, in such numbers that the police would surely be summoned. Once that had been achieved . . . Peroni tried to imagine the extent of Franco Malaspina's home. It covered a huge area, extending by first-floor bridges beyond neighbouring streets, as far as the studio in the Vicolo del Divino Amore where this tragedy, one that had such powerful, continuing personal dimensions for them all, had begun.

It was impossible to guess where to start looking. Then they turned a corner, one that looked much like any other – gleaming stone, carved heads on plinths, sterile splendour everywhere – and saw her. Peroni stopped, breathless. Just one look at the woman on the floor, terrified, clutching her clothes to her, made him realize exactly what they were seeking. Somewhere within this vast private empire was Franco Malaspina's clandestine lair, the sanctum where he felt free to do whatever he liked. This cowed and frightened woman in front of him understood where it lay. He could see that in her terrified features.

One of the other officers got there first, dragged her roughly to her feet and started to throw a series of loud, aggressive questions into her frightened face.

'Shut up,' Peroni barked at the man and pushed him out of the way, found a chair – all ornate gilt and spindly legs – by the window, brought it for her and let her sit down. Then he kneeled in front, making sure he didn't touch her, even by accident, and said, 'Please, Signora. We need your help. We must find Franco Malaspina, the master of this palace, now. There are people in danger here, just as you were. We must know where he is.'

'Yeah,' the officer who got there first butted in. 'Start talking or we start asking for papers.'

Peroni glowered at him and pointed at the broad glass panes next to them.

'If you utter one more moronic word,' he said quietly, 'I will, I swear, throw you straight out of that window.' He looked at the woman. In truth she was little more than a girl, a slim, pretty creature, with scars on her cheeks and short hair caught and braided in beads, now dishevelled. She was terrified still, but perhaps not as much as before. 'Please,' he repeated. 'I am begging you. This is important. This man has hurt people in the past.' He hesitated, then thought: why not? 'He's killed people. Women like you. Perhaps you've heard . . .'

Her eyes were astonishingly white and broad, fearful but not without knowledge and some strength too. Her body, which was lithe and athletic, shook like a leaf as she clutched her cheap, skimpy hooker's clothes more tightly as he spoke those words.

'He's a rich man,' she muttered in a strong African accent.

'You heard about those women who were murdered,' Peroni replied immediately. 'You must have done. We've had officers out on the streets telling everyone.'

She nodded, the gesture barely perceptible.

'Rich and powerful he may be,' Peroni continued, 'but he killed those women and a good friend of mine too. Where is he?'

Her eyes grew bright with anger.

'I show you,' she said, and led the way, down a set of

stairs at the end of the hallway, down a long, dark, narrow corridor, over a footbridge, with the bright chilly December morning visible through the stone slats, like emplacements for imaginary archers, open to the air, then on into a distant sector of the palace they would never have found so quickly on their own.

– 10 –

Costa edged back towards the drape and the corpse of the 'Ndrangheta thug, making sure Agata stayed out of range by forcing his right hand down behind and guiding her along the wall. When they were close enough – he could feel the man's body hard against his foot, he could smell the rank odour of the wound – he turned and caught her gleaming eye.

'Go down the corridor as fast as you can and make your way outside. Keep running,' he whispered. 'Leave this to me.'

She didn't move.

'Not now,' he insisted, beginning to feel desperate.

Malaspina was taking his time. He was no more than a few steps away, playing with the sword, watching them, an athletic, powerful figure in a place where he felt confident, secure.

'What do you take me for?' she murmured softly, her breath warm in his ear. 'I didn't come here to run away.'

'Agata . . .'

She was moving, slipping out from beneath him in a way he couldn't prevent. With a couple of short, deliberate steps, Agata Graziano worked herself free, then paced into the circular hall to set herself between him and Malaspina.

The gleaming blade ceased moving in the man's hands. He looked . . . interested.

'How many years have you known me, Franco?' she asked. 'Will you kill me? Will you kill me now?'

He shrugged, amused, in control.

'After . . .' he said, half laughing. 'Sorry. Needs must.'

'Why?'

He blinked as if it was a stupid question.

'Because I can.'

She took one more short stride to stand in front of him, thrust her slender, dusky arm in front of his face, pinched her own skin on her wrist.

'Not because of this? Because of the shade of some-one's skin? A sport in the blood? Some small thing inside you've come to hate and a painting that obsesses you?'

Malaspina's eyes strayed to the canvas in the centre of the room.

'You're a fool, Agata,' he murmured. 'You understand nothing.'

'I understand everything! My father was an African. My mother was a Sicilian whore. I am a little more black than you, Franco. But not much. Does it matter that Ippolito Malaspina shared my race? *Our* race?'

Costa couldn't take his eyes off the man's face. There was nothing there. No recognition. No feeling what-soever.

The machine pistol lay in the dead thug's arms, no more than one step away.

'No,' Malaspina answered, almost with sadness. 'It doesn't.'

'Caravaggio . . .' she began.

'We were here before Caravaggio,' he interrupted. 'We were here before Christ, before Caesar. We are what man was meant to be, before you and yours came to poison us.'

She shook her head and the dark hair moved. Agata was lost, her eyes flying around the chamber with its sunken floor, its obscene statues and paintings, the paean to brutality that was everywhere.

'You hate them,' she insisted. 'You hate me. You hate yourself.'

Malaspina stared at her and there was contempt in his eyes.

'Not for that,' he murmured. 'So much wisdom, Agata, and so little knowledge . . .'

'I forgive you everything,' she said, trembling like a leaf in the wind. 'Those poor women. Everyone.' She glanced in Costa's direction for a moment. 'Even Nic can forgive you. He's a good man. Everything can be atoned for if you wish it. Accept who you are, what you have done. Ask for justice and it is yours.'

He shook his head and cut the knife through the air in front of her, unmoved by a single word.

Costa rolled left, eyes never leaving the weapon that lay in the dead man's bloodied hands. He turned as quickly as he could, snatched the metal stock up, rose to a crouch, felt for the trigger, gripped it, played once with the metal stub, heard a single shot burst from the barrel and exit through the drape behind. Then he rolled sideways once again, trying to avoid any attack that was coming, landing on his knee, a firm position, one that would take him out of Agata's way and give him a direct line to Malaspina, an opportunity he would take on the instant, without a second thought.

It was all too late. By the time Costa wheeled round with the weapon in his hands, Agata was in the man's grasp, his strong arm around her throat, the stiletto tight to her neck. Her eyes shone with terror.

'Drop it,' Malaspina ordered.

Agata screamed. Malaspina had curled the blade into her flesh in one short, cruel flick, fetching up a line of blood.

'Drop it or I will slit her like a pig,' he declared with no emotion, then turned the knife further into her neck as she struggled helpless in his arms.

The weapon slipped from Costa's hands. To drive home the point, he kicked it away, watching, listening as the black metal screeched across the shiny marble, fetching up near the circular boundary wall opposite, well out of reach.

He could hear something from above. Footsteps, short and feminine, and the rushing of long robes. It was the sound Agata made across the polished tiles of the Doria Pamphilj.

Then something louder. The heavy approach of men. And another noise he recognized, and welcomed.

'Nic!' Peroni bellowed down from above.

Costa looked upwards, to the gallery that circled this strange Pantheon in miniature. They were gathering there, police officers and nuns, a crowd of witnesses, an audience which spelled a certain end for the last of the Ekstasists.

'The lawyers won't get you out of this, Franco,' the big man bellowed from above, scanning the gallery, trying to work out some way down to the ground floor. 'We're in this place now. Legally. There are more officers on the way. Even you can't walk away now.'

There was fury on Malaspina's face. Nothing more. Not fear, not an acceptance that this was the end, which was what Costa wanted. The knife was still hard on Agata's neck. The blood there welled like a river ready to burst its banks.

'Little men, little women,' Malaspina shouted, head jerking from side to side, taking in the flood of visitors now racing onto the balcony. 'All of you. No idea of your place. No idea of the . . .'

His face contorted until there was nothing there but hatred, a black, dead loathing for everything.

'. . . impudence.'

The knife moved again. Agata yelled, more faintly. A second wound line started to appear beneath her ear. The balance had shifted, Costa sensed. In Malaspina's mind, the dark, savage place where he imagined himself to live supreme, this was the endgame, the rich knight's final hour, the moment of death and dissolution, the final opportunity to place a bloody mark against a world he detested.

She was, to him, as good as dead already.

Costa strode forward to confront him, stopping within reach of the sharp, deadly stiletto that never strayed from her neck, tempting the blade away from her dusky skin towards his own.

The idea had been buzzing in his head now for days. He had never discussed it with anyone, with Agata least of all, and it was her opinion, more than any, that he had come to value about Franco Malaspina.

Yet Agata Graziano was wrong. Costa understood this instinctively and he believed he knew why. He and Malaspina shared the same pain.

He leaned forward until his own features were so close to Malaspina's he could see the wild, crazed determination in his eyes, smell the sweat of anticipation on him, and feel the sense that there was no going back now, not for any of them.

'What about Véronique Gillet?' he asked quietly, eye to eye with the man, close enough for him to switch his attention away from Agata if he wanted, if this taunting did its work.

'Véronique is dead,' Malaspina murmured, black eyes burning with fury.

'Would this have been part of the game too? If she were still alive?'

There were more sounds from above. More men. He thought he heard Falcone's voice. Malaspina's features were locked in bleak determination.

'Do not come near,' Costa ordered in a loud, commanding voice. 'Count Malaspina has a hostage and a weapon.'

Falcone's voice began to object.

'No!' Costa shouted.

There was quiet.

'They listen to you,' Malaspina murmured. 'That's good. There'll be many people at your funeral. There was a crowd for your wife, wasn't there? I read it in the papers. I sent a man to take photographs. They amused me.'

'Did they comfort you, Franco?' he asked.

'You speak in riddles.'

'I don't think so,' he disagreed. 'Will there be many mourners for Véronique?'

'I have no idea.'

Costa could see the interest in Agata's eyes, detect, perhaps, a loosening of Malaspina's grip on her neck.

'Her body is in the morgue still. Autopsies . . .' Costa shrugged. 'It's not a pretty event. We cannot release her for a burial, naturally. Not with the case open. She must stay stiff in that cabinet, perhaps for years.'

The point of the stiletto twitched in his direction.

'I may kill you first,' Malaspina murmured. 'Just for the pleasure.'

'It's all in the blood,' Costa said, wondering.

'You bore me. You both bore me, and that is dangerous.'

'It wasn't the black gene at all, was it?' Costa demanded. 'You checked your ancestry too. That was merely curiosity. The arrogance of proving you are what you are.'

He watched the point of the knife, tried to measure how Malaspina might move if he managed to goad him enough for Agata to get free.

The man said nothing. The circular chamber was silent, save for the breathing of Malaspina and the captive Agata Graziano.

Costa pointed to the painting: the naked goddess, the eternal sigh, the moment the world became real.

'What took her was all much more simple, much more human, which is why you hate it so,' he continued. 'Your game. Véronique's game. The game of Castagna, Buccafusca and Nino Tomassoni when you drew them into it.'

He took one step back and traced a finger along the outline of the naked figure's fleshy thigh. Malaspina stiffened, infuriated.

'Was that your idea or Véronique's?' There were so

many questions, so many possible answers. He didn't care what Malaspina said. He only cared that soon, very soon, he might get Agata away from the knife.

'You're guessing,' Malaspina growled.

'I'm guessing it was yours. She was a weak, difficult woman. Beautiful, I think. Not unwilling to play as you dictated.' He stepped back to them, close again. 'The whores. The violence, sham perhaps at first, all part of the price to be paid. Then . . .'

In the distance, above the shining floor and the bright painting that seemed so alive, he could see Falcone watching from the gallery, listening to every word.

Costa moved yet closer.

'Something changed. An obvious thing. But something you believed could never happen to you and your kind. This game caught up with you.' He leaned forward. 'It came with a price.'

'Shut up,' Malaspina muttered.

'You have sex with poor, miserable street whores. And one day you catch a disease. The disease. It's not some black gene that gets passed down from generation to generation. You don't care about that. You like to fool yourself you care about nothing at all. Then the sickness comes and it's the worst sort, the sort that can kill you. HIV. Aids, in Véronique's case. A disease that's not supposed to affect people like you. Aristocrats, lords with money and power, little gods in your own private world. And when it does . . .'

He reached for the man's jacket, watching the blade all the time. There was a shape behind the breast pocket. One he had noticed before, in the farmhouse. A shape that could be one thing only.

Costa dipped his fingers quickly into the pocket and

withdrew a small silver case, popped it open, revealed the pills inside.

'Véronique had something like this,' he went on. 'Drugs. Expensive drugs, I imagine. Not ones they give to street whores because they can't afford them and they're just animals in any case. Special drugs. Ones that work. Mostly.'

The man's face was stiff and ugly with strain and hate. Costa looked into those black, dead eyes and knew this was the truth.

'You paid for them for yourself, naturally. And for the others too. I imagine you paid for them for Véronique, but – ' he smiled, deliberately, as he continued – 'even the richest man in the world cannot buy a cure for death. With Véronique, they didn't work. She was ill already. The drugs made her worse. They shortened a life that was in jeopardy to begin with. In the end they killed her—'

'Shut up, shut up, shut up,' Malaspina repeated through clenched teeth.

Costa caught Agata's attention. Her eyes were glassy with tears. She stared at him in horror. This was an explanation from a world she had never known, one that would never have made sense if she had stayed where she thought she belonged, quiet and safe inside a sister's plain, coarse uniform.

'All your money, all the drugs and treatment . . . They weren't enough for Véronique, were they? She'd left it too late,' Costa said simply. 'You could save yourself and the others. But you couldn't save her, the very woman you wished to keep alive. And what was worse, so much worse, was that, as she began to die . . . as you *killed her* . . . a part of you thought this might be love. Some stray strand of humanity inside of you looked at her wasting away and regretted that fact.' He watched the man's reaction, prayed he saw some dim sign of recognition in his eyes. 'But this being you, that small part spoke to the larger part and all it could think of was blood and murder and hate. To take some cruel vengeance on the innocent that should, by rights, have been directed at yourself.'

'You will die,' Malaspina murmured, his voice low and lifeless.

'How did you work the others into your scheme?' Costa asked. 'Did you murder some poor black hooker who failed you all one night, then tell them they were a part of it anyway? Did you promise them lawyers too, the way you promised them drugs?'

The knife flashed back and forth in Malaspina's clenched fist, cutting through thin air a finger's length from Costa's eyes.

'Most of all, Franco,' Costa asked lightly, 'I would like to know what you told her. When Véronique knew she would surely die. Did you offer her one last chance to indulge you, in front of your painted goddess, as a . . . reward somehow? Was that supposed to be some kind of comfort? Do you really believe this passes as love?'

He folded his arms, waiting for the explosion.

'I know what love is, Franco. Most people do. But not you. Never you. She was simply an obsession. Something you owned. Like this palace. Like the painting you forced Nino Tomassoni to give you. One more beautiful object you've torn apart as if it were worthless . . .'

He was screaming, moving, releasing Agata Graziano, throwing her to one side in his fury. Costa backed up, watching the stiletto flash through the air, feeling it make one arc in front of his chest, just close enough to cut a scything line through the fabric of his jacket.

Another sweep, another blow. There was nothing he could do, no weapon, no physical manoeuvre he knew that would offer any defence against a man like this.

Then the growing hubbub from the gallery above, the sound of racing footsteps, shouts, screams, disappeared beneath a deafening, cataclysmic clamour.

The blade swept through nothing and fell from view. The rage was gone from Franco Malaspina's face. In its place was shock and surprise . . . and fear.

Costa looked beyond the figure stumbling towards him and saw her now. Agata Graziano had withdrawn something from the pocket of the cheap office girl's jacket. It was the gun Rosa Prabakaran had given her, a weapon Costa had never expected to see again. Grey smoke curled from the short snub barrel. As he watched, Agata raised the pistol again and fired one more shot at the falling figure between them, then a third.

Malaspina jerked with pain and the physical blow of the impacts. Blood rose in his mouth. His eyes turned glassy. The knife fell to the floor with a hollow echoing ring, followed by the stricken man, who clutched at the legs of the stand on which Caravaggio's naked goddess rested, watching the scene, unmoved, her throat locked in a cry that was lost in the clamour of Franco Malaspina's death.

A pebble-sized hole, surrounded by broken shards of skull, gaped above Malaspina's ear. The dun, viscous matter Costa could see beneath the man's hairline matched that which now ran in a spraying line, mixed with blood, across the naked figure of Eve like the splash of a murderous graffiti artist seeking something beautiful to defile.

Agata was shouting, screeching, was not herself, was quite unlike the woman he knew.

He watched in dismay as she emptied every last shell from Rosa's gun into the still, frozen form on the canvas, painted by the artist she had come, in her own fashion, to love, watched as the mouth and its inaudible eternal sigh disappeared beneath the blast of a shell.

When the bullets ran out she began to tear at the canvas with her bare hands, ripping into four-hundred-year-old pigment with her nails, weeping, screaming.

He strode over and pulled her away.

Her face stole into his neck, damp with tears. His hand fell on her rough, tangled hair and held her small, slim body close.

Agata Graziano looked up and the power of her gaze was unmistakable. She was staring at him and there was something in her expression – a kind of dislike, bordering on hatred – that was reminiscent, for a moment, of Franco Malaspina.

'This is done now,' Costa said, and wondered, seeing the look persist in her eyes, what it was that she saw.

Part 19

FRESH BEGINNINGS

– 1 –

Fiumicino was always busy just after the New Year. Families on the move, businesses returning to life. Part of the daily round of modern life. They were together at a small table in the cafe drinking coffee, an awkward silence between them, one he was desperate to break.

It was the mother superior of the convent who had called and asked if it was possible for him to give Agata a lift to the airport. The sisters were, she said, too upset about her decision to be trusted. He didn't have to think twice before saying yes.

Now they sat, she with two carrier bags full of personal detritus on the floor after checking in a small, cheap canvas tote for the flight. Costa with . . . nothing but regrets and thoughts he found difficult to turn into words. He wished she wasn't leaving so soon and was determined not to burden her with that knowledge. Agata had enough to carry now.

'What's the order like there?' he asked finally, unable to bear the thought that they could part in a few minutes without having exchanged more than a few perfunctory words. 'Is that the right word, "order"?'

She smiled weakly. Her face seemed to have aged over

these past few weeks. She now looked like the person he would have met had she never worn the black robes of a sister: a beautiful woman just turning thirty, with flawless dark skin, high cheekbones and eyes that shone with intelligence, and a new sense of sadness that had never been there before.

'There is no "right word",' she said. 'I left. Didn't they tell you that?'

'No . . . I mean, I assumed you wanted to move to a convent somewhere else. Away from Rome.'

'I'm not just going somewhere different,' she replied emphatically.

'Oh . . .'

She reached over and touched his wrist. Automatically – he knew this gesture so well by now he never thought about it – he turned it so she could see his watch.

'I only have a few minutes before I need to go. I can't explain everything. I don't want to. Talk about something else.'

'I don't want to,' he objected. 'You spent your entire life in that place. I don't understand.'

Her eyes widened with outrage.

'I killed a man. How can I be a sister after that? It's impossible.' She looked at her hands, as if remembering the moment Rosa Prabakaran's weapon sat in her fingers. 'I feel no guilt either. That's the worst thing.' She stared at him. 'He would have killed you. Instead of me, because your friends, Gianni, Leo, would have been there in time to stop that. But why do I tell you this? You know already. This is what you do, isn't it? Put yourself in the way instead.'

He tried to pull a wry smile.

'It seems to work most of the time.'

'No, it doesn't. Not really.'

He stirred the sugar in the grounds of his coffee a little harder, hearing that.

'What will you do?' Costa asked.

She seemed relieved to be able to shift the focus of the conversation.

'There are many illegal immigrants coming to Malta each month. Mostly from Africa. They want to come to Italy. One way or another most of them will. The Church has a programme trying to help them. I will teach. Children, young men and women. These are people who need me. They're desperate. As my father must have been once. I can't sit by and ignore them. It's unthinkable.'

He had no difficulty imagining her excelling at that kind of work. Or being in Malta.

'Will you go to Valletta? And the co-cathedral? You said you always wanted to see those paintings.' An image of the Caravaggio flashed through his own mind. 'John the Baptist. And St Jerome of course.'

The laugh returned, and it was still light, still mostly untroubled.

'I'm there to try to help people in difficulty. Why would I walk away from that to see a painting? I spent too long in that daydream. I was like Franco Malaspina, obsessed with something that was unreal. Trapped in a world that had nothing to do with the way people actually live.'

He shook his head firmly.

'Caravaggio's real, Agata. Those people he portrayed . . . You said it yourself. They came from the streets. They're you and me.'

'Oh, Nic.' Her hand crossed the table and almost fell briefly on his before returning to the plastic bag by her side. 'I have work to do.' The amusement in her face disappeared. 'Sins to atone for . . .'

'What you did was self-defence,' he replied instantly. 'Not a sin.'

'That's not for you to decide. Or me. It's a question of faith.'

'Faith,' he snapped without thinking, his voice rising so that the woman at the next table raised an eyebrow in their direction.

'Yes,' she went on. 'Faith. You think I lost it? No. Not for a moment.' Her eyes stayed on him, clear, insistent, knowing. 'I found more. I found real faith was awkward and uncomfortable. It asked questions I didn't want to hear. Demanded sacrifices I didn't want to make.' She shook her head. The stray black curls flew around her neck in a way that mesmerized him. 'I discovered it existed for my salvation, not my enjoyment. That it was awkward and uncomfortable and occasionally – ' she peered at the empty coffee cup on the table, her eyes misty – 'that it meant I had to avoid . . . forgo things I might come to want for myself.'

'And I don't have that?' he asked.

'Not in the same way,' she answered carefully. 'I've watched you. Your faith lies in others. Not in politics. Not in religion. Not even in the law or justice, I think, any more. It's rooted in the people you love.' Her voice caught with emotion. 'More than that. I envy it. I look at you and think, "I wish I could feel that way too." But I can't.'

'Love isn't something you can control or call up on demand. None of us knows when it might happen. I didn't with Emily. I had no idea and nor did she.'

Her slender lips curled in a deprecating smile.

'You're not listening. This isn't about that kind of love. I'm trying to stay away from my beliefs for a while in the hope I might find some answers to my doubts. You're making the same journey, but in reverse. We're moving in opposite directions. It's not Emily you're looking for, it's God, and since you think he doesn't exist, that makes it all the worse for you.' Her shining eyes held him. 'Also, people die. Everyone in the end. Does this small, plain faith of yours die with them?' Her fingers reached out and touched his hand, for the briefest of moments. 'Did it?'

'For a while,' he answered honestly.

He felt so inadequate, so tongue-tied, and had no idea whether he believed what she said, about him or about herself.

Over the hubbub of the busy airport they were calling the plane. He could see from her face she had heard the announcement.

'If I came to visit in Malta . . .'

'I don't think that would be a good idea.'

Costa sighed and said nothing.

'I have to go,' she murmured. 'There's no need to see me to the plane. I have a little time, I think. I would like to spend it on my own.'

She was standing, picking up her two carrier bags, an independent young woman entering a world she barely understood, alone, determined to explore its dark corners and intricacies without the help of another.

'Here,' he said, getting up too. 'You'll need one of these at some stage.'

He took off his watch and passed it to her. She tried to put it on. The leather strap was too large and needed

another hole. She'd no clue how to make one, no idea
that a man would simply push the spike hard through the
old soft leather and find some new purchase that way.

'Let me . . .'

Gently, he wound the strap around her soft, warm
wrist, worked out the size, removed it, forced through
the hole and wound it back around her dusky skin again,
fastening the strap, making sure it fitted well.

They stood there, so close.

Nervously, Costa extended his right hand and waited.

Agata Graziano closed her eyes and there was a single
line of moisture beneath each dark lid.

'Oh my, oh my,' she whispered, laughing, crying, he
wasn't sure quite which. 'For God's sake, Nic. My hand?'

She opened her arms and walked forward, enclosing
him, waiting as his own arms fell, hesitantly, around her
slender shoulders.

Outside the dead, half-forgotten nightmare of the
funeral, it was the first time he had embraced anyone
since Emily had died. He was crying now, he knew that,
not much, but enough to feel some tight interior knot
inside him relax, release, then, if not disappear, begin to
dissipate somehow.

Costa held her, tightly, his face against her dark hair,
acutely aware that she was unlike any woman he had ever
known, simple, pure, innocent. There was no fragrance
about her, nothing but fresh soap, and her skin against
his, as young and smooth and perfect as that of a child.

'Enough of this,' she said, her voice breaking a little,
pushing him away. 'Farewells are something new to me
also, and clearly I am as terrible at them as you.'

They looked at one other, lost for words. Then, very
quickly, she came close again, reached up and kissed him

once, tenderly, on the cheek, with a swift, embarrassed affection.

'Goodbye, Nic,' she murmured, then, without looking back, scooped up her bags and scurried off down the corridor towards the gate.

– 2 –

Two hours later Costa was sitting in the kitchen. It was a chill, bright afternoon. Through the window he could see planes high in an eggshell sky leaving vapour trails in their wake. Beyond the lines of black, dormant vines crows bickered in the trees by the road. Bea had returned to her apartment with the little dog. The house was empty. He was alone again, back in the sprawling farmhouse his late father had built with his own hands, a place where every brick and tile was familiar, every angle and corner carried a cherished memory.

Grief was a journey, a transition through opposing phases, of knowledge and ignorance, togetherness and solitude, pain and consolation. What counted was the passage, the recognition that at the heart of life lay motion. Without that there was nothing but stasis, a premature quietus that rendered everything and everyone it touched meaningless.

Here, surrounded by Emily's lingering fragrance, the shelves with the food and drink only she would eat, her music by the hi-fi system, her jars and bottles still lurking in cupboards in the bathroom, it was to his dead wife that his thoughts turned constantly, and would for years to come. Her presence was everywhere, a benevolent ghost forever active in his conscience. He had lost her, but not entirely. When he closed his eyes he could hear her voice. When he called up those precious memories of their time together, he could sense the soft grip of her fingers in his, the warmth of her breath as she whispered in his ear.

As she whispered now, calling, *Live, Nic, live.*

He felt the shiny marble urn in his fingers, its smooth surface as cold as a statue's skin, the way it was the day he'd taken it home from the crematorium.

Costa got up from the table and went outside into the cold, walking on until he was among the rows of vines they had tended together, so carefully, and with such rudimentary skill. As he reached that point he began to let her go, to let the stream of dust and ashes tumble from the vessel's grey marble neck, out into the air, to scatter among the slumbering black trunks, across the dun, chill earth.

He walked on and on, the horizon rising and falling with his steps, blurred by the tears that flooded his eyes in a way they never had before. It took no more than a minute. Then he threw the empty container as far as he could, out towards the road and the distant outline of the tomb of Cecilia Metella.

In the field, shaking with fierce emotion, lost, blind, choking, he found himself consumed by a swirling plume of grey dust raised from the earth by a sudden fierce squall. It clung to his head. Like a sandstorm in miniature, a miasmic cloud of pale particles, it swirled around his head, danced in his eyes, his mouth, his nostrils, clung briefly to his fingers like a second, shedding skin.

Then a fresh blast caught and it was gone.

– Author's Note –

This is a work of fiction constructed around some certain facts, so I feel it is important to give a few guidelines on where this division is drawn. There is no painting entitled *Evathia in Ekstasis*, by Caravaggio or any other artist of the same period. Canvases close to its subject matter certainly did exist, however, among them Annibale Carracci's *Venus with a Satyr and Cupids*, which remains in the possession of the Uffizi today. Erotic paintings, some by well-known artists, others pure, graphic pornography, were popular throughout sixteenth- and seventeenth-century Rome among the richer classes and with influential men of the Church. The more risqué works would be kept in private rooms, covered by a curtain, and shown only to close and discreet friends. This penchant for private interests bordering on vice was not uncommon. Cardinal Francisco Maria del Monte, Caravaggio's patron and landlord for a while, did indeed tinker with the forbidden art of alchemy in the privacy of the casino of the Villa Ludovisi, and paid the artist to produce a unique fresco associated with his experiments there.

Caravaggio lived in turbulent and hypocritical times, variously fêted as the new saviour of the coming generation of Roman artists and declaimed as a dissolute sinner who used prostitutes as the models for saints. His output while he lived in Rome – from 1592 until he fled a sentence of death for murder in 1606 – was prolific but is in part uncharted. Like many of his colleagues and rivals, he veered between pious works commissioned by the Church and smaller, often more daring canvases paid for by private collectors seeking something for their galleries and intimate chambers where visitors were allowed only by invitation.

The reputation of Caravaggio today stands, to a great extent, upon his religious paintings, some of which, such as *The Martyrdom of St Matthew* (San Luigi dei Francesi, Rome), *The Beheading of St John the Baptist* (Oratory of the Co-Cathedral of St John, Valletta, Malta) and *The Crucifixion of St Peter* (Santa Maria del Popolo, Rome), remain on the very walls for which they were first painted. But the artist accepted private commissions as well. There is no doubt that he embraced a wider range of work when the money and the job interested him. The poet Giambattista Marino certainly owned a painting of *Susannah* by Caravaggio, now lost, which is assumed to have been a rare female nude. Caravaggio was prolific and temperamental, a difficult and violent man, willing to walk away from valuable projects simply because they failed to interest him. At the height of his career he was celebrated as the most famous artist in Rome, and hailed by poets as the defining spirit of a new age of painting. Within the space of a few years, however, he was impoverished, living in simple conditions with a single servant in the alley now known as the Vicolo del Divino Amore.

The Palazzo Malaspina depicted here is entirely fictional, though sprawling palaces similar to it do exist in

Rome today. One of the most famous still in original hands is the Palazzo Doria Pamphilj, which contains the canvases mentioned in the book and is, in part, open to the public. A palace more reminiscent of the imaginary home of Franco Malaspina is the Palazzo Altemps in the Piazza San Apollinare. The former residence of a powerful cardinal related to the papacy by marriage, this ornate and glorious property, now a museum, is on the edge of the area once known as Ortaccio, a red-light district created by the Vatican to be a zone for the city's prostitutes. In the sixteenth and seventeenth centuries the inns and lodgings of Ortaccio came to be popular with artists and writers, and were the scene of many brawls and arguments, feuds and vendettas.

Long-running enmities were common in this volatile community and gangs such as the fictional Ekstasists depicted here certainly existed, taking their cue from the real-life knight's handbook written by Domenico Mora, which argued for a violent, arrogant attitude towards others. It was a street fight that cost Caravaggio his career in Rome when, in 1606, he killed Ranuccio Tomassoni close to the Piazza di San Lorenzo in Lucina. The circumstances remain a mystery. Contemporary accounts are coloured by bias and riddled with lacunae, though the popular modern theory that the brawl stemmed from a dispute over a game of tennis is probably a myth. Tomassoni was indeed the *caporione* of his district and closely involved, sometimes intimately, with several of the women Caravaggio knew, among them the notorious Fillide Melandroni.

Alessandro de' Medici ruled Florence for five years briefly before his assassination in 1537. It is generally accepted that he was the son of a black kitchen maid named Simonetta and the seventeen-year-old Giulio de' Medici, who was to become Pope Clement VII. His lineage was carefully hidden in most portraits, though his enemies frequently referred to him as '*il Moro*', the Moor. Ippolito Malaspina was a real figure and a genuine patron of Caravaggio in Malta; his coat of arms can be seen on the artist's *St Jerome*, which remains in the co-cathedral in Valletta, for which Malaspina commissioned it. The Malaspina family was at one time powerful in Tuscan politics; an ancestor of Ippolito receives a mention in both Dante's *Purgatorio* and Boccaccio's *Decameron*. The aristocratic Malaspina dynasty disappeared in the eighteenth century. In the time of the Medici, however, the Malaspina clan had a visible and important presence in Florence. The favourite mistress of Alessandro de' Medici was Taddea Malaspina. The depiction of Alessandro by Pontormo, which is now in the Philadelphia Museum of Art, was originally his gift to her. In turn, she bore Alessandro's only children.

Apart from the canvas of *Evathia* and the imagined lost portrait of the man pretending to be Ippolito Malaspina in Malta, all the paintings mentioned in this book are real and mostly on public view.

David Hewson
Rome, Kent and San Francisco

THE PROMISED LAND

TUESDAY

TUESDAY

The gurney wheels stop squealing. I dare to look. There's someone new there. He's got the face of an Andy Warhol doll: bright eyes gleaming like glass, a shock of white, spiky hair and yellow tombstone teeth locked into a smile that has all the sincerity of a cosmetics salesman peddling cheap aftershave.

'Hi!' he says brightly. 'Good day to you, sir. It's a fine day. A sunny day. Outside the birds are singing.'

His speech is too old for his looks. I remember voices like that, back from before, from outside. It's the jaundiced, bored intonation of the wage slave trundling through his daily routine.

'Very loudly I might say.'

He pauses theatrically, as if waiting for a sound. I can't hear a thing except the hum of air conditioning and electrical equipment, the stupid tinnitus that's lived alongside me for twenty-three years, three months and four days.

All the same, I try to speak. The words come out incomplete, a mumbled half-sentence mashed by the sedative shot I got before they strapped me to the gurney.

3

'Yeah, yeah, yeah . . .'

He's cross. He doesn't appreciate being interrupted.

'I like birds too. Don't we all? Please don't talk. Some of us are working here. Or trying to.'

The fierce rays of the surgical lighting dazzle me. For a moment the bright white hair looks like a halo, like a shining mantle rising from a slender, almost girlish neck.

'My . . . name . . . is . . . Martin . . .' The man in the green gown says this very slowly, very precisely, as if speaking to an idiot. 'Call me Martin the Medic. Call me God. Call me anything you like. I am merely your willing attendant on this short but meaningful journey. It's a job, chum. Someone's got to do it.'

I just manage to see as he retrieves something from a place beneath my range of vision: a silver kidney-shaped bowl sitting on a trolley alongside a line of implements and containers inside, neatly arrayed, ready for use.

Martin the Medic raises his right hand. In it sits a syringe, long, gleaming and, as yet, empty.

'This is just beer money, a part-time thing, you understand,' he says, then reaches down and plunges a needle deep into my right arm, piercing the flesh, hunting for the vein, finding it, then holding the metal spike there as he reaches round with his other hand and firms it down with tape.

'Killing people, I mean,' Martin adds, working the needle into my flesh till it hurts. Then, brightly, 'Oh!'

The yellow teeth gleam.

'We do have something in common.'

I mumble again and I can't even hear the words. Martin has replaced the syringe and picked up some ampoules. He's talking to himself. I'm just some eaves-dropper here.

'Sodium thiopental. *Check!* Saline. *Check!*'

He touches two slender, feminine fingers to the line in my arm again and dabs the area with a piece of cotton wool.

'Old nursing habits. Crazy, I know. Here I am swabbing and flushing with all this clean-up routine. As if it matters.'

He picks up two more ampoules and flicks a finger-nail against the labels.

'Fifty ccs of pancuronium bromide. Fifty ccs of potassium chloride.'

He seems satisfied. The glassy blue eyes are back on my face.

'Listen to me, friend. This is important. It's prob-ably the last important thing you'll hear. First, I pump in the thiopental. Which sends you to sleep, straight off pretty much, just like a baby. Not that they sleep easy all the time, but you were a father once. *Before* . . . So I imagine you know that.'

The vial comes up close to his face. He stares at it myopically.

'Then I flush the line clean. After that it's the pancuronium.'

He holds up another glass bulb for me to see, then, for show, turns round to some people I can just make out behind a glass screen to the left. They're not clear but somehow I know what they're wearing: dark suits and grim faces because there's a dress rule for such occa-sions, even though a good half of them think this is a day to throw hats in the air, scream a little joy from the rooftops.

Martin lets them see the vial because it's why they're here. In a way, the thing belongs to them.

After this he returns to face me and speaks, in a rapid, businesslike voice, 'You may know this already, but pancuronium is very neat stuff. It paralyses the diaphragm, the lungs. All quick, all clean. Given the choices, you picked the right place to be, let me tell you. This is *so* much better than electrocution. More hygienic. Let me tell you a secret. Want to know what happens when they fry a man? Everyone shits themselves. *Everyone.*'

He sighs.

'Where's the dignity? I ask you. If we *have* to do this work – and when I look at you, I know we do – let's manage it with a little decorum. You agree?'

It feels as if a ball of cotton wool is stuck in my throat. I couldn't scream if I tried.

'Behold.'

A syringe is in his hand again, with a different vial. I can just read the details on the bottle: a pharmaceutical company, one that's vaguely familiar. Once, a long time ago, in a different lifetime, we bought cough medicine for Ricky that bore this same logo. It tasted sweet. The boy loved it so much he'd pretend-cough sometimes just to get some.

'Progress . . .' the medic goes on. 'So the thiopental here is in. The pancuronium's chasing it. You don't breathe too well but – and this is important, follow me here – you're still not dead. OK?'

One more vial. One more familiar brand on the paper covering the glass.

'I flush with the saline again. And finally we come to

the potassium chloride. This – *listen to me when I'm talking*!'

Something had popped into my head at that moment. Some memory: an image from the last time Ricky suffered a cold. I remember the small room he commandeered the moment he was old enough to talk. The wallpaper had cartoon characters running up and down it. There was a full-size bed, too big for the boy, but that was what Ricky wanted. So we gave in, and on his fifth birthday I lugged the thing up the old wooden stairs of the house in Owl Creek, then stood by my son, holding his hand, as Miriam made the bed: white cotton sheets, tight and perfect, by the window where the apple tree had recently come into bloom.

The bed. Another memory enters my head. The two of us between creased white sheets, hovering on the edge, me wondering whether she wants this or not. Then Miriam smiling, saying, 'Sometimes it's good slow. Sometimes fast. Today . . .'

Ricky would be twenty-eight now. Maybe we'd have had grandchildren. Then one more memory starts to rise from the dust.

'Listen to me!' Martin orders once more, and he's winding the needle of the line round and round in my arm, stirring some deep, hard pain to get my attention.

The recollection – a five-year-old boy in bed, while I read him Dr Seuss, still in my police uniform – fades into darkness and I wish, more than anything, I had the strength to claw it back from the lost, damaged part of my mind where it's now cowering.

The vial is in front of my eyes. Closer up, I see the logo has changed. When it was on a bottle of kid's cough medicine it had more colour.

'This,' Martin the Medic insists, 'kills you. After a little while, thirty seconds maybe, you get hit by cardiac arrest. You're long unconscious by then. You don't feel a thing. Sadly. In total I guess we're looking at . . .'

He examines his watch. It's a fake Rolex, too fat and shiny for the real thing, with a metal band, big and bulky. I can see the second hand ticking away, faster than it ought.

'Oh . . . two minutes from now. Three max. Then I'm away for breakfast, and you're getting cleaned up for the box. Nothing fancy. No one wants to pay. I guess you know that. You're incinerator fuel, Bierce. Nothing more, nothing less.'

The man in the green gown puts a finger to the dimple in his chin and thinks about something.

'Orange juice. And fruit. Mango and citrus. Got to stay healthy. Any questions?'

I struggle again, trying to speak, but the sedative's really kicking in. My head's thick with dope and formless, swirling thoughts.

The medic laughs.

'No, no, no. That was rhetorical. I've heard it all a million times. You know. Is there life after death? My opinion? People who ask that should really be thinking: is there life *before* death? Honestly . . .'

He picks up a second syringe, inserts the long needle into a vial and checks the level.

'Here's another I get all the time. You want to know how much I'm getting paid for this modest little professional appointment?'

Martin shakes his head, as if he can't quite believe it himself.

'A hundred and fifty an hour, less tax. It's the

operating theatre plus twenty or something. Not a lot, my friend.'

He pauses. The bright eyes are no longer gleaming. 'Still, let me tell you something,' he adds.

The needle's coming closer, a glittering silver spear in front of my face, with not a tremor, not the slightest sign of hesitation.

'I would do this for free. I would *pay*, for God's sake. This . . .'

He has flawless skin. Pale and lightly tanned.

I can feel him grip the line in my arm once more, harder than ever this time, twisting it, lifting the needle until it runs tight against the inner wall of the vein.

I fight to pull in enough breath to shout, to say anything. The heavy weight of the sedative keeps me still, a straitjacket in the blood doing everything to paralyse me except remove the pain.

'. . . is for your wife and kid.'

Somewhere – in my imagination or the frantic flickering of my eyes as I struggle to shake my head – I see a man move, rise from the seats beyond the glass.

Not a harbinger of hope. After all this time they're gone, every last avenue of appeal extinguished, every channel of possible life closed. Except one, a simple act of mercy. The last thing anyone in this city would grant for a man called Bierce.

From the corner of my eye I see the needle enter the line.

Martin the Medic leans over, peers into my eyes and says, 'It's been a pleasure working with you, sir.'

A cold, hard sensation begins to creep along my arm. It makes a ringing noise at the back of my head, like the distant chimes of the old Chinese church, half a mile from home.

The Warhol face closes in for a last good look. His breath is stale and fetid. His smile has returned. It's different: eager and hungry.

'For in that sleep of death,' he whispers, yellow teeth shining, lips damp, blue eyes feasting on his work, 'what dreams may come?'

He pauses. A smile. I wish I had the time and the strength to tell him what I think of quoting Shakespeare out of context. The trouble is, a part of me doesn't care. About anything much at all.

There's a new pain now, a fierce chemical dagger rising from my spine, chasing upwards.

I shriek. I can hear myself. I flex my muscles against the tight surgical bonds, steel my body for the coming embrace.

We're in the kitchen, looking out on the garden that final summer. Wild briar roses bloom in the strong wire fence that runs on all three sides. A string of honeysuckle rises yellow and fragrant among the thorns. These are the barriers, one sweet and perfumed, one hard and painful, between ourselves and the bleak, dark tenements beyond.

A letter sits on the table.

It's the force annual medical. *Again.*

I want to avoid it. *Again.*

Her fingers touch the back of my hand, her soft warm mouth falls lovingly against my cheek for one bitterly brief moment.

'You think you're immune from all this, don't you?' she asks in a teasing, gentle voice, the one I first heard that day when I went, in a fresh new uniform, to her school. 'You think that all the physical things that happen to other people are beyond you somehow. That it's all different inside. Nothing to go bad. Nothing to go wrong. Bierce?'

I'm not really listening. There's a shadow in the garden. I see it now and wonder: *is this real or not?*

I squint. I cough into my fist. I do all the things I do when I'm trying to make up my mind. Then I open my eyes, and it's hard this time, harder than ever before.

This is not the garden, the piece of paradise belonging to a house we once owned, a place that stood for family and warmth and contentment. This is the death room in the grim, antiseptic prison that is Gwinett, and Martin the Medic is there leering at me, triumphant. He grins then winks then turns, pirouetting by the flat table, twisting, twirling, singing a little song I can't quite hear for the roaring rushing sound in my ears, blowing kisses towards the figures behind the glass, writhing like a dancer racked with glee, the star of some small, private show, a performer taking his bow.

I can see them all now. Four ranks of men and women, sober suits, sober faces. Watching me, waiting for my death to release them.

No one moves. Not even the one figure I thought I recognized earlier: the thin black man in a tight black suit, with the familiar long face and heavy jaw, the gloomy eyes and a head of wavy hair. He looks so much older, and as miserable as sin.

'Stapleton,' I try to scream.

I can't hear the sound of my own voice. I can't believe that among the last words I shall utter on this earth will be the name of a once-crooked police officer I turned into a straight man, in a different world, another time.

'I saw . . .'

I saw what?

Nothing I could remember. That was the problem. That was always the problem. But not now.

A shadow moves through the garden.

Something is shooting into my brain, some wild, stark compound, chasing down my consciousness, extinguishing everything it meets with the subtlety of a chemical jackhammer stomping on living cells.

The seated man in black doesn't move, not a muscle, not a finger. Then my vision is gone altogether, ripped away by some black falling sea of nothingness. It grows from inside the crude searing presence of the drug, roaring up from my veins, fighting to extinguish the last living part of my being, a place where some faint, fading memories of Miriam still lurk.

I'm afraid.

I'm relieved.

This was always coming. Always.

'Bierce?' her dead voice says.

My heart races. The rhythm of my lungs locks into a single, solid beat. This sound is now the warmest thing in the universe and I know full well that behind it lies an empty space, a void that goes on forever.

It's Owl Creek again and I know what day it is without looking at the newspaper that lies, unopened, on the table.

Thursday, 25 July 1985, part of a memorable month,

one that has stayed frozen in my memory, its events trapped like a scorpion suspended in amber.

A lot happened in the world that month. Coca-Cola gave up on new Coke. The French bombed the *Rainbow Warrior* in New Zealand. George Bush Senior stood next to a bright-looking teacher called Christa McAuliffe and announced she'd be the first woman ever to ride aboard the Space Shuttle, a particular one too, called *Challenger*. Six months later, in the Gwinett TV room, I'd watch that burn up in the sky like a fiery spear, after which I pretty much gave up on the news for good. They were asking for the death penalty by then. Seven months later they had it, and the long stay in the execution wing, twenty-two years in all, began.

Not that any of this matters. What does is this. That very afternoon my real five-year-old was supposed to be taken by his mother to see his – *their* – last movie: *Pee-wee's Big Adventure*. And it hadn't happened, for some reason I don't know, can't work out in the sullen silence between them.

Stupid thoughts dog you when people you love die. This one had eaten away at me for years: I just wish the movie they hadn't seen could have been something better.

We sit in the kitchen, Miriam and me. At this moment there is high pressure out over the distant water that lurks just a little under two miles away, beyond the line of apartment blocks straggling the horizon like bad teeth. Desiccated, stifling weather has been hanging in a bright pall over the city for days. There was a riot two days ago in the tenements of St Kilda. An entire building burned down during a turf scuffle between the

gangs. One teenager was dead; thirteen more were licking their wounds. It was another short-staffed week in
the station. I'd seen none of this. For reasons I never
did understand, they'd had me out of uniform for seven
weeks, on surveillance watching an empty warehouse
on the edge of the docks, twenty-seven hours with
scarcely a break on this last shift while other men and
women tried to push the lid back down on something
that stemmed from the simplest of causes. The heat.
The poverty. The boredom.

Exhausted, I close my eyes, and at that moment I
understand this same dank lethargy is everywhere. This
is my city, a part of my character. Every inch of it is
known to me, its small beauties and large blemishes,
its people, good and bad and indifferent. I see them
now in Greenpoint, out by the clean sea just a few
miles south, beyond the industrial outflows, where
four beaches, two marinas, and the estates of white
apartments and luxurious villas allow the rich to live
unmolested. I see them in Yonge, down by the docks,
where stevedores and truck drivers, drunks and street
women all hide beneath the shadows of the idle cranes,
too exhausted to work or play or do much except drink
beer and grow more surly, more resentful with each
passing hour.

They populate my mind as they have for years, since
I started to ride these streets on a police department
motorcycle, a badge and a gun visible on my person if I
can make it that way, because the uniform is a part of my
personality, one I refuse to hide. I never wanted to sneak
inside a suit. I never wanted to be invisible, peering in
to try to see what was going wrong inside their lives.

The law needs to make its presence known, and when I am there that presence is me.

Along the broad business streets of Westmont men in black suits, white shirts, ties tight into a button-down collar, scuttle between their offices like beetles fleeing the sun, snatching glances at the pretty girls in their skimpy dresses, both too weary to make or take a pass. On the deserted hills of Eden, the old, original quarter, now a declining residential area of decaying houses and shuttered stores, with the polyglot mess of Chinatown at its heart, the trams travel half empty, squeaking iron wheels on ancient tracks, shuttling between stops with names that have lost their meaning, Fair Meadow and Leather Yard, God's Acre and Silent Street, carrying a meagre load of the poor and the elderly, passengers tracking the old metal road for want of anything else to do.

This is summer, mirror image to the hard freezing days of December and January. For these few brief months the marina yachts should have been out on the blue, blue water. The single remaining piece of green in Eden, Wicker Park, ought to have filled with families watching the ducks and geese on the pond, eating ice creams from the Italian *gelati* stands, imagining they could smell the sea over the stink of smog from the traffic and the factories by the Yonge docks. But the city is in stasis, for rich and poor, black and white, young and old. This scorching, heartless weather recognizes neither colour nor class, poised as it is, airless, without a breath of wind, over everyone.

It's always like this in July and only some interior sense of self-deception manages to keep a perpetual truth at bay: *no one escapes the city easily*. Going north, there's the long, viewless drive the length of the peninsula, then three hours through endless spruce forests before another metropolis rises into view. South, across the De Soto bridge, it takes almost as long to reach civilization, following the winding line of A1A, past abandoned coastal hamlets and dead fishing ports, just, in the end, to find another city much like the one left behind.

And turning away from the coast, going west, lies the dead wasteland of the plains, a sprawling, barren region where a few farmers eke out a living, their numbers winnowed each year as their children gravitate to the cities, looking for work in the factories and offices, the fast-food stores and the malls, dreaming, all the time, that something will snatch them from the daily tedium, give them what the young always want: celebrity, status, money.

We never had the cash to travel, but in truth it hadn't mattered. In the end you always wind up where you started: a place where rich and poor and the middling masses in between fight each other for the right to go home in the evening, having survived another day. If they're lucky, with a scrap of dignity and a little something to show.

We haven't been outside the city in the seven years since we married. There was never the time, never a bill that didn't need paying. Sometimes it irks her. But not a lot. She's been here most of her adult life. She knows it lives like a rogue gene in the blood.

'Bierce?' she asks that last morning, reading my thoughts easily, the way she can.

I hold a cup of coffee. It doesn't taste rich and comforting, the way her coffee normally does.

Then I look at Miriam, enjoying this small moment of intimacy, as I always do. She has on a long, loose scarlet cotton dress, low at the neck. Her bare arms are suntanned from so much time in the garden with the boy. This is the kind of thing she wears at home. Her face, dark and beautiful, a little Spanish-looking I always think, doesn't seem to own a care in her world. She has eyes the colour of expensive chocolate, beautiful eyes, full of interest and consideration and, in the presence of her family, love. Miriam is an attractive, striking woman. We never go anywhere without some man taking a second look. She never believes me when I tell her it was the eyes I noticed first, that time I went round to the school to check up on some small case of theft, a childhood prank she'd found amusing when I pulled her out of class to talk about it.

No matter what she believes, it's true. I could stare into those eyes forever.

Mine are fixed on the garden. It looks more beautiful than ever. The place was a tip when we moved in, taking a mortgage we can still scarcely afford, most of it for renovation, on one of the last remaining original houses in Eden, the first city district, created back when the settlers came and took the land without asking who'd lived there first. Miriam found it on the agency lists, talked to the authorities to save it from demolition, negotiated the loan and a long pay-back period, one that seems endless, and still manages to bleed us dry. When we finally took possession she went through every last mid-nineteenth-century corner, restoring wood and plasterwork, removing vile modern paint, stripping the place back to the plain, pristine condition it once had when it was an upper-middle-class mansion, next to the small stream that gave the cul-de-sac in which it sat a name.

Owl Creek.

The last time I'd slept, in the big bedroom at the front, I thought I heard an owl, shuffling, screeching low from its sharp beak, hooting secretly to itself on the roof. The Pocapo natives said that birds – all birds – were harbingers of death, couriers that flitted between this world and the next. When it came to owls, I could almost believe it. Later that night I listened as the bird returned with some kind of prey, a small animal that squealed and screamed as it was torn apart and consumed alive just a few feet above our heads, as we lay in the big iron-framed bed, on the soft mattress, just a sheet to cover us during the long hot night.

Sometimes it's good slow. Sometimes fast. Today . . .

Miriam hasn't heard a thing. It's a dream. It has to be. There are no owls these days. Ours is the only residence in Owl Creek. Next door, just thirty feet away, is a deserted warehouse that has lain unoccupied for thirty years. On the other side sits a small two-storey factory occupied during the day by immigrants, mainly illegals. They make cheap clothing and handbags that get sold, for the most part, in the sprawling local market in St Kilda. None of them ever looks me in the eye, though I do nothing about them. Still, they know. Everyone does. That's part of the job. You don't become a cop for anonymity.

In those first few months I lugged barrowloads of junk – scrap metal, an old bath, rotting furniture – out of the back yard. I watched the way she coaxed back to life the old plants and trees there, as if some magic lived in her fingers. While I was working, she built a swing for the boy, made this small patch of life in the grey, faded landscape of the city her own.

One August morning, three years after she began, when the long, patient time she'd spent pruning and repairing the old tree began to bring rewards, Miriam put fresh fruit on the table in a new olive-wood bowl she'd bought from the immigrants next door. Ricky was too young to try them raw, so she cooked some and mashed them up into a pulp he devoured, sitting giggling in his high chair, next to the kitchen table. The apples tasted a little of the city smoke, even after several dowsings under the tap. Neither of us mentioned it. The house and the garden were our private places, though a century and a half of constant development had transformed, completely, the area around them.

The stream now runs in a hidden culvert, its water polluted by industrial filth. The fields and orchards beyond Owl Creek, of which our fruit tree is a solitary survivor, have been consumed by the uncontrolled, haphazard growth of St Kilda, transformed into housing blocks and clumps of low, grimy lock-ups, workshops and shanty huts where, from shadowy doorways, the dope dealers hang out, looking for trade.

Something moves in the garden, beyond the apple tree, hidden by its heavy, leafy branches, which contain green gems of bright round fruit growing, but still bitter, dangling from thick stems, like ornaments attached to an out-of-season, out-of-shape Christmas tree.

'Where's Ricky?' I ask.

Silence. The kind we get before an argument. I don't understand.

'You never listen.'

'Please,' I say, exasperated. 'Where's Ricky?'

I look at her when there's no reply. Miriam seems different. The room seems different.

Out in the garden the shape moves. I see more of it this time. It looks like a man, someone who must have got across the high wire fence, through the wild briar and the thick tangle of honeysuckle, finding a way into our small, private haven.

'Stay here,' I say, and get up from the table.

A stray finger catches the coffee cup. Liquid falls on my hand. It contains no heat whatsoever – nor cold. It merely exists.

I open the solid timbered door, a modern one – I'd insisted on that. Security is important. Then I go outside and look around.

The place seems more lush, more luxuriant than I recall. The apple tree is covered in flowers and tiny fruit the size of elongated cherries. Ferns and fennel and green, spiky artichokes rise from a vegetable bed down near the end fence, close to the old well and the covered creek culvert, now a hard concrete vein rising from the earth.

I walk forward and stand on the drain for a moment. The water inside is beating, pulsing, roaring. For reasons I can't understand, this disturbs me. I blink, I fight to stop myself keeling over, then step off, stumbling, trying to scan the garden, the house, anywhere, everywhere.

Someone could have walked inside during that brief

period in which I wasn't watching. Lapses like these cost you everything in the end.

Feeling a sudden foreboding, I look behind me. The kitchen door is wide open, thrown back on the hinges.

I never leave it this way.

My eyes shift upwards to the first-floor room, Ricky's, with its white cotton sheets and the over-sized bed. We let him use the one at the back because there was less noise. The cul-de-sac gives on to the busy main thoroughfare of De Vere. Our own bedroom shakes sometimes when a heavy vehicle roars down the road in the middle of the night, rattling the iron manhole covers, slipping a gear for the hill ahead, rising towards north St Kilda.

The double windows are open. Ricky's favourite mobile – plastic dolphins dancing over ripples of blue cardboard waves – moves gently in an invisible breeze there, then, as I watch, almost on cue, begins to go round and round, faster and faster.

I close my eyes again and try to breathe. There's no wind. There's scarcely any air. Just the dusty city smog, so meagre it's hard to believe anyone can find oxygen inside it.

Then I look at the house again, just starting to think, cursing my slowness. The kitchen is empty. This is wrong. She was there. Ricky was in bed. She wouldn't disturb him. Not without good reason.

For the first time I feel some real sensation, some genuine emotion, chilling the blood in my veins, making my teeth chatter with fear.

Suddenly, it's cold, bitterly cold, even in the harsh late-afternoon sun, and none of this matters: Miriam is upstairs now and this is wrong. I can hear it. Not a scream. Not a cry for help. It's Miriam's voice and she is furious with someone, filled with an anger I've never heard, not in the entire time we've been married.

She's yelling with all the force her lungs can muster, with a fear and a rage I barely believe can exist.

Though if she yelled at anyone like this, it would surely be at me.

I begin to run for the kitchen. When I'm partway through the door something falls, a weight so heavy I expect and believe its mass will run straight through the top of my skull, keep on going, down and down, until it enters the throat and the neck or works its way clean out through my body.

I fall to my knees, starting to sob silently with the pain, an agony so harsh, so cruel, so intensely internal that, for a moment, I think only of myself, not of them.

For a moment.

My arm reaches out. There is blood on the hand, thick and red, from wrist to fingertip.

'Miriam . . .' I say.

Then no more, because from above come other sounds, other noises.

Screaming and the slow, blunt rattle of blows, something hard and heavy on flesh and bone. Ricky's voice, her voice, both among the damaged, these I hear, and they make me want to rise from the ground, full of hate and vengeance, if only my limbs could move, if only I possessed the strength to save them.

Miriam's voice grows higher, louder, reaches a crescendo and then is silent.

A thick line of blood begins to move down my vision like some red stain descending from an unseen sky.

I fall backwards, can't help it, find myself flat on the

floor in the old kitchen, hard on the ochre tiles she recovered from the dump one day, cursing someone else's lazy ways before laying them herself, patiently fitting each one.

I stare at the ceiling. It stares back, perfect white, the way she painted it, now tinted with the blood flooding into my vision.

A foot obscures everything, stamps on my face, stamps again near one eye.

I feel nothing. I can think of nothing but the agonizing sound coming from above . . .

Daddy, Daddy, Daddy, Daddy.

I want to die now. Or I would if the same damn thought didn't keep running through my head.

There are three.

This is new. Before, in all the long years waiting in a cell, trying to recover some memories from the black, pained past, there had been just an empty well of not-knowing, a void that, before long, filled itself with my own self-doubt.

That infuriated them – judge and jury, even one-time friends – more than anything.

I never revealed the single truth of which I was certain: it infuriated me too, made it impossible to sleep most nights, to close my eyes without seeing their faces, the way I found them, when I discovered the strength and the courage to crawl upstairs, then wait there, too weak to reach the phone, for how long I never knew, until the screaming squad cars arrived, threw themselves across the dead-end road, between the deserted warehouse and the little factory, outside what had once been a simple wooden porch in a country field on the outskirts of a nascent, new-born city made alive by ingenuous hope.

I couldn't tell them what happened because I simply didn't know. Even, in the blackest moments, whether I was victim or the perpetrator they believed.

'There are three of you,' I murmur through lips that can barely speak, lips that feel swollen and useless, like those of a man with the plague. 'Three . . .'

'"There are three of you." What in God's name is that supposed to mean?' I was still on the hard, flat, surgical bed, in the same white medical gown I wore into the death room. This place was different. There was a window, a hard summer sun streaming through it, past a high fence topped by a watchtower with three crows on the roof, then, in the distance, what looked like skyscrapers and gleaming towers in the direction of Westmont. Not that they seemed how I remembered them. Thanks to the time I'd spent in the Gwinett jail, the last twenty-two years in the third of the jail reserved for condemned men, I had no idea what the city looked like now.

The ragged line of corporate monoliths, like upright gleaming tombstones, disappeared just as I was beginning to recall the low, smoke-stained office blocks I thought should have been there. A black man in a tight-fitting dark blue suit walked into my line of vision, reached down, then unfastened the fabric restraining straps that still held me tight to the table.

His voice was familiar.

'Stapleton? Is that really you?'

My throat felt raw and painful. My head was still

spinning. I wasn't sure whether this was part of the dream or not. Or how I found out which.

'What? Of course it's me. Who else gets dumped with this kind of shit job? You're babbling to yourself, man. Get it together.'

The straps fell free. I pushed myself up and slid round to sit on the edge of the bed. There was a throbbing pain in my arms. I looked. The line was no longer there. All I could see was a red mark over the vein and a livid yellow bruise stain spreading out from under it. Martin the Medic, with his shock of white hair and bright blue eyes, must have undone his work while I was unconscious. There was just Stapleton, the individual who once used to ride the squad bike next to mine, the lean black man who'd come out from St Kilda, put some dark, messy past behind him and clawed his way to some respect on the force before getting promoted out of the mundane place the rest of us worked.

'How long have I been out?'

Stapleton glanced at his watch.

'Three hours. They kept you under just to make sure there was no permanent damage.'

'If there was I guess I would never have woken up.'

'You were always too quick for your own good. They just wanted to do things right. These people are trained to finish lives, not revive them. They needed a little specialist help.'

Thinking, I reached over quickly and pinched his arm, finding flesh between thumb and forefinger, squeezing hard.

'Hey!' Stapleton yelled. 'What the hell do you think you're doing?'

'Just checking. I might be dreaming this.'

'Yeah. You might be. You're just the kind of screwed-up jerk who'd invite the likes of me into your dreams.'

'You didn't say welcome back, Stape.'

'You noticed?'

He looked unhappy. He often used to. Just not this way. About me.

'What am I doing here. What . . . ?'

Stapleton silenced me with a fierce stare.

'I talk. You listen. This is one short and very rare opportunity for a second chance. I don't care one way or another if you think this is real or not. I say my piece. Then I'm gone. You've got a decision to make. Be smart or be stupid. Either way it means nothing to anyone except you.'

He retrieved a sheaf of printed documents out of a leather briefcase. This interested me. The Stapleton I knew before he left the force never owned a briefcase. He moved papers around in a supermarket bag. Then he took out some pages, flicked through them, handed them over and sat down on a metal chair by the window.

'Sign these and you get to walk out of here today. Free. It's a great deal. The best you'll ever get. *All* you'll ever get.'

He'd aged. A lot. We all had, I guessed, though on those rare moments when I looked into the plastic mirror in the communal shower rooms in jail I didn't detect much change. Prison stopped my clock running in many ways. I was twenty-nine when I went inside, fifty-two now. The rest of the world got on with its business, not knowing, not caring, just getting older while I ran through all the rounds of predictable emotions: bewilderment, anger, fear, then finally a dull acceptance.

Maybe that last preserved me somewhat. Stapleton was one year younger than me yet his once-black hair was grey with white streaks. His long, miserable face fell down in two jowls from his cheeks. There were bags beneath his sad, staring eyes. He used to be about my size, just under six foot tall, muscular, fit. Sometimes, when we were in uniform on the road together, we'd mixed up each other's jackets. Either fitted. Once we had a few issues out of the way, I'd liked this man, mostly, during the couple of years we worked together, before he got promoted to detective work, then left the force altogether. I believed he felt the same way about me.

That was then. *Before*. We wouldn't swap clothes any more. He'd got a gut on him, a pouch of belly that jutted out over his belt. His chest had sunk in some-what, in an old man's way. There was a hint of envy in his eyes when he looked in my direction. I don't think he meant to hide it. This new Stapleton had found one more reason to hate me and that seemed to give him a buzz.

'I thought I was supposed to be guilty,' I protested.

'This is about the law, Bierce. Not justice. Two different things. You taught me that. Remember?'

Stapleton used to be on the take from some of the drug runners we were supposed to look out for. One day I found him getting paid off in a parking lot on the edge of the Yonge docks. After I watched the scurvy brother who'd been financing him flee the scene in some shiny new Toyota sports car, I delivered a brief lecture, part spoken, part physical, about honesty and what it meant to be a cop, even when most of those around you still hadn't quite received the message. I got through to him back then. It wasn't hard. There'd always been something to get through to, and I'd recognized that in the man all along.

I took the papers from his hand and looked at them. Page after page of legal bullshit, that mix of English, arcane and real, we always had to wade through before going to court.

There were three places for me to sign.

'What are these?'

'Waivers. Statements that say you're willing to forgo your right to sue anyone – the mayor, the chief of police, judges, lawyers, the prison people, me if you feel cranky, *everyone* – in return for getting out of here.'

I stared at the print and tried to take in the details.

'Why?'

Stapleton swallowed, got up. The gut apart, he looked thinner all round, and more than a little unwell. This question had been inevitable, and he hadn't been looking forward to it.

'What does "why" matter? Can't you just put your arrogance to one side for a change, take a gift and walk away with it?'

'No. That was your speciality if I remember correctly. Until I taught you otherwise.'

'Oh, Christ! Are you going to play the insufferable pain-in-the-ass all over again? After what you've been through? After what's on your record? Give me a break.' He was standing next to me now.

I put a hand on Stapleton's jacket and gripped the lapel. The material was a lot better than anything he wore when we worked the streets.

'I want to know,' I said very carefully.

What I got in return was a look I'd learned to

recognize over the last two decades, one that said: *but you know already, you bastard, just stop pretending*.

'So it's still that game, is it?' Stapleton grumbled miserably. 'Let's get this straight. I am not here to plead with you. I am not here to convince you one way or the other. I am merely a messenger from people who, for reasons beyond me, are feeling a touch generous in your direction right now. Are we clear on that?'

'Sure,' I agreed. 'After this I hope never to see your ugly sick face again too.'

His mouth curled up in a timid little snarl. I remembered what was wrong. Stapleton used to have a pencil moustache above his thin upper lip. There was just rough stubble there now, flecked with white and grey.

'I am assuming,' he went on, 'that your supposedly damaged memory does not extend to forgetting Frankie Solera?'

Names. Faces. Sometimes they came back quickly. Sometimes it was as if I'd never heard them before in my life. This was a familiar one.

'Dopehead,' I said. 'We put him inside in the summer of '83. "We" being you and me. Armed robbery in the company of one Tony Molloy. We chased them over the De Soto bridge until they ran out of gas on the highway. They came without protest if I recall correctly. Twelve months with parole.'

Solera and Tony Molloy were a team, both violent street hoods who belonged to one of the gangs smuggling goods – dope, contraband, anything worthwhile – through the docks. Not that they didn't take on freelance work when it came along.

'So?'

'Two nights ago Solera died in hospital. Cancer of

the colon, in case you're interested. It was a long and painful time coming, so perhaps there is a god. We 've been talking to him for a while. About what happened at Owl Creek. About other things. We thought maybe you and him . . .'

I just looked into his sick face. Stapleton got the message.

'You said there were three,' he pressed.

'You said I was babbling. How many times do I have to tell you this? I don't remember a thing.'

Barely, I added, but to myself.

'So you say. Anyway, he confessed. Said it was just him.'

'What about Molloy? Was he around or in jail?'

'I don't know! Do you think we've got nothing better to do than chase old ghosts?'

'I didn't realize you'd developed the giving-up habit.'

'Don't get smart with me, Bierce. Or I may just walk straight out of here and let you stew for the rest of your pathetic little life. Solera said there was no one else. Then he died. Personally, I don't believe him, not for a second. It doesn't matter. The legal department thinks your conviction could go before a judge if someone pushed it. There's some procedural shit involved no one but a lawyer would understand. So maybe it's best we come to some quite private arrangement. *If* you're willing.'

Stapleton's eyes flashed at me and there was some hesitation, maybe even some hate, there.

'Why you?' I asked. 'Why not some lawyer?'

He twisted his mouth into a kind of a smile.

'In case you don't know, I saw that house after-

wards. I just wanted to see what you looked like when you walked out of here thinking you'd got off scot-free.'

This was interesting. This made me think.

'You weren't police then, were you?'

'Your memory's still working there too! My, is it one selective organ. This is none of your business. Whatever I was, I saw that house. One man couldn't do all that damage. Forensic said so. Common sense said so. But I'm not paid to make those kinds of judgements.'

'You're not paid to make private arrangements either. What happened to the law?'

He hesitated, wondering whether to say what was on his mind.

'There's something you have to understand, Bierce. I'm saying this just once, so that I can tell myself you've been warned. Not that I imagine it will make a difference. You're an obstinate son of a bitch and always will be. But hear this anyway. Life is different now. A lot different. All the rules you thought existed, such as they were . . . Don't assume anything. That would be stupid, and stupidity is one thing I never thought you guilty of.'

I rubbed my arms. Some life was coming back into them. Maybe.

'Is there any evidence linking Solera to the house?' I asked.

'What does it matter? What do you care?'

'That was my wife and son. I care.'

Stapleton pushed the papers at me again.

'If it means anything, he said he still had the knife in his apartment. The moron kept it as a trophy all these years. The blood was hers. And Ricky's.'

I thought about what he said. Thought about the

dream too. It seemed oddly ironic that it took a shot of dope designed to soften me up for execution to start to loosen all those locked memories from years ago.

'You found my blood on it?'

'No!' Stapleton spat back at me. 'You know damn well where we found your blood. Underneath Miriam's fingernails. You used to be a police officer once, how do *you* think it got there?'

'I have no idea,' I answered. 'And that's the truth.'

'The truth . . .' he muttered. 'I don't really care about that. These are strange times, and forgiveness is a part of that strangeness, I guess. So are you signing those papers or not?'

I'd been glancing through them in the few minutes while we talked. Even wrapped in legalese, the release came with heavy conditions.

'This doesn't make me innocent,' I pointed out. 'It just puts the conviction on ice. It's like parole without the conditions.'

'Listen to me,' Stapleton replied. 'Guilty or not, you get to walk out of here. Also you pick up four hundred and sixty thousand in cash as recompense for the time you spent in jail. Twenty thousand a year for twenty-three years.'

'I'd have earned more than that on the force.'

He smiled.

'Only if you'd lived. To get this you need to sign on the line, go your way quietly, keep your mouth shut, stay away from stirring the shit with lawyers or anyone else. Plus the usual condition we'd impose on any ex-con. Do not touch any kind of firearm whatsoever, on pain of immediate reimprisonment. This is all, by the way, non-negotiable and comes with the shelf life of a mayfly. Take it now or lose it forever. Everything's off the table if I walk out of this door without your name on those documents.'

He pulled a gold pen out of his jacket and placed it on the table.

'Maybe I ought to talk this over with someone,' I stalled.

'Do that and it's gone. Here's the deal and it's the only deal there'll ever be. Sign and you get a little of your life back. All that money and a little upfront. Twiddle your thumbs for one second beyond my limits and you're back in Gwinett, staring at the wall forever and ever amen. Well?'

He reached into his jacket, took out a fat wad of used notes and threw the money on the table. It looked like a lot.

'Here's twenty thousand cash to be going along with. The rest we'll pay into one account you get to specify. This could buy you a few nights of heaven out there. Alternatively, you can be some stuck-up, stupid prig and you stay in solitary for life. Without parole. It's your choice. And if you're thinking you can call in a lawyer later and try to revive this deal, let me enlighten you now. These papers . . .'

Stapleton waved them in my face.

'. . . they don't exist. They came out of some private safe on the way here. They go back in if you sign. Or hit the shredder if you don't. This is all happening outside the judge's rooms, Bierce. Bear that in mind. If you want to get prissy we're talking years and years of argument and in the end you'll lose. We'll make sure of that. Think on this. There's enough circumstantial evidence

33

to let us treat Solera's confession as that of your accomplice if we want. Remember Miriam's fingernails. I do.'

I shook my head.

'Didn't I teach you anything? This is the law you're dealing with. You can't cut deals like that, Stape. It doesn't work this way.'

He sighed.

'I keep telling you. These are different times. Don't argue with them. It's not productive. Also . . .' He pointed a finger straight in my face. 'Don't get familiar with me again. Should we meet in the street after this, ignore me, 'cos I will surely ignore you. Should we meet professionally – and I pray for your sake that does not occur – it's Agent Stapleton these days. I get some respect.'

I smiled.

'Agent? Congratulations. I guess you're glad I punched your lights out when I caught you taking money that time. You might have stayed in the police. And prospered.'

He laughed. Briefly there was a little sparkle in his tired eyes.

'Jesus, Bierce.' His voice went down to a whisper. His eyes flickered nervously round the room. 'I could have been up for commissioner right now. Different times. Bear it in mind.'

This man was once my friend. It was hard to believe everything was gone.

'You don't honestly believe I killed them, do you?'

The smile dropped like a stone.

'Can you honestly say you didn't?'

That was the problem, and had been all along. I told them the truth. What else was there to say? They found me unconscious, my wife and son battered to death upstairs. All the physical evidence pointed to a struggle with Miriam before she died. My blood and prints were on the sledgehammer used in their murders. And I didn't remember a thing, not a single moment of the events leading up to the killings. I didn't deny the facts of the murder because I couldn't. All I could rely on was my own emotional instinct, which told me, without a possibility of error, that I couldn't have committed the acts of which I stood accused. That was the only honest answer and, as a stratagem in court, it was disastrous.

There was no remaking the past. Only a possibility of its recovery. Of comprehension.

So I took the pen and signed three times, promising to be quiet from now on, not to talk to the media, break the law or be anything but the good citizen that, in my mind, I always was. Four hundred and sixty thousand dollars, more money than I'd ever owned in my entire life, ought to be enough to work out what to do next.

My name looked odd on the paper. It had been a long time since I'd written anything.

'I will organize transport,' Stapleton said, watching. 'Where do you want to go?'

'Home.'

There was a brief silence.

'You mean Owl Creek?'

'I mean Owl Creek. It's the only home I have.'

I didn't let them sell it, not even when my lovely lawyer, Susanna Aurelio, was moaning, very sweetly, for money. Nor could they make me. Through some odd irony, the insurance money had paid off the mortgage automatically, before the court case. Susanna expected the insurance people to come hunting me for the money once I was convicted. For some reason they never did. It was just one more question that bugged me for a while. But not long. The endless days in Gwinett saw to that. Owl Creek was 100 per cent mine two months before I was sentenced to death for the murder of Miriam and Ricky, and stayed that way throughout my time as a condemned man, not that I ever expected to see it again.

'That house has been empty for twenty-three years, Bierce. With all the money I'm handing you, why not go to a decent hotel for a few days?'

'Because I want to go home.'

'Fine,' he snapped. 'I rather thought you'd say that. It can pass for now, though I seriously suggest you find yourself somewhere more healthy soon. That neighbourhood is not coming up in the world. Particularly for a friendless individual like you. I'll make some calls. It's in both our interests that the media stay off your back. They've been warned already. Doesn't do any harm to be a little more emphatic.'

I tried to think straight. This didn't ring true. So much of what he said didn't.

'Warned? How the hell can you warn people like that?'

'There are only so many times I can say this. Things have changed. Do yourself a favour. Remember that. Do yourself a bigger favour.'

The man in the suit stood up and took my arm. For a few seconds I thought I saw a flicker of sympathy, some concern, in his eyes.

'Take a plane out of here. Go to the other side of the country. The world. The universe. Somewhere no one has a clue who you are. As long as you stay here you're just a man in limbo, Bierce, and limbo's not a nice place to be.'

I nodded. I knew how to be cooperative when it felt right.

'I'll think about that. So what took you?'

'Excuse me?'

'Solera died two nights ago. You had the confession then. This morning you had me on the slab, thinking I was about to get dead. Events like that kind of mark you.'

I pointed to the documents on the table.

'If you'd been a little later with those . . . Even with your lousy timing that was cutting it fine, Agent Stapleton, don't you think?'

He picked up the papers, examined the signatures, then placed them in a plastic folder which he inserted into the briefcase.

'Oh! You mean these?' he asked, wide-eyed, sarcastic. 'No. I had these last night. I was just asked to put them aside for a while. Where were you going anyway?'

I felt my fists clench. It was a long time since I'd hit anyone.

Stapleton took my right hand in his lean black fingers, pushed it down, smiled, just briefly.

'Hey. You taught me something once. Now it's my turn. This is educational, friend. Think about it. There are people out there who want to see you sweat a little. To make sure you understand how the land lies in the hope you will adjust your future behaviour accordingly.'

He nodded at the money on the table.

'I wonder if it worked. I'll send out for some clothes

before the car arrives. After that, you're back where you always were. On your own.'

It was dark by the time the car pulled into the narrow dead-end turning that was Owl Creek. Stape was right. From what little I could see, the area hadn't come up the way Miriam had expected. I'd slept most of the way, still doped. No dreams. Nothing. I still felt wiped out when the car's movement jolted me awake as it negotiated the ragged cobblestones of the short dead end that led towards my front door. The warehouse on the left looked even more decrepit than I recalled. There wasn't a window or a door intact in the place any more. From the back seat of the vehicle I could see straight into the interior: broken walls, missing floorboards. We told Ricky never to play in the place. He'd done as we said. He always did. The factory opposite looked unchanged. There was a light in one room on the first floor, a single bare, yellow bulb, and the silhouette of someone working at a desk. Apart from that, the building seemed empty.

I got out of the car and gazed at the single street lamp in front of the house. It was flickering into life, looking as if it might never quite get there. I thought I heard an owl hoot somewhere nearby, but perhaps I was dreaming.

'Thanks,' I said to the driver, some plain-clothes guy Stapleton had called.

'Don't walk around here at night,' the man said, still gunning the engine.

I hardly heard him. I was staring at the house, feeling its presence come back into my life, the good and the bad. But mainly the good. People are made that way. Sane people anyway, and in spite of the years in jail, and the dope Martin the Medic had pumped inside me that morning, I still felt sane.

It would be just a few steps up the broken paving stones to the front door. I could see a heavy, rusting police padlock and chain there, now hanging loose and broken, a clear, perhaps deliberate, indication that some-one had been inside of late. Stapleton had given me my old set of house keys from the belongings bag they'd stored for twenty-three years. There were no clothes, of course. They, and their attendant bloodstains, had gone into the evidence file. Just a set of keys and a wallet with nothing but an expired driver's licence and police ID card inside. I'd left the latter for him as a souvenir, but now I couldn't help but think about what he'd said. I could have gone somewhere else, some anonymous hotel, placed my head on a comfortable pillow for the first time in a third or so of the average lifetime, and for-gotten about the past. The trouble was, I didn't feel I had a choice. This old house, with its rotting weather-boarded timbers and cobwebbed windows, looked grey and old and dead, but I still saw it in another way too, as somewhere my family once lived, in a semblance of brief happiness. One night of horror doesn't obliterate seven years of normality. Not quite.

'I'll bear that in mind,' I said, then walked up to the wooden porch, removed the shattered chain, found my old key, amazed how it still felt familiar in my fingers, unlocked the door after a struggle with the rusty, stiff lock, took a deep breath – smog and ocean, drains and, from somewhere out back, the slightest hint of apple blossom – and walked inside.

*

It didn't smell old or dead. The house still had the odour I'd noticed the first day we moved in: drying, antique wood, on the floors, the stairs, around the long, generous windows. Cedar maybe, or something else aromatic. I never did find out.

Instinctively, I reached for the light switch. To my surprise, it worked. Quite why, in a house that had been empty all this time, all bills, except the city taxes, unpaid, was beyond me. But this was a new century, a new world. A lot would be beyond me, I guessed, and standing there, in the place that had once been the focus of the only family I'd ever have, I realized I couldn't care less. What mattered was then, not now, and maybe it would always be that way.

What I saw in front of me was both foreign and familiar. The house had been in legal limbo since my conviction, incapable of being sold or rented, visited only by lawyers and the police over the years. Cobwebs ran everywhere, geometric grey skeins with a covering of dust like the first frost of winter stored somewhere dusty, somewhere it could grow old. A line of yellow police tape still ran across the foot of the stairs. I strode up and brushed it to one side with my hand. As I did so, something rose in my memory. It came from my working days. The touch of the plastic tape, so distant yet so familiar, brought back a mental picture of a case I'd handled once, many years before. The rape and murder of a young girl found in the rocky, seaweed-strewn dead land beneath the Greenpoint side of the De Soto bridge. Stapleton and I had been the first to the scene. I could recall the sight of her ruined, broken body, the smell of the place, the sound of the waves lapping over the algaed rocks where she was found. I could recall, too, Stape gagging into the bushes, choking as he threw up, moaning about how unjust it was that this job had fallen on his shift.

We never did catch that girl's killer, not while I was out on the streets. Still, that was a memory in itself. They did keep coming back, which gave me pause for thought.

I glanced up the wooden staircase and thought: not yet.

Then I turned round and walked through the ground-floor rooms, slowly, methodically, trying to recover the mental map stored somewhere deep in my head.

The parlour faced on to the street. I went in. Nothing had changed. I walked to the upright piano that sat against the end wall, lifted the lid and played a chord: G minor seventh, the one I always remembered from a couple of months of lessons at school because it was my favourite, sad, resigned yet not entirely devoid of hope. The instrument was hideously out of tune. The chord didn't sound right. I crossed the hall, went past the foot of the stairs and entered the dining room. Only one light bulb worked here. It cast a hard shadow across the large, eight-place mahogany table, still with the set of high-backed chairs tucked in between its legs as if awaiting guests.

It had been a standing joke between us: the Bierces only ever had eight guests at Christmas, when Miriam's small and argumentative family descended. We found it hard to fill this house with family at other times, until Ricky came along, and after that it didn't much matter.

I ran a finger through the dust and spiders' webs on the table. Beneath it lay the hard, polished shine she'd put there through days of dedicated labour after we found it languishing, half wrecked, in a St Kilda junk yard.

It made me try to remember the last meal we ate here. It was impossible. All of a sudden I felt giddy, aware that I was deeply exhausted, maybe a little unbalanced and prone to hallucinations from the stuff still circulating in my veins. I was desperate to lie down and sleep. Just not ready. And not upstairs either. Not yet.

There was a sofa in the parlour, beneath the window out on to the street. When I needed it, that would do.

These two rooms were untouched by the savagery. I knew in my heart that was why I came here first. But self-deception was never one of my talents. So I turned round and walked to the back of the house, into the big kitchen, with its French windows out on to the garden, a pool of semi-blackness now, just illuminated by the washed-out lighting from the nearby tenement blocks.

The bright fluorescent tubes came on, flickering, as if nothing had ever happened here. I saw what I knew I'd see, and still it made me catch my breath, fight to stem the nausea rising with the memory of the pain, that all-consuming agony that came when the blows, from an unremembered hand, rained down.

There were blue chalk marks on the floor and scribbled annotations from the investigating officers. I moved my foot across them quickly. The ochre tiles had lost their warmth under a dusty azure film. These stains wouldn't go easily.

Through the windows, in the garden, I could just make out the shape of the apple tree. It seemed huge, a sprawling, low mass of branches. Miriam pruned this thing carefully each spring, brought it back to shape. It needed that. So many things did. Perhaps I could do the same again, and in five or six years it would look like it used to. Or – this thought wouldn't go away – perhaps I could do what Stapleton wanted, turn my back on everything here and run, for good. I had the money. I could walk out to De Vere, pick up a cab, book into a clean, bright, antiseptic place with no memories, nothing to keep me awake at night. Then, in the morning, go to the airport. Take the first flight out, to anywhere.

All this was possible, I thought, and then my mind seized on itself, like an engine abruptly starved of oil.

There was a sound upstairs. It was someone moving, softly, as light as a cat.

I thought for a moment, then walked back into the hall, placed my hand on the warm wood of the banister and started taking the steps, two at a time.

When I reached the top I heard the sound again: the bare wooden floorboards, once polished, creaked under a step that was light. Like a woman, not like a child.

There were more chalk marks on the landing. I tried to move my foot to obliterate them but there was too much blue dust, too many scrawls on the floor. I fought to remember what this level was like in detail. A design still lived in my head, but it wasn't specific. The house had become a part of us, almost a member of the family too, a jumbled-up, rambling collection of rooms, running from the cellar, where Miriam had made some small den for herself, up to this bedroom floor in a crooked, illogical tangle of half-staircases and dead-end corridors. I was never a man to work on a home; Miriam did that or found someone. So it became something close, accepted for what it was, not broken down into some kind of precise, visual inventory. And this section of it always puzzled me more than anywhere else. It should have been bigger, not just three bedrooms – ours, Ricky's and a third for rare guests – along with a bathroom, a closet and, on the blind side of the building, looking out on to a small scrappy field of scrub kept in permanent shadow by high walls on both sides, so it was invisible from the house, a tiny boxroom for storage.

I flicked the landing light switch. One more burnt-out bulb. The entire garden end of the house – Ricky's room, the guest bedroom, the boxroom – was still in darkness.

I walked forward and said, in what I took to be a calm, flat voice, 'Who's there?'

Feet scampered ahead in the gloom, making swift, light movements across the boards. A shape flitted through the shadows, got lost in the gloom so thoroughly I couldn't see where she came from or where she went.

My heart skipped a couple of beats. My mouth went dry. Noticeable physical symptoms, proof I was alive. That hadn't happened in a while.

I'd seen enough to know she was wearing a dress, scarlet probably, loose and flowing, open at the neck. Like all those dresses Miriam kept on buying because they were so comfortable in the scorching summer heat.

Like the dress she died in. I'd never forget the pictures. Bendinck, the sour-faced detective who led the investigation, seemed to take a particular pleasure in thrusting them into my face, even in hospital, when

I could scarcely open my eyes. Those shots, taken from every angle, unforgiving in their brutal honesty, had stayed with me, would stay with me, always. The colour of the blood and the fabric seemed so closely matched.

I walked forward, turned left into the boy's room and hit the light. The sight made me want to weep. The bed was still there, stripped of sheets. The cartoon characters remained stuck to the walls, each in mid-flight, hitting, running, chasing, doing what cartoon people did: things we weren't supposed to in real life. Many were now marked by the work of the forensic men, whose pens and crayons had disfigured everything, everywhere. In places there was a fine spray on the paper. It jogged a phrase at the back of my memory: blood spatter.

Blue chalk lines ran across the floor, the walls, on to the cupboards and the low table where Ricky used to work, crouched over a book, head lolling on the desk-top, pencil in hand.

Like slender, writhing snakes, they all ran outwards from the chalk silhouette of a small body curled on the floor, a single arm raised defensively to his head, a curving, organic shape that looked as if it was scrawled there in one single, sweeping movement.

Ricky died here. This stark blue impression on the bare floorboards was the only physical evidence our son existed, a moment snatched from a single human life and pinned to the ground as if to say: *here*.

My foot reached out to touch the shape. Then I stopped. There was so much blue chalk. I couldn't obliterate it all, not with a simple gesture.

From somewhere behind came a sound again. I went back to the landing, trying to locate it in the darkness that squatted like a black, dead pool in the corner, out of reach of the bulb in the stairwell.

I knew where it came from. The bedroom. Nowhere else. And as I watched, something skipped through the door: in and out, teasing. I saw the briefest of glimpses of a scarlet cotton dress, a lithe naked leg, an outstretched bare arm, shifting tentatively into the light, then disappearing.

She had so many of those dresses. She couldn't stop buying them. They were like a uniform, like a second skin.

I went forward, past the guest room, past the boxroom, over the lines of blue chalk on the floor, like tattoos on the face of some primitive being, and entered, holding my breath, determined to see this through.

Something tried to burst into life by the Victorian metal bed where we'd slept. A smell reached me: it was dry and vile and burning. I looked and saw a gigantic moth trapped inside the bowl of the upright tungsten lamp she kept on the cabinet, stuck to the burning glass by its own dissolution, struggling, flapping, to get free.

In the corner, she was dancing.

Round and round the scarlet dress turned, revealing the long, loose limbs, bare and brown, tanned from the summer sun.

Her hair flew about her head, a brown, shining mantle over her face and the dark, slender stalk of her neck.

There was another blue outline on the floor. A larger shape, contorted in agony. I stepped over it, towards the figure, trying not to shake.

She skipped round me, round the bed, past the

mirror, hair flying, long, slender hands curving, curling in theatrical gestures.

The cassette in the clock radio was playing a song from a tape I'd owned in jail for a while, until they took it away when I did something wrong, like breathing in six/eight instead of four/four.

It was Bruce Hornsby's rolling piano and soft, sad voice.

> *This is no fond farewell.*
> *You can be sure I could wish it was no farewell at all.*

I tried to remember the title, cursed my own failed memory. Then the music told me anyway.

> *This is my swan song. I'm gone, gone.*

I walked up to the head of the bed, hit the stop key and punched the eject button. The tape sat in its little hole, pale plastic. Scrawled on the top, with the cheap black felt tips they gave us in Gwinett, my writing said: *Property of Bierce. Steal me and die.*

The scarlet figure moved towards the door. My hand swept the air in front of me, touching nothing except cobwebs falling long and loose from the old fan in the ceiling down to the iron bedstead. It fell hard on the burnished bronze frame at the foot. The springs squeaked, a sound I hadn't heard in more than two decades, one that filled me with despair and a sad longing.

> *Sometimes it's good slow. Sometimes fast.*

In a low voice, one filled with some fear and fury I hadn't expected, I murmured, 'Who are you?'

Then I sprang forward, caught hold of the scarlet cotton, pulled, feeling a body, a real body, exert momentum in return.

I was grateful for that.

The mantle of brown hair subsided. She had her back to me. I placed my hands on her naked shoulders and turned her round.

Two green, unfamiliar eyes stared into mine.

'Hi.'

The girl was about twenty-five, slim, beautiful in a marked, damaged way. There was a hint of something Oriental in the oval shape of her face. A small horizontal scar ran above one eye. She smiled: even white teeth and a silver stud in the tip of her tongue.

She stood there, her body twisted into the inviting curve of some dancer in a cheap St Kilda sex dive.

'Who the hell are you?'

The girl's face fell. It was still pretty.

'You don't look pleased to see me.'

Her voice didn't quite match her slightly foreign appearance. It had the hard city inflection to it, the mark of a local.

'Get out of my dead wife's clothes,' I said. 'Then get out of my house.'

She touched the scarlet fabric.

'So many things to wear here. They don't do her any good now. Do they?'

'Get out,' I said, and didn't feel mad for some reason. Someone had sent her, and if she was the kind of woman who could be bossed around that way, it wasn't hard to guess the rest.

'Hey, Bierce. Don't be so prissy. Why shouldn't someone live here? No one else does. Who do you think put back the electricity and the water and the gas? Who washed a few things so they don't smell musty and bad? Me. That's who. A big house like this needs a woman around.'

She reached out. Her fingers touched my hand, stroking the skin gently. Almost with tenderness.

'My name's Alice. If you let me stay you won't regret it.'

'Out,' I said, and I could hear how weak it sounded. I felt exhausted, screwed up by Martin the Medic's dope and the events of the day. I was alive but I didn't feel it.

Also, I was aware I couldn't take my eyes off her. The girl's body was so like Miriam's, slim, lithe, like an athlete's but a little worn down and damaged by use. If I didn't look into her face, if I couldn't remember or imagine . . .

'You want the dress,' she said. 'You take the dress.'

With that easy two-handed movement a woman has, she reached down and pulled the scarlet cotton past her head, dragging it over her hair. Then she stood in front of me, slouching a little, her mouth midway between anger and a pout.

She pressed the dress into my hands. I felt the soft seersucker fabric, smelled its freshness, so familiar, once a part of the ritual that began here, ended here, sometimes made me believe this room was where we'd live forever, locked into each other, not moving, scarcely daring to breathe, in rapture that two people could become one like this, could find so much in each other that nothing else in the world beyond the shutters mattered at all.

I let it go. The thing fell through my fingers and drifted to the floor. She watched it land gently on the old carpet, then picked it up, carefully I thought, and threw it on the bed, looking at me, leaning her slim, bronzed body the way she did before.

She had small upright breasts with dark nipples, almost black. The triangle of hair at the apex of her long, slender legs had been fashioned into an artificial geometric shape, like some twisted astrological symbol. A small green and red dragon tattoo nestled above the final curls in the soft curve of her lower stomach.

She reached out and stroked me through the cheap pants the prison had provided.

'I think you're going to need some work there,' the girl whispered tentatively, with no confidence at all. Almost shy, I thought. And reluctant.

It didn't seem to be an offer, even if she thought that was what was expected of her.

'I've got work aplenty,' I said, then turned round and walked down the stairs.

Just the touch of her fingers had broken some spell. With that came a memory.

It was in the garden and it mattered.

Two of the four security floods came on like small silver suns. Shaded by high walls on all three sides, the garden was unrecognizable.

The lawn was thigh deep in long grass and weeds. The roses had defeated the honeysuckle in the wire fences, which were now thickets of thorns and white, simple flowers, rambling down to the ground.

The broad crooked path of broken paving that led to the end wall, and the old wooden door to the scrub land beyond, was barely visible beneath the weeds and wild flowers that covered it. Then there was the tree.

Uncared for, uncut for more than twenty years, it had grown into a behemoth of heavy branches, stooping low on one side under a surfeit of fat green fruit, a rough, misshapen giant, bent in on itself, malformed by the shade.

Things thrived, after a fashion, in spite of neglect. It didn't always work out for the worse.

I heard a sound behind me and looked back. It was the girl, Alice, skipping across the kitchen. She was wearing jeans and a cheap white T-shirt now. She looked more natural.

'I never went in here,' she said quietly, coming to a stop by my side. 'I never lived anywhere with a garden before. What's it for?'

I walked up to the good side of the tree and pulled off a couple of apples. They were just like the first ones Miriam had picked for me. Half green, half rosy red. I gave her one. She watched me, cautious. I rubbed the shiny skin with the arm of my shirt and took a bite. She did the same, not taking her eyes off my face for a moment.

They still tasted a little of smog, not quite sour, not quite sweet. I didn't mind. It was better than anything I'd eaten in Gwinett.

'Gardens exist to remind you there's something else in the world apart from buildings and cars and money.'

She laughed.

'There is?'

The memory was firm now. It could wait.

'I'd like the key,' I said.

The green eyes glittered, a little resentful. She didn't like being found out.

'Take 'em.'

She kept the bunch in her pocket. They were new and still had a label on them from the shop where they were cut.

'Was it a black guy who put you up to this? Stapleton? Old. Grey-white hair. Stubble where he used to have a moustache.'

She nodded.

'I didn't know his name but it sounds like him. You don't ask when it comes to this kind of work. I just heard they were putting it round they needed someone who'd be happy to make up a welcoming party. They let me in last night. Said to clean up the worst places. Get things going.'

She folded her arms. The next thing didn't come easily.

'Part of the deal was that, when you got here, I'd do whatever you liked. I think he wanted you to be happy. Sorry. I didn't mean to upset you.'

'You didn't,' I answered honestly.

'They gave me five hundred, Bierce. That's a lot of money.'

No, it wasn't. Not even twenty-three years ago.

'You could make that with two tricks in Westmont,' I guessed.

'What?' Her face lit up with anger. It looked keen and intelligent when that happened. 'I'm no hooker.'

'So what are you?'

She thought before answering.

'Someone who scrapes along. Or tries to. This is a profession followed by the masses these days. Maybe a man in jail forgets that. Besides, I've got reasons.'

I reached forward and took her by the wrists, turned them over and looked, slowly. There were no marks.

'What particular reason happens to be yours?'

'Huh?'

They always kept it about them. I patted the pockets of her tight jeans, ignoring her struggles. The bottle was in the left-hand one. I took it out and waved it in front of her face. Brown-coloured glass. A pharmaceutical label. Something about this didn't make me feel smart.

'It's for hay fever, you jerk,' she squealed, wriggling out of my hold. 'Talk about once a cop, always a cop. Can I have my medicine back now? Jesus, getting accused of being a hooker and a junkie in two consecutive sentences is a little tough to take. Even for me. How'd you get married in the first place? Was your wife allergic to charm or something?'

The funny thing was, Miriam used to say something very like that at times. When we lay back in bed, after. I was feeling sleepy. She was feeling talkative.

Is that what got you here, Bierce? Charm?

No. I never did unlock that secret.

I looked at the label, then opened the bottle. It was half full of white, innocuous-looking pills. There had to be something, I thought. A real reason. A good one.

'Thanks for the apple,' she said, then pulled back her arm and threw the spent core straight ahead as hard as she could. It flew through the bright beam of the security lights and went over the high wall, into the dead land behind the abandoned warehouse. A good shot. A powerful shot.

'You're right. I should go now.'

'Stapleton gave you the Hornsby tape? The one you put on in the bedroom.'

'Is that who it was? Some of this old guy stuff is really cool.'

I blinked.

'It's not old. Eighties. Early nineties at the most. I was in solitary all the time after that. I never got anything.'

Alice licked her lips, wondering whether she ought to say it.

'Bierce, that's old. *You're* old.'

I looked at my hands, my arms. Looked at the parts of me I could see.

'I don't look any different. I don't feel any different.'

'OK,' she agreed. 'You haven't changed. It's just the rest of the world. Same thing.'

'Did he ask you to keep tabs on me?'

'No.'

'What did he ask for?'

'Nothing. I told you. He wanted you to be happy. That was all.'

'So for five hundred you'd just go and spend the night with a man convicted of killing his own wife and child? In the house where he was supposed to have murdered them?'

She blushed.

'All the dress stuff was my idea. I said I'm sorry. Sometimes . . .' She winced. 'Look. Being physical is the easiest way to converse with most men. It gets round the awkward questions. It's a way of saying hello.'

I laughed. I really did, though it took me a moment to recognize the sound that came out of my own throat.

'That's a hell of a way of saying hello.'

She was peering at me. She looked worried.

'Twenty-three years?' she asked.

'Plus forty-seven days,' I added. 'And just for the

54

record, I do not, and never have, fallen into the category "most men".'

'God, you have a lot to learn. You said you didn't kill them anyway.'

I nodded towards the high wall at the end of the garden.

'Tell the people out there that.'

'I don't need to. It wouldn't mean a thing anyway. They don't know who you are, Bierce. They don't care.'

She didn't like the way I was looking at her.

'Besides,' she added, 'you got let out. They don't do that to guilty people. Remember?'

'No, I don't,' I said honestly. 'That's the problem.'

I strode over to the small lean-to by the south wall where we kept all the garden stuff. There was a rusting shovel next to a tangle of rakes and sieves. I dragged it out of the trumpet vine tangle that held it down, then walked through the mess of weeds and high grass to the end of the garden, close by the cement culvert, where the creek would have run back when it was something real, not an imaginary line on a map.

Most cops in the city had a private store. It was a dangerous profession. Occasionally it took a ride home with you. What I remembered in the bedroom, when Alice's fingers brushed against me, was where I'd kept mine. In the foot of the concrete stump I'd put in place to keep the bird table Miriam had always wanted.

It made a kind of sense. If there was trouble, I said, just run to the garden, find the table, look for the little handle in the cement block at the foot.

It was overgrown now: thick, heavy weeds and rye grass covered the metal hook I'd buried into the cement slab I made for the lid. I turned away the earth with the shovel, found what I was looking for, pulled hard until it moved, then peered into the small rectangular hole I'd dug into the hard clay earth all those years ago.

It wasn't quite as I remembered. A little deeper, and the metal box sitting in the bottom, rusting slowly, seemed rather more visible than I recalled. But there were leaves and dead beetles and all manner of stuff stuck above it. No one had been around here in more than two decades. So I got my shoulder to the ground, reached down with my right arm and pulled out the box. After several attempts on my own, Alice groaned and loaned me a coin. With that I managed to open the waterproof seal and put my hand inside. It was still there, a service revolver, already loaded, and three boxes of ammunition. Stock-keeping had never been good on the force range. Most officers managed to smuggle a gun out of there when they needed one.

'Wow,' Alice gasped. 'Are you sure you've got memory problems?'

'Some,' I replied, and let the weapon hang in my hand. It felt strange. Wrong somehow.

'There's a law in the city these days,' she said. 'If they find you with a gun and no licence you go straight to jail. No arguments. Unless you've got friends. If you've got friends you can do any damn thing you like. I thought you ought to know.'

In that case I'd go back to jail twice over if they found me carrying a piece. I'd bear it in mind.

'Do you have a vehicle?' I asked her.

'I got a bike. A 1993 Kawasaki 500 twin. Looks like a wreck.'

She smiled. A real smile. It changed her.

'It isn't,' Alice added. 'I did a hundred and forty on it on the big road south from the bridge last summer.'

She hesitated.

'Is this a job or something?'

'Fifty a day. Cash. A hundred when it gets into over-time.'

'For what exactly?'

'Let's call it personal assistance. I want transporta-tion. And a little advice when I need it.'

She was smirking.

'What's so funny?'

'You wanting advice. What's that they say about alcoholics? Acknowledging the need is the first step on the road to recovery.'

'You really don't know me,' I said ruefully.

At that moment I wasn't sure I knew me either.

'You didn't kill them, Bierce,' she said again force-fully.

She looked convinced. It was ridiculous.

'I am grateful for your trust.'

'It's not that.'

She nodded behind her.

'My mom used to work in that little sweatshop next door. With all the other illegals turning out cheap crap for some crooked jerk in Chinatown.'

'So . . . ?'

'So she saw you. Every day, when she was slaving over her stupid sewing machine, praying it wouldn't bite half her arm off like it did some of the others. You wonder why I do what I do?'

I shook my head.

'You never said what you did.'

'Don't play the smartass. She saw you come home

on that big shiny police motorcycle you had. She thought that was really brave back then, given the neighbourhood. Now . . .'

She stepped forward and looked into my eyes.

'She saw you with them too. Your wife. Some lovely little white kid. My grandma, Lao Lao, told me all about this. More than once. My mom watched you and your wife and your boy and she thought . . . one day. I will have something like that. I will make it for myself. I will have that kind of family, that kind of house. All this *will* be mine.'

'Oh,' I said.

The reason was here somewhere.

'What made your grandma so talkative about me?'

'She brought me up. She was OK, even if she did think I was something slightly less than human as a result of my mom getting knocked up by some white guy who took the next train the moment the test tube came back blue.'

'Well, Alice. What's your last name?'

'Loong. Don't bother asking one of your police friends to look me up. I don't have a record. Nothing interesting anyway.'

'Good. I don't have any police friends either.'

I held out my hand for her to shake. She took it and laughed.

'Do I get a little cleaning for that money too?' I asked.

'For that money you get any . . .'

'No.'

I didn't want her to say it. I didn't want to hear it, even as a joke.

'Get rid of the chalk, will you? All of it. Every last

piece of police crap in there. This is a home, not a carnival show.'

Miriam never lived in the past. She thought it was a sin. It always seemed a crazy idea to me back then. Experience makes you, breaks you sometimes. But I knew now what she was getting at.

'No blue lines,' I said again.

My eyelids felt like lead. My head was aching. I was already dreaming of a quiet, uneventful night on that big, fat sofa downstairs.

'No dust. No cobwebs. I woke up dead today, Alice. This gives a man pause.'

'Huh?' she asked, green eyes wide with puzzlement.

'It's a private joke. I'll let you in on the secret some time. Where are you going?'

I watched her amble into the kitchen and thought for a moment: this could have been Miriam. But it wasn't. She was just some desperate young woman who'd been press-ganged by Stapleton into doing something that maybe half interested her in the first place.

For a reason I still didn't understand.

She stopped and looked back at me over her shoulder. Miriam never did that. She always turned to face you. These two were different. Every last person on this planet was.

'You'll need a pillow, Bierce. Even on a sofa like that.'

A small shadow of uncertainty crossed her face.

'Does it bother you if I sleep upstairs?' she asked. 'In the big room? If it freaks you out . . .'

'No. I don't mind if you don't.'

'Never had much time for ghosts,' she said, then

walked on until she was out of sight, leaving me to the smell of apple blossom and the buzzing cloud of mosquitoes swirling in the bright hard beam of the security lights.

The pillow was there when I made it to the sofa. I was so tired I thought nothing in the world could keep me from sleep.

I was wrong.

After tossing and turning for the best part of an hour I went up those old familiar creaking stairs. Something had happened. I walked around, through each part of the floor, before going into the back bedroom. The chalk marks were gone already, along with the tape. Alice Loong had been working before going to bed, which I hadn't, in truth, expected. Also, it meant she hadn't got out of her jeans and T-shirt by the time I walked into our old room. Not quite.

She stood by my old double bed, staring back at me, hands on her undone belt, puzzled, not wanting anything, probably not refusing anything either.

'It could have waited until tomorrow,' I said. 'But thanks.'

'I should have done it before. It was thoughtless of me.'

'No . . .'

'I wanted you to wake up to a new day or something,' she interrupted.

'Thanks. Why did your grandma bring you up?' I asked.

'That took a while,' she observed.

'I've had other things on my mind. Why?'

Alice Loong sat down on the bed and looked up at me. She could have been a teenager at that moment.

'Do we have to do this now, Bierce?'

'Yes.'

'Why?'

'Because you're in my house and it matters.'

I must have let a little cop attitude drift into my voice then. She didn't like it.

'Please,' I added.

She folded her arms, which seemed skinny but strong too.

'The same day someone killed your family, my mom got murdered. Grandma was out working. My mom had called in sick for work because I was down with a cold or a headache or whatever.'

'I'm sorry,' I replied. 'And?'

'Someone beat her to death with a sledgehammer. Just like happened here. She knew they were on the way somehow. I was three. She pushed me into a cupboard, told me not to say a word, not to breathe even, not till she said it was OK.'

Alice took a deep breath.

'I listened for a while until I managed to stuff my fists into my ears so hard it kind of stopped. Not everything. I was there three hours, Grandma said. I didn't start screaming until she came and found me. I don't remember much and what I do remember . . . I don't know if it's real or not.'

'I'm sorry.'

She came up and stood in front of me. She looked really small and young, not the twenty-six or so she had to be.

'You're fired,' I said.

'What?'

'You heard. I hired you to clean up around here and lend me your bike. I don't want someone sticking their nose into my affairs, thinking some personal reasons give them that right.'

'Bierce!'

'You can stay the night. In the morning I want you gone.'

'Look . . .' She was shaking her head, fighting for the words. There were tears of rage in her eyes. 'You stuck-up dinosaur. You haven't been in the outside world for more than twenty years. You don't know what it's like here. You don't even belong.'

'Hey,' I replied, opening my hands. 'This is my city. I was born here. I know this place.'

'Really?'

She walked out to the landing, marched over to the little boxroom we used for junk, stepped through the cases and stuff on the floor, then, with me following, watching, threw open the curtains and waited in silence while I caught my breath. It took a while before I could stop shaking, and in that while, that long while, I thought of only one thing: how easy it would be, how comfortable, to be back in Gwinett, even in the same old twelve by ten cell that stood just stumbling distance from Martin the Medic's death room.

I still remembered the view we used to have when Miriam and Ricky were alive. That gave on to one piece of open green scrub, the last remnant of pasture from the old days of Eden, not that long ago, when cows must have grazed within the city limits. True, it was in shadow from the high walls of the warehouse in Owl

Creek to one side and something similar on the other. But it was grass, real grass, and beyond that was nothing but scrappy single-storey homes and lock-ups.

I cursed myself for sleeping all the way here. The grass was gone. I was blinking at a sea of winking lights rising so high they went beyond the window: floor upon floor of apartments or offices, or both for all I knew, a massive wall of stone and glass where once there was nothing but scrub and kids playing ball.

She came back from the window and stuck a finger in my face.

'You need me, Bierce.'

'My mentoring days are over. The answer's no.'

'Whoever killed your family killed my mom,' she insisted.

'Tell the police.'

'The police *knew*! They didn't care then. Why are they going to care now? This was all in St Kilda. No one cares. No one gives a shit. That's how animals like us are supposed to live.'

There had to be a reason they let me out. A part of me – the thinking part – was screaming that I ought to focus on this. Finding someone to blame. A part of me also said I needed to be wary of Alice Loong too. Perhaps she was what she appeared now, nowhere near as tough as she thought, and naive enough to walk into a situation that might get dangerous. Perhaps that was part of the act too. Stapleton recruited her, and he was one sneaky beast.

I didn't much care what happened to me so long as someone paid for Miriam and Ricky, if that someone was still alive. I didn't need any other corpses on my conscience.

'So what the hell do you think I can do?' I asked.

'I want them. I want to know who they are. If they're still alive, I want to look them in the face and ask why. Don't you want that too?'

I closed my eyes for a moment and thought of this place in the happy times. And of that big black hole in my memory. Not knowing could drive you crazy, but it couldn't kill you.

'I know my wife and my son are dead. I know I wasn't responsible. That's more than I was sure of this morning.'

She was in the shadows. I couldn't see her eyes. She said, 'Are you really certain of that?'

'Yes.'

It didn't sound so convincing.

'You mean you know it? You *remember* it wasn't you?'

I didn't want these questions. They sounded too much like the ones people had been throwing at me for more than two decades in jail.

The lights in front of the window disturbed me. I moved forward and closed the tiny curtain. They were so bright they shone straight through the fabric.

'I mean I know. And that's enough.'

I was lying to her. And to myself, I think. Sometimes, when you're dog tired, it's hard to tell.

'I wonder,' she said quietly.

Alice Loong, who wasn't a hooker, I now knew, but would have given herself to me that night, if that was what it took, walked out to the landing.

I waited, listening to her footsteps travel the familiar path across the creaking floorboards to the bedroom.

The door closed with a groan so distantly familiar it tore at my ragged memories.

Then I went downstairs, found the sofa and closed my eyes.

Twenty-three years. An entire generation had passed while I was stuck in a stinking cell in Gwinett beating my head against the wall. I was fifty-two. How many more chances did a man get?

WEDNESDAY

They didn't used to nail dead men to telegraph poles when we first moved into Owl Creek. They didn't even used to do that in the worst parts of St Kilda, the back streets where stray cats walked around on tiptoe, skeetering from trash can to trash can, trying to stay in the shade.

I inhabit a world in motion. Alice Loong had reminded me of this on several occasions. So had the man I still thought of as Stape. All the same, neither of them quite prepared me for what I saw that morning, my first day of freedom, after the caterwauling klaxon dragged me from sleep and sent me staggering out of the door.

It was bright, so bright my eyes hurt a little after all those years inside. There was a squad car there, dirtier and a little more beat up than I remember, and two slouching patrol monkeys in ill-fitting uniforms mooching around the first telegraph pole on the right, outside the abandoned warehouse, the one that Ricky liked to use in his counting games, touching the tips of his little fingers.

Pole, wire, rose bush, trash can, gate, fence . . .

He hit ten on our front door.

Things still kept coming back slowly, when they felt like it.

This was my first day outside a prison cell in more than twenty-three years. I dimly acknowledged the fact that it was a beautiful morning: a fiery sun sat in a sky the colour good summer skies were supposed to be. There was a keen, cool breeze coming in from the ocean, full of enough fresh salt and ozone to disguise most of the industrial pollution. This was the taste of freedom. A part of me liked it.

And there was a dead man nailed to telegraph pole number one, stuck there like flesh in a sack. I walked over. The nondescripts took an interest but clearly lacked the energy to move or say anything. A spike of metal, red and rusty, joined their stationary charge together at the ankles and through the palms, stapling him to the black wood of the pole so he hung there, limp in a bloodstained T-shirt and shapeless jeans, head drooping down so that his fleshy chin sat on his grey, scrawny, whiskered neck. He wore a black hood, like a velvet bag over the head, the kind they used to put on people before they hanged them, at least in the movies. Not that we got that kind of touch today. What we got, in this modern, civilized world, was Martin the Medic.

Even so, this was something new. Just like the voice I kept hearing at the back of my head. It was Ricky's and he was singing . . .

Pole, wire, rose bush, trash can, gate, fence, dead guy, cops, dead guy, cops, dead guy, cops . . .

Be quiet now, Ricky, I thought. Daddy's got things on his mind.

Pole, wire, rose bush, trash can, gate, fence, dead guy, cops, dead guy . . .

Things like this. You're dead too. And so is your mother. Maybe I killed you. Maybe I didn't.

Pole, wire, rose bush . . .

And if I didn't, then who did? That was all a blank, even after a long night in my own house for the first time in twenty-three years. So much was just a big black hole in my imagination hunting for facts to fill it. In truth the only certainties I had at that moment were about what had happened since the strange perform-ance that got me released from the death room at Gwinett, with Stape looking as if he was going through the motions of some deed he hated to the core, just as he hated me for some reason. Not that it was a good enough one to stop him handing over all that money and a ride home.

Here was the kicker. The only things I could remem-ber with any clarity were nasty, malevolent, scary little recollections, each of them bleakly insignificant on its own, but, when I strung them together, they got me shaking the way I should have been when Martin the Medic was standing over me, looking for the right vein to match his needle.

Here was the bigger kicker. Martin's tombstone teeth apart, there was, for some reason, little I had found scary about lying on a hard steel bed waiting to die. I'd had more than a couple of decades to get ready. It all seemed natural in a way. Someone might have felt cheated had the show been cancelled.

But now . . .

Now I was scared.

My kid was chanting in my ear, a high-pitched laughing voice rising from a grave I'd never seen.

Pole, wire, rose bush, dead guy, dead . . .

Inside my house was a pretty young half-Chinese woman called Alice Loong who turned up out of nowhere, offered me her body and some cheap, unlikely story about her mom that made no sense whatsoever, then just nodded like a rear-window dog when I said no, but it would be really useful if she could clean up the chalk marks that outlined where the battered, bloodied corpses of my wife and child once lay.

I felt naked and stupid, the most stupid man in the world, a dumb willing target with a bullseye on my chest, waving it at anyone who ventured near, be that Stape or Alice or some vicious, dread bastard I'd yet to meet in this strange new world that seemed so unlike the one I remembered.

Also – and this was the worst by far – this was the first time in twenty-three years that I'd seen a dead person. They tidied them away in jail, swept into bags in the morgue like unwanted dust in need of disposal. Back when I wore a uniform the sight of a body wasn't so rare. They weren't usually lying around the street, waiting for you to trip over them. But they were there, part of the landscape, still and stiff, looking up at the sky through blank eyes that always, to me anyway, seemed to ask: *why?*

But here, in the grubby little street outside the house that was the closest I'd ever got to home . . . here was wrong. Here was a place I felt I knew, had some duty to defend. The city was never kind or sensitive or compassionate. Still, it had its limits, and nailing bodies to poles in some ordinary suburban street was one of them.

I looked at the poor bastard, all that pain, all that blood and agony, and when I did I saw something back from *then* again, something that hurt. I listened . . .

Pole, wire, bush, cops, dead guy, dead guy, dead guy . . .

. . . and I thought, and then I saw myself nailed there, out in the hot dry day for all to see, in just the pose they wanted me, taking the blame, carrying the guilt for something I didn't do, maybe.

I closed my eyes and when I did I saw it all: me on the pole, Miriam there in front, staring, not laughing, not quite, saying nothing, just with that expression on her face, the one that said: *this time you really screwed up*.

That was the truth. I did. I had. I always would. They should have stuck the right ampoule on the end of the needle in Gwinett, because what happened there really was that I died in some way I didn't quite understand yet. Everything after . . . the voices, the memories, Alice Loong, Stape and these ugly drone cops huffing and puffing at some stinking corpse hanging by nails stuck through old wood . . . was irrelevant. I cared about one thing only. *Knowing*. What happened. What I did or didn't do. How, maybe, I could make amends, then sit back and let the big black rush begin.

Nothing really mattered any more apart from that.

So I looked at the uniforms in front of me and said, 'Good day to you, sirs. It's a fine day. A sunny day. Could you kindly keep the noise down, please? A man's trying to sleep.'

The two cops were of identical size: fat. They had the same blank, angry faces and dead, tired eyes. At some point, probably on the operating table, someone had surgically excised what little charm, wit and intelligence birth had given them and left nothing in their place except a physical tic that jerked one side of their mouth up to the nearest eye in a permanent squint and seemed to say: *what*?

In the way of the modern world – I had learned this in jail, on the few occasions I spoke with my fellow guests – this was uttered, always, rhetorically. I recognized men like this from the old days. They didn't ask questions. They waited for answers to fall from the sky and slap them round the face, screeching, *Look at me! Look at me!*

Curiously, too, their shared tic was symmetrical: one mouth rising on the left side, one on the right.

They had thick black leather belts, the kind power-line repairmen used to wear, but these contained big guns, cans of what I took to be some kind of nasty substance, radios and other gear I couldn't recognize, all hanging on neat little clips where the hammers and screwdrivers used to be. Progress. It made me feel like scampering back into the house, finding the bedroom and hiding under the sheets. Except someone, Alice Loong to be precise, was there already.

'Huh?'

Right Tic didn't look mad at me. He looked mad at everything, his own stupefied bewilderment most of all.

'This is a residential neighbourhood,' I suggested. 'I seem to remember from somewhere that you only hit the sirens and the flashing-light stuff when you're going on a call to the living. This, on the other hand . . .'

I looked at the body nailed to the pole. The bloodstains were dry and black. Rigor was setting in. It was now just after eight a.m. Sunrise must have been well before seven. He hadn't just been there for most of the night. He'd been hanging like a lone human scarecrow out in broad daylight for a good hour and a half before someone – a small crowd of faces at the broken and dusty factory windows told me who – had called the cops.

'I claim no expertise in these matters, but some small trace of ancestral memory tells me this guy's dead.'

They'd hardly looked at the man pinned to the pole. It was as if this kind of thing happened all the time.

'OK,' I said. 'I was just passing the time of day and that's done. It wasn't me, I swear, scout's honour. Do you think I can go now?'

Left Tic slapped his stick in his slack fat hand. It occurred to me then that he just might really hit me with the thing. Here, out in the bright light of day, a day I recognized, but only dimly. I shivered. I was trembling. It wasn't cold. A lot had happened since I last hung out with a squad car.

'That would be a very good idea,' he muttered. 'We're just waiting till the detectives . . .'

He pronounced that '*dee*-tectives', just like a little kid.

'. . . arrive. You don't have anything to hide now, do you?'

'Officers,' I said, opening my hands, 'if I was that kind of a person, would I be out here talking to you?'

They stared at each other, wondering.

'So why *are* you here?' Right Tic asked at last. 'Be truthful now. We will find out. We will.'

I smiled, trying to look both harmless and stupid. 'I've lived an uneventful life. I've never seen a dead man. Not a murdered man anyway, and – I'm guessing here – that same ancestral memory suggests this guy didn't nail himself to the pole.'

The two of them nodded. I felt they'd got about that far for themselves.

'Honestly?' I added. 'This sounds sick, I know. But I simply wanted to get a closer look.'

'Understandable,' Left Tic said with a shrug.

I winced.

'Trouble is . . .'

They still didn't get it.

'It's that hood. It's like . . . if you go into an adult movie and find they keep their clothes on. It provokes and unprovokes. Simply awful.'

Right Tic moved his head from side to side and chanted in a childish monotone rhythm, 'He wants to see the dead man, he wants to see the dead man, he wants to see . . .'

His hand was making a gesture. Finger and thumb, rubbing together greedily.

The last police officer I saw doing that was Stapleton, a quarter of a century ago. He regretted it deeply shortly afterwards.

This time round, though, I reached into my pocket, took out the wad, which, like an idiot, I'd failed to separate into smaller bundles, and passed over a fifty.

'Please,' I said. 'Pretty please.'

Left Tic took out something from his belt. It looked like a Swiss Army knife that had mated with a pair of bolt cutters: blades and screws and gadgets protruded from every inch of its squat little body. He clicked his podgy fingers and a pair of tiny scissors materialized out of nowhere. Then, with more care than I would have expected, he snipped his way up the left half of the hood, stopped to stare briefly at the two hands pinned together by the long sharp nail above him, before working his way down the other side.

It took a little tug. There was some blood keeping the fabric glued to a face that had, it turned out, taken a big punch to the mouth at some stage.

We all of us stared at the dead man's features. I'd done enough murder scenes to know what always tended to come out at this time. So I said it.

'He looks like he's sleeping.'

'He looks like he's dead,' Left Tic muttered, which made his partner crease over and hold his fat gut, consumed by an overdose of glee.

What I was unable to tell them was this: Tony Molloy always did look dead, even when he was a living, breathing, slouching six-foot streak of semi-human slime working the Yonge waterfront. He still had the same grey acne-scarred skin, the same dyed black hair, bushy eyebrows and bulbous nose, a little more pockmarked than I recalled. The crooked mouth, frozen on one side, from a knife fight back in his teens, though now it looked like a middle-aged man's stroke, hadn't improved. The truth was, if you knew the man, he simply looked *more* dead than usual, and that annoyed me greatly, because of all the people I had on my list to talk to that day, Tony Molloy was close to the top.

Stape would have second-guessed my interest in Tony Molloy. Anyone who knew me and the case and possessed an IQ edging just a touch south of three digits would have guessed that.

This was interesting, if a little depressing too.

A man who'd been the partner of the creature that

77

had confessed, supposedly, to slaughtering Miriam and Ricky was dead outside my home, killed the night I happened to get out of jail. The sequence of events facing me was beginning to contain far too many subtly prolix personal elements for it to enter the comprehension of either of the uniformed amoebae who were my present company.

There were too many coincidences here and coincidences could kill me for good. There was also a stolen police department handgun sitting by the side of my bed with three equally illicit boxes of shells.

'It's a pleasure to know we still have officers of your insight and respectability in the police,' I said quietly.

The Tics twitched at me in silence.

'Presumably, gentlemen, you'd rather I didn't go anywhere for a while. Not until the *dee*-tectives arrive.'

Right Tic sneered at me, 'This is a gang thing, man. Always killing each other for fun. You don't have the tattoos. Or the colour.'

'Gangs,' I said, raising a finger. 'Excuse me. We don't have them back home.'

'Where the hell is that?' Left Tic asked, bemused. 'The moon?'

'East,' I said immediately, as if that explained everything.

He and his partner shared the look called 'caustic'.

'I should be surprised,' Left Tic grunted. 'But you *will* have to talk to someone. Unless . . .'

The fingers made that gesture again.

'That money came out easy,' Right Tic observed.

'I guess it did. I await your pleasure, sirs,' I replied with a little bow, then turned and walked back to the house.

Alice wasn't sleeping. She was smart and observant. I imagine she hadn't been sleeping for a while. Now she was watching me carefully from behind a curtain in the sitting room. She had a duster in her hand.

Shame. The cleaning was going to have to wait.

Maybe it was the half-Chinese gene, but a part of me wondered whether Alice Loong could read minds. By the time I'd walked back into the house, she had a light bag packed and ready to go. The gun was on the top.

'What's the rest of the stuff?' I asked. 'The gun is all I have.'

Her hands were flying over the fabric. It occurred to me she took a very professional approach to fleeing the impending arrival of the law.

'If you're in trouble – and judging by the smug, "nothing's going on here" look you were showering over those idiots you *are* – I am out of here too. I gave that Stapleton guy a phoney name. That's what you do with people who pay cash. I don't want him in my face, asking where the hell you've got to.'

This was not a good idea. Or rather it was an excellent idea, and one I felt I couldn't go along with.

'No, no, no. Listen to me. There's a dead man nailed to a pole out there. He is not unknown to me. Some people might even say I'd be prime candidate for making him that way.'

The green eyes glared at me.

'Stupid people you mean? Why would you dump the corpse outside your own home? Are you putting out an ad campaign too? Got a website?'

I shook my head.

'A what?'

She was checking through the bag. From what I saw she didn't own much either.

'You've been in jail, Bierce. Not in suspended animation.'

There was an important point to be made here.

'Look,' I said, watching her pick up the bag, ready to go. 'This is important. I am the person I was when I went inside. I intend to remain that way. All that modern stuff leaves me cold. When I communicate with a fellow human being I wish to see into their eyes.'

Alice Loong gave me a withering look.

'In that case you might as well go out there again and sit in the police car. They will walk all over you, Bierce. They will kill you. And me if they like. This is the world now. The one we live in, not the one in your head. They've got . . . things.'

'Things like what?'

'Things that know where you are! Things that can track you down just 'cos you used an ATM machine.'

'A what?'

'Oh, for Christ's sake! This isn't 1985 or whenever. You can't live like you did then. You need money.'

I reached into my pocket and waved some of the remaining hundreds.

'Gone in two days,' she snapped back. 'And you with it. We need more information!'

I'd thought about that already. It was on my list.

'What about libraries? You're telling me they're gone already?'

'Jesus,' she said with a long, pained sigh. 'This is like having a child in tow. Or a caveman.'

I snapped my fingers.

'The keys. I won't damage the bike, I promise. Not if I can help it.'

She folded her arms.

'You're not fit, caveman.'

'I rode motorcycles for a living, Alice. In uniform. Also, you don't know where I want to go.'

'Tell me!'

'The keys . . .'

'*No!* And I'll scratch your eyes out if you try to take them. I came here for a reason. We have the same problem if only you saw it. If I'd known you were the selfish, arrogant, macho, antiquated pig you are, maybe I'd have stayed at home. But there you go. This Stapleton guy's seen me. If you think they're going to come for you, then you surely know they're going to come for me. I will *not* be abandoned. Understood?'

I held out my hand.

'Understood. But like I said. I know where we're going and it's a place you couldn't even find. The keys.'

She hesitated.

'Trust me,' I pleaded.

'In this century,' she said, 'men normally say that just before they disappear.'

'It's your century, not mine.'

I pulled back the curtain a little further. More vehicles were arriving outside. Two marked cars, two plain ones. The *dee*-tectives were surely here.

She reached into her pocket, took out a single stub of battered old metal and held it in front of my face. I glanced at it. If this was the key I could probably have started the thing with a paper clip.

'This is my bike,' Alice Loong said. 'You ride on the back or not at all.'

81

I could see two men walking towards the house. Men in dark suits. They didn't look stupid.

'A word of advice,' she added, picking up the bag and throwing it into my arms. 'Hold on tight.'

The battered, grubby blue and rust Kawasaki was in the garage, leaning on its prop stand like a drunk struggling to stay upright. When I saw it I was almost glad she didn't want me up front.

The problem was obvious to both of us straight off. If we opened up the doors and roared out into the street, past the Tic Twins, we'd be facing a roadblock within minutes. Even in the eighties I wouldn't have expected to make it far. If they really had these new toys now . . .

We had five miles to travel and even then I'd no idea what we might meet at the other end. Miriam's kid brother, Sheldon, was the family failure. He ran a low-grade motor repair shop, principally for people too poor to run a vehicle legally, out beyond Yonge, where the docks melted into the grey polluted estuary mud of the Pocapo river, an area I'd known well since childhood. I was sure he was still there because once a year he wrote me a letter that said nothing much at all, except, after a page of rambling self-pity: *sorry*.

Sheldon never visited me once in jail. Still, for all I knew, during those years he was the only living person on the planet who believed I wasn't responsible for murdering his sister and nephew. Even my own lawyer, the lovely, cold and utterly ineffective Susanna Aurelio (she preferred her maiden name, possibly because she was now on her fifth husband in the two decades she'd owned me as a client), had some doubt in her eyes from time to time.

Susanna usually delivered Sheldon's annual letter. That thought came back to nag me when I was in the garage looking at the bike, wondering how fast the thing might go. I couldn't work out why, but now, with my mind freed from the dumbing effect of being locked in a cell pretty much twenty-four hours a day, and wandering illogical places it sought just because it could again, the Susanna–Sheldon link seemed odd. There was precious little in the way of a professional reason for a big-time lawyer to keep in touch with a man like him. Socially they were planets apart, she slowly working her way through the moneyed husbands in Greenpoint, picking and choosing as she pleased, while Sheldon, unmarried, with never a girlfriend that I ever saw, lived over his repair shop next to the stinking grey flow that the Pocapo became once it worked its way into the city.

'Bierce!' Alice hissed at me through clenched teeth, and I came back down to earth.

Someone was hammering on the front door. No. I was wrong. Someone was beating down the front door with a hammer. Which, in the circumstances, seemed both impolite and ominous. Even in this strange new world, cops surely rang the bell first.

Starting to shake again, a physical side effect, it seemed to me, of Martin the Medic's dope, I went to the rear of the garage, opened the rickety screen door there and took one last look at the garden.

'You can see the gate?' I asked.

It was rotten, almost off its hinges, with under-growth behind. We didn't even have time to open it, but that didn't matter. The thing was barely usable when Miriam and Ricky were alive. Today it would just shatter the moment the bike edged through it.

'Where does it go?' she demanded.

It took a moment for me to remember, and when I did a low, nagging bell began to ring at the back of my head, singing . . . *but that was then*.

'Just scrub land,' I said, with some false authority. 'We can make our way out to the back roads. Trust me. I'll show you.'

If luck was on our side – and statistically I felt it was about time the old bitch stirred herself and put in a little work on my case – we'd be able to make our way out to Sanderton on the largely deserted minor road that mirrored the busy trawl of De Vere just half a mile south.

I walked over to the bench, blew dust off my old helmet and put it on. The fit was a little loose for some reason and the strap didn't close well. When I turned round she was straddling the bike, helmeted, arms crossed, with a look behind the visor I was beginning to recognize.

I retrieved the handgun from the bag, checked it was loaded, stuffed it into my belt, filled my pockets with shells and climbed on behind.

The bike started first push, though the battery sounded a little weak. Alice raised the engine a little and worked it slowly out of the garage into the bright morning. She blipped the throttle once out of habit. Mistake. Someone in the house started shouting. I heard a window getting opened. The back door was rattling.

It was locked.

It was strong.

They had a sledgehammer.

She turned and looked at me. She was scared.

'Now . . .' I said, and wished to God she'd let me ride.

Alice opened the engine wide and let loose the lever.

She was right. I did need to cling on tightly. The old Japanese bike came out of the shade of the garage like a crazed animal, so quickly my arms fought to keep a grip on the slim body in front of me. She held the Kawasaki down in first all the way, found the trellised gate, aimed straight at it and barrelled through. Brambles and vines and tall, flowery weeds consumed us.

Alice started screaming. So did I. The earth was falling away in front of us, and it wasn't supposed to be like this, this *wasn't* the scrub land I imagined. We'd roared through the old planked door and found ourselves on the summit of some new, steep hill, one that disappeared from beneath our wheels the moment the screaming bike came over the edge.

I leaned out and looked down, still thinking . . . So far so good. All she has to do now is land the thing amid the mess of abandoned refrigerators and other junk that must still litter this dead, deserted land, festering like an old scab right behind my home, thirty or forty feet lower than it should have been.

Someone else started screaming, and then there were more voices.

Young ones too.

As the bike flew forward through thin air, I pumped myself up on the foot stands, took hold of Alice's slim shoulders and looked down in front of us. There was a sea of faces there, none of them much older than five or six, hundreds of them maybe, or, on second glance, at least a dozen.

My mind did what it usually does on such occasions: wound itself into a congealed, swirly, sticky mass where fast and slow don't mean much but simply bump into one another, over and over again. It didn't help that I could see the neighbourhood now, and it might as well have been Mars for all I could recognize it. Streets and buildings, factories and low grey offices, spread in every direction where, in what I thought of as 'my day', there'd been nothing but endless green scrub and the odd illegal tin shack.

As we flew joyfully through the air, I saw a small swing, some other brightly coloured little rides, and toys everywhere: dolls and animals and board games and a line of blue buckets next to a sandpit.

But more than anything I saw children: boys and girls, in summer shorts and T-shirts, happily playing in that tiny world which only they can inhabit until two lunatics on an ancient motorcycle come roaring out of nowhere, like a monster falling from the sky.

Someone had turned my dead land into a kindergarten and never thought to drop me a line.

The sensible ones started to scatter.

Alice kept screaming, frozen on the handlebars. A chubby kid stood there like a human target, a blob of flesh in the path of the bike, oblivious to the fact that several hundred pounds of metal and adult flesh were, at this very moment, plummeting towards him at something like forty miles an hour.

Yelling 'Out of the way, fat kid' seemed somewhat pointless in the circumstances. I thought of the tricks I used to try out on the flats near the Pocapo river, all those years ago. In the scant microseconds that flashed by as we descended, it occurred to me that these were always performed as individual acts of derring-do. Passengers never really came into the equation.

But then neither did overweight infants who stood rooted to the spot a few feet from you, mouths wide open dripping kiddie-drool.

So I flicked my weight hard over to the right and angled the bike down with me. There was screaming at the front and some hard, desperate tugging. Alice didn't want me to tip the bike over. In truth, she didn't have much choice.

The Kawasaki hit the ground at a forty-five-degree angle. Dirt scuffed up in all directions. I put my left arm round her waist and held tight, then forced myself forward till I had hold of one bar, stomping down hard with my right leg, trying to do a decent impression of a speedway skid. Somehow, in the shock of the impact and all this strange, retro momentum, my helmet came flying off and whizzed straight into the sandpit.

We travelled maybe ten feet thereafter, at the same drunken angle, till the bike finally came to a stop, without touching a single child, which must have surprised them as much as it did me.

Alice marked this wondrous event by flying head first over the bars, hitting the ground, hands in the dirt, surrounded by plastic bricks and a couple of small ride-on animals, screeching in sudden pain, then aiming in my direction an expression full of an anger that was so deeply, unfailingly female I had to focus for a moment to work out what it truly was.

'Christ, Bierce,' she screamed, holding on to her left arm, tears of pain in her eyes. 'I broke my wrist. *You* broke my wrist.'

Through some miracle of gravity and fortune I was still on the bike. Its gutsy little engine continued to rattle beneath me. The fat kid walked up to the front, eyes wide open. He looked a little older than I thought. Perhaps seven.

Then he stuck out a hand and said, 'Cool. My name's Tim.'

'Tim!' I said, pointing a finger in his face. 'Don't you *ever* do this at home. You hear me?'

I looked at Alice. She was clutching her left arm and staring back at the wall. I did the same. Some guy in a suit was there, struggling through the brambles of the shattered gate. He looked mad. In his right hand a gun was waving erratically.

There was no time to discuss this. I shuffled forward, took the bars and blipped the throttle. It felt odd to hear the sound of a twin exhaust again, and at that moment I was far from confident I could fall back into riding one of these machines after almost a quarter of a century out of the saddle. Not that there was much choice.

'Are you coming?' I asked quickly. 'Or do you want to stay and play with the rest of the children?'

She said something I rather wished Tim hadn't heard, then leapt on the back, clutching me tightly with her good arm.

Nothing looked right. That is to say, nothing looked the same or felt the same.

Alice screeched and I couldn't work out whether it was my terrible handling of the machine or the instant shock of my reaction to this new world, transferred to her by our enforced closeness. I was in an alien world, a land that had once been mine and now belonged to other people, people I didn't know except to understand I wasn't much going to like many of them.

I glanced back and found some old, lost emotion rising up from a place it had slumbered for a couple of decades, one I only recognized when I thought about it, and remembered the name: anger.

The dark suit was standing in a crowd of kids, right arm raised, black pistol pointed straight in our direction. As I watched, his arm jerked and a loud, distantly familiar noise cut through the kiddie-screaming.

For the first time in years someone was shooting at me, and that at least provoked something I knew, the same old feeling of fear I got on the streets, sweating in a tight uniform, over two decades before.

It made me mad as hell.

'Bierce!' Alice yelled again, then ducked down hard into my back. 'Will you get us out of here?'

Sure, I thought. And just leave these kids to some maniac letting loose with a handgun in their midst. A maniac who, the small, rational part of my head reminded me, ought, by the looks of things, to be a plain-clothes cop.

I took my old handgun out of my belt. She grabbed hold of my arm. Her hand was covered in blood. She was in pain.

'You want to start shooting?' she yelled. 'With all these kids around? Would that make you feel better, huh?'

The man in the suit was running towards us in a way that looked very professional, his gun held upright all the way, as if it was attached to a child's gyroscope.

'No,' I answered, and stuffed the police revolver back where it came from.

I wound the bike wide open and we tore out of the side passage by the school, towards the road that had to be there, somewhere ahead, fighting to keep us upright, because riding a bike wasn't, I learned at that moment, a talent you never forget. I was relearning it all the time we were disappearing from the suit with the gun, racing into somewhere that was not now, and never had been, a part of any planet known to me.

Whatever street this was curved downhill, past line after line of low industrial blocks that looked like bricks from a child's toy box, heading roughly in what I assumed to be the direction of Sanderton, though nothing, not a single brick or yard of asphalt, sparked a moment of recognition in my fevered head. There was the sound of a gunshot behind me. Alice started screaming again, holding on ever more tightly. I jumped the bike down a gear and opened the throttle. Some four hundred yards later the road angled sufficiently to put us out of sight of anyone on foot emerging from the kindergarten. Once we'd rounded the bend, I eased the power down a little, aware that I had two visible accoutrements that were, perhaps, not good for someone seeking to remain anonymous.

I wasn't wearing a bike helmet in an alien city where this was now, in all probability, a capital offence. And that handgun in my belt looked all too visible out here in the penetrating light of day.

Not that there was anyone to notice at the moment. I couldn't see a single house or everyday human being anywhere. Just buildings and office windows, and one lone delivery van parked in the street. We were, I felt sure, near to Sanderton, though. Something that seemed half familiar was finally looming up ahead, a junction where a local farmer once sold fruit and vegetables from a stall by the side of the road. There was a video store there now, but I saw the name sign and, when we finally reached the crossroads, I turned left, as confident as I could be that this was the right direction. They could erect new buildings, create new roads, change names and places entirely. But rivers stayed around longer than a single life, and this route had to take us down to the Pocapo, where I could think of getting this thing off the road, then disappearing into some kind of territory I surely still knew.

That last, welcome thought, and the rattle of the bike over the road, just about quelled my internal shakes, for a few seconds anyway. Then I stopped thinking about the future altogether, because I looked around me and everything Alice Loong had said about me being some kind of a dinosaur was finally starting to make sense.

The Sanderton I recalled was a long, straight, dusty road of low, single-storey economy homes, plain, unpretentious boxes for plain, unpretentious working people, with picket fences around tiny patches of lawn, each with a single beat-up automobile on it.

This place was gone, long gone by the looks of things, though I couldn't believe so much could change in twenty years. There were parts of Eden, the peripheral parts with the adult stores and girlie bars, that seemed similar. But Sanderton wasn't that kind of neighbourhood. Quite. All I saw were long lines of identical single-storey shops and offices running down each side of the road, mirror images of each other complete with gaudy, over-sized signs: for pawn shops and bail-bond merchants, gun stores and tiny neighbourhood food outlets.

Most of the places had wire frames over their windows and metal doors that let through just a crack of light, though by this time it was ten in the morning or so. The places had to be open. Just scared open. Also, they were dirty, that special kind of grubbiness that's limited to cheap places that haven't been built long.

This ragged string of grubby development ran in a dismal strip of concrete in both directions, as far as my eyes, dashing front and back, checking out the best view of this nice new world, could see. Maybe the whole of the city looked this way these days. Or the world even. I was a foreigner in a place I once knew, a place that bred me, and for one brief moment I found myself pining once again for that plain twelve by ten cell in Gwinett. At least there I knew where I was.

I toed the Kawasaki into fourth and cut a steady speed, hovering around forty. Alice's arm relaxed, then I felt her move, get more comfortable behind me. We had to tough this out until we could find some place to hide. Still, I couldn't take my eyes off this different world that had supplanted all those innocent little homes of twenty years ago. There was nothing of that remaining now, just stores and auto lots, repair shops and places selling electronic gear I doubtless wouldn't understand. Someone had come down from on high, taken away the gardens and the little painted porches, deciding to colour this entire neighbourhood grey, sixteen shades of it maybe, not a lot more.

And then there were the people. I slowed down just to make sure of this.

Did we smile in the eighties?

I believe so. Not often, perhaps. Not without reason. But we did smile, and we walked along with our heads up straight, looking around us, talking to strangers from time to time, eye to eye. The latter was something I was very good at, and not only because it was part of the job. Talking to people always seemed to me to be an integral part of being awake, being alive. I lost the opportunity in Gwinett, but never the memory.

These people looked as if they didn't talk much at all, not even when they were meandering down the sidewalk in pairs. They just stared down at their feet, dreaming of nothing in particular, I guess, yammering from time to time into little black phones that they glued to the side of their head as if nothing mattered more to them than this call, this brief snatch of conversation, which would be so much more important, more vital, than a couple of simple words with someone, friend or stranger, a few feet away.

I rode idly through Sanderton, mouth open, collecting flies, trying to stop myself gawping at the men and women walking along the street, to force myself to rebuild a mental map of this part of the city in my head, and the way down to the Pocapo river, because the cops would surely come, and soon, with new toys I couldn't possibly hope to defeat.

I gunned the bike and went on, feeling ever more disconnected from the semblance of life I saw around me. A little further down the street there was another crossing and I just found myself drifting through the red light, wondering whether to abandon the bike and Alice Loong right here, take a cab back to Gwinett, hold out my hands at reception and plead for a cell.

A man of about thirty, in a well-cut khaki linen suit, one that made him look very elegant indeed, wandered out into the road. I pressed the horn. The Kawasaki made a sound like a baby seal crying feebly for its mother.

He had the regulation phone, but this time it was attached to his belt by some fancy leather holster. Over his ears were little white headphones, a fraction the size of anything I'd ever seen, joined by a thin white cable to some tiny white box pinned to his chest like a badge.

He was doing a bad boogie dance to some stupid rhythm only he could hear, which doubtless made it more precious, because if you looked at him you'd have thought the music coming into his ears, his music, no one else's please, was the finest ever made, so fine it didn't make him look twice to see if some idiot from another century had ridden the red light of his toy-town pedestrian crossing and was perilously close to mowing him clean down to the asphalt.

I braked hard, listening to the squeal, feeling Alice get squashed, hard and cursing, into my back. The bike came to a halt one foot in front of khaki suit.

He stared at me, affronted. So much so he actually pulled the little white things out of his head and started yelling in total outrage, using the kinds of words that, once upon a time, were not supposed to be available to people who had the wit to put together clothing that matched.

Then he leapt out of the way because another vehicle had arrived to join the party now, and it was just a touch bigger, a low, bright red sports car, not bad-looking either, like a Ferrari that had got shrunk in the wash. It screeched sideways on to the pedestrian crossing, tyres screaming, smoke coming up from the road, sending an acrid smell into my nostrils.

The smell was good. It woke me up.

The khaki suit took one look at the vehicle, ceased swearing, then dashed for the pavement on the far side, terrified, those little white ear cables dangling from his chest.

Strange.

I looked into the shrunken Ferrari. It was a two-seat coupé, both of them occupied. Men, judging by the way they seemed to fill up the meagre space behind the dashboard.

The driver had white hair and yellow tombstone teeth, grimacing not grinning this time. He had the window down and was hanging out, staring at me, looking as angry as a man might get at that time on a beautiful August morning.

Just seeing him brought back the medical smell and the pain in my arm.

'Martin,' I said pleasantly, and took a good grip on the throttle. 'To what do I owe the privilege? Are you here for a second attempt?'

He smiled, an ugly sight.

'If you don't pull over, I will be,' he said, and nosed the barrel of a black pistol out of the window, pointing it loosely in my direction. 'Off the bike. Wait for me over there,' he ordered.

Ordinarily I listen to people with guns. But there were four of us in this conversation now. Martin had just a two-seat coupé. Whatever was on his mind, it didn't involve an escorted tour of this new, changed city of mine.

'Sure,' I said, and twisted the plastic grip as hard as I could, let loose the left clutch lever and took Alice's Kawasaki veering in front of the coupé's red hood, which gave us a couple of seconds I reckoned, at least.

In my century, anyway.

By the time I reached the left intersection, praying it still went down towards the deserted mud flats by the Pocapo, we had a couple of hundred yards on Martin and his unseen companion. The trouble was, this was territory made for pursuit, not escape: level, open and visible in every direction. And I had an inkling that whatever breed of shrunken Ferrari Martin owned, it would, in the end, outrun a battered old bike.

I steered left towards the river, foot hard on the gravel, taking it as quickly as I dared, still jumpy from the power this little machine seemed to have, more than its size merited, more than a man of my age and rusty skills could handle. Then Alice began to chatter some scared refrain into my back. Somehow Martin had made up ground in the couple of seconds it took me to navigate that corner. His machine went faster than I could have guessed too. Everything did in this inexplicable new world in which I found myself. And what lay ahead looked bad: the same dead streets, everything so easy to see, not a sign of some sneaky little turn-off where two wheels might prove good and four bad.

Alice clung to me throughout. I regained a little distance coming out of the corner but I could sense it wasn't going to last. My legs hurt, my wrists were aching from the unaccustomed strain of throwing around a bike with two people on it. If I could have wound the clock back, found my old self, my old machine, then maybe . . .

Something moved behind me. I just managed to glance back. Alice had taken off her helmet and launched it out into the slipstream, towards the red coupé. It struck the windshield and bounced off harmlessly. The only visible effect was that it got Martin waving the gun out of the window again.

'Congratulations,' I yelled into the wind. 'Can't you just sit back and enjoy the ride while I try to figure this out?'

'Bierce!' she shrieked. 'Who the hell are these people in the Hyundai?'

Maybe it was all that time inside. Or maybe Martin the Medic's dope had done something to my head. Whatever the reason, words could have odd effects sometimes.

This road was a dead end. It had to be. The long, straight, quarter-mile-wide mud-stained stretch of the Pocapo had to lie somewhere at the end of it. A new century couldn't consume an entire river without leaving a trace. As I saw the line of high wire fencing come to greet us in the distance, I started to get a good idea of where it ought to be.

'That was a *Hyundai*?' I asked, not quite believing her.

She clung on more tightly and, when I looked back, had just managed to get a fraction of her face round my shoulder.

'*What?* We're talking automobiles now?'

No. Not really. We were talking about this strange century of hers. One where people walked down the street, eyes on the pavement, with white hearing aids in both ears, phones clamped to the belts of their khaki suits, thinking themselves immortal as a result. Where Sanderton, poor pathetic lost Sanderton, a quiet district old people lived in after they retired from the steel plant and working the railways, got turned into some bland, grubby and doubtless dangerous portion of homogeneous suburbia, a grey dusty nothingness that could, for all I knew, be anywhere on the planet.

We all have our limits and I felt I'd reached mine. The fast-approaching margin of the Pocapo river, which had a drop of around twenty feet from land to the bank around here, if I recalled correctly, only served to confirm my sentiments on this matter.

Martin and his new-fangled Hyundai didn't, couldn't, know this district. Otherwise the two of them wouldn't be shredding rubber on the asphalt behind me with such gleeful abandon at that moment.

I slammed on the brakes and wheeled the bike round in a badly handled curving skid, realizing my jail shoes had probably worn through judging by the growing pain that kept biting into the soles of my feet. When we circled to a halt I took both hands off the bars, turned towards the oncoming sports car, got out my gun and aimed carefully, the way the police range taught me, because it occurred to me that we were now a little like the fat kid in the kindergarten playground, a stationary target facing a mass of metal racing through space with a momentum that would take out anything dumb enough to stand in its way.

You can't flip a sports coupé round just by leaning over the side, even if this had been on Martin's mind at that moment.

I saw the bright white hair twitch as his hands began to work the wheel.

Then I let loose all six shells from the gun, the first into the hood, close to where the badge was supposed to be, the rest towards the tyres, since shooting people was not, at this point anyway, a part of my game.

A puff of smoke burst from the near front. The shiny red vehicle went down on that side, then began to slowly career sideways, sliding out of control. I could see Martin fighting desperately with the wheel. Whoever it was in the passenger seat had, wisely, slid down below the dashboard, out of view, and had every right to be wondering what it was like to be a crash-test dummy in Korea.

Enough, I thought, and popped the bike back into gear.

Badly. So badly the engine made a single loud metallic hiccup, then stalled, dead in an instant.

Alice swore, something about clumsy men.

I popped the starter button. It grumbled once, then nothing. I fumbled round for the kick-start, pumped wildly at it, banging my leg hard against the frame. The engine didn't even cough.

The Hyundai was starting to look big now, and I just knew from the way Alice's Kawasaki was sulking underneath me we weren't going anywhere.

There wasn't time to say a thing. I let loose of the bars, turned round, grabbed hold of her and half dragged, half pushed us out of the path of the oncoming metal beast as swiftly as I could. We fell into some low scrubby bushes by the edge of the wire fence. Martin the Medic's sports monster encountered some pothole in the dead end of the road, bounced once, bounced twice, then turned on its side, screaming sparks and smoke and debris as it flew towards the ragged cliff edge above the river.

'My bike!' was the first thing Alice got round to saying, once we'd picked ourselves out of the thorn bushes where we landed.

The coupé clipped the Kawasaki as it lay on the ground, sent it spinning out past the far side of the flimsy wire fence, bouncing off one lone, stripped eucalyptus tree, after which the bike somersaulted down into the river, falling with a loud, noisy splash and the sound of fractured metal.

I wasn't watching much. I was trying to see what was going on in the car. Something had exploded behind the dashboard. Two big white cushions that dimly brought back the memory of a fancy new contraption I'd read about in the prison library, back when they still let me in there. A concept I'd never quite understood: airbags.

Martin and his passenger would live, I guess. Which meant we didn't have much time to waste.

'We need to be going,' I said, leading Alice down the winding dust and rock path that several decades of kids had made from this cul-de-sac to the river bank.

It looked half familiar. There were cut-throughs like this along the length of the Pocapo. I'd probably used this one more than once back in that mythical era of my youth. We were some way from the estuary too. The water looked clean and lively, even with a dying Kawasaki steaming away in some low rock pool to one side.

Alice looked at the bike, tears in her eyes, and I felt, at that moment, worse than at any time since Martin the Medic had poked his little needle into my vein. My feet crumpled under me. I don't know whether it was exhaustion, Martin's dope or the air in this strange new world of theirs. But at that moment I felt as weak as a baby, and just as likely to burst into tears as Alice Loong. This was *not* my world.

It must have knocked the spirits out of her too. I never was good at hiding things.

'Shit,' she said softly, then hugged herself with her one good arm, staring down at the ground. I wasn't sure whether that was aimed at me or not.

She walked over and sat down next to me. I pulled myself together as best I could and took a look at her wound. Like a child, she let me examine it, gingerly. Tenderly, I might almost have said. She had a long, shallow scratch running from her wrist to her elbow. A big bruise was building. But as I gently squeezed around the unmarked skin it was clear nothing was broken, though it must have hurt like hell. I tore off one of the lower sleeves of my shirt and wrapped it round the cut, tying it carefully.

'Try to keep the dirt out,' I said. 'It feels worse than it is.'

She looked at what I'd done as if it was the work of a spaceman, with puzzlement bordering on gratitude. I don't think many men had behaved like that around Alice Loong, perhaps not in her entire life.

The riverside path was littered with stuff that could have been here forty years – candy wrappers and old newspapers, discarded fishing line, cigarette ends. And items I'd never associated with the banks of the Pocapo before. Just a quick visual sweep showed me two syringes and a couple of spent condoms. Then a heron flew lazily along the river like a slender grey spear, just a couple of feet above the surface, eyeing what lay beneath, looking for food.

'How beauteous mankind is,' I muttered to myself. 'O brave new world, that has such people in it.'

'What?' she asked, shaking her head.

'I got a little carried away with my reading for a couple of decades.'

The Hyundai had come to rest caught between two trees leaning drunkenly into the low cliff above us. I could hear people there. One voice, a familiar male one, sounded fit and healthy and deeply pissed off.

'We need to go,' I said, then waded into the water, recovered the bag from the bike, opened it and stuffed some shells into my pockets, planning on reloading the handgun as we moved.

'Where?' she asked.

'A good place,' I answered. 'For a little while anyway.'

When I was ten years old my parents went out for a drive and didn't come back. Some lumber truck shed its load running a narrow two-lane on the Peyton peninsula. They had the misfortune to be following meekly behind. In a Hyundai Pony as it happens. My dad never was one for expensive automobiles. Or overtaking. It just caused trouble, he said. Best wait patiently for everything to improve, as surely it would. Unless some trucker had failed to chain his load properly, in which case the wait would be very long indeed.

Had I not been in bed with flu, watched over from a

distance by a friendly neighbour, I would have been in the back seat, dead too.

I wasn't a good foster kid. I wasn't a bad one. I just didn't give much back in the way of love and affection, for the very good reason, it seemed to me, that these were two things you couldn't invent at will, turning them on or off when you felt like it. The whole point about emotions was that they were beyond your control. Beyond your comprehension sometimes.

That was how it seemed to me anyway, at the age of ten, when two cops in uniform arrived to tell me my parents were 'gone', and did it with such quiet sympathy and skill I can still remember their faces now. And that was what made every foster home I went to move me on after a while, even though I behaved impeccably, being polite and helpful and always willing to clear away the dishes and wash whatever vehicle in the drive required my attention.

The river helped a lot in those years. Wherever I was fostered in the city I could reach this place on a push-bike and spend hours down by the slow, swirling waters, watching, waiting, thinking. My dad had taken me fishing here when I was so young I could barely walk. We'd sit for hours, never catching a lot to begin with. In time I got so much better than him that, by the age of eight, I was the one bringing home the trout, which both my parents found so amusing they could be reduced to tears just talking about it.

I can still recall the smell of fish frying in a pan in the kitchen as they sat around laughing at how hopeless he was at everything practical, while I became the one who fixed things, caught things, made a few modest repairs to the minor flaws in our small, small world.

The river wasn't about the fish, though. It was about us, about talking and looking at the water and the wild, green river bank that hadn't changed at all in hundreds of years, and would still have been recognizable to any of the natives who'd lived here back then, if the brute emergence of the city and the modern world hadn't wiped them out like back-yard pests needing eradication.

My dad liked music. Frank Sinatra, Mel Tormé, Perry Como, anyone from the era. He had a good voice too, and a feel for the occasion. One time we stayed so late the stars came out. I remember he began singing, word perfect, note perfect, 'The Night Has a Thousand Eyes', the whole song, including a little jazz riff in the middle, all while we packed away the gear and a couple of big fish suppers.

I never told him this at the time, but I didn't like that song. Not the words anyway. I was still just a little kid, whatever he thought, and the idea of all those eyes, in a deep black velvet sky, however beautiful, didn't make me feel good at all.

This was three weeks before he died. The first foster home I went to had that song on some compilation album. I played it over and over again until the man in the house went a little crazy and called the childcare people, asking for me to be moved on.

While we walked I told Alice Loong a little of this, for two reasons. First, she wouldn't stop asking questions. But second, and most important of all, I wanted to hear her talk about herself. I had heard a kind of reason for what she'd done the night before. She thought Miriam and Ricky's deaths were somehow connected with that of her mother. I still found that idea improbable, but I wasn't about to say it.

We walked that river bank, east, towards the ocean and the flat, industrial land that would surely engulf us soon, since no one could possibly build homes on these muddy grey flats, even in this dark century. After an hour or so we were both hungry.

'Do you eat fish?' I asked.

'When I can afford it.'

'Find me some dry wood, enough for a fire. Then wait for me here.'

She watched me take off my ragged shoes, roll up my suit pants, then wade into the river. It was a trick I'd learned to tease my dad. Most of the time he couldn't catch a thing even with line, a hook and bait. It used to drive him crazy that I knew how to stand in the slow, cool flow of the river, wait until the trout took me for granted, then scoop them out with my hands, straight on to the bank, where he'd club them quickly with the little toy he'd made at work, a lead weight on a short steel rod.

I waited in the river, not worrying about Martin the Medic or Stape or anyone, because they were city people, now of the twenty-first century, and nothing would suggest to them we'd be making our way along a narrow, little-used path through bulrushes and bramble thickets, down by the Pocapo river. The water swam around my toes and ankles. It reminded me I was young once. It also made me realize how much I needed some food.

The first dark shape wriggled my way after fifteen minutes or so. I scooped it straight out of the river with both hands, just as I used to, sent it flying to the bank, where Alice danced around it giggling, kicking the flapping thing with her feet, trying to stop it struggling back to the water. I watched, pleased. She didn't notice her hand much any more. I was right about that at least.

'What am I supposed to do now, Bierce?'

'Kill it,' I yelled back, not focused on her entirely, because another fat shape was stupidly wandering in my direction.

'I can't kill it! What with?'

'Bear with me . . .'

The second trout swam close enough for me to scoop that out of the water. It flew through the air and hit her clean on the chest, which provoked a little commotion. I climbed out of the river, picked up the wriggling fish and beat their heads a couple of times on the path.

The way women do, she looked at me as if I were some kind of animal, not the provider of much-needed nutrition. I smiled back all the while, aware of two things. I rather liked Alice Loong. And something told me not to trust her an inch, because there was a part of her story that didn't add up. Perhaps a very large part.

Once the disapproval had given way to hunger, it turned out she'd put a pocket knife in the bag, which was the kind of forward-looking act I'd never even have considered. After a little gutting, and the retrieval of her lighter – she was, she explained, 'in the process' of giving up smoking – we had two silver-head trout on twigs, cooking nicely over a small fire. The smell took me back to the kitchen in the only place I ever called home. This was disconcerting, but in a pleasant way, unlike most of that day.

'It's the caveman thing again,' she said after a while, as we squatted upwind of the smoke, me turning the fish to get them good and golden.

'Yes,' I agreed. 'It is. You have me named, labelled and pinned to a display board in some museum some-where. So how about you?'

'Me what?'

'Who are you? What do you do?'

'You keep asking this, Bierce! There's nothing to say.'

'Come on.'

I moved the trout away from the flames a little and put on a listening face.

'I'm nothing. Just one more pair of hands in the minimum-wage economy, trying to get by. You want someone to work a few hours in your store? Alice will comply. You want a barmaid who'll dress nice and skimpy so the men in suits will get a little thrill on the way home from work? Done, provided they don't expect their hands to wander. How do you think I got to hear all the cop gossip?'

'I still don't know,' I said very seriously, 'how you came to hear all the cop gossip. Tell me.'

'Oh, right. You wreck my bike. You basically kidnap me. And now *I* have to provide the trust.'

'You came to me.'

The finger stabbed at me.

'I am twenty-six years old.'

'You don't look it. That is merely an observation, nothing more.'

'Well, I am. Also, I share – or perhaps this should be *shared* – an apartment with two other females of similar attributes. They worked the bars I wouldn't work. They got approached by this black cop and asked if someone would throw a welcome party for an ex-con who was secretly coming out of jail. Good money. He wasn't too specific about what was required. I was improvising there. How was I to know cavemen had scruples?'

'Scruples being something the human race has acquired in greater quantity over time?' I asked, trying to puzzle this out for myself.

'Darwin,' she said. 'There. See. You're not the only one who's read books.'

'I never much believed in evolution. Sounds good in principle. But the more people you meet, the more you realize it doesn't add up. It's just . . .'

It felt strange having someone smart and contrary to talk with after a couple of decades in which the longest conversations I had were brief arguments with prison wardens about how the toilet was blocked. Again.

'Just what?'

'The idea of the human race getting gradually more intelligent, more *humane*, over time seems to defy analysis. When I was in jail I read people who've been dead two thousand years and still seemed brighter than most of the idiots penning editorials on big newspapers today. Also social things . . . Marriage. What is it? Half the time it ends in misery and hatred. If we're constantly evolving socially, how come we don't get better at it?'

'We are,' she insisted. 'By doing it less and kicking out the jerks when we don't need them any more.'

'Great for the kids,' I said.

She prodded the fish with a long twig. She was right. They were done. I was wandering, and I knew why. I took them off, wrapped each in some cleanish newspaper I'd found nearby and we ate two fresh Pocapo trout that ranked among the finest food I've ever tasted. Some dimension of life returned to me at the moment, one that had been long absent. It was this: food can taste good, plain simple good most of all.

'Anyway,' she went on, wiping away some grease from her mouth, 'you were married. Happily. So what's the problem?'

'Maybe none,' I lied. 'Why do you think your mother's death and Miriam and Ricky's murders are linked?'

She hunched up her body and looked a little desperate.

'I don't know. They have to be, don't they? The timing. A sledgehammer . . .'

'The timing may just be coincidence. You can buy a sledgehammer in any hardware store. It doesn't take a genius to realize they can be used for pounding things that are not naturally inanimate.'

'She knew you!'

This puzzled me.

'You didn't say that. You said she saw me come home from work.'

'She felt she knew you. And she worked in that factory next to your place. That's a hell of a coincidence, isn't it? You're a cop. I thought things like that pushed your buttons.'

'I *was* a cop.' She had a point, though. 'What was her name?'

'Everyone called her May. It's fancier than that in Chinese, but May will do.'

May Loong. It didn't ring a bell. Not the tiniest of ones.

'You've no idea why she was killed? Still?'

She stared at the fish bones, picking through them, not eating any more.

'None.'

Alice Loong was very focused on the silver-head trout in her fingers when she said that.

'Was anything taken?'

'I don't think so. All I know is . . .'

She put down the fish. This conversation was ruining her appetite, and I blamed myself for that.

'. . . it didn't happen quickly. I was just three years old but I know that. It went on for a long time. They didn't kill her quickly.'

'They?'

She peered into my eyes. This woman possessed the kind of stubborn, steadfast determination that got people into trouble.

'Two voices. Two men.' Her voice went quiet. Her face became flat and emotionless. 'I suppose what I'm saying is I think they tortured her, judging by all the screaming.'

That ruined my appetite too.

'Do you remember what they were asking about?'

She shook her head.

'I'm not sure. Maybe I'm dreaming it. I don't know, Bierce.'

'Tell me.'

She hesitated, and that seemed strange.

'I thought they kept asking her about something called Sister Dragon. It doesn't mean a thing to me. Not a single thing. You?'

I was glad the fire was between us. It meant she couldn't see my hands shaking like dead leaves caught in the powerful, swirling current of the Pocapo, gripped by something that surrounded them, from which they couldn't shake free.

'No,' I said, and it was both true and a lie. I'd no idea who or what Sister Dragon might be. But I had heard that phrase before. It rang a bell from back in the black time, like Miriam's scarlet dress dancing around Alice's lithe body the night before and the taste of the red-green apple from the tree in the garden. These things were important, if only I could understand.

'It's probably my imagination,' she murmured, a sentiment to which I immediately agreed.

'Listen,' I added. 'This is crazy. My problems are nothing to do with yours. They're big problems. Maybe so big . . . You saw what happened back there. You don't look like the kind of girl who deserves to get shot at.'

'I am *not* a "girl".'

'Choose your own honorific. The point remains the same.'

'You're firing me again.'

'I don't ever remember unfiring you.'

'You stole my bike. You kidnapped me . . .'

I took out Stape's odd, tainted gift of the day before and laid the wad down by the fire.

'I want you to have this. You can use it. I can't. I never counted but there's supposed to be twenty thousand there. You could buy yourself several new bikes. Or, being a smart person, a ticket out of here. Go somewhere else. Find a new life.'

She stared at the money. I could see it looked like a lot to her.

'I've got a life already,' she answered.

This made me a little impatient.

'Well try and make sure you keep it. Let me put this less politely. There are people I may have to deal with, people who won't take kindly to having amateurs around. Nor will I if it comes to it. I thought you might have gathered that already.'

She didn't blink.

'No. I don't leave men, not even men I don't like or much care for. They leave me. That's the way it's supposed to be. Besides, you're just mad at me for mentioning marriage.'

'What?'

'I saw the way your face screwed up when that came into the conversation. What's the idea? You get rid of me and hope it'll just go away?'

'Hope what will go away?'

She picked up the trout again, ripped off a chunk of flesh from the side and stuffed it into her mouth, looking pleased with herself.

'That part always puzzled me,' she said, still eating. 'I went to the library a few times and read the court reports. Not that they were very detailed. I would have thought a city cop killing his wife and kid would have made more than half a column on page thirty-three or whatever.'

This was interesting.

'That's all I got?'

'Six, eight paragraphs. Nothing more. Not in any of the rags. They only mentioned the motive thing once too, which I didn't get either.'

'"The motive thing"?'

'They said Miriam was having an affair and you found out.'

'Ah,' I replied, nodding, head suddenly spinning. '"The motive thing". That.'

I bundled up the fish and threw them in the river. Trout were cannibals. My dad had told me that.

Then I walked back into the water, washed my hands, and stayed there, staring upstream. There was nothing to see. Seeing wasn't the point.

'I'm sorry.' She looked it, a little. I'd made her wait ten minutes. We didn't really have that time. By now Martin the Medic and whoever else was chasing us would surely have started to narrow down the options on where we were. 'I shouldn't be bringing this up, but it's best I get it out of the way. I was always puzzled by the idea they could nail you on what seemed pretty flimsy evidence and amnesia alone. They needed a motive. A reason why you'd do such a terrible thing.'

She hesitated.

'Was it true, Bierce? Was she unfaithful?'

'I honestly don't know,' I answered without a second thought. 'I've no recollection that Miriam had a lover.'

'And on the day?'

'On the day, I remember nothing.'

'So if you'd found out. If what they said was true . . .'

'Then I'd still be in the dark. Did they use his name? In the papers?'

'No. Do you know it?'

I watched her closely.

'I remember the name they kept throwing at me in the interview room. Kyle McKendrick. Some cheap little crooked city councillor. I'd busted him once trying to pick up whores in St Kilda. He'd walked away scot-free for some reason, probably because he had friends. I don't know any more about him than that.'

Her tanned face went a little paler at the mention of that name.

It was my turn to be puzzled. Kyle McKendrick had never really entered my life except as a brief and unsuccessful customer of the city police department, and a name I kept hearing during interrogations where I couldn't really focus on much except what I'd lost. He seemed unimportant, irrelevant, whatever the angry faces across the table had said.

'You've heard of him?' I asked.

'Kyle McKendrick? Didn't you read *any* newspapers while you were in jail?'

'Not for a couple of decades. What was the point? I was never coming out.'

She still wasn't looking me in the eye.

'Bierce . . . Kyle McKendrick *is* this city now. He owns everything one way or another. The newspapers. The TV station. All the public services got privatized years back. Transportation. Health care. Some of the jails and the police system.'

'Jails?' I asked, bewildered.

'This is the enterprise era. Even the prisons. Why deprive convicts the privilege of getting a corporate logo on their dinner plates or whatever?'

'I didn't get a corporate logo on my dinner plate.'

'Are you sure?'

No, I wasn't. I'd stopped looking at everything for a while. They had moved me around for some reason, from solitary cell to solitary cell, which didn't help. A good decade and a half of my life was one big, fuzzy blur. I know I went into Gwinett. I assumed I came out of there, though that view from the window the previous day, when Stapleton offered me the deal, still puzzled me. It seemed *wrong*. The truth was they could have done anything they liked with me all that time inside. I wouldn't have known or cared.

'I see,' I said lamely.

'I doubt it. So they thought Kyle McKendrick was screwing your wife and that was why you killed her?'

'That's what they said. Is this guy really that important?'

'He's the new royalty. Big family man. If he doesn't own something himself, one of his kids owns it on his behalf. McKendrick could have got you out of prison just by clicking his fingers.'

'Why would he have done that?'

'I don't know. He could have got you killed too.'

'Oh,' I said. 'So he's that kind of royalty? The old-fashioned sort.'

'Word has it, not that polite or sensible people ask.'

I had to raise the question.

'Do you think . . . maybe . . . he knew your mother?'

'What, some cheap Chinese single parent working in an illegal flophouse sweatshop twelve hours a day?'

'She must have been pretty.'

'Oh, please . . .'

'That was simply another observation. I'm looking for strands here. That's all.'

She screwed up her face in disappointment.

'I thought you were supposed to be a good cop.'

'Is that good in the sense of "decent"? Or just highly competent?'

'Both.'

I shrugged.

'Oh, great,' she moaned. 'You don't even remember that either.'

'I have some intimations on the subject. You know if this is McKendrick, it can't be him alone now, can it?'

'Excuse me.'

'Someone set me free, maybe to line me up to take the rap for something. Me carrying twenty thousand in cash ought to be enough to raise a little suspicion in the first place. I don't know. But if that was McKendrick, why would he nail Tony Molloy to a post outside my house this morning? And who were the pair in the Hyundai? Not cops. They didn't feel like cops. They felt like . . .'

'Like what?'

She seemed interested.

'I don't know. I've been out of things for a while, remember? Someone wanted me out of jail, dripping in money, and knew I'd be in Owl Creek last night, hoping to get something out of it. On the other hand, maybe some other people want me . . .'

Dead, I thought, for no particular reason, and I wasn't sure whether I said the word or not.

'Ergo . . .' I went on.

'Please stop using words like that. You've read some books. I've got the message.'

'Ergo, I need a place to start. And that place has to be finding out whether McKendrick and Miriam really were an item, I guess.'

I hadn't told her about my brother-in-law Sheldon and his little motor shop, which probably lay less than a mile back up over the river bank, in the scrappy industrial landscape I hoped still existed there, unchanged by the years. It was always best to introduce Sheldon to people unawares.

'I concur,' she said. 'Now you'll have to excuse me.'

'Why?'

'The bathroom. Or the bushes, if you prefer. Do I have to spell it out?'

I tipped my hand to forehead in a little salute and watched her disappear behind a large clump of vegetation: wild rose and elder, fighting it out to see who could win. Four rowdy greenfinches burst from the branches, screaming at her approach. They were very loud little birds.

Alice Loong seemed intelligent and selflessly dogged in her determination to get what she wanted, whatever that might be. These were both good reasons not to have her around.

When she was out of sight, I took out the wad of money again, retrieved a couple of hundred for possible future expenses and deposited the rest in her bag. Then, very quickly, I found a pen and scrap of paper and scrawled, 'He went thataway . . .' on it, with an arrow, which I pointed downstream, to the grey estuary and, eventually, the ocean at Blue Oyster Point.

Maybe she'd believe it. Maybe not. Either way she'd spend a couple of minutes puzzling over whether this was bluff or double bluff. Alice Loong was like that. She liked to understand things, or hoped to, before she made a decision. I have never felt shackled by such sensible constraints.

Though I hadn't mentioned it, I knew this particular section of the river very well indeed, which was why I'd stopped here in the first place. This was where we'd fished many a time when I was young, the very place where my old dad had sung 'The Night Has a Thousand Eyes' to a young moon trapped among a celestial coverlet of twinkling stars. When he was gone, it remained one of my favourite places, alone or with the one good childhood friend I had, Mickey Carluccio, whose father owned the city fish market, where I worked for pocket money from time to time. Until that bond got broken up too. I hadn't thought about Mickey in years. There hadn't seemed any point. But the memories were starting to come back, in their own time. Some of them had to be useful.

It was easy to hoist myself up the bank using the low branches of the shrubs struggling to hold on to the red clay earth there. At the top there was another path leading to the low, ragged outlines of the industrial zone, all just as I remembered, only a lot bigger. Big enough for the nearest block to be just a short walk away, so I could get there and disappear behind it in less than a minute.

I didn't have a watch but I guessed it was now early afternoon. Sheldon would be dozing over the first beer of the day.

Ricky was just turned three when he got his Uncle Sheldon right. It was one day down at the beach, with Miriam secretly eyeing the fancy houses in Greenpoint, wondering if we'd ever make it there. She thought I never noticed but I did. There seemed nothing wrong in dreams at that time. On this particular day Ricky looked up from his large and rather complex sand castle – more a fortress really, there was a touch of his dad there even then – pointed at Sheldon and declared, 'The Amazing Mumford. A la peanut butter sandwiches!'

Miriam had to help me out with the reference. I didn't watch daytime TV much. Or the evening stuff either.

But the next day I sat down with my son and we watched an entire hour of *Sesame Street*, both screaming with joy when the Amazing Mumford did hop on screen to perform a very passable impersonation of Sheldon Jay Sedgwick.

The long, black, greasy hair was a little weirder, the baldness somewhat more apparent and the moustache more sleazily crooked. But I guess it was difficult to put all those real-life details on something as simple as a stuffed puppet made out of felt and cardboard. Still, the Amazing Mumford was damn close, most notably in the cack-handed way he approached even the simplest of tasks, starting out with one thing, ending up with something else altogether. From that point on, Sheldon *was* Mumford as far as I was concerned, though it was a year before Miriam took me to one side and asked me to stop using the name, because Sheldon had finally plucked up the courage to complain.

He was that kind of human being. Timorous yet full of his own small self-importance. Utterly incapable of holding down a real job, yet convinced the low-grade, incompetent motor shop he'd run since getting kicked out of engineering school would one day make his fortune.

Sheldon – I've lost the habit of calling him Mumford, even if I still think of him that way – inhabited a world that existed inside his head alone, and as far as I could see he was reasonably happy there. He lived over the shop, which kept down costs. He had a steady stream of customers who couldn't afford to take their

119

DAVID HEWSON

vehicles anywhere but a place where the primary fixing
tool for any problem, large or small, was simple brute
force. Nor did he have much in the way of friends –
particularly female ones – who might introduce such
awkward things into his life as relationships and human
contact.

And he was the only person who wrote to me in jail.
Now who would have predicted that?

The city may have been transformed while I was in jail
but not Shangri-La Motor Repair. Six gutted automobiles stood on the forecourt, rusting away, either
because the owners hadn't paid or come to collect, or
because their problems were simply beyond Sheldon's
rudimentary mechanical skills. Half the neon sign
Sheldon had bought, at great expense, was now out.

At the time he acquired it I had queried this purchase on the grounds that, since he opened only during
the day, and then sporadically, a bright neon hoarding was, perhaps, something of a luxury. Miriam had
thrown a large object in my direction. There was, you
see, no way of offering Sheldon advice. He and Miriam
were non-identical twins, the only offspring of a charming farmer from the Peyton peninsula whose wife had
died when they were young. Their father doted on the
pair, understandably in Miriam's case, expensively in
Sheldon's. By the time old man Sedgwick died, Sheldon
had run through the family's entire savings and mort-
gaged the farm too. I know because that was the one
letter I got in jail in which he actually told me something. This said more about Sheldon than he realized,
I suspect. He wasn't just indolent, untrustworthy and

utterly friendless in life. He was also happy to let every-one know about it.

I worked my way past one half-burnt-out Volks-wagen and a Volvo that looked as if rodents had taken up residence in the rear. There was, to my complete lack of surprise, not a sound coming out of the work-shop, the doors of which were wide open to the sun, inviting any passing thief to enter and help themselves to whatever worthless junk lay inside. There was a clock just inside the door, though, and I was minded to think it half accurate, since the time there said just after three p.m., about what I'd reckoned.

If Alice Loong was sensible she'd be halfway to the airport now, thinking of somewhere to go. A part of me hoped it would be a long way away, perhaps in another country altogether. A part of me thought this improbable, and was both pleased and sorry. Alice had told me only half the story, maybe not even that, and I wasn't sure I wanted to know the rest, or understand its implications.

A TV was playing somewhere: familiar sounds, grunts and sighs. I turned the corner into the office and there was Sheldon, feet up on a desk covered in sheets of paper, many of them with shouting red type on them, beer in hand, gawping at a porn video featuring two highly pneumatic women and a couple of plastic imple-ments that would never make it on to *Sesame Street*.

'A la peanut butter sandwiches,' I said, then walked over and popped the off switch on the grubby little portable perched on top of a rickety filing cabinet.

Sheldon's grease- and oil-stained features creased in fear and disbelief.

'Oh, crap,' he muttered, and took a gulp of beer,

most of which went down the front of his grimy blue overalls. 'Oh, shit and crap and . . .'

The beer can went up again.

He'd put on weight and, to my amazement, lost so much hair that all he had left were a couple of lank, black strands attached to the lower portion of his gleaming skull, like pigtails stuck on with drawing pins. The moustache had got bigger and uglier, but not so big it obscured much of Sheldon's flabby face, which was a shame.

He looked terrible. Old and fat and sick. And scared now too.

'What the hell are you doing here, Bierce?' he asked finally.

'Just looking up my last remaining relative. What do you expect a man newly released from jail to do?'

'Released?' he asked, seemingly amazed. 'When the hell did that happen? How?'

I brushed the remains of a long-expired pizza from the only other chair in the room, pulled it up and sat down next to him.

'Don't you keep up with the news?' I asked. 'I was under the impression that was my failing.'

'What news?'

There was a paper on the desk. I'll give him that. I picked it up and shuffled through the front pages and the local ones. The previous day's too. Nothing.

'They let me out of jail yesterday. Someone confessed. Frankie Solera. You heard of him?'

'Frankie Solera?'

He shook his head. The lank pigtails moved behind his shiny skull, one second out of sync.

'Never,' he insisted. 'Never!'

'Then this morning I found some guy called Tony Molloy nailed to a telegraph pole outside the house. Dead.'

He gulped on the beer and choked some.

'But,' I went on, 'since Tony Molloy was some kind of associate of Frankie Solera, someone you don't know, I guess he's a stranger to you too.'

'They let you *out*?'

'It's because I'm innocent, Sheldon. I thought you understood that. I thought that was why you wrote me that letter once a year.'

To his credit, he put down the can.

'I wrote you because I never thought you did it, Bierce. But I never worked out why you couldn't convince them of that either. You seemed to do everything else so easy.'

I said nothing.

'I wondered,' he added, 'whether that was because you hadn't quite convinced yourself.'

'That's an interesting observation.'

I looked around the office. One phone. Lots of bills. No obvious work. Cheap porn on the TV.

'So,' I asked, 'how are things in Shangri-La?'

'Lull before the storm,' he said, then leaned over, picked up a filthy computer keyboard, one which had no wires attached, and started punching it with his stubby fingers.

Something began to flash up on the tiny thin screen on the desk. It meant nothing to me, any of this.

'See, this business today is about knowledge. Being one step ahead of the pack. What those bums in the big auto shops out there don't know *will* kill them. You remember the second-series VW Sports Polo GTI hatch-back, 97–2001?'

'We talked of little else on death row.'

He typed in something, then pointed to an unread-able page of text on the screen.

'Out of warranty now, natch. But there's a problem with the overhead valves on some of them. Not widely known yet. You have to understand where to look to get this info. The maker won't fix it, not without a lot of money. It needs a mod which you only get from Germany. Unless . . .'

More beer, and a broad grin which revealed that regular dental visits had not been part of Sheldon's medical regime in some time.

'. . . you know me. I have the parts. I have the knowledge. When those babies start coughing and wheezing and falling apart all over town, people are going to be beating a path to my door to fix them. *Big* money.'

I glanced at the empty workshop.

'When's this gold rush likely to start?'

He frowned.

'Six weeks. Eight at the most. The guy who sold me the mod parts says the problem only starts big time when the weather goes from hot to cold. Come the end of September, the streets out there will be littered with dead VWs and no one to fix them, short of paying a fortune to some dealer, except me.'

There were seven or eight cardboard boxes stacked in the corner of the office with Korean and Japanese writing on them, and a picture of a vehicle that looked as if it had been drawn by a three-year-old.

'You get these on sale or return?' I asked.

Sheldon's beetle brows curled in bafflement.

'What?'

'Nothing. Listen, Sheldon. I need . . .'

'I don't have any money.'

'I don't want money.' I looked up the little set of stairs that led to the loft that had been Sheldon's home since he left the farm. In desperate circumstances . . . 'The Airport Ramada is unexpectedly full. I need a place to stay, just for tonight. I need to talk to you about some things too.'

He shuffled and looked worried. Then he cracked open another beer and didn't think to offer me one.

'Things?' Sheldon asked, with that little nervous squeak in his voice I'd forgotten.

I came straight to the point.

'Were we happy, Sheldon?'

He wriggled in his seat.

'How the hell should I know? It was your marriage.'

'Did we *look* happy? Miriam, I mean.'

'Yeah,' he replied, nodding. 'I never saw her look as happy as she did the day you got married.'

'And after?'

'She looked pretty happy too. We didn't talk regular. I think she would have liked you to be home a little more. Maybe earning a decent wage. The Sedgwicks always had a thing about money, you know. Family failing.'

He cast a jaundiced glance around him.

'Miriam knew I was burning up the old man's inheritance big time ever since I started this business. That pissed her off. As she made clear to me on more than one occasion.'

Miriam and I had run through that conversation ourselves, several times.

'That was about you, Sheldon. Not the money.'

'No.' He said this carefully, as if he was scared of getting the words wrong. 'It was about both. Miriam had ideas, Bierce. Maybe you didn't notice that, but she did.'

I shook my head. This didn't fit the picture I'd stored in my mind, one that was, in many respects, very clear, since I'd taken it out and polished it so often while sweating in a cell in Gwinett.

'What kind of ideas?'

'Ordinary ones. A big house. A big garden. A pool maybe and a view of the beach.'

'She wasn't going to get to Greenpoint married to a cop. Not an honest one.'

'No.' He was speaking carefully again. 'I guess she wasn't.'

'Was she cheating on me?'

'Of course not! What the . . . ?'

He threw the half-empty beer can in my direction, which for Sheldon was tantamount to extreme violence.

'Hey. I don't have to listen to you insulting my dead sister's memory. OK?'

'I had to ask. You know what they hinted at in the trial. Not that they ever put a face to him.'

'I never came to the trial. I never read a word about it in the papers. I couldn't. Pop was getting sick by then, not that I expect you to be aware of that fact. I just . . .' He hung his head and sighed. 'I just wanted to be near him.'

'Inheritance time,' I said, and hated myself the moment the words floated out.

'There wasn't any left by then,' he said sourly.

'They said she was cheating. You must have heard that.'

'I heard it. I don't want to know any more.'

'With some jerk called Kyle McKendrick. That part never got into court somehow. But they ran the name past me all the same.'

He shivered and picked up the newspaper.

'Could that be true, Sheldon?'

He creased an inside page in half and thrust it in front of me. There was a long story, half the available space, about some charitable foundation and a gift it was making to one of the city hospitals. I scanned the details. Kyle McKendrick had come up in the world since I busted him for trying to talk cheap hookers into his Honda in one of the crappier parts of St Kilda.

The article described him as 'the city billionaire and philanthropist'. His foundation was giving the hospital twenty million for a new children's ward. There was a picture of him – a middle-aged man with well-kept grey hair and a face like that of some fallen angel, young and old at the same time – handing over the cheque to some pretty young nurse. I was surprised they used this particular photo. Mr McKendrick was leering straight down her neckline as he passed over the piece of paper. Maybe someone on the photo desk had a sense of humour.

'Seems a nice guy now,' I observed. 'A nice, generous guy.'

Sheldon grunted.

'He can afford to be. The only things in this city Kyle McKendrick doesn't own are the churches and the graveyards, and he's probably planning a takeover bid for them as we speak. You know who I pay the rent to on this place? When I pay it.'

'In person?'

'Nah! He's rich, Bierce. Rich people don't do things the straight way. It goes to his daughter's company, out on some Caribbean island, then straight back to him. I'll tell you one thing, though.'

He hesitated, as if he wished he hadn't thought of this.

'I'm listening,' I said by way of encouragement.

'It all comes back to Kyle in the end. Everything. He's a hands-on man. Doesn't delegate anything easy. Even the crooked stuff. Why should he bother? He's got everyone in his pocket anyway.'

'I understand. So was it true what they said? About Miriam?'

'How the hell would I know? Tell me that.'

There was a phone book on the desk. I just about recognized it. They'd changed the way things looked, the way things got organized. Also, judging by how thick the thing was – I noticed, after a couple of flicks through, that this was merely volume one – it appeared every last person on the planet now owned at least one phone number, if not several.

'Where can I call him? We need to talk.'

Sheldon was over in an instant, grabbing the book out of my hands.

'Are you insane?'

'Possibly. I'd still like to sit down with this guy all the same. We've things that need clearing up. Surely you can see that?'

'No, no, no, no, no. You do not call Kyle McKen-drick. You don't go anywhere near someone like that.

I don't know how the hell you got out of jail, but he could sure put you straight back in there, no questions asked.'

People kept saying stuff like this and it was starting to bother me.

'Did someone change the nature of the legal system while I was in prison? I still have this phrase "independent judiciary" running round my head. Is it an anachronism?'

'*You're* an anachronism. In this world money is everything. If you have it, you do what you like. If you don't, you stay alive by keeping your head down, getting on with the day and feeling glad when it's over. We're all just little fleas feeding off one another, then passing on a few of the spoils to bigger fleas because they *are* bigger. And Kyle McKendrick is the biggest of them all.'

'How did this happen?' I asked, genuinely bewildered.

Sheldon shook his head.

'I don't know. I really don't.'

'Then why the hell do you take it?'

'Because that's how things are! Listen. I don't want you getting any stupid ideas. I know what a stubborn bastard you are and on this point, brother-in-law, you are wrong. You may think the pinnacle of human civilization happened some time in the spring of 1985, and ever since then we've just been going downhill . . .'

'You put that with a remarkable eloquence . . .'

'Well, it's bullshit! What we are is what we were all along. It just took us a while to realize it.'

'Cynicism does not become a man. Are you ever going to offer me a beer?'

It was the last one. That was why he kept shuffling his tubby body in front of it.

Sheldon Sedgwick sighed and threw the can across to me. I tried to open it and failed. A little swearing started.

'Gimme!' Sheldon yelled, then got up and snatched the thing from my fingers. He was furious all of a sudden. Over a can of beer. Or rather, over me. 'If you can't even open a beer, what the hell hope is there?'

I watched. It was different. In my day tabs got ripped off completely and came with razor-sharp edges that could stripe your fingers if you weren't careful. The opening on this thing just sort of turned in on itself, then hung there, meek and mild.

'Progress,' Sheldon said, and sat down. 'See.'

'Yeah,' I agreed. 'Now you can get shit-faced without fear of cutting yourself to ribbons.'

Nevertheless, I took a swig. The beer was warm but wonderful. And the first small kick of alcohol I'd tasted in twenty-three years suddenly brought on a moment of epiphany, a small one this time.

The revelation being . . . I could scarcely keep my eyes open.

'I'll go out and get some more,' Sheldon promised.

'Something to eat might be a good idea too.'

'Any other requests?'

I thought about this.

'Bread. Straight from the oven, so you can smell it. Roast beef. Apples. Some salad. Fresh. Fragrant. Those are your shopping watchwords for this evening, Sheldon. Here . . .'

I threw over fifty from my remaining wad. I was

feeling generous towards him. It must have been good beer.

Then, without even thinking, I asked, 'Does the name "Sister Dragon" mean anything to you?'

He didn't blink. He was thinking. I was willing to give this some time, because saying the actual words prodded some subterranean mental rock inside my head that had been liberated by the presence of alcohol. Beneath it lay the conviction that I only remembered Sister Dragon because someone, perhaps in interrogation, had thrown around the phrase repeatedly, and drawn a total blank from me then too. Even so, there was something about the context – *my* context, the situation in which the question got asked – that made me feel scared and more than a little shaky, just as I had when Alice had uttered that same phrase. If it was an interrogation, it surely wasn't an ordinary one.

'You mean you never went?' Sheldon asked.

'Went where?'

'It was a place on Humboldt Street. Got closed down twenty years ago, all of a sudden. Overnight, as if something bad happened. Wasn't open for long but . . . wow. Started off as some smart cocktail bar, all straight and nice and above board. Went sleazy really quick. The way of the world. Dancing. The strip part turned a little . . . participatory if you get my meaning.'

It didn't ring any bell I recognized.

'Miriam took me there!' Sheldon continued. 'I remember now. We had margaritas. They were good.'

'Miriam? Margaritas?'

I never remembered her drinking anything but wine, and that in delicate, studied moderation.

'Yeah. She knew the people who ran it or something.

I don't recall. This was a long, long time ago. She must have taken you, Bierce. It looked like she was at home in the place.'

'Maybe,' I agreed, knowing I had never, in a million years, stepped through the door of some bar-cum-strip joint called Sister Dragon.

'What kind of a name is that anyway?' I wondered.

'It was something to do with the woman who ran it, I think. Who the hell knows? This was twenty years ago. More. What does it matter?'

'Not much, I guess. Buy me some flowers too. White roses.'

My head hurt. Too much information.

'Flowers?'

'I just want to smell them. Wake me when you get back. And thanks.'

I crawled off towards the steps to the loft, trying not to think about what dank, bachelor pit lay up there.

He wasn't such a bad guy. Nor was his tiny pad, with its mattress on the floor, boxes full of half-folded clothes, and stacks of magazines laid up against the roof walls, as squalid as I expected.

There were probably worse brothers-in-law in the world, I thought, and went to sleep on the wrinkled sheets of the mattress on the floor, to dream about the Pocapo river, and not from the old days either, but as it was now, with the syringes and the condoms, the silver-head trout and Alice Loong there smiling, unworried, pleased because I was standing in front of her, nervous like a kid, holding a bunch of white, white roses.

She looked as if no one had ever given her flowers in her life, which seemed a shame, and maybe a little unbelievable. Also she appeared to be holding a small and very real-looking handgun, one that hung its short snout very loosely in my direction. And when I looked into her face I realized why she was smiling. She was pleased to see me again, and that was not good news, not at all.

The last part notwithstanding, I was happy in that dream until something shook me out of it. Muzzy-headed and with the beer smog still hanging around my mouth, I opened my eyes.

There was a silver-haired man seated on a chair in front of me. He wore an expensive-looking suit, silk maybe, a white shirt and a red necktie pulled up tight, the way business people liked. On the chair next to him was some huge black guy with the build and muscles of a wrestler who'd been squeezed into a uniform that was similar, though slightly inferior, to that of the individual by his side. This gentleman had my service pistol in his hands and was staring at it as if the thing was an antique. Behind the pair, standing, fiddling with a dark leather bag, was a serious-looking doctor type whose myopic eyes twitched nervously inside thick, rimless glasses.

Sheldon was there to one side of them and he looked even more nervous than the one with spectacles.

'You s-s-s-said you wanted to meet Mr McKendrick,' my lying, treacherous brother-in-law stuttered nervously. 'I was hoping we could talk this through nice and polite.'

'Oh, Sheldon . . .'

To my surprise, I genuinely did feel more disappointment than anger at that moment. Except about his persistent abuse of grammar.

'And who the hell killed the adverb during my

incarceration? Is there a death notice I can read some-where?'

He hung his head and mumbled a word I seem to have associated with him for most of his sad little life.

'Sorry.' He gulped. 'Those parts weren't. You reminded me.'

'Weren't what?'

'Sale or return.'

Me and my mouth.

The doctor figure was holding a hypodermic syringe in his hand and, just like my new-old friend Martin, was poking it inside a little glass bottle, when he wasn't casting scrutinizing glances in my direction.

I was, I began to realize, starting to lose my child-hood fear of needles.

'Is there something I can do to help you gentlemen?' I asked.

'For your sake,' McKendrick said, in a low, coarse voice that didn't match the silver-haired appearance and the suit, 'I hope so.'

'So, Kyle,' I answered amicably. 'It's been more than twenty years since I busted you for chasing street whores in St Kilda. What kind of stuff are you into these days?'

McKendrick reached inside his grey jacket and took out a small, shiny handgun.

Then he turned round to Sheldon and casually shot him twice in the chest.

My brother-in-law flew backwards five or six feet, a look on his face that was half fury, half shock. A couple of dark shiny patches started to show through his over-alls. They were the colour of the old oil that lived there most of the time anyway.

'That kind of stuff, when I feel like it,' McKendrick said, and watched Sheldon close his eyes and go still, propped against a large pile of *Playboy* magazines of some vintage, stacked tidily against the leaning loft wall.

I'm a reasonable man, particularly when there are guns and needles around, and people who've tied me tight to a chair with some nylon rope they appear to have brought for the occasion.

So I looked, first at Sheldon, who didn't appear to be moving a muscle, then at Kyle McKendrick and said, 'You know, you could always ask.'

McKendrick stared at me as if I were some kind of idiot.

'Ask? *Ask?* What the hell do you think we've been doing all this time?'

I shook my head. This was beyond me.

'I'm sorry. I don't understand.'

'Sir.'

Dr Rimless spoke hesitantly, as if worried he might say the wrong thing without knowing it.

'What?'

'He wouldn't remember,' the doctor type said. 'Not necessarily.'

'Remember what?' I asked. 'You people keep talking in riddles. How am I supposed to help if I don't know what it is you want?'

McKendrick sat and looked at me. Then he put a finger up to his cheek, the way TV people used to do when they wanted to look thoughtful.

'Who else have you talked to since they sprung you?' he asked.

'They? You mean like the judge.'

'None of my judges let you out of that jail.'

This sounded strange.

'You mean I escaped?'

'Somehow.'

'Sleepwalking. That's all it can be. See, I was under the impression someone from the law office or whatever came along, let me loose, gave me some money and a drive home. And then . . .'

What the hell had Stape been up to, I wondered? He had those papers, but he kept them. There was the money, but that was plain bills. The truth was I didn't have a scrap of proof that I'd got out of jail legally at all.

'Then what?' McKendrick asked.

'Then somebody nailed some dirtbag called Tony Molloy to a telegraph pole outside my front door, which seemed to have got the real police, and several other parties, chasing me like I'm a fugitive or something.'

He didn't speak.

'OK,' I said. 'So I understand. I *am* a fugitive. Also the person who nailed Tony Molloy up there was you.'

'Me,' the black guy interjected, pointing a finger at his own chest.

'I stand corrected.'

'Frankie Solera never confessed to killing my wife and kid then?'

'Of course the moron confessed!' McKendrick snarled. 'Who'd have thought a jerk like that would get religion?'

'Strange things happen on a man's deathbed.'

'You're in a good position to judge, Bierce.'

'I take your word on that. Just so's I know . . . you're saying those two *did* kill Miriam and my boy?'

Kyle McKendrick sighed.

'You're still playing the innocent, Bierce? This is so

tedious. I could stiff you just for that. What the hell did she see in you?'

There were three of them. I am not a man given to fantasies. All the same, a part of me was wishing I could shrug off those ropes, step right up and rip off their heads in one easy movement.

'You and Miriam . . . ?' I asked, not really wanting to know the answer.

'Where did she hide it?' he demanded.

'Hide what?'

Dr Rimless found the courage to intervene again.

'He really doesn't remember,' he said. 'We've tried too many times for him to be hiding that.'

'Maybe he never knew in the first place,' the black guy grumbled. 'In which case, why are we wasting our time?'

McKendrick closed his eyes, the way people did when they were dealing with children.

'Because we don't know for sure. Or whether he's spoken to anyone else.' Then to me. 'Have you spoken to anyone else?'

'I went home. I got up. People started chasing me. Then I came here and talked to my brother-in-law about family stuff until you shot him. What else can I tell you?'

The black guy glowered at me.

'Man says there was someone on the back of that bike you used.'

'Man needs to get his eyesight checked. I haven't been outside a jail cell in twenty-three years. How many friends do you think I have here?'

'None,' McKendrick muttered. 'None coming either. All the same . . .'

He scowled. He was stuck for a course of action and this seemed to be a situation that was new to him.

'Maybe,' the hood suggested, 'they're still looking for him too. We could just pop him here and have done with the damn thing.'

McKendrick put his head in his hands and swore, freely, profusely, worse than a street hood did a quarter of a century ago. I never moved much in billionaire circles, but I didn't expect them to use words like that.

'Jesus,' the boss man moaned. 'I am surrounded by idiots. He *knows*, moron. I was banging his wife for a little while. Maybe that's why he doesn't feel coopera-tive.'

I wriggled in my ropes, mind blank, not scared, not angry. Just stuck there, wondering.

'If you tell me what I'm supposed to know . . .' I said.

'Miriam took something that was important to me,' McKendrick said flatly. 'I want it back.'

'Something like . . .?'

The man in the silk suit sighed.

'Stick him now,' he said to Dr Rimless. 'I can't hang around here dealing with this shit. I got a school to open. Then I got to see the ad agency about some corporate branding session at four-thirty. That gives me a diary window in one hour forty-five. Make sure he has something to fill it.'

The grass is short, newly mown, with the lovely fresh green smell I always found ample reward for the tedious task of cutting it. Ricky's running around the garden, kicking a ball. Something sits in the branches of the apple tree. A large animal. Maybe a cat. Maybe something bigger.

I look more closely. It's some kind of bird, grey and shapeless, with a long sharp beak and wearing rimless spectacles behind which lie two cold black eyes watching me, gleaming. In its claws there's a syringe, from which a line leads straight across the flower bed, through neat rows of lilies and white roses, up the table leg, into my arm.

The creature's listening. I know what it can hear.

My blood boiling in my veins. My mind racing a million miles an hour, searching for something, matching what I think I know against what I'm trying to dig up from my damaged memory.

'Ignore him,' Miriam suggests.

She's in the loose red dress, which is odd, since this is day. Her arms look more tanned than normal. Her face seems tired and a little lined.

'That's easy for you to say. You're dead. Or imaginary. Or both.'

She smiles, a sad smile, one I haven't seen much.

'Did I ever really know you?' I ask.

'How can you say that? We were married for seven years.'

'And for the last few months you were banging some city councillor I'd picked up once in St Kilda, hunting for a whore.'

She folds her arms and gives me a cold, disappointed look.

'You should ask more questions. Those two facts are mere coincidence. Surely you recognize that? Besides, it's always about you.'

Her arms are skinnier than I remember. There are

marks on them. Scratch marks. They look old and some are a little scabby.

'What do you mean?' I say, offended. 'I *am* asking questions. I'm asking about *us*. About the fact we were married.'

I glance at Ricky, who isn't really Ricky at all. His features are blurred and unrecognizable. He's just a shadow with a little colour, chasing over the short grass, like a cartoon character running in a loop in the background.

'And the rest,' I add.

She uncrosses her arms. One hand reaches out and touches me. Or so my eyes tell me. I can't feel a thing.

'No, Bierce. I didn't mean it that way. This *is* all about you. Surely you understand that?'

'Kind of.'

A part of me appreciates what she is saying very precisely. I'm not in the garden in Owl Creek, back in 1985. I'm in Sheldon Sedgwick's loft, with him, dead probably, a couple of yards away, and some bird-impersonating creep in rimless glasses feeding dope into my arm in the hope he can force me to remember something that disappeared the night she and Ricky died, in the beating I took too, from Frankie Solera and Tony Molloy, who were working, probably, at Kyle McKendrick's behest, though it's hard to be sure.

Maybe Miriam is really the creature in rimless glasses, though I doubt that. More likely she's part of me, asking questions of myself, throwing them at some black, empty part of my memory that died over the years, trying to find some answers before Dr Rimless prises them out with his needles and dope.

'I thought I would have known,' I say.

'Known what?'

'That you were having an affair.'

'Cops,' she answers, with a shrug. 'You spend so much time peering into the lives of other people you never really notice what's going on in your own. You weren't there a lot of the time, Bierce. You never realized, I know. And it wasn't deliberate neglect. But you were gone. Days and nights. For a long time on occasions.'

I try to squeeze her hand, wondering if there's any warmth in the flesh.

'So you went to Sister Dragon?'

'Among other places,' she agrees.

'Where was Ricky?'

She looks at the boy. He is my son at that moment. *Our* son. I can see this in her imaginary face.

'Dreaming of seeing penguins,' she says quietly. 'Dreaming . . .'

'They can fly,' Ricky, suddenly sharply in focus, says, except it isn't his voice, it's mine, and hearing it emerge from his young, unspoiled mouth makes me feel more miserable than at any other moment in my too-long life, makes me feel as if I've stolen the breath from my child's lungs and placed my own there in its stead. 'They can fly. I know it.'

'Penguins,' Miriam says, with the careful intonation of the schoolteacher she once was, 'cannot fly. We have been here a million times.'

'Just because you haven't seen them . . .' Ricky or I, it's unclear which, objects.

'Their wings are too short and stubby,' Miriam goes on. 'There are physical laws that mean you don't have to see them not flying to know they *can't* fly. In the

141

promised land, maybe. Here, no. This is the way the world works. This . . .'

She looks into my face and the pupils of her eyes are black, bottomless pools.

'This is the gravity that holds us all down. Cops do not prosper. Penguins do not fly. Children believe day-dreams until one day they know better. And then they turn into us.'

She waves Ricky away.

'Also there are these people called "baby-sitters". I believe I explained the concept to you one time.'

'And while Ricky was with a baby-sitter, you were out screwing a thing called Kyle McKendrick. I don't understand.'

'No,' she says, without emotion. 'You don't. I realize that.'

'Did I? Once?'

Miriam closes her eyes, and this is her, in a way, even if she happens to be nothing but stitched-together memories fired up by Dr Rimless and his assistant, Mistress Dope.

'No. You never understood. Not really.'

'But I knew, right? That night when . . . it all happened. You told me then.'

'I believe so.'

There's nothing there, nothing in my memory to support the question I ask next.

'And we fought? You against me, not the other way round? Which is why they found my skin under your nails?'

I need to know this, desperately. She recognizes that. She says nothing.

'Why?'

It isn't me talking. It's the creature in the tree. Its voice has an inhuman metallic ring to it. If I could move – the line that leads from his syringe into my arm keeps me rooted to the spot for some reason – I would get up and wring his fat feathery neck, long sharp beak notwithstanding.

'Why what?' she asks, of me, not it.

'Why did we fight?' I interrupt, because this is my dream, not his. 'Over McKendrick?'

'What do you think, Bierce? How would you react if you thought I was sleeping with another man? That perhaps I even *loved* another man?'

She makes the distinction very clear. That puzzles me. Either way I'd be heartbroken. I'd sit where we are, at the battered wooden table, staring out at the garden, wondering how we might put our lives back together again, struggling for the means, determined they would, at any cost, be found.

There were women before Miriam, but none came close. She was . . . is the one. I thought she felt the same way about me. I'm wrong but, even now, when I know, it doesn't make any difference. If you can choose love, it isn't love at all. What more is there to say?

'Where did you hide it?' the creature demands.

'Hide what?' she replies.

'You know.'

She looks at me and we say the words together.

'Do I?'

Something happens in my arm. A cold rush of chemical comes running through the hole there. Some unknown instrument, a bell maybe, or a drone, begins singing at the back of my head, one note, not a word, not even a sound I can recognize.

'You know,' the grey spectacled bird in the tree repeats.

'Tell me,' I ask her.

There are tears in her eyes. Not grief. Fury, with herself I guess.

'I don't believe in ghosts, Bierce, and nor do you. Think about it. Either you have the understanding. Or you don't. Some things you can only do on your own.'

'Then help me.'

She shrugs.

'How?'

She takes my fingers more tightly in hers, winding them round and round, the way she used to.

Miriam, dead Miriam, Miriam out of a dream, can't take her eyes off me, and for a moment I envy whatever place it is she occupies.

'All you have is what you have. You're the only person who can find it. Not through some chemical fix or a blow to the head or anything artificial like that. You find it by being yourself. There's no other way.'

Then she adds, never breaking her hard, fixed gaze, 'If you really want to, that is. Some things are best left buried.'

'Bierce,' says the other voice, 'it's . . .'

She starts howling. She puts her hands to her ears and the crazy thing is, when she does that *I* am the one who can't hear a sound.

The Rimless Thing falls out of the tree, on to the hard bare ground beneath its branches. It drops the syringe. It's yelling something, over and over again, but my lip-reading talents, such as they are, have deserted me. All I can hear is Miriam, yelling and yelling

and yelling, hands tight to her – my? – head, so the
sound of her voice stays inside me, fills up everything
there, every corner, every dark, fleshy passageway.

I say something and don't detect the sound of my
own voice.

I look in the direction of the tree again. The Rimless
Thing is gone completely.

Something is changing with Miriam too, and even
though I know this is just a dope dream, it makes me
want to weep. The image of her isn't so definite. It's
fading slowly, her sad eyes, the real eyes now, glassy with
tears, slipping back where they came from, down into
the lost depths of my consciousness.

My head's starting to roll sideways, towards some
abyss that's opening up beneath the garden table.

I feel rotten. I can't keep upright at the table. When
I next try to look at her there's nothing on the other
side but bright, filmy dust, floating in an unreal breeze.

From out of the line of my vision comes the sound
of a man, Rimless I guess, yelling something I can hear
but not comprehend. The thought of getting my shaking hands tight around his neck refuses to go away.

'Bierce?' says a distant female voice, and I don't even
have the strength to twitch my head around, trying to
find where it's coming from.

'I don't know what you're talking about,' I mumble.
'If I did know some time, it's gone. And it's not
coming back, not ever. So just kill me now. Who the hell
cares anyway?'

'Bierce!'

'Quit shouting, start shooting. *I don't give a shit.*'

I try to find the bird but he isn't anywhere. There is
no tree. There's a grubby room with grubby furniture,

a body I kind of recognize, heaped against some magazines. It's Dr Rimless, who is back to being a man. He's
slumped on Sheldon's floor mattress, looking shocked
and hurt. His spectacles lie on his chest, shattered. A
large red wound has sprung up from somewhere on his
wide forehead.

'Listen, dinosaur,' the hidden woman says. 'We're
getting out of here now. Before anyone comes back.
Can you hear me? Can you even move?'

'Bierce!'

Her shape stops swimming. A long, slender hand the
colour of a fading golden rose comes out from the fuzzy
part of my universe and starts slapping me hard around
the cheek.

'We are going. Now. And who's this?'

The hand is pointing at Sheldon. His eyes are open.
He appears to be conscious and breathing. I envy him
on both counts.

'Brother-in-law. Treacherous stinking asshole.'

'Then he's coming too,' she says, and jerks me to my
feet, an act that leads to my head wobbling wildly on
my shoulders, looking for a spare place on the floor,
between the beer cans and porn mags, where it can roll
off and lie still for a while.

Alice Loong looks me straight in the eye.

'You *will* help me pick up the shot guy,' she orders.
'There are four vehicles downstairs and a million sets of
keys. Something's got to work around here. We *need*
him.'

Dr Rimless moans and says something colourful.

My slender half-Chinese friend walks over and wal-
lops him hard on the head with the largest mechanic's

wrench I have ever seen in my life. He doesn't move or say anything after that.

I struggle to pull together a smile for her.

'I tried to buy you flowers,' I say with a sorry slur, hating Sheldon all the more because I know he never got them.

'You're the most generous man in the world,' she replies. 'Now take his legs. We're gone.'

The thing about pharmaceuticals is that, unlike booze, they usually wear off quickly. Or so I kept trying to tell myself.

We drove out of the Pocapo flats industrial zone in the ancient brown Volvo estate wagon I saw on the way in, now newly vacated by rodents, selected by Alice from Sheldon's small fleet of vehicles deemed too far gone to be collected by their true owners. I sat bolt upright in the passenger seat, suddenly feeling pretty high and talkative. The miracle of chemicals. Sheldon was sprawled out in the back, moaning. Alice Loong was behind the wheel, angerometer touching ten on the Richter scale.

'Where are we going?' I asked.

'I'm dumping your friend off at the hospital. Then I'm taking you somewhere quiet.'

'When will we be there?'

'Shut up, Bierce. I am thoroughly pissed off with you.'

I gave up struggling to put my seat belt on and stared at her.

'For why?'

'You abandoned me, for God's sake! While I was taking a leak. What kind of man does that?'

'Maybe a man who thinks you're better off that way. Besides, I left you money, didn't I?'

A silver Mercedes came speeding the other way, with a now-familiar black figure behind the wheel.

'Uh-oh,' I muttered, and quickly ducked down behind the dashboard.

When I got back up, the Mercedes was still sailing on in the direction of the Shangri-La.

'Evil bastard McKendrick fooling with my wife,' I grumbled under my breath.

'What?' Alice barked.

'You heard.'

'You're full of that stuff they gave you. Why don't you shut up and go to sleep or something?'

'Can't. Thinking. Besides, maybe he was fooling with your mom too.'

She slammed on the brakes. We came to a halt by a couple of newspaper stands that had been vandalized by someone learning how to spell.

'That's it. Get out. Now.'

'I'm serious! Tell her about Sister Dragon, Sheldon.'

He was groaning like crazy on the back seat. But he wasn't bleeding so much. Even doped up as I was, I felt pretty sure Sheldon Sedgwick would live to cheat and lie another day.

'I've been shot,' he whined.

'You got two tiny bullets from a ladies' gun. They clearly hit nothing of any importance, otherwise you wouldn't be squawking like you are now.'

'*I've been shot!*' he squealed again.

'Don't worry. You're made of lead-absorbent lard. We'll drop you off at the hospital, they'll give you some-one else's blood, then you'll pass for an ordinary decent human being for an hour or two before your own stuff starts to kick in again.'

Alice swore, put the car in gear and swerved back into the road.

'How the hell could you sell me like that, Sheldon?' I asked, and sounded a little pathetic too, I could tell. 'Me. Your own brother-in-law, who comes to you for help, *and* passed over a fifty for beer and flowers.'

'Flowers?' Alice asked, bewildered.

'Yeah. Flowers. Never got them either. How could you do it, Sheldon?'

He was well enough to drag his bleeding frame up off his seat, lean over the back of mine and stab an accusing finger at me.

'I didn't know they were gonna pull stuff like that, did I? Otherwise I wouldn't have said nothing.'

'Use one more double negative and I'll shoot you myself, O brother. Why?'

'The landlord guy called this morning. Said they were just interested in knowing if you showed up. One whole month's rent in it for me.'

I brushed off his arm. He fell back on to the seat.

'Oh, wonderful,' I moaned, and looked at Alice in the driver's seat. 'I am cash-flow positive. That excuses everything. And you?'

She glared back at me.

'Me?'

'Yeah. Who *are* you?'

'What do you mean "who am I"? I'm the person who just saved your life.'

'But why?'

She reached down into her bag, pulled out the wad I'd left there and threw it at me.

Sheldon sighed in the back. The presence of so much cash within smelling distance seemed to me the greatest threat his health was likely to encounter all day.

I still couldn't work out whether I felt super-smart or super-stupid.

'I don't like being abandoned,' Alice added. 'And I don't like being patronized. What the hell did you mean by that?'

My head really wasn't running on the right lines. I shook it to see if that would help.

'What?'

'About my mom? And McKendrick.'

'Oh.' It took a second or two. '*Tell* her, Sheldon. About Sister Dragon.'

He didn't say anything. He was hiccuping. Or throwing up. Or both. He did have two bullets in him. He did need medical help.

'Fine,' I announced. 'Leave this to me too.'

I tried to pull myself together and looked at her. She glanced back at me, a little nervous. This wasn't going to be nice, for either of us, and somehow Alice Loong understood that already.

'Sister Dragon was some sleazy cocktail bar pick-up joint on Humboldt,' I said, speaking very precisely. 'It got closed down years ago. Unbeknown to me, my wife used to go there before she climbed into the back of Kyle McKendrick's Taurus for a quick hump or some-thing.'

'For Christ's sake, Bierce. How can you possibly know that?'

'I *know*. Just trust me. McKendrick virtually rubbed it in my face for one thing. It's not the kind of stuff you'd lie about.'

She winced.

'I'm sorry.'

I waved an arm around loosely.

'No. It's OK really. A part of me knew already. It just doesn't want to vomit up all the rest of the crap it's got hiding down there.'

'Wait . . .' she said.

We'd passed some kind of medical station by the side of the road. There were a couple of ambulances there and an office with – I could just make this out – some people in white nylon coats inside.

'Sheldon,' Alice said, 'it is time for you to discover the joys of private medicine.'

I turned round. His eyes were looking bleary. There was blood all over the back seat.

'Huh?' he moaned. 'I don't have insurance. Don't leave me here. They'll cut me up for parts.'

'No,' I found myself saying. 'They'd only do that if you were the same species as the rest of us.'

Then she helped him out and got him to sit on a trash can by the front door. The white coats inside didn't notice a thing. They all seemed to have their faces stuck to computer screens, one per head, or so it looked like.

Alice went round the corner, where I couldn't see her. It took a minute or so before she came back, but at least we didn't have Sheldon any more.

'Let's go,' she said.

She'd made a phone call. I saw her putting her tiny little pink plastic handset into her bag when she came back. Had I possessed more of my wits, I would have mentioned this. But I didn't, and that, I guess, was why she thought she could get away with it.

'Such efficient, detached care,' I observed instead. 'You could get a job in medicine yourself.'

Alice drove off slowly. She looked as if she wasn't sure where to go. She looked uncertain of herself, if I'm being honest. Somehow I found this reassuring.

'So,' she asked, 'your wife used to go to a cocktail bar and screw McKendrick? And you knew nothing about this?'

'No,' I corrected her. 'My present self did not know knowingly. That is not to say my previous self did not, at some stage, know, not that he's telling. If you follow me.'

'I'm trying. How are you, Bierce? Is there anything I can get you?'

I thought about this.

'I have a serious thirst for a Long Island Iced Tea, a bucket of buttered popcorn and a plate of steak tartare. Which probably means I'm not good at all. If you could find me some real food and water that would be nice. Before . . .'

She had very nice eyes, the colour of the green you used to get in signet rings. I noticed something else too, when she opened her mouth and half smiled at me. The tongue stud was gone. This was one more invention of the twenty-first century. You could stick lumps of metal in your mouth and make it look as if they'd been nailed there. Then take them out the following day and no one would ever have guessed.

'Before what?'

'Before we visit Sister Dragon or whatever it's called these days. I just want to see. Find out if it sparks any pictures in my head or something.'

She shook her head.

'I don't know Humboldt. Isn't that a really long street? If you don't have a number we'll need to ask.'

I said nothing and hunched up in the passenger seat. A small store – with the iron grille and warning notices about alarms that I was now getting used to – hove up on the right. We weren't a mile from Humboldt in any case.

'Pull over, will you?' I said. 'I need to get some sugar or something inside me.'

She did, without a moment's hesitation.

I dragged a note out of my pocket and walked through the door. I liked this place immediately, with that warm, tears in the eye affection only the truly doped up or drunk can have. It looked as if it hadn't changed much in twenty-five years or more. Just the prices, and the security cameras that seemed to be poking at everyone who entered.

Lurching up to the counter, I started counting through the candy bars, picking ones I recognized, throwing in some potato chips and sundry assorted junk snacks.

There was a time for fine food. There was a time to fill the face.

I picked up several specimens, then let them loose in front of the man behind the counter, a small, elderly individual of wiry build and Mediterranean appearance. Behind him was a large wire cage with a green parrot inside. It kept talking in what sounded like Greek. Dirty Greek.

'Party time,' the counter man said, and laughed.

'Yeah . . .'

I hadn't even noticed the newcomer who'd slid in behind me and walked straight up to pay. I looked at

him now. He was about my height, in the familiar uniform of a patrol car monkey, with shorn golden hair
and sunglasses tucked back on to his head, like a bad TV
cop.

He eyed me up and down carefully, then grinned.

'Don't you go crazy with all that,' he advised, in a
slow, stupid drawl.

To this day I have absolutely no idea whether he was
serious or not.

Still, if the cops were looking for me hard even this
bozo should surely have known. So whoever the other
party on my case was – Kyle McKendrick's rivals, that
much was clear – they didn't appear to be wearing a
badge. Which made me think it would be very interesting to have a talk with my old friend Stape some time
soon.

'You have any flowers?' I asked. 'White roses.'

The shop guy's eyes rolled back into his head, thinking.

'Out back maybe,' he said, then looked at me, as if
trying to work out whether I was the type to purloin his
entire stock of confectionery and potato snacks once
his back was turned. 'Ah, there's a cop here. What's to
worry about?'

He went through a little door behind him. The
patrolman and I exchanged vapid glances.

I pointed to the security cameras sprouting everywhere, and the signs about alarms and time locks and all
kinds of stuff I didn't begin to understand.

'What's the world coming to?' I asked. 'Where are
the values?'

He nodded.

'I believe, for economy shopping, sir, you may be

better served by a larger establishment such as a super-market chain. You don't come visit Mr Thanatos for bargains, now do you?'

I closed my eyes and thought about weeping.

'Just a little retail advice,' he added.

When the store keeper came back I saw the roses were getting a little grubby at the edges. I paid what he wanted, though, which seemed an extraordinary amount, then asked, 'Either of you two heard of a place called Sister Dragon on Humboldt? It closed down years ago. A cocktail bar or something. A friend of mine was in town once. Said it was quite something.'

The uniform looked blank. The store man stared at me, not pleasantly either.

'That was a whore joint,' he said eventually. 'What kind of friend was he?'

'It was a she, actually. You wouldn't happen to know the address? She's a nun now. I thought it might be funny to send her a photo or something.'

'Corner of Vine, south side,' he said.

'And now?'

He said something that made no sense to me at all, then added, with some finality, 'Good night.'

Back in the car she stared at the roses, then picked out a couple of chocolate bars and took a big bite of one.

'What the hell did those people do to you, Bierce? These are the worst flowers I've ever seen.'

'Limited choice. Sorry.'

'And why?'

'Why'd I go in there? Because I was hungry. And because I wanted to know if anyone around here had heard of this Dragon Sister place?'

Her face was taut with interest. I wasn't so doped up I didn't notice.

'And?'

'I got an address. Humboldt on Vine. The south side.'

'Tomorrow maybe.'

'No. Now. I insist.'

She laughed.

'I'm driving this stolen vehicle, Bierce. You're in no position, or condition, to insist on a thing.'

She put the car into gear. I put my hand on the wheel, firmly, to stop her going wherever she thought we ought.

'No, Alice. I am. I want to go see this place. I want to think about it. And then I want to know the truth.'

Alice Loong sighed and stared at me.

'You're tired and doped up and stupid.'

'All true, but only of late. Just a couple of hours ago I was feeling quite bright and breezy, to be frank with you. Here's one thing I thought back then. You said you knew they were asking your mom about Sister Dragon when they killed her. Which maybe was true. And maybe not. But this I *do* know. I worked China-town for a couple of years. I had friends there. I went to parties and festivals. And this I remember.'

She'd put down the chocolate bar and was looking young and worried again.

'The Chinese for dragon is "*loong*". You've got to know that. You said yourself you got brought up by your grandmother who's all Chinese. So why's it so puzzling that someone would be asking youR mother about Sister Dragon?'

'Tell me, smartass,' she murmured.

'Because it isn't. I'm putting two and two together

here and maybe getting five and a half. But the way I see it is this. Your mom didn't know Miriam and Ricky because she worked in that factory in Owl Creek. She knew them through the bar. Maybe she and Miriam were friends. Maybe she was some secret baby-sitter while I was out at work. Or maybe the place was called Sister Dragon after the person who ran it, which seems to me to make the most sense, since everyone was just beginning to embark upon the cult of self-worship you people all know and love so well today.'

She didn't hit me. She didn't say no.

'So . . . my bet is that Sister Dragon was called that because the person who ran it *was* your mother. And if that's true, then what follows next is obvious. It was called *Sister* Dragon because the guy who owned it was her brother. Your uncle.'

I stared at her.

'Is he dead too?'

She didn't say a thing, just looked a little crestfallen.

I picked up the flowers, which had tumbled to the floor by her side.

'I can get out of the car if you like. I can leave you that money. Whichever, I don't care.'

'No . . .' she said, shaking her head.

I thought of what the man in the store had said.

'It's something called Starbucks now. Do you know what that is?'

'Oh, my God, Bierce . . . You're not fit to be on the streets. It's a coffee place. There are millions of them.'

That sounded a pleasant bell in my head.

'Coffee?' I said. 'That would be nice.'

That, I thought, and the truth.

*

I have no idea what a double skinny latte mocha with a tangerine shot or something is. But coffee it is not. I sat in this smoke-free, squeaky clean, sanitized dump on Humboldt, squeezed between a launderette and what looked like an appealing book store, feeling I'd wandered into some adolescent's dream of what grown-up life ought to be like.

There were cushions of many colours, meaningless paintings on the wall, soft unmemorable music, and cups of drink the size of Bavarian *Bierkeller* mugs. Most people seemed to be sipping on gallons of warm sweet milk while chewing tiny fancy biscuits that cost the price of a meal the last time I had walked down Humboldt. In between sucks, they played around with little computers on their laps, spoke on their tiny phones and even, in a couple of rare, misfit cases, read something that had once been a tree. I believe I saw one young man and woman indulging in a conversation too, though that may well have been a hallucination. Every last one of them looked fit and well and deeply grateful to have escaped the ravages of the world beyond the door. This was a communal womb with caffeine – or at least a pretence of it – on tap, and I wondered if some of them ever went home at all.

I smiled at the young girl behind the counter as she tried to interest me in some incomprehensible extras.

'Sorry,' I apologized. 'English is my only language. I gather this place used to be a strip dive called Sister Dragon. I don't imagine there would be an adult around here who could confirm such a theory.'

I thought she was about to burst into tears for a moment. Then she just turned her back on me and upped the volume on the Muzak. In my day it came without fuzz guitar, which at least seemed somewhat more honest.

Alice led me to the one free sofa. I sat in it and sank three feet deep into soft, plushy foam.

I tried the liquid in the cup and felt a little nauseous. It was impossible to believe a coffee bean had expired in its making. Also, I wondered how it would get along with whatever else was still floating in my veins. With hindsight, I suspected Martin the Medic's little pro-cedure the day before hadn't entirely slipped my bloodstream before Dr Rimless came along and added his intravenous cocktail to the mix. Pouring a double skinny latte or something on top was, perhaps, unwise. On the other hand, it did just seem to be mainly warm milk.

'I think maybe I should get a doctor to look at you,' Alice suggested.

'A good night's sleep is all I need. If I'm still weird in the morning, nag me then.'

She sighed. Alice Loong was a quick young woman. She knew by now there was no point in arguing.

Instead she looked around the cafe.

'It's hard to believe, isn't it?' she said.

It was just about possible to imagine it as a cocktail bar. The windows must have been expanded somewhat for its present purpose. When I imagined them replaced by the little square panes of glass that were *de rigueur* for drink joints back in my own time, a picture started to form. Bars always had some kind of magic about them that meant the more people came through the door, the bigger the space inside seemed. Empty, the place would have looked tiny. Crammed with fifty or so thirsty customers, it would, I imagine, have sought to attain the status of being intimate. There were also, I suspected, other rooms out back, now used to store millions of cardboard coffee cups and cinnamon aerosol sprays.

I'd never be able to confirm this last part, not without breaking in. The moment Alice parked the old Volvo outside – something she did without even having to check the street intersection – I became ever more sure of one thing. Miriam had never taken me inside Sister Dragon, doubtless for some very good reasons.

'Everything's hard to believe until you start working on it,' I said. 'So let's begin. Your uncle first. Did he have a name?'

'Everyone called him Jonny. That wasn't his real name, naturally. But not many people speak Cantonese.'

I nodded.

'Jonny Loong. Jonny Loong.'

'Say it, Bierce.'

'I told you. I worked Chinatown for a while. It was standard training when you were new to the department.'

'And?'

She knew what I was going to come out with anyway.

'I heard the name Jonny Loong once or twice. He was a crook. Not a big crook, not in Chinatown terms. Just street lowlife, the kind of man you'd put in front of something to hide who really owned it.'

My memory was very good about some things.

'He owned, or claimed to, a restaurant in Eden. Some of the cops used to eat there cheap, lunch and dinner.'

'Cheap being free. Were you among them?' she asked.

I shook my head, with some insistence.

'No. I pay the same price as everyone else. Either that or I don't eat at all.'

'That must have cut down the availability of dining partners.'

'A little. So what? Did I get Jonny wrong?'

Her green eyes lit up with a touch of fury.

'I was three years old when he disappeared. When my mom died. How the hell am I supposed to know?'

Unbeknown to her, I'd smuggled in a crappy rose in my pocket. I took it out and placed it on her lap.

'Alice,' I said, 'if we're to do anything together, we have to learn to be honest with each other. If we can't do that, nothing works. Not when it comes to finding out what happened to your mom or my family. Nothing else either.'

Her face creased with puzzlement.

'What "else"? Don't mistake what happened in your house for something real, Bierce. I was just trying to get you on my side.'

'No, no, no.' I cursed myself for being so stupid. 'That wasn't what I meant at all. What I'm trying to say is . . . we have to have some trust between us. So we can talk frankly. There's no alternative.'

She did the smart thing. She turned the trust question back on me.

'So you won't stuff a wad of cash in my bag and run off again?' Alice asked sweetly.

'No,' I said, and crossed my heart. 'That's a promise. Now it's your turn. Tell me about your family, please.'

*

It was, I imagine, a pretty standard immigrant story, with one significant twist. The Loongs had come out of Hong Kong in the sixties, penniless, like most people in their circumstances, but willing to work every minute of the day to make a go of things. They wound up in the city, in Chinatown, slaving everywhere, from the restaurants to the little factories that made tourist junk, and sending what they could back home to help.

The one unusual thing was this: old man Loong never came with them. For some reason Alice didn't know, he stayed in Hong Kong and died there, of lung cancer she said, when her mother was still young.

'So your grandma was on her own with two kids, in a strange city, with no work except what she could pick up on the streets?'

'Correct. Lao Lao had no relatives either. I just heard stories from time to time. She never wanted to talk about it much. It must have been awful. The thing is, people of that generation don't think about the past. She's fine now. Got her own little apartment. Enough money to get by. It doesn't bother her any more. I'm not sure how much that part of things ever did.'

'Losing your two kids would, though. Were they her only children?'

'Yes,' she said warily. 'The rest is difficult, Bierce. I've never had this conversation with her direct. I daren't do that with Lao Lao. We don't have that kind of relationship.'

'So this is just what you've picked up over the years?'

'Correct.'

There was quite a lot there, though. Jonny Loong was a typical teenage jerk, the kind you got when there was no father around to exercise a little discipline. May

Loong, Alice's mother, was less inclined to mix with criminal types. Instead, she hung around with the left-overs from the hippie fad that had once taken over the east side of St Kilda. This flirtation with the beautiful people left her briefly in hospital for heroin addiction, busted for softer drugs on a couple of occasions, and, from a passing relationship with someone Alice never knew, owner of a daughter.

Motherhood, it seems, had put May on the straight and narrow – mostly – in the way it sometimes can. She went back to live with Lao Lao, started studying for some kind of college qualification that would one day get her a job as a nurse and looked set to become what, in some quarters, is known as 'a good citizen'.

Alice went quiet.

'And then?' I prompted her.

'She still needed to work to pay for the classes. Jonny came back and said he had a business idea. A bar. Here. He wanted my mom to run it. He wanted lots of pretty women. It was going to be that kind of bar.'

'Meaning?'

'Meaning a bar with pretty women! My mom wasn't a hooker. I *know* that, Bierce.'

'I knew my wife was my wife, and never even thought of looking at another man. I was wrong. Maybe . . .'

'No!' she yelled, so loud that the youth at the next table gasped in horror and stuffed a pair of white plugs – the kind I'd seen on the idiot walking across the road earlier that day – into his ears.

It takes a while to accept ideas like that. For me it had proved easy, in the end. I'd seen Kyle McKendrick now and knew that, while he was an ugly, lying, murderous lump of crime-slime, on that subject he was telling the truth. There'd been no reason not to.

'What happened?' I asked.

She closed her eyes. I thought there was the ghost of tears there.

'There's a bar four doors down. A real bar. I can't do this without a drink. Are you OK with that?'

I didn't touch my beer for fear of what it might do to me. Alice downed half her Bloody Mary, then let the glass rest on the counter. We were the only customers in there. I wasn't surprised. The place smelled of stale smoke, spilled beer and fryer fat. The solitary bartender lurked out back most of the time, switching seventies rock tracks on the hi-fi system: the Doobie Brothers, ZZ Top and some things I only half remembered. It felt like home.

'As far as I can tell,' she began, 'they only ran Sister Dragon for a few months. I went down and looked at the liquor control records. There's not a lot there. The licence was taken out on 13 May 1985. It was revoked on the grounds that the business had gone bankrupt on 29 July.'

'Four days after your mom and my family got killed? They didn't wait long, did they?'

'I asked about that. The licensing people say they revoke licences the moment someone points out a business has gone under.'

I was about to ask a question.

'No. There's no record of who reported that,' she said, anticipating me.

'Who was the licensee? Jonny?'

'My mom.'

Alice caught something in my expression.

'Is that significant?'

'Was Jonny ever convicted of anything?'

'Not that I'm aware of.'

'So he could have been the licensee but preferred not to be. That means the money wasn't his, and he didn't want anyone to see where it really came from. If he made your mom the licensee, it would be one more obstacle to clear if people started to get nosy.'

I think she'd worked this out already.

'My mom had two drug convictions.'

'Then Jonny had important friends. I don't know what the rules are now – maybe a criminal record is a primary requirement to run a bar these days. But back then any conviction that could attract imprisonment ruled you out as a licensee.'

'Fine,' she snapped. 'My mom and my uncle were crooks. I have the message.'

'It's not exactly big time, Alice,' I pointed out. 'There are millions of people out there doing a little cheating on the side.'

'It doesn't matter anyway. What matters is what happened on 25 July. Your family died. My mom died. And my uncle disappeared for good. Dead, I imagine. It's hard to think of anything else.'

I would be lying if I said I wasn't expecting the last part.

'It's taken me five years to piece this much together,' Alice continued. 'Lao Lao never went near the place. I get the impression she hated the idea from the outset, which, if you knew her, meant it basically didn't exist. I couldn't find anything in the papers either.'

'Any stories about a fire? A fight or something?'

'No, Bierce! *I couldn't find anything in the papers about my mom and my uncle*. I know she got killed. I was there, hiding, when it happened. Lao Lao saw her body too. But then these people who called themselves detectives came round. They took my mom away. They cleaned the place up. And after that . . .'

She finished the rest of her Bloody Mary. I waved away the bartender when he came hovering in the hope she'd have another.

'After that?'

'Nothing. Not in the newspapers. Not from the police. Not a word. There was no funeral. No mourning.'

This seemed incredible.

'What about the detectives who came round?'

'We never saw them again. When Lao Lao finally went to the police, they denied it had ever happened. They just said my mom and Jonny were logged under "missing persons". I imagine they still are.'

'I worked in the police department then. No one could have hidden something like that.'

'Dammit, Bierce, they did! In case you haven't got the message yet, my mom and Jonny were born in Hong Kong. They were illegals. A little less than human. It goes without saying, Lao Lao still *is* illegal, at least in her own head. Amnesties and stuff like that don't count with people of her generation. They always think someone might come along in the middle of the night and kick them out. That's why they daren't ask questions.'

She pointed a finger in my direction, as if I was the enemy.

'But not me,' she added. 'I was born here. There's not a thing they can do.'

I was starting to appreciate the enormity of what she was saying.

'They – whoever "they" happen to be – can kill you. I think we both know that much by now.'

'Maybe. But they have some weak points, don't they? When it comes to killing a nice white family, where the man just happens to be a cop, they couldn't cover that up.'

'No,' I agreed. 'They just unloaded it on me.'

'I wasn't taking a pop at you.'

'Thanks. Do you know what time of day they came round to kill your mom?'

She took a deep breath. It occurred to me that Alice Loong had never had this conversation with another human being in her life, which I found deeply interesting.

'I'm pretty sure it was about one-thirty in the afternoon. I used to go to some free kindergarten for immigrant kids so she could work. I was able to check that. It ran from ten in the morning through till eight in the evening weekdays for those who needed it. On Saturdays it closed at noon, so my mom would collect me and we'd be home for the afternoon. I remember being there a lot, so I guess my mom did need it. Lao Lao worked in a Chinese herbal store till five every day. She still does from time to time. So it must have been in the afternoon.'

She glanced at me, a little nervous.

'The court report said police came round to your house after someone – anonymously – reported screaming around seven p.m.'

'That would be correct,' I agreed. 'I was on duty till four. I had paperwork to do. I wouldn't have got home till six or so.'

'What do you remember?'

I took a look at the beer going flat in front of me. A little sip seemed in order.

'The last thing I'm sure of is leaving work. I think I recall parking in the garage. I *think* – though this may just be imagination – I had logged the fact there was a strange car in Owl Creek. Something modern and shiny. Since we were the only house, that would have appeared a little strange. The industrial places nearby had their own lots. But I'm not sure about any of this. The trouble is, when you try so hard to remember things, events appear in your head anyway, and you're not sure what's real and what's not. The next certain thing I have is waking up in hospital surrounded by people I once thought were my friends looking at me as if I were some kind of monster.'

She reached over and put her hand on mine.

'You said that very easily,' Alice observed. 'It's good to talk about it, I guess.'

'It would be if I had more to talk about. You, on the other hand . . .'

I gritted my teeth. We both knew it had to be said.

'The likelihood,' I went on, 'is they came for your mom first, beat something about Miriam out of her, killed her, then came for us. I imagine you worked that out a long time ago.'

'They took three hours killing my mom, Bierce. She didn't give it up easily.'

'I wasn't blaming her. I'm of a disposition where you could beat something out of me with a feather. If I knew what McKendrick and these others were looking for I'd tell them right now, then catch the first flight out of town.'

Alice laughed.

'I'm sure you would.'

'No. Really. It's just that it's not an option. They wanted something out of your mom and beat her until she gave it them. After that they wanted something out of Miriam. And they didn't get it.'

'Your little boy . . .' Her green eyes watched me carefully. 'No mother would keep something inside her and lose her own child.'

I shook my head.

'She didn't have the choice. I went over the autopsy reports time and time again, trying to understand what had happened. It wasn't like your mom. They killed Miriam really quickly. Too quickly, I imagine. I think she was dead before the bastards even got around to offering the option. After that, Ricky was a witness. And I was an easy scapegoat.'

Something flashed in my memory. Something unpleasant I didn't want to think about, let alone face or discuss with Alice Loong.

'It wasn't hard to make it look as if she'd hit me in self-defence. In a crude way, at least. Some of the forensic stank to high heaven, but by the time I realized that I was past caring. What was there left to fight for?'

She was ordering up another drink anyway. This sudden rush of income brought half a smile out on the face of the bartender. I felt a deep, deep thirst coming on me, slaked down the small glass of beer and ordered a big one to follow.

*

When he'd gone, I turned to her and said, 'You need to think really hard, Alice. About what you heard when they came for your mom. I know it hurts, but that's the only contemporary evidence we have.'

She stared at my beer, picked up the glass, then leaned over the counter and poured three-quarters down the sink. The bartender watched in horror, but said nothing, nor did a thing to help a thirsty man.

'I've tried. Really I have. I just remember them going on and on about Sister Dragon.'

'They spoke Chinese?'

'No. Not a word. I thought . . .'

She shook her head. Alice's long hair moved gently around her shoulders. I think she was exhausted too.

'It just sounded to me as if they were asking, "Where is it? Where is it?" I thought they meant where was the place. It couldn't have been that, of course. If they'd come to see my mom, they *knew* where the bar was. So she had something of theirs. Or they thought she had. And I guess she must have told them it was round your house.'

She was still keeping something back.

'How do you know she knew Miriam? You said your grandma told you. Then you said she didn't talk about the bar at all. I don't get it.'

Alice frowned and looked guilty.

'I lied. It happens. Lao Lao's never really told me a thing. But I've lived with her from time to time, when I couldn't afford a room of my own. When she's out I've looked around. Even traditional old Chinese grannies keep photographs. I found some of my mom and Miriam and your boy, at least I assume it's Ricky.

A bright sunny day outside a place that's got a fresh-painted sign. The two of them look as if they own it.'

One more link back to the past. Alice seemed to be a positive well of them.

'Do you still have the photos?'

'They're at Lao Lao's in the little room she keeps for me. She doesn't know I have them. Otherwise she'd go crazy.'

'I would like . . .' I began.

'I know. They're as much yours as they are mine. Maybe more. Bierce, we can't stay drinking in a bar all night long. We have to find somewhere to stay. There are cheap motels. What are we going to do?'

I wondered how far I could push it.

'You're absolutely sure that, whoever these people are, they've no way of tracing you.'

'You bet. Whoever that fake cop is, he thinks my name is Jenny Wong and I live out in a trailer park on the Peyton peninsula. Stupid I am not.'

'I never doubted that for a moment.' I paused, hoping. 'Lao Lao. Will she put us up for the night? I'll sleep on the floor. Wherever. I'd like to see those photos. Maybe if I talk to her . . .'

She was creased with laughter. I'd never seen her like this. Some small, stupid, doubtless doped-up part of me wished I had some decent flowers in my possession.

'You can't call her Lao Lao,' she said when she got her breath back. 'It means "maternal grandmother". I can say that. You can't.'

'So what do I call her?'

'I don't know. I never took a man back there who stayed long enough for me to find out. How about

"Grandma"? If you see knives come flying in your direction, you know it isn't working.'

One last thought struck me in the car, as we drove through deserted streets, past empty clanking trams, down into the tacky scented neon jungle in Eden that was Chinatown.

'I have a question,' I said as we crawled lazily past an empty tram headed for the terminus. 'How did you find me?'

'That beer was a bad idea, Bierce. I told you this already. One of my bargirl friends heard they were looking for someone.'

'No. I meant, how did you find me today? At Sheldon's.'

I must have been looking over-suspicious.

'Oh, that.'

She reached into her bag and took out something using one hand. To me it looked like one of those odd little boxes people of this century stuck into the white cable plugs they liked to stuff in their ears. I was becoming familiar with them now. One day I'd need to find out what they were.

'It's easy. You can buy these tracker gizmos in drug stores. They're invisible unless you know. I stuck one on you when we were down the river, when I realized I didn't like the sneaky look on your face. After that I can track you anywhere. Today. Tomorrow. For the rest of time. You can never escape me now, Bierce. Never.'

I found myself brushing the grubby suit furiously, cursing this creepy modern world in all manner of flowery ways. I couldn't find the damn thing anywhere. I was about to get *very* mad indeed.

Then I noticed she'd started laughing again.

'Great joke,' I barked.

'You had it coming,' she answered with a shrug. 'Besides, I was making a point.'

'Thank you. So how?'

We were in a back street of Chinatown now. One of the places visiting white people wouldn't go too often, not because it was dangerous, but because the local restaurants hereabouts served things – chicken's feet, thousand-year-old eggs – nice white people stayed away from.

'Listen and learn,' she said, parking the car. 'I knew you had to be going to those industrial places because there was nothing else downriver, and scary people up. So I just walked round banging on a few doors, asking if anyone had seen a man who looked like an extra escaped from an episode of *The Rockford Files*. It didn't take long.'

'Oh. Why didn't I think of that?'

'You would have,' she said. 'In the end.'

It was hard to tell how old Alice Loong's Lao Lao truly was. She was a small, rotund woman, with tiny gleaming eyes that shone out of a face the shape of a shrunken melon. Her black hair looked as if it had been copied from Davy Jones of the Monkees. Home was the top of a three-storey apartment block that had a drunken lean on it and some kind of all-night traditional drug emporium, all stinking dried snakes and pots of rhino horn, on the ground floor.

When we arrived she was wearing a dark, old floral dress and, for no good reason I could see, since the place was frankly a little grubby, a bright pink polyester cleaner's apron.

'Very kind of you, Grandma,' I said, extending a hand in which I had one remaining faded rose bloom. 'I – *we* – appreciate it greatly.'

She looked me up and down and said, in a highly accented voice that sounded as if it was being filtered through several packs of hard-core tobacco, 'I not your freakin' grandma, jerk.'

Then, to Alice . . .

'How come all your men are jerks? You can't find no real men out there or wha'?'

One more brutally appraising look flew in my direction.

'This one *old* jerk too. Jeessuss . . .'

I decided the kiss on the cheek and the general chit-chat about the lousy state of the world could maybe come later. I was so tired I could barely keep my eyes open, so I made a few noncommittal noises, then asked to be shown somewhere to sleep.

The room was a shoebox littered with old junk and cases of Chinese books and tiny paintings. There was a rickety double bed and a threadbare rug by the side of it.

Alice followed me in and closed the door.

'Can I see the photos?' I asked, remembering.

'You don't like waiting for anything, do you?'

'I've been waiting twenty-three years.'

She swore mildly, then fetched an envelope from one of the plastic storage boxes.

'In fact,' I said, 'at heart I am a very patient man.'

She kept quiet. That was nice of her.

There were six pictures in all. Miriam and May

Loong were in each, standing outside Sister Dragon, with a fresh-painted sign in the background. Alice's mother had no make-up on and stood there, smiling at the camera, looking beautiful, a plain, easy, elegant beauty that didn't need any artificial help on its way out into the light of day. Miriam was beautiful too, but then I knew that all along. The two of them were wearing the same kind of clothes. Bright, shiny silk cheongsams with colourful flowing serpents embroidered all over them. May Loong's was purple. Miriam's was pure white. The dresses were slashed way up the leg. In a couple of the photos, the two women were making a point of showing off some thigh. Ricky was in one of these, looking a little baffled. I didn't blame him. I'd never seen a piece of clothing like this anywhere in the house. Miriam never bought anything Chinese, not that I knew of. Nor, or so I thought, was she the type to flaunt herself like this, even for some unknown cameraman, who had to be Jonny Loong, I guessed, and that made me feel distinctly uncomfortable.

I sat cross-legged on the rug and stared at the photos for so long I lost track of time. Alice came back in some kind of nightgown and brought me some long, navy-blue cotton pyjamas, a large fluffy towel, a disposable razor and a tiny throwaway toothpaste set. Then, after some prompting, I put down the pictures and she showed me the bathroom, where I did what I was supposed to, before coming back to look at the photos again.

Lao Lao was downstairs listening to Cantonese TV at full volume.

'I'm OK sleeping on the floor,' I said. 'It's good for my back.'

'Bierce,' she said softly from the bed.

'No, Alice. Please. I'm tired and confused and I feel like crap, what with beer and God knows what else running through me. I just want to close my eyes and disappear somewhere.'

Martin the Medic's words came back then, ringing in my ears.

For in that sleep of death what dreams may come?

Kyle McKendrick surely never employed anyone with a passing knowledge of Shakespeare. A part of me understood that already, implicitly. I'd been improvising when I told Alice there were two parties involved in this particular game, but the more I thought about it, the more convinced I became. There was Kyle's side and there was the side where Stape, good old generous Stape, now lived.

Also, there was a third. The cops. Who surely, even in this new world, must have taken an interest in a convicted killer who appeared to have slipped jail illicitly.

I looked up from the floor at Alice, young, damaged Alice, whose position on most things seemed to be set in sands that shifted beneath her constantly, in ways she couldn't comprehend.

I wondered which of the three, if any, she worked for.

'For pity's sake,' she said to me crossly. 'This is not last night. I know I don't need to go there again. But we need a good night's sleep. Who the hell knows what we have to deal with tomorrow?'

'Bierce?' she whispered again after a while.

'Oh, lord,' I moaned. 'What was that you said about sleeping?'

'I just want someone to hold me, that's all. I don't see anyone else around.'

'That's flattering.'

I put one arm around her and left it at that. She moved her head closer to me. That was all. We lay there chastely, because it really wasn't about anything else. I can say that in all honesty. Alice Loong, twenty-six, tough, but not as tough as she thought, wanted some simple physical comfort.

Her hair had the wonderful fresh smell a woman's hair has, something I'd completely forgotten. After a while I could sense something else that had submerged in my memory too: the dampness leaking from her eyes on to my neck.

She wriggled into my chest more closely. I shut my eyes tight and tried to think of what the night was like in Gwinett; the howls down the corridor, the rattle of plates on bars, the sound of men getting beaten up.

'Bierce,' she whispered again, so close into me I found it very difficult to stop my arms curling round her slender, tense shoulders, hugging her tightly.

Somehow – I swear I have no idea how this occurred – the ancient springs of the bed creaked.

In an instant, Lao Lao was hammering on the door with her tight little fist, yelling, 'No making out in there. *No making out, you hear?*'

We lay there, unable to speak, giggling like two schoolkids caught necking on the veranda.

Then, unable to stop myself, I kissed Alice Loong on the forehead, just once, for no more than one and three-eighths of a second, or possibly less.

She was as surprised as me, I think. Not that she protested.

Her skin tasted sweet and soft against my lips. The one small act, and the way she didn't flinch from it, made me feel as if someone had dragged me out of the grave and breathed new life back into my old, tired lungs. Which maybe wasn't far from the truth.

My head swelled with a mix of competing emotions: guilt and pride, certainty and confusion, hope and, behind it, always, the distant siren wail of the onset of despair.

It couldn't stay like this. I knew it. Nothing could be this simple.

THURSDAY

When I woke the sunlight was streaming in through the windows, a little too yellow and faded for my liking, the kind of sun you got at the dying of the day, not its birth. Turtle doves were cooing noisily on the roof. Outside, the racket of the traffic had an afternoon cadence to it, the kind of slow-burn anger people got on the way home.

I looked at the clock by the side of the bed. It was four p.m. and I was alone. Drenched in dope, and just a touch of alcohol, I must have slept for the best part of seventeen hours.

I was still in my fresh cotton pyjamas, for which I was grateful. From downstairs came the loud bark of the TV, an English channel, one which, to my dismay, appeared to be mentioning my name.

Oh, I thought, and walked down the rickety stairs.

The two of them sat in front of the little TV, which was perched on some silver box I failed to recognize. Alice looked horrified. Lao Lao clucked like an old, incomprehensible hen.

The newscast was coming to an end.

'Did I hear that right?' I asked.

Lao Lao threw me a dirty look, picked up a remote control and, to my astonishment, wound back a live TV programme just as if it was on tape.

'How the hell did you do that?' I asked, amazed.

She shook her head in disgust.

In a couple of seconds she'd reached the start of the bulletin. It was the local station. Their lead story was about the execution that morning of a former city police officer who'd been on death row for nearly twenty-three years.

My lawyer ever since, the lovely Susanna Aurelio, was there on camera, live from outside some place I had never heard of, 'the McKendrick County Correctional Facility', tears in her eyes, shaking her head, saying something about how cruel and unnecessary capital punishment truly was.

'But Officer Bierce killed his wife and five-year-old son,' the interviewer objected. 'Doesn't a man like that *deserve* to die?'

Susanna dabbed at her face with a tissue. She looked as if she'd come straight from the opera: all silk and pearls and on-cue sobbing.

'Many may believe so, Bruce. But I watched that man go to his death today. I listened to the confession he finally made, and the true and heartfelt remorse he showed at the very end. Had you witnessed those final moments . . .'

'Sure,' the interviewer interrupted with a sneer. 'And there we must leave it. Now, on A1A this morning . . .'

Lao Lao picked up another remote – she seemed to be collecting them – and hit the off button.

'This some kind of record,' she said, looking at me

and shaking her head. 'Not only new guy a jerk who's an old jerk. Now he's *dead* old jerk too.'

Being beyond the realm of the living isn't all bad news. For one thing I knew the cops – the *real* cops, like the Tic Twins and my blond-haired friend from the grocery store – definitely wouldn't be scouring the streets, trying to hunt me down. The only people I had to worry about now were the ones I thought of as McKendrick's people and Stape's. The former were, it seemed pretty clear to me, murderous. The latter had, unless I was much mistaken, freed me from jail illegally in the hope either of jogging my memory about the events of twenty-three years ago or pinning some new crime to my chest.

It didn't seem entirely impossible that I could, with no support except that of Alice – for what it might turn out to be worth – no information or intelligence, real weapons or other firepower, defeat the two of them. I could blow the twenty thousand in my possession on an Uzi or some such toy and try to do a kind of real-life Clint Eastwood impersonation. But it didn't seem right. It wasn't me. What's more, I was beginning to think I was getting a feel for this new century. People weren't that different really. They were just a little more miserable and fearful. And they relied on inanimate objects and nebulous procedures to tell them how to act. When I was a cop and heard someone had done some bad thing, it was easy. All I did was ride round to their home, knock on the door, stare them in the face and ask, straight out loud . . . *Well?*

I'd talked this through with Alice already. What she said confirmed my initial impressions. In this world the first thing anyone did before tackling *anything* was turn on the computer, hunt around for the right instructions, then try to follow them to the letter. Don't think, just do as you're supposed to. As your peers expect. That, to me, seemed to be motto of the century, and if I was in luck, then perhaps it left a little space into which a caveman could throw the odd spanner. Predictable people have predictable weaknesses, if you can find them.

There was one other excellent piece of news, too. When Alice told me she thought no one had any idea who she was, it seemed clear she'd been right. Had Stape or McKendrick possessed the merest hint of Lao Lao's address, they'd have been round while I was sleeping, all guns and noise, with badness to follow. Even the postman hadn't come to call, as Lao Lao mentioned several times in her long litany of moans to her granddaughter, spelled out so loud I could hear them from every room of the apartment.

The truth was this. In Grandma Loong's cramped third-floor apartment, breathing in the smell of dead lizard and God knows what else from the pharmaceutical store below, we were, for the time being, safe.

Or, perhaps, where Alice, and anyone behind her, wanted us to be. I had racked my brain trying to work out whether I trusted her or not. The plain answer was: not. Every piece of her story had leaked out so slowly, requiring such careful extraction, I just knew there had to be more. But was this simple reticence on her part, with some good reason I couldn't guess? Or was there a bigger secret in Alice's life? I couldn't get away from the fact that she was in my house in Owl Creek that night, looking at home, and ready for anything, just a few hours after they let me out of Gwinett. Or more accurately, the McKendrick County Correctional Facility, whatever and wherever that was.

My old dad always said it wasn't worth worrying about problems you couldn't solve. He was right. I should have listened to him more. Over the past three days I'd been shot at, mock-executed and now declared officially dead on public TV. A man becomes sanguine about such things after a while. Alice had saved me from the needle of Dr Rimless. She'd done her best to get me away from the men I assumed to be McKendrick's in Owl Creek too. Whatever other secrets lay inside her smart young head, I didn't want to leave her and miserable old Lao Lao exposed when the smoke cleared.

And that would still require some work.

They watched me slink off to the bedroom, ostensibly to think, after I watched the newscast one more time through Lao Lao's magic silver box. While I was sleeping Alice had gone out and bought me some clothes: cotton pants, a couple of shirts, all the other practical stuff a woman would think about, knowing it would pass me by completely. I dressed, looked at myself in the mirror, and was surprised by what I saw: a middle-aged man, not fat, not thin, not remarkable in any way, dressed in the kind of clothes that seemed to go down well in the twenty-first century. I was anonymous, which was, as Alice, smart, lovely Alice, had quickly realized, definitely look of the month for me.

After a while I went downstairs and joined her. It was now gone six in the evening. A wonderful smell of Chinese food was coming from the minuscule kitchen squeezed next to the bathroom. Lao Lao was working away in there with a wok. Eventually she came over with two plates of noodles and meat and vegetables, dumped them in front of us and said, 'Even dead people gotta eat. I work downstairs for a while now. Old Fred need me.'

I tried the food and, for a moment, couldn't say a word. It contained all the flavours and colours that had been methodically removed from everything that ever went on a plate in jail. I wanted to put it in a box and carry it around, ready to sniff when I started to feel sorry for myself again. For a moment, I thought this new century couldn't be all bad.

When I got my voice back, I said, 'People. She called me "people". Not jerk. I'm coming up in the world.'

Alice shook her head. She'd gone out and got her hair cut that afternoon, the way women did at such idle, uneventful points in their lives.

Or – and I hated myself for this suspicious, conniving thought – when you'd fixed some secretive meeting with the boss.

'She's not so bad. She kept me alive when no one else was interested.'

'How the hell could that have happened? You're smart. You're beautiful.'

'Bierce . . .'

'No. I mean it.'

This had to be asked. She was in a fresh white cotton shirt and pale fawn slacks. Almost business gear. Looking at her, she could have been a tour guide or an office receptionist. Talking to her, you might have upped that to some kind of postgrad student still working her way through college. Her hair was so clean and shiny, and her face, long and intriguing, in an imperfect, half-Chinese way, was definitely the most interesting I'd seen in a long time. Something had happened to Alice Loong and I needed to know what it was.

'Where did your dad come from?' I asked.

'A boat.'

The hard stare told me that wasn't going any further. I pointed to the small scar above her left eye.

'And that?'

'That what?'

'The scar.'

'Oh. The scar. Fight. A man, naturally. I wouldn't lower myself to fighting other women.'

I waited for more. When she saw I wasn't leaving the subject she went upstairs to the bedroom and came back down with another photograph. This one was more recent. I turned it over and it even had the date printed on the back: five years ago, almost to the day. It was just a kid by the beach, near the larger Greenpoint marina, I think. The ocean was a lovely shade of blue. The same colour as her hair, though I wouldn't have said that was lovely. This was Alice Loong too, I realized. A different Alice, though perhaps one who still lived inside the same skin somewhere.

She was as thin as a rake, bones sticking out from inside a ragged T-shirt and torn jeans. There was hardware everywhere: in her eyebrows, her ears, her nose. Worst of all, she was staring at the camera wearing an expression of intense hatred. For herself, naturally. It couldn't have been anything else.

I put the photo face down on the table.

'The past is done with. I'm surprised you didn't come out of that period with more tattoos.'

'Hated needles,' she said. 'I just got the one.'

'I know,' I pointed out.

'Oh.'

I guess she'd forgotten how she'd briefly stood naked in the old bedroom in Owl Creek that first night. It seemed a long time to me too.

'So what changed?'

'I got older. Got sick of waking up feeling ill and cold and poor. The poor part hasn't changed much. But at least I can function, even if it's only working behind a bar in a miniskirt.'

'You've done a little more than that of late.'

She grinned and scooped up some noodles with her chopsticks, in that expert way some people have. Lao Lao had thoughtfully provided me with a fork and spoon.

'Yes, Bierce, I have. It was my grandma too. She got to me in the end. I think she knew she always would. It didn't matter how bad things were. How lousy the company. How stupid, selfish and offensive the behaviour. She always came along to pick me up from the hospital, bail me out, whatever.'

'She's your family now. And you're hers. She doesn't have a choice.'

'But she does! That's the point. She could have abandoned me.'

There was a flicker of anger in those green eyes.

'You did.'

'No,' I said carefully. 'I left you behind. I thought it was in your best interests.'

'Do you think that now?'

'I don't know,' I answered honestly. 'I'm not sure there's a choice. You need to understand what happened to your mom. Just as I need to find out what the hell went wrong between Miriam and me.'

'Thank you.'

'You're welcome. Besides, if this doesn't work out, I know I'll be walking down some street in Chinatown five years hence and you'll be standing across the road, slumped up against the wall, with blue hair and iron-work in your face again. That I could not stand.'

She nodded.

'I'll try my best. What do we do now?'

The big question.

'I would,' I confessed, 'really love to spend some quality time with my old friend Stapleton. The guy who roped you into all this. I don't imagine he left a phone number or address or something.'

She shook her head.

'How were you going to get paid the rest of your money?'

'He said he'd drop it round the bar where my friends worked. It was all cash. I was supposed to trust him.'

All these answers came so glibly. I wish she could have hesitated, just a little.

'And you talked to him at the bar? Nowhere else?'

'That's right. He didn't feel like a cop. I think my antennae are pretty good on that front. It comes from growing up around here. He didn't feel like a cop at all.'

We'd stopped working as partners some eighteen months before Miriam and Ricky were killed. He'd disappeared from the police department after that. I assumed this was because he'd moved to another precinct, or perhaps joined one of the fast-car and Ray-Ban squadrons people kept putting together trying to tackle organized crime. A certain type of cop couldn't watch enough *Miami Vice* episodes around then.

'OK. I'll have to find him some other way. But we do need to speak to someone. This isn't going to unravel from us sitting around talking or punching computer keyboards.'

'Who?' she asked, shrugging.

There was, I knew, only one answer.

'I think,' I said, 'it's time I saw my lawyer.'

The last time I saw Pelican Bay it was a small, protected cove that sat between the southern end of the Greenpoint rich persons' neighbourhood and the ragged, unspoilt coastline that ran down to the De Soto bridge. We used to take Ricky there to play and watch the birds and seals. I believe it may be where his penguin obsession started. There was one parking lot, restricted to no more than a hundred and fifty vehicles, a warden's lodge where you could pick up free brochures that described the wildlife, and a single coffee and ice-cream stall, open summer weekends only.

Susanna Aurelio lived here with husband number five, in something called Ocean Vista Gardens. It was getting dark by the time Alice drove the Volvo down the hill, on a brand-new private highway, towards the shoreline. I could see from the twinkling zigzags below that things had changed somewhat. There were hundreds of them: street lights and home illumination, all in that irregular pattern that spoke of money. When they build for the poor and the lower-income classes streets run in straight lines, homes look much like one another. The affluent need to convince themselves they're different from the rest. Even their equally rich neighbours. So I'd no idea where to begin, or where the address we'd found for Susanna, from some law directory Alice had picked up through her computer, was located.

'Swing by the beach first, will you?' I asked. 'I haven't walked on sand in a while.'

'How romantic. Unfortunately that won't be possible. This is private now. I told you.'

She pointed up ahead. We were approaching a large, half-circle iron gatehouse with what looked like a prison warden's cabin by the side of it. There were camera lenses poking in every direction, naturally, and a man in a dark uniform already eyeing us, beginning to get out of his booth. Beyond the rungs I could see wisps of moonlight running across the dark ocean waves and the sheen of the long, flat, perfect sand we used to sit on, breathing in the salt sea smell.

'What the hell is this?' I demanded, feeling more than a little angry.

'It's called a gated community. This is how rich people live today. Actually, it's how anyone with any money lives, if they can afford it.'

'Behind bars, you mean?'

'That pretty much sums it up.'

'The beach. I want to walk on the beach.'

'Well, you can't. That's part of the community. They own it.'

No one can own a beach, I thought. That was just obscene.

I'd imagined I would just walk down Susanna's street, check the house names – hers was called Bellagio – ring the bell and wait for the maid to answer. Some hope. The guy in the uniform was out walking towards us already. He had a truncheon. And a handgun. If I squinted hard I could have mistaken him for a cop, which was, I guess, the point.

'This is private security, right?'

She nodded.

'They get to walk around with weapons wherever they feel like?'

'They get whatever they want. It's just ordinary people who don't get guns. The rich want protection.'

'Don't we all?' I asked idly. 'No. That was rhetorical. No need to answer. I'll handle this. It's best no one saw you. Go drive around. Take in a movie or something. I'll call when I'm done.'

She smiled at me in that slightly condescending way I was beginning to recognize.

'How exactly?'

'Er . . .'

Alice reached into her bag and pulled out a little plastic gadget which I took to be some kind of phone. A ladies' model, since it was that same horrendous shade of pink as the one I saw her use earlier, only somewhat bigger.

'Put that in your pocket,' she ordered. 'If I don't hear in two hours, I'll call. If you need me, just hold down the 1 button till it rings out. It'll call me.'

I said thanks or something and got out quickly. The fake cop was getting near and I really didn't want him to see Alice for a moment. She was gone, not too quickly, not too slowly either.

I stood there, smiled at him and said, 'I'm hoping to see Susanna Aurelio, sir. Would you happen to know if she's at home?'

He was a surly-looking sort in his mid-twenties, clearly pleased to get both uniform and a gun all in the same job. He had the same build as McKendrick's heavy: fat running to muscle.

'She expecting you?'

'Absolutely not. This is a surprise visit. I'm a cousin from out east. We were at school together. Haven't seen each other in five years. My flight got overbooked while I was passing through. So I thought . . .'

I smiled, which was a waste of effort.

'Is her husband at home too?' I asked.

He turned back to the gatehouse, expecting me to follow him I guess.

'You can call her on the video phone,' he said, not answering my question. 'If she says you're in, you're in. If she doesn't know you from Adam, you and me are going to have an interesting conversation.'

Susanna came into view, looking as preciously gorgeous as ever. The light came on and lit up my face.

I yelled, 'Surprise!'

She started screaming.

The security guy gave me a cold, hard stare.

'I told you this would be a hoot,' I said, smiling.

It took a couple of minutes. I had to say a few things to convince her I wasn't a ghost. Though quite why a ghost would want to use a video phone . . .

Finally, the gate buzzed. He pushed it open for me. I walked into Ocean Vista Gardens and followed his directions for Bellagio.

It was nice in there. Leafy and smelling of oleander and pool ozone drifting up from the shining blue rectangular mirrors I could see floating around in the back gardens of the vast low villas, each with yet another iron gate in front, that someone had built on my one-time pelican-viewing station.

Mr Security was phoning someone from inside the booth. I couldn't miss that fact.

She greeted me at the door, looking as if she'd dressed for the occasion: long silk blue evening dress, low-cut, tight around her still-perfect figure, and a double pearl necklace around her swan-like, unwrinkled throat. I first knew Susanna Aurelio when she was a twenty-one-year-old law student hanging around the city courts, looking for some attorney, any attorney, to 'take her under their wing'.

She was beautiful then, with gentle, innocent, 'who, me?' movie-star looks, short, glossy red hair that bordered on chestnut, perfect white skin, bright, seemingly sensitive eyes that always made you feel you were the only person that mattered in the world. She also possessed a mind so sharp you could open evidence packets with it. Which happened, from time to time, since the wings the lovely Susanna got taken under were many and varied. The police department gossip was that she had the scalps of judges, fellow attorneys, city and state politicians, plus a couple of movie stars and well-known rock guitarists hanging from her bed head by the time she was twenty-five.

Not mine, I hasten to add, though she had tried. This occasion did give me an insight into the Aurelio love technique. I got lured back to her little bachelor-girl apartment on a work pretence. It had all, or mostly, been about me giving her an illicit look at some evidence due to be introduced into court about a young teenage kid she was representing on a dope charge. I let her see it anyway. The kid was innocent and, I suspected, getting fitted up by someone in narcotics because they didn't like his face and background, neither of which came with the word 'white' stamped upon them. She didn't need me in her bed to get that and I told her so, and couldn't work out whether she was happy or deeply offended that she'd finally found a man who turned her down.

Not that I cared. That was Susanna all over. Lots of the cases she took on were good, principled *pro bono* stuff, often on behalf of poor, underprivileged people who may well have been innocent. That didn't stop her pulling every last underhand trick she could imagine in order to get her way. The perfect case for Susanna – the young Susanna anyway – involved social injustice and a pile of suspect evidence that could miraculously be made to go away by some smart wheeler-dealing in the judge's rooms and the simple and judicious application of copious quantities of sex, exploits that were, on occasion, capable of being performed simultaneously.

On pillars such as these are legal careers made.

'Oh, Bierce,' she whispered, covering my face and neck with kisses. 'What the hell's happened here? Come in, come in . . .'

The house could have been described as a 'mansion', but only if it had been made a little smaller. There were two circular staircases winding up on each side of a massive entrance hall, and rooms going off in all directions, doors open so you could see into each.

The floor was shining Mediterranean terracotta or something. Paintings and masks and bits of porcelain hung on the walls. Lots of little tables, all in very dark, almost black wood, stood around, bearing vases full of vast bouquets of roses and lilies. At the end was a long internal window that let visitors see across the grown-up amusement park outside – pool, tennis court, statuary and the rest – straight down to the beach. *My* beach, once upon a time.

I did not feel at home.

'Where's your husband, Susanna?' I asked.

'Out on some Caribbean cruise banging his junior partner,' she said. Her hair had lost none of its fire, maybe through a little cheating. It still hung around her head loose to her slender neck. In truth, as I stared at that oh-so-innocent face I was amazed to realize she'd hardly changed in all the time I knew her, apart, that is, from the ever more expensive wardrobe. 'It's just fine by me. I sent the servants out for the night too when I saw it was you. Seemed best.'

'Dead people don't need servants.'

She was gazing into my eyes with so much love and affection I felt a little queasy.

'Oh, baby,' she moaned, soft hands back on my cheeks again. 'I dreamed of getting you out of that horrible, stinking place all those years. And I never did. And now you're here. What the hell happened, Bierce? Here . . .'

She took my arm and led me through to some kind of living room. There was a tiger print sofa that could have slept a family of six and a flat, thin TV the size of a private cinema screen.

'A drink,' she said.

'I'm fine.'

'Who's talking about you?'

'Maybe a beer.'

She went in the kitchen and came back with two glasses. Mine contained something fancy and foreign.

Hers smelled of vodka which had made the passing acquaintance of a thimble of tonic along the way.

I toasted her. She pulled me to the sofa and sat down in the next cushion, very close.

'*Salute*,' she murmured. 'I never said that to a ghost before.'

'You still haven't. It's me, Susanna. Really.'

'I have *eyes*,' she said in the low yet very distinct voice she had.

'And yet . . . I have to ask.' This was a difficult and unusual question to phrase.

'Ask away.'

'I caught up with the TV this afternoon. You seeing me dead and all.'

Susanna Aurelio took a large sip, put her drink on the table and looked at me.

This was more than a little unnerving, because I felt it was the same look I'd had all those years ago, in her tiny Eden apartment, when she was starting out, hunting for sneak peeks of evidence the easiest way she knew.

'Oh,' she said, almost forgetfully. '*That*.'

'First things first,' I began. 'When I saw you on TV you were standing outside something called the McKendrick County Correctional Facility. Where the hell is that and what does it have to do with me?'

'Are you kidding? McKendrick is where you've been these last eighteen months.'

A little bubble burst in my mind. It was utterly empty.

'I think I would have known that, Susanna.'

'They moved you there from Gwinett. They heard someone was going to kill you. They didn't like cops in jail, I guess.'

No, no, no, screamed some small voice inside my head.

'I went into solitary in Gwinett years ago,' I insisted. 'I stayed there, all the way into the execution wing. No one was going to kill me. They'd have been robbing the state of that privilege, and the state wouldn't have liked that.'

She shrugged.

'I'm a lawyer. Not a penal expert. That's what they said. You didn't object.'

'I didn't know! For God's sake . . .'

The words wouldn't come quite right. She waited for me to calm down.

'They had you sedated in Gwinett. It was for your own good. I went along with that, Bierce. You were terribly distraught, for years. People feared for your sanity.'

'I was an innocent man in jail for murdering my own wife and kid, and about to die for it. What do you expect of a morning? A rousing chorus from *Oklahoma?*'

Her eyes went watery. She stared at her drink. In spite of everything, I felt like a jerk.

'I'm sorry,' I said. It was hard to believe Susanna was pushing fifty. She had the appearance of someone fifteen years younger. But it was more than that. She had the mannerisms and the easy charm to match too. 'It's been a hard couple of days.'

She sighed and placed her hands in my lap. A cloud of something expensive filled the air.

'What do you think it's been like for me? I know you didn't kill them. I couldn't convince anyone. You didn't help. Not with your high and mighty, "If I can't remember, I *can't* remember" act. All the same, I always thought I'd get you out of there in the end.'

There were so many avenues available for further exploration in that conversation. I just leaned forward, took another mouthful of foreign beer and said, 'I know you did. And I appreciate everything. Now tell me why you think you saw me die this morning, please. Because for the life of me – if you'll excuse the expression – I swear I missed it.'

The story was this. At eleven the previous night she'd been called at home by the correction facility's legal representative, who'd told her that every last avenue of appeal had been exhausted and I was, without a shadow of doubt, going under the death needle at eight the following morning. This was, of course, some twenty-odd hours after I'd actually been driven out of the place, not that I was going to complicate matters for my faithful, gorgeous attorney at this stage.

Susanna had, naturally, spent most of the night phoning around every last judge and contact she knew – something that had happened a dozen times before, and ended in stays of execution for an ever-diminishing and more inexplicable array of legal niceties. This time round no one was playing. Dead meant dead, and there wasn't a single string she could pull, not one last remaining past lover she could twist around her slender fingers.

So at seven in the morning she'd driven out to Kyle McKendrick's private penitentiary-cum-murder farm, hoping there might be some last stunt she could try on the spot, such as a plea of insanity or – this seemed so bizarre I could only believe her – by claiming I was suffering from some physical ailment that made it improper for me to be executed until I got better. She was always a resourceful woman. The way she told it, I began to believe she felt some genuine remorse at my impending end, though how much was grief and how much fury at losing a case was hard to tell.

She stopped. Her drink was empty. She went to the kitchen and came back with fresh ones for both of us. I accepted, on the grounds it was mine by right; it's not every day a man hears a description of his own death.

'And then?' I prodded her.

'I blew a tyre on the freeway. Would you believe it? That thing cost more than a quarter of a million. Supposedly the best six-litre sports coupé to come out of Italy. Then that.'

'You were late for my execution, Susanna? How could you?'

'I tried and I tried. Hell, Bierce, they shouldn't have gone ahead with the execution without me there.'

'Maybe they thought you were trying to stall them.'

She patted my knees and gave me a brisk, business-like peck on the cheek.

'You bright, bright baby. That's exactly what that bastard Johansson said to me when I finally got there. Smug as hell with that "You're too late for this one, bitch" look on his ugly face.'

'Johansson?'

'He was the governor. You met him. I promise you met him. He was there when I came to see you. Eleven months ago, I think it was.'

'In this McKendrick place?'

'Yes! We had to talk. About the money. A couple of decades of representation now. It doesn't come cheap.'

I shook my head.

'I don't remember any of this.'

'It happened,' she insisted. 'You signed the papers. They were witnessed.'

'What papers? No. *No*. Later. I saw you on the TV, Susanna. You stood there telling them how I went out all brave and that.'

She nodded.

'I did.'

'You went in front of the camera and made all that up?' I asked, and tried not to let my voice squeak too much.

'What the hell did you expect me to say?' she snapped. 'I missed my own client's execution because I got a flat on the way? Be realistic, Bierce. As far as I knew you were dead. I have a career.'

This was, I now recalled, the real Susanna.

'But you didn't ask to see a body?'

She looked at me as if I were stupid.

'Why the hell would I want to see a dead body? I'm a lawyer. I represent people who are still breathing. You think I'm some ambulance-chasing ghoul trying to squeeze money out of a corpse or something?'

She looked around the room.

'Does this look like what ghoul work gets you?'

She had her standards, you see. They just weren't those of normal, civilized human beings.

'You said,' I pointed out, 'that I felt remorse.'

She put down her drink at that, took my hands in hers and stared deep into my eyes.

'Bierce,' she murmured, working on the huskiness so that I got sexy on top of sincerity. 'I know you didn't murder Miriam and your boy. But the world out there made up its mind on that subject years ago, and you didn't win. I agonized over what I was supposed to tell those TV people. That you went screaming your innocence all the way into the killing room? No. I wouldn't have been doing you any justice that way. What I said, I said out of respect for you. If people thought you showed remorse at the end, then some of them would think, well, maybe he wasn't all bad. If I said you just kept screaming "not guilty", they'd put you down for an asshole. Which would you prefer?'

'The truth,' I said straight away.

She laughed, then went back to the drink again.

'The truth being what?' my beautiful lawyer asked, dispatching a whiff of raw, expensive vodka in my direction.

She had a point. I wanted to punch holes in her story. It deserved that kind of treatment. But for the life of me I couldn't work out how.

'Your turn,' she said.

I told her, as much as I wanted, and watched her eyes widen all the while.

The funny thing was that, when I was done, she didn't ask a single question. That was left to me.

'The man I saw on the way out of Gwinett . . . I mean McKendrick, or wherever it was. His name was Stapleton. Do you know him?'

'Stapleton, Stapleton, Stapleton . . . Do you want a sandwich or something? Damn, I shouldn't have sent those servants away.'

'Stapleton. Also known as Stape. He was a detective alongside me for a while. Then he went somewhere else. The secret people, maybe.'

She shook her head.

'It may ring a bell. I don't know. You say he put some money into your bank account?'

'Just a little. Four hundred and sixty thousand. It ought to be there now.'

'I can check if you want,' she said, as if this was the easiest thing in the world.

'How the hell can you check my bank account?'

She actually looked sorry for me at that moment.

'Oh, my. They really did pump you full of stuff in there, didn't they? I've had power of attorney over all your accounts, all your assets, for a long, long time. I can look up your account online. To all intents and purposes, I own Owl Creek. It's held in escrow against your legal bills. Why else do you think the mortgage people didn't foreclose? They'd have been coming up against me if they did.'

'My house?'

'We discussed this. That last time I saw you in McKendrick. You signed the papers.'

'I signed away my house?'

'Don't worry, Bierce. I'm not taking anything away from you. I couldn't be that cruel. You're alive. That's what counts.'

'My *house* . . .' I said again.

'Let's find out about this money first,' she interrupted. 'Then I can look up some private places you might find this Stapleton individual. Would you like that?'

I answered, truthfully, that I'd like that very much indeed.

'In that case, you've got to come upstairs. I work in my bedroom. It's the one place I can guarantee my asshole husband will never disturb me.'

*

I could have fitted most of the ground floor of Owl Creek into Susanna Aurelio's bedroom and left space for a Jacuzzi or three. The place had a huge bed, with its slate sheets, opened up, ready for use. A couple of sofas. A grand fireplace with what looked like a fake Adam but real marble surround, and above it the statutory painting of the owner, looking gorgeous and, naturally, naked. Then a small kitchen off, and a door that led to a bathroom that appeared to be stocked with porcelain and shiny marble fittings that could have been stolen from an Arab prince's palace.

I got a good view of the veranda too. I walked up and opened the doors. There was a terrace with several tables, more chairs, a large telescope on a pedestal, then a gentle line of steps down to the garden, the pool, lit by underwater lights, and, at the end, the silver ribbon of beach and the sea, moving with a solitary grace under the moonlight.

'This is what I call the mistress bedroom,' Susanna announced with no small measure of pride.

'You mean the master's is smaller?'

'Just. And pretty soon I'm going to own that too. When Frank gets back from the islands I serve papers. After which . . .'

She came and stood by me, slipping the palm of her hand into the small of my back for one brief moment.

'. . . I am available.'

'Quite,' I said, and moved away. 'Now about this guy Stapleton.'

Susanna's face fell and, just for a second or two, she looked her age. A woman like her wasn't used to getting knocked back and I'd done it twice. She walked over to the long, gleaming desk just a little way from the bed and flicked a switch on the stretched-aluminium box there, pulling up the lid to reveal a screen.

She pushed a button on the keyboard and the panel became alive. It was covered in photos, mostly of Susanna. At the podium, speaking. On TV. Handing out prizes of some kind. It was all a long way from that little apartment where she'd tried to seduce me for a packet of papers from the prosecution files.

'First name?' she asked.

'Radley,' I said. 'Or maybe it was Ridley. It was a long time ago.'

'Never mind. Neither's common. Which is good.'

She typed something, very quickly.

'I have a Radley Stapleton who's a wireless op in the navy. Oh. No good. He's serving abroad.'

'You what?' I asked.

'Bear with me, Bierce. I'm not done yet.'

She typed again.

'Correction. I am. I can't find a single Ridley Stapleton in Google. Which means he doesn't exist.'

'Google? This is this special place you mentioned?'

'No. But generally speaking the special place just has a little more of what Google has. I can try.'

I watched her, feeling like a Neanderthal who'd just walked in on Einstein.

'Nothing,' she said after tapping a few more keys.

'So where does that leave me?' I sighed.

'You said he promised you money?'

It was instructive, I thought, that Susanna's mind, in these circumstances, turned not to the fact that a convicted killer, apparently out of jail illegally, was now standing in her bedroom, but instead to hard lucre.

'He gave me twenty thousand cash. He said there'd

be another four hundred and sixty thousand in my bank account this morning.'

'Let's see . . .'

'But . . . ?'

I wanted to scream. This was my bank account. Well, *our* bank account, since Miriam and I did everything jointly, had done ever since we got married.

Susanna Aurelio sat there, let her fingers fly across the keyboard, and shot up the whole thing on to the screen of the machine in her grandiose bedroom in just a second or two.

'No,' she said, pointing at the paltry figure there. 'You have less than three hundred in the account. It's been like that for twenty-three years. If there'd been anything more I could have got you into something interest-bearing . . .'

'W-w-wait a minute! We had more than eighty thousand saved when I went into jail. I put some by every month. For Ricky's college fund. For the future. It was hard. Miriam used to give me a tough time for putting all that aside.'

She wheeled round the leather chair in which she sat and eyed me seriously.

'Do we really want to talk about this?'

'Yes! Where the hell's my money?'

'OK,' she answered, shrugging her bare shoulders.

She tugged on the pearl necklace for a moment, then started hammering the keys again.

'They don't have statements from the eighties online. But I'm your attorney. I digitized everything to do with your case. To do with you. Standard practice with everyone. Here . . .'

Something else popped up. It looked like a paper

bank statement, the kind I recognized from when the world was real.

Except this one could not be true.

It showed a cash withdrawal of eighty thousand, dated Wednesday, 24 July 1985. Just about every last cent we owned had been withdrawn from our joint bank account the day before Miriam and Ricky got killed.

'This is not possible,' I said, shaking my head. 'That kind of thing can't happen without my knowing. Why didn't anyone tell me? Why the hell didn't you say something?'

'Because I was trying to keep you alive, Bierce!' she snarled. 'That's what attorneys are for.'

I was quiet. Susanna didn't lose her temper without reason.

More buttons got slapped around on the keyboard. Another piece of paper appeared on the screen.

I stared at it and, not for the first time, wondered if this was all really just one long dream, a bunch of illusions filtering through my mind in the brief moment between Martin the Medic putting in that last needle and the long, dark, empty place rising up to claim what it was owed.

There was no way of knowing. Right then, I wouldn't have minded either way.

What was on screen were two cheques. The first moved eighty thousand in cash from our joint account into the private one I'd held from my single days. It was signed by both of us, as it would have to be, since sums of this nature required mutual agreement. The second appeared to move this selfsame money, our life savings, on to some account I'd never even heard of.

'This is a fake,' I said. 'I never signed either of these.

Also, that doesn't look like Miriam's signature. Not if I recall right.'

Susanna nodded.

'I have handwriting analysis on it. They said there's a 90 per cent possibility your signature is genuine. Just 10 per cent on hers.'

'This is ridiculous. What the hell would I do with all that money?'

'I can tell you that too. You tried to transfer it abroad. The second cheque only needed your signature of course.'

She pulled up a letter from a bank in Liechtenstein, one that had some sort of mythical bird with spiky wings and a dragon's head at the top.

'It never got there. They froze your money trans-actions the Monday after the murders. Then they seized it for costs.'

'Where the hell is Liechtenstein? *What* is Liechtenstein?'

'It's a small principality in Europe. Between Switzer-land and Austria. Back in the eighties, some people used it for laundering cash they didn't want anyone else to see.'

I put my finger right on the screen. She looked at it until I took it away again. This was apparently bad manners.

'I did not take money out of our joint account. I did not try to move it to some country I've never even heard of. This is someone else trying to forge my signa-ture, Susanna. You know that.'

She nodded.

'I would have tried to argue that if I'd needed it. Handwriting analysis isn't foolproof.'

'So why the hell didn't you?'

'Christ, Bierce! Stop making me repeat myself. I was trying to keep you alive, and God knows, with what they had against you, that was hard enough. Did you really expect me to introduce into court something that suggested you'd raided the family bank account and moved all that cash abroad one day before they died? Think about it.'

I did, and she was absolutely right.

'I was trying to paint you as a good and responsible husband and father,' she went on. 'Putting stuff like this in front of a jury just places more doubts into their heads, and there were plenty there already. Besides, even if they believed me, that these signatures were fakes, what did it do for you? This was a real bank account. Someone opened it. Unless I'm mistaken . . .'

She flailed the keys. Something popped up on screen. It had the same fancy bird logo on it and a line of figures.

'It's still sitting there.'

Even a financial idiot like me could read what was on the screen. On 2 July 1985, three weeks before my family died, it appeared I'd opened the account with a deposit of a couple of hundred. Bank charges over the years had reduced this to a mere thirteen and fifty cents. I guess the Liechtensteinians, or whatever they called themselves, were still hoping.

'What this shows is someone was messing around with us.'

'Who?' she demanded.

'I don't know! That was the job of the cops.'

The words got out of my throat before I could throttle them.

'You were a cop,' she pointed out. 'If anyone should have been able to prevent this kind of thing, it was you. Right or wrong – and I think it was right – I felt this would have done us a lot more harm than good.'

Her incisive and apparently guileless eyes bore down on me.

'And by the way, you really don't want to know what I had to do *personally* to keep all this out of court. It was above and beyond the call of duty. Even for me.'

I felt miserable. I felt stupid. I walked over to the bed, sat on the edge, rested my elbows on my legs and struggled to understand just one iota of what she'd told me. Susanna had seen the truth all along, and kept it from me for my own good. Someone had ripped the heart out of my family, in more ways than I knew, and done it with a methodical, deliberate, calculating audacity, right under my unsuspecting nose.

She came over, sat next to me.

'Don't give up, sugar,' she insisted. 'That was then. This is now. Things are different.'

'I noticed,' I observed drily. 'So I'm broke. I'm an illegal fugitive who's skipped jail. Except I also appear to be dead from getting executed this morning.'

She nodded.

'That about sums it up. I can work with this. If we play it right, it could turn out fine.'

I shook my head.

'What happened this morning, Susanna? Why would they announce I was dead?'

'Maybe because they want to cover up the fact you're free. What other reason could there be?'

'No . . . Stapleton said that Solera had confessed. It was there. A judge had seen it.'

She took my face in her hands and shook my head gently.

'Stop thinking so hard, Bierce. You'll explode. No one's been talking to me about your case since I saw you last year. It can't have gone in front of a judge. Whatever they've been telling you was a bunch of lies for some reason. I mean . . . four hundred and sixty thousand dollars. If you'd done twenty-three years in jail on a wrongful conviction we'd have been coming at them for *much* more than that.'

She corrected herself.

'We *will* come at them for much more than that. I mean it.'

'And now?'

She smiled at me. Susanna could look so innocent sometimes, so full of sympathy and understanding too, that it was impossible to believe she was thinking about anyone else in the world, herself least of all.

'Now I keep you safe and sane. Tomorrow, we drive south to a house I own. It's just over the state line, so if anyone starts throwing writs around I can drown them in paper from a safe distance. Even if they found you I'd have a year, maybe two, before they could put a thing in court here. You're not going back inside, Bierce. That I promise. I take on people for life. Rain or shine.'

I nodded. A part of me wanted to sit back and do whatever she wanted.

'Now,' she said. 'I'll be back in a moment with some food and drink. In the meantime, you go raid Frank's wardrobe for some decent clothes. The Gap-reject look doesn't suit you.'

While she was gone I wandered along the corridor to another, slightly smaller bedroom, where I went through everything husband Frank owned, thinking. I picked out a pair of impeccably pressed blue linen slacks and a white polo shirt. Then I went and showered before putting them on.

Water made my head start to work again, or at least believe it was doing so.

I walked back into Susanna's bedroom, framing a few questions.

Susanna was there with an empty glass and a look that said: enough booze for now.

She patted the cushion beside her on the sofa and said, 'You know, you're the only man who's ever – *ever* – turned me down.'

She pondered this statement for a second or two.

'Apart from my Uncle Joe and he doesn't count.'

'I'm flattered by these intimate confidences. What about Kyle McKendrick?'

Her faultless features wrinkled up with disgust.

'Please! A lady doesn't tell. But in the case of that creep, no. I do have standards. Maybe they weren't high enough for you back then . . .'

'I was married,' I reminded her.

'That stopped a lot of men.'

'Happily married.'

Or so I thought.

'Well, you're not married now. You've not been near a woman for twenty-three years. How does that feel?'

She dented the soft sofa again. I shook my head and stayed where I was.

'I haven't given it much thought.'

'You will.'

Something made a noise, and vibrated too, in my pocket.

I took out the pink phone Alice had given me. There wasn't a button to push anywhere. I hadn't a clue where to begin. Finally, with Susanna looking on, awestruck by my inability to cope with such a simple device, I managed to lever the bottom edge free. The phone opened up like two seashells on a hinge. I could even hear a voice coming out of the earpiece.

'Yes?' I said.

'I don't want to worry you.' Alice sounded anxious. 'But I've done something stupid. Some people came looking for Lao Lao's apartment. She's safe round the corner for now. We need to pick her up. Also . . .'

She didn't seem keen to say this.

'I could be wrong but I thought I saw that black cop guy of yours go past me in a car, headed your way. Just a minute or two ago. I found a parking space by the public road at the end of the beach. Just walk to the shore, turn right and I'll be there.'

'Fine,' I said, unsurprised, and put the phone back in my pocket.

'So you do have friends,' Susanna murmured.

'Only in ways you wouldn't understand.'

I walked over, bent down, kissed her softly on the cheek, reached round the back of her warm, slender neck and gently unhooked the string of pearls from her throat. She made small, soft squealing noises in my ear.

Then, while her eyes were still screwed shut with

anticipation, I took both her hands in mine. I'd removed the cord from the silk dressing gown I found in husband Frank's bedroom. I looped her left hand through the noose I'd made there, then the right, and finally pulled her up and round so she had her back to me, managing to gently tie her together at the wrists, just like I once did with suspects and plastic cuffs a quarter of a century ago, before she could begin to say much at all.

I turned my lovely lawyer round and sat her back on the sofa, as comfortably as I could manage. I genuinely believe Susanna thought this might all have been some kind of foreplay for a moment. But the silence didn't last long.

'Bierce! *Bierce!*' she began to yell, flailing her legs around, up and down in fury, trying to struggle free.

'I'm sorry . . .' I began to say.

'No man says no to me twice,' she yelled. '*No* man.'

That was Susanna. The refusal hurt most of all.

A fake electronic bell chimed. Then a small video screen lit up by the side of the bed. Stapleton – *Ridley* Stapleton, I recalled – was there, looking both puzzled and mad.

I walked up to the screen and gazed into the little lens above it.

'Stape,' I said. 'I am in dire need of male company, friend. There are so many women in this world of yours. Meet me tomorrow morning, Pier Twenty-seven, the one for the Stonetown ferry. Eight-thirty. Come alone or the deal's off.'

'What deal?' he bawled, wide-eyed and furious.

'I got my memory back. *That* deal.'

He didn't say a thing.

'And by the way,' I added, 'the price is now a million. Cash. Paid into an account in Liechtenstein. Maybe you know the number.'

Susanna's fury was building up nicely. Until something happened that defeated even her.

It was a deep, growing, roaring sound, like two gigantic jet engines strung on wires, getting dangled low over the roof of her mansion in Pelican Bay, so close, and so powerful, they shook the room. I could feel my skin vibrating over my bones. I watched as a couple of paintings worked themselves off their hooks and tumbled to the floor.

She looked a little scared at that moment. I'd already guessed she'd called Stape when she went downstairs. The wide-eyed ignorance she'd shown at his name, and that little game with the computer, never really came across as convincing. I don't imagine she expected, for one minute, that some vast, dark helicopter would materialize in the night sky as a result.

'You know,' I yelled above the racket, pointing upwards at the beast in the sky, '*that* has really ruined the mood.'

I walked over to the desk, unhooked the computer and the power cord and stuffed them under my arm. Then I hopped through the French windows and down towards the beach.

I'd love to say I eluded Stapleton and his flying machine through a combination of low athletic cunning and intellectual guile. But I'd be lying. By the time I made it to Susanna's pool, breathless, panting and finally realizing I was either out of condition or old or both, Stapleton's helicopter appeared to be hovering just a couple of inches above my head. Beams of bright silver light were beginning to swoop across the perfect clipped lawn and a voice was coming out of a loudspeaker, barking commands I couldn't decipher.

Then, as I leapt over the iron gate at the beach end of the garden, the sensible part of my mind asking, somewhat drily, why the hell I was headed for the only place nearby where a helicopter could land, something happened. The painful hot downdraught of the rotor blades stopped. The chemical stink of avgas disappeared, a little anyway. For some reason the helicopter decided it had better things to do than chase an out-of-condition escaped convict struggling through the back lot of a private paradise in Pelican Bay.

I stood on the soft sand, beneath the fringe of a palm tree, coughing and wheezing, fighting to get my breath back, listening in amazement as the machine flew off south, away from the lights of the city, to some private landing strip hidden from view in the dead flat lands along A1A, I guessed.

They were gone, and there could be just one explanation. Stape called them off. Something I'd said over the video phone gave him pause for thought. It could only be the one thing, of course: *I knew*. And the fact this made him send his scary buzzing thing home could, naturally, mean just one thing too: it wasn't there as luxury transportation to take me to some desert island where we might discuss the state of the world over cocktails and canapés. It was there to scoop up my awkward ass once and for all, until the moment I let on that I now recalled what it was both my former colleague and the charming Mr McKendrick wanted so much to hear.

The latter was a lie, naturally, though I had fast come

to the conclusion of late that lying – and stealing Susanna's valuables – seemed small sins next to everything else happening around me. It felt bad enough being dead, without having people wanting to kill me. What are a little untruth and theft next to that?

Also, my head hurt, in a way I was coming to recognize. Not so much pain as muzzy confusion, a state of mind that hovered between the real world, if I could call this strange place that, and some dark corner of my imagination trying to poke its way through to take a look around. I'd felt like this ever since waking up after Martin the Medic's needle. If that's what I did. The needle from McKendrick's Dr Rimless hadn't helped. Nor had the beer Susanna had come up with either.

'I need a break,' I murmured to myself, then looked up, towards the gentle incoming tide, with the rippled reflection of a full moon on the small, regular wavelets, and felt my heart sink straight through my boots and bury itself deep in the sand, whimpering all the while.

When I say I saw Miriam standing in the water I don't actually mean she was *there*. This wasn't my sanity taking flight. It was the lost part of my mind trying to crawl back into place and find some perspective by running through a few games it thought might help me comprehend. Miriam had been dead for twenty-three years. The only place any fraction of her survived was in the memories of those who loved her. Recent discoveries taken into consideration, I still counted myself among that club. She cheated on me somehow. But then someone cheated on both of us, big time, in a way I'd yet to comprehend. They gave Jonny Loong money to start Sister Dragon. They roped in Alice's mom as smiling front of house, and somehow Miriam signed up too, putting on her sexy cheongsam with the slit up the side before getting down to business.

And while doing that, my wife and Alice's mom and uncle found out something that got them all killed; Ricky too, as what the military men like to call 'collateral damage'. I am not a naive man. When Susanna showed me those cheques and the bank account in some far-off country I still couldn't picture, I saw one possible explanation instantly. Miriam had faked my signature on cheques before. Several times. It was necessary, she'd said, when she needed to pay for something big that went over the single-signature limit on the joint account and I was out working somewhere. Occasionally she had good reason.

It was entirely possible she had written both signatures on the joint account – making mine good and hers bad in case things went wrong. And then forged my name again to move the money from my personal account – which normally had just a couple of hundred in, a hangover from my single days – before transferring it offshore.

But why? And where was she getting all the help from? She was a smart woman, but setting up bank accounts in foreign countries required the kind of knowledge that was surely beyond her. Was she planning on running off with someone she'd met through Sister Dragon, leaving me to deal with the awkward questions? Or was it possible a figure from outside had done all of this, without her direct knowledge, and killed her and Ricky and the Loongs when the truth trickled out?

'Well?' I asked of the figure standing in the waves,

holding her scarlet skirt up out of the water that lapped around her knees.

She didn't look dead. She looked beautiful. But that was only to be expected. This wasn't Miriam. It was my memory of her, ripped from my mind by the various chemicals floating round my bloodstream, then turned into some kind of simulacrum of my long-dead wife because she was the person I wanted to see more than anyone else at that moment.

This Miriam made by my memories looked at me, smiled and said, 'Not now, Bierce. You don't have the time.'

'Prevarication is an ugly thing after all these years.'

'My, you learned a lot of long words in jail. Here's a short one. *Run.*'

'Yeah, right, Miriam,' I snapped. 'Here I am, trying to work out whether I'm alive or what. Whether you loved me or hated me or . . . I don't know. And all you can say is . . .'

There was another sound too. Several of them. Voices. Shouting. Some way off, but loud too.

'Run.'

It wasn't her voice at all, that last time most definitely. When I looked up from my sudden fury there was no Miriam there. Just a ghostly white kid's paddle boat bobbing up and down on the rippling black waves, with a transistor radio on the seat, still playing, its tinny voice singing a song I remembered from back when. A lone pelican sat on the back, beak on chest, eyeing me miserably.

Music's odd. It defies time. It sits in your synapses, apparently forgotten, then jumps back out of nowhere when you hear two notes on a guitar or a lone male voice singing a single word from a refrain that should have been lost over the years.

This time it was Fleetwood Mac and 'Go Your Own Way' and the sound of it dragged me out of whatever stupid, selfish hole I'd fallen into, straight back into the dark, threatening night of the now I so wanted to avoid.

Something in my pants pocket started vibrating just at the moment a high-pitched voice began singing.

She'd adored that album, had played it over and over again, until the needle scratched the surface – we were still a pre-CD family – and I had to go out and buy a new copy.

I pulled out the pink phone.

'Run, Bierce,' Alice screamed. 'Run!'

To my right, close to where I said I'd meet her, a vehicle was flashing its lights. To my left I could hear another engine gunning over the beach. I looked. It was some huge thing, like a Jeep on junk food, churning through the sand with floodlights attached to its two front corners, searching, lost, I was glad to see, for where to begin.

I loped steadily towards her, thinking about what I'd seen, what I'd heard these last few hours.

'Let me drive,' I said, when I got to the car. 'I know the lanes around here.'

'Bierce . . .'

'Please.'

She watched me throw the computer into the back seat and then went ominously quiet. The gigantic lights on the beach had seen us and were roaring our way.

This time round there was no argument. Alice shuffled along the bench seat and let me drive. I put the old

Volvo into gear, was relieved to discover my head was working well enough for it not to worry too much about driving again, and turned off the concrete parking slab by the shore, heading inland and uphill, wondering how long the lead we had on them, a quarter of a mile at best, might last.

Away from the carbuncle of Ocean Vista Gardens, this area hadn't changed much at all. Tiny single-track roads criss-crossed the hills that led back to the city, a remnant of the time this was poor farmer land for settlers trying to stake a claim to a couple of acres and dig a living for their families out of the ground. My mind began to work overtime, recalling all the occasions we'd got lost here, looking for picnic places, even before Ricky came along. I had half an idea of where we were going, and the right direction to follow. In a warren of tracks like this, that was worth a head start or several.

At times we could hear the Jeep thing bellowing angrily below. But these were still little more than lanes made for the horse and cart era. It didn't belong, and pretty soon we heard its ugly voice no more.

After fifteen minutes of slow, patient driving, we were clear of Pelican Bay altogether and Alice still hadn't said a word. This couldn't go on. I drove into a deserted lay-by in one of the public park stops near the summit of the hill, close to the highway, turned off the engine and the lights, then looked at her.

'So what happened?' I asked.

'I did something stupid. I called the ambulance service to see how Sheldon was.'

'You what?'

'He'd been shot. We took him in. I needed to know.'

221

'Sheldon is a lying, cheating, venomous scumbag who tried to sell me to Kyle McKendrick.'

She looked miserable and grumpy. But she also looked as if she was telling the truth. I was starting to get an inkling for these things. It was all to do with the eyes, whether they peered straight at me or not. A simple thing, I know, but I hadn't stared into many faces for quite a while.

'He regretted what he did, don't you think?' she said. 'He's doing OK in hospital, in case you're interested.'

'I knew he'd be OK! How many shot people do you think I got to see when I was on the streets?'

All the same, it shouldn't have exposed us.

'How did they know?' I asked.

She frowned.

'I think I heard it in their voices when I called the ambulance people to check out where they'd taken him. I told you it was a privatized service. They'd been ordered to listen out for someone calling about Sheldon, I guess.'

'Privatized? You mean McKendrick?' I asked.

'Who else? I guess they tracked back the phone number. Lao Lao phoned me soon after I dropped you off. She's pretty smart, you know. The people in the medicine store called up from downstairs to say someone was asking. She went out by the fire escape and walked round to some bar a friend of hers runs. We need somewhere to stay, Bierce.'

'I'm thinking,' I lied.

'Well, that's good.'

For the life of me I couldn't work out why she seemed so angry with me.

'What did you do after you left?' I asked.

'You mean after getting the call from my grandma saying some people with guns were out looking for us? I drove around a little. Then I found that way down to the beach.'

She hesitated.

'After that I walked along the beach. They don't seem to patrol it so much at night.'

'No.'

That had struck me. But that part of the bay was pretty difficult to reach by any major public road. I guess they felt secure behind whatever sea of electronic devices they'd installed in their fake palaces.

'Your lawyer isn't much of a one for closing the curtains, is she?' Alice stated. 'Also you smell somewhat . . . fragrant. If you don't mind my saying.'

'Ah.'

If you'd been someone peering in through an open window it must have looked pretty damning.

'Did you used to kiss her in jail too?'

So that was why she was mad with me.

'No. I was trying to work out how to get what I wanted out of her, and then get free before the goons answered her call. That's all. Susanna knows things about me I don't know myself, though I ought to.'

I told her about Gwinett and the supposed move to McKendrick, Susanna's account of my 'execution', a little of the missing-money tale, and not a word about the meeting I hoped I'd set up with Stapleton the following morning.

She thawed a little.

'What did your lawyer tell you to do?'

'Go south with her, over the state line, and engage

in long-range fisticuffs with the legal system. What do you expect? But then, while she was out getting a beer, she called Stapleton. The rest . . .'

I opened my arms wide.

'Alice,' I said, 'I'm sorry. I am not the kind of man you think. Part of me's still locked to what happened twenty-three years ago, and I can't stop that part talking in my head, much as I'd like to. I don't have whatever it is men of this century are supposed to possess in terms of manners or morals or charm. For instance . . .'

I reached into my pocket and pulled out the double string of pearls.

'I stole these along with Susanna's computer. I wanted to give them to you. I thought they'd be a present. I now realize what a dumb, thoughtless idea that was.'

She looked at the two rows of luminous spheres shining in the dark.

'Are they real?'

'You saw the house. Do you think she'd own fakes?'

Alice ran her fingers along them, then took her hand away.

'They're not me, Bierce.'

'No,' I agreed, and a part of me was glad, because it was thinking, if you give her a present and she takes it smiling, you'd *have* to trust her, wouldn't you? We were both, men and women, made that way.

'I got a little of what I wanted out of Susanna, then left. And here I am talking to you, still feeling like some slow-witted fool who's got the big picture waiting inside his head and just can't see it.'

I pulled the creaking Volvo back out into the road.

There was only so much time and energy I could expend on banging my head against that particular wall. I needed to think about somewhere to stay, somewhere Ridley Stapleton and Kyle McKendrick would never find us.

Lao Lao was waiting for us in a Hawaiian bar in Eden, three blocks from home. She had a plastic bag with some belongings in it, a drink that looked more fruit and paper umbrella than liquid, and an expression that suggested an evening of pleasant banter around an open fire, with the odd glass of good cognac, was probably not scribbled on her to-do list.

'Thanks, jerk,' she muttered as I helped her into the car.

I didn't hear another word from her, even when we pulled into the Seaview Motel. Lao Lao shuffled off to her room without another word. Alice hung around as I raided the vending machine for soft drinks and snacks and a way into the awkward conversation which now had to ensue.

We'd passed the Seaview on the way back from Pelican Bay. Some part of my childhood said there was a rule about 'hiding in plain sight' or something. They wouldn't be looking for us just three miles from Susanna Aurelio's mansion, I thought. In fact, I doubted Stapleton would be looking for me at all. I'd made the appointment for the following morning. Being a man of substantial resources – as the helicopter showed – Stape doubtless thought he could keep this meeting, hear me out, then, if need be, grab me there to shake out any facts which remained undisclosed.

Which was perhaps true, though I planned to do my best to avoid that particular eventuality.

The Seaview was a place teenagers of my generation took their girlfriends for a few hours of shared privacy. You could rent rooms by the afternoon or the evening. If you were feeling exceptionally generous you could stay overnight, though this was not a common event. It was more than thirty years since I'd set foot in the place, for professional reasons – that missing teenager I later found dead under the De Soto bridge. Nothing much had changed in that time. It still was furnished in garish red velvet with plastic furniture and cheap prints of places – Paris, Rome – that hadn't seemed so exotic even back in my youth.

I asked for three separate rooms, which surprised the gawky youth behind the desk. It didn't take more than a moment to prise out of him the fact that we were the only guests that night. In fact, I rather suspected the Seaview hadn't enjoyed an overnight paying customer in some time, judging by the way he made us wait in the lobby while he went to check the rooms were actually fit for human habitation.

They weren't, of course, but I wasn't going to argue. The place was a classic of its type, little more than a line of low single-storey cabins running either side of the reception, each with a door opening out on to the wooden deck in front. It would do.

'Was the Bates Motel full?' Alice asked, as we walked outside towards the accommodation. The three rooms were in the left row, with Lao Lao at the end, and me willing to go wherever was empty and quiet enough to sleep.

'A cultural reference to the twentieth century,' I

noted. 'I am impressed. When this is over and done with I will take you to the Overlook. Or its equivalent.'

'I don't know that one, Bierce. Don't push your luck.'

I reached the first cabin. 'I wouldn't dream of it. Can I borrow you for a moment?'

I held up Susanna's computer.

'Instinct tells me there might be something in here that's useful for us. And that perhaps I could communicate with the outside world if necessary.'

She frowned. The skinny receptionist was out of his cubbyhole watching us, looking suspicious.

Alice walked over and asked, 'You got wi-fi?'

He looked at us with an expression that I believe was meant to appear tough.

'It's twenty a day. Cash.'

I handed over a note and got some grubby voucher in return.

He shuffled around on his cheap sneakers.

'No web cams in the room. That's one of the rules. We don't want no one pushing out live porn from here. Someone down A1A got busted for that last month. I don't want trouble.'

I put my hand on his arm. He jumped, just a little.

'I promise you. No web cam.'

'Unless,' he added, looking her up and down and licking his lips, 'you need an extra or something. I got some acting experience, if you know what I mean.'

She looked ready to hit him, which was all we needed.

'I wish you well with your career,' I replied, and opened the door of the first cabin, ushering her in front.

'The places you take me, Bierce,' she grumbled. 'Will I ever forget them?'

'In time,' I said, holding out the computer. 'You now have twenty minutes to teach a stupid old man everything he needs to know about how to survive in the twenty-first century. After that you go next door and we both get a decent night's sleep. Agreed?'

It was easy really. You just clicked things and pushed things and typed here and there. Then Susanna's computer coughed up its secrets all in a rush. And, if it couldn't find any answers there, it went hunting and pulled them out of thin air from this distant, amorphous place even I'd heard of in jail. Somewhere known as the internet, which I asked Alice to explain to me, then waved her into silence after thirty seconds.

We started off with my financial affairs. How she did it I'll never know – or, I hope, need to – but Alice somehow managed to find everything that Susanna had shown me, and a little more. It lived, she said, inside this silver thing, along with countless other letters and case files and messages and faxes . . . It seemed most of Susanna's entire professional life of the past twenty-three years was in there somewhere.

Alice hammered away at the thing, typing furiously, running her finger across some strange little pad, watching the screen like a hawk every second of the way.

After a while I could only ask, in astonishment, 'How the hell do you learn this stuff? Do they teach it at school?'

'Only to old people. How did you learn to use the phone?'

'I picked it up and started talking.'

'Snap. You know, I can't believe she's got all this just sitting there. No password. No security. Nothing.'

That made sense to me anyway.

'Susanna's obscenely rich and lives behind big iron gates. This thing never sets foot outside the bedroom.'

'I'll take your word on that,' she said slyly.

'It's psychology, a much-neglected art in your century if you ask me. Rich citizens of Susanna's persuasion believe security is something they pay other people to do. She *knows* no one can break into her beautiful mansion and start tapping away at the keys of this thing. So why worry?'

'It's a generational thing,' she said, shaking her head. 'She's about your age, isn't she?'

'A little younger.'

'Really beautiful too. From what I saw on the TV. She does a lot of TV. I remember seeing her before.'

'Yes,' I agreed. 'She's very beautiful.'

Alice waited, her fingers still for the first time in several minutes.

'Fine,' I sighed. 'I will say this just the once and never return to the subject again. A very beautiful woman is not necessarily a sure-fire signal that a man should turn off, even temporarily, all sentient thought for the well-being and security of himself and those he admires in return for nothing more or less than thirty minutes of predictable, albeit usually pleasurable, physical activity. You may find it hard to believe, but many of my sex also think this way.'

'You haven't met many of your sex in a while,' she muttered, shaking her head.

'That is the end of the Susanna Aurelio discussion, Alice. I appear to be damned if I want the woman and damned if I don't. The truth is I don't. Never have and never will. You just work out which of those two possibilities you'd prefer to believe, then take it as read I agree, absolutely, that was the way it was.'

I took her hands off the keyboard. They'd started fidgeting, not typing.

'Well?' I looked her in the eye.

'I know you didn't do anything. It's just . . . twenty-three years. People have needs.'

'Agreed. I need you to tell me everything that's in that machine. Now, will you look at my case records? Please.'

She swore, then got back to typing. I watched the screen. It filled with line after line of impenetrable jargon.

'How the hell am I supposed to read this stuff?' I grumbled.

'You can't. These are just file names. Lists of all the documents that have been lodged as part of your case. They're all there. Look.'

She pointed to the names scrolling down the screen.

'Witness statements. Forensic reports. Officer reports.'

'I was awake when all that stuff came in. I heard it in court. It's no use to me.'

'Then . . . what can I do?'

One thing that puzzled me still. Why were they convinced so absolutely I was the one who killed Miriam and Ricky? The bank account had never made it into the trial. All I got thrown at me was the fact they didn't like my line about not remembering anything to do with the attack. Plus they had traces of my skin underneath Miriam's fingernails, and some bloody prints of mine on the floor and the stairs. This was flimsy material on which to hang a murder prosecution. The skin could have got there a variety of ways. Through making love even. The prints might have been the result of me crawling upstairs after being attacked myself.

'Can you narrow this down to reports from the DA's office? Before they went ahead with the case?'

She did something magical. Three documents appeared on the screen.

'There's got to be more than this,' I pointed out. 'I've worked murder inquiries. We used to drown in paper when we were trying to persuade these people to go ahead with a prosecution.'

'In that case, they're missing,' Alice said. 'It's a computer, Bierce. They can't fall behind a filing cabinet. These are the only documents from the DA's office which mention your name.'

It wasn't hard to guess what I'd find there either. They were all about the money movements, out of our joint account, into this thing in Liechtenstein. The first two reports were wailing on in excited terms about how this was cast-iron proof that I'd been planning to murder Miriam all along, spirit away our money, then, I assume, enjoy a life of untold abandon in Austria, wearing short leather pants presumably and gorging on sausage. There were caveats even then. As a motive, this was all a little neat and tidy. Some anonymous individual had pointed out we had the reputation for being a loving, devoted couple. If they wanted to pursue this line, they really needed something that burst that particular illusion. They didn't have it, which was a shame, because right then I would have very much liked to have known myself.

In any case, it all became irrelevant. By the time of the third report the money evidence had been shelved, through a bunch of legal technicalities only someone with several degrees in gibberish would have understood. Susanna's wiles – whatever they had been – had worked. There was one interesting thing there, though.

Someone had scribbled in the margin, close to the end: *And we can't use the call either. Great work, surveillance!*

'The call?' Alice asked.

'I have no idea. None whatsoever. The law directory that listed Susanna's address did that because she works from home. It only listed an office number. Can you find her private phone number on this thing? She's got to be ex-directory. Also, can you see if she's been in touch with McKendrick recently?'

'Yes . . .' she replied cautiously. 'But you're being uncharacteristically slow here, Bierce. If you call her on the mobile I gave you, or worse, on the hotel phone, you can be traced.'

'I know that. I know Susanna too. Trust me. Please.'

She gave me a long, somewhat worried look. Then, shaking her head, to herself I think, not me, she began typing again.

It took her three seconds to find the number. After a minute I could see that there were indeed contacts between her and McKendrick, but they appeared to be the kind of social things rich people liked. Invitations to public occasions and charitable events. I knew Susanna well enough to recognize her tone. With McKendrick it was distanced, even chilly.

I used the little pink phone, interrupting her on the

first syllable of 'Hello', and said, 'I don't want to know why you called Stapleton. I just need to know this. Did you phone McKendrick too? Was that his giant Jeep thing chasing me up and down the sand?'

The line went quiet. Alice was glowering at me.

'I did not . . . I *would not* phone that man.'

'Well, that's a relief. You only called in one person to kill me. Please don't do that right now, will you? I'm hiding in a convent full of saintly nuns and it would be a real shame if they got wasted by that big black helicopter of his.'

There was an ominous silence on the phone. Alice was giving me the 'nice try, smartass' look.

'Bierce,' Susanna said eventually, 'what the hell have you got yourself into? What am I supposed to do in these circumstances?'

'Listen to your client, I would have thought.'

'I have more than one client. Sometimes their needs conflict.'

Ah. Something clicked.

'I had no idea he'd call in the air force or whatever,' she went on, oozing her special kind of sincerity. 'I thought he was coming to get you out of trouble. The Jeep was nothing to do with him. I swear that's the truth. Please believe me.'

'I'll try. Here's one more question. When you kept out the evidence about the cheques, there was something else. Someone's scribbled on the file. Something about "the call". What was the call, Susanna?'

It would have been so easy to have objected . . . *Search me. You want perfect recall of a scrawl on a piece of paper from twenty-three years ago?*

Instead she said, 'They never told me, Bierce. And

believe me I asked. There was a lot they never told me about you. And you know something? There was a lot you never told me, although you wanted me to believe that was because you really couldn't remember. Was that true too?'

'I believe so, but after all this time I really don't know. And that's the honest truth.'

'Can I still help?' she asked quietly. 'Or did I screw everything this evening?'

'Probably,' I said, and cut the call.

I didn't master the twenty-first century in twenty minutes. But, thanks to Alice Loong's patient and skilful tuition, I did learn how to find things, fetch things and even send the President of the United States an email, from something called a Hotmail address which Alice kindly set up for me.

After which we went through everything we'd found among my attorney's private files, cursed the fact that blackmail wasn't our calling and decided that, the scribble on the third DA's memo apart, there really wasn't much of interest at all.

'It's just a machine, Bierce,' she said, and yawned.

I couldn't help but notice she looked at the bed at that moment. She noticed I'd noticed and both of us pretended we hadn't.

I pulled the pearls out of my pocket and held them out in my hand.

She stared at them, close up this time, seeing them for what they were, not a part of the image of me and Susanna she'd had in her head when we were in the Volvo.

'They're beautiful,' she said, not really able to look away.

I reached up and fastened them round her neck. They nestled against Alice's smooth olive skin, seemingly at home.

'They look a million times better on you than they ever did on their owner,' I said truthfully. 'Go see. Keep them if you like.'

We got up and stared into what reflection remained among the cracks and stains of the motel mirror. Alice looked lovely just then. Composed and intelligent and completely in control of herself. I seemed old and out of place next to her, and that was both a shock and a disappointment.

'I'll think about it,' she said, fingering the two lines of shining oyster spit balls. 'Tomorrow . . .'

Tomorrow I had an appointment.

'Let's talk about that over breakfast,' I said. 'Just now, Alice, I need some sleep.'

There was suspicion in her eyes again. She wanted me to see it.

'You'll be here, won't you?'

'Where else would I be?'

'I don't know. You're sneaky sometimes.'

'Not at all. I'm a very old-fashioned man,' I insisted. 'I thought you might have noticed.'

I hesitated. This needed to be said.

'You've got a gun,' I said. 'I saw it in your bag this evening. In the Volvo. It wasn't there before.'

She blinked, took her cheap little plastic bag off her shoulder, opened it and pulled out an old automatic.

'Lao Lao gave it to me,' she explained. 'She thought I might need it.'

235

'For me? Or someone else?'

Alice Loong sighed.

'How many times do I have to save you before you give up on this fantasy? If I wanted to shoot you, I could have done it that first night.'

She put the gun back into her bag. For some reason, that made me feel scared. Alice looked vulnerable at that moment. I had the horrible feeling she was going to tell me something, and I didn't want to hear it. No confession. No sudden truth or revelation. The shifting semblance of some plan was starting to hatch at the back of my damaged brain, and it had taken so long to get there I couldn't countenance anything – particularly not something personal – getting in the way.

'You're not what I expected,' she began to say. 'You're not . . .'

Before she could utter another word I kissed her, very quickly, on the cheek, then, for just a microsecond, on her full, pink lips, in a way, I hoped, that could have denoted either attraction or affection. Or maybe, in truth, a mixture of both.

'G'night . . .' I whispered, and, to my relief, she said nothing, leaving without another word.

I waited until I heard the door to the adjoining cabin slam before opening up the computer, trying to remember everything she'd told me. Finally I tracked down Kyle McKendrick's email address and began hunting and pecking across the keys.

> Kyle! You rogue, you. Shooting my miserable SOB brother-in-law like that (he's still alive, friend, you should take gun tuition, soon please).
>
> And making out with my wife all those years

ago! How'd you do that? Did the cheongsam help
or hinder? No. This is your secret. Keep it. I never
had a clue. Not the slightest. Talk about dumb cops.
Here's one more thing. I don't care. If Miriam
wanted to cheat on me that was her right, just as
it's mine to say: to hell with the bitch, she had it
coming.

All this is in the past. I am a forgiving man. And
I forgive you everything. Well, almost everything.
You go eat the food in that correctional facility of
yours and see how you like it.

Most of all, though, I am alive and I would like to
keep things that way. To this end I can offer you a
bargain, the best you'll ever get.

You post a million dollars in cash into my
account in Liechtenstein, the details of which I'll put
at the end of this message. You do this first thing in
the morning. Then around noon I'll give you the little
secret you want, because – here's the rub – Dr
Rimless and his magic needle worked. If you'd just
turned up before my rescue party I'd have poured
out everything, heart and soul, right there in the loft
of Shangri-La Motor Repair, where you could have
listened, taken notes, then popped me just like you
popped Sheldon, except with more care.

Such is fate. But here's the thing. Now I have
experienced once more what it's like being alive, I
quite like it. So as well as the money I want your
assurance that, once we both have what we want,
no one's going to come looking for me – or anyone
else among the few people I happen to know in this
shiny new world of yours – with a gun or a syringe
or anything. I have researched your present status

on this marvellous toy you call the internet. You are, I see, a man of great renown. A charitable human being, with many generous endowments and political connections that must make for a lot of tedious dinners. I wish you well in all your many ventures. But should you break this part of my munificent bargain, there is a cost. Just the usual. Some incriminating documents and the rambling story of my life, in every last damning detail, deposited this night with a lawyer, to be dispatched to every mainstream media outlet in the country should I expire of anything other than the most natural of causes at any period over the next ten years.

Being rich, I'm sure you'd stay out of jail, of course. But here's the bad news. You'd be a pariah. Look it up if you don't know already. No more society receptions and free champagne. No nights at the opera. When you open the post in the morning all you'll see is bills not invitations. Hell, you'd be just like the rest of us. Nasty, huh?

I'll book a table at Loomis and Jake's for twelve-thirty (just to take away the taste of that prison food of yours). If you're amenable, this is over. Expect my call.

Yrs, Bierce

PS The lobster's on you

I hit send and wondered how long it took for these things to arrive. Were there morning and afternoon deliveries? Did Kyle pick up these things for himself or have a secretary read them out loud from the computer?

However quickly they turned up, I didn't expect him

to be sitting, waiting for them, at thirty minutes past midnight. I had time, to think, to plan and, most of all, to prepare.

Kyle McKendrick would not, unless I was very much mistaken, put one million dollars into that bank account in Liechtenstein. Though he no longer knew it, he was a crook first and a businessman second. Had it been the other way round, things might have been different.

Still, I would settle for some guarantee that I – and Alice and Lao Lao – got out of this safely, maybe by leaving the city altogether, though even at this stage I found that idea unappealing. I'd never lived anywhere else. Where would I go? Also I deserved that meal at Loomis and Jake's. The place had memories for me and an ad in the restaurant guide I'd found in that grubby room revived them. They hadn't even changed the art-work: badly drawn lobsters and crabs and a promise of the best food in town from a kitchen that had been run by the same family for nearly eight decades. The father of Mickey Carluccio, my one childhood friend, owned the place along with the city fish market, where he employed me when I was a school kid chasing pocket money. He had other connections I didn't know about till later too. Miriam and I used to go to eat there before we were married, when money hadn't seemed so tight. Ricky came along once or twice when he was old enough, and got his face covered in tomato sauce when we bought him his favourite, the *cioppino*. It was a land-mark that had sat down by the Piers for half a century or more, with a view of the boats and the ferries, the sea lions and the gulls. It was impossible to think of the city without thinking about Loomis and Jake's, at least for me. And when this mess was over, I would, I swear, buy Alice Loong one good, expensive meal there, before working out what happened next.

There was just one obstacle along the way.

I had no idea, not the slightest clue, what it was that Stape and McKendrick lusted after so badly they seemed willing to kill anyone to get it.

Bringing McKendrick into the loop came from the stated wisdom of my old man on the subject of mad dogs. Never fight them yourself or try to run away. Just find another mad dog and let the two of them sort it out between themselves.

It was the kind of advice I would have handed out to Ricky when he was old enough, since fathers are supposed to come up with that kind of plain, sensible fare, even though I doubt anyone spouting such nonsense has ever tried it out in real life.

Weren't these creatures mad to begin with? In which case how could you apply any logic whatsoever to their actions? And what if they decided they liked each other and turned on you instead?

The Fleetwood Mac song I'd heard on the beach came back to taunt me.

Go Your Own Way.

That was what I was trying to achieve really. Something, anything that was the opposite of Stape's and McKendrick's expectations. These two men had money and organizations and access to gadgets and stuff a caveman from the eighties couldn't begin to imagine. There was no way I could play them at their own game; I needed them to play me at mine.

And here's the truth. I was a lousy cop at most things. I couldn't shoot straight. I was never much good in a fight.

My one talent was this: I could talk to people, high and low, big and small, crooked and straight. This was no small gift for one very good reason. When I became a cop there was one thing I noticed very quickly. People don't shoot you while they're speaking. Guns only come into their own when the talking stops.

To this end I tried to develop a little sly charm and persuasiveness. Now it was time to gauge how much had survived the years in jail.

When I went outside my heart was up in my mouth. I walked along to her room, knocked twice, gently, so as not to wake the person next door, and waited.

Lao Lao opened the door in a lurid violet floor-length nightdress. She was smoking a cigar and had a glass of amber spirit in her hand.

'What took you?' she muttered, and ushered me into the room.

'Do you believe in ghosts?' I asked.

'What kind of question's that?'

'The simple kind,' I said, shrugging. 'Like, "Can I call you Lao Lao?" Alice does. It makes things easier for me.'

'Sure you can. I just wanted you to ask.'

'Your English is good.'

'When I want it to be. It's useful being some dumb Chinese grandma occasionally. You got a first name?'

'Bierce works either way. Let's not complicate things.'

She sat down on the bed, pulled out her bag from beneath the mattress, brought out a bottle of cheap whiskey and poured some into a plastic tooth mug she'd kept by the chair.

I politely turned it down.

'I need a clear head for the morning. Big day.'

'Every day's a big day.'

'Some are bigger than others. You didn't answer my question.'

She gulped at the whiskey and winced.

'Lots of Chinese believe in ghosts. Me, I dunno. Someone once said, if you believe in them, they exist. If you don't, they never pester you. Why'd you ask?'

There was no point in hiding it.

'I keep seeing my wife.'

Lao Lao looked interested.

'Does she say anything?'

'Nothing useful. Not so far.'

She stubbed out her stinking cigar in the sink by the bed.

'Alice says your memory's not so good. Maybe this is one way it's trying to make itself better.'

'That had occurred to me.'

'Best listen, then. Best get it talking.'

'How?'

She held up the bottle.

'I've had more stuff pumped into me than you can begin to imagine, Lao Lao. It didn't work. And I don't want any more.'

She hunched her shoulders and stared at her knees.

'What would really help,' I went on, 'would be some information.'

'I'm just an old woman. Why do you tell me this?'

'Because whatever happened, it began with that club that Jonny and May started. Sister Dragon.'

She waved a compact, wrinkled fist at me.

'Just Jonny. You leave May out of it.'

'She was there. She ran it. The licence was in her name.'

'No! She was just doing her stupid brother a favour. She had a good heart. Like her daughter.'

'It killed her. It killed them both. And my wife. And my son.'

Lao Lao was starting to look as if she regretted allowing me into the room.

'What do you want from me, Bierce?'

'Something that can help me understand what these people need so much.'

'They think you know that!'

Clearly Alice talked to her grandma rather more than she let on. Either that or . . . I didn't want to think too much about the alternative just then.

'They're wrong. And tomorrow I've got to tell them something. I don't know what. This has got to come to an end. We'll run out of places to hide. We'll run out of patience with each other.'

'You're a smart man in some ways,' she said, which was, I believe, quite a compliment.

'I've spent a lot of time in jail for something I didn't do. How smart is that?'

'You should have seen some of the jerks she brought home. So what's wrong with my granddaughter? You too good for her?'

'There's nothing wrong with her. I've other things on my mind right now. I need some help.'

She shuffled her round body on the bed, steeling herself to say something awkward.

'You got to remember, Bierce. I came here illegal, forty-four years ago, when May was two and her brother just a couple of years older. I thought my husband would follow in a few months. Instead the stupid man died. I was on my own. I didn't get protection from no one. Not the police. Not my own people. That's good education. You learn to stay out of the way. To talk stupid when you're around people you don't know. You learn to make yourself invisible.'

'I can understand that,' I agreed.

'Yeah, but try telling it to your kids. Jonny and May didn't think they were Chinese at all, not really. This was their home. They could do what they wanted. Except . . . they were still illegal. They just didn't know it. So they walked around pretending they were something they weren't, and when it all went wrong they had nothing. Except me, yelling at them. What else could I do?'

She put down the drink. Lao Lao was an interesting woman. That didn't surprise me.

'Listen, Bierce. I'm saying this once and once only. I tried to put them straight. Then I gave up. When your kids go bad, you can talk till you've got no voice left. If that don't work, all you can do is wait and hope. I couldn't fix Jonny. He was a loser, always was. Never did a thing for anyone. But May was the sweetest kid I ever knew. She was always getting him out of trouble and never a word of thanks, nothing. That was how she was. Everyone loved her. She would have come good once she'd got all the nonsense out of her system. She *was* coming good when Alice came along, and Alice is her daughter through and through. A few years ago you wouldn't have recognized *her*. She was just a bum, living with bums, a real mess. Then she changed.'

I'd a good idea what had done that too.

'When she decided she needed to find out more about her mom?' I asked.

'Like I said, you're a smart man.'

'And if she doesn't work this out?'

She picked up the whiskey glass again and just looked at me.

'Alice doesn't tell me everything. She's her mother's daughter in that way.'

That had occurred to me already.

'Is she in trouble?' I asked.

'We're all in trouble, aren't we?'

That wasn't good enough.

'You know what I mean, Lao Lao. Alice came to me. It wasn't the other way round.'

She knocked back some more of the drink.

'I already told you, Bierce. If a child doesn't want to tell you, there's no making them. Not a way that works.'

That particular avenue was clearly closed, though it was apparent Lao Lao knew full well what I was talking about. I tried something different.

'Who gave Jonny the money to open the club?' I asked.

'I don't know.'

'If you lie to me I can't help anyone. Alice. Me. You. It's too late for that. Don't you see?'

'We've got money. We can move somewhere else.'

'Then Alice won't know, will she? And maybe these people she's been working with will get even madder than they must be at the moment.'

'Don't try this emotional stuff on me, Bierce.'

'Emotions matter. You love Alice. She loves you. That matters more than anything else in the world.'

'Really?' she snapped. 'What do *you* love? Huh? Not

even yourself from what I see. Where do you think that's going to get you? Fix yourself before you think you're good enough to fix the rest of us.'

'I'm just like Alice. I want to know what happened,' I said weakly. 'After that . . .' I honestly hadn't given it a thought, but I wasn't going to let her bludgeon me out of the room before I'd pushed a little further.

'Jonny mixed in bad company. Alice told me. Did he get the money for the club from some local crooks? Kyle McKendrick, say?'

She laughed.

'Kyle McKendrick. Some stuffed-up white guy in a fancy suit. I'm Chinese, Bierce. We got crooks, real crooks. People who could pick up Kyle McKendrick by his ankles right now and throw him in the ocean. All these white guys . . . they want it both ways. Want to be crooks and big citizens, in the paper, everywhere. Chinese crooks know who they are. They don't need dinner dates with politicians to pump up their egos.'

In some roundabout way Lao Lao was, I believe, trying to tell me something.

I'd worked that part of the city. I knew the four rival triad groups who fought to control it. I could still remember their names. They weren't the kind of thing you'd forget: Wo Shing Wo, San Yee On, 14K-Hau and 14K-Ngai.

'So if it wasn't crooked white money, maybe it was crooked Chinese money?'

'This was Chinatown! Half the restaurants and bars there were opened on crooked money. You think I'd be worried about *that*?'

What few working gears remained in my mind crashed at that moment.

'I give up. What's left? The National Rifle Association? Opus Dei? The Boy Scouts?'

She was staring at her old, gnarled hands, looking deeply miserable. I wasn't proud of myself for not letting this go, but there wasn't an option.

'Tell me, Lao Lao,' I said. 'Tell me now or I walk out of this room, out of this place, for good. I had a wife who lied to me once. I never knew it at the time but it screwed us all up. Cost her and my son their lives. Maybe it killed May too. I don't know, but I know this: I am not dealing with that kind of deceit again. I can't.'

I sat down on the bed next to her, took her old hands and peered into her face.

'I won't,' I said. 'I mean that.'

She dragged her fingers from out of my grip and hugged herself.

Then she looked at me, half resentment, half relief perhaps, because I don't think this was a secret Lao Lao liked much either.

'It was the gov'ment,' she murmured, then poured herself some more of the whiskey.

She looked scared. Truly scared, and it even came through in her speech, which wandered back into the crude, half-English I imagine she used among most white people.

I wanted to stand up and find some way of kicking myself. Lao Lao had been trying to tell me this all along. She was an illegal immigrant, in her own head, still. She'd die that way. A woman like her would spit in the shadow of made-up hoods like Kyle McKendrick. She probably took tea with the wives and mothers of the four triads and listened to them moaning about how hard it was to get out the bloodstains from their men's best suits.

When every other possibility has been laid to rest, look at the most improbable.

'Tell me,' I said.

'Nothing much *to* tell! I scream and scream at Jonny not to get involved in this shit. He so stupid. By the end it like he not my son at all. He just live in some dream world where he was this big shot who could have anything he wanted. Then one time, when I'm yelling at him again, he turns round on me, like I'm an idiot or something, and says, "What do you know, you old witch? It's the gov'ment that's giving me the money. It's all some big, secret thing the gov'ment's doing, and when it's all over, you just look at me. I'm a big man. So big I won't even have to talk to some miserable immigrant bitch like you."'

The glass bobbed up and down, got emptied, got filled again.

'Three weeks later Jonny's gone for good. And I'm coming home and my little girl's dead on the floor, just some bloody mess there I don't really recognize, and that half-white kid of hers is going crazy in a cupboard.'

There was a shine in her round black eyes and I felt deeply, sickeningly guilty for putting it there.

'That's all I know,' she added. 'All he ever told me. It was enough. I can't explain to Alice. She wouldn't understand, would she?'

'Probably not,' I agreed.

'Besides . . .' she added, and didn't need to say more. There was a secret Alice didn't want to share either, and it concerned me.

She'd given me a clue herself. She wasn't an immigrant. She wouldn't lie back and take the kind of humiliation a woman of Lao Lao's birth and generation would swallow, then try to forget. She'd make noise. She'd do what it took.

'Tell me, Lao Lao. Are the Wo Shing Wo still the big people in Chinatown? Or did one of the other three steal their thunder while I was in jail?'

She stared at me, then laughed.

'What the hell kind of man are you? How do you know people like that?'

'I'm the sociable kind. I talk to everyone. High and low. Good and wicked. It's the one small skill I own.'

'Small?' She had a hold on her emotions again. The question interested her. 'Wo Shing Wo are the men. No one messes with them. Also, they never harm anyone outside the societies. Not if they can help it. It's a matter of principle. If you got to have criminals, best you have people like them.'

I nodded. In my time Wo Shing Wo were also the biggest importers of hard drugs through the Yonge docks. If they were still in charge, that couldn't have changed. But I wasn't in a position to be picky.

'You still know a few people there?'

'Not for a long time, Bierce. Not since Jonny got killed.'

'You can call someone, though?'

She shook her head.

'You can never beat the gov'ment, Bierce. Never.'

One way or another I seemed to be kissing a lot of women since I left jail. So it seemed only natural that I leaned over and placed a gentle, filial one on her wrinkled, walnut cheek.

'We don't need to beat them,' I said. 'We just need to know their game.'

I walked outside, past Alice's door, back to my own room. Then I waited an hour, thinking, before quietly sneaking outside.

The weather forecast Alice had found for me was turning out to be dead right. When I walked to the edge of the parking lot I could see a long finger of fog rolling in across the bay from the north. It would reach the city by sunrise. Tomorrow the sun would be gone for most of the day, trying to burn off this grey shroud that would trap every district, rich and poor, in a cold, damp sea mist of the kind anyone who'd grown up here had come to know from an early age.

I wished I could have left them the gun; the weapon Lao Lao had given Alice was so old-looking it maybe didn't work well, and was doubtless the only one she had. But I did count out ten thousand from my stash, then placed the rest in an envelope that I pushed beneath Alice's door on the way out.

I left a note by the computer. It said, 'Believe me when I say this. I am not abandoning you. Whatever it is you want, I will try to find it for you. Wait for my call.'

They could have the car too. I noticed on the way in that the spotty receptionist appeared to keep a pushbike at the back of the property. We were so out of the way here – and the thing was so decrepit – that he didn't even bother to lock it.

So I hopped on the hard, worn saddle, felt my muscles seize as they tried to accustom themselves to a form of physical exercise they hadn't encountered since we'd been teenagers together, and pushed myself out of the drive of the Seaview Motel, grateful for the bright silver light of a full moon that shone in fat beams through the conifer forest that ran all the way to the city outskirts.

It was a good thing it was downhill. I didn't feel too short of sleep, but I was stiff and out of condition. I freewheeled as much of the way as I could, first through the deserted business streets of Westmont, then on through Eden, where the Chinese restaurants and gambling parlours were still operating, even in the morning hours, and the odd tram clanked its way noisily along the road.

Susanna Aurelio and Lao Lao had given me a few answers, ones that begged more questions, naturally. But there was a limit to the number of places I could pose them. Everything, I was coming to believe, hinged on one place. The house where Miriam died, where they found me afterwards. The house where something crucial in our lives had gone deeply, irrevocably wrong, and I'd never noticed, not for a moment.

I couldn't imagine Stapleton or McKendrick had the interest or the resources to keep Owl Creek under surveillance day in and day out. They didn't need it now either. They had an appointment with me, and, being the big, important men they were, they understood that was all they needed. They could come along with their guns and their might and everything would roll over straight into their laps.

For all I knew, they might be right.

I didn't mind. Something told me I needed to go back to Owl Creek that night. When I wheeled the pushbike into the cul-de-sac, there was nothing there.

Not a vehicle. Not a sign that anyone was watching, or much interested in my presence.

I let myself in. Then, using a flashlight I'd picked up at an all-night store along the way, I finally plucked up the courage to go back up to our old bedroom and lie down, exhausted, on the mattress.

A few of Alice's things – cheap clothes and under-wear – still lay on the floor. A tang of her perfume, something exotic, continental, and unsophisticated, continued to hang around the room.

A part of me missed her already. A part of me wished I could sit down with her and beg her for the truth, not that I thought it would come easily. There was some internal struggle going on inside her too.

You're not what I expected.

Someone had given her a few ideas beforehand.

I tried to force these thoughts from my mind. I came back to Owl Creek because this was the place to find answers. The place to stare the ghost that lived inside me straight in the eye and ask: *why?*

So I lay down and fell asleep almost instantly, expectant, waiting for Miriam to appear.

What was it that Lao Lao had said? If you believe in them, they'll come. If you don't, they won't.

Miriam never entered my mind at all that night, though I seemed to spend a lifetime searching for her, in the kind of landscapes a Dalí on dope might have painted in his strangest dreams.

Then the phone was ringing, the little pink one Alice gave me, sitting by the bed, buzzing like an angry wasp.

I dragged myself off the sheets, still dressed. It wasn't yet dawn.

'Yes?' I said, not quite awake.

Someone was screaming. A female voice, yelling something wordless, over and over again.

This went on for a good minute or more. They wanted to make sure I got the message.

I felt cold. I felt small and stupid and powerless.

Eventually the shrieks stopped and I knew why. Someone had dragged her away from the phone.

'McKendrick here,' said an amused, cold voice.

'Morning, Kyle.'

'I have your girlfriend. Make me happy today, Bierce. I hate it when I have to put down something beautiful.'

FRIDAY

They gave her the phone when I asked. Kyle McKendrick was, you see, a professional. At least in his own eyes. He only resorted to kidnapping, torture and murder when there was no commercial alternative. I believe that, in his own head, he was simply a highly successful entrepreneur who'd managed to circumvent the conventional venture capital route to power and affluence.

I listened for a minute or more, then asked for McKendrick.

'Kill her, Kyle,' I said. 'If that's what turns you on. We're supposed to be doing business with one another. I feel deeply disappointed you should attempt to complicate matters in this way. This isn't personal, is it? Please . . .'

He spluttered for a moment. With people like this, it's always best to say and do the opposite of what they expect. And let's face it, what else did I have?

'You talk to her again,' McKendrick yelled when he'd got his voice back. 'I'm through listening.'

The screaming started once more and I wasn't sure whether he meant he was through listening to me or her. I'd half recognized what was going on the first time round, once the initial shock had subsided. The clue was this: it was fury, not fear that was causing all that volume. And now it was flying in my direction.

When the swearing had stopped, she yelled, 'What the hell do you think you're playing at, Bierce?'

'Me? *Me*? You're my lawyer, Susanna. Not my girlfriend. Why don't you explain *that* to him. It might put a different complexion on things. Also what are you doing there?'

'I am trying to clear this mess up, you moron! That's what I do.'

A part of me felt sorry for her. A very small part. Susanna Aurelio was out of her depth, very possibly for the first time in her life. No amount of cooing and cajoling was going to help. I doubt Kyle McKendrick cared whether she was clothed or not. All this must have hurt.

'Did you call him? Or did he come for you?'

'Number two,' she answered, with a little less heat.

I thought of the big Jeep wheeling around on the beach. And the guard on the gatehouse, too nosy for his own good. Just one more minion on the McKendrick payroll, I guess. It was obvious he'd be watching Susanna. I should have seen that.

'What kind of mess are you *in*?' she asked. 'I had no idea . . .'

For Susanna, I realized, life basically boiled down to reading torts in between sex. There was no real connection between what was happening out there and the insular existence she enjoyed in her pampered mansion or three. It hadn't always been like this.

'My kind of mess.'

'Well, that's informative. So what do you want?'

'Kyle knows that. I want him to buy me lunch. No. Correction. Now I want him to buy *us* lunch. It's the least he can do. I mean . . . does he want to piss off the Bar Association or whatever? How's that going to play the next time there's a vacancy on the Opera House board?'

Susanna went off the phone. I could still hear a little of what was going on. It sounded pretty bad-tempered. I'll say this for the woman. She had guts.

'He says no,' she said when she came back. 'Either you come up with whatever it is he wants. Or . . .'

'Or what? Put him on.'

After a second or two McKendrick's voice began to blare out of the earpiece. I waited till he had to pause for breath, then broke in.

'Quiet. *Quiet.* Please. Listen. Threatening to kill well-known telegenic lawyers is beneath you. If you don't know that, you need to change your PR people. The situation is simple. I have something you want. I have stated my price. This is just a case of supply and demand. Either we come to some agreement, or we don't. In which case I look for another buyer. Did your guys in the Jeep see the helicopter last night? Jesus, what is that Stapleton guy spending your hard-earned taxes on now? If he can afford that, he can afford to buy a little something from me, don't you think?'

It went quiet for a while. Then . . .

'Don't *dare* threaten me, Bierce.'

'Kyle, Kyle,' I said, in a hurt voice. 'You are one amazing individual. I've been in jail for the best part of my life. I've lost my wife and my kid. I've been stabbed with needles and filled with dope. And now, as far as I can work out, I am officially *dead* thanks to you. And what happens? I come up with a nice, simple solution to all of our problems, and you just turn nasty. This is not the behaviour of a gentleman.'

'Bierce!'

'Listen to me. There is no rule in the world which says that, in order for you to win, I have to lose. Or vice versa. I am offering you a way out of this mess, one that doesn't pose any legal risks for either of us, and will make all our present problems go away. You get what you want. I start all over again. A little late, being fifty-two, but it's better than my prospects were a few weeks ago. What's wrong with all that?'

He didn't come back straight away. This was good.

'So?' I asked after a while, cautiously but with a degree of firmness that told him, I hoped, I wasn't budging. 'Are we doing lunch?'

'There's no window at twelve-thirty! You think I don't have better things to do than deal with all this crap?'

'Window? *Window*? What the hell are you talking about? Whoever it is you're supposed to meet, are they really more important than me? Well? Are they?'

'Yes,' he answered. 'They are.'

'But at that particular moment in time . . . ? Think about it. Ask yourself this too. How long is it since you ate at an ordinary place like Loomis and Jake's? Checked tablecloths with yesterday's stains on them. Waiters who spill your beer and dare you to complain. Fresh cooked lobster and clams. Nothing fancy. The world like it used to be. One relaxing hour, some nice food, a little pleasant conversation and then we're done. Both happy, both safe. You give me what I want. After which I point you to where you can find your heart's desire.'

Silence.

'So . . . Where's the harm in that?'

'I'll get a table for two. You don't get a penny in that stupid bank account of yours until I have it.'

'I can agree to that. Make that a table for three, though. Buy Susanna something nice and I think we can both guarantee not a word of this will go on the cocktail circuit. We can make it for twelve-fifteen, if you like,' I added graciously. 'Outside. Don't you love the sea air?'

'Don't push me, Bierce. I have my limits.'

As have we all, I thought, and cut him off.

He could probably trace me back to Owl Creek just from that. But somehow I didn't think Kyle McKendrick would bother now. He was in the same position as his opposite number, Ridley Stapleton. Both men knew they were going to meet me. Both felt sure they'd get what they wanted. Their older, baser parts were probably already imagining what they'd do to me once all that was over.

Crooks had changed while I was in jail. The ones like Kyle McKendrick had put on airs and graces. Some of them anyway.

I picked up my watch and stared at the phone. It was four-fifteen. Business people worked weird hours these days. Perhaps everyone did.

Unable to help myself, I called.

'Where are you?' she asked softly.

'What happened to "Who are you?"'

'Let me add caller ID to the "must teach him" list. Where *are* you?'

'Owl Creek. I had to. I can't explain it. There's a note by the computer. You should talk to Lao Lao too.'

'Too late. I've done both. You made a hell of a racket when you left this morning.'

'The only thing I do well is talk. And I'm not so sure about that any more.'

'Have no doubts.'

'Thanks. McKendrick's got Susanna Aurelio.'

'Oh, my God!'

'I thought it was you.'

I really would have been lost if that had been the case. What would Kyle McKendrick have cared about a struggling cocktail bar waitress whose one prize possession in life, a 1993 Kawasaki 500, was now dead and bent and rusting in the Pocapo river, all thanks to me? What would he have done to squeeze out of her the secret that I didn't even dare ask for?

'We have to get her out of there, Bierce.'

'I know. I know.'

'How?'

'Working on it. Talk to Lao Lao. Make those calls she'll tell you about. Let me know when you're done.'

She didn't drop the line.

'Did you see any ghosts?' she asked.

'Not a one,' I answered. 'But I'm looking.'

And look I did. Everywhere. In the garden. In the shed. In the garage and the cellar where I'd been planning to build Ricky a model train network on the old dining table when he was old enough to appreciate it. Or when I found the time. I worked my way through every bedroom cupboard, through sheets and dirty clothes that had gone musty and damp over more than two decades, through boxes of toys that made me weep remembering them, and all the assorted junk seven years of married life had accumulated in the timbered loft.

Forty-five minutes later, when it was supposed to be daybreak, I was covered in dust and scratches, cursing everything I could point my tongue at. I'd looked everywhere, in every stupid hidden corner, all the fancy, pointless places that attracted Miriam to Owl Creek to begin with.

It didn't help that I had no idea what I was searching for in the first place. It didn't help that Miriam's shade refused to crawl out of my ear, materialize in front of me and say, with a sweet, self-deprecating smile, 'Oh, *that*? You mean the thing that got us killed? Third cupboard on the right.'

I needed a coffee. I needed to think.

I went into the kitchen. On a good summer day the sun would be filtering down at this moment, sending golden shafts between the ugly, thick branches of the lumbering apple tree. If it had been like this while Ricky was around I'd have been ordered to take a saw to the branches.

I walked out into the garden and picked a couple of apples, came back in, still eating one. There was a jar of instant coffee by the sink. Alice had come prepared, as best she could. So I made myself a cup, black, strong, sat down to finish my apple, and began to accept there was going to be no sudden flash of revelation, no moment of epiphany in which everything fell into place.

The finger of fog I'd first seen in the distance from the Seaview Motel was now working its way into the city. I could feel its chill, damp presence already. Soon it would drift everywhere. I'd grown up with this kind of weather. It interested me. When I was on duty it meant I could set my motorcycle on its stand anywhere in the city and sit there, unseen, even in uniform, listening to the invisible gulls cawing from the rooftops and the trams working their way through the tight, narrow streets of Eden, bells ringing, wheels squealing, the old-fashioned sound of metal upon metal.

The fog was good. An acquaintance, if not a friend. I'd been living with it in my head for so long it didn't bother me any more. But for people like Kyle McKendrick and Ridley Stapleton it must have seemed foreign and threatening. They thought they were better than the rest of us, different, immune. But when the fog came we were all equal, just walking animals with a few clothes on our backs, stepping through its chilly, opaque embrace, trying to work out what was happening up ahead.

I bit into the apple and sipped the coffee. Instant, like I used to make for myself when Miriam wasn't home, but out somewhere, with Ricky – was that true? – shopping or visiting or doing one of the many things she cited as 'getting out of the house'.

Such as putting on a cheongsam and taking Kyle McKendrick into a back room at Sister Dragon for a little quiet time together.

It was twenty minutes, twenty-five, no more, down to the Piers on my stolen pushbike. In this weather no one would see me. No cop would complain about the lack of lights. No street hood would get interested in what I was carrying: a wad of ten thousand, an old police handgun and a little remaining ammunition.

I was free. Kind of.

The coffee tasted better than it should have done. In fact, it tasted just like the coffee used to back then.

The fog was closing in, and it was thick and curling, a fat sinuous cloud of grey that seemed to want to make its way everywhere.

The kitchen door was still open. The shroud of mist began to work its way into the house.

'Nice timing, Miriam,' I said, and cursed the coffee.

'The coffee?'

'Yeah,' he says. 'Where'd you get it? I don't own any that tastes this good. Mind you . . .' Ridley Stapleton casts me a look that says, *lucky man*. 'I'm just a bachelor living on my own. If I had some beautiful wife to find me these things—'

'Colombian,' I interrupt. 'We pick it up with the coke and smack we get from the Yonge gangs. They deliver now, Stape. I thought you might have known that. What with you being in this all-new secret-squirrel thing the government's setting up.'

'Secret squirrel?' he asks. 'I never heard it called that before.'

He's wearing a dark suit cut very tight and has that moustache I always thought he'd copied from some bad black cop movie. He thinks it makes him look good.

'So what should we call you?' Miriam asks.

'I am a public servant,' he replies coyly, and picks at a morsel of pizza. 'You don't want to know. Trust me.'

It's the end of April. That last year. We've invited people round, colleagues, friends, a few neighbours from our old days when we lived in Miriam's studio apartment. The spring is so warm we take them into the garden, about twenty adults or so, and Ricky with a couple of friends riding their bikes around the apple tree.

'Secret squirrel?' she asks. 'Is that why you're drinking coffee when we went to the expense – the unusual expense – of buying in wine?'

'Strictly speaking, I'm on duty,' Stape says. 'You know, I can't believe they never gave the police department a decent raise this year. How do you people live on that kind of money?'

I lift my glass of white Pinot Grigio, trying to forget how much it cost, and say, 'Mostly I take bribes. Though I continue to hope the male prostitution market will pick up again soon.'

'But why secret squirrel?'

Miriam's feeling persistent.

'Because,' I go on, 'they all have nice clean coats and bushy tails. And they scurry around from tree to tree, so you know they're there but you can't quite see them. Listening. Looking. That right?'

'*You* have never seen my tail,' Stape says, grinning, and a part of me thinks he has actually thrown a wink in Miriam's direction. 'Oh. Excuse me.'

He pulls something out of his black jacket pocket. It's the size of a brick but black too. With white buttons, numbers on them.

He walks away from us and starts to talk into the thing.

I am getting mad.

'What's wrong?' she asks.

'Manners.'

'It's a phone, Bierce. They say we'll all have them some day.'

266

'Not me.'

'What's the big deal?'

There's an exasperated inflection to her voice, not far off anger.

'Everyone needs somewhere they can be on their own,' I point out. 'Privacy. Somewhere they can think.'

'Everyone needs money. How much do you think a secret squirrel gets?'

'I have no idea. We have a house, don't we?'

She glances back at the white timber garden frontage, then kisses me, just.

'My own pet caveman. When do you start dragging me around by the hair?'

'He doesn't do that already?' Stape asks, now he's finished the call.

He's still holding the big, brick phone, just so we can see it.

'Only in private,' Miriam says. 'How do you like it normally?'

He grins and it's ugly.

'Sometimes it's good slow,' he says. 'Sometimes fast. Today . . .'

'Ridley!' she says, laughing. 'I meant the coffee.'

I can't quite grasp what I'm hearing. She knows his first name. He's learned this little refrain of hers.

'Gimme that . . .' I say, and try to grab the phone from his hands.

'Bierce . . .' Miriam whines.

'*Gimme that!*'

I snatch the big, ugly hunk of plastic from him and dash it to the ground. It bounces on the soft grass. Ricky is watching, with his friends, still on their little bikes, eyes shining with shock and disbelief.

I kick it to one side, hard, and I'm screaming mad now. The rest of them, all these strangers, are going quiet. They're looking at me as if they half expect this. It's not just the noise either. There's something in my hands.

A sledgehammer.

I didn't know we owned that. I've no idea where it comes from. Still . . .

I swing it once. It bites the paving stone in the slender winding path where the brick phone now lies. Dust and dirt rise up from the ground, make a small storm cloud in the unnaturally warm spring air.

'You'd think,' Stape's voice says behind me, 'a man would know his station.'

I look at the phone. This time the hammer doesn't miss. The thing breaks into a million flying pieces, cheap plastic and wire, circuit boards and buttons bursting everywhere.

The funny, not-funny part is this: there's blood spurting up from this shattered piece of junk. Gouts of it, small rivers. I can feel the spots hot and sticky hitting my face, smell them too.

I stop. I'm tired. I'm sweating and I'm cold.

'Miriam?' I murmur, closing my eyes.

When I open them they've disappeared. Every last dead one of them. All that remains is the cold breath of her voice deep within my ear.

'And you thought it was all about me?' she asks, teasingly.

I sit in the kitchen, the real kitchen, cold coffee in front of me, not daring to touch it or finish the apple.

I'm shaking and shivering, miserable and afraid.

The little pink phone rings. I stare at it, wishing I had a hammer right now.

Then I pick it up.

'Bierce? Are you OK?'

'Never better,' I say after a long moment. 'How's things?'

'Good,' Alice replies. 'I think we're ready. How about you?'

In the shadow of the apple tree I can see something moving.

I hold my breath. A large grey cat leaps into the lower branches and seizes a sparrow picking at the heart of a half-rotten apple dangling there. The dying bird struggles in its sharp claws, a cloud of soft, insubstantial feathers now stained with blood.

'Ready.'

I cycled through the fog, navigating on memory and the sound of the trams, listening to their iron wheels clanking, old bells chiming, through the invisible streets of Eden, past Fair Meadow and Leather Yard, God's Acre and Silent Street, on into Westmont, where gigantic black limousines were starting to vomit up their breakfasts of suited executives looking to rule the coming day.

These streets used to be my life. The red-brick squares of late Victoriana, the long, narrow lanes of timbered stores and homes. Beyond the grey shroud it was, I knew, changed. In Westmont, huge shapes loomed above me, dark monoliths, with dim yellow lights burning in offices that probably never slept. On the low, two-lane carriageway of Broad Street, once a grassy plain for cows and linking Eden with the port, video stores and fast-food outlets shone like neon spectres risen from what was once parking lots and storage areas, a place the sensible never went.

Everywhere vehicles glided past me, oblivious to my presence. Only the middle classes cycled these days, I guessed. They started work late. And few would be found at the Piers.

That change had begun in my childhood. As the Yonge docks grew steadily grubbier and more dangerous, the city stepped in to preserve a little of its 'heritage'. The unions were losing their power. More and more ships arrived, from Japan and Europe, bringing their wares in containers, not open holds. That meant fewer men and less pier space. Eventually the full extent of the commercial waterfront – thirty-seven piers – was too much. So they hived off everything except the first nineteen, demolished twenty and twenty-one to build a new concert hall, as a landmark between the good part of the city and the bad, and dubbed the rest 'the Piers'.

Some were commuter ferry stops, bringing in workers from the islands and suburbs along the coast. The rest were tourist attractions: restaurants and bars, fairground arcades and rides, stores selling everything from kids' toys to Chinese furniture and Russian furs.

Only Pier Twenty-six stayed the same in all of this. It was here, for three-quarters of a century, that the city's fishing fleet had brought its catch. In the great glass hall of the fish market locals and visitors crowded to buy salmon and scrod, mussels and oysters, and, as its fame grew, fancier stuff from further afield, Alaskan spider crab and Maine lobster, South American tilapia and red snapper from Jamaica.

I knew this place well from when I was a school kid.

During the holidays I used to come down and earn a little cash, scrubbing mussels and scraping out the meat from fresh boiled crab. Then, when the morning's work was done, I'd wait around for the real reward, which was a seafood stew, made with tomatoes and garlic and wine, just the things your mom would never use at home, thrown together by the stall bosses themselves, and handed out for nothing to anyone who'd put in a good morning's work.

They fed me every time, on two accounts. I always earned my money. More importantly, my best friend, the one who got me into this tight little community, which was almost exclusively Italian, was Mickey Carluccio, son of the man who owned this part of town.

The Carluccios were a sprawling second-generation family from Salento in Puglia and proud of the fact. Their fiefdom covered Pier Twenty-six and the tourist candy and drink stands that roamed the entire area, from one end to the other, selling identical junk food to identical dumb tourists gasping for a sugar refill.

If you wanted to trade in Pier Twenty-six you saw Mickey's old man, Arturo, a large, smiling individual who had a habit of patting my head every time he saw me.

If you wanted to hawk your goods to the dullards meandering the piers and the waterfront, you hired your cart from the Carluccios too. Breaking either of these rules was a sure-fire way to get yourself roughed up a little, then dumped back in town with a reminder to be more polite next time round. They also owned Loomis and Jake's, after Loomis, who'd long ago bought out his partner, defaulted on some gambling debts. This was before my time, but everyone said the food, which was wonderful before, just got better and better after the Carluccios arrived.

The month we discovered Miriam was pregnant, a porter looking to get paid found Arturo at his desk in Pier Twenty-six. His face had been shot off. Before that happened someone had removed his fingers with the large, curved knife he often used to gut big fish like tuna and halibut. Arturo liked to mix with the real men in the market hall, doing what they did, all his life.

We never got a soul in court, naturally. The gossip was that one of the bigger crime firms, a *real* crime firm, had walked in and asked Arturo to front some kind of a dope-smuggling operation through the boats he used to bring in imported species from South America. Arturo had a family the size of a small country. Like Liechtenstein in all probability. From what little I recalled of him, drugs would be something he wouldn't touch, not from a mile.

So they took off his fingers, then shot away his face. Remembering this reminded me it wasn't all sunshine and lemonade in my time after all.

I'd lost touch with my schoolfriend Mickey long before that. When I chose my particular calling the relationship had cooled on both sides. But I'd phoned him a few days after, asking whether he minded if I came to the funeral. I always loved being around his old man, particularly after my own father was gone. He was funny. Alive and real in a way most of the Italians on Pier Twenty-six seemed to be. They didn't have much money, in truth, and what they did have they spent on food and drink and family.

Mickey said he thought it best I stay away. I got the

message. He kept the business the way it was. As far as we knew in the police, no one ever came to him asking the Carluccios to front a dope operation. Unless Mickey had changed greatly over the years, he would have told them where to go, especially after what happened to his old man.

Never threaten the *Salentini*, Arturo told me once, when he'd had a few glasses of wine. It was just counter-productive.

He was fifty-four when they killed him. A different generation, I thought, as I cycled down to the water-front.

Or, my head reminded me, someone just two years older than I was at that moment.

Time has a habit of catching you unawares on occasion.

I leaned my stolen pushbike against the corrugated ironwork of the market and peeked inside. It was seven-thirty in the morning. The only living things around at this time would be the professionals: fish merchants and restaurateurs looking to steal the best prizes before Joe Public arrived and got sold the rest, and flocks of white cawing gulls screaming for the scraps of flesh that found their way out of the building and into the water below.

The smell of raw fish and the sea hit me in the face and flung me back forty years in an instant. If I'd had an ounce of Italian blood in me I could probably have got a job here myself, under Mickey's wing. And then what would have happened?

Maybe something worse.

I walked through the doors. The place was bustling with people haggling over white trays of fish and clams and scallops. The layout looked much the same. In the corner where they made the stew, someone was frying down tomatoes and onions already. The vast iron crockpot, black and burnt on the base, looked like the same one Arturo used to tip fish scraps into, singing some song in Italian, with a bottle of cheap wine hanging from his left hand all the while. The sight and the smell made my stomach start to rumble.

The Carluccios' office was in the same place too: on the first floor, overlooking their territory through long wooden-framed windows. I wondered what Mickey would say when someone he hadn't seen in almost three decades walked through the door, a dead man at that.

I was still thinking that when an arm grabbed me, rough and hard, dragged me under the first-floor overhang of the office above, so quickly I couldn't even protest.

By the time I'd got round to wondering what was happening I found myself pinned up against one of the ribbed metal pillars the Italians used to strike their matches on in the old days, before smoking and food got divorced.

A man I didn't recognize had me by the throat. He looked old: almost completely bald, with a florid, pockmarked face and watery eyes. He was strong, though, and big. I couldn't move an inch.

'Bierce?' he asked, not letting go of me for a moment.

'Mickey?'

'Who the hell else?'

'Apologies. It's been . . . what?'

'A long time.'

'Right. You know what puzzles me?' I asked.

He shook his head.

'Why everyone gets older. And I just stay the same.'

'Maybe,' he said, 'that's because you're dead.'

He relaxed his grip. I held out my hand.

'Aren't you?' he added.

'Very. Does that mean we can finally talk?'

Five minutes later I was sitting in Mickey Carluccio's office with a big cup of steaming cappuccino and a warm sausage ciabatta in front of me. He had a picture of his old man on the wall. Apart from that, the office didn't look different at all. Good coffee, good food and a small, comfortable room that had scarcely changed since I was a child. I could have stayed here for the rest of my life.

I told Mickey as much as I thought wise. He listened carefully, nodding his head, thinking. It *was* him, too. The same gestures, the same thoughtful, considered habit of letting someone get through a story without interruption. He'd just got older, that was all, in a way that was much more marked than anything that had happened to me. I'd kept my hair, my teeth, my physique. Probably thanks to the regime in jail and the regular check-ups they kept giving me there. Very regular, now I thought about it. I guess if they were pumping me full of dope to a schedule, it was important to understand how I was holding up under the strain.

Mickey had been out here in the real world all along. Which for him meant two marriages, both now over, six kids, all of them still beloved, and a young girlfriend who worked as the front of house manager for Loomis and Jake's. I didn't ask which came first, the job or her.

When I finished, he gulped down the last of his

coffee, shook his head and said, 'Why you, Bierce? That's what I don't get. Of all the people I ever knew, you seemed the straightest. The one who'd end up retiring at fifty-five, living off a comfortable state pension, watching the grandchildren. You seemed so *stable*.'

Miriam and I had gone out for dinner with him and his first wife, just a couple of times. It hadn't been easy.

'I don't know,' I answered honestly. 'One day it all seemed to be there. The next . . .'

He stopped shaking his head and walked over to the long window overlooking the market.

'I never liked her,' he said, his back still turned to me.

'What?'

'Your wife.'

He came back and sat down, so that he could look me in the face.

'It was always as if she was waiting for something to come along. As if what she was doing with you was the warm-up. I don't know. It's a stupid thing to say. Ignorant too.'

'No, no. I'm interested.'

I'd told him how screwed my memory was when it came to certain periods.

'Did the two of us argue much?' I asked.

He shook his head, vigorously.

'No. Nothing like that. I'm talking crap, Bierce. Tell me to shut up.'

'I don't want you to shut up. Did I ever look as if I could have been violent to her?'

'You? Give me a break. I don't remember you getting heavy with anyone. It just wasn't the way you were. Always. I remember when we were ten, eleven.

There were jerks around at that school. I was little then. None of this fat. You stuck up for me. You didn't need to punch anyone to do it. You just told them what a bad idea it would be if they didn't go along with what you wanted. That was enough.'

I racked my brain.

'I don't remember that.'

'I do. It was the reason I stuck with you to begin with. That and the way you could gut sand dab twice as fast as anyone I knew. I *never* did like that job. Still don't.'

I laughed. It was easy.

'And when you heard Miriam and Ricky were dead?'

He squirmed in his captain's chair, spinning it from side to side, playing with a pen. The very image of his father, though I doubt he knew it.

'I don't believe for one minute you could have killed a child, Bierce. Not anyone's.'

'And Miriam?'

This had to be dragged out of him.

'Like I said, I didn't much care for her. I could imagine how she could drive a man a little crazy. Perhaps even you. She had that beautiful smile some women use the moment before they take everything you have. You want to know what I wondered?'

I did.

'I wondered whether she had done anything to that boy of yours. And that what happened then was . . .' He sighed. '. . . some kind of consequence. Is that possible?'

'I don't think so. No. I don't believe it's possible.'

'Then . . . I'm sorry. What do you need? Money? A way out? What the hell is your status anyway? Are you on the run or what?'

I shrugged.

'I'm dead, I guess. On paper. So if a couple of people come along and make that for real, who's going to know?'

'That's all I need. I'm getting you out of here.'

'Not yet,' I said quietly.

'Bierce!'

'There are people who know what happened, Mickey. I think one of them's responsible too. I can't just leave it at that.'

He groaned.

'These people being?'

'Half of them are hoods, though I imagine they'd tell you they were businessmen now, at heart.'

Mickey Carluccio swore. He seemed familiar with that concept, which I found interesting.

'And the other half?'

'Some kind of government team. Federal, I guess. Fill in the spaces. The kind of people you never hear about, not even when . . . or if . . . something comes to court. They exist. They're necessary. They're just not the sort who like you getting in the way.'

He went quiet.

'Mickey?' I asked.

He stayed quiet.

'OK,' I said. 'I understand. It was stupid of me to think I could come and pester you like this. Stupid and rude.'

I got up. His hand was on my shoulder. He was a strong man. I wasn't leaving, not yet.

'Don't rush me,' Mickey Carluccio grumbled. 'There's something we need to get out of the way.'

He didn't look happy having to say this.

'I know you thought my family were involved in all that mob stuff. It wasn't that simple. My pop was no hood, for God's sake. He was just on the edges of it all, a little guy who made good food for people the rest of town preferred to think didn't exist. He was their clown, for God's sake. He never did a serious thing for any of them. All he did was fool around and talk too much from time to time, when the wine got flowing.'

He glanced at the photo on the wall.

'So a couple of them listened to him in his cups, came round asking for something he'd never deliver and this got him killed. I have six kids, two wives and a girl-friend to feed. I am not going the same way.'

'I appreciate that,' I said, feeling a little anxious. 'I don't want your money. I just wanted a little assistance. I'm going to be having a conversation with someone important very soon.'

I looked at my watch.

'In thirty-five minutes to be precise.'

'Oh! *Oh!* I appreciate the advance notice.'

'I'm a dead man trying to walk here, Mickey. I want to have this conversation undisturbed. Your guys can make sure of that. Especially in weather like this.'

'No shooting,' he said. 'Nobody dead.'

'That I guarantee. If it all goes well, the person concerned won't even be on your territory after eight-thirty.'

'And if it doesn't?'

'Then who's to know? I'll be gone anyway. And the Chinese won't talk to anyone.'

His watery eyes lit up with alarm.

'The Chinese! What the hell do they have to do with this?'

279

'Nothing that matters to you. Are they so bad?'

'How the hell do I know? It's hard enough keeping a bunch of Italians happy without messing around with the Chinese. Get 'em in and out quick.'

He stared at me. I liked what Mickey Carluccio had become. He had authority and style. He looked like the boss around here.

'And the rest?' he demanded.

I opened my hands.

'What do you mean?'

'That sounds much too small a thing to have you come sneaking into my fish market at this time in the morning, looking guilty and scared as hell.'

'Just the one thing. I have a lunch appointment at twelve-thirty. Loomis and Jake's. Table for three.'

'You have good taste. I will make sure the food's superb. You can have some wine from my private cellar. Italian wine you won't see in the shops. The lunch is on me.'

'I'm dining with a man and a woman. The woman you can forget about. The man is, I think, something big in the mob, not that he likes to let on about that these days.'

'You didn't have to tell me that, Bierce. You already got a free meal and the best wine we have.'

'I intend to deal with the mob guy's protection, kidnap the man himself, then bring him and the other one together so that, between us, we can sort things out.'

Mickey was fidgeting on his chair, rubbing his brow with one big fist.

'I'll need you to do more than look the other way for that,' I added.

He kept on staring at me.

'*What*? After all I've said . . .'

He looked ready to throw his old schoolfriend out of the place that very instant.

'After all this you want me to help you snatch some kind of *capo* or whatever they call them? Have you listened to a single word I've said?'

'I don't have a choice, Mickey.'

He sighed.

'I am truly sorry to hear that. The answer's still no. Ask me for something I can give. It's yours.'

He looked around the room, the hall outside.

'This has been ours for seventy-eight years. The two sons I have who are of an age to run it don't want to know. Law and medicine, would you believe? How does that stack up to gutting a sand dab?'

'Mickey . . .'

'No.'

I glanced at the photo of his pop on the wall.

'The guy concerned was just some rising politico back then. I'm sure the people who knew him understood what he really was. Ambitious mostly. The kind of ambition that wasn't good for anyone who stood in his way. Do you know who killed your old man?'

'I know,' Mickey snapped. 'This conversation is coming to a rapid end now. Get out of here! Or I'll call one of the big guys.'

He had his hand on the phone. Throwing out bums was beneath this Mickey Carluccio.

'The man I'm having lunch with,' I added, 'is called Kyle McKendrick. One way or another, he's going to be in jail or dead by the end of this day. Him or me.'

He stared at me the way someone stared at a madman. But he put down the phone.

'McKendrick?'

'I think maybe it was him who had Miriam and Ricky killed. He was building some big empire back then. Don't ask me why he did it. I can't tell you. I was wondering. Did he . . . ?'

'Don't ask!' Mickey yelled. 'Don't *dare* ask. Christ, Bierce. I've spent half my life trying to swallow down what happened to my pop. Do you think that's easy?'

'I had a wife and a kid. I know it's not.'

'Oh, yeah! Oh, great! Lay that on me too. Jesus, what did I do to deserve this? You walking in looking like you've been stuck in a freezer for a couple of decades. I'm an old guy, Bierce! I got responsibilities. People looking up to me.'

'I'm sorry. If there was an alternative.'

'Find one!' he bellowed at me.

'I can't. Besides . . .'

'Besides what?'

'When someone kills a person you love you have to find some way of balancing it out. I don't think you ever did that. Did you?'

He kept quiet. He was staring at the photo on the wall, tears starting to run down his cheeks, shaking his head, grinding his teeth, swearing and gulping for breath.

I felt inordinately ashamed of myself at that moment.

'You know why they cut off his fingers?' Mickey asked after a while.

'I've no idea.'

'They said it was a question of taste. He had this

party trick. He used to play the piano. Really badly. *It was a joke!*'

My old friend Mickey Carluccio thumped his big fist on the desk and sent the contents, bills and pens, a mobile phone and some loose change, scattering all over.

'It was a joke,' he said again softly. 'McKendrick watched while that evil old bastard Guerini butchered my pop. A few years later Guerini's dead in a car somewhere out on the peninsula and everything's McKendrick's. He owns the whole damn city.'

'That was after I'd gone to jail.'

'I guess. Guerini was a buffoon. If people wrote histories of these scum they'd say McKendrick was the main man all along. They'd say it was all changing anyway, and men like my pop were just part of the dead generation who never understood that. This isn't the world we were kids in, Bierce.'

'I noticed.'

'I wish it was. That's a place you can't go back to. Not me. Not you. Not anyone.'

'I don't want to go back there,' I said emphatically. 'I just want things set straight. And I want my memory back. Nothing more.'

Mickey shrugged. He was in control again.

'Those were the things I heard,' he added. 'I think they're true. I can't guarantee it. What I *can* tell you is that McKendrick's a big man. Bigger than ever today.'

I nodded.

'He's a hood in a silk suit, fooling himself he's something else,' I said. 'Your pop would have said that was a sure sign of weakness. That a man should be what he is, not what he thinks he should be.'

Mickey grimaced, then reached into his desk and pulled out two cigars. I turned down the offer and watched him light up.

'We used to get up to some stuff, didn't we?' Mickey said with a shadow of a grin.

'I believe so.'

He laughed, a wreath of smoke curling round his bald head.

'Why the hell does it have to be me, Bierce? Do you really have no other friend in the world?'

'Not a one,' I lied.

He got to his feet, looked out of the window and stared down at the market floor.

'Keep talking,' he said.

Alice was outside, next to the chowder stall by the gate, shivering in a blue Chinese jacket. The fog was turning into a bad one. Somewhere over the curved roof of the market hall I could just make out the hazy silver disc of the sun struggling to fight its way through the thick grey haze. It wasn't making much impact. The city got cold in weather like this. It always fooled the tourists, who came out, spent thirty minutes shivering on the streets and the trams, then fled back to the hotels and cafes of Eden to try to stay warm, wondering how they'd fill the rest of the day.

This suited me wonderfully. Also, there was a steady rush of long-faced commuters dribbling off the ferry piers and starting on the long walk to their cubicles in Westmont, a small river of humanity flowing in one direction, unwilling, for a moment, to stop for anything in its way. Stape might have lots of hardware and knowledge. He wouldn't come alone either, though, because he understood I was no fool. But his helicopter wouldn't be flying. I had opportunity and more than a couple of surprises up my sleeve.

And I had Alice and her gang. Six surly, slovenly Chinese youths who stood by her, sniffing at the chowder getting made, snarling at the girl preparing it because there wasn't a bowl yet ready to eat.

They didn't look the smartest, nicest people on the planet, but right then I wasn't in much of a position to get picky.

One, the tallest, about twenty, with a long, arrogant face and the aggressive demeanour of a street punk, came up to me and said, 'Money. Mr Ho say you got money.'

I smiled.

'Who the hell is Mr Ho?'

He glanced at Alice. She gave him a vicious look in return.

'Boss,' he said simply.

'Mr Ho is a well-informed man.'

'You pay now. Cash in advance.'

'Do I get a receipt? Is this tax-deductible?'

He stared at me, unable to work this out.

I took his arm.

'Here's the deal, er . . . I didn't catch your name.'

'No name.'

'OK. Here's the deal, No Name. You do the work.'

I took out my wad and waved it under his nose.

'You get paid. You do it exceptionally well and I hand over a little more, not that I'm telling Mr Ho that. Agreed?'

He looked me up and down, smiled, nodded, then

walked back to talk to the rest of them. They didn't return. I took this as a sign they were in agreement.

'Where the hell did you find these people?' Alice hissed at me when they were still mumbling among each other, out of earshot.

'I didn't. I thought you did.'

'You and Lao Lao put this together, Bierce. Don't blame me.'

This would have been interesting had I possessed the time.

'I can't imagine Lao Lao knows little punks like this,' Alice continued.

'She called someone for me. Maybe that person called someone else. Who cares?'

Alice waved a finger in my face.

'I don't know who these kids are, Bierce. Bear that in mind. I don't know . . .'

There. It happened again. One more moment where I could have stepped in and torn down the walls between us.

Instead I said, 'All this plan needs is a little muscle.'

She brightened up a little at that. We were both relieved, I guess. Then she slapped her gloved hands together.

'There's a *plan*? Well, that's a relief. I thought we were just making this up as we went along.'

I refused to rise to that particular bait.

'Am I to be allowed to share in this information?' she asked.

'Sure. Today, I – *we*, if you like – kidnap two people. One being the government agent I suspect talked Jonny and May and Miriam into the whole Sister Dragon idea in the first place. The second is Kyle McKendrick.'

'Because . . . he was having an affair with your wife?'

'No. Because one of these two people ordered a couple of lowlife crooks-to-rent called Frankie Solera and Tony Molloy to kill your mom and my family in order to keep them quiet about what had been going on.'

She nodded.

'Which one?'

'I don't know. Plus, there's a personal matter too. One of them somehow talked Miriam into thinking he was going to run away with her. Or maybe set her up in some new life in Europe, with all the money they were stealing from our joint account, and whatever else they could take from the Sister Dragon scam.'

Alice considered these possibilities.

'And when you – *we* – find out? Then what?'

'I don't know that either,' I answered honestly. 'Do you have any suggestions?'

'Not legal ones.'

'Me neither,' I agreed. 'Can we trust these Chinese kids?'

She smiled and shrugged.

'I'm just a cocktail waitress with a background. How would I know?'

'Can you understand them?'

'It's Cantonese. I can get it up to a point. They speak really quickly. These are gang members.' A shadow crossed her face. 'I guess they're what my Uncle Jonny was once.'

'Talk to No Name. Get him on our side.'

'All that takes is money.'

'Then that's what he gets. As much as it takes.'

She hesitated.

'Do you really want to do all this at Owl Creek? Won't that be the first place they'll look?'

I'd thought about that already. I was beginning to have a feeling for this time I was living in. It felt it was smart. In some ways, perhaps. In others . . .

'These people aren't like that. They'll stare at their computers, call a meeting or three. Try to think it all through. We used to just blunder in and hope everything worked out OK in the end. I think that's considered a little . . .'

'Neanderthal?' she asked.

'Your word not mine.'

'Neanderthal,' she said again, and stared at the ocean, which was fast disappearing behind a wall of grey mist.

The eight-twenty-five ferry from Stonetown was for people who planned to start work late. Maybe they were lucky or hung-over or just plain idle. But there were plenty of them. I had to fight against a struggling tide of besuited, shivering, unhappy humanity as I tried to make my way up Pier Twenty-seven for my appointment with Ridley Stapleton, glancing around me to see what kind of interested company I might be picking up.

None that was obvious. The secret squirrels were good at their job. The problem they had was one they shared with all the covert people I'd briefly encountered during my time as a uniform cop. They lived inside their own little world, so much they thought it was real, and the rest of us were just marionettes going through the motions.

The squirrel mentality demanded, too, that there

could be no easy way to do anything. You had to check out everything first.

I didn't have time for that. Neither did Stape. The difference was I knew it. I also knew why I was there. Not to deal with Stape, or kill him, which was probably what he believed. But to snatch him from right under the noses of his colleagues. Here was my strong point. They were focusing on me when, in truth, they should have been focusing on him.

I'd borrowed a fisherman's jacket from the market and a woollen hat I pulled down low over my face. There were scores of men dressed this way in the fog. I didn't look out of place for a second.

Once I'd pushed through the throng of commuters I made my way slowly towards the head of the pier, stopping by the rusty gangplank where the passengers came off. I took a good look around. Stape was no fool. There were men – and women – hanging about. The next ferry back to Stonetown left at twenty to nine, another, to the larger suburban town of Rainport, five minutes later. Some of the bodies nearby would be people waiting to travel home against the normal flow of traffic this time of day. Some would be his.

Naturally, I made myself late. Stape was desperate to meet me. If I didn't turn up he would have to face the possibility I'd bumped into Kyle McKendrick along the way. If I was late, he would start to get uncomfortable, and the first rule in dealing with anyone you're trying to do bad things to is . . . make them feel as awkward and ill at ease as possible.

After five minutes of hanging around the gang-plank, though, I was starting to get a bit restless myself. Mr Ho's little gang was there, crowded together by the billboards on the jetty, ostensibly checking out the latest movie posters. The ferry was making moves to go. This being the 'wrong' direction, and Stonetown barely more than a village, the return trip at this time of the morning would often be almost empty apart from the crew. On a day like this you could sit outside, up front, wreathed in mist, listening to the foghorn all the way on the steady ten-minute trip across the water to Stonetown. It should have been perfect.

Then I saw a dark crook-backed figure wending its way through the huddle of coated bodies on the jetty.

About time, I muttered to myself, and carefully slipped my old police handgun out of the pocket of my jacket, into my tight fingers.

He was looking. The ferry was getting ready to go. Any second now the gangplank would go up and the grubby little tug-like ferry would be on its way.

I nodded to Mr Ho's gang. They saw their man. I waited until the ferry crew started walking towards their ropes.

Then I let off two shots into the grey foggy air and yelled, 'Stape, Stape, you murdering bastard, you . . .'

Fill in the obscenities as you see fit. Most of the ordinary men and women didn't hear them, not clearly anyway. Because, you see, I was screaming them out loud while racing as fast as I could along the jetty *back* to dry land.

By my count there were a good five squirrels following in my tracks. One of them had bright white hair and a limp. I guess Martin the Medic didn't walk away from the wreck of his Hyundai completely unscathed.

The sight of him, the memory of his sharp, pricking

needles, inspired me to let loose a couple more shots up into the fog when I got back to the chowder stand, where Alice was screaming blue murder. Sheldon's old Volvo was up on the sidewalk, revving, ready to go.

'Get in,' she screeched.

When we turned south, driving very slowly and carefully, towards the Stonetown jetty, fifteen minutes or so away at this time of the morning, just a little slower than the ferry, I allowed myself a look back.

Mickey had been as good as his word. It looked as if the entire population of the fish market, a couple of hundred people by that time of day, had emptied out on to the wharf and were now milling around, looking lost and angry, blocking the narrow exit of the pier, spreading out on to the cobblestones of the pierside road.

However many little silicon toys they had tucked away in their furry pockets, the secret squirrels would be struggling against that unforeseen eventuality for an hour or more. From what insight I'd gained into their management methods, it seemed quite probable to me that, before they settled upon their next course of action, it might well be necessary to convene a meeting, with someone to take notes, and run through a re-evaluation of their goals and targets, their *modus operandi* and tradecraft.

At some stage – though not soon, in all this murky fog and human confusion – they might work out that Ridley Stapleton was missing. At some stage they might even come to realize that a small party of Chinese youths hopped on to the departing Stonetown ferry very, very quickly, with such a rapid, deliberate motion they just might have swept up an unsuspecting middle-aged man in their midst, and sat on him, lightly, but not too much I hoped, outside on the front deck for the short journey across the water to Stonetown.

Not that any of this mattered, I thought, as Alice drove carefully to the pier stop, where, dimly, we could now see the ferry moored, silent for the morning, with a handful of crew seated outside the terminal, cigarettes beaming like small orange beacons through the fog.

There was a rusty red van with some Chinese writing on it parked a little way along from the exit. I left Alice, then opened the van doors and got in. Stape was there, his hands in front of him, bound with rope.

He had a black eye and a bloodied mouth.

'Hey,' I said to No Name, 'I told you not to damage the goods.'

'Stupid old guy got punchy,' he muttered, and hit Stape lightly on the shoulder.

The vehicle began to move, with the awkward bumping motions old vans have.

'That is *so* out of character,' I said, shaking my head. 'His stuff?'

No Name passed over a handgun, a mobile phone, some kind of radio, a set of headphones with a curly wire coming out of the back and what looked like a mike dangling down beneath. Plus something that looked like a shrunken video cassette made out of aluminium. It was just big enough to fit into a pocket. The thing had a large screen blinking colourful patterns and a few silver buttons on the front.

'What the hell is this?' I asked him, and got no reply.

'Palmtop,' No Name answered.

'A what?'

'Palmtop.'

He pressed a button. The screen filled with a street map. A red star was flashing on it, moving gently along the selfsame road we ought to be using.

'What the hell are they giving you squirrels these days, Stape?' I asked.

'Nothin' special,' No Name interjected. 'My uncle got electronics shop. He sell this shit. Cheap too. Palmtop. GSM. GPRS. GPS. You can play videos and MP3s on it too.'

He tapped Stape on the shoulder, gently this time.

'Next time your boss want some more, come to Chinatown. We do a good deal.'

'You don't want to get involved in government purchasing schemes,' I said. 'It's not your field.'

They all stiffened at the g-word. I reminded myself not to use it again.

After which I took out my gun and placed it on Stape's temple. The Chinese boys stiffened even more at that. Someone turned up the radio. It was playing old Western pop.

'The suspicious part of me keeps saying there must be something in this magical device that tells people where you are. For your sake I hope this isn't true. Because if we get disturbed, Stape, I will, I swear, put a bullet through your temple before I even so much as consider what to do next. So?'

He pointed a finger at the side of the thing. I held it closer to him. He pushed at a little slot. A black plastic card the size of a thumbnail popped out.

'Oh . . .' No Name grinned, grabbing it. 'SIM card! Free gov'ment phone calls!'

They laughed.

'Where are we going?' Stape asked after a while.

'Please,' I answered, and gave him a playful pat on his shoulder. 'You're kidding me. You mean you really don't know?'

'What do you want, Bierce?' he murmured.

'I want . . .'

The radio was damn loud. A familiar tune. One that was starting to get to me.

The van stank of old perfume and Chinese herbs. I closed my eyes. She was there.

Sing to me, Bierce.

I can't sing.

Then pretend.

'I want to bury Miriam, Stape. Don't you?'

I was never a den man. No time and, if I'm being honest, no interest. Work and family were what mattered to me. The basement of Owl Creek belonged to Miriam. It was her territory and I knew to keep out unless invited. She had a desk down there, for what she called her 'house routine'. She put in an old TV and a VCR. I never got the attraction myself. The room was the length of the house, undivided, but dusty and always damp. There was scant light coming in from the narrow ground-level windows that sat above the damp-course collecting algae and mud. It always felt to me like a grave with electric lighting. Ricky didn't want to go in there either. It scared him. Ghosts or demons or bogey-men lurked behind the cobwebbed corners.

Perhaps that was why she liked it.

We passed Alice's Volvo, parked in the street, then Mr Ho's young acolytes drove their red van into my drive. I hopped out, opened up the garage. They reversed in and, thanks to the wonders of house design in the 1890s, we were able to take our captive straight to the basement through a side door that led down from inside the garage.

No one saw or knew a thing as far as I was aware. It couldn't have gone more smoothly.

Every last light bulb worked. They should have done. I'd checked them that morning, changing two for the replacements Alice had brought that first night, when she was trying to make the place liveable in. I told No Name to tie Stape to one of the six old kitchen chairs tucked beneath the ancient wooden table we found here when we moved in.

I walked round the room and ran a finger through the thick dust on the table.

'Sorry,' Alice said, with a smile. 'I never even knew this place existed.'

'And you?' I asked of my guest.

Stape didn't seem much interested in a conversation. He sat there, No Name's rope around his chest, under his arms, his hands tied in front of him. He was hovering between being awkward and being scared, with the former winning at that particular moment.

'You are *so* out of your depth here, Bierce. Trust me. The best thing you can do is let me go now and pray I'm feeling generous once I get outside this dump.'

No Name had sent the others back to the van. He was wandering around with a big, stupid smile on his face, looking at all the junk, the washing machine, the central heating furnace, the typewriter sitting in the middle of the kitchen table, touching stuff, pressing keys and buttons, laughing to himself. Judging by the amused look on his face, he thought he'd stepped into a time machine. He wasn't even in the womb the last time I'd been in this place. So maybe he was right. It was from another world.

'Best you go see what your boys are doing,' I suggested.

He was, I now tended to believe, a distinctly creepy individual.

'No. We done a good half of the job. We get good half of the money.'

'When the . . .' I started to say.

Then I stopped. No Name had walked up to the old TV, a junk thing even in our day, with a mechanical rotary dial and a picture that shook from time to time. He'd punched some buttons on the front. A picture came up, bright and good. Black and white, but who'd complain? They built things well back then.

It was a newscast. It seemed the biggest story of the day was the fog. That was good to hear.

'Turn it off,' I ordered. '*Turn it off!*'

No Name was hunting round the kitchen table. It struck me after a second or two. He was looking for a remote.

I walked over to the TV and pressed the power button. Miriam had put a VCR next to it not long before the sky fell down on us. It was still there, still dusty.

It rang a bell, one I couldn't place.

I pulled out something like a thousand in notes, showed No Name there was lots more where that came from and said, 'I am, by nature, a generous individual. But only for good boys who do as they're told.'

He took the cash, grinning.

'I want watch you, Bierce. You interesting guy. This

better than chasing rent down Chinatown. I learn from you.'

'Yeah. You can learn how to end up in jail. Alice?'

She stared at me, a little mad because she knew what was coming.

'Take him upstairs. I'll be along in a little while. Then we go back down the Piers.'

'This involves me,' she insisted.

'We need a few moments of private time.'

I patted Stape on his grey rodent's head.

'That's right, now. Isn't it?'

He muttered something obscene.

They went. I took out my gun, held it loosely in my fingers, angling it in his direction.

'The first time you lie to me, Stape,' I said, 'I will shoot you in the knee. The next time in that busy little groin of yours. The last time in the head. Do those three statements leave *any* room for misunderstanding between us? Because if they do, best we clear it up now.'

I should have remembered something. Ridley Stapleton had, by this time, been a government employee, a fully fledged secret squirrel no less, for a quarter of a century. He was institutionalized by that experience just as much as I was by the time I'd spent in Gwinett and Kyle McKendrick's private convict quarters, sweating and staring at the walls.

What guile and imagination he'd once possessed had been surgically squeezed out of him by some endless round of focus groups, managerial assessments and bonding sessions. He thought like a robot. A scared, sneaky robot with the moral backbone of a jellyfish, but a robot all the same.

All I had to do was press the right buttons and off he went. For one very good reason. Stape, my old patrol-bike buddy, the man I thought I'd saved from a life of corrupt policing, genuinely believed me guilty. He just wasn't quite sure of what any more.

We began with Sister Dragon, since that was something I was beginning to get a feel for anyway. There were only a limited number of reasons the squirrels would set up a sleazy nightclub in St Kilda and governmental privatization was not among them. It was a sting operation. They'd got their sights on someone they wanted very badly indeed. Someone smart enough to stay out of legal harm in the natural way of things.

So they did what smart squirrels did in the eighties – and ever since, for all I knew. They invented a situation in which crime could flourish and be seen to flourish, then they sat around, collecting all the evidence, waiting for the day they could jump out from the wings and say, *Surprise!*

It didn't come, of course. What did arrive was 25 July, killing day for the Bierce and Loong families. Stape didn't look too happy about that outcome either when we went over it. I'll give him that.

Ridley Stapleton looked at me and asked, 'Why are we going through all this, Bierce? Am I really expected to believe it's all news to you?'

'Yes . . . Because it *is*. What do I have to do to convince you?'

'Find a time machine,' he said instantly. 'She had your skin under her nails. You don't get that through a handshake.'

'Married people do not shake hands. Did you find my skin under May Loong's fingernails too?'

He lost his temper and yelled, 'It wasn't just Miriam and May!'

I blinked, wondering whether this really was news to me. My old partner was staring at me as if I were the devil incarnate or something.

'We lost seven other people that day. Some bastard tipped off McKendrick's people. You want to see? Pull that gadget out of my pocket. Give it here.'

I took out the thing that had the street map on it and put it in his right hand. He had just enough movement to hit the buttons and press at the screen.

'Here. This is Sister Dragon. The way we found it.'

I let him flick through the photos on the little screen while I looked. It was the kind of scene you used to see on the news in Beirut and places. Bodies and blood everywhere. Arms and legs sprawled out in that awkward, crooked way dead people fall.

'This is supposed to mean something to me?' I asked. 'I didn't know any of these people.'

'Is that so? The only two of our operatives who didn't get killed were May and Miriam,' Stape went on. 'They weren't there at the time. Not that it did them much good.'

'Were you screwing Miriam too?' I asked, not really wanting to know.

He closed his eyes.

'It was a business relationship. Nothing more.'

Something in his face made me rest the gun on his knee and play with the trigger.

He squeezed his eyes tight, then screeched, 'OK! *OK!* It was just the twice. In that damn club.'

'Why?' was all I could manage.

'Because she was beautiful! Because she wanted it. Because . . .'

The sweat was starting to bead on Stape's face. He went quiet, scared.

'Because . . . ?' I prompted.

'Because it was in that place. Don't ask me for an explanation. Or an apology. You don't get either. We set up that club to be somewhere people could check in their identities at the door, then become someone else. We – and I give most of the credit to Miriam – did that very well. You left it behind when you walked out.'

I wanted to laugh.

'You don't honestly believe that, do you?' I asked. 'Still?'

'I slept with your wife twice, in some squalid little sex club in Humboldt Street. She seemed pretty pleased with how it went at the time. That's all there is to say on the subject. Besides . . .'

He wasn't scared any longer. He was just full of hate.

'You got her into all this, Bierce. Or is that a part of your memory that got burned out too?'

The gun was starting to feel a little damp in my fingers. I put it down, wiped my hand on my pants and took it up again. A part of me wanted a drink.

'You're saying I came to you and *asked* you to whore my wife for whatever faceless grey-suited bureaucrats pushed your buttons?'

He nodded.

'Pretty much.'

'I did this in person? Was I buying the beer or was it you?'

He wriggled. This was something he had to remember.

'No. Miriam came to me. She said it was your idea.'

The weapon twitched in my hand.

'Oh, right . . .'

'She said you told her there was some civilian under-cover work going. She didn't specify what interested her. Neither did I. When we spoke it was kind of obvious . . .'

'*What* was kind of obvious?'

'She was bored. Bored stupid. She said you knew that. You'd talked about it. You both thought a little . . . experience might help your marriage.'

'So you never heard it directly from me?' I asked.

'This was Miriam! Why the hell would she make up something like that? Why the . . . Jesus, Bierce. *Jesus!*'

I let loose two rounds close to his right leg. The shells bounced off the hard stone floor and winged their way around the basement, whistling in different directions. Then they buried themselves in the woodwork somewhere. I wasn't looking. It didn't seem important.

'That wasn't a lie!' Stape screamed.

'Correction,' I said calmly. 'It was not *your* lie. It was Miriam's. That's why I missed.'

'What is it you want?' I asked. 'A memory? A cassette? A photograph? What?'

Stape sighed and shook his head. I lifted the gun again.

'You are seriously starting to get to me,' I warned. 'There's something missing here. You think I know about it. I swear I don't.'

'OK,' he snapped. 'I'll play this game. I should be used to it by now. We had some fancy state-of-the-art surveillance system in there. No one had ever used it before. There were these little cameras, big cameras, all kinds. The mob people weren't stupid. They had stuff they could sweep a place with too.'

He frowned. The memory was painful.

'The big local man at the time was Guerini. Mc-Kendrick was just his puppet on the council. But he had ambitions.'

Stape stared at me.

'Guerini was in some deal to get into bed with people from the east. We had one room, very private, all wired up through a video chamber behind in a way they couldn't detect. Miriam and May worked that with their clients, then dealt with the tapes after. When they weren't using it, the mob people would go in and talk. Sometimes it got a little mixed up. A bit of both. That was when it turned really valuable.'

'And?'

'Don't look so freakin' bored, Bierce. We weren't talking about a bunch of mid-rank punks running local rackets. They were all going to hook up, become something *huge*. Maybe legitimate mostly.'

I shook my head.

'What place is there in this world for the little man?'

'We could have taken them all. Guerini. McKendrick. Those bastards from the east. We had agents from all over waiting and watching for the day. Then, when our backs are turned, someone walked in and slaughtered every last one of them.'

He was glaring at me now.

'We got it all down on two tapes Miriam had cut for us in the video room. When we'd washed up the blood we found they were gone. All our work. All our evidence.'

I got the accusing look again.

'Which means,' Stape went on, 'they knew where to look.'

'That must have been a blow. You shouldn't have turned your backs.'

'Screw you,' he grumbled. 'We lost everything. The mobs merged. Guerini got blown away by his underling one day after playing golf. McKendrick became the local don and the city benefactor too. Result? This is the Wild West now and no one knows it. The trains and the buses run on time. If you walk down the street you'd think the crime rate wasn't too bad at all. It doesn't need to be. *They own it all anyway.*'

Which was, in a very fuzzy way, very much what I'd begun to think for myself.

'So,' I asked carefully, 'if I did all these favours for them, how come I wound up in jail, sitting on death row, getting needles up me all the time?'

'You tell me.'

'I do not know.'

'How many answers can there be, Bierce?'

'Just the one, I guess. I was trying to screw them. Or someone was.'

'Correct.'

'With these tapes?'

He didn't need to say a thing.

'And if you had them now?' I asked.

'There'd be people falling down all the way from here to the Atlantic, McKendrick being one of the smaller ones. Why do you think he kept you alive in jail all those years? He needs the things, still.'

I must have been getting smarter at that moment.

Because the next question worked so well it made me think I could have been a decent detective – sorry, *dee*-tective – once upon a time.

'And when Frankie Solera got religion and coughed this all up to his priest or someone?' I asked.

Stape's mouth creased with the ghost of a smile.

'Then bingo. McKendrick knew you'd be coming out soon. Which to us meant that one way or another you'd be dead before long. He'd had you for more than two decades, pumping you for what he wanted. If he couldn't get it and you had a ticket to freedom, then . . .'

He frowned. I think he couldn't work out whether to say what was on his mind or not.

'We'd prior warning Solera was going to get talking before he croaked. We lifted you out of the correctional facility six weeks ago and put you in some fake jail rooms we made out some place we have in the forest,' he continued, and for some reason that news depressed me deeply. I really had been out of things not to notice such an event. 'All that crap on the TV about the execution was just McKendrick trying to cover his tracks. We tried our best to . . . get through to you too. It didn't work. Still, you're alive. For the moment.'

Inside No Name's ropes my old partner shrugged, the way a doctor might if some cough medicine hadn't worked correctly.

'We thought we'd try a few last tricks. No luck. Then we thought we'd let you come home. See what happens.'

His two rheumy eyes never left me.

'You always were a smug bastard, Bierce. It was your name on that bank account. And the rest.'

I thought about the document on Susanna Aurelio's computer. And that scribble in the margin.

'I saw something on the court documents. About a call I supposedly made. Which you couldn't use. Why was that?'

'Illegal phone tap. I thought maybe it was admissible because Miriam knew about it. She put the bug on your line.'

'*Our* line.'

'Your line,' he said, gripping his little toy. 'Do you want to hear?'

'Sure,' I said, and I knew from the quick and easy grin on his sick face that this was probably the last thing I'd want, ever.

His fingers started working the screen.

'We picked this up four hours after the shootings at Sister Dragon. Straight after May Loong was murdered. We don't know where the call was made from. Back in those days we couldn't work that out so easily. This was you calling Miriam, after you'd worked out she wasn't going to play your game.'

Coming out of the tinny speaker of his little gadget it sounded scratchy, the way old recordings do. But it was me all right. And I sounded mad. Very mad.

'Miriam. *Miriam!*'

There was a silence on the line. Then, 'Bierce? Where are you? What's wrong? Please come home. We can work this out. I love you, sweetheart. I love you.'

The terror in her voice sounded so real.

'*Damn your love!*' this old me on Stape's gadget roared.

'Ricky's going to bed soon, darling. Don't wake him. He hates it when we argue. Please . . .'

'*Damn your lies!*' I bellowed.

The call ended suddenly. Someone, me supposedly, had slammed down the phone somewhere.

Stape stayed quiet, looking smug.

The basement felt alive with her presence, strong and pervasive, like the sweet damp wood smell of the old timbers rising with the dust.

The TV's on. She has the VCR hooked up to it and something new. A large, shiny video camera.

'Miriam! *Miriam!* Where'd this come from? We can't afford things like that.'

It sits on a tripod, staring back into the room, big and ugly, connected to the VCR by cables. I've no idea why it's there. Ricky's at school. I've come home a little early. She isn't around when I arrive. When she turns up she looks flustered, excited. Perhaps a little embarrassed.

She rushes me down to see the camera when I ask her where she's been.

'It's not bought, silly. You know Caitlin Sanderson?'

'No.'

'You do. You just don't recall. Her husband works for Sony or someone. He has these things coming out of his ears. They hand them out. To get consumer feed-back or something.'

'You mean it's free?'

'It's free.' She sighs. 'What's the problem? Look . . .'

She messes with the buttons on the VCR. It seems to me as if it was recording already and she stopped it. I know nothing about these toys, though it occurs to me that Miriam loves playing with them more than any-thing. Then a picture comes on the TV, Ricky fiddling with his face, looking bored. Finally he sings a song, something from *Sesame Street*. He seems embarrassed.

'How cute can something be?' she asks. 'Think of the memories.'

I tap the side of my head.

'This works just fine for me.'

'You're prehistoric, Bierce. Look . . .'

She puts a tape in the hi-fi, something I only half recognize, then stands in front of the microphone doing her best impersonation of a rock chick, wildly throwing her hair around, screeching the lyrics.

After a minute she stops and looks at me.

'Your turn,' she says, pointing at the camera.

'No, no, no.'

I'm not in uniform. I'm in plain clothes, and have been for a couple of weeks, staking out a dead and empty warehouse on the edge of Yonge. It had got so boring I even told Miriam a little of what I was doing. I *complained*. This was not like me.

'Do this for me,' she says. 'I like this new stuff. Cameras and things. There's so much you can do. It's like Hollywood.'

'Hollywood's a bunch of dreams. Or nightmares.'

'It's cool.'

'I find it hard enough dealing with what we have already.'

'Don't worry. I'll deal with it for you. Stand there.'

I get pushed in front of the camera, stare into its dead glass eye. She fast-forwards the tape. I listen to it squealing. Then the monotonous thump of a bass drum, some scratchy banjo, harmony singing, male and female in unison, so high and perfect I couldn't imagine how people would even think of something like that, let alone perform it.

The bass falls in. The anguished voices roll.

'Sing it, Bierce,' she orders over the music.

'I don't know the words. I can't sing . . .'

'Listen. *Sing!*'

She turns down the volume of the hi-fi. It's almost like a backing track now. Inviting me.

'Come on. Just for me. *Please.* Then we can go upstairs and I'll do *anything* you want. Even . . . I don't know. You name it.'

This isn't like her at all.

'Miriam . . .'

She lifts up her scarlet dress, starts swirling it around her long, tanned legs, lifting it to the insistent rhythm of the music. I blink. She's got nothing on underneath.

'Here's an idea,' she snaps. 'If you don't want to sing it, just *say* it. Imagine I'm a movie director or something. *Act*, Bierce. Pretend for once in your life. Do this for me. *Please.*'

I hate disappointing her, even when I feel like a fool. But we're in our dusty old basement where no one can see. And afterwards she'll hide it, in the drawer behind the TV, which sits on a table facing the wrong way towards the wall, because the front legs are so weak and rickety that's the only position in which it can stay upright.

I mumble the refrain and they're words full of anguish and hatred.

'*Act*, Bierce,' She yells at me. 'Get mad. Get human.'

'Don't want to,' I complain like a child.

'Give me feeling! Give me fury, goddammit!'

She walks up and slaps me hard in the face.

I stare into the camera and yell, loud and hurt and angry now, hearing the refrain of the song, trying to match my pained grunting in time to the music, the way she wants it.

And I sing, because these are the words coming out of the hi-fi over and over again, '*Damn your love, damn your lies.*'

She hits the off button, for the VCR and the hi-fi, before the end of the song. The room falls into a sudden, stark silence.

'That was good,' Miriam says. 'Now we can go upstairs and . . . Oh.'

She's looking at her watch.

'I'm sorry. It's late. I have to go fetch Ricky.'

She kisses me quickly on the cheek.

'You don't mind, do you?'

'No,' I say, and mean it.

She points at the camera.

'Play with the thing some more if you like.'

'No,' I say firmly. 'It's beyond me.'

'Poor Bierce,' she says, and walks up the steps to the garage. Soon after I hear the sound of her car, gunning hard and loud, as the vehicle lurches noisily out into the road.

Stape regarded me carefully for a few moments, then said, 'Forty minutes or so after you made that call they were dead. It wasn't us. I don't think it was McKendrick. It was you and Solera and Tony Molloy, doing what you did at the club, and at May Loong's, trying to screw us all.'

This was interesting. Not what he was saying but the uninterrupted way he said it. I thought I'd been out for a good five minutes or so. To him it had all happened in an instant. The miracle of jail dope flashbacks. Or something.

'I was on duty that day,' I replied quietly.

'Kind of. We checked. You were on plain-clothes surveillance. You had been for weeks. On your own. No supervision. You could do what the hell you liked.'

When I closed my eyes I could see Miriam bending over the VCR, punching the buttons, hooking wires up to the hi-fi, doing clever things, copying and editing, words and pictures and sounds, managing to change things, meld things in ways I could never begin to understand.

I like this new stuff, she said.

I walked over to the table, leaned around the back, found the drawer that didn't really look as if it existed at all. There were only so many places you could hide something in Owl Creek, and the squirrels clearly didn't have the imagination to find any of them. The tape was still there, inside its cardboard case. I turned on the VCR, wondering how reliable these things were after two decades, and pushed the plastic slug through the dusty slot. It took a minute of button punching to get something on the screen. The picture was crackly and coarse, from all the dust I guess. But I'd found the right one.

Ricky, dead Ricky, just a few ghostly shapes now, trapped on a piece of tape, was singing his song from *Sesame Street*.

The poor kid didn't look cheerful. With the benefit of twenty-three years' hindsight I thought there was, perhaps, something in his face I'd never noticed at the time, and should have. Some unhappiness. Some awkward, inner fear.

My captive squirrel was struggling against his ropes, excited all of a sudden.

I found I was crying. I wiped the tears from my eyes with the sleeve of Susanna's errant husband's shirt.

'Sorry,' I said. 'Wrong tape.'

Then I hit the stop button and went upstairs.

'Are you OK?' Alice asked.

I didn't answer straight away, so No Name jumped in for me. He was driving. The two of us were upfront. His underlings bounced around in the back of the van with all the restaurant smells.

'He's fine,' No Name insisted. 'I watch this man. He handle himself good.'

We were heading through the business district, downtown Westmont, all tall office buildings and anonymous grey people on anonymous grey sidewalks.

I looked at her and said, 'I keep remembering. It's the house, I guess.'

Her fingers wound their way into my hand. I looked her straight in the face and wondered how long it was going to be before I knew exactly what it was she was lying about.

'Did he tell you anything?'

'Not really.' That's the thing about lies. They're infectious.

A few minutes later No Name stopped the van by the goods entrance. Mickey Carluccio was there already, as he promised. Loomis and Jake's sat round the corner, on its own small pier overlooking the sea lions and the gulls, just far enough away from the fish market to escape the smell.

I checked my watch. We had twenty minutes to spare.

'How are you feeling now?' Alice asked, and I think she was worried.

I thought about it, wondering how I might inform her politely that this question was starting to bother me.

'Hungry,' I replied.

Mickey gave us an outside table. It stood at the end of the miniature wharf, with three gigantic lampposts pumping out heat and light from gas canisters in their feet. It was cold, but only when you strayed away from the table. The fog had cleared just enough for me to be able to see the black, slug-like shapes of the sea lions basking on the rocks below and the gentle wash of an incoming tide over the long hanks of green seaweed around them.

I was enjoying a glass of tomato juice laced with some comforting Tabasco when a large, white individual, twice as wide at the shoulders as he was at the feet, walked over towards me very purposefully.

He kept his hands stuffed deep in the pockets of his grey suit. I had a momentary flash of fear as they came out when he reached the table.

'Mr Bierce?' he asked in a slow, patient voice.

'No one else.'

I stuck out a hand.

'May I be of assistance?'

'I am Paul,' he announced. 'Mr McKendrick will be here momentarily.'

He had just the one earpiece with a curly cable coming out of it, then running down to the collar of his jacket. His face had a bland babyish appearance that was almost fetching. Paul didn't look threatening at all. He was front-of-house security, not the muscle guy I'd met the day before.

'What work do you do, Paul?'

'I am Mr McKendrick's engagements officer, sir,' he replied.

I pointed at the earpiece and the curly cord.

'Can you get sports scores on that?'

'No, sir,' he replied very seriously. 'I regret that is not a possibility.'

'Seems a shame. I was thinking of hiring an engagements officer myself. How much does a man like you expect to earn these days?'

He wriggled inside his suit, uncomfortable.

'I guess the . . . going rate is thirty thousand up.'

'*Thirty thou?* All that responsibility. You having to carry a gun and all?'

He swallowed. For such a large man he had a remarkably small Adam's apple.

'You *do* have a gun, don't you? Kyle and I have made a few enemies over the years. I'd hoped you were here to protect me as well.'

He nodded.

'I do own a gun, sir,' he said quietly. 'Legally.'

Poor Paul. He really was just front-of-house security. He'd no idea why he was there at all.

'Now will you excuse me for a moment?' he added.

He went back to the fire escape that led down to the lower level of the pier. A couple of feet along was the end of the kitchen block. The double wooden door still stood there as I remembered it. Waiters would bounce through at regular intervals with plates of steaming soup and seafood stew. It was a little early for that now, though. And from the brief conversation I'd enjoyed with Mickey Carluccio on the way in, I gathered that Kyle McKendrick's special of the day was likely to be more special than most.

I was just finishing the tomato juice when they arrived. Susanna appeared tired, perhaps a little worried even. McKendrick just looked angry. He sat down, shouted for a vodka, then got round to moaning about the fact we were outside, in the fog, listening to the horns of the nearby ferries and the gulls squawking on the railings from the piers beyond.

'I thought you'd want privacy, Kyle,' I said when the rant ended. 'We can go inside if you like.'

'No,' he snapped. 'This isn't going to take long.'

The waiter had turned up. It was Mickey himself, servile inside a striped shirt and blue apron.

'Gimme a plate of something hot and a glass of New Zealand Sauvignon,' McKendrick ordered. 'Plus some peanuts.'

'You know they make this wonderful seafood stew here,' I said. 'It's what the bosses used to prepare for the market men once the work was over. Fish, shrimp, mussels, clams, tomatoes, wine, garlic . . .'

'Yeah, yeah, yeah. Three of them.'

'Thank you,' Susanna said coldly, then put down her menu.

I smiled at her. It was a one-way thing. From the expression on her exquisite face you'd have thought I was the one who'd organized that morning's kidnap.

'First things first, Kyle,' I said the moment Mickey

314

had gone off with the orders. 'I don't want anyone involved with this except us. It's nothing to do with Susanna. Or any other people you might get to hear I've encountered during my brief sojourn in this outside world of yours. Is that agreed?'

He pulled a sour face. A weird noise came out of his jacket pocket, like a tinny, fake symphony. McKendrick pulled out a silver phone, spoke on it as if we weren't even sharing the same planet, then came back to us just as Mickey returned with the drinks. Our genteel host downed a shot of vodka, then a mouthful of Sauvignon, and threw in a handful of peanuts along the way.

'Listen to me, Bierce. This is beneath me. *You* are beneath me. Give me what I want. Then nothing will drag your miserable sorry ass into my consciousness ever again.'

Susanna took a sip of wine, leaned over and said, 'I would venture the opinion that sounds like a yes.'

'How clear do you want it?' he asked. 'Please me and you live. Piss me off and I'll feed you to those damned birds out there. Her too if she jumps into the conversation one more time without getting invited.'

'No,' Susanna interrupted. 'I am not listening to this. I will *not* negotiate under this duress.'

'Shut up,' McKendrick ordered.

'Shut up,' I echoed.

She did, but not without the filthiest of glances in my direction.

'The money?' I asked.

He laughed.

'The money. *The money!* Here you are, eating my food, nothing in your hands, no proof or anything, and you're talking about money.'

315

'You wouldn't expect me to bring you the tape straight out or something. All those people getting shot in a little sex club you and your friends used for screwing and talking business. Come on, Kyle. Let's not be foolish here.'

He stared across the table, brows furrowed, eyes close to being crossed with fury. It occurred to me there were several things you weren't supposed to do around people of his stature, one being to call them fools.

Mickey arrived with three deep bowls of steaming stew. Just the smell made me want to take one to a corner somewhere with a whole bottle of semi-frozen wine, then eat and drink myself into oblivion.

After the plates were on the table and we were alone again, McKendrick asked, 'So when did you remember that?'

I laughed.

'You're a smart guy. I always knew that. Miriam did too. She never underestimated you, Kyle.'

'When did you remember?' he asked again. 'At that bum's garage?'

I shook my head.

'Keep trying.'

'This is not some stupid game!' he yelled, leaning across the table, spitting red tomato and fish pieces everywhere.

'See,' I said quietly. '*That* is why we're eating out-side.'

An interesting thing: Paul, the engagements officer, didn't move a muscle during this outburst. He surely knew his place.

'When did you know?' he asked one more time.

'Always,' I said. 'Right from go. But what's a man supposed to do?'

He was spitting food again.

'We pumped you full of so much dope! I even got you moved to that correctional facility so's they could do things we couldn't get away with in Gwinett.'

Susanna was staring at me wide-eyed and with a flattering degree of sympathy. I have to say that dressed, with no make-up, and a glass of wine in her hand she did look wonderful. Back in my bachelor days I would have dreamed of dining at Loomis and Jake's with a woman like her sitting across the table, particularly if someone else was paying.

'Sorry,' I said. 'See it my way, Kyle. If I gave you everything in jail I was dead.'

He was slurping down his stew. He seemed to like it.

'Well?' I went on. 'Wasn't I?'

'Of course you were dead,' he snarled.

'So I kept it to myself.'

'Those doctors pumped you full of such shit . . .'

'The medical profession. Can you believe a word they say? This isn't a proposition from Wittgenstein. I just wanted to live.'

I raised my glass.

'Now I'm out again I just want to live a lot more. Also, I have had the opportunity to check the tapes were where I left them. And in good condition. No one likes selling shoddy goods. A satisfied customer is a happy customer. I want you to be happy, Kyle. Is that so wrong?'

He grunted. Susanna was still eyeing me with a mixture of shock and alarm.

'The money,' I said again.

317

'I put a thousand in that bank account you gave me,' he said. 'Just to see if it was active.'

Then, without warning, he belched. A loud one.

'Excused,' I said. 'And is it?'

'Yeah, yeah, yeah. You don't get a million, Bierce. You get . . .' He belched again, and this one sounded even worse than the last. 'Twenty thou and your life,' McKendrick finished weakly.

'I need more than that.'

'OK you get fifty thou and I leave the life out. And . . .'

The belching came back.

Susanna reached over and patted his arm.

'Kyle, dear. Are you OK? Would you like to go to the bathroom or something?'

'Stinking fish,' he snarled. 'Stupid Italians can't even cook right.'

Mickey was hovering at his elbow.

'Is everything well with your food, sir?' he asked, laying on the toadying a little heavily for my taste.

But Kyle McKendrick was dashing for the double doors to the kitchen, clutching his guts, letting loose an Uzi-like burst of gas along the way.

Mickey followed. I took a good look at Paul. He was shuffling on his tiny feet, seeming lost. I could see his hand hovering over some hidden button in his jacket. This was not good.

'Bierce!' Susanna snapped at me. 'What the hell is going on here?'

I took her hand.

'Just walk away quietly now,' I said. 'Take a cab home. Stay inside. Don't let in any strangers. Not till I call.'

'I haven't finished my food!' she yelled.

'Did you not see what it did to our good friend Kyle?'

'Yeah, but that's because you and your Italian friend put some stuff in it or something. Kyle may be stupid and blind but I'm not. I will not . . .'

There was a commotion beyond the doors. Loud and violent.

'I'm gone,' she said, and by the time I'd reached Paul she was nowhere to be seen.

He had his hand on his little hidden button. I had mine on my gun.

'Please,' I said, and ripped the thing out of his ear, then reached inside his jacket and retrieved the piece nestling in the holster there.

It was as clean and shiny as a cop's badge the first day they give it to you.

Paul stared at my weapon, gulped, sending that tiny Adam's apple on a long journey up and down his very large throat, and asked, 'Are you going to shoot me, sir? Because if you are I should tell you I have a girlfriend. And we were hoping to start a family real soon.'

'Of course I'm not going to shoot you, Paul,' I snapped back at him. 'What kind of man do you think I am?'

'I dunno. Sometimes Mr McKendrick meets people . . . I don't know at all.'

'Did you call anyone? With that magic earpiece of yours?'

'No,' he replied instantly, with a sad, earnest openness. 'If I'd been a little quicker like I should have been

I would've, though. That's why Mr McKendrick pays me.'

The noises in the kitchen next door were getting a little less loud. Pretty soon they ought to have Mc-Kendrick down in No Name's van. I just hoped that whatever stuff Mickey had put in his food had stopped making him throw up by that stage. It smelled bad enough already.

Mickey walked out of the kitchen, wiping his hands.

He stared at Paul.

'What are you going to do with him?'

'Can't he stay here?'

'No! We got a full house. What do you think this is? Some holding tank for hoods?'

'He's not a hood,' I objected, before Paul was able to make that point for himself.

'Well, he's not a waiter and he's not a cook. So he can get the hell out of here.'

'For God's sake,' I muttered. 'Paul, hold out your hands.'

Mickey went and got some rope from one of the lobster-pot decorations to tie him.

'What's going to happen to me?' Paul asked, with his gigantic hands stuck out in front of him.

'We're going for a ride,' I said automatically.

His big featureless face turned a deathly shade of white.

'No, Paul. I didn't mean it that way. We're just . . . going somewhere.'

I barked at him to get down the back stairs, then go round to the trade entrance, where we found No Name's van.

Kyle McKendrick hadn't heaved in it, thankfully. But he didn't smell very good at all.

Thirty minutes later we were back in the basement, Stape and McKendrick and Paul, bound on chairs, Paul to one side because to be honest I really hadn't planned on having him there.

Alice was watching me. So was No Name, who'd now had his second stab at my remaining money and still looked as if he was waiting on a tip.

Whatever it was Mickey put in McKendrick's stew seemed to have worn off, judging by the way his mouth had rediscovered its purpose in life. He was yelling and cursing and shouting the kind of language that came most naturally to him.

I looked at Paul and shrugged. Even he was a little embarrassed. Come tomorrow he'd be looking for a new job, that was for sure. If he got out of this alive, a qualification that had to be running round the heads of everyone in this room, except perhaps for No Name.

It was bothering me more than most. Because now I had them here – Stape and McKendrick, one of whom *must* have sent Frankie Solera and Tony Molloy round to kill Miriam and Ricky, and me along the way – now they were seated in our old basement, tied to chairs, there was something wrong.

It was this. *They didn't look guilty.*

Mad. Puzzled. Expectant. But neither of them was acting the way I'd expected, the way that could have got me out of this mess.

Alice said it. Once a cop, always a cop. I know what guilty men look like. I can spot that shifty look in their eye, the way they wriggle and squirm when you talk to them.

Guilty men act the way they do for one reason and one reason alone. All along they're thinking . . . *does he really know?*

And I wasn't getting that kind of self-conscious doubt from Stape or the jumped-up hood pretending to be some big-time businessman.

There's only one person I was getting it from.

Me.

McKendrick finished his latest bile-laden tirade and yelled, 'Do you even *have* this God-damn tape, Bierce?'

I didn't answer.

Stape was glowering at me too.

'You know,' he added, 'I was sort of wondering that too. Sooner or later my people will find their way here. You're already looking at kidnap and conspiracy charges, along with all the rest. If I had the tape maybe I'd have something to bargain with. If not . . .'

'What is it with you people?' I asked.

I nodded towards Alice.

'One of you got her mother killed. My wife, my kid, at least one of whom was innocent. Both probably, if I'd been a better husband.'

'I didn't order them dead,' McKendrick insisted. 'Maybe when the smoke had cleared and I'd worked out what kind of stunt you bastards had been playing in that club I would have done. But not then.'

I pulled up a chair in front of him and looked Kyle McKendrick in the face.

'But you did send Solera and Molloy round to the club to . . . clean up, right?'

He winced.

'What if someone did? This is supposed to be a free country. No one wants the government setting up places to spy on its own citizens.'

Stape laughed.

'Yeah, right. "Citizens". Let me tell you something, Kyle. Citizens are people who pay taxes, go to work every morning and generally get through their lives trying to stick to the law.'

'I know,' McKendrick snapped. 'I employ plenty.'

'Well, then . . .'

'Hey, hey,' I interrupted. 'This is not the time or place. The point I am endeavouring to establish is this. Did you send those two murderous bastards round to Sister Dragon, Kyle?'

He pulled a sour face and said, 'OK. Listen to this. You get an anonymous call saying people have been making movies of you screwing and talking private to your buddies. What would you do?'

'I'd try to buy them back,' I said.

'Not first off you wouldn't. You'd try to *get them*. That's all the answer you're gonna get.'

'And after the club you went for May Loong?' I persisted. 'Then here?'

'Are you serious? After we'd trashed the damn place we realized the tapes that mattered weren't there anyway. We were way too busy making preparations to get out of town to start chasing a couple of women. No one went after them.'

'Someone did!' I yelled.

'Seems to me,' McKendrick said with a smug look on his face, 'that's a question you should be asking a little closer to home.'

They were only looking in one direction at that moment, even Alice. My direction.

'Oh, no, no, no,' I shouted. 'I did not go to extra-ordinary lengths to put you two in my basement in order to hear this. Alice! Join me, please.'

She watched me storming towards the stairs.

'Where are we going?'

'To give the men what they want,' I barked back at her, then pushed the gang of Chinese teenagers out of the way and stormed into the garden.

I couldn't help but notice she gave No Name a look at that moment and said something short and low in Chinese, something that sounded very like an order.

It was cold and foggy and the only noise I could hear through the mist was the distant shrieks of hungry gulls. I couldn't even make out the silhouette of the apple tree or the line of the surrounding walls.

'Is this the right thing to do?' she asked, and came close to me.

'I don't know any more,' I answered. 'I thought I'd just get those creeps here and it would be . . . maybe not simple, but apparent. Something I could touch and feel.'

I stared around the garden, then back at the outline of the timbered house behind me.

'Maybe the answers are here. But if they are they're not what I expected.'

Or, I realized, wanted either.

Alice was shivering. If I thought she'd do as I suggested I would have given her every last piece of money I owned and told her to get out of the city for good. But it wasn't going to work and I knew it. We'd come too far.

She put her hand on my arm.

'Do you really know where these things they want are?'

'I think so.'

'Will they help?'

'I have no idea. But there's nothing else left. Not that I can think of.'

When I got out of Stape's fake jail I'd been in a haze. It had never really lifted. Owl Creek had swallowed me up, tried to hug me tight to what I dreamed were my memories of the place. Were they lies? No, not really. They were just parts of a bigger truth, one that was more ugly and more complicated than I wanted to remember.

Some details still grated, though. And one of them was of picking up my old gun from the place I'd left it, the place Miriam and I had both agreed upon.

My memory was always good until I got hit that black night all those years ago, and then spent a couple of decades having dope shot into me. I had a feel for things. People. Places. Objects.

Even after twenty-three years, something had felt wrong when I went to retrieve my old police handgun watched by an Alice Loong I no longer recognized. It just took a while for the realization to sink in.

'Here,' I said, giving her Paul's shiny pocket piece, showing her how to take off the safety catch and then handing over a small oyster knife I'd taken from the kitchen in Loomis and Jake's. 'I took a gun off Stapleton too. You'll find it underneath an upturned fruit bowl on the sideboard next to where I parked Paul,

McKendrick's bodyguard. Take that when you get back too.'

She stared at the lump of metal I'd placed in her hand.

'I already have a gun.'

'That thing Lao Lao gave you belongs in a museum. Use these.'

'I'm not sure I *want* to, Bierce.'

Here we were again. Dancing around the same old unasked question: what was it she was chasing really?

'That's very sensible but you have to think ahead. If it turns awkward in there for some reason we may not be able to cope. I want you to get Paul's ropes off and give him a weapon. The shiny one. Since it's his he'll be more familiar with it. I don't think he's a bad guy. We may need him.'

'Why?'

That made me angry.

'Will you stop throwing questions at me?'

She stood there and let the gun droop in her fingers. Her eyes were glassy.

'Bierce . . .' she said softly.

It was coming. All at the wrong time. And I didn't want to hear it.

I took hold of Alice Loong, I put my arms around her and held her tight. She was frightened. I think there was something in her face that told me she was a little ashamed too.

'There's something I have to tell you.'

'No,' I said, and put a finger to her warm, smooth lips. 'I don't want to hear it.'

'You do. I can't . . .'

'*Please*. What's done is done. I don't care about it. All I care about is . . .'

I ran out of words. I kept thinking . . . all I care about is you, which is exactly the way I felt about Miriam, who betrayed me somehow, set me up for all this black nonsense and paid for it with her life.

Alice Loong looked at me steadily, with that calm, self-assured wisdom I was fast beginning to appreciate.

'What if it *was* you?' she asked. 'Neither of those two look worried.'

'You noticed?'

'So why don't we just walk away? Take the money. Buy a bike. If you don't remember, would you still be the same man?'

'I think so,' I answered straight away.

She put her arms round my neck and looked into my face, hopeful, uncertain.

'We could leave them to the Chinese. Drive somewhere. Right now.'

'How far would we have to go?' I asked.

She thought about it and answered, in a quiet, pained voice, 'Forever.'

The tapes were there. They had to be there. I remembered the way things felt. It was Miriam who was the forgetful one.

'That's too far,' I said.

We walked down the path to the lean-to by the south wall, close to the shattered door we'd left behind when we made our swift exit with Alice's now-deceased Kawasaki two days before. I didn't need the shovel this time. The cement lid was on neat and square. I picked it up by the rusty hook and threw it to one side, then peered down, as far as I could.

There was something there, beneath where the box, with my old spare gun inside, had lain. It was a good place to hide things. Only two people knew about it. One of them was dead.

I got down on the ground and strained with my right arm, deeper and deeper. Finally I got my fingers round a soft, familiar object covered in dirt and mouldy leaves. I pulled it out.

Ricky's old school bag, the blue one with plastic red piping, fell on the lawn. The school was on vacation when he died. I guess it hadn't been needed.

She watched me as I brushed away the cobwebs and the dirt. Then I undid the buckles and prised it open.

Miriam had bundled everything up in three plastic trash bags, bound in duct tape, tight so no water would get in. It took me a minute to rip them open. Inside were three video cassettes in plastic covers.

'You knew?' she asked, and I didn't feel comfortable about the tone in her voice.

'I guessed. At least, I think . . .'

You knew.

How many times had I been asked that question for more than two decades, almost a quarter of a century now? Did I know? And if I didn't, was that what Alice was coming round to thinking?

'How could you guess something like that?' she insisted.

'Because when you live with someone you start to understand a little of how their head works.'

Even someone who turns into another person, in a flimsy cheongsam, when you're gone.

Alice didn't look convinced. To be honest I didn't blame her. All the same she said, 'You don't have to . . .'

'No. I do. *We* do.'

I carried what I'd found down into the basement. Alice followed. Stape and McKendrick sat quiet, watching me as I held up what I'd found.

No Name was still there and for some reason this seemed wrong. This was a private matter. Paul, quiet, baffled Paul, I could live with. No Name . . .

I threw some more money at him.

'There's the tip,' I said. 'Go outside. Listen to the radio. Tell your buddies there's a little more to come after we've done some private business.'

'What private business?' No Name asked.

I held up the tapes.

'Private, private business. OK?'

'OK.' He shrugged and walked off.

Two of the tapes had dates. One didn't. Not knowing quite why, I picked the one without a label, removed the tape that was already in the VCR, slotted the new one in its place, then pressed the play button.

Alice stood by me all the while. I watched the screen flicker. I think she squeezed my hand but I'm not sure. After a moment or two she'd walked away in any case, to stand on the far side of the room, beyond McKendrick and Stape, close by the scared, confused Paul.

All things considered, I was grateful for that.

It's the club, can't be anywhere else. There's a date stamp running along the bottom like some small tattoo: 25 July 1985, 12.52. No wonder Ricky never made it to

Pee-wee Herman. I still don't know where he really went.

Miriam, my wife, I now know about. I see her, naked on some kind of single bed, face up to the camera, hair splayed back against the pillow. A man is over her. They are . . . making love is the polite term but it's not the right one. They're screwing. Hard and physical like animals, and the noises that are coming out of Miriam's mouth aren't the sounds I know. Soft and loving, excited and intimate. They're grunts, not pleasure, not pain but some strange place in between where all the notions that are supposed to go along with this act – passion, affection, some shared pleasure in a small common miracle – are entirely absent.

I can't work out who the man is. All I can see is the back of his head. Dark hair, pale skin. The video's black and white. That doesn't help. But a part of me's convinced I'm not meant to see him either. This is about Miriam, about seeing some part of her I've never witnessed before.

I start to shake. I walk over to the VCR and try to stab at the buttons. Nothing works.

They're driving at it hard now. The sounds increase. She's using words that don't fit right in her mouth. She's screaming and yelling and rolling her eyes.

My fingers flail at the machine. I start to think I could shoot it maybe.

Then the images stop anyway. There are white crackly lines like static and a hissing noise.

'That was worth a million dollars?' Kyle McKendrick says, and before I know it I have the gun in his face and I'm fighting to stop myself blasting his ugly head off.

But something's coming back on the screen. It's

Miriam again. The time stamp says 16.11. Not long before I got home, if what they said in court was right. She and Ricky have maybe an hour left to live.

'You see, you see, you see . . .' she whispers.

Her face is in the camera. This is somewhere else. She's frightened, terrified. Her hair sticks to her skull. She can't stop brushing it back with her shaking fingers, frantically, more often than it needs.

'Listen', she says. 'I don't know who you are or whether anyone will ever get to look at this. I just want it *down*. OK? I don't know . . .'

She goes out of view of the camera. We see the basement. It's cleaner. A little. There are things on the table: clothes and stuff. And in the corner a case and some travel bags, though I'm the only one who'd really notice. To everyone else they might as well be junk.

'He'll be back some time. If I'm lucky me and Ricky will be gone. I know I shouldn't . . .'

She pauses, does the neurotic shuffle with her hair again.

'I want someone to *know*. It was him. It was Bierce who told me to do this. I didn't want to . . .'

Miriam stops. There are real tears in her eyes. She looks as if she can't control herself.

'He *forced* me to do these . . . things. With all those other men. Crooks. Their friends.'

Her mouth makes a pained, crazy O-shape.

'I didn't want to, Bierce. For God's sake, why'd you make me do that? We didn't need the money that bad. I feel so . . .'

She wrings her hands and shakes them as if they're wet and the water won't come off, not that it's doing anything at all.

'Filthy.'

She looks straight into the lens. A serious expression. Miriam is saying: *I have a hold on myself again*.

'He sent me down to see those government men. He said to do what they say. Everything.'

A pause. The hair.

'*Everything*. And wait and wait. Because some time at the end of it there's a kind of prize so valuable someone will pay big money for it. More money than a uniform cop could earn in ten lifetimes. Money he could use to do anything. Go abroad. Be someone else. Take Ricky and me anywhere in the world so we can live in a big house by a beach or something. He says . . .'

She gulps, as if this is difficult.

'. . . we just sell this thing to whoever comes up with the most. The crooks. The government. Anyone. And . . .'

Miriam sighs, tired, frightened.

'I don't believe him any more. I never should have. Bierce is crazy.'

She leans into the lens.

'Listen to me. *Bierce is crazy*. He doesn't look that way. Everyone sees him and thinks he's more normal than normal. But it's not like that. You don't see what I see. Here. In the house. He's mad and bad and violent and . . . I don't think he means this at all. I don't think he wants me and Ricky along. I don't wanna go anyway. *This is wrong*. I did . . .'

More tears. The O-shaped mouth again for a few seconds.

'I did these things. In that place . . . And now I'm just scared I'll disappear. He could do that. He could do anything he wants and no one would know.'

She stops. From somewhere there's a noise, though a part of me, the small, still-sane part, says maybe it's just her kicking hard with her foot on the floor.

'Oh, my God. I think he's here. He said he'd get these people killed. We'd hold out for some money. But he *scares me*. And now he's here. Jesus . . . *Jesus*. I've got to hide us somewhere. Hide . . .'

The TV goes black. White noise comes out of the tinny old speaker again. Crackly lines run across the dark, empty screen.

They look at me, each in their different way.

Stape, saying: *I knew it was you all along.*

McKendrick, thinking: *this is certainly screwing up my schedule.*

And Alice. Poor, lost Alice.

Alice stares across the room, eyes glazed with tears and rage, mouth trembling, trying to say something . . .

'No, no, no, no, no . . .'

The word just trickle out of her mouth in a conjoined mumble.

I don't hear. I don't want to hear.

Then she yells, 'It's not true, Bierce. Tell me it's not true and I'll believe you.'

The old question, the one that always catches me out.

I lift the gun. I put the nose against my temple.

I stutter what I always stuttered, the words that come out so easily now it's as if they're programmed into my head.

'I don't remember. I don't recall.'

And all it takes is something simple. A little light

pressure on that warm stub of metal nestling against my index finger, a flash of momentary agony.

Then there is no such thing as memory. No pain. No chance of it again.

Something falls hard against the back of my skull. The old hurt, the familiar one.

I open my eyes. I'm falling. There's the sound of people, a babble of voices.

And a man standing over me, a weapon in his hand, with blood on the butt.

I look at his Chinese face and think, 'Ah . . .'

Lying on the floor of the basement, slugged by some hood's pistol, I finally realize. This face has a name. Two in fact. And I am stupid, the stupidest man on earth.

I roll upright. My weapon's gone, scattered across the floor. No Name and the rest of the Chinese kids are there, nervous and a little scared, because this whole thing has surely taken on a dimension they never envisaged, not in all their teenage fantasies. This is out of their league. Someone is going to die, and that is both frightening and fascinating at the same time.

The individual who stands above me is staring straight at Alice Loong, who's walked across the room to stick a gun down at my face, hesitantly because the barrel's wavering, between me and the empty, grubby floor, to an unnerving degree. His own weapon is down by his side. He holds it there, confident.

'Be nice to your Uncle Jonny,' I find myself saying, quietly, and hear the catch in her voice, see the terrified look in her eyes. 'Or Mr Ho. Take your pick. Which was he to you?'

'You knew,' she says, and it's not a question. 'I think . . .'

Her face is troubled, perhaps even undecided.

'. . . think you're good at hiding those things, Bierce. From yourself sometimes too.'

Is that true? I've no idea. All I know at that moment is I can't take my eyes off the figure next to her, the Chinese man with the lean, damaged face, skinny body tight in a dark hood suit. A man who is wearing a grin that could frighten children from half a mile away, not that Alice sees this, because that's what family does to you.

Jonny takes a little bow.

'Course he knew,' he says. 'One smart guy. Like I told you, girl. He worked this out himself, all those years ago. When he killed your mom and those other people.'

Jonny walks over and kicks me hard in the gut. It doesn't hurt as much as it ought to.

'Bierce knew I ran away, now didn't you? He just didn't expect me to come back.'

There's now a fresh stabbing ache in my stomach. It's not the worst thing happening at that moment.

'No,' I sigh. 'I don't know him. I never did any of that . . .'

I look Alice straight in the eye.

'I *am* sure. The amnesia only works for that afternoon, Alice. Nothing longer. This man's a stranger to me, not you, and I should have realized that. It took getting hit on the right part of my head. Sorry . . .'

Her gun is pointed more at me at this moment and it isn't wavering.

'Not that you or anyone here's going to believe it,' I add. 'I can't blame you.'

I shake my head, trying to clear it, then take a good look at him.

'So you went away? And then you came back?'

'Right first time.'

He strokes his face.

'Got this done in Singapore. You like it?'

Jonny has a short, snout-nosed automatic by his side and can't decide who to laugh at more. Me or his niece, who, for once, is uncharacteristically blind to what's going on. Alice has tears in her eyes and a part of me thinks she likes that because it blurs the fury of acceptance in her face as she stares at me.

'Nothing to compare it with,' I say. 'You mind if I stand up?'

'Sure,' he answers, grinning. 'You finally got round to handing out the tapes?'

'Finally,' I say, and point to the two remaining ones sitting on top of the VCR.

Stape is trying to barge his way into the conversation. He has his serious, let's-do-business face on. I feel like weeping with mirth.

'I still represent a federal agency in all this,' my treacherous one-time partner says, with a marked quiver in his cracked old-man's voice.

He tries to look dignified inside the ropes.

'I promise you we can cut you a deal. Money. Witness-protection programme. You name it.'

'Witness protection?' Jonny laughs, and kicks me again.

Alice keeps her gun pointed in my direction. Jonny has a genial-seeming, carefree nature. I can imagine he'd be a lot more fun, in the short term anyway, than me.

'Why the hell would I wanna mess with crap like that?' he wants to know.

'Security, sir,' Stape answers very seriously.

Jonny didn't say anything. Getting lectures on security from a man strapped to a chair in someone's basement, with a room full of armed Chinese teenagers waiting to do what they like . . . I can understand that.

'Tell them, though, will you?' I ask. 'Please. Do this for me. No. Do it for Alice.'

'Tell 'em what, Bierce?' Jonny replies, not quite understanding.

'What happened,' I say, and just the words make me feel cold and scared and angry.

The big grin gets bigger, like that on the Cheshire Cat I once imagined lived in the apple tree outside, pouncing on birds it thought too fat and lazy to live.

'Oh. What *happened*?'

He makes a little bow to her. It all looks very nice.

'See, Alice,' Jonny Loong says kindly. 'You're a grown-up girl. A good girl. Who helps her family. So you can hear grown-up things. The truth is, we were all friends together. Your mom and me and Miriam and Bierce. Good friends. Sometimes I'd bang Miriam. Sometimes Bierce'd bang your mom.'

'No, no, no, no, no,' I start, but then his gun comes up and I fall silent. Not so much for the gun, but out of respect for the pain visible on her beautiful face.

'We had this little deal together. We work for the man here. We take his money. We get something precious of his. Then we sell it. Except . . .'

337

He shrugs.

'Stupid white jerk gets greedy. Wants it all for himself. Gets these hoods in. Kills your mom. Kills Miriam.'

'Ricky too,' I interject. 'Don't leave him out.'

'Yeah. Would've killed me if I hadn't run.'

She glances at me. Some small part of her still doesn't know what to make of this. She'd like that part to go away.

'You see?' Jonny asks her. 'I told you. Right from the start. Bierce is a bad man. Would kill us all if he could.' He puts a hand on her shoulder, an uncle interested in his niece's welfare.

'And now?' I ask.

He shrugs.

'Now Alice knows.'

He looks at the VCR.

'Now I got something to sell.'

He looks at me.

'Now you get dead.'

'Shoot this jerk after,' McKendrick interrupts. 'Look, Loong. Get me out of here. I'll arrange double anything this fed moron offers. And you don't get to pay tax on it either.'

'Lot of money for a couple of tapes,' Jonny observes.

'It is indeed,' McKendrick agrees.

'Thing is,' my new Chinese friend goes on, 'I talked to some people out east this morning. They say they could be very embarrassed if those tapes start getting round.'

McKendrick nods, listening carefully, looking very corporate.

'Damned right. That's why I'm prepared to be very, very generous.'

'They say, only some kind of real jerk could lose that kind of thing in the first place. Then screw up getting it back. They pay better than anyone too.'

'Hey!' McKendrick yells, straining at his ropes, the old part of him coming to the surface now. 'Cut the crap, Chinaboy. Get me out of here so we can talk business.'

'Here's business,' Jonny says, then empties four bullets into Kyle McKendrick's silk-clad torso.

The room's quiet after that, except for a gentle little sobbing coming by way of Paul in the corner.

'What happened . . .' Jonny repeats quietly, looking at Alice, not me. '*What happened?* You screwed us, Bierce. We had a deal and you broke it. I gonna kill you. I wait years for this.'

The short black barrel of Jonny's piece rises up to greet me. Two bullets left, I guess. Not that he needs more than one at this distance.

'No.' He checks himself. 'Alice?'

She's just a couple of feet away, glaring in my direction in a way that makes me feel worse than anything else I've experienced in the last few days.

'He murdered your mom. You got the right. You kill him. That way it all gets even. Yin, yang. All that shit. We take our money, we do what we like with it after. You're a good clever girl. I been watching you a long time. I know. We can do things.'

Alice Loong can't take her eyes off me. I pull an old dusty chair out from beneath the table, sit on it and open my hands.

'Say something,' she murmurs.

'Like what? I'm out of answers, except the obvious ones. How about this? It was Jonny and Miriam. They put it all together in bed or somewhere. Maybe they were both planning on cheating each other too. Maybe Miriam was going to dump him the way she planned to dump me. When he found out . . .'

'You . . .' Alice began to say.

'Me? *Me*? I just walked in on the whole horrid party, an idiot at the feast. What else can I tell you?'

'Listen to family, Alice,' Jonny says. 'You think I'd murder your mom? My own sister? What kind of man could do that?'

'Yeah, listen to family,' I suggest. 'Ask Lao Lao. Ask his own mother. Does she know who Mr Ho is? That he's been talking to you all along? Did she know it was his bunch of charm merchants she was calling into this party today? Or was that down to you?'

Alice says nothing and thereby gives me her answer.

'Is she even aware this lying, murdering, blood-thirsty offspring of hers is still alive?' I add, just for good measure.

Jonny walks over and slaps me hard around the face. I wipe away blood from the edge of my mouth. Broken lip. I don't even feel it.

'Just tell me you didn't do it,' she says.

'I didn't do it! Any of it!'

'The tape, Bierce. We *saw* the tape.'

'I can't explain that. I know myself, who I am.'

Two words, a vicious caveat, form in my head: *I think*.

The big question, the biggest, one so many people have thrown at me over the years, is forming at the back of her mind. I just know it. I understand, too, what I'll say.

'Do you *know* you didn't do any of these things?' she asks, and the room goes quiet, because they understand, even dead Kyle McKendrick wherever he may be, what my answer will be, *must* be. The one it's always been.

'Oh, my God, Alice,' I whisper, hearing my voice break with exasperation. 'How many times do I have to go through this? With people I hate. With people I love. I don't remember. Not much. I don't . . .'

I close my eyes. What does it matter?

'Kill me for being so stupid I never saw this coming, then or now. But not for that. Unless you don't believe me, in which case do what the hell you like. The truth . . .'

There's an important point to be made here, though I'm not entirely sure what it is. Last words often come this way, I guess.

'The truth . . .'

I begin to say, the smells of dry old wood and Kyle McKendrick's blood feeling their way into my nostrils, so strong I start to shake, while, from the peripheral edge of my vision, a black cloud begins to work its way ever inwards.

'The truth,' I repeat, and no one hears, least of all me, because there's a sound rushing towards me, fast and hot and angry, a roaring, devastating blast that can be one thing and one alone.

The truth is this, nothing but, world without end, amen, and now, in these closing moments, it comes racing into my mind, so vicious and vivid nothing can squeeze it back into the closed compartment in my head where it's stayed hidden, festering all these years.

It's that afternoon. I park in the drive and walk through the garage to the garden. I can hear voices there, angry voices. Miriam and Ricky, arguing.

It's hot. I'm tired. I feel stupid from all those long hours staring at an empty building, pointless work, work I don't understand.

When I get there he's punching her, little fists hammering on her knees. He's screaming and, as I look at them, I feel my head getting heavy because this is something new, a side to them I've never seen before.

They are my family and family spells love. These things do not happen.

'Ricky,' I say, and he stops hitting her, clings to my legs, crying, furious.

I look at Miriam and there's something in her face I don't recognize. Plain, bitter fury. With the boy. With me for interrupting them maybe.

'You're early,' she says accusingly.

She's covered in dust and cobwebs. It looks as if she's been scrabbling around in the cellar for some reason. She's been doing that a lot of late.

'I couldn't keep my eyes open any longer. What's wrong?'

'Bad mommy, bad mommy, *bad mommy*,' he screams, and tries to go back to thumping her with his small tight fists, though I stop him, pulling him back, bending down to look into his eyes.

My son's more full of grief and rage than I've ever known. This is all so foreign.

'She said we'd go to a movie!' he spits at me.

'Well, Ricky. Sometimes grown-ups say things they can't always deliver. Life gets busy.'

'She said to tell you we did.'

'You know I . . .'

My mind goes blank. There's nothing to say. I can't imagine what's happening here.

She's got Ricky by the hair now.

'Go to your room, you little bastard,' Miriam screeches at him. 'Go to your room. *Go now!*'

And I blink at what I see. She hits him. Not hard, but hard enough, a slap across his pale, flawless face. There are more tears, on his part, more screaming, then he runs, over the too-long grass, past the scattered toys, the second-hand bike with stabilizers I got down the charity shop because we didn't have the money to buy new, the cheap balls and tin trucks, into the house, screaming, screaming, all the way through the kitchen and up the stairs.

I look above me. The curtains of his room are drawn in a sudden sweep. Angry, bitter words fly down at her, not me. Then a kind of silence.

There are birds on the roof. Three black crows, watching me, watching us all.

This is like a bad dream. Or coming back to a place that looks like home, smells like home, has people in it that seem like family, but it's all wrong, foreign. Nothing's real or as it should be.

She's tense and tired-looking too. Her face is gaunt. She's wearing a white shirt and long dark slacks, grubby from the basement, and a part of me thinks: *she dresses like this when we go places.*

Not that it happens very much, and I'm ashamed by that thought.

Her hair's a mess. I don't see that often either.

'You're early,' she says again. 'Is it too much to call?'

'I live here,' I say gently, not as some kind of admonition.

'Me too. It's just . . .'

She's struggling to work out what to say.

'I thought you and Ricky were going to the movies?'

'Pee-wee Herman,' she snaps. 'I decided I'd save that joyous occasion for you. Though I guess that particular masterpiece may be long gone by the time the opportunity comes around.'

'Miriam . . .'

'This isn't convenient. I've got to go.'

'Go where?'

'Somewhere else.'

'When? For how long? Why?'

'Forever!' she yells.

I don't know what to say or do.

'I get bored easily, Bierce. You mean you never noticed?'

I shake my head. I feel stupid.

'I don't understand.'

'This is over,' she says, waving her hand horizontally across the tall grass and the scattered toys, a look of intense fury in her eyes I simply do not recognize. 'Everything. Me, you, Ricky. Owl Creek. All gone for good, never to return. And you know the best news?'

I stare at her, not a single word forming in my mind.

'They'll put it all down to you. I'll be somewhere else, with a different name. And all they'll think of is putting you in jail while I have the time of my life. *My* life.'

She turns. I put a hand on her shoulder. She flies round, hands tearing through the hair at my face. I feel her nails scratch deep into my skin.

'Don't touch me! Don't *ever* touch me!'

I try to hold her and then she's gone, in through the open kitchen door, looking for something, racing round the room, frantic. I stand there, mind frozen, immobile with shock.

Finally I follow in her footsteps, bleating, 'Miriam. *Miriam?*'

She's not there. But someone is. Not one visitor either. Two. Possibly more.

Then I hear it. Ricky screaming again, loud and frightened this time, not the anger of before.

Ricky is screaming, and somewhere upstairs so is Miriam. It's her voice, even more than his, that makes my blood run cold, for the way it's veered from hatred to terror in just a few short breaths.

There are men in the house and they're murderous.

And before I can do a thing, raise a fist or a voice even, something falls upon me, so heavy I tumble, groaning, to the floor.

I roll over and stare upwards. It's a new face, one I have never seen before in my life, though some insidious cerebral connection takes me from that moment to now and says: *Jonny Loong.*

'She was expecting you,' I say, tasting the blood in my mouth.

'Stupid white bitch,' he mutters. 'Thinks she can screw with me.'

In his hand there's a sledgehammer. There's blood on it. Lots.

'Get the hell . . .' I start to say, then my vision goes black, my head feels as if it's about to fly off my shoulders.

It sounds as if the biggest church bell in the world has rung between my ears. I roll, I tumble, try to scream and know my voice means nothing in this place.

When a little of my vision returns I see him reach down and straighten my face so he can look into my eyes.

'Where are they?' he asks.

'Miriam,' I mumble.

'She dead. Can't tell me.'

My breathing's not working right. My whole body's pulling in on itself to try to disguise the pain.

'Dead like you,' he says, and pulls back his two arms, the hammer rising behind his head.

No, I think. Not say, because the words have gone from my throat now, scattered like gulls fleeing the city waterfront when the foghorns start to bellow through the mist.

Struggling, rolling around on the floor, waiting to die, I can see his face, try to freeze it in memory. And I think . . .

I remember it all.

Four simple words, an entire universe inside them. These thoughts and recollections and fragments of a life as it was lived . . . they embrace everything. They give my dead parents a semblance of life. They let me think of my little lost child and wonder what he might have become.

They make me wonder about Miriam too, and how I failed her. In what small, invisible ways I allowed our marriage to fall apart and never noticed a thing.

I open my eyes, desperate to speak, to say those few short words I never thought I'd be able to utter.

'I didn't kill anyone,' I mutter. 'I *know* I didn't kill anyone.'

Except something's happening already.

Jonny Loong is looking at his long-lost niece, holding on to his chest with two hands, staring at the pumping red wound there in disbelief, staring at her too.

Alice extends the gun towards him.

'You lying bastard,' she says, and fires one more time, straight into his torso, and I try to think, hard, because there's No Name in the room, and six green but troublesome Chinese youths, who are surely more than a match even for Alice Loong and the weapon in her oh-so-steady hand.

'Paul,' she yells.

On the far side of the cellar I see the big figure in his grey suit. My baby-faced, wedge-shaped captive is out of his seat already, shiny firearm tight in hand, roaring at No Name, who's screaming and shouting on the floor, clutching his leg, backing into his little band of fake warriors, face contorted with pain and fury.

'I am in control,' Paul bellows at them. 'I *am* in control.'

I just know there must be an instructor in some training school somewhere who would look at this young man and see a job well done, because there are six young thugs crawling in the dust, doing every last thing he asks, throwing knives and guns across the stone tiles, pleading for mercy.

Alice walks over and lands a fast, hard kick into Uncle Jonny's torso.

I get up, brush myself down and take a look at him.

'Doctor . . .' Jonny begs, beginning to cough up thick red blood. 'Family.'

She's got the gun up again. I take it quickly. She doesn't object. Not much anyway.

'Not my family,' she spits at him. 'Not mine.'

He isn't listening.

'Mr Bierce?' someone asks from across the room.

I blink. I haven't heard the 'Mr' part in a very long time.

'Paul?'

He waves his weapon towards No Name and his terrified companions.

'What do I do with them?'

I stare at the gangly youth. His bravado has departed, for a while anyway.

'No Name. Go. Do not cross our path again. Tell no one a word of what you saw here. Otherwise . . .'

He's shaking, nodding his head, terrified.

Paul watches them struggle up the stairs in silence. He's doubtless deeply aggrieved Kyle McKendrick isn't going to make his next appointment, and the anger that has put on his cherubic features gives me pause.

I am, I realize, a terrible judge of character.

I look into Alice's cool green eyes.

'You didn't wait for me to say it?'

'Say what?'

'That I didn't do it.'

She sighs.

'For pity's sake, Bierce. Do I have to explain everything?'

She's shaking her head, unable to believe I finally got round to pressing this matter, the delicate shifting bond of trust between us.

Alice looks at Jonny, who's groaning in a lot of blood on the floor, and says, 'I had to shoot someone. It felt better shooting him than it would have done you. Is that good enough?'

'I guess,' I say, feeling stupid.

'I never really thought you killed them,' she adds. 'Not from the moment you wouldn't sleep with me. It's just . . .'

She glowers at her stricken uncle on the floor and for a moment I think she might be about to kick his wounded gut again.

'Sometimes it's easier to believe a lie than accept the truth,' she says carefully. 'Because the truth causes more pain, I think.'

This is a conversation for another time. I turn to my old colleague. He must have been out of the front line for a while. He's sweating and scared and looking as if he might throw up at any moment.

With this last in mind I see the little oyster knife from Mickey Carluccio's kitchen sitting on the table, where Alice must have dropped it when she freed Paul. I cut him free. He wriggles his arms, struggling to get back some feeling.

'Bierce . . .' he begins to say.

'Shut up and listen.'

I point to the VCR and the tapes.

'The deal is this. You get these and Jonny Loong,

who's yours to deal with as you see fit. You clean up this mess. You get everything off my record. You never come looking for any of us, me or Alice or Paul. We saved your life here and if you *ever* show a lack of gratitude for that I will be very pissed off indeed. Are we agreed on this?'

He's looking at the gun in my hand, the one I took from Alice. He's suspicious.

'How much?' he asks.

Alice rolls her eyes.

'C'mon,' Stape goes on. 'I need to know. This is government. We got to raise paperwork and stuff. If it's a real lot of money – and I'm not saying that's impossible – you may have to get it in instalments. Offshore, natch.'

I look at her and say, 'Tell him.'

To my delight, Alice picks up the spare video cassette and drops it daintily in his lap.

'Mister,' she says, 'we'd pay *you* to take this crap away. If we had any money, that is.'

He's speechless, then he's nodding. A little voice at the back of my head is screaming at me for being an idiot, but I soon silence it. There is still one thing left.

Jonny Loong is on his back, gasping, in pain, but nothing necessarily fatal. This can be altered.

I place the barrel of my large police weapon square in his face, between his scared eyes, and say, 'How did you know, Jonny?'

'Wha'?' he squawks. 'Get me a doctor, for God's sake.'

'You won't need a doctor if you don't talk to me right now. Miriam thought she had this all pat. She left all this evidence. My blood under her nails. The bank account. Everything. It fell apart because you found out.'

He wriggles, not wanting to look at the gun.

'How did you know?' I ask again.

'Stupid women,' he spits. 'She called May at the club and told her to go home, play sick or something, 'cos something bad might happen. Next thing McKendrick's people coming round shooting everyone, screaming the tapes aren't there. I got out of the back, went home, saw May. Solera and Molloy wanted more money than McKendrick threw their way. So we got it all out of her in the end. She was a stubborn bitch. Tapes gone. Miriam gone. Always was one greedy, crazy bitch. Not hard to work out, huh?'

'And for that,' I say, feeling the trigger get hot and sticky under my finger, 'you beat your own sister to death? My wife, my kid too?'

'I was mad at them!' he bawls. 'OK? We were supposed to be partners, selling it all together! Didn't I screw her scrawny white hide enough or something?'

I mutter something bad and out of character, then pull the trigger. Jonny Loong screams and puts his bloodstained hands over his eyes. The hammer falls on nothing. It's my gun. I haven't fed it any more bullets since loosing off the four shots in the fog when we took Stape that morning. The two slugs Alice put in her Uncle Jonny were the last ones. I never was good with numbers.

'Please,' Alice says quietly, and takes the weapon from me. I am still wondering if it's worth beating Jonny Loong to death when she places her strong, purposeful hand on my arm and turns me.

'Please,' she says again.

There's a noise from the TV behind. I turn.

The crackly lines have disappeared. There's a picture again.

There's more.

'Bierce?'

She's back on screen and she's laughing. After all these event-filled minutes when nothing but inter-ference and white noise came on the screen, Miriam's there on the TV again.

'Note to self,' she says in a dead, robotic voice that's foreign to me. 'Must erase end of tape.'

My dead wife shakes her head.

'So much to do, so little time.'

She closes her eyes tight shut, concentrating. Then she goes . . .

'Listen. I don't know who you might be or whether you ever get to see this. I just want it *down*. OK? I don't know . . . Oh.'

There's a line of vivid cursing. She did an amateur theatre production once. The rehearsals never came easy.

Miriam looks into the camera and her eyes have a genuine, deep sadness that cuts into my heart.

'How many takes do I have, Bierce? You'll be home soon.'

She folds her arms, the way she did when we had a conversation and the point she had to make was serious. To her anyway.

'What will you say when I tell you? Shout? Scream? Cry? Try to stop me?'

She shakes her head.

'You know something? I could do anything to you. I could beat you half to death and you still wouldn't put a finger in front of your face to stop me. I could ball half the men down the Yonge docks, one after the other, right in front of your eyes, and you'd just watch, puzzled, waiting for an explanation you could live with. You're like a little dog. Always coming back for more.'

She makes tight, harsh claws of her hands, as if to mark me with her nails.

'I'll scratch you and you'll never notice. They can convict a man for homicide, even without a body. I looked it up. I can screw you. I can screw Jonny. All of them. There's people out there who want these things so badly . . .'

There's a tape in her hand.

'I took them. Me. The little homemaker. The mother of your child. The woman who fills your refrigerator and irons your stupid khaki shirts. I took them, then I phoned Kyle, who's been in every last part of me and still doesn't know my voice. I said a friend needed for him to hear something. Bye-bye, Jonny. Not that you'll ever know. Exciting, huh?'

She laughs. Then she's serious. All this happens in a split second.

'More exciting than a lifetime of living off a cop's wages. Dreaming of the time we can take a vacation in some dump all the other drones go. Me driving the kid to school, then driving him back. Did you never wonder why there wasn't another one?'

She's scrabbling in her bag. Something comes out. She waves it furiously in front of the lens.

'It's called the pill, Bierce. I've been taking it for four years, all the while we've "been trying". And you never noticed. You're not the kind of man who'd look in a woman's bag or think to ask a personal question.'

I think, as I look at this dead woman on the screen, that you only remember the good elements of a person, the parts that have a place in your heart. It is Miriam and it isn't. At that moment it's principally a stranger, full of hate.

Her face comes closer.

'You know what *I* want. No. You never asked. I want to go to Paris when I feel like it. I want to pick up a man, screw him and wake up to find him gone. I want everything, now, instantly, and then I want something else in its place when I'm bored.'

Everything drains from her at this moment. All life. All feeling. All humanity.

'I *hate* you, Bierce. I hate what you and Ricky and *this fucking life* have done to me.'

She stops. Something inside is choking her. I recognize this woman again. I knew her.

Her eyes close. When they open again she's back to being herself, what I lazily, stupidly think of as her 'real' self.

Then, almost as an aside, 'Look after Ricky. He's a sweet kid if a kid's what you want, and it always was. A kid. Not me.'

There's a sound from somewhere out of view.

'Note to self,' she says, a little anxiously. 'Must erase end of tape.'

LATER

The fog never lasts. It didn't come back again that summer at all. The day we ate lunch at Loomis and Jake's – real lunch, by which I mean Susanna Aurelio was paying, so we managed our way through three courses – I wouldn't have wanted to be anywhere else in the world. The temperature was moderate enough to walk around without feeling uncomfortable. You could see miles in every direction. There were crowds of boats bobbing on the water, white sails, big and small, fluttering in the gentle ocean breeze. And the company was . . . interesting.

Partway through the first course Susanna watched Alice walk off to take a call, pushed aside her plate of Mickey Carluccio's finest lobster and said, 'She's too young for you, Bierce. It won't work.'

I shook my head.

'Oh, no. I'm not going there.'

'Come on. Are you seriously telling me you two aren't doing it?'

I nearly choked on my halibut.

'Doing it? *Doing it*? Not that it's any of your damn business but no . . . we're not "doing it".'

She winked at me.

'You're figuring it won't take long, though.'

'No! Enough! You make too many assumptions. You add up everything correctly, then push on an extra one just for good measure. Which makes you wrong, in case you hadn't noticed.'

'Is that a denial? That would be rich. A real denial. Not the "don't know but think so" I've been getting for a quarter of a century or so.'

'It's a "what the hell does it have to do with you?", OK?'

'It's got everything to do with me! I'm your lawyer, remember? Your closest friend. Your only true ally. None better. Also you're into me for a quarter of a million dollars in unpaid fees. So I have a personal interest too.'

There had to be a reason for the lunch, naturally.

'Send the bill to Stape. Tell him if he doesn't pay I'll throw the mother of all lawsuits at him.'

Susanna smiled. She was wearing a two-piece red business suit and something gold and heavy around her neck. She was looking very pleased with herself. The divorce papers had been filed two days before. According to a story in the newspaper that morning, one she'd doubtless leaked, the prenuptial agreement – one more modern concept I was still trying to grasp – had been primarily written by her firm on her husband's behalf. So it was going to be an expensive summer for Frank.

'I *love* lawsuits. I'm so good at them. Give me a chance. No win, no fee. Just 20 per cent on the nose when I come through, all expenses included.'

It ought to have been tempting. I'd managed to claw

back the freehold of Owl Creek from her, on the grounds that I was clearly not compos mentis when I signed it over. In return she'd seized the thousand Kyle McKendrick had deposited in the Liechtenstein bank account. So all Alice and I had between us was what remained of Stape's original twenty thousand, which was disappearing at a speed I still found hard to believe.

Susanna did what she always did. Persisted.

'What do you have to lose?'

'How about my chance to get back into the world? It's not *my* world. Not really. But it's the only one there is. Either that or slip into being a hermit. Or . . .'

Or what? I really didn't know. A uniform and a badge worked for me then, but they wouldn't now. I was fifty-two. I felt pretty fit and well now my head had cleared. Not quite seventeen again. Or at least in one way only, in that I was staring at this big empty thing called the future stretching out in front of me, wondering.

Mickey Carluccio came over with a couple of plates of extras: sautéed razor shells and clams. I picked at them. It must be nice to live like this every day.

He gave Susanna a knowing glance.

When he was gone I said, 'You know, I think the owner's got his eyes on you. I'm not sure the present girlfriend will last.'

She slapped down her napkin.

'I don't do retail.'

I nodded down at the fish market.

'Mickey's wholesale too. Also, he cooks. That stew you just ate? He learned it from his father. Have you ever dated a man who could cook?'

She was peering at me as if I'd transferred down from Mars.

'One word, Bierce. *Restaurants.*'

I wasn't listening.

Alice was coming back, beaming. She'd spent some of our diminishing money on clothes that morning, specially for lunch. She had a cream shirt, silk, but from somewhere in Chinatown where it cost a fraction of the price of the stores. Plus some sleek blue slacks that looked as if they were tailor-made.

She seemed as happy as anyone could be. We both had plenty of reasons for that, I guess. Stape was as good as his word when it came to the law. Neither of us had a black line against our names. I got a fresh start. Alice now knew she'd never be going back to blue hair and chains. And Jonny Loong, the man responsible for the deaths that had haunted us for so long, had disappeared from the face of the planet, into the arms of Stape's men, presumably to work up a prosecution some time. Not that I expected to see that happen. I was at one with this world now. I had come to appreciate how it worked.

She sat down and said, 'It's outside.'

'What's outside?' Susanna demanded.

'A 1993 Kawasaki 500 twin,' I answered.

My lawyer shook her head.

'This is a lawnmower or something?'

'A bike,' Alice replied. 'Not the colour I'd prefer. But it'll do.'

'Wow,' Susanna gasped. 'You bought her an antique used motorcycle. You surely know how to treat a woman, Bierce. Back to business . . .'

She took a folder out of her bag.

'The thing is . . . I have a certain amount of discovery work I need doing on a couple of cases. I could put this out to the usual agencies. But you need a break. And I've got to give you this: you're resourceful.'

She glanced at Alice.

'Both of you. Hire her as a secretary or something. What you do with the money is up to you.'

'Susanna . . .' I tried to say.

'All legal and above board. Also, as long as you're working for me, I'll happily put *my* claim against your assets to one side.'

The Aurelio smile shone across the table.

'That *is* a good idea. Believe me.'

Alice looked businesslike and efficient.

'Are you seriously asking us to do some sort of investigation work for you?'

'Why not?' Susanna demanded. 'Listen, kid. There are a million agencies out there with long names and fancy offices and all they do for my money is stare at a computer. I can Google myself if I want. You two are a neat combination, professionally anyway. You can do the modern stuff. Bierce here can go out and talk to people face to face, and frankly that's becoming a lost art.'

Alice gave me a knowing look and got back to eating.

'Maybe later,' I said.

Susanna stared at me in disbelief.

'When you work for me, Bierce, you soon come to appreciate the word "later" is not in the approved vocabulary.'

I leaned forward, picked up a razor shell, slipped it on to my plate and repeated, very firmly, 'Later.'

Alice looked up from her plate and the two of them caught each other's eye for a moment. I'm not sure I liked what I saw there. It resembled two predators agreeing on which part of the herd they were each going to eat.

'An office, a salary, a guarantee of six months' work plus free legal indemnity insurance,' Susanna said.

Alice sighed and shook her head.

'Not even close. An investment of two hundred thousand, for which you get a minority stake in the firm,' she said. 'Plus the work guarantee, the legal indemnity insurance, and something else I haven't dreamed up yet.'

Susanna thought for a moment then nodded. 'OK.'

Then the two of them were staring at me, a little cross, because I'd got up from the table and was starting to leave.

In unison, both pairs of eyes firmly set in my direction, they said slowly, carefully, 'Bierce?'

I turned back, smiling, waved the keys and kept on walking.

'Where the hell are you going?' Susannah yelled across the crowded terrace.

Having no idea what penguins say or do, I replied simply, 'Oink, oink,' and flapped my arms.

It was beautiful outside. I sat on the saddle of the old green Kawasaki, thinking about the open road, waiting.